THE YEAR'S BEST DARK FANTASY AND HORROR

2012 EDITION

THE YEAR'S BEST DARK FANTASY AND HORROR

2012 EDITION

Edited By Paula Guran

○
PRIME BOOKS

Contents

THE THIRD TIME MAY BE A CHARM, BUT IT'S NOT NECESSARILY DEFINITIVE

Paula Guran

—◆—

This is the third volume of *The Year's Best Dark Fantasy and Horror,* and I still feel I need to introduce it by pointing out that there is really no definition of "dark fantasy." Beauty is in the eye of the beholder; dark fantasy is in the mind of the reader.

I mean that literally. Neuroscience can now identify the particular parts of the brain affected by reading. According to Maria Nikolajeva, director of the Cambridge/Homerton Research and Training Center for Children's Literature, fiction with a very dark theme "creates and amplifies a sense of insecurity . . . but it can also be a liberation, when readers 'share' their personal experience with that of fictional characters . . . readers' brains are changed after they have read a book . . . " (quoted by Valerie Strauss, "The Answer Sheet," *The Washington Post*/washingtonpost.com: 2010 September 4.)

But what makes one brain sense insecurity may not affect another in the same way. What our minds perceive as "dark" varies. Dark fantasy, in general, can evoke a wide range of responses and those may differ by degree. It can be slightly unsettling, a bit eerie, profoundly disturbing, or just generally convey a certain atmosphere. Since darkness itself can be many things—shadowy and mysterious, deep and unknowable, paradoxically illuminating—it can be used in fiction in innumerable ways. Stories need not even remain dark throughout. They can be journeys through the dark with a positive, even uplifting, outcome. The dark can amuse even as it disturbs.

"The dark" can be found in any number of literary forms—weird fiction (new or old), supernatural fiction, magical realism, the mythic, fairy tales, adventure, mystery, surrealism, or the *fantastique.* Since it is fantasy, something of the supernatural needs to be involved, or the story can be set in a world where what is ordinary is, in our world, extraordinary.

As for horror: horror is a subjective and personal emotion. Again, what you feel is not necessarily what I feel. Not everyone agrees—there is no exact definition—but I do not think horror fiction needs to be supernatural. Life itself—and our fellow humans—can be far more terrifying than the extramundane. And when we speculate on the darker possibilities of our future, that, too, can be horrific.

As far as this series of anthologies is concerned, you will encounter scary stories, but the intent is not to *always* frighten the reader. Nor is it to make you constantly feel subconsciously insecure—although some of you may. Certainly you will feel slightly uneasy at times, perhaps apprehensive, possibly unsettled, even disturbed. Thoughts may be provoked. But you'll also smile here and there, maybe even laugh out loud.

Perhaps you can consider *The Year's Best Dark Fantasy and Horror* an exploration of the shadowy places and darker paths of the imagination. These stories—all published in 2011—will take you to a great many of those locations. It will take you back in time to several eras (not all of which are part of our history), forward into several futures, down mean streets, just next door or perhaps over the next hill, inside minds quite unlike (I hope) yours, to places you don't quite recognize but are still somehow familiar, and into many otherworlds.

In some instances, you may visit some tenebrous locales that are quite similar, but since there are different guides, the peregrinations each prove unique.

Each reader will, no doubt, take an entirely different trip—choosing, feeling, reacting individually; abandoning some adventures, lingering for a while elsewhere.

The authors whose work you encounter include some of whom you've probably never heard; some you may have read before, but don't know well; others whose work you already acknowledge as masterful.

Of course, a single book can gather only a small portion of the great new dark fiction being published each year in anthologies, collections, and periodicals on paper with ink or in pixels on screens. This is far from *all* "the best" published in one year.

To repeat what should be obvious: Anthologies with titles including phrases like *Year's Best*, *Best of*, *Best (fill in the blank)* are what they are. When compiling such a volume, no editor can completely fulfill the inference of the title. Fiction is not a race to be won, there are no absolutes with which to measure it. Yet those of us who edit such anthologies exert tremendous effort in a genuine attempt to offer books worthy of their grandiose monikers. Decisions are arrived at with sincere intention, but personal taste is, of course, involved, and—like it or not—compromises must be made.

One compromise I made this year was to not include what I felt was certainly one of the finest dark stories of last year ("The Adakian Eagle" by Bradley Denton) because my fellow Prime Books editor, Rich Horton, chose it first. Rich, infinitely more organized than I, invariably meets his deadline long before I do, and announced his table of contents before I did. Fair and square! But since his *The Year's Best Science Fiction and Fantasy* and my *The Year's Best Dark Fantasy and Horror* are companion volumes published at same time, I thought it best not to duplicate.

And, with timeliness in mind, for next year's volume, it is best to make sure any recommendations or material published in 2012 reach me by February 1, 2013—*preferably sooner.* Information on previous volumes of the series can be found on the Prime Books website (www.prime-books. com) and the current "Call for Submissions" can be found at www.prime-books.com/call-for-submissions-years-best-dark-fantasy-horror-2013. You can e-mail me at paula@prime-books.com.

Paula Guran
April 2012

She knew she had been here before. It was the strongest wave of déjà vu she'd ever felt, a sickening collision between two types of knowledge: she knew it was impossible, yet she remembered . . .

OBJECTS IN DREAMS MAY BE CLOSER THAN THEY APPEAR

Lisa Tuttle

Since we divorced twenty years ago, my ex-husband Michael and I rarely met, but we'd always kept in touch. I wish now that we hadn't. This whole terrible thing began with a link he sent me by e-mail with the comment, "Can you believe how much the old homestead has changed?"

Clicking on the link took me to a view of the cottage we had owned, long ago, for about three years—most of our brief marriage.

Although I recognized it, there were many changes. No longer a semi-detached, it had been merged with the house next-door, and also extended. It was, I thought, what we might have done ourselves given the money, time, planning permission and, most vitally, next-door neighbors willing to sell us their home. Instead, we had fallen out with them (they took our offer to buy as a personal affront) and poured too much money into so-called improvements, the work expensively and badly done by local builders who all seemed to be related by marriage if not blood to the people next-door.

Just looking at the front of the house on the computer screen gave me a tight, anxious feeling in my chest. What had possessed Michael to send it to me? And why had he even looked for it? Surely he wasn't nostalgic for what I recalled as one of the unhappiest periods of my life?

At that point, I should have clicked away from the picture, put it out of my mind and settled down to work, but, I don't know why, instead of closing the tab, I moved on down the road and began to discover what else in our old neighborhood was different.

I'd heard about Google Earth's "Street View" function, but I'd never used it before, so it took me a little while to figure out how to use it. At first all the zooming in and out, stopping and starting and twirling around made me queasy, but once I got to grips with it, I found this form of virtual tourism quite addictive.

But I was startled by how different the present reality appeared from my memory of it. I did not recognize our old village at all, could find nothing I remembered except the war memorial—and that seemed to be in the wrong place. Where was the shop, the primary school, the pub? Had they all been altered beyond recognition, all turned into houses? There were certainly many more of those than there had been in the 1980s. It was while I was searching in vain for the unmistakable landmark that had always alerted us that the next turning would be our road, a commercial property that I could not imagine anyone converting into a desirable residence—the Little Chef—that it dawned on me what had happened.

Of course. The Okehampton bypass had been built, and altered the route of the A30. Our little village was one of several no longer bisected by the main road into Cornwall, and without hordes of holiday-makers forced to crawl past, the fast food outlet and petrol station no longer made economic sense.

Once I understood how the axis of the village had changed, I found the new primary school near an estate of new homes. There were also a couple of new (to me) shops, an Indian restaurant, wine bar, an Oriental rug gallery, and a riding school. The increase in population had pushed our sleepy old village slightly up-market. I should not have been surprised, but I suppose I was an urban snob, imagining that anyone living so deep in the country must be several decades behind the times. But I could see that even the smallest of houses boasted a satellite dish, and they probably all had broadband internet connections, too. Even as I was laughing at the garden gnomes on display in front of a neat yellow bungalow, someone behind those net curtains might be looking at my own terraced house in Bristol, horrified by what the unrestrained growth of ivy was doing to the brickwork.

Curious to know how my home appeared to others, I typed in my own address, and enjoyed a stroll around the neighborhood without leaving my desk. I checked out a few less-familiar addresses, including Michael's current abode, which I had never seen. So *that* was Goring-on-Sea!

At last I dragged myself away and wrote catalogue copy, had a long talk with one of our suppliers, and dealt with various other bits and pieces before knocking off for the day. Neither of us fancied going out, and we'd been consuming too many pizzas lately, so David whipped up an old favorite from the minimal supplies in the kitchen cupboard: spaghetti with marmite, tasty enough when accompanied by a few glasses of Merlot.

My husband David and I marketed children's apparel and accessories under the name "Cheeky Chappies." It was exactly the sort of business I had imagined setting up in my rural idyll, surrounded by the patter of little feet, filling orders between changing nappies and making delicious, sustaining soups from the organic vegetables Michael planned to grow.

None of that came to pass, not even the vegetables. Michael did what he could, but we needed his income as a sales rep to survive, so he was nearly always on the road, which left me to take charge of everything at home, supervising the building work in between applying for jobs and grants, drawing up unsatisfactory business plans, and utterly failing in my mission to become pregnant.

Hard times can bring a couple together, but that is not how it worked for us. I grew more and more miserable, convinced I was a failure both as a woman and as a potential CEO. It did not help that Michael was away so much, and although it was not his fault and we needed the money, I grew resentful at having to spend so much time and energy servicing a house I'd never really wanted.

He'd drawn me into *his* dream of an old-fashioned life in the country, and then slipped out of sharing the major part of it with me. At the weekend, with him there, it was different, but most of the time I felt lonely and bored, lumbered with too many chores and not enough company, far from friends and family, cut off from the entertainments and excitement of urban existence.

Part of the problem was the house—not at all what we'd dreamed of, but cheap enough, and with potential to be transformed into something better. We'd been jumped into buying it by circumstances. Once Michael had accepted a very good offer on his flat (*our* flat, he called it, but it was entirely his investment) a new urgency entered into our formerly relaxed house-hunting expeditions. I had loved those weekends away from the city, staying in B&Bs and rooms over village pubs, every moment rich with possibility and new discoveries. I would have been happy to go on for months, driving down to the west country, looking at properties and imagining what our life might be like in this house or that, but suddenly there was a time limit, and this was the most serious decision of our lives, and not just a bit of fun.

The happiest part of my first marriage now seems to have been compressed into half a dozen weekends, maybe a few more, as we traveled around, the inside of the car like an enchanted bubble filled with love and laughter, jokes and personal revelations and music. I loved everything we saw. Even the most impossible, ugly houses were fascinating, providing material for discussing the strangeness of other people's lives. Yet although I was interested in them all, nothing we viewed actually tempted me. Somehow, I couldn't imagine I would ever really live in the country—certainly not the practicalities of it. I expected our life to continue like this, work in the city punctuated by these mini-holidays, until we found the perfect house, at which point I'd stop working and start producing babies and concentrate on buying their clothes and toys and attractive soft furnishings and decorations for the house as if money was not and could never be a problem.

And then one day, traveling between the viewing of one imperfect property to look at another which would doubtless be equally unsatisfactory in its own unique way, Blondie in the cassette player singing about hanging on the telephone, we came to an abrupt halt. Michael stopped the car at the top of a hill, on one of those narrow, hedge-lined lanes that aren't even wide enough for two normal sized cars to pass each other without the sort of jockeying and breath-holding maneuvers that in my view are acceptable only when parallel parking. I thought he must have seen another car approaching, and taken evasive action, although the road ahead looked clear.

"What's wrong?"

"Wrong? Nothing. It's perfect. Don't you think it's perfect?"

I saw what he was looking at through a gap in the hedge: a distant view of an old-fashioned, white-washed, thatch-roofed cottage nestled in one of those deep, green valleys that in Devonshire are called coombs. It was a pretty sight, like a Victorian painting you might get on a box of old-fashioned chocolates, or a card for Mother's Day. For some reason, it made my throat tighten and I had to blink back sentimental tears, feeling a strong yearning, not so much for that specific house as for what it seemed to promise: safety, stability, family. I could see myself there, decades in the future, surrounded by children and grandchildren, dressed in clothes from Laura Ashley.

"It's very sweet," I said, embarrassed by how emotional I felt.

"It's exactly what we've been looking for," he said.

"It's probably not for sale."

"All it takes is the right offer." That was his theory: not so much that everything had its price, as that he could achieve whatever goal he set himself. It was more about attitude than money.

"But what if they feel the same way about it as we do?"

"Who are 'they'?"

"The people that live there."

"But you feel it? What I feel? That it's where we want to live?"

I thought about the children—grandchildren, even!—in their quaint floral smocks—and nodded.

He kissed me. "All right!" he cried, joyously, releasing the hand-brake. "Let's go!"

"Do you even know how to get there?"

"You've got the map. Direct me."

My heart sank. Although I had the road atlas open in my lap, I never expected to have to use it. Michael did not understand that not everyone was like him, able to look at lines and colored patches on a page and relate them to the real world. His sense of direction seemed magical to me. Even when the sun was out, I had no idea which way was north. On a map, it was at the top. In the world, I had to guess at right or left or straight ahead.

"I don't know where we are *now*," I objected. "We need to stop and figure it out."

Fortunately, we were approaching a village, and it offered parking space in front of the church, so that was easily done. Michael had no problem identifying which of the wriggly white lines was the road we'd been on, and where we'd stopped and seen the house, and with that and the location of the village we were in, he was able to perform some sort of mental triangulation that enabled him to stab a forefinger down on a blank place within the loops of spaghetti representing the nameless country roads. "There," he said with certainty. "It's got to be there. An OS map would show us exactly, but anyway, it shouldn't be hard to find. We'll just drive around until we spot it."

We drove around for the next two or three hours. Round and round and round. The same route, again and again, up and down the narrow roads, some of them like tunnels, they were so deep beneath the high-banked hedges, until I was dizzy, like a leaf swept away in a stream. Deep within those dark green lanes there was nothing to see except the road ahead, the deep, loamy earth with roots bursting through on either side, and the branches of trees overhead, through which I caught pale, gleaming shards of sky. The house remained hidden from view except when Michael drove up to higher ground, and found one of the few places where it was possible to see through, or over, the thick, ancient hedgerows that shielded nearly every piece of land from the road.

There it was, so close it must be just beyond the next curve of the road, yet forever out of our reach. The faint curl of smoke from the chimney inspired another yearning tug as I imagined sitting cozy and warm with my dear husband beside a crackling fire. I could almost smell the wood-smoke, and, closer, hot chocolate steaming in a mug.

I was hungry, thirsty and tired of stomping my foot down on an imaginary brake every time we met another car. There was a chill in the air as afternoon began to fade towards evening, and I wondered if we'd be able to get lunch anywhere, and made the point aloud.

He was impatient with my weakness. "We'll get something afterwards.

Surely they'll invite us in for a cup of tea when we get there. They can't have many visitors!"

"If we could find that house by driving around, we would have found it already. You've already taken every turning, and we've seen every farmyard and tumble-down shed and occupied house in the whole valley."

"Obviously we have missed one."

"Please, darling. It'll be dark soon. Look, we need to try something else. Why not go to Okehampton and ask an estate agent?"

"So now you're assuming the house is for sale."

"No. I assume it was for sale some time in the past and will be again in the future, and it is their business to know the local market. It's a beautiful place. We can't be the first people to have asked about it."

"No, but we will be the ones who get it!"

No one knew the house in the offices of the first two estate agents, and the man in the third one also stated there was no such cottage in the valley where we claimed to have seen it—that area was all woods and fields, he said—but there was something in his manner as he tried to fob us off with pictures and details of ever more expensive houses located twenty miles away that made me think he was hiding something, so we persisted, until, finally, he suggested we go see Mr. Yeo.

Mr. Yeo was a semi-retired property surveyor who had been in the business since before the War, and knew everything worth knowing about every house in this part of Devon. He lived still in the village where he had been born—Marystow—a name we both recognized, as it was one of the places we'd passed through a dozen times on our futile quest. So off we went to find him.

He was an elderly man who seemed friendly, happy to welcome us in to his home, until Michael revealed what we had come about, and then, abruptly, the atmosphere changed, and he began to usher us out again. The house was not for sale, we would not be able to visit it, there was no point in further discussion.

"But surely you can give us the name of the owners? An address to write to?"

"There b'ain't owners. He's not there."

I thought at first "he" referred to the owner, unused to the way that older inhabitants of rural Devon spoke of inanimate objects as "he" rather than "it." But Mr. Yeo made his meaning clear before sending us on our way: the perfectly desirable house we'd seen, nestled in a deep green coomb, did not exist. It was an illusion. We were not the first to have seen it; there were old folk and travelers' tales about such a house, glimpsed from a hilltop, nestled in the next valley; most often glimpsed late in the day, seemingly near enough that the viewer thought he could reach it before sunset, and rest the night there.

But no matter how long they walked, or what direction they tried, they could never reach it.

"Have you ever seen it?"

Mr. Yeo scowled, and would not say. "'Tis bad luck to see 'im," he informed us. "Worse, much worse, to try to find 'im. You'm better go 'ome and forget about him. 'Tis not a good place for you'm."

Michael thanked the old man politely, but as we left, I could feel something simmering away in him. But it was not anger, only laughter, which exploded once we were back in our car. He thought Mr. Yeo was a ridiculous old man, and didn't buy his story for an instant. Maybe there was some optical illusion involved—that might explain why we hadn't been able to find the house where he'd expected it to be—but that was a real house that we'd seen, and someday we would find it.

Yet we never did. Not even when Michael bought the largest scale Ordnance Survey map of the area, the one for walkers that included every foot-path, building and ruin, could we find evidence that it had ever existed. Unless he'd been wrong about the location, and it was really in a more distant coomb, made to look closer by some trick of air and light . . . Even after we moved to Devon—buying the wrong house—we came no closer to solving the mystery. I think Michael might have caught the occasional glimpse of it in the distance, but I never saw it again.

I shouldn't pretend I didn't know what made Michael's thoughts return to our old home in Devon, because I had been dreaming about it myself, for the same reason: the Wheaton-Bakers Ruby Anniversary Celebration. We'd both been invited—with our respective new spouses, of course—to attend it at their house in Tavistock in four weeks' time. I didn't know about Michael, but I had not been back to Devon in over twenty years; not since we'd sold the house. The Wheaton-Bakers were the only friends from that period of my life with whom I'd kept in touch, although we saw each other no more often than Michael and I did.

I'd been pleased by the invitation. The party was in early October. David and I had booked a room in an inn on Dartmoor, and looked forward to a relaxing weekend away, with a couple of leg-stretching, mind-clearing rambles on Dartmoor book-ending the Saturday night festivities. And yet, although I looked forward to it, there was also a faint uneasiness in my mind attached to the idea of seeing Michael again, back in our old haunts;

an uneasiness I did not so much as hint at to David because I could not explain it. It was irrational and unfair, I thought. My first marriage had not worked out, but both of us, or neither, were responsible for that, and that failure had been come to terms with and was long in the past. There was no unfinished business between us.

When the weekend of the party arrived, David was ill. It was probably only a twenty-four-hour bug (it was going around, according to our next-door neighbor, a teacher) but it meant he couldn't consider going anywhere farther than the bathroom.

I should have stayed home and tended to him, like a good wife—that is what I wish I had done. But he insisted I go. The Wheaton-Bakers were my friends. They would be sorry not to see me. We wouldn't get our money back for the hotel room—that had been an Internet bargain. And he didn't need to be tended. He intended to sleep as much as possible, just lie in bed and sweat it out.

So I went. And I did enjoy myself. It was a lovely party; the Wheaton-Bakers were just as nice as I remembered, and they introduced me to other friendly, interesting people, so I never felt lonely or out of place for a moment. Michael was there, but he'd been seated at a different table, and struck up conversations with a different set of people, so although we'd exchanged greetings, we'd hardly done more than that. It was only as I was preparing to leave that he cornered me.

"Hey, you're not leaving!"

"'fraid so."

"But we've hardly spoken! You're driving back to Bristol tonight?"

"No, of course not." I told him where I was staying.

"Mm, very posh! I'm just up the road, nylon sheets and a plastic shower stall. Want to meet and have lunch somewhere tomorrow?"

I was happy to agree. We exchanged phone numbers, and he offered to pick me up at my hotel at ten. "If that's not too early? It'll give us time to drive around a bit, see how much the scenery has changed, before deciding what we want to do."

There was a familiar glint in his eye, and I was suddenly certain he meant to take me back to look at our old house, and maybe one or two other significant sites from our marriage. I didn't know why he felt the need to revisit the past like that—the past was over and done with, as far as I was concerned—but I didn't say anything. If he needed to go back and see with his own eyes how much time had passed, to understand that we were no longer the people who had fallen in love with each other, then perhaps I owed him my supportive, uncomplaining companionship.

Anyway, I thought it would be more fun than going for a walk by myself or driving straight back home.

The next morning, I checked out, and left my car in the car park. There was no question that we'd go in his: I remembered too well that he'd always disliked being a passenger. His car was better, anyway: a silver Audi with that new-car smell inside, soft leather seats and an impressive Sat-Nav system. Something by Mozart issued softly from hidden speakers as we he headed down the A386 before leaving the moor for the sunken lanes I remembered, winding deep into a leaf-shadowed coomb.

"Remember this?" he asked, as the car raced silently along. It was a smoother ride than in the old days.

"I'm glad they haven't dug up all the hedgerows," I said. "I was afraid Devon might have changed a lot more."

He frowned, dissatisfied with my answer. "Didn't you click on that link I sent you?"

"Yes, I did. I saw our old house—didn't I send a reply?"

He shrugged that off. "I thought you might have explored a bit more widely. Not just the village, not just the street view, but moving up and out, looking at the satellite pictures."

"It's a busy time of the year for us, with Christmas coming. I don't have much time to play around on the Internet. Although I'm sure it's very interesting."

"It's more than just 'interesting.' You can see things that aren't on other maps. The aerial shots—do you remember how we had to go up to the top of the hill to see it?"

I understood. "You're not talking about our house."

"You know what I'm talking about." He touched the screen of his navigation system and a calm, clear female voice said, "You are approaching a crossroads. Prepare to turn right."

"You found it?" I asked him, amazed. "How?"

"Turn right. Follow the road."

"Satellite view on Google. I zoomed in as much as I could—it wasn't easy to get a fix on it. Street View's no good—it's not on a road. But it's there all right; maybe not in exactly the place we kept looking for it. Anyway, I have the coordinates now, and I've put them into my system here, and—it will take us there." He grinned like a proud, clever child.

"How, if it's not on a road?"

"Prepare to turn left. Turn left."

"It will take us as close as it can. After that we'll walk. Those are good, sturdy boots you have on."

"Take the first turning to the right."

"Well done, Sherlock," I said. "Just fancy if we'd had GPS back in those days—we'd have found it, and . . . do you think they'd have accepted our offer?"

"Bear left. At the next crossroads, turn right."

Despite the smoothness of the ride, as we turned and turned again— sometimes forced to stop and back up in a *pas-de-deux* with another Sunday driver—I began to feel queasy, like in the old days, and then another sort of unease crept in.

"Haven't we been along here already? We must be going in circles," I said.

"And when did you develop a sense of direction?"

"Prepare to turn right. Turn right."

The last turn was the sharpest, and took us off the road entirely, through an opening in a hedge so narrow that I flinched at the unpleasant noise of cut branches scraping the car, and then we were in a field.

There was no road or path ahead of us, not even a track, just the faint indication of old ruts where at some point a tractor or other farm vehicle might have gone, and even they soon ended.

"Make a U-turn when possible. Return to a marked road."

Michael stopped the car. "So that's as far as she'll take us. We'll have to rely on my own internal GPS the rest of the way."

We got out. He changed his brown loafers for a pair of brilliant white sports shoes that looked as if they'd never been worn, took an OS map out of the glove-box, and showed me the red X he had marked on an otherwise blank spot. "And this is where we are now."

"Why isn't it on the map?"

He shrugged. I persisted. "You must have thought about it."

He shrugged again and sighed. "Well, you know, there are places consid- ered too sensitive, of military importance, something to do with national security, that you're not allowed to take pictures or even write about. There's an airfield in Norfolk, and a whole village on Salisbury Plain—"

"They're not on maps?"

"Not on any maps. And those are just the two examples I happen to know. There must be more. Maybe this house, or the entire coomb, was used for covert ops in the war, or is owned by MI5, used as a safe house or something."

My skin prickled with unease. "Maybe we shouldn't go there."

"Are you kidding? You're not going to wimp out on me now!"

"If it's so secret that it's against the law—"

"Do you see any 'No Trespassing' signs?" He waved his arms at the empty field around us. "It's a free country; we can walk where we like."

I took a deep breath, and thought about that airfield in Norfolk. I was pretty sure I knew the place he meant; it was surrounded by barbed wire fences, decorated with signs prohibiting parking and picture-taking on the grounds of national security. It was about as secret as the Post Office Tower. I nodded my agreement.

It was a good day for walking, dry and with a fresh, invigorating breeze countering the warmth of the sun. For about fifteen minutes we just walked, not speaking, and I was feeling very relaxed when I heard him say, "There it is."

Just ahead of us, the land dropped away unexpectedly steeply, and we stopped and stood gazing down into a deep, narrow, wooded valley. Amid the turning leaves the golden brown of the thatched roof blended in, and shadows dappled the whitewashed walls below with natural camouflage. If we hadn't been looking for it, we might not have seen it, but now, as I stared, it seemed to gain in clarity, as if someone had turned up the resolution on a screen. I saw a wisp of smoke rise from the chimney, and caught the faint, sweet fragrance of burning wood.

Michael was moving about in an agitated way, and it took me a few moments to realize he was searching for the best route down. "This way," he called. "Give me your hand; it's a bit tricky at first, but I then I think it should be easier."

I was suddenly nervous. "I don't think we should. There's someone there."

"So? They'll invite us in. We'll ask how long they've had the place and if they'd consider selling."

I saw that the notion of an MI5 safe house was far from his mind, if he had ever believed it. He wasn't even slightly afraid, and struggled to comprehend my reason for wanting to turn back.

"Look, if you want to wait for me here . . . "

I couldn't let him go by himself. I checked that my phone was on, and safely zipped into my pocket, and then I let him help me down to the first ledge, and the one after that. Then it got easier, although there was never anything as clear as a path, and on my own I'm certain I would have been lost, since my instinct, every time, was to go in a direction different from his. He really could hold a map in his head. At last we emerged from a surprisingly dense wood into a clearing from which we could see a windowless side wall.

I fell back and followed him around towards the front. Pebbles rolled and crunched gently underfoot on the path to the front door. I wondered if he had a plan, and what he would say to whoever answered the door: was he really going to pretend we were interested in buying?

Then I looked up and as I took in the full frontal view, I knew I had been here before. It was the strongest wave of *déjà vu* I'd ever felt, a sickening collision between two types of knowledge: I knew it was impossible, yet I remembered this visit.

The memory was unclear, but frightening. Somehow, I had come here before. When my knock at the door had gone unanswered, I'd peeked through that window on the right, and saw something that made me run away in terror.

I could not remember anything of what I had seen; only the fear it had inspired was still powerful.

Michael knocked on the door, then glanced over his shoulder, impatient with me for hanging back.

I wanted to warn him, but of what? What could I say? I was in the grip of a fear I knew to be irrational. I managed to move a little closer to Michael and the door, telling myself that nothing could compel me to look through that window.

We waited a little while, but even after Michael knocked again, more loudly, almost pounding, there was no reply. I relaxed a little, thinking we were going to get away with it, but when I spoke of leaving, he insisted, "Not until I find out who lives here, what it's all about. There is someone here—I can see a light—look, through that window—"

I moved back; I wouldn't look.

"I think I can smell cooking. They're probably in the kitchen. Maybe a bit deaf. I'm going to try the back door. You coming? Suit yourself."

I didn't want to stay, but wanted even less to follow him around the back, so I waited, wrapping my arms around myself, feeling a chill. The sun didn't strike so warmly in this leafy hollow. I checked my phone for the time and was startled to see how much of the afternoon was gone. I wondered if I should call David to warn him I'd be late, but decided to wait for Michael.

I didn't like to keep checking the time because it made me more nervous, but at least five minutes had passed when I felt I had no choice but to walk around to the back of the house to look for him.

I had no sense of *déjà vu* there; I was certain I'd never seen the peeling black paint that covered the solidly shut back door, or the small windows screened by yellowish, faded curtains that made it impossible to see inside.

"Michael?" I didn't like the weak, wavering sound of my voice, and made myself call out more loudly, firmly, but there was no reply. Nothing happened. I knocked as hard as I could on the back door, dislodging a few flakes of old paint, and as I waited I listened to the sound of leaves rustling in the wind; every once in awhile one would fall. I felt like screaming, but that would have been bloody stupid. Either he had heard me or he hadn't. Either he was capable of reply—could he be hiding just to tease me?—or he wasn't. And what was I going to do about it?

As I walked back around to the front of the house I was assailed by the memory of what I had seen when I looked through the window the last time I was here—if that had ever happened. I'd seen a man's foot and leg—I'd seen that there was someone inside the house, just sitting, not answering my knock, and the sight of some stranger's foot had frightened me so badly that I'd run away, and then repressed the memory of the entire incident.

Now I realized it must have been a dream that I recalled. It had that pointless, sinister atmosphere of a bad dream. Unfortunately, it now seemed like a precognitive dream.

Nothing had changed in front of the house. I got out my phone and entered the number Michael had given me. As I heard it ringing in my ear, I heard the familiar notes from *The William Tell Overture* sounding from inside the house. I clenched my teeth and waited. When the call went to his voicemail, I ended it and hit re-dial. Muffled by distance, the same tinny, pounding ringtone played inside the house, small but growing in volume until, once again, it was cut off by the voicemail program.

I knew what I would see if I looked through the window, so I didn't look. I wanted to run away, but I didn't know where to go. It would be dark soon. I had to do something.

The front door opened easily. Tense, I darted my gaze about, fearful of ambush although the place felt empty. To my right, I could see into a small, dark sitting room where an old man sat, or slumped, in an armchair.

He was a very, very old man, almost hairless, his skin like yellowed parchment, and appeared to have been dead for some time. It would have been his foot I would have seen if I'd looked through the window: his feet in brand new, brilliantly white sports shoes. But even as I recognized the rest of the clothes—polo shirt, jeans, soft gray hooded jacket, even the phone and car keys in his pockets—I clung to the notion of a vicious trick, that someone had stolen Michael's clothes to dress an old man's corpse. How could the vigorous fifty-eight-year-old that I'd seen a few minutes ago have aged and died so rapidly?

I know now that it is what's left of Michael, and that there is no one else here.

I am not able to leave. I can open the door, but as soon as I step through, I find myself entering again. I don't know how many times I did that, before giving up. I don't know how long I have been here; it seems like a few days, at most, but when I look in the mirror I can tell by my hair that it must be two months or more.

There's plenty of food in the kitchen, no problems with plumbing or electricity, and for entertainment, besides all the books, there's an old video-player, and stacks of videos, as well as an old phonograph and a good collection of music. I say "good collection" because it might have been planned to please Michael and me, at least as we were in the eighties.

Having found a ream of paper in the bottom drawer of the desk in the other parlor (the room where Michael *isn't*) I decided to write down what has happened, just in case someone comes here someday, and finds my body as I found his. It gives me something to do, even though I fear it is a pointless exercise.

While exploring the house earlier—yesterday, or the day before—I found evidence of mice—fortunately, only in one place, in the other sitting room. There were droppings there, and a nest made of nibbled paper, as if the mouse had devoted all its energy to the destruction of a single stack of paper. One piece was left just large enough for me to read a few words in faded ink, and recognize Michael's handwriting, but there was not enough for me to make sense of whatever he was trying to say.

⊰⊱

*There were rumors that there was a refugee camp for homeless
outside of Toronto. So they were walking to Detroit . . .*

AFTER THE APOCALYPSE

Maureen McHugh

Jane puts out the sleeping bags in the backyard of the empty house by the
toolshed. She has a lock and hasp and an old hand drill that they can use to
lock the toolshed from the inside, but it's too hot to sleep in there, and there
haven't been many people on the road. Better to sleep outside. Franny has
been talking a mile a minute. Usually by the end of the day she is tired from
walking—they both are—and quiet. But this afternoon she's gotten on the
subject of her friend Samantha. She's musing on if Samantha has left town
like they did. "They're probably still there, because they had a really nice
house in, like, a low-crime area, and Samantha's father has a really good
job. When you have money like that, maybe you can totally afford a security
system or something. Their house has five bedrooms and the basement isn't
a basement, it's a living room, because the house is kind of on a little hill,
and although the front of the basement is underground, you can walk right
out the back."

Jane says, "That sounds nice."

"You could see a horse farm behind them. People around them were rich,
but not like, on-TV rich, exactly."

Jane puts her hands on her hips and looks down the line of backyards.

"Do you think there's anything in there?" Franny asks, meaning the
house, a '60s suburban ranch. Franny is thirteen, and empty houses frighten
her. But she doesn't like to be left alone, either. What she wants is for Jane to
say that they can eat one of the tuna pouches.

"Come on, Franny. We're gonna run out of tuna long before we get to
Canada."

"I know," Franny says sullenly.

"You can stay here."

"No, I'll go with you."

God, sometimes Jane would do anything to get five minutes away from

Franny. She loves her daughter, really, but Jesus. "Come on, then," Jane says.

There is an old square concrete patio and a sliding glass door. The door is dirty. Jane cups her hand to shade her eyes and looks inside. It's dark and hard to see. No power, of course. Hasn't been power in any of the places they've passed through in more than two months. Air conditioning. And a bed with a mattress and box springs. What Jane wouldn't give for air conditioning and a bed. Clean sheets.

The neighborhood seems like a good one. Unless they find a big group to camp with, Jane gets them off the freeway at the end of the day. There was fighting in the neighborhood, and at the end of the street, several houses are burned out. Then there are lots of houses with windows smashed out. But the fighting petered out. Some of the houses are still lived in. This house had all its windows intact, but the garage door was standing open and the garage was empty except for dead leaves. Electronic garage door. The owners pulled out and left and didn't bother to close the door behind them. Seemed to Jane that the overgrown backyard with its toolshed would be a good place to sleep.

Jane can see her silhouette in the dirty glass, and her hair is a snarled, curly, tangled rat's nest. She runs her fingers through it, and they snag. She'll look for a scarf or something inside. She grabs the handle and yanks up, hard, trying to get the old slider off track. It takes a couple of tries, but she's had a lot of practice in the last few months.

Inside, the house is trashed. The kitchen has been turned upside-down, and silverware, utensils, drawers, broken plates, flour, and stuff are everywhere. She picks her way across, a can opener skittering under her foot with a clatter.

Franny gives a little startled shriek.

"Fuck!" Jane says. "Don't do that!" The canned food is long gone.

"I'm sorry," Franny says. "It scared me!"

"We're gonna starve to death if we don't keep scavenging," Jane says.

"I know!" Franny says.

"Do you know how fucking far it is to Canada?"

"I can't help it if it startled me!"

Maybe if she were a better cook, she'd be able to scrape up the flour and make something, but it's all mixed in with dirt and stuff, and every time she's tried to cook something over an open fire it's either been raw or black or, most often, both—blackened on the outside and raw on the inside.

Jane checks all the cupboards anyway. Sometimes people keep food in different places. Once they found one of those decorating icing tubes and wrote words on each other's hands and licked them off.

Franny screams, not a startled shriek but a real scream.

Jane whirls around, and there's a guy in the family room with a tire iron. "What are you doing here?" he yells.

Jane grabs a can opener from the floor, one of those heavy jobbers, and wings it straight at his head. He's too slow to get out of the way, and it nails him in the forehead. Jane has winged a lot of things at boyfriends over the years. It's a skill. She throws a couple of more things from the floor, anything she can find, while the guy is yelling, "Fuck! Fuck!" and trying to ward off the barrage.

Then she and Franny are out the back door and running.

Fucking squatter! She hates squatters! If it's the homeowner they tend to make the place more like a fortress, and you can tell not to try to go in. Squatters try to keep a low profile. Franny is in front of her, running like a rabbit, and they are out the gate and headed up the suburban street. Franny knows the drill, and at the next corner she turns, but by then it's clear that no one's following them.

"Okay," Jane pants. "Okay, stop, stop."

Franny stops. She's a skinny adolescent now—she used to be chubby, but she's lean and tan with all their walking. She's wearing a pair of falling-apart pink sneakers and a tank top with oil smudges from when they had to climb over a truck tipped sideways on an overpass. She's still flat-chested. Her eyes are big in her face. Jane puts her hands on her knees and draws a shuddering breath.

"We're okay," she says. It is gathering dusk in this Missouri town. In a while, streetlights will come on, unless someone has systematically shot them out. Solar power still works. "We'll wait a bit and then go back and get our stuff when it's dark."

"No!" Franny bursts into sobs. "We can't!"

Jane is at her wit's end. Rattled from the squatter. Tired of being the strong one. "We've got to! You want to lose everything we've got? You want to die? Goddamn it, Franny! I can't take this anymore!"

"That guy's there!" Franny sobs out. "We can't go back! We can't!"

"Your cell phone is there," Jane says. A mean dig. The cell phone doesn't work, of course. Even if they still somehow had service, if service actually exists, they haven't been anywhere with electricity to charge it in weeks. But Franny still carries it in the hope that she can get a charge and call her friends. Seventh graders are apparently surgically attached to their phones. Not that she acts even like a seventh grader anymore. The longer they are on the road, the younger Franny acts.

This isn't the first time that they've run into a squatter. Squatters are cowards. The guy doesn't have a gun, and he's not going to go out after dark. Franny has no spine, takes after her asshole of a father. Jane ran away from home and got all the way to Pasadena, California, when she was a year older than Franny. When she was fourteen, she was a decade older than Franny. Lived on the street for six weeks, begging spare change on the same route that the Rose Parade took. It had been scary, but it had been a blast, as well. Taught her to stand on her own two feet, which Franny wasn't going to be able to do when she was twenty. Thirty, at this rate.

"You're hungry, aren't you?" Jane said, merciless. "You want to go looking in these houses for something to eat?" Jane points around them. The houses all have their front doors broken into, open like little mouths.

Franny shakes her head.

"Stop crying. I'm going to go check some of them out. You wait here."

"Mom! Don't leave me!" Franny wails.

Jane is still shaken from the squatter. But they need food. And they need their stuff. There is seven hundred dollars sewn inside the lining of Jane's sleeping bag. And someone has to keep them alive. It's obviously going to be her.

Things didn't exactly all go at once. First there were rolling brownouts and lots of people unemployed. Jane had been making a living working at a place that sold furniture. She started as a salesperson, but she was good at helping people on what colors to buy, what things went together, what fabrics to pick for custom pieces. Eventually they made her a service associate, a person who was kind of like an interior decorator, sort of. She had an eye. She'd grown up in a nice suburb and had seen nice things. She knew what people wanted. Her boss kept telling her a little less eye makeup would be a good idea, but people liked what she suggested and recommended her to their friends even if her boss didn't like her eye makeup.

She was thinking of starting a decorating business, although she was worried that she didn't know about some of the stuff decorators did. On TV they were always tearing down walls and redoing fireplaces. So she put it off. Then there was the big Disney World attack where a kazillion people died because of a dirty bomb, and then the economy really tanked. She knew that business was dead and she was going to get laid off, but before that happened, someone torched the furniture place where she was working. Her boyfriend at the time was a cop, so he still had a job, even though half the city was unemployed. She and Franny were all right compared to a lot of people. She didn't like not having her own money, but she wasn't exactly having to call her mother in Pennsylvania and eat crow and offer to come home.

So she sat on the balcony of their condo and smoked and looked through her old decorating magazines, and Franny watched television in the room behind her. People started showing up on the sidewalks. They had trash bags full of stuff. Sometimes they were alone; sometimes there would be whole families. Sometimes they'd have cars and they'd sleep in them, but gas was getting to almost ten dollars a gallon, when the gas stations could get it. Pete, the boyfriend, told her that the cops didn't even patrol much anymore because of the gas problem. More and more of the people on the sidewalk looked to be walking.

"Where are they coming from?" Franny asked.

"Down south. Houston, El Paso, anywhere within a hundred miles of the border." Pete said. "Border's gone to shit. Mexico doesn't have food, but the drug cartels have lots of guns, and they're coming across to take what they can get. They say it's like a war zone down there."

"Why don't the police take care of them?" Franny asked.

"Well, Francisca," Pete said—he was good with Franny, Jane had to give him that—"sometimes there are just too many of them for the police down there. And they've got kinds of guns that the police aren't allowed to have."

"What about you?" Franny asked.

"It's different up here," Pete said. "That's why we've got refugees here. Because it's safe here."

"They're not *refugees*," Jane said. Refugees were, like, people in Africa. These were just regular people. Guys in T-shirts with the names of rock bands on them. Women sitting in the front seats of Taurus station wagons, doing their hair in the rearview mirrors. Kids asleep in the back seat or running up and down the street shrieking and playing. Just people.

"Well, what do you want to call them?" Pete asked.

Then the power started going out, more and more often. Pete's shifts got longer although he didn't always get paid.

There were gunshots in the street, and Pete told Jane not to sit out on the balcony. He boarded up the French doors and it was as if they were living in a cave. The refugees started thinning out. Jane rarely saw them leaving, but each day there were fewer and fewer of them on the sidewalk. Pete said they were headed north.

Then the fires started on the east side of town. The power went out and stayed out. Pete didn't come home until the next day, and he slept a couple of hours and then when back out to work. The air tasted of smoke—not the pleasant, clean smell of wood smoke, but a garbagey smoke. Franny complained that it made her sick to her stomach.

After Pete didn't come home for four days, it was pretty clear to Jane that he wasn't coming back. Jane put Franny in the car, packed everything she could think of that might be useful. They got about 120 miles away, far enough that the burning city was no longer visible, although the sunset was a vivid and blistering red. Then they ran out of gas, and there was no more to be had.

There were rumors that there was a refugee camp for homeless outside of Toronto. So they were walking to Detroit.

Franny says, "You can't leave me! You can't leave me!"

"Do you want to go scavenge with me?" Jane says.

Franny sobs so hard she seems to be hyperventilating. She grabs her mother's arms, unable to do anything but hold onto her. Jane peels her off, but Franny keeps grabbing, clutching, sobbing. It's making Jane crazy. Franny's fear is contagious, and if she lets it get in her, she'll be too afraid to do anything. She can feel it deep inside her, that thing that has always threatened her, to give in, to stop doing and pushing and scheming, to become like her useless, useless father puttering around the house vacantly, bottles hidden in the garage, the basement, everywhere.

"GET OFF ME!" she screams at Franny, but Franny is sobbing and clutching.

She slaps Franny. Franny throws up, precious little, water and crackers from breakfast. Then she sits down in the grass, just useless.

Jane marches off into the first house.

She's lucky. The garage is closed up and there are three cans of soup on a shelf. One of them is cream of mushroom, but luckily, Franny liked cream of mushroom when she found it before. There are also cans of tomato paste, which she ignores, and some dried pasta, but mice have gotten into it.

When she gets outside, some strange guy is standing on the sidewalk, talking to Franny, who's still sitting on the grass.

For a moment she doesn't know what to do, clutching the cans of soup against her chest. Some part of her wants to back into the house, go through the dark living room with its mauve carpeting, its shabby blue sofa, photos of school kids and a cross-stitch flower bouquet framed on the wall, back through the little dining room with its border of country geese, unchanged since the eighties. Out the back door and over the fence, an easy moment to abandon the biggest mistake of her life. She'd aborted the first pregnancy, brought home from Pasadena in shame. She'd dug her heels in on the second, it's-my-body-fuck-you.

Franny laughs. A little nervous and hiccupy from crying, but not really afraid.

"Hey," Jane yells. "Get away from my daughter!"

She strides across the yard, all motherhood and righteous fury. A skinny, dark-haired guy holds up his hands, palms out, no harm, ma'am.

"It's okay, mom," Franny says.

The guy is smiling. "We're just talking," he says. He's wearing a red plaid flannel shirt and T-shirt and shorts. He's scraggly, but who isn't.

"Who the hell are you," she says.

"My name's Nate. I'm just heading north. Was looking for a place to camp."

"He was just hanging with me until you got back," Franny says.

Nate takes them to his camp—also behind a house. He gets a little fire going, enough to heat the soup. He talks about Alabama, which is where he's coming from, although he doesn't have a Southern accent. He makes some excuse about being an army brat. Jane tries to size him up. He tells some story about when two guys stumbled on his camp north of Huntsville, when he was first on the road. About how it scared the shit out of him but about how he'd bluffed them about a buddy of his who was hunting for their dinner but would have heard the racket they made and could be drawing a bead on them right now from the trees, and about how something moved in the trees, some animal, rustling in the leaf litter, and they got spooked. He's looking at her, trying to impress her, but being polite, which is good with Franny listening. Franny is taken with him, hanging on his every word, flirting a little the way she does. In a year or two, Franny was going to be guy crazy, Jane knew.

"They didn't know anything about the woods, just two guys up from Biloxi or something, kind of guys who, you know, manage a copy store or a fast-food joint or something, thinking that now that civilization is falling apart they can be like the hero in one of their video games." He laughs. "I didn't know what was in the woods, neither. I admit I was kind of scared it was someone who was going to shoot all of us, although it was probably just a sparrow or a squirrel or something. I'm saying stuff over my shoulder to my 'buddy,' like, 'Don't shoot them or nothing. Just let them go back the way they came.'"

She's sure he's bullshitting. But she likes that he makes it funny instead of pretending he's some sort of Rambo. He doesn't offer any of his own food, she notices. But he does offer to go with them to get their stuff. Fair trade, she thinks.

He's not bad looking in a kind of skinny way. She likes them skinny. She's tired of doing it all herself.

The streetlights come on, at least some of them. Nate goes with them when they go back to get their sleeping bags and stuff. He's got a board with a bunch of nails sticking out of one end. He calls it his mace.

They are quiet, but they don't try to hide. It's hard to find the stuff in the dark, but luckily, Jane hadn't really unpacked. She and Franny, who is breathing hard, get their sleeping bags and packs. It's hard to see. The backyard is a dark tangle of shadows. She assumes it's as hard to see them from inside the house—maybe harder.

Nothing happens. She hears nothing from the house, sees nothing, although it seems as if they are all unreasonably loud gathering things up. They leave through the side gate, coming nervously to the front of the house, Nate carrying his mace and ready to strike, she and Franny with their arms full of sleeping bags. They go down the cracked driveway and out into the middle of the street, a few gutted cars still parked on either side. Then they are around the corner and it feels safe. They are all grinning and happy and soon putting the sleeping bags in Nate's little backyard camp made domestic—no, civilized—by the charred ash of the little fire.

In the morning, she leaves Nate's bedroll and gets back to sleep next to Franny before Franny wakes up.

They are walking on the freeway the next day, the three of them. They are together now, although they haven't discussed it, and Jane is relieved. People are just that much less likely to mess with a man. Overhead, three jets pass going south, visible only by their contrails. At least there are jets. American jets, she hopes.

They stop for a moment while Nate goes around a bridge abutment to pee.

"Mom," Franny says. "Do you think that someone has wrecked Pete's place?"

"I don't know," Jane says.

"What do you think happened to Pete?"

Jane is caught off guard. They left without ever explicitly discussing Pete, and Jane just thought that Franny, like her, assumed Pete was dead.

"I mean," Franny continues, "if they didn't have gas, maybe he got stuck somewhere. Or he might have gotten hurt and ended up in the hospital. Even if the hospital wasn't taking regular people, like, they'd take cops. Because they think of cops as one of their own." Franny is in her adult-to-adult mode, explaining the world to her mother. "They stick together. Cops and firemen and nurses."

Jane isn't sure she knows what Franny is talking about. Normally she'd tell Franny as much. But this isn't a conversation she knows how to have. Nate comes around the abutment, adjusting himself a bit, and it is understood that the subject is closed.

"Okay," he says. "How far to Wallyworld?" Fanny giggles.

Water is their biggest problem. It's hard to find, and when they do find it, either from a pond or, very rarely, from a place where it hasn't all been looted, it's heavy. Thank God Nate is pretty good at making a fire. He has six disposable lighters that he got from a gas station, and when they find a pond, they boil it. Somewhere Jane thinks she heard that they should boil it for eighteen minutes. Basically they just boil the heck out of it. Pond water tastes terrible, but they are always thirsty. Franny whines. Jane is afraid that Nate will get tired of it and leave, but apparently as long as she crawls over to his bedroll every night, he's not going to.

Jane waits until she can tell Franny is asleep. It's a difficult wait. They are usually so tired it is all she can do to keep from nodding off. But she is afraid to lose Nate.

At first she liked that at night he never made a move on her. She always initiates. It made things easier all around. But now he does this thing where she crawls over and he's pretending to be asleep. Or is asleep, the bastard, because he doesn't have to stay awake. She puts her hand on his chest, and then down his pants, getting him hard and ready. She unzips his shorts, and still he doesn't do anything. She grinds on him for a while, and only then does he pull his shorts and underwear down and let her ride him until he comes. Then she climbs off him. Sometimes he might say, "Thanks, Babe." Mostly he says nothing and she crawls back next to Franny feeling as if she just paid the rent. She has never given anyone sex for money. She keeps telling herself that this night she won't do it. See what he does. Hell, if he leaves them, he leaves them. But then she lies there, waiting for Franny to go to sleep.

Sometimes she knows Franny is awake when she crawls back. Franny never says anything, and unless the moon is up, it is usually too dark to see if her eyes are open. It is just one more weird thing, no weirder than walking up the highway, or getting off the highway in some small town and bartering with some old guy to take what is probably useless US currency for well water. No weirder than no school. No weirder than no baths, no clothes, no nothing.

Jane decides she's not going to do it the next night. But she knows she will lie there, anxious, and probably crawl over to Nate.

They are walking, one morning, while the sky is still blue and darkening near the horizon. By midday the sky will be white and the heat will be flattening. Franny asks Nate, "Have you ever been in love?"

"God, Franny," Jane says.

Nate laughs. "Maybe. Have you?"

Franny looks irritable. "I'm in eighth grade," she says. "And I'm not one of those girls with boobs, so I'm thinking, no."

Jane wants her to shut up, but Nate says, "What kind of guy would you fall in love with?"

Franny looks a little sideways at him and then looks straight ahead. She has the most perfect skin, even after all this time in the sun. Skin like that is wasted on kids. Her look says, "Someone like you, stupid." "I don't know," Franny says. "Someone who knows how to do things. You know, when you need them."

"What kind of things?" Nate asks. He's really interested. Well, fuck, there's not a lot interesting on a freeway except other people walking and abandoned cars. They are passing a Sienna with a flat tire and all its doors open.

Franny gestures toward it. "Like fix a car. And I'd like him to be cute, too." Matter of fact. Serious as a church.

Nate laughs. "Competent and cute."

"Yeah," Franny says. "Competent and cute."

"Maybe you should be the one who knows how to fix a car," Jane says.

"But I don't," Franny points out reasonably. "I mean maybe, someday, I could learn. But right now, I don't."

"Maybe you'll meet someone in Canada," Nate says. "Canadian guys are supposed to be able to do things like fix a car or fish or hunt moose."

"Canadian guys are different than American guys?" Franny asks.

"Yeah," Nate says. "You know, all flannel shirts and Canadian beer and stuff."

"You wear a flannel shirt."

"I'd really like a Canadian beer about now," Nate says. "But I'm not Canadian."

Off the road to the right is a gas station/convenience store. They almost always check them. There's not much likelihood of finding anything in the place, because the wire fence that borders the highway has been trampled here so people can get over it, which suggests that the place has long since been looted. But you never know what someone might have left behind. Nate lopes off across the high grass.

"Mom," Franny says, "carry my backpack, okay?" She shrugs it off and runs. Amazing that she has the energy to run. Jane picks up Franny's backpack, irritated, and follows. Nate and Franny disappear into the darkness inside.

She follows them in. "Franny, I'm not hauling your pack anymore."

There are some guys already in the place, and there is something about them, hard and well fed, that signals they are different. Or maybe it is just the instincts of a prey animal in the presence of predators.

"So what's in that pack?" one of them asks. He's sitting on the counter at the cash register window, smoking a cigarette. She hasn't had a cigarette in weeks. Her whole body simultaneously leans toward the cigarette and yet magnifies everything in the room. A room full of men, all of them staring.

She just keeps acting like nothing is wrong, because she doesn't know what else to do. "Dirty blankets, mostly," she says. "I have to carry most of the crap."

One of the men is wearing a grimy hoodie. Hispanic yard workers do that sometimes. It must help in the sun. These men are all Anglos, and there are fewer of them than she first thought. Five. Two of them are sitting on the floor, their backs against an empty dead ice cream cooler, their legs stretched out in front of them. Everyone on the road is dirty, but they are dirty and hard. Physical. A couple of them grin, feral flickers passing between them like glances. There is understanding in the room, shared purpose. She has the sense that she cannot let on that she senses anything, because the only thing holding them off is the pretense that everything is normal. "Not that we really need blankets in this weather," she says. "I would kill for a functioning Holiday Inn."

"Hah," the one by the cash register says. A bark. Amused.

Nate is carefully still. He is searching, eyes going from man to man. Franny looks as if she is about to cry.

It is only a matter of time. They will be on her. Should she play up to the man at the cash register? If she tries to flirt, will it release the rising tension in the room, allow them to spring on all of them? Will they kill Nate? What will they do to Franny? Or she can use her sex as currency. Go willingly. She does not feel as if they care if she goes willingly or not. They know there is nothing to stop them.

"There's no beer here, is there," she says. She can hear her voice failing.

"Nope," says the man sitting at the cash register.

"What's your name?" she asks.

It's the wrong thing to say. He slides off the counter. Most of the men are smiling now.

Nate says, "Stav?"

One of the guys on the floor looks up. His eyes narrow.

Nate says, "Hey, Stav."

"Hi," the guy says cautiously.

"You remember me," Nate says. "Nick. From the Blue Moon Inn."

Nothing. Stav's face is blank. But another guy, the one in the hoodie, says, "Speedy Nick!"

Stav grins. "Speedy Nick! Fuck! Your hair's not blond anymore!"

Nate says, "Yeah, well, you know, upkeep is tough on the road." He jerks a thumb at Jane. "This is my sister, Janey. My niece, Franny. I'm taking 'em up to Toronto. There's supposed to be a place up there."

"I heard about that," the guy in the hoodie says. "Some kind of camp."

"Ben, right?" Nate says.

"Yeah," the guy says.

The guy who was sitting on the counter is standing now, cigarette still smoldering. He wants it, doesn't want everybody to get all friendly. But the moment is shifting away from him.

"We found some distilled water," Stav says. "Tastes like shit but you can have it if you want."

Jane doesn't ask him why he told her his name was Nate. For all she knows, "Nate" is his name and "Nick" is the lie.

They walk each day. Each night she goes to his bedroll. She owes him. Part of her wonders is maybe he's gay? Maybe he has to lie there and fantasize she's a guy or something. She doesn't know.

They are passing by water. They have some, so there is no reason to stop. There's an egret standing in the water, white as anything she has seen since this started, immaculately clean. Oblivious to their passing. Oblivious to the passing of everything. This is all good for the egrets. Jane hasn't had a drink since they started for Canada. She can't think of a time since she was sixteen or so that she went so long without one. She wants to get dressed up and go out someplace and have a good time and not think about anything, because the bad thing about not having a drink is that she thinks all the time and, fuck, there's nothing in her life right now she really wants to think about. Especially not Canada, which she is deeply but silently certain is only a rumor. Not the country, she doesn't think it doesn't exist, but the camp. It is a mirage. A shimmer on the horizon. Something to go toward but which isn't really there.

Or maybe they're the rumors. The three of them. Rumors of things gone wrong.

At a rest stop in the middle of nowhere they come across an encampment. A huge number of people, camped under tarps, pieces of plastic, and tatters, and astonishingly, a convoy of military trucks and jeeps including a couple of fuel trucks and a couple of water trucks. Kids stop and watch as they walk in and then go back to chasing each other around picnic tables. The two groups are clearly separate. The military men have control of all the asphalt and one end of the picnic area. They stand around or lounge at picnic tables. They look so equipped, from hats to combat boots. They look so clean. So much like the world Jane has put mostly out of her mind. They awake in her the longing that she has put down. The longing to be clean. To have walls. Electric lights. Plumbing. To have order.

The rest look like refugees, the word she denied on the sidewalks outside the condo. Dirty people in T-shirts with bundles and plastic grocery bags and even a couple of suitcases. She has seen people like this as they walked. Walked past them sitting by the side of the road. Sat by the side of the road as others walked past them. But to see them all together like this . . . this is what it will be like in Canada? A camp full of people with bags of wretched clothes waiting for someone to give them something to eat? A toddler with no pants and curly hair watches solemnly like one of those children in those "save a child" commercials. He's just as dirty. His hair is blond.

She rejects it. Rejects it all so viscerally that she stops and for a moment can't walk to the people in the rest stop. She doesn't know if she would have walked past, or if she would have turned around, or if she would have struck off across the country. It doesn't matter what she would have done, because Nate and Franny walk right on up the exit ramp. Franny's tank top is bright, insistent pink under its filth and her shorts have a tear in them, and her legs are brown and skinny and she could be a child on a news channel after a hurricane or an earthquake, clad in the loud synthetic colors so at odds with the dirt or ash that coats her. Plastic and synthetics are the indestructibles left to the survivors.

Jane is ashamed. She wants to explain that she's not like this. She wants to say, she's an American. By which she means she belongs to the military side, although she has never been interested in the military, never particularly liked soldiers.

If she could call her parents in Pennsylvania. Get a phone from one of the soldiers. Surrender. You were right, Mom. I should have straightened up and flown right. I should have worried more about school. I should have done it your way. I'm sorry. Can we come home?

Would her parents still be there? Do the phones work just north of Philadelphia? It has not until this moment occurred to her that it is all gone.

She sticks her fist in her mouth to keep from crying out, sick with understanding. It is all gone. She has thought herself all brave and realistic, getting Franny to Canada, but somehow she didn't until this moment realize that it all might be gone. That there might be nowhere for her where the electricity is still on and there are still carpets on the hardwood floors and someone still cares about damask.

Nate has finally noticed that she isn't with them and he looks back, frowning at her. *What's wrong?* his expression says. She limps after them, defeated.

Nate walks up to a group of people camped around and under a stone picnic table. "Are they giving out water?" he asks, meaning the military.

"Yeah," says a guy in a Cowboys football jersey. "If you go ask, they'll give you water."

"Food?"

"They say tonight."

All the shade is taken. Nate takes their water bottles—a couple of two-liters and a plastic gallon milk jug. "You guys wait, and I'll get us some water," he says.

Jane doesn't like being near these people, so she walks back to a wire fence at the back of the rest area and sits down. She puts her arms on her knees and puts her head down. She is looking at the grass.

"Mom?" Franny says.

Jane doesn't answer.

"Mom? Are you okay?" After a moment more. "Are you crying?"

"I'm just tired," June says to the grass.

Franny doesn't say anything after that.

Nate comes back with all the bottles filled. Jane hears him coming and hears Franny say, "Oh, wow. I'm so thirsty."

Nate nudges her arm with a bottle. "Hey, Babe. Have some."

She takes a two-liter from him and drinks some. It's got a flat, faintly metal/chemical taste. She gets a big drink and feels a little better. "I'll be back," she says. She walks to the shelter where the bathrooms are.

"You don't want to go in there," a black man says to her. The whites of his eyes are yellow.

She ignores him and pushes in the door. Inside, the smell is excruciating, and the sinks are all stopped and full of trash. There is some light from windows up near the ceiling. She looks at herself in the dim mirror. She pours a little water into her hand and scrubs at her face. There is a little bit of paper towel left on a roll, and she peels it off and cleans her face and her hands, using every bit of the scrap of paper towel. She wets her hair and combs her fingers through it, working the tangles for a long time until it is still curly but not the rat's nest it was. She is so careful with the water. Even so, she uses every bit of it on her face and arms and hair. She would kill for a little lipstick. For a comb. Anything. At least she has water.

She is cute. The sun hasn't been too hard on her. She practices smiling.

When she comes out of the bathroom, the air is so sweet. The sunlight is blinding.

She walks over to the soldiers and smiles. "Can I get some more water, please?"

There are three of them at the water truck. One of them is a blond-haired boy with a brick-red complexion. "You sure can," he says, smiling back at her.

She stands, one foot thrust out in front of her like a ballerina, back a little arched. "You're sweet," she says. "Where are you from?"

"We're all stationed at Fort Hood," he says. "Down in Texas. But we've been up north for a couple of months."

"How are things up north?" she asks.

"Crazy," he says. "But not as crazy as they are in Texas, I guess."

She has no plan. She is just moving with the moment. Drawn like a moth.

He gets her water. All three of them are smiling at her.

"How long are you here?" she asks. "Are you like a way station or something?"

One of the others, a skinny Chicano, laughs. "Oh, no. We're here tonight and then headed west."

"I used to live in California," she says. "In Pasadena. Where the Rose Parade is. I used to walk down that street where the cameras are every day."

The blond glances around. "Look, we aren't supposed to be talking too much right now. But later on, when it gets dark, you should come back over here and talk to us some more."

"Mom!" Franny says when she gets back to the fence, "You're all cleaned up!"

"Nice, Babe," Nate says. He's frowning a little.

"Can I get cleaned up?" Franny asks.

"The bathroom smells really bad," Jane says. "I don't think you want to go in there." But she digs her other T-shirt out of her backpack and wets it and washes Franny's face. The girl is never going to be pretty, but now that she's not chubby, she's got a cute thing going on. She's got the sense to work it, or will learn it. "You're a girl that the boys are going to look at," Jane says to her.

Franny smiles, delighted.

"Don't you think?" Jane says to Nate. "She's got that thing, that sparkle, doesn't she?"

"She sure does," Nate says.

They nap in the grass until the sun starts to go down, and then the soldiers line everyone up and hand out MREs. Nate gets Beef Ravioli, and Jane gets Sloppy Joe. Franny gets Lemon Pepper Tuna and looks ready to cry, but Jane offers to trade with her. The meals are positive cornucopias—a side dish, a little packet of candy, peanut butter and crackers, fruit punch powder. Everybody has different things, and Jane makes everybody give everyone else a taste.

Nate keeps looking at her oddly. "You're in a great mood."

"It's like a party," she says.

Jane and Franny are really pleased by the moist towelette. Franny carefully saves her plastic fork, knife, and spoon. "Was your tuna okay?" she asks. She is feeling guilty now that the food is gone.

"It was good," Jane says. "And all the other stuff made it really special. And I got the best dessert."

The night comes down. Before they got on the road, Jane didn't know how dark night was. Without electric lights it is cripplingly dark. But the soldiers have lights.

Jane says, "I'm going to go see if I can find out about the camp."

"I'll go with you," Nate says.

"No," Jane says. "They talk to a girl more than they'll talk to a guy. You keep Franny company."

She scouts around the edge of the light until she sees the blond soldier. He says, "There you are!"

"Here I am!" she says.

They are standing around a truck where they'll sleep this night, shooting the shit. The blond soldier boosts her into the truck, into the darkness. "So you aren't so conspicuous," he says, grinning.

Two of the men standing and talking aren't wearing uniforms. It takes her a while to figure out that they're civilian contractors. They aren't soldiers. They are technicians, nothing like the soldiers. They are softer, easier in their polo shirts and khaki pants. The soldiers are too sure in their uniforms, but the contractors, they're used to getting the leftovers. They're *grateful*. They have a truck of their own, a white pickup truck that travels with the convoy. They do something with satellite tracking, but Jane doesn't really care what they do.

It takes a lot of careful maneuvering, but one of them finally whispers to her, "We've got some beer in our truck."

The blond soldier looks hurt by her defection.

She stays out of sight in the morning, crouched among the equipment in the back of the pickup truck. The soldiers hand out MREs. Ted, one of the contractors, smuggles her one.

She thinks of Franny. Nate will keep an eye on her. Jane was only a year older than Franny when she lit out for California the first time. For a second she pictures Franny's face as the convoy pulls out.

Then she doesn't think of Franny.

She doesn't know where she is going. She is in motion.

The protection of the devil you know is preferable to being meat to something else. Besides, you never know when a giant mutant possum might change the situation . . .

SUN FALLS

Angela Slatter

I tap the fingers of one hand against the steering wheel, beating out a rhythm to replace the one that went missing when we got beyond the reach of any radio reception. It helps me to ignore the noises from the back seat.

The window is down so I can blow away the smoke from a hand-rolled ciggie. Barry hates it when I smoke in his car. Few things in the world Barry loves more than this old Holden, with its mag wheels, racing stripes, flames painted on the bonnet, and the fluffy dice dangling from the rear view mirror like a pair of square, furry testicles. He adores it better than any woman. I wouldn't be allowed to drive if it weren't an emergency of the most urgent kind.

Me? I think he looks like an idiot driving it, like some clueless pimp. But I'm not stupid enough to tell Barry that. Nope, not stupid enough at all. And it's not as if I'm paid for my opinion. In fact, I'm not paid. Just here to shut up and earn my keep, as Barry says. Just like my Mum did before me and her mum before that, all serving Barry for as long as we can remember.

Two hundred years give or take. It's a long time to be a slave.

Outside it's cooling down, which is a blessing because the air-con died a few hours back. The sky is splashed garish pink by the setting sun and now it's low enough to not hurt my eyes. I push the cheap sunnies to the top of my head, hook the earpieces into my hair so they stay put. I enjoy the rush of the breeze moving in and out of the car. In those brief moments when the engine doesn't howl, I can hear the sounds of the night: cicadas, possums, snakes, lizards, hares, wallabies. All manner of nasties that don't come out in the sunlight.

Kinda like Barry.

I can't hear the words he's shouting, but he knows the dark's come and he wants out. I've got a fair idea what he's saying. *Terry, open the fucking box.*

There'll be that for a few more k, then *Teresa, love, sweetie, please open the box. Please let me get some fresh air. It's cold in here.*

I leave it just until I sense he's about to move to threats, then I reach behind, keeping my eyes on the road, feel around on the back seat, find the cooler and flip the lid off. It lands on the floor with the sort of noise only falling polystyrene can make, both offended and humble, a sort of squeal like it's not happy but doesn't want to bother you.

"Thank fuck for that!" Barry's got quite a voice on him for someone currently without lungs. "Are you deaf?"

"Couldn't hear you, Barry. Engine's too noisy." And the machine doesn't make a liar of me—it rumbles and protests like an old man with emphysema. It's been a long trip.

"Well, this thing better keep going, I can't afford to get stuck out in the middle of nowhere in this state."

Barry's "state" has been a cause of concern for a couple of days now. There have been gang fights on the streets of Sydney—not the usual sorts, not the drug peddlers or the slave traders, not the gunrunners or the money launderers. Not this time anyway. Rival gangs of bloodsuckers, all trying to survive, to reach the top of the tree. All trying to be the big dog and negotiate with the breeders, those few Warm who are in the know (even with the current state of societal decay, there are some things you don't want the general populace to find out). But there are those who understand the night isn't a safe place, never has been, not since the First Fleet came and nicked the nation from under the nose of the indigenous population. That even on those ships, the greatest enemy wasn't scurvy or the lash, it was the things, just one or two, that roamed the lonely hours picking off the weak so as not to draw attention to themselves. Those who slept nestled in hidden compartments until the daylight passed.

Barry was one of them. Nasty bastard by all accounts (I've read the diaries my grandmothers kept). Didn't make too many of his own kind initially, just found a thin girl, none too bright, pregnant and fearful, someone he could bully and boss, someone who could do what was needed when the sun ruled the sky and who thought his protection worth the price of her liberty. Minnie: my ever-so-great-grandmother, a silly little pickpocket too slow to not get caught, who sold all our freedoms with her one stupid decision.

She couldn't read or write, but her daughter could, so Minnie told the story and her girl wrote it down. And so on and so on—we've all kept notes of some kind, some more literary than others. The Singleton women have quite a collected work now.

After Minnie's dimness, Barry decided we'd be more useful if educated, so fancy schools for his girls, university if you wanted it (I have a science degree for all the good it did me). He never turned any of us, just keeps us, generation after generation, like family retainers . . . or pets. We don't run. I asked my Mum why, but she just gave me that sleepy junkie smile. In her own way she did run—she just found her escape at the pointy end of a needle.

I've thought about it a lot in the years since and I reckon we stay put because we're told from the cradle there's nowhere else to go. How do you outrun the night? How do you go on living when closing your eyes means you might wake with a weight on your chest that doesn't go away? It's easier to live in the eye of the storm than to try and outrun it. And, ashamed as I am to say it, the protection of the devil you know is preferable to being meat to something else. There are worse things in the dark than Barry.

Of course there's always the theory that girls without fathers will attach themselves quite willingly to father-figures. Barry's a bad dad if ever there was one, but he's always looked after us. Can't argue with that.

So we shut up, do what's expected or find a way out. I'm never quite sure if Mum intended things to go the way they did. The drugs numbed her, but she could function, and Barry turned a blind eye. I guess I always thought it would go on like that forever until I got the call to say Barry had found her one night, stiff and cold under the pergola, propped against the BBQ with the little silver happy stick still in her arm. So, the big recall for me. Goodbye, uni; goodbye, honors degree; goodbye, normal life.

But I digress.

Barry and his state.

He thought himself safe; thought himself well-protected. He'd built up his empire and believed himself king of the vampires. Didn't occur to him that his bodyguard—not me, I'm just a kind of housekeeper—might not be content with the status quo. That Jerzy might want a change of pace, of lifestyle, of regime. That Jerzy might take the great big Japanese sword Barry liked to keep hanging on the wall of his study and use it to separate Barry's head from the rest of his body before the other bodyguards had a chance to tear Jerzy up like a hunk of shredded pork. Then, untethered, they all bolted out of the big house with its Greek columns and stamped concrete driveway, its seldom-used-in-daytime swimming pool, blackout blinds, and luxuriously appointed cellar, leaving the wrought iron gates open and me to wander in from the kitchen to find all the excitement had passed.

What should I see but Barry's head still intact? His body nothing but a pile of cinders and ash, but the head was all in one piece. And talking. Well, less talking than screaming and yelling obscenities. That's when I went to find the cooler, as much ice as I could, and Barry's car keys.

And here we are, heading towards the arse-end of nowhere because Barry says so. Because he says there's a place he can find help, a place where life begins again.

The road is more dirt than black stuff now and it's starting to rise, just a little. Around each bend, the incline gets steeper and the car protests more loudly. Soon, I should imagine, it will make its wishes known with the mechanical equivalent of a big *fuck you*.

"So, tell me how this is going to go again, Boss."

Dawn is starting to gray the sky and Barry's gotten lethargic as you might expect. He's quietened down and I should probably put the lid back on his box—the last of the ice I'd dumped in the esky turned to warmish water hours ago, but I don't guess he'll drown. Looks like he's immortal, if not invulnerable.

"It'll all be sweet, Terry. I'll be good as new," his voice is low and sleepy.

"Fine and dandy, Barry, but what are the details? What about me?"

"What about you? This isn't about you, you dopey bitch." More awake now.

"Never said it was, Barry, but: point of order. We're walking into this place. What's out there? More of your brethren? You're not really in a position to protect me, are you? I'm a canapé on legs. So, *what's out there*?"

"Nah, Terry," he says but he doesn't sound very sure. "It'll be okay, nothing there, no one. Nothing to worry about."

And for the first time in my life I don't believe Barry. I don't trust him to look after me and it gives me a funny feeling in the pit of my stomach. Of course, that could be hunger—that last apple was three hours ago and I'm down to a packet of muesli bars and a tube of Pringles. "Sure, Barry. Sure."

No one, my arse. I know enough about bumps in the night and deserted dead hearts to know nothing's ever really empty. If Barry knows about this place, so does someone else. *You're not king of the vampires here, Bazza, you're just a talking head*. I pull over to the shoulder of the road, reach back and put the lid on Barry and his polystyrene swimming pool. I get out of the car and look around, stretching my long body as my back protests and my worn-too-long cargos and tee stick to my skin. I can smell my own sweat and the determined stink of the cigarettes that ran out not far out of Sydney. I stare into the bush. It's changing as we head up the mountains, getting greener, darker, denser, wetter. More like a rainforest. Not sure what I expect to see . . . nothing there, no movement, not even the twitch of a leaf in the breeze. I feel weird though; I feel watched. *Imagination*, I tell myself. *Bullshit*, I tell myself.

I slide back into the driver's seat and turn the key in the ignition.

The only answer I get is the exhausted metallic grinding of a thing that's gone as far as it can go. I lean forward and rest my head against the steering wheel, smelling the stale-sour scent of hands gripped too long about the leather cover. My spidey senses tell me this road trip will not end well.

I've got Barry's box in one hand and in the other is the long Japanese sword that parted him from his body. It seemed like a good idea to bring it along— just made sure Barry didn't see it, sore point and all that. The water bottle hanging at my waist is making sad little wishy-washy sounds. Not much more than a mouthful left and I'm thirsty. The need for nicotine is dancing under my skin.

The air is cool and damp, the clouds are sitting on the road and it's hard to see too much in front of me. The condensation is plastering the fringe to my forehead. It's mid-afternoon and I don't know where I'm going, I'm just following the road. Can't open the box to ask Barry; he's been in deep sleep for hours now. I just keep walking, although my boots have rubbed blisters onto my soles and the outer edges of my little toes.

Up ahead I can hear a sound, sweet and clear. Running water.

I pick up my pace and stumble off the road, down a slight slope to find a clearing, a little creek running through it. There's a fire pit that looks like it hasn't been used in a long, long time. I refill the water bottle, drink deeply, then peel off my boots and socks and plunge my feet in. It's icy and hurts only for a little while before the numbing cold makes everything seem okay. I lean back, raise my face to where the sun should be and imagine it on my skin. Problem with being in service with a night crawler is that you don't tend to see too much daylight. Oh, you have to run errands and some of those are unavoidably day-oriented. But mostly, you become as nocturnal as your master. Feels like shift-work. Do it long enough you either get used to it or go nuts. Or a bit of both.

Behind me there's a sound; behind me, where I dropped Barry's box (the katana I kept close). There's that distinct polystyrene noise and I turn to see the biggest freaking possum I've ever seen in my life. It looks like a large dog, a Labrador maybe, on its hind legs and it's got the lid off the cooler and one paw buried deep inside. It pulls Barry's head out by the messy black hair.

There it dangles at the end of possum claws, eyes closed, lips slack and a little open, the neck so cleanly severed you could almost admire it as a nice tidy job. I stand slowly. The possum sniffs at Barry's nose, licks it, then opens its mouth and sinks sharp white teeth into the substance of Barry's pert little snoz.

I take a good few fast steps and bring the katana sweeping upward and the possum paw drops to the ground, which leaves Barry hanging briefly by his nose in the grip of the teeth of a very unhappy marsupial. Possum spits out its meal and gives me a look that makes me think twice about getting any closer. Then I remember that I've got the sword and about four feet in height on the thing. But it's fast and the remaining claws sharp; my cargos and the leg underneath get a nasty gash before I manage to take the stinking thing's head off.

I have a rest, bent over, hands on knees, breathing hard while I watch blood dribble out of my injured flesh. There's a yell and I fear a possum support column may have arrived. But it's only Barry, waking up.

"What the fuck happened to my nose? Do you have any idea how much this hurts? What the hell did you do to me?"

"Oh, Barry, you don't want to know. Now, which way? There are no signs for Sun Falls."

"Just keep following the road." The he pitches his eyes downwards, trying to get a good look at the state of his nose. I manage not to laugh as he goes a little cross-eyed. "Fuck this hurts."

A bonfire and five figures gathered around it: a woman, an old man, two young men, and a teenage girl. Raggedy stragglers, left out here with orders to guard the place, I guess. They're vampires, though, so it doesn't matter if there are five or a hundred. The rush and roar of water is clear from somewhere in the darkness. I can feel a damp spray I think might come from the falls.

I washed the wound and wrapped my leg up tight, but I know they can smell it before I step into the circle of light. There's a collective growl that must be something like a gazelle hears before a pride of lions brings it down. I might be able to take out a couple before they get to me. The fire catches the edge of the katana and pinwheels in Barry-unboxed's wide open eyes. The pack stays back, however. I must look as though I know what I'm doing—well, you can fool some of the vampires some of the time, I guess.

The woman stands and takes a few steps towards me.

"Hello, dinner," she says. "How obliging of you to turn up."

"You might want to re-think that," I say, and raise my boss's head.

Barry pipes up, "Lynda, keep your hands off her. She's no one's meal."

"Is that you, Barry?" The woman squints. Her hair is wound into filthy dreads, not all of her teeth remain and the breeze tells me she's not washed in some time. Hillbilly vamps, who'd have thought it? Feeding on the occasional lost tourist, stray cattle, giant possums. "Aw, Barry. What the fuck happened?"

"Long fucking story. I need to use the pool," he says shortly.

"The pool? No one's done that in a hundred years—you dunno what's gonna happen." She gets a cunning look in her eye. "What's it worth to ya?"

"How about a snack?"

Told you Barry was a nasty piece of work. But you know what, I'm less afraid of him than I am of them. One thing I do know is this: no matter how much he lies to everyone else, he's always kept his word to my family. He said I would be safe. He's also the only thing protecting me from the cast of a bloodsucking *Deliverance*.

I'm flanked by two underfed youths with straggly beards and, if I didn't know better, a look that says "Inbreeding keeps it in the family." One of them carries a torch plucked flaming from the fire. They don't need it to see, hell, they don't need fire at all, but I recognize in the building of the bonfire a remnant of their warm days, a little thing to hang onto. A memory of *back when*, of kids playing at grown-ups, of a time when heat meant comfort, meant life. Creatures pretending one day there might be light.

The falls are a couple of minutes walk away, down a path strewn with sticks and pebbles, occasionally hidden by touchy-feely ferns. When we reach the bottom, there's a shallow pool and a whole lot of spray where the water crashes down. One of my escorts points to a break in the foliage, right next to the cataract; the other pushes me roughly forward. My Docs slip and slide on the damp rocks. I keep my balance though; with a head in one hand, a sword in the other, and Barry cursing me the whole while it's no mean feat. I walk around behind the curtain of wet and see an entrance, a glow coming from inside it like a jack-o'-lantern.

There are no torches here, I notice, but the walls glow. Phosphorous? I wait until we're far enough down the tunnel for my guard of honor to not hear.

"Barry, you ungrateful bastard. I carry your sorry metaphorical arse all the way here, nearly get eaten by a mutant possum, and this is the thanks I get?" I shake him by the hair and glare into his blue eyes. "You think I'm an *hors d'oeuvre*?"

"Calm down. Wait—possum? Is that what happened to my nose? You let a possum eat my fucking nose?"

"Focus, Barry. Seriously, do you think I'm going to drop you in the all-healing, all-fixing pond so you can serve me up to that lot?" I shake him again and he winces. "Or are you gonna snack on me yourself?"

"Don't worry about it. Once I'm whole again, no one's going to mess with you."

"You didn't answer me!"

"I might need a little blood when I'm done," he admits. I give his head a good rattle and a few choice profanities, and he yells, "Not much! Not much! Just a little to top up. I promise!"

"What are we talking? A thimbleful? A shot glass?"

"Just a—bit. Terry, I promise I won't drain you, I won't turn you."

What choice do I have? The devil I know or the ones I don't.

The pool is at the bottom of the slope, in roughly the center of a small cavern. The liquid in it is milky-white with the same sheen as mother-of-pearl, and the smell is a little like household cleaner. A bit bleachy—more *Domestos* than *Dettol*.

"What's that?" I ask, trying not to breathe too deeply.

"Stuff. You know—stuff."

"You knew about this how?"

"Stories, Chinese whispers, old diaries—your lot aren't the only ones who keep records, you know. Nothing precise, nothing exact, just hints."

"You *read* our diaries?" I shouldn't be surprised.

"Yeah, yeah, yeah, I'm a bad person. Throw me in."

"But what if it doesn't work?"

"Not really in a position to be picky, am I? Fountain of youth, a wellspring, a cauldron of plenty. There are legends and they all say it brings life."

I don't point out to Barry that strictly speaking he has been for some time well and truly beyond the usual span of any creature. Well and truly outside the spectrum of what we call "life."

"So," I say, "life?"

"Life. Now hurry the fuck up and toss me in."

I walk around the edge. It's about five meters across and bubbling enthusiastically. If I drop him, maybe he'll just drown—this is a bit deeper than the esky—which still leaves me with a problem.

"Here's the deal, Barry: I'll put you in but in return you let me go. I'm no one's lunch, I'm no one's slave, I'm gone. I'm out. I do whatever I want."

"Terry . . . "

"You want life or not?"

"Yes, fuck it!" He gives a growl of frustration. "Alright. Agreed. I can find better than you at the local whorehouse anyway."

"Touché."

I kneel beside the pond and lower Barry in, resisting the impulse to drop him from a height to see how much of a splash he'll make. Some of the fluid leaps up like a nipping fish and lands on my fingers. It stings like ice. I grit my teeth and keep going, don't release the head until he is thoroughly submerged.

I try to straighten up, withdraw my arm, but I feel sharp teeth in my wrist. Barry, you bastard. That, however, is the least of my problems: the water has me. Blood spurts from my nose and turns pink as it hits the milky pond. It's like I'm in the grip of an electrical current. It tugs at me and tugs at me until I over-balance and it pulls me beneath the surface.

I feel as if I'm dying forever.

My last sight before I'm overwhelmed is Barry's head tossed and churned, jumping about like popping corn. Angry fingers of fluid force their way into my mouth and race down my throat, filling my lungs like inhaled fire. My skin seems to peel off, each hair follicle is a tiny pin in my scalp. Surely my eyes burst.

When it stops hurting, the water lets me go.

I crawl out and lie on the surprisingly warm rock. I'm whole, intact if somewhat soaked. I rub a hand against my shin, right where the possum bite was and feel . . .

And feel . . .

Nothing.

I roll up the leg of my cargos and strip away the bandage. There's just a pink mark that might have been a scar but fades as I watch. The katana is where I left it, and I pick it up, prick at my finger with its sharpness. Something silver oozes out from the cut and just as quickly the opening closes over.

A great spout of water comes from the pool and a body lands not far from me, gives a displeased groan.

Barry, whole again, tall and handsome and muscular and . . .

And no longer pale as if he tries to tan beneath the moon.

He rolls on his back, coughing, making a noise like an espresso machine. He breathes. I poke at him with the katana. A tiny drop of blood blossoms on his skin and he swears. Rich, fresh, oxygenated, *living* blood.

"Oh, Barry," I say. "You were right."

He sits up, runs his hands over his arms and legs, wondering, not understanding. "But . . . "

"It does give life, Barry. You've been dead a long time." I can't keep the laughter out of my voice.

"But . . . Fuck!" He stands up, pacing. "Okay. I don't have to outrun them, I just have to outrun you."

"Here's the thing, Baz, I don't think they're going to be interested in me anymore." I rise, do the thing with the poking and the quick silvery bleed. "Close as I can figure it, nature abhors a vacuum. The pond finished what you started, taking my blood and all, then . . . replaced it."

I start up the path, cast a look behind, "Long time since you've been meat. How's it feel?"

There was something inside the music; something that squished
and scuttled and honked and raved, something unsettling,
like a snake in a satin glove.

THE BLEEDING SHADOW

Joe R. Lansdale

I was down at the Blue Light Joint that night, finishing off some ribs and listening to some blues, when in walked Alda May. She was looking good too. Had a dress on and it fit her the way a dress ought to fit every woman in the world. She was wearing a little flat hat that leaned to one side, like an unbalanced plate on a waiter's palm. The high heels she had on made her legs look tight and way all right.

The light wasn't all that good in the joint, which is one of its appeals. It sometimes helps a man or woman get along in a way the daylight wouldn't stand, but I knew Alda May enough to know light didn't matter. She'd look good wearing a sack and a paper hat.

There was something about her face that showed me right off she was worried, that things weren't right. She was glancing left and right, like she was in some big city trying to cross a busy street and not get hit by a car.

I got my bottle of beer, left out from my table, and went over to her.

Then I knew why she'd been looking around like that. She said, "I was looking for you, Richard."

"Say you were," I said. "Well you done found me."

The way she stared at me wiped the grin off my face.

"Something wrong, Alda May?"

"Maybe. I don't know. I got to talk, though. Thought you'd be here, and I was wondering you might want to come by my place."

"When?"

"Now."

"All right."

"But don't get no business in mind," she said. "This isn't like the old days. I need your help, and I need to know I can count on you."

"Well, I kind of like the kind of business we used to do, but all right, we're friends. It's cool."

"I hoped you'd say that."

"You got a car?" I said.

She shook her head. "No. I had a friend drop me off."

I thought, Friend? Sure.

"All right then," I said, "lets strut on out."

I guess you could say it's a shame Alda May makes her money turning tricks, but when you're the one paying for the tricks, and you are one of her satisfied customers, you feel different. Right then, anyway. Later, you feel guilty. Like maybe you done peed on the Mona Lisa. 'Cause that gal, she was one fine dark skin woman who should have got better than a thousand rides and enough money to buy some eats and make some coffee in the morning. She deserved something good. Should have found and married a man with a steady job that could have done all right by her.

But that hadn't happened. Me and her had a bit of something once, and it wasn't just business, money changing hands after she got me feeling good. No, it was more than that, but we couldn't work it out. She was in the life and didn't know how to get out. And as for deserving something better, that wasn't me. What I had were a couple of nice suits, some two-tone shoes, a hat, and a gun—.45-caliber automatic, like they'd used in the war a few years back.

Alma May got a little on the dope, too, and though she shook it, it had dropped her down deep. Way I figured, she wasn't never climbing out of that hole, and it didn't have nothing to do with dope now. What it had to do with was time. You get a window open now and again, and if you don't crawl through it, it closes. I know. My window had closed some time back. It made me mad all the time.

We were in my Chevy, a six-year-old car, a forty-eight model. I'd had it reworked a bit at a time: new tires, fresh windshield, nice seat covers and so on. It was shiny and special.

We were driving along, making good time on the highway, the lights racing over the cement, making the recent rain in the ruts shine like the knees of old dress pants.

"What you need me for?" I asked.

"It's a little complicated," she said.

"Why me?"

"I don't know . . . You've always been good to me, and once we had a thing goin'."

"We did," I said.

"What happened to it?"

I shrugged. "It quit goin'."

"It did, didn't it? Sometimes I wish it hadn't."

"Sometimes I wish a lot of things," I said.

She leaned back in the seat and opened her purse and got out a cigarette and lit it, then rolled down the window. She remembered I didn't like cigarette smoke. I never had got on the tobacco. It took your wind and it stunk and it made your breath bad too. I hated when it got in my clothes.

"You're the only one I could tell this to," she said. "The only one that would listen to me and not think I been with the needle in my arm. You know what I'm sayin'?"

"Sure, baby, I know."

"I sound to you like I been bad?"

"Naw. You sound all right. I mean, you're talkin' a little odd, but not like you're out of your head."

"Drunk?"

"Nope. Just like you had a bad dream and want to tell someone."

"That's closer," she said. "That ain't it, but that's much closer than any needle or whisky or wine."

Alma May's place is on the outskirts of town. It's the one thing she got out of life that ain't bad. It's not a mansion. It's small, but it's tight and bright in the daylight, all painted up canary yellow color with deep blue trim. It didn't look bad in the moonlight.

Alma May didn't work with a pimp. She didn't need one. She was well known around town. She had her clientele. They were all safe, she told me once. About a third of them were white folks from on the other side of the tracks, up there in the proper part of Tyler Town. What she had besides them was a dead mother and a runaway father, and a brother, Tootie, who liked to travel around, play blues, and suck that bottle. He was always needing something, and Alma May, in spite of her own demons, had always managed to make sure he got it.

That was another reason me and her had to split the sheets. That brother of hers was a grown-ass man, and he lived with his mother and let her tote his water. When the mama died, he sort of went to pieces. Alma May took mama's part over, keeping Tootie in whisky and biscuits, even bought him a guitar. He lived off her whoring money, and it didn't bother him none. I didn't like him. But I will say this. That boy could play the blues.

When we were inside her house, she unpinned her hat from her hair and sailed it across the room and into a chair.

She said, "You want a drink?"

"I ain't gonna say no, long as it ain't too weak, and be sure to put it in a dirty glass."

She smiled. I watched from the living room doorway as she went and got a bottle out from under the kitchen sink, showing me how tight that dress fit across her bottom when she bent over. She pulled some glasses off a shelf, come back with a stiff one. We drank a little of it, still standing, leaning against the door frame between living room and kitchen. We finally sat on the couch. She sat on the far end, just to make sure I remembered why we were there. She said, "It's Tootie."

I swigged down the drink real quick, said, "I'm gone."

As I went by the couch, she grabbed my hand. "Don't be that way, baby."

"Now I'm baby," I said.

"Here me out, honey. Please. You don't owe me, but can you pretend you do?"

"Hell," I said and went and sat down on the couch.

She moved, said, "I want you to listen."

"All right," I said.

"First off, I can't pay you. Except maybe in trade."

"Not that way," I said. "You and me, we do this, it ain't trade. Call it a favor."

I do a little detective stuff now and then for folks I knew, folks that recommended me to others. I don't have a license. Black people couldn't get a license to shit broken glass in this town. But I was pretty good at what I did. I learned it the hard way. And not all of it was legal. I guess I'm a kind of private eye. Only I'm really private. I'm so private I might be more of a secret eye.

"Best thing to do is listen to this," she said. "It cuts back on some explanation."

There was a little record player on a table by the window, a stack of records. She went over and opened the player box and turned it on. The record she wanted was already on it. She lifted up the needle and set it right, stepped back and looked at me.

She was oh so fine. I looked at her and thought maybe I should have stuck with her, brother or no brother. She could melt butter from ten feet away, way she looked.

And then the music started to play.

It was Tootie's voice. I recognized that right away. I had heard him plenty. Like I said, he wasn't much as a person, willing to do anything so he could lay back and play that guitar, slide a pocket knife along the strings to squeal out just the right sound, but he was good at the blues, of that, there ain't no denying.

His voice was high and lonesome, and the way he played that guitar, it was hard to imagine how he could get the sounds out of it he got.

"You brought me over here to listen to records?" I said.

She shook her head. She lifted up the needle, stopped the record, and took it off. She had another in a little paper cover, and she took it out and put it on, dropped the needle down.

"Now listen to this."

First lick or two, I could tell right off it was Tootie, but then there came a kind of turn in the music, where it got so strange the hair on the back of my neck stood up. And then Tootie started to sing, and the hair on the back of my hands and arms stood up. The air in the room got thick and the lights got dim, and shadows come out of the corners and sat on the couch with me. I ain't kidding about that part. The room was suddenly full of them, and I could hear what sounded like a bird, trapped at the ceiling, fluttering fast and hard, looking for a way out.

Then the music changed again, and it was like I had been dropped down a well, and it was a long drop, and then it was like those shadows were folding around me in a wash of dirty water. The room stunk of something foul. The guitar no longer sounded like a guitar, and Tootie's voice was no longer like a voice. It was like someone dragging a razor over concrete while trying to yodel with a throat full of glass. There was something inside the music; something that squished and scuttled and honked and raved, something unsettling, like a snake in a satin glove.

"Cut it off," I said.

But Alma May had already done it.

She said, "That's as far as I've ever let it go. It's all I can do to move to cut it off. It feels like it's getting more powerful the more it plays. I don't want to hear the rest of it. I don't know if I can take it. How can that be, Richard? How can that be with just sounds?"

I was actually feeling weak, like I'd just come back from a bout with the flu and someone had beat my ass. I said, "More powerful? How do you mean?"

"Ain't that what you think? Ain't that how it sounds? Like it's getting stronger?"

I nodded. "Yeah."

"And the room—"

"The shadows?" I said. "I didn't just imagine it?"

"No," she said, "Only every time I've heard it, it's been a little different.

The notes get darker, the guitar licks, they cut something inside me, and each time it's something different and something deeper. I don't know if it makes me feel good or it makes me feel bad, but it sure makes me feel."

"Yeah," I said, because I couldn't find anything else to say.

"Tootie sent me that record. He sent a note that said: Play it when you have to. That's what it said. That's all it said. What's that mean?"

"I don't know, but I got to wonder why Tootie would send it to you in the first place. Why would he want you to hear something makes you almost sick . . . And how in hell could he do that, make that kind of sound, I mean?"

She shook her head. "I don't know. Someday, I'm gonna play it all the way through."

"I wouldn't," I said.

"Why?"

"You heard it. I figure it only gets worse. I don't understand it, but I know I don't like it."

"Yeah," she said, putting the record back in the paper sheath. "I know. But it's so strange. I've never heard anything like it."

"And I don't want to hear anything like it again."

"Still, you have to wonder."

"What I wonder is what I was wondering before. Why would he send this shit to you?"

"I think he's proud of it. There's nothing like it. It's . . . original."

"I'll give it that," I said. "So, what do you want with me?"

"I want you to find Tootie."

"Why?"

"Because I don't think he's right. I think he needs help. I mean, this . . . It makes me think he's somewhere he shouldn't be."

"But yet, you want to play it all the way through," I said.

"What I know is I don't like that. I don't like Tootie being associated with it, and I don't know why. Richard, I want you to find him."

"Where did the record come from?"

She got the sheaf and brought it to me. I could see through the little doughnut in the sheath where the label on the record ought to be. Nothing but disk. The package itself was like wrapping paper you put meat in. It was stained.

"I think he paid some place to let him record," I said. "Question is, what place? You have an address where this came from?"

"I do." She went and got a large manila envelope and brought it to me. "It came in this."

I looked at the writing on the front. It had as a return address, The Hotel Champion. She showed me the note. It was on a piece of really cheap stationery that said The Hotel Champion and had a phone number and an address in Dallas. The stationery looked old and it was sun faded.

"I called them," she said, "but they didn't know anything about him. They had never heard of him. I could go look myself, but . . . I'm a little afraid. Besides, you know, I got clients, and I got to make the house payment."

I didn't like hearing about that, knowing what kind of clients she meant, and how she was going to make that money. I said, "All right. What you want me to do?"

"Find him."

"And then what?"

"Bring him home."

"And if he don't want to come back?"

"I've seen you work, bring him home to me. Just don't lose that temper of yours."

I turned the record around and around in my hands. I said, "I'll go take a look. I won't promise anything more than that. He wants to come, I'll bring him back. He doesn't, I might be inclined to break his leg and bring him back. You know I don't like him."

"I know. But don't hurt him."

"If he comes easy, I'll do that. If he doesn't, I'll let him stay, come back and tell you where he is and how he is. How about that?'

"That's good enough," she said. "Find out what this is all about. It's got me scared, Richard."

"It's just bad sounds," I said. "Tootie was probably high on something when he recorded it, thought it was good at the time, sent it to you because he thought he was the coolest thing since Robert Johnson."

"Who?"

"Never mind. But I figure when he got over his hop, he probably didn't even remember he mailed it."

"Don't try and tell me you've heard anything like this. That listening to it didn't make you feel like your skin was gonna pull off your bones, that some part of it made you want to dip in the dark and learn to like it. Tell me it wasn't like that? Tell me it wasn't like walking out in front of a car and the headlights in your face, and you just wanting to step out there even though it scared hell out of you and you knew it was the devil or something even worse at the wheel. Tell me you didn't feel something like that."

I couldn't. So I didn't say anything. I just sat there and sweated, the sound of that music still shaking down deep in my bones, boiling my blood.

"Here's the thing," I said. "I'll do it, but you got to give me a photograph of Tootie, if you got one, and the record so you don't play it no more."

She studied me a moment. "I hate that thing," she said, nodding at the record in my hands, "but somehow I feel attached to it. Like getting rid of it is getting rid of a piece of me."

"That's the deal."

"All right," she said, "take it, but take it now."

Motoring along by myself in the Chevy, the moon high and bright, all I could think of was that music, or whatever that sound was. It was stuck in my head like an ax. I had the record on the seat beside me, had Tootie's note and envelope, the photograph Alma May had given me.

Part of me wanted to drive back to Alma May and tell her no, and never mind. Here's the record back. But another part of me, the dumb part, wanted to know where and how and why that record had been made. Curiosity, it just about gets us all.

Where I live is a rickety third floor walk up. It's got the stairs on the outside, and they stop at each landing. I was at the very top.

I tried not to rest my hand too heavy on the rail as I climbed, because it was about to come off. I unlocked my door and turned on the light and watched the roaches run for cover.

I put the record down, got a cold one out of the ice box. Well, actually it was a plug in. A refrigerator. But I'd grown up with ice boxes, so calling it that was hard to break. I picked up the record again and took a seat.

Sitting in my old arm chair with the stuffings leaking out like a busted cotton sack, holding the record again, looking at the dirty brown sheave, I noticed the grooves were dark and scabby looking, like something had gotten poured in there and had dried tight. I tried to determine if that had something to do with that crazy sound. Could something in the grooves make that kind of noise? Didn't seem likely.

I thought about putting the record on, listening to it again, but I couldn't stomach the thought. The fact that I held it in my hand made me uncomfortable. It was like holding a bomb about to go off.

I had thought of it like a snake once. Alma May had thought of it like a hit and run car driven by the devil. And now I had thought of it like a bomb. That was some kind of feeling coming from a grooved up circle of wax.

Early next morning, with the .45 in the glove box, a razor in my coat pocket, and the record up front on the seat beside me, I tooled out toward Dallas, and the Hotel Champion.

I got into Big D around noon, stopped at a café on the outskirts where there was colored, and went in where a big fat mama with a pretty face and a body that smelled real good, made me a hamburger and sat and flirted with me all the while I ate it. That's all right. I like women, and I like them to flirt. They quit doing that, I might as well lay down and die.

While we was flirting, I asked her about the Hotel Champion, if she knew where it was. I had the street number of course, but I needed tighter directions.

"Oh, yeah, honey, I know where it is, and you don't want to stay there. It's deep in the colored section, and not the good part, that's what I'm trying to tell you, and it don't matter you brown as a walnut yourself. There's folks down there will cut you and put your blood in a paper cup and mix it with whisky and drink it. You too good looking to get all cut up and such. There's better places to stay on the far other side."

I let her give me a few hotel names, like I might actually stay at one or the other, but I got the address for the Champion, paid up, giving her a good tip, and left out of there.

The part of town where the Hotel Champion was, was just as nasty as the lady had said. There were people hanging around on the streets, and leaning into corners, and there was trash everywhere. It wasn't exactly a place that fostered a lot of pride.

I found the Hotel Champion and parked out front. There was a couple fellas on the street eyeing my car. One was skinny. One was big. They were dressed up with nice hats and shoes, just like they had jobs. But if they did, they wouldn't have been standing around in the middle of the day eyeing my Chevy.

I pulled the .45 out of the glove box and stuck it in my pants, at the small of my back. My coat would cover it just right.

I got out and gave the hotel the gander. It was nice looking if you were blind in one eye and couldn't see out the other.

There wasn't any doorman, and the door was hanging on a hinge. Inside I saw a dusty stairway to my left, a scarred door to my right.

There was a desk in front of me. It had a glass hooked to it that went to the ceiling. There was a little hole in it low down on the counter that had a wooden stop behind it. There were fly specks on the glass, and there was a man behind the glass, perched on a stool, like a frog on a lily pad. He was fat and colored and his hair had blue blanket wool in it. I didn't take it for decoration. He was just a nasty son-of-a-bitch.

I could smell him when he moved the wooden stop. A stink like armpits and nasty underwear and rotting teeth. Floating in from somewhere in back, I could smell old cooking smells, boiled pigs feet and pigs tails that might have been good about the time the pig lost them, but now all that was left was a rancid stink. There was also a reek like cat piss.

I said, "Hey, man, I'm looking for somebody."

"You want a woman, you got to bring your own," the man said, "But I can give you a number or two. Course, I ain't guaranteeing anything about them being clean."

"Naw. I'm looking for somebody was staying here. His name is Tootie Johnson."

"I don't know no Tootie Johnson."

That was the same story Alma May had got.

"Well, all right, you know this fella?" I pulled out the photograph and pressed it against the glass.

"Well, he might look like someone got a room here. We don't sign in and we don't exchange names much."

"No? A class place like this."

"I said he might look like someone I seen," he said. "I didn't say he definitely did."

"You fishing for money?"

"Fishing ain't very certain," he said.

I sighed and put the photograph back inside my coat and got out my wallet and took out a five-dollar bill.

Frog Man saw himself as some kind of greasy high roller. "That's it? Five dollars for prime information?"

I made a slow and careful show of putting my five back in my wallet. "Then you don't get nothing," I said.

He leaned back on his stool and put his stubby fingers together and let them lay on his round belly. "And you don't get nothing neither, jackass."

I went to the door on my right and turned the knob. Locked. I stepped back and kicked it so hard I felt the jar all the way to the top of my head. The door flew back on its hinges, slammed into the wall. It sounded like someone firing a shot.

I went on through and behind the desk, grabbed Frog Man by the shirt and slapped him hard enough he fell off the stool. I kicked him in the leg and he yelled. I picked up the stool and hit him with it across the chest, then threw the stool through a doorway that led into a kitchen. I heard something break in there and a cat made a screeching sound.

"I get mad easy," I said.

"Hell, I see that," he said, and held up a hand for protection. "Take it easy, man. You done hurt me."

"That was the plan."

The look in his eyes made me feel sorry for him. I also felt like an asshole. But that wouldn't keep me from hitting him again if he didn't answer my question. When I get perturbed, I'm not reasonable.

"Where is he?"

"Do I still get the five dollars?"

"No," I said, "now you get my best wishes. You want to lose that?"

"No. No, I don't."

"Then don't play me. Where is he, you toad?"

"He's up in room 52, on the fifth floor."

"Spare key?"

He nodded at a rack of them. The keys were on nails and they all had little wooden pegs on the rings with the keys. Numbers were painted on the pegs. I found one that said 52, took it off the rack.

I said, "You better not be messing with me?"

"I ain't. He's up there. He don't never come down. He's been up there a week. He makes noise up there. I don't like it. I run a respectable place."

"Yeah, it's really nice here. And you better not be jerking me."

"I ain't. I promise."

"Good. And, let me give you a tip. Take a bath. And get that shit out of your hair. And those teeth you got ain't looking too good. Pull them. And shoot that fucking cat, or at least get him some place better than the kitchen to piss. It stinks like a toilet in there."

I walked out from behind the desk, out in the hall, and up the flight of stairs in a hurry.

I rushed along the hallway on the fifth floor. It was covered in white linoleum with a gold pattern in it; it creaked and cracked as I walked along. The end of the hall had a window, and there was a stairwell on that end too. Room 52 was right across from it.

I heard movement on the far end of the stairs. I had an idea what that was all about. About that time, two of the boys I'd seen on the street showed themselves at the top of the stairs, all decked out in their nice hats and such, grinning.

One of them was about the size of a Cadillac, with a gold tooth that shown bright when he smiled. The guy behind him was skinny with his hand in his pocket.

I said, "Well, if it isn't the pimp squad."

"You funny, nigger," said the big man.

"Yeah, well, catch the act now. I'm going to be moving to a new locale."

"You bet you are," said the big man.

"Fat ass behind the glass down there, he ain't paying you enough to mess with me," I said.

"Sometimes, cause we're bored, we just like messin'."

"Say you do?"

"Uh huh," said the skinny one.

It was then I seen the skinny guy pull a razor out of his pocket. I had one too, but razor work, it's nasty. He kept it closed.

Big guy with the gold tooth, flexed his fingers, and made a fist. That made me figure he didn't have a gun or a razor; or maybe he just liked hitting people. I know I did.

They come along toward me then, and the skinny one with the razor flicked it open. I pulled the .45 out from under my coat, said, "You ought to put that back in your pocket," I said, "save it for shaving."

"Oh, I'm fixing to do some shaving right now," he said.

I pointed the .45 at him.

The big man said, "That's one gun for two men."

"It is," I said, "but I'm real quick with it. And frankly, I know one of you is gonna end up dead. I just ain't sure which one right yet."

"All right then," said the big man, smiling. "That'll be enough." He looked back at the skinny man with the razor. The skinny man put the razor back in his coat pocket and they turned and started down the stairs.

I went over and stood by the stairway and listened. I could hear them walking down, but then all of a sudden, they stopped on the stairs. That's the way I had it figured.

Then I could hear the morons rushing back up. They weren't near as sneaky as they thought they was. The big one was first out of the chute, so to speak; come rushing out of the stairwell and onto the landing. I brought the butt of the .45 down on the back of his head, right where the skull slopes down. He did a kind of frog hop and bounced across the hall and hit his head on the wall, and went down and laid there like his intent all along had been a quick leap and a nap.

Then the other one was there, and he had the razor. He flicked it, and then he saw the .45 in my hand.

"Where did you think this gun was gonna go?" I said. "On vacation?"

I kicked him in the groin hard enough he dropped the razor, and went to his knees. I put the .45 back where I got it. I said, "You want some, man?"

He got up, and come at me. I hit him with a right and knocked him clean through the window behind him. Glass sprinkled all over the hallway.

I went over and looked out. He was lying on the fire escape, his head, against the railing. He looked right at me.

"You crazy, cocksucker. What if there hadn't been no fire escape?"

"You'd have your ass punched into the bricks. Still might."

He got up quick and clamored down the fire escape like a squirrel. I watched him till he got to the ground and went limping away down the alley between some overturned trash cans and a slinking dog.

I picked up his razor and put it in my pocket with the one I already had, walked over and kicked the big man in the head just because I could.

I knocked on the door. No one answered. I could hear sounds from inside. It was similar to what I had heard on that record, but not quite, and it was faint, as if coming from a distance.

No one answered my knock, so I stuck the key in the door and opened it and went straight away inside.

I almost lost my breath when I did.

The air in the room was thick and it stunk of mildew and rot and things long dead. It made those boiled pig feet and that shitting cat and that rotten-tooth bastard downstairs smell like perfume.

Tootie was lying on the bed, on his back. His eyes were closed. He was a guy usually dressed to the top, baby, but his shirt was wrinkled and dirty and sweaty at the neck and arm pits. His pants were nasty too. He had on his shoes, but no socks. He looked like someone had set him on fire and then beat out the flames with a two-by-four. His face was like a skull, he had lost so much flesh, and he was as bony under his clothes as a skeleton.

Where his hands lay on the sheet, there were blood stains. His guitar was next to the bed, and there were stacks and stacks of composition note books lying on the floor. A couple of them were open and filled with writing. Hell, I didn't even know Tootie could write.

The wall on the far side was marked up in black and red paint; there were all manner of musical notes drawn on it, along with symbols I had never seen before; swiggles and circles and stick figure drawings. Blood was on the wall too, most likely from Tootie's bleeding fingers. Two open paint cans, the red and the black, were on the floor with brushes stuck up in them. Paint was splattered on the floor and had dried in humped up blisters. The guitar had blood stains all over it.

A record player, plugged in, setting on a nightstand by the bed, was playing that strange music. I went to it right away and picked up the needle and set it aside. And let me tell you, just making my way across the room to get hold of the player was like wading through mud with my ankles tied

together. It seemed to me as I got closer to the record, the louder it got, and
the more ill I felt. My head throbbed. My heart pounded.

When I had the needle up and the music off, I went over and touched
Tootie. He didn't move, but I could see his chest rising and falling. Except
for his hands, he didn't seem hurt. He was in a deep sleep. I picked up his
right hand and turned it over and looked at it. The fingers were cut deep,
like someone had taken a razor to the tips. Right off, I figured that was from
playing his guitar. Struck me, that to get the sounds he got out of it, he really
had to dig in with those fingers. And from the looks of this room, he had
been at it non-stop, until recent.

I shook him. His eyes fluttered and finally opened. They were bloodshot
and had dark circles around them.

When he saw me, he startled, and his eyes rolled around in his head like
those little games kids get where you try to shake the marbles into holes.
After a moment, they got straight, and he said, "Ricky?"

That was another reason I hated him. I didn't like being called Ricky.

I said, "Hello, shithead. You're sister's worried sick."

"The music," he said. "Put the music back on."

"You call that music?" I said.

He took a deep breath, rolled out of the bed, nearly knocking me aside.
Then I saw him jerk, like he'd seen a truck coming right at him. I turned. I
wished it had been a truck.

Let me try and tell you what I saw. I not only saw it, I felt it. It was in
the very air we were breathing, getting inside my chest like mice wearing
barbed wire coats. The wall Tootie had painted and drawn all that crap on,
shook.

And then the wall wasn't a wall at all. It was a long hallway, dark as
original sin. There was something moving in there, something that slithered
and slid and made smacking sounds like an anxious old drunk about to
take his next drink. Stars popped up, greasy stars that didn't remind me of
anything I had ever seen in the night sky; a moon the color of a bleeding
fish eye was in the background, and it cast a light on something moving
toward us.

"Jesus Christ," I said.

"No," Tootie said. "It's not him."

Tootie jumped to the record player, picked up the needle, and put it on.
There came that rotten sound I had heard with Alma May, and I knew what
I had heard when I first came into the room was the tail end of that same
record playing, the part I hadn't heard before.

The music screeched and howled. I bent over and threw up. I fell back against the bed, tried to get up, but my legs were like old pipe cleaners. That record had taken the juice out of me. And then I saw it.

There's no description that really fits. It was... a thing. All blanket wrapped in shadow with sucker mouths and thrashing tentacles and centipede legs mounted on clicking hooves. A bulb-like head plastered all over with red and yellow eyes that seemed to creep. All around it, shadows swirled like water. It had a beak. Well, beaks.

The thing was coming right out of the wall. Tentacles thrashed toward me. One touched me across the cheek. It was like being scalded with hot grease. A shadow come loose of the thing, fell onto the floorboards of the room, turned red and raced across the floor like a gush of blood. Insects and maggots squirmed in the bleeding shadow, and the record hit a high spot so loud and so goddamn strange, I ground my teeth, felt as if my insides were being twisted up like wet wash. And then I passed out.

When I came to, the music was still playing. Tootie was bent over me.

"That sound," I said.

"You get used to it," Tootie said, "but the thing can't. Or maybe it can, but just not yet."

I looked at the wall. There was no alleyway. It was just a wall plastered in paint designs and spots of blood.

"And if the music stops?" I said.

"I fall asleep," Tootie said. "Record quits playing, it starts coming."

For a moment I didn't know anything to say. I finally got off the floor and sat on the bed. I felt my cheek where the tentacle hit me. It throbbed and I could feel blisters. I also had a knot on my head where I had fallen.

"Almost got you," Tootie said. "I think you can leave and it won't come after you. Me, I can't. I leave, it follows. It'll finally find me. I guess here is as good as any place."

I was looking at him, listening, but not understanding a damn thing.

The record quit. Tootie started it again. I looked at the wall. Even that blank moment without sound scared me. I didn't want to see that thing again. I didn't even want to think about it.

"I haven't slept in days, until now," Tootie said, coming to sit on the bed. "You hadn't come in, it would have got me, carried me off, taken my soul. But, you can leave. It's my lookout, not yours . . . I'm always in some kind of shit, ain't I, Ricky?"

"That's the truth."

"This though, it's the corker. I got to stand up and be a man for once. I got to fight this thing back, and all I got is the music. Like I told you, you can go."

I shook my head. "Alma May sent me. I said I'd bring you back."

It was Tootie's turn to shake his head. "Nope. I ain't goin'. I ain't done nothin' but mess up sis's life. I ain't gonna do it."

"First responsible thing I ever heard you say," I said.

"Go on," Tootie said. "Leave me to it. I can take care of myself."

"If you don't die of starvation, or pass out from lack of sleep, or need of water, you'll be just fine."

Tootie smiled at me. "Yeah. That's all I got to worry about. I hope it is one of them other things kills me. Cause if it comes for me . . . Well, I don't want to think about it."

"Keep the record going, I'll get something to eat and drink, some coffee. You think you can stay awake a half hour or so?"

"I can, but you're coming back?"

"I'm coming back," I said.

Out in the hallway I saw the big guy was gone. I took the stairs.

When I got back, Tootie had cleaned up the vomit, and was looking through the notebooks. He was sitting on the floor and had them stacked all around him. He was maybe six inches away from the record player. Now and again he'd reach up and start it all over.

Soon as I was in the room, and that sound from the record was snugged up around me, I felt sick. I had gone to a greasy spoon down the street, after I changed a flat tire. One of the boys I'd given a hard time had most likely knifed it. My bet was the lucky son-of-a-bitch who had fallen on the fire escape.

Besides the tire, a half dozen long scratches had been cut into the paint on the passengers side, and my windshield was knocked in. I got back from the café, I parked what was left of my car behind the hotel, down the street a bit, and walked a block. Car looked so bad now, maybe nobody would want to steal it.

I sat one of the open sacks on the floor by Tootie.

"Both hamburgers are yours," I said. "I got coffee for the both of us here."

I took out a tall, cardboard container of coffee and gave it to him, took the other one for myself. I sat on the bed and sipped. Nothing tasted good in that room with that smell and that sound. But, Tootie, he ate like a wolf. He gulped those burgers and coffee like it was air.

When he finished with the second burger, he started up the record again, leaned his back against the bed.

"Coffee or not," he said, "I don't know how long I can stay awake."

"So what you got to do is keep the record playing?" I said.

"Yeah."

"Lay up in bed, sleep for a few hours. I'll keep the record going. You're rested, you got to explain this thing to me, and then we'll figure something out."

"There's nothing to figure," he said. "But, god, I'll take you up on that sleep."

He crawled up in the bed and was immediately out.

I started the record over.

I got up then, untied Tootie's shoes and pulled them off. Hell, like him or not, he was Alma May's brother. And another thing, I wouldn't wish that thing behind the wall on my worst enemy.

I sat on the floor where Tootie had sat and kept restarting the record as I tried to figure things out, which wasn't easy with that music going. I got up from time to time and walked around the room, and then I'd end up back on the floor by the record player, where I could reach it easy.

Between changes, I looked through the composition notebooks. They were full of musical notes mixed with scribbles like the ones on the wall. It was hard to focus with that horrid sound. It was like the air was full of snakes and razors. Got the feeling the music was pushing at something behind that wall. Got the feeling too, there was something on the other side, pushing back.

It was dark when Tootie woke up. He had slept a good ten hours, and I was exhausted with all that record changing, that horrible sound. I had a headache from looking over those notebooks, and I didn't know anymore about them than when I first started.

I went and bought more coffee, brought it back, and we sat on the bed, him changing the record from time to time, us sipping.

I said, "You sure you can't just walk away?"

I was avoiding the real question for some reason. Like, what in hell is that thing, and what is going on? Maybe I was afraid of the answer.

"You saw that thing. I can walk away, all right. And I can run. But wherever I go, it'll find me. So, at some point, I got to face it. Sometimes I make that same record sound with my guitar, give the record a rest. Thing I fear most is the record wearing out."

I gestured at the notebooks on the floor. "What is all that?"

"My notes. My writings. I come here to write some lyrics, some new blues songs."

"Those aren't lyrics, those are notes."

"I know," he said.

"You don't have a music education. You just play."

"Because of the record, I can read music, and I can write things that don't make any sense to me unless it's when I'm writing them, when I'm listening to that music. All those marks, they are musical notes, and the other marks are other kinds of notes, notes for sounds that I couldn't make until a few days back. I didn't even know those sounds were possible. But now, my head is full of the sounds and those marks and all manner of things, and the only way I can rest is to write them down. I wrote on the wall cause I thought the marks, the notes themselves, might hold that thing back and I could run. Didn't work."

"None of this makes any sense to me," I said.

"All right," Tootie said, "This is the best I can explain something that's got no explanation. I had some blues boys tell me they once come to this place on the South side called Cross Road Records. It's a little record shop where the streets cross. It's got all manner of things in it, and it's got this big colored guy with a big white smile and bloodshot eyes that works the joint. They said they'd seen the place, poked their heads in, and even heard Robert Johnson's sounds coming from a player on the counter. There was a big man sitting behind the counter, and he waved them in, but the place didn't seem right, they said, so they didn't go in.

"But, you know me. That sounded like just the place I wanted to go. So, I went. It's where South Street crosses a street called Way Left.

"I go in there, and I'm the only one in the store. There's records everywhere, in boxes, lying on tables. Some got labels, some don't. I'm looking, trying to figure out how you told about anything, and this big fella with the smile comes over to me and starts to talk. He had breath like an un-wiped butt, and his face didn't seem so much like black skin as it did black rock.

"He said, 'I know what you're looking for.' He reached in a box, and pulled out a record didn't have no label on it. Thing was, that whole box didn't have labels. I think he's just messing with me, trying to make a sale. I'm ready to go, cause he's starting to make my skin crawl. Way he moves ain't natural, you know. It's like he's got something wrong with his feet, but he's still able to move, and quick like. Like he does it between the times you blink your eyes.

"He goes over and puts that record on a player, and it starts up, and it was Robert Johnson. I swear, it was him. Wasn't no one could play like him. It was him. And here's the thing. It wasn't a song I'd ever heard by him. And I thought I'd heard all the music he'd put on wax."

Tootie sipped at his coffee. He looked at the wall a moment, and then changed the player again.

I said, "Swap out spots, and I'll change it. You sip and talk. Tell me all of it."

We did that, and Tootie continued.

"Well, one thing comes to another, and he starts talking me up good, and I finally I ask him how much for the record. He looks at me, and he says, 'For you, all you got to give me is a little blue soul. And when you come back, you got to buy something with a bit more of it till it's all gone and I got it. Cause you will be back.'

"I figured he was talking about me playing my guitar for him, cause I'd told him I was a player, you know, while we was talking. I told him I had my guitar in a room I was renting, and I was on foot, and it would take me all day to get my guitar and get back, so I'd have to pass on that deal. Besides, I was about tapped out of money. I had a place I was supposed to play that evening, but until then, I had maybe three dollars and some change in my pocket. I had the rent on this room paid up all week, and I hadn't been there but two days. I tell him all that, and he says, 'Oh, that's all right. I know you can play. I can tell about things like that. What I mean is, you give me a drop of blood and a promise, and you can have that record. Right then, I started to walk out, cause I'm thinking, this guy is nutty as fruitcake with an extra dose of nuts, but I want that record. So, I tell him, sure, I'll give him a drop of blood. I won't lie none to you, Ricky, I was thinking about nabbing that record and making a run with it. I wanted it that bad. So a drop of blood, that didn't mean nothin'.

"He pulls a record needle out from behind the counter, and he comes over and pokes my finger with it, sudden like, while I'm still trying to figure how he got over to me that fast, and he holds my hand and lets blood drip on—get this—the record. It flows into the grooves.

"He says, 'Now, you promise me your blues playing soul is mine when you die.'

"I thought it was just talk, you know, so I told him he could have it. He says, 'When you hear it, you'll be able to play it. And when you play it, sometime when you're real good on it, it'll start to come, like a rat easing its nose into hot dead meat. It'll start to come.'

"What will?" I said. "What are you talking about?"

"He says, 'You'll know.'

"Next thing I know, he's over by the door, got it open and he's smiling at me, and I swear, I thought for a moment I could see right through him. Could see his skull and bones. I've got the record in my hand, and I'm walking out, and as soon as I do, he shuts the door and I hear the lock turn.

"My first thought was, I got to get this blood out of the record grooves, cause that crazy bastard has just given me a lost Robert Johnson song for nothing. I took out a kerchief, pulled the record out of the sleeve, and went to wiping. The blood wouldn't come out. It was in the notches, you know.

"I went back to my room here, and I tried a bit of warm water on the blood in the grooves, but it still wouldn't come out. I was mad as hell, figured the record wouldn't play, way that blood had hardened in the grooves. I put it on and thought maybe the needle would wear the stuff out, but as soon as it was on the player and the needle hit it, it started sounding just the way it had in the store. I sat on the bed and listened to it, three or four times, and then I got my guitar and tried to play what was being played, knowing I couldn't do it, cause though I knew that sound wasn't electrified, it sounded like it was. But, here's the thing. I could do it. I could play it. And I could see the notes in my head, and my head got filled up with them. I went out and bought those notebooks, and I wrote it all down just so my head wouldn't explode, cause every time I heard that record, and tried to play it, them notes would cricket-hop in my skull."

All the while we had been talking, I had been replaying the record.

"I forgot all about the gig that night," Tootie said. "I sat here until morning playing. By noon the next day, I sounded just like that record. By late afternoon, I started to get kind of sick. I can't explain it, but I was feeling that there was something trying to tear through somewhere, and it scared me and my insides knotted up.

"I don't know any better way of saying it than that. It was such a strong feeling. Then, while I was playing, the wall there, it come apart the way you seen it, and I seen that thing. It was just a wink of a look. But there it was. In all its terrible glory.

"I quit playing, and the wall wobbled back in place and closed up. I thought, Damn, I need to eat or nap, or something. And I did. Then I was back on that guitar. I could play like crazy, and I started going off on that song, adding here and there. It wasn't like it was coming from me, though. It was like I was getting help from somewhere.

"Finally, with my fingers bleeding and cramped and aching, and my voice gone raspy from singing, I quit. Still, I wanted to hear it, so I put on the record. And it wasn't the same no more. It was Johnson, but the words was strange, not English. Sounded like some kind of chant, and I knew then that Johnson was in that record, as sure as I was in this room, and that that chanting and that playing was opening up a hole for that thing in the wall. It was the way that fella had said. It was like a rat working its nose through red hot meat, and now it felt like I was the meat. Next time I played the record, the voice on it wasn't Johnson's. It was mine.

"I had had enough, so I got the record and took it back to that shop. The place was the same as before, and like before, I was the only one in there. He looked at me, and comes over, and says, 'You already want to undo the deal. I can tell. They all do. But that ain't gonna happen.'

"I gave him a look like I was gonna jump on him and beat his ass, but he gave me a look back, and I went weak as a kitten.

"He smiled at me, and pulls out another record from that same box, and he takes the one I gave him and puts it back, and says, 'You done made a deal, but for a lick of your soul, I'll let you have this. See, you done opened the path, now that rat's got to work on that meat. It don't take no more record or you playing for that to happen. Rat's gotta to eat now, no matter what you do.'

"When he said that, he picks up my hand and looks at my cut up fingers from playing, and he laughs so loud everything in the store shakes, and he squeezes my fingers until they start to bleed.

"A lick of my soul?" I asked.

"And then he pushed the record in my hand, and if I'm lying, I'm dying, he sticks out his tongue, and it's long as an old rat snake and black as a hole in the ground, and he licks me right around the neck. When he's had a taste, he smiles and shivers, like he's just had something cool to drink."

Tootie paused to unfasten his shirt and peel it down a little. There was a spot half way around his neck like someone had worked him over with sand paper.

"'A taste,' he says, and then he shoves this record in my hand, which is bleeding from where he squeezed my fingers. Next thing I know, I'm looking at the record, and it's thick, and I touch it, and it's two records, back to back. He says, 'I give you that extra one cause you tasted mighty good, and maybe it'll let you get a little more rest that way, if you got a turntable drop. Call me generous and kind in my old age.'

"Wasn't nothing for it but to take the records and come back here. I didn't have no intention of playing it. I almost threw it away. But by then, that thing in the wall, wherever it is, was starting to stick through. Each time the hole was bigger and I could see more of it, and that red shadow was falling out on the floor. I thought about running, but I didn't want to just let it loose, and I knew, deep down, no matter where I went, it would come too.

"I started playing that record in self-defense. Pretty soon, I'm playing it on the guitar. When I got scared enough, got certain enough that thing was coming through, I played hard, and that hole would close, and that thing would go back where it come from. For awhile.

"I figured though, I ought to have some insurance. You see, I played both them records, and they was the same thing, and it was my voice, and I hadn't never recorded or even heard them songs before. I knew then, what was on those notes I had written, what had come to me was the counter song to the one I had been playing first. I don't know if that was just some kind of joke that record store fella had played on me, but I knew it was magic of a sort. He had give me a song to let it in and he had give me another song to hold it back. It was amusing to him, I'm sure.

"I thought I had the thing at bay, so I took that other copy, went to the Post Office, mailed it to Alma, case something happened to me. I guess I thought it was self defense for her, but there was another part was proud of what I had done. What I was able to do. I could play anything now, and I didn't even need to think about it. Regular blues, it was a snap. Anything on that guitar was easy, even things you ought not to be able to play on one. Now, I realize it ain't me. It's something else out there.

"But when I come back from mailing, I brought me some paint and brushes, thought I'd write the notes and such on the wall. I did that, and I was ready to pack and go roaming some more, showing off my new skills, and all of a sudden, the thing, it's pushing through. It had gotten stronger cause I hadn't been playing the sounds, man. I put on the record, and I pretty much been at it ever since.

"It was all that record fella's game, you see. I got to figuring he was the devil, or something like him. He had me playing a game to keep that thing out, and to keep my soul. But it was a three-minute game, six if I'd have kept that second record and put it on the drop. If I was playing on the guitar, I could just work from the end of that record back to the front of it, playing it over and over. But it wore me down. Finally, I started playing the record nonstop. And I have for days.

"The fat man downstairs, he'd come up for the rent, but as soon as he'd use his key and crack that door, hear that music, he'd get gone. So here I am, still playing, with nothing left but to keep on playing, or get my soul sucked up by that thing and delivered to the record store man."

Tootie minded the record, and I went over to where he told me the record store was with the idea to put a boot up the guy's ass, or a .45 slug in his noggin. I found South Street, but not Way South. The other street that should have been Way South was called Back Water. There wasn't a store either, just an empty, unlocked building. I opened the door and went inside.

There was dust everywhere, and I could see where some tables had been, cause their leg marks was in the dust. But anyone or anything that had been there, was long gone.

I went back to the hotel, and when I got there, Tootie was just about asleep. The record was turning on the turntable without any sound. I looked at the wall, and I could see the beak of that thing, chewing at it. I put the record on, and this time, when it come to the end, the thing was still chewing. I played it another time, and another, and the thing finally went away. It was getting stronger.

I woke Tootie up, said, "You know, we're gonna find out if this thing can outrun my souped-up Chevy."

"Ain't no use," Tootie said.

"Then we ain't got nothing to lose," I said.

We grabbed up the record and his guitar, and we was downstairs and out on the street faster than you can snap your fingers. As we passed where the toad was, he saw me and got up quick and went into the kitchen and closed the door. If I'd had time, I'd have beat his ass on general principles.

When we walked to where I had parked my car, it was sitting on four flats and the side windows was knocked out and the aerial was snapped off. The record Alma May had given me was still there, lying on the seat. I got it and put it against the other one in my hand. It was all I could do.

As for the car, I was gonna drive that Chevy back to East Texas like I was gonna fly back on a sheet of wet newspaper.

Now, I got to smellin' that smell. One that was in the room. I looked at the sky. The sun was kind of hazy. Green even. The air around us trembled, like it was scared of something. It was heavy, like a blanket. I grabbed Tootie by the arm, pulled him down the street. I spied a car at a curb that I thought could run, a V-8 Ford. I kicked the back side window out, reached through and got the latch.

I slid across the seat and got behind the wheel. Tootie climbed in on the passenger side. I bent down and worked some wires under the dash loose with my fingers and my razor, hot-wired the car. The motor throbbed and we was out of there.

It didn't make any kind of sense, but as we was cruising along, behind us it was getting dark. It was like chocolate pudding in a big wad rolling after us. Stars was popping up in it. They seemed more like eyes than stars. There was a bit of a moon, slightly covered over in what looked like a red fungus.

I drove that Ford fast as I could. I was hitting the needle at a hundred and ten. Didn't see a car on the highway. Not a highway cop, not an old lady on the way to the store. Where the hell was everybody? The highway looped up and down like the bottom was trying to fall out from under us.

To make it all short, I drove hard and fast, and stopped once for gas, having the man fill it quick. I gave him a bill that was more than the gas was worth, and he grinned at me as we burned rubber getting away. I don't think he could see what we could see—that dark sky with that thing in it. It was like you had to hear the music to see the thing existed, or for it to have any effect in your life. For him, it was daylight and fine and life was good.

By the time I hit East Texas, there was smoke coming from under that stolen Ford's hood. We came down a hill, and it was daylight in front of us, and behind us the dark was rolling in; it was splittin', making a kind of corridor, and there was that beaked thing, that . . . Whatever it was. It was bigger than before and it was squirming its way out of the night sky like a weasel working its way under a fence. I tried to convince myself it was all in my head, but I wasn't convinced enough to stop and find out.

I made the bottom of the hill, in sight of the road that turned off to Alma May's. I don't know why I felt going there mattered, but it was something I had in my mind. Make it to Alma May's, and deliver on my agreement, bring her brother into the house. Course, I hadn't really thought that thing would or could follow us.

It was right then the car engine blew in an explosion that made the hood bunch up from the impact of thrown pistons.

The car died and coasted onto the road that led to Alma May's house. We could see the house, standing in daylight. But even that light was fading as the night behind us eased on in.

I jerked open the car door, snatched the records off the back seat, and yelled to Tootie to start running. He nabbed his guitar, and a moment later, we were both making tracks for Alma May's.

Looking back, I saw there was a moon back there, and stars too, but mostly there was that thing, full of eyes and covered in sores and tentacles and legs and things I can't even describe. It was like someone had thrown critters and fish and bugs and beaks and all manner of disease into a bowl and whipped it together with a whipping spoon.

When we got to Alma May's, I beat on the door. She opened it, showing a face that told me she thought I was knocking too hard, but then she looked over my shoulder, and went pale, almost as if her skin was white. She had heard the music, so she could see it too.

Slamming the door behind us, I went straight to the record player. Alma May was asking all kinds of questions, screaming them out, really. First to me, then to Tootie. I told her to shut up. I jerked one of the records out of its sheath, put it on the turn table, lifted the needle, and—

The electricity crackled and it went dark. There was no playing anything on that player. Outside the world was lit by that blood-red moon.

The door blew open. Tentacles flicked in, knocked over an end table. Some knick knacks fell and busted on the floor. Big as the monster was, it was squeezing through, causing the door frame to crack; the wood breaking sounded like someone cracking whips with both hands.

Me and Alma May, without even thinking about it, backed up. The red shadow, bright as a camp fire, fled away from the monster and started flowing across the floor, bugs and worms squirming in it.

But not toward us.

It was running smooth as an oil spill toward the opposite side of the room. I got it then. It didn't just want through to this side. It wanted to finish off that deal Tootie had made with the record store owner. Tootie had said it all along, but it really hit me then. It didn't want me and Alma at all.

It had come for Tootie's soul.

There was a sound so sharp I threw my hands over my ears, and Alma May went to the floor. It was Tootie's guitar. He had hit it so hard, it sounded electrified. The pulse of that one hard chord made me weak in the knees. It was a hundred times louder than the record. It was beyond belief, and beyond human ability. But, it was Tootie.

The red shadow stopped, rolled back like a tongue.

The guitar was going through its paces now. The thing at the doorway recoiled slightly, and then Tootie yelled, "Come get me. Come have me. Leave them alone."

I looked, and there in the faint glow of the red moonlight through the window, I saw Tootie's shadow lift that guitar high above his head by the neck, and down it came, smashing hard into the floor with an explosion of wood and a springing of strings.

The bleeding shadow came quickly then. Across the floor and onto Tootie. He screamed. He screamed like someone having the flesh slowly burned off. Then the beast came through the door as if shot out of a cannon.

Tentacles slashed, a million feet scuttled, and that beaks came down, ripping at Tootie like a savage dog tearing apart a rag doll. Blood flew all over the room. It was like a huge strawberry exploded.

Then another thing happened. A blue mist floated up from the floor, from what was left of Tootie, and for just the briefest of moments, I saw Tootie's face in that blue mist; the face smiled a toothless kind of smile, showing nothing but a dark hole where his mouth was. Then, like someone sniffing steam off soup, the blue mist was sucked into the beaks of that thing, and Tootie and his soul were done with.

The thing turned its head and looked at us. It made a noise like a thousand rocks and broken automobiles tumbling down a cliff made of gravel and glass, and it began to suck back toward the door. It went out with a snapping sound, like a wet towel being popped. The bleeding shadow ran across the floor after it, eager to catch up; a lap dog hoping for a treat.

The door slammed as the thing and its shadow went out, and then the air got clean and the room got bright.

I looked where Tootie had been.

Nothing.

Not a bone.

Not a drop of blood.

I raised the window and looked out.

It was morning.

No clouds in the sky.

The sun looked like the sun.

Birds were singing.

The air smelled clean as a newborn's breath.

I turned back to Alma May. She was slowly getting up from where she had dropped to the floor.

"It just wanted him," I said, having a whole different kind of feeling about Tootie than I had before. "He gave himself to it. To save you, I think."

She ran into my arms and I hugged her tight. After a moment, I let go of her. I got the records and put them together. I was going to snap them across my knee. But I never got the chance. They went wet in my hands, came apart and hit the floor and ran through the floorboards like black water, and that was all she wrote.

⬥

This retelling and expansion of "The Tinderbox" by Hans Christian Andersen inside the mind of a soldier. Such a point of view can be cruel and brutal—but so is war.

CATASTROPHIC DISRUPTION OF THE HEAD

Margo Lanagan

Who believes in his own death? I've seen how men stop being, how people that you spoke to and traded with slump to bleeding and lie still, and never rise again. I have my own shiny scars, now; I've a head full of stories that goat-men will never believe. And I can tell you: with everyone dying around you, still you can remain unharmed. Some boss-soldier will pull you out roughly at the end, while the machines in the air fling fire down on the enemy, halting the chatter of their guns—at last, at last!—when nothing on the ground would quiet it. I always thought I would be one of those lucky ones, and it turns out that I am. The men who go home as stories on others' lips? They fell in front of me, next to me; I could have been dead just as instantly, or maimed worse than dead. I steeled myself before every fight, and shat myself. But still another part of me stayed serene, didn't it. And was justified in that, wasn't it, for here I am: all in one piece, wealthy, powerful, safe, and on the point of becoming king.

I have the king by the neck. I push my pistol into his mouth, and he gags. He does not know how to fight, hasn't the first clue. He smells nice, expensive. I swing him out from me. I blow out the back of his head. All sound goes out of the world.

I went to the war because elsewhere was glamorous to me. Men had passed through the mountains, one or two of them every year of my life, speaking of what they had come from, and where they were going. All those events and places showed me, with their color and their mystery and their crowdedness, how simple an existence I had here with my people—and how confined, though the sky was broad above us, though we walked the hills and mountains freely with our flocks. The fathers drank up their words, the mothers hurried to feed them, and silently watched and listened. I wanted to bring news home and be the feted man and the respected, the one explaining, not the one all eyes and questions among the goats and children.

I went for the adventure and the cleverness of these men's lives and the scheming. I wanted to live in those stories they told. The boss-soldiers and all their equipment and belongings and weapons and information, and all the other people grasping after those things—I wanted to play them off against each other as these men said they did, and gather the money and food and toys that fell between. One of those silvery capsules, that opened like a seed-case and twinkled and tinkled, that you used for talking to your contact in the hills or among the bosses—I wanted one of those.

There was also the game of the fighting itself. A man might lose that game, they told us, at any moment, and in the least dignified manner, toileting in a ditch, or putting food on his plate at the barracks, or having at a whore in the tents nearby. (There were lots of whores, they told the fathers; every woman was a whore there; some of them did not even take your money, but went with you for the sheer love of whoring.) But look, here was this stranger whole and healthy among us, and all he had was that scar on his arm, smooth and harmless, for all his stories of a head rolling into his lap, and of men up dancing one moment, and stilled forever the next. He was here, eating our food and laughing. The others were only words; they might be stories and no more, boasting and no more. I watched my father and uncles, and some could believe our visitor and some could not, that he had seen so many deaths, and so vividly.

"You are different," whispers the princess, almost crouched there, looking up at me. *"You were gentle and kind before. What has happened? What has changed?"*

I was standing in a wasteland, very cold. An old woman lay dead, blown backwards off the stump she'd been sitting on; the pistol that had taken her face off was in my hand—mine, that the bosses had given me to fight with, that I was smuggling home. My wrist hummed from the shot, my fingertips tingled.

I still had some swagger in me, from the stuff my drugs-man had given me, my going-home gift, his farewell spliff to me, with good powder in it, that I had half-smoked as I walked here. I lifted the pistol and sniffed the tip, and the smoke stung in my nostrils. Then the hand with the pistol fell to my side, and I was only cold and mystified. An explosion will do that, wake you up from whatever drug is running your mind, dismiss whatever dream, and sharply.

I put the pistol back in my belt. What had she done, the old biddy, to annoy me so? I went around the stump and looked at her. She was only disgusting the way old women are always disgusting, with a layer of filth on her such as war always leaves. She had no weapon; she could not have been dangerous to me in any way. Her face was clean and bright between her dirt-black hands—not like a face, of course, but clean red tissue, clean white bone-shards. I was annoyed with myself, mildly, for not leaving her alive so that she could tell me what all this was about. I glared at her facelessness, watching in case the drug should make her dead face speak, mouthless as she was. But she only lay, looking blankly, redly at the sky.

She lied to you, my memory hissed at me.

Ah, yes, that was why I'd shot her. *You make no sense, old woman,* I'd said. Sick of looking at her ugliness, I'd turned cruel, from having been milder before, even kind—from doing the old rag-and-bone a favor! *Here I stand,* I said, *with Yankee dollars spilling over my feet. Here you sit, over a cellar full of treasures, enough to set you up in palaces and feed and clothe you queenly the rest of your days. Yet all you can bring yourself to want is this old thing, factory made, one of millions, well used already.*

I'd turned the Bic this way and that in the sunlight. It was like opening a sack of rice at a homeless camp; I had her full attention, however uncaring she tried to seem.

Children of this country, of this war, will sell you these Bics for a packet-meal—they feed a whole family with one man's ration. In desperate times, two rows of chocolate is all it costs you. Their doddering grandfather will sell you the fluid for a twist of tobacco. Or you can buy a Bic entirely new and full from such shops as are left—caves in the rubble, banged-together stalls set up on the bulldozed streets. A new one will light first go; you won't have to shake it and swear, or click it some magic number of times. Soldiers are rich men in war. All our needs are met, and our pay is laid on extra. There is no need for us to go shooting people, not for cheap cigarette-lighters—cheap and pink and lady-sized.

Yes, but it is mine, she had lied on at me. *It was given to me by my son, that went off to war just like you, and got himself killed for his motherland. It has its hold on me that way. Quite worthless to any other person, it is.*

In the hunch of her and the lick of her lips, the thing was of very great worth indeed.

Tell me the truth, old woman. I had pushed aside my coat. *I have a gun*

here that makes people tell things true. I have used it many times. What is this
Bic to you? or I'll take your head off.

She looked at my pistol, in its well-worn sheath. She stuck out her chin,
fixed again on the lighter. *Give it me!* she said. If she'd begged, if she'd wept,
I might have, but her anger set mine off; that was her mistake.

I lean over the king and push the door-button on the remote. The queen's men
burst in, all pistols and posturing like men in a movie.

It was dark under there, and it smelled like dirt and death-rot. I didn't want
to let the rope go.

Only the big archways are safe, she'd said. *Stand under them and all will*
be well, but step either side and you must use my pinny or the dogs will eat you
alive. I could see no archway; all was black.

I could *hear* a dog, though, panting out the foul air. The sound was all
around, at both my ears equally. I knew dogs, good dogs; but no dog had
ever stood higher than my knee. From the sound, this one could take my
whole head in its mouth.

Which way should I go? How far? I put out my hands, with the biddy's apron
between them. I was a fool to believe her; what was this scrap of cloth against
such a beast? I made the kissing noise you make to a dog. *Pup? Pup?* I said.

His eyes came alight, reddish—at the far end of him, praise God. Oh, he
was enormous! His tail twitched on the floor in front of me, and the sparse
gray fur on it sprouted higher than my waist. He lifted his head—bigger
than the whole house my family lived in, it was. He looked down at me over
the scabby ridges of his rib-cage. Vermin hopped in the beams of his red
eyes. His whole starveling face crinkled in a grin. With a gust of butchery
breath he was up on his spindly shanks. He lowered his head to me full of
lights and teeth, tightening the air with his growl.

A farther dog woke with a bark, and a yet farther one. They set this one
off, and I only just got the apron up in time, between me and the noise
and the snapping teeth. That silenced him. His long claws skittered on the
chamber's stone floor. He paced, and turned and paced again, growling deep
and constantly. His lip was caught high on his teeth; his red eyes glared and
churned. The hackles stuck up like teeth along his back.

Turning my face aside I forced myself and the apron forward at him. Oh,
look—an archway there, just as the old woman said. White light from the
next chamber jumped and swerved in it.

The dog's red eyes were as big as those discs the bosses carry their movies
on. They looked blind, but he saw me, he saw me; I *felt* his gaze on me, the

way you feel a sniper's, in your spine—and his ill-will, only just held back. I pushed the cloth at his nostrils. Rotten-sour breath gusted underneath at me.

But he shrank as the old woman had told me he would, nose and paws and the rest of him; his eyes shone brighter, narrowing to torch-beams. Now I was wrapping not much more than a pup, and a miserable wreck he was, hardly any fur, and his skin all sores and scratches.

I picked him up and carried him to the white-flashing archway, kicking aside coins; they were scattered all over the floor, and heaped up against the red-lit walls. Among them lay bones of dog, bird, sheep, and some of person—old bones, well gnawed, and not a scrap of meat on any of them.

I stepped under the archway and dropped the mangy dog back into his room. He exploded out of himself, into himself, horribly huge and sudden, hating me for what I'd done. But I was safe here; that old witch had known what she was talking about. I turned and pushed the apron at the next dog.

He was a mess of white light, white teeth, snapping madly at the other opening. He smelled of clean hot metal. He shrank to almost an ordinary fighting dog, lean, smooth-haired, strong, with jaws that could break your leg-bone if he took you. His eyes were still magic, though, glaring blind, bulging white. His heavy paws, scrabbling, pushed paper-scraps forward; he cringed in the storm of paper he'd stirred up when he'd been a giant and flinging himself about. As I wrapped him, some of the papers settled near his head: American dollars. *Big* dollars, three-numbered. Oh these, *these* I could carry, these I could use.

For now, though, I lifted the dog. Much heavier he was, than the starving one. I slipped and slid across the drifts of money to the next archway. Beyond it the third dog raged at me, a barking fire-storm. I threw the white dog back behind me, then raised the apron and stepped up to the orange glare, shouting at the flame-dog to settle; I couldn't even hear my own voice.

He shrank in size, but not in power or strangeness. His coat seethed about him, thick with waving gold wires; his tongue was a sprout of fire and white-hot arrow-tips lined his jaws. His eyes, half-exploded from his head, were two ponds of lava, rimmed with the flame pouring from their sockets—clearly they could not see, but my bowels knew he was there behind them, waiting for his chance to cool his teeth in me, to set me alight.

I wrapped my magic cloth around him, picked him up and shone his eye-light about. The scrabbles and shouting from the other dogs behind me bounced off the smooth floor, lost themselves in the rough walls arching over. Where was the treasure the old biddy had promised me in this chamber, the richest of all the three?

The dog burned and panted under my arm. I walked all around, prodding parts of the walls in case they should spill jewels at me or open into treasure-rooms. I reached into cavities hoping to feel bars of gold, giant diamonds—I hardly knew what.

All I found was the lighter the old biddy had asked me to fetch, the pink plastic Bic, lady-sized. And an envelope. Inside was a letter in boss-writing, and attached to that was a rectangle of plastic, with a picture of a foreign girl on it, showing most of her breasts and all of her stomach and legs as she stood in the sea-edge, laughing out of the picture at me. Someone was playing a joke on me, insulting my God and our women instead of delivering me the treasure I'd been promised.

I turned the thing over, rubbed the gold-painted lettering that stood up out of the plastic. Rubbish. Still, there were all those Yankee dollars, no? Plenty there for my needs. I pocketed the Bic and put the rubbish back in the hole in the wall. I crossed swiftly to the archway, turned in its safety and shook the dog out of the cloth. Its eyes flared wide, and its roar was part voice, part flame. I showed it my back. I'd met real fire, that choked and cooked people—this fairy-fire held no fear for me.

Back in the white dog's chamber, I stuffed my pack as full as I could, every pocket of it, with the dollars. It was *heavy*! It and the white fighting dog were almost more than I could manage. But I took them through and into the red-lit carrion-cave, and I subdued the mangy dog there. I carried him across to where rope-end dangled in its root-lined niche, and I pulled the loop down around the bulk of the money on my back, and the dog still in my arms, and hooked it under myself.

There came a shout from above. Praise God, she had not run off and left me. *Yes!* I cried. *Bring me up!*

When she had me well off the floor, I cast the red-eyed dog out of the apron-cloth. He dropped; he ballooned out full-sized, long-shanked. He looked me in the eye, with his lip curled and his breath fit to wither the skin right off my face. I flapped the apron at him. *Boo,* I said. *There. Get down.* The other two dogs bayed deep below. Had they made such a noise at the beginning, I never would have gone down.

And then I was out the top of the tree-trunk and swinging from the branch, slower now than I'd swung before, being so much heavier. The old woman stood there, holding me and my burden aloft, the rope coiling beside her. She was stronger than I would have believed possible.

"Do you have it?" She beamed up at me.

"Oh, I have it, don't worry. But get me down from here before I give you it. I would not trust you as far as I could throw you."

And she laughed, properly witch-like, and stepped in to secure the rope against the tree.

She is not the first virgin I've had, my little queen, but she fights the hardest and is the most satisfying, having never in her worst dreams imagined this could happen to her. I have her every which way, and she urges me on with her screams, with her weeping, with her small fists and her torn mouth and her eyes now wide, now tight-closed squeezing out tears. The indignities I put her through, the unqueenly positions I force her into, force her to stay in, excite me again as soon as I am spent. She fills up the air with her pleading, her horror, her powerless pretty rage, for as long as she still has the spirit.

I left the old woman where she lay, and I took her treasure with me, her little Bic. I walked another day, and then a truck came by and picked me up and took me to the next big town. I found a bank, and had no difficulty storing my monies away in it. There I learned what I had lost when I put the sexy-card back in the cave wall, for the bank-man gave me just such a one, only plainer. The card was the key to my money, he said. I should show the card to whoever was selling to me, and through the magic of computers the money would flow straight out of the bank to that person, without me having to touch it.

"Where is a good hotel?" I asked him, when we were done. "And where can I find good shopping, like Armani and Rolex?" These names I had heard argued over, as we crouched in foxholes and behind walls waiting for orders; I had seen them in the boss-magazines, between the pages of the women some men tortured themselves with wanting, during the many boredoms of the army.

The bank-man came out with me onto the street and waved me up a taxi. I didn't even have to tell the driver where to go. I sat in the back seat and smiled at my good fortune. The driver eyed me in the mirror.

"Watch the road," I said. "You'll be in big trouble if I get hurt."

"Sir," he said.

At the hotel I found that I was already vouched for; the bank had telephoned them to say I was coming and to treat me well.

"First," I said, "I will have a hot bath, a meal, and some hours' sleep. I've traveled a long way. Then I will need clothes, and this uniform to be burned. And introductions. Other rich men. Rich women, too; beautiful women. I'm sure you know the kind of thing I mean."

When I was stuffing my pack full of dollars underground, I could not imagine ever finding a use for so much money. But then began my new life. A long, bright dream, it was, of laughing friends, and devil women in their devil clothes, and wonderful drugs, and new objects and belongings conjured by money as if by wizardry, and I enjoyed it all and thoroughly. Money lifts and floats you, above cold weather and hunger and war, above filth, above having to think and plan—if any problem comes at you, you throw a little money at it and it is gone, and everyone smiles and bows and thanks you for your patronage.

That is, until your plastic dies. *Then* I understood truly what treasure I'd rejected when I left that card in the third cave. There was no more money behind my card; that other card, with the near-naked woman on it, behind *that* had been an endless supply; *that* card would never have died. I had to sell my apartment and rent a cheaper place. Piece by piece I sold all the ornaments and furniture I'd accumulated, to pay my rent. But even the worth of those expensive objects ran out, and I let the electricity and the gas go, and then I found myself paying my last purseful for a month's rent in not much more than an attic, and scrounging for food.

I sat one night on the floor at my attic window, hungry and glum, with no work but herding and soldiering to turn my fortunes around with. I went through my last things, my last belongings left in a nylon backpack too shabby to sell. I pulled out an envelope, with a crest on it, of a hotel—ah, it was those scraps from the first day I had come to this town, with all my money in my pack. These were the bits and pieces that the chamber-boy had saved from the pockets of my soldiering-clothes. *Shall I throw these away, sir?* he'd said to me. *No,* I told him. *Keep them to remind me how little I had before today. How my fortunes changed.*

"Ha!" I laid the half-spliff on my knee. A grain fell out of the tip. That had been a good spliff, I remembered, well-laced with the fighting-powder that made you a hero, that took away all your fear.

"And you!" I took out the pink lighter, still fingerprinted with the mud of that blasted countryside.

"Ha!" One last half-spliff would make this all bearable. A few hours, I would have, when nothing mattered, not this house, not this hunger, not my own uselessness and the stains on my memory from what I had done as a rich man, and before that as a soldier. And then, once it was done . . . Well, I would just have to beggar and burgle my way home, wouldn't I, and take up with the goats again. But why think of that now? I scooped the grain back into the spliff and twisted the end closed. I flicked the lighter.

Some huge thing, rough, scabby, crushed me to the wall. I gasped a breath of sweet-rotten air and near fainted. Then the thing adjusted itself, and I was free, and could see, and it was that great gray spindly dog from the underground cave, turning and turning on himself in the tiny space of my attic, sweeping the beams of his red movie-disc eyes about, at me, at my fate and circumstances.

I stared at the lighter in my hand. A long, realizing sound came out of me. So the lighter was the key to the dogs! You flicked it, they came. And see how he lowered his head and his tail in front of me, and looked away from my stare. He was mine, in my power! I didn't need some old apron-of-a-witch to wrap him in and tame him.

Sweat prickled out on me, cold. I'd nearly left this Bic with the old biddy, in her dead hand, for a joke! Some other soldier, some civilian scavenger, some child, might have picked it up and got this power! I'd been going to fling it far out into the mud-land around us, just to laugh while she scrabbled after it. I'd been going to walk away laughing, my pack stuffed with the money I'd brought up from below, and the old girl with nothing.

I looked around the red-lit attic, and out the window at the patched and crowded roofs across the way, dimming with evening. I need never shiver here again; I need never see these broken chimneys or these bent antennae. Now I *enjoyed* the tweaking of the hunger pangs in my belly, because I was about to banish them forever, just as soon as I summoned that hot golden dog with his never-dying money-card.

I clicked the lighter three times.

And so it all began again, the dream, the floating, the powders and good weed, the friends. They laughed again at my stories of how I had come here from such a nowhere. For a time there my family and our goats had lost their fascination, but now they enthralled these prosperous people again, as travelers' tales had once bewitched me around the home fires.

I catch the queen by the shoulders. One of her men dives for his gun. I shoot him; his eye spouts; he falls dead. The queen gives a tiny shriek.

I heard about the princess from the man who fitted out my yacht. He had just come from the tricky job of making lounges for the girl's prison tower, which was all circular rooms.

"Prison?" I said. "The king keeps his daughter in a prison?"

"You haven't heard of this?" He laughed. "He keeps her under lock and key, always has. He's a funny chap. He had her stars done, her chart or whatever, right when she was born, and the chart said she'd marry a soldier. So he keeps her locked up so's this soldier won't get to her. She only meets people her parents choose."

Oh, does she? I thought, even as I laughed and shook my head with the yacht-man.

That night when I was alone and had smoked a spliff, I had the golden dog bring her. She arrived asleep, his back a broad bed for her, his fire damped down for her comfort. He laid the girl on the couch nearest the fire.

She curled up there, belonging as I've never belonged in these apartments, delicate, royal, at peace. She was like a carved thing I'd just purchased, a figurine. She was beautiful, certainly, but not effortfully so, as were most women I had met since I came into my wealth. It was hard to say how much of her beauty came from the fact that I knew she was a princess; her royalty seemed to glow in her skin, to be woven into her clothing, every stitch and seam of it considered and made fit. Her little foot, out the bottom of the nightdress, was the neatest, palest, least walked-upon foot I had ever seen since the newborn feet of my brothers and sisters. It was a foot meant for an entirely different purpose from my own, from most feet of the world.

Even in my new, clean clothes, like a man's in a magazine, I felt myself to be filth crouched beside this creature. These hands had done work, these eyes had seen things that she could never conceive of; this memory was a rubbish-heap of horrors and indignities. It was one thing to be rich; it was quite another to be born into it, to be royal from a long line of royalty, to have never lived anything but the palace life.

The princess woke with the tiniest of starts. Up and back from me she sat, and she took in the room, and me.

Have you kidnapped me? she said, and swallowed a laugh.

Look at your eyes, I said, but her whole face was the thing, bright awake, and curious, and not disgusted by me.

Perhaps your name? she said gently. Her nightwear was modest in covering her neck-to-ankle, but warmth rushed through me to see her breasts so clearly outlined inside the thin cloth.

I made myself meet her eyes. *Can I serve you somehow? Are you hungry? Thirsty?*

How can I be? said the princess, and blinked. *I am asleep and dreaming. Or stoned. It smells very strongly of weed in here. Where was I before?*

I brought a tray of pretty foods from the feast the golden dog had readied. I sat beside her and poured us both some of the cordial. I handed it to her in the frail stemmed glass, raised mine to her and drank.

I shouldn't touch it, she whispered. *I am in a story; it will put me under some spell.*

Then I am magicked too, I said, and raised again the glass I'd sipped from, pretending to be alarmed that half was gone.

She laughed, a small sweet sound—she had very well-kept teeth, just like the magazine women, the poster-women—then she drank.

Now, tell me, what is all this? I said of the tray. *These little things here—they must be fruit by their shape, no? But why are they so small?*

She ate one, and it clearly pleased her. *Who is your chef?* she said, with a kind of frown of pleasure.

He is a secret, I said, for I could hardly tell her that a dog had made this feast.

Of course. She took another of the little fruits, and ate it, and held her fingers ready to lick, a delicate spread fan.

She touched her fingers to a napkin, then put the tray aside. She knelt beside me, and leaned through the perfume of herself, which was light and clean and spoke only quietly of her wealth. *Who are you?* she said, and she put her lips to mine, and held them there a little, her eyes closing, then opening surprised. *Do you not* want *to kiss me?*

I sit with my fellows in the briefing-room at the barracks. Up on the movie screen, foreign actors are locked together by their lips. Boss-soldiers groan and hoot in the seats in front of us. We giggle at the screen and at the men. "And they call us 'tribals,'" says my friend Kadir who later will be blown to pieces before my eyes. *"Look at how wild they are, what animals! They cannot control themselves."*

The princess was poised to be dismayed or embarrassed. *Oh, I do want to,* I said, *but how is it done?* For, except for my mother in my childhood, I had never kissed a woman—even here in my rich-man life—in a way that was not somehow a violence upon her.

So handsome, and you don't already know? But she taught me. She was gentle, but forceful; she pressed herself to me, pushed me (with her little weight!) down onto the couch cushions. I was embarrassed that she must feel my desire, but she did not seem to mind, or perhaps she did not know enough to notice. She crushed her breasts against me, her belly and thighs. And the kissing—I had to breathe through my nose, for she would not stop, and there was no room for my breath with all her little lively tongue, and her hair falling and sliding everywhere, and eventually I dared to put my hands to her rounded bottom and pull her harder against me, and closed my eyes against the consequences.

Hush, she said over me at one point, rising off me, her hair making a slithering tent around our heads and shoulders, all dark gold. Her breasts hung forward in the elaborate frontage of the nightgown—I was astonished by their closeness; I covered them with my hands in a kind of swoon.

I told her what I was, in the night, over some more of that beautiful insubstantial food. I told her about the old woman, and the dogs; I showed her the Bic. *That is all I am,* I said. *Lucky. Lucky to have lived, lucky to have come into this fortune, lucky to have you before me. I am not noble and I have no right to anything.*

Oh, she said, *but it is all luck, don't you see?* And she knelt up and held my face as a child does, to make you listen. *My own family's wealth, it came about from the favors of one king and one bishop, back in the fourteenth century. You learn all the other, all the speaking and manners and how to behave with people lower than yourself; it can be learned by goatherds and by soldiers just as it can by the farmers my family once were, the loyal servants.*

She kissed me. *Certainly you look noble,* she whispered and smiled. *You are my prince, be sure of that.*

She dazzled me with what she was, and had, and said, and what she was free from knowing. But I would have loved her just for her body and its closeness, how pale she was, and soft, and intact, and for her face, perfect above that perfection, gazing on me enchanted. She was like the foods she fancied, beautiful nothingness, a froth of luxury above the hard, real business of the world, which was the machinery of war and missiles, the flying darts and the blown dust and smoke, the shudder in your guts as the bosses brought in the air support, and saved you yet again from becoming a thing like these others, pieces of bleeding litter tossed aside from the action, their part in the game ended.

With the muzzle of the pistol, I push aside the queen's earring—a dangling flower or star, made of sparkling diamonds, a royal heirloom. I press the tip in below her ear, fire, and drop her to the carpet. It's all coming back to me, the efficiency. "Bring me the prince!" I cry.

The women of the bosses' world, they are foul beautiful creatures. They are devils, that light a fire in the loins of decent men. One picture is all you need, and such a picture can be found on any boss-soldier's wall in the barracks; my first time in such a place, all my fellows around me were torn as I was between feasting their eyes on the shapes and colors taped to the walls, and uttering damnation on the bosses' souls, and laughing—for it was ridiculous, wasn't it, such behavior? The taping itself was unmanly, a weakness—but the posturing of the picture-girls, I hardly knew how to regard that. I had never seen *faces* so naked, let alone the out-thrustingness of the rest of their bodies. I was embarrassed for them, and for the boss-men who looked upon these women, and longed for them—even as the women did their evil work on me, and woke my longings too.

We covered our embarrassment by pulling the pictures down, tearing one, but only a little, and by accident. We put them in the bin, where they were even less dignified, upside down making their faces to themselves, of ecstasy and scorn, or animal abandon. We looked around in relief, the walls bare except for family pictures now. Someone opened a bedside cupboard and found those magazines they have. Around the group of us they went, and we yelped and laughed and pursed our mouths over them, and some tried to whistle as the bosses whistled; I did not touch one at all, not a single page, but I saw enough to disgust and enliven me both for a long time to come.

Someone raised his head, and we all listened. Engines. "Land Rover! They are coming!" And we scrambled to put the things back, made clumsy by our laughter and our fear.

"This is the best one! Take this one with us!"

"Straighten them! Straighten them in the cupboard, like we found them!"

I remember as we ran away, and I laughed and hurried with the rest, another part of me was dazed and stilled by what I had seen, and could not laugh at all. Those women would show themselves, *all* of themselves, parts you had never seen, and did not want to—or did you?—to any man, any; they would let themselves be put in a picture and taped up on a wall for any man's eyes. I was stunned and aroused; I felt so dirtied that I would never be clean, never the man I had been before I saw what I had seen.

And now I was worse, myself, even than those bosses. I lived, I knew, an unclean life. I did not keep my body pure, for marriage or any other end, but only polluted myself and wasted my good seed on wanton women, only poisoned myself with spliffs and powders and liquors.

It is very confusing when you can do anything. You settle for following the urge that is strongest, and call up food perhaps. Then this woman smiles at you, so you do what a man must do; then another man insults you, so you pursue his humiliation. While you wait for a grander plan to emerge in your head, a thousand small choices make up your life, none of them honorable.

It is much easier to take the right path when you only have two to choose from. Easiest of all is when you are under orders, or under fire; when one choice means death, you can make up your mind in a flash.

These things, about the women and my impurity, I would not tell anyone at home. This was why my family stayed away from the greater, the outer world; this was why we hid in the mountains. We could live a good life there, a clean life.

Buzzz. I go to the wall and press the button to see out. Three men stand at the door downstairs. They wear suits, old-fashioned but not in a dowdy way. *You thought you had run ahead of us,* say the steep white collars, the strangely-fastened cuffs, and the fit, the cut of those clothes; even a goat-boy can hear it. *But our power is sunk deep, spread wide, and knotted tight into the fabric of all things.*

The closest one takes off his sunglasses. He calls me by my army name. I fall back a little from the screen. "Who are you and what do you want?"

"We must ask you some questions, in the name of His Majesty the King," he says. He's well fed, the spokesman, and pleased with himself, the way boss-soldiers are, the higher ranks who can fly away back to Boss-Land if things get too rough for them.

"I've nothing to say to any king," I say into the grille. How is he onto me so quickly? Does *he* have magic dogs as well?

"I have to advise you that we are authorized to use force."

I move the camera up to see beyond them. Their car gleams in the apartment's turning circle, with the royal crest on the door. Six soldiers—spick and span, well armed, no packs to weigh them down if they need to run—are lining up alert and out of place on the gravel. Behind them squats an armored vehicle, a prison on wheels.

I pull the sights back down to the ones at the door. I wish I had wired those marble steps the way the enemy used to. I itch for a button to press, to turn them to smoke and shreds. But there are plenty more behind them. By the look of all that, they know they're up against more than one man.

I buzz them in to the lobby. In the bedroom, I take the pistol from my bedside drawer. In the sitting-room lie the remains of the feast, the spilled throw-rug that the princess wrapped herself in as she talked and talked last night. I pick up the Bic and click it twice. "Tidy this up," I say into the bomb-blast of silver, and he picks up the mess in his teeth and tosses it away, and goggles at me for more orders. He could deal with this whole situation by himself if I told him. But I'm not a lazy man, or a coward.

The queen's men knock at the apartment door. I get into position—it feels good, that my body still knows how. "Shrink down, over there," I say to the silver dog. The light from his eyes pulses white around the walls.

Three clicks. "Fetch me the king!" I shout before the gold dog has time to properly explode into being, and they arrive together, the trapped man jerking and exclaiming in the dog's jaws. He wears a nice blue suit, nice shoes, all bespoke as a king's clothes should be.

The knocking comes again, and louder. The dog stands the king gently on the carpet. I take the man in hand—not roughly, just so he knows who's running this show. "Sit with your friend," I say to the dog, and it shrinks and withdraws to the window, its flame-fur seething. The air is strong with their spice and hot metal, but it won't overpower me; I'm cold and clever and I know what to do.

I lean over the king and push the door-button on the remote. The queen's suits burst in, all pistols and posturing. Then they see me; they aren't so pleased with themselves then. They scramble to stop. The dogs stir by the window and the scent tumbles off them, so strong you can almost see it rippling across the air.

"You can drop those," I say. The men put up their hands and kick their guns forward.

I have the king by the neck. I push my pistol into his mouth, and he gags. He doesn't know how to fight, hasn't the first clue. He smells nice, expensive.

"Maybe he can ask me those questions himself, no?" I shout past his ear at the two suits left. I swing him around to where he will not mess me up so much. "Bring me the queen!" I shout to the golden dog, and blow out the back of the king's head. The noise is terrific; the deafness from it wads my ears.

The queen arrives stiff with fear between the dog's teeth. Her summery dress is printed with carefree flowers. Her skin is as creamy as her daughter's; her body is lean and light and has never done a day's proper work. I catch her to me by the shoulders. One of the guards dives for his gun. I shoot him in the eye. The queen gives a tiny shriek and shakes against me.

The dogs' light flashes in the men's wide eyes. "Please!" mouths their captain. "Let her go. Let her go."

I can feel the queen's voice, in her neck and chest, but her lips are not moving. She's trying to twist, trying to see what's left of the king.

"What are you saying, Your Majesty?" I shake her, keeping my eyes on her men. "Are you giving your blessing, upon your daughter's marriage? Perhaps you should! Perhaps I should make you! No?" My voice hurts in my throat, but I only hear it faintly.

I take her out from the side, quickly so as not to give her goons more chances. I drop her to the carpet. It's all coming back to me, the efficiency.

"The prince!" I command, and there he is, flung on the floor naked except for black socks, his wet man wilting as he scrambles up to face me. I could laugh, and tease him and play with him, but I'm not in that mood. He's just an obstacle to me, the king's only other heir. My gaze fixes on the guards, I push my pistol up under his jaw and I fire. The silent air smells of gun smoke and burnt bone.

"Get these toy-boys out of here," I shout to the dogs, even more painfully, even more faintly. "Put the royals back, just the way they are. In their palace, or their townhouse, or their brothel, or wherever you found them. My carpet, and my clothes here—get the stains off them. Don't leave a single clue behind. Then go down and clear the garden, and the streets, of all those men and traffic."

It's not nice to watch the dogs at work, picking up the live men and the dead bodies both, and flinging them like so many rags, away to nothing. The filthy dog, the scabbed one—why must *he* be the one to lick up the blood from the carpet, from the white leather of the couch? Will he lick me clean too? But my clothes, my hands, are spatter-free already; my fingertips smell of the spiciness of the golden dog, not the carrion tongue of the mangy one.

Then they're gone. Everything's gone that doesn't belong here. The carpet and couch are as white as when I chose them from the catalogue; the room is spacious again without the dogs.

I open the balcony windows to let out the smells of death and dog. Screams come up from the street, and a single short burst of gunfire. A soldier flies up past me, his machine-gun separating from his hands. They go up to dots in the sky, and neither falls back down.

By the time I reach the balcony railing, all is gone from below except people fleeing from what they've seen. The city lies in the bright morning, humming with its many lives and vehicles. I spit on its peacefulness. Their king is dead, and their prince. Soon they'll be ruled by a goatherd, all those suits and uniforms below me, all those bank-men and party-boys and groveling shop-owners. Everyone from the highest dignitary to the lowliest beggar will be at my disposal, subject to my whim.

I stride back into the apartment, which is stuffed fat with the dogs. They shrink and fawn on me, and shine their eyes about.

"I want the princess!" I say to the golden one and he grins and hangs out his crimson tongue. "Dress her in wedding finery, with the queen's crown on her head. Bring me the king-crown, and the right clothes, too, for such an occasion. A priest! Rings! Witnesses! Whatever papers and people are needed to make me king!"

Which they do, and through everyone's confusion and my girl's delight—for she thinks she's dreaming me still, and the news hasn't yet reached her that she is orphaned—the business is transacted, and all the names are signed to all the documents that require them.

But the instant the crown is placed on my head, my rage, which was clean and pure and unquestioning while I reached for this goal, falters. Why should I want to rule these people, who know nothing either of war or of mountains, these spoiled fat people bowing down to me only because they know I hold their livelihoods—their very lives!—in my hands, these soft-living men, these whore-women, who would never survive the cold, thin air of my home, who would cringe and gag at the thought of killing their own food?

"Get them out of here," I say to the golden dog. "And all this nonsense. Only leave the princess—the queen, I should say. Her Majesty."

And the title is bitter on my tongue, so lately did I use it for her mother. King, queen, prince, and people, all are despicable to me. I understand for the first time that the war I fought in, which goes on without me, is being fought entirely to keep this wealth safe, this river of luxury flowing, these chefs making their glistening fresh food, these walls intact and the tribals busy outside them, these lawns untrampled by jealous mobs come to tear down the palaces.

And she's despicable too, who was my princess and dazzled me so last night. Smiling at our solitude, she walks towards me in that shameful dress, presenting her breasts to me in their silken tray, the cloth sewn close about her waist to better show how she swells above and below, for all to see, as those dignitaries saw just now, my wife on open display like an American celebrity woman in a movie, like a porn queen in a sexy-mag.

I claw the crown from my head and fling it away from me. I unfasten the great gold-encrusted king-cape and push it off; it suffocates me, crushes me. My girl watches, shocked, as I tear off the sash and brooches and the foolish shirt—truly tear some of it, for the shirt-fastenings are so ancient and odd, it cannot be removed undamaged without a servant's help.

Down to only the trousers, I'm a more honest man; I can see, I can *be*, my true self better. I take off the fine buckled shoes and throw them hard at the valuable vases across the sitting room. The vases tip and burst apart against each other, and the pieces scatter themselves in the dogs' fur as they lie there intertwined, grinning and goggling, taking up half the room.

The princess—the queen—is half-crouched, caught mid-laugh, mid-cringe, clutching the ruffles about her knees and looking up at me. "You are different," she says, her child-face insulting, accusing, above the cream-lit cleft between her breasts. "You were gentle and kind before," she whispers. "What has happened? What has changed?"

I kick aside the king-clothes. "Now you," I say, and I reach for the crown on her head.

My mother stirs the pot as if nothing exists but this food, none of us children tumbling on the floor fighting, none of the men talking and taking their tea around the table. The food smells good, bread baking, meat stewing with onions.

It is a tiny world. The men talk of the larger, outer one, but they know nothing. They know goats, and mountains, but there is so much more that they can't imagine, that they will never see.

I shower. I wash off the blood and the scents of the princess, the bottled one and the others, more natural, of her fear above and of her flower below that I plucked—that I *tore,* more truthfully, from its roots. I gulp down shower-water, lather my hair enormously, soap up and scrub hard the rest of me. Can I ever be properly clean again? And once I am, what then? There seems to be nothing else to do, once you're king, once you've treated your queen so. I could kill her, could I not? I could be king alone, without her eyes on me always, fearful and accusing. I could do that; I've got the dogs. I could do anything. (I lather my sore man-parts—they feel defiled, though she was my wife and untouched by any other man—or so she claimed, in her terror.)

I rinse and rinse, and turn off the hissing water, dry myself and step out into the bedroom. There I dress in clean clothes, several layers, Gore-Tex the outermost. I stuff my ski-cap and gloves in my jacket pockets, my pistol to show my father that my tale is true. I go into my office, never used, and take from the filing drawers my identifications, my discharge papers—all I have left of my life before this, all I have left of myself.

Out on the blood-smeared couch, my wife-girl lies unconscious or asleep, indecent in the last position I forced on her. She's not frightened any more, at least, not for the moment. I throw the ruined ruffled thing, the wedding-dress, to one side, and spread a blanket over her, covering all but her face. I didn't have to do any of what I did. I might have treated her gently; I might have made a proper marriage with her; we might have been king and queen together, dignified and kind to each other, ruling our peoples together, the three giant dogs at our backs. We could have stopped the war; we could have sorted out this country; we could have done anything. Remember her fragrance, when it was just that light bottle-perfume? Remember her face, unmarked and laughing, just an hour or so ago as she married you?

I stand up, away from what I did to her. The fur-slump in the corner rises and becomes the starving gray, the white bull-baiter, the dragon-dog with its flame-coat flickering around it, its eyes fireworking out of its golden mask face.

"I want you to do one last thing for me." I pull on my ski-cap. The dogs whirl their eyes and spill their odors on me.

I bend and put the pink Bic in the princess's hand. Her whole body gives a start, making me jump, but she doesn't wake up.

I pull on my gloves, heart thumping. "Send me to my family's country," I say to the dogs. "I don't care which one of you."

Whichever dog does it, it's extremely strong, but it uses none of that strength to hurt me.

The whole country's below me, the war *there*, the mountains *there*, the city flying away back *there*. I see for an instant how the dogs travel so fast: the instants themselves adjust around them, make way for them, squashing down, stretching out, whichever way is needed for the shape and mission of the dog.

Then I am stumbling in the snow, staggering alongside a wall of snowy rocks. Above me, against the snow-blown sky, the faint lines of Flatnose Peak on the south side, and Great Rain on the north, curve down to meet and become the pass through to my home.

The magic goes out of things with a snap like a passing bullet's. No giant dog warms or scents the air. No brilliant eye lights up the mountainside. My spine and gut are empty of the thrill of power, of danger. I'm here where I used to imagine myself when we were under fire with everything burning and bleeding around me, everyone dying. Snow blows like knife-slashes across my face; the rocky path veers off into the blizzard ahead; the wind is tricky and bent on upending me, tumbling me down the slope. It's dangerous, but not the wild, will-of-God kind of dangerous that war is; all I have to do to survive here is give my whole mind and body to the walking. I remember this walking; I embrace it. The war, the city, the princess, all the technology and money I had, the people I knew—these all become things I once dreamed, as I fight my frozen way up the rocks, and through the weather.

"I should like to meet them," she says to me in the dream, in my dream of last night when she loved me. She sits hugging her knees, unsmiling, perhaps too tired to be playful or pretend anything.

"I have talked too much of myself," I apologize.

"It's natural," she says steadily to me, "to miss your homeland."

I edge around the last narrow section of the path. There are the goats, penned into their cave; they jostle and cry out at the sight of a person, at the smells of the outside world on me, of soap and new clothing.

In the wall next to the pen, the window-shutter slides aside from a face, from a shout. The door smacks open and my mother runs out, ahead of my stumbling father; my brothers and sisters overtake them. My grandfather comes to the doorway; the littler sisters catch me around the waist and my parents throw themselves on me, weeping, laughing. We all stagger and fall. The soft snow catches us. The goats bray and thrash in their pen with the excitement.

"You should have sent word!" my mother shouts over all the questions, holding me tight by the cheeks. "I would have prepared such a feast!"

"I didn't know I was coming," I shout back. "Until the very last moment. There wasn't time to let you know."

"Come! Come inside, for tea and bread at least!"

Laughing, they haul me up. "How you've all grown!" I punch my littlest brother on the arm. He returns the punch to my thigh and I pretend to stagger. "I think you broke the bone!" And they laugh as if I'm the funniest man in the world.

We tumble into the house. "Wait," I say to Grandfather, as he goes to close the door.

I look out into the storm, to the south and west. Which dog will the princess send? The gray one, I think; I hope she doesn't waste the gold on tearing me limb from limb. And when will he come? How long do I have? She might lie hours yet insensible.

"Shut that door! Let's warm the place up again!" Every sound behind me is new again, but reminds me of the thousand times I've heard it before: the dragging of the bench to the table, the soft rattle of boiling water into a tea-bowl, the chatter of children.

"You will have seen some things, my son," says my father too heartily— he's in awe of me, coming from the world as I do. He doesn't know me any more. "Sit down and tell us them."

"Not all, though, not all." My mother puts her hands over the ears of the nearest sister, who shakes her off annoyed. "Only what is suitable for women and girl-folk."

So I sit, and sip the tea and soak the bread of home, and begin my story.

=⟩—

*Perhaps death is neither as easily defined
nor quantified as we might think . . .*

TELL ME I'LL SEE YOU AGAIN

Dennis Etchison

◄══►

Say it happened like this:

All the lawns were dry and white that day. Cars hunkered in driveways or shimmered like heat mirages at the curb. Last summer the four of them had tried to fry an egg on the sidewalk. This year it might work. As she walked past Mrs. Shaede's rosebush she noticed a cricket perched on the bleached yellow petals. When she stopped for a closer look the insect dropped off and fell at her feet. She studied it, the papery body and thin, ratcheted legs, but it did not move again. So she reached down, picked it up and slipped it carefully into her shirt pocket.

At that moment there was a rumbling in the distance.

She knew the sound. Mr. Donohue's truck had a bad muffler. She glanced up in time to see it pass at the end of the street. A few seconds later a bicycle raced across the intersection, trying to catch the truck. The spokes flashed and the tires snaked over the hot pavement.

"David!" she shouted, and waved, but he pedaled away.

The muffler faded as the pickup headed for the boulevard. Then she heard a faint metallic clatter somewhere on the next block. It could have been a bicycle crashing to the ground.

She hurried for the corner.

Vincent came out of his house, drinking a Dr Pepper. "Where you going?" he said.

"Did you hear that?"

"Hear what?"

Now there was only the buzzing of bees, the raspy bark of a dog in a backyard.

"I think it was David."

"What about him?"

"He's in trouble," she said, and hurried on.

Vincent followed at a casual pace. By the time he caught up she was squinting along the cross street.

"What happened?"

"I don't know!"

"Don't worry about it." He showed her the can of soda. "Want one? I got some more in the basement."

"Not now!"

"Aw, he's all right."

"No, he's not. Look."

A couple of hundred feet down, before the turn onto Charter Way, the bicycle lay on its side in the grass, the front wheel pointing at the sky and the spokes still spinning. David was twisted under the frame, the handlebars across his chest.

She ran the rest of the way, stopped and waited for him to move.

"Not bad." Vincent walked around the crash scene. "I give him a seven."

"This isn't a game." She studied the boy on the ground, the angle of his neck. She watched his eyelids. They remained shut.

"Sure it is," said Vincent. "We used to play it last summer. Remember?"

She got down on her knees and pressed her ear to his chest. There was no heartbeat. She unbuttoned his shirt to be sure. Then she moved her head up until her cheek almost touched his lips. No air came out of his nose or mouth. This time he was not breathing at all.

"Help me," she said.

"I don't see any blood."

Vincent was right about that. And the bike seemed to be undamaged, as if it had simply fallen over.

"David? Can you hear me?"

"It looks pretty real, though. The way he's got his tennis shoe in the chain . . . "

"Are you going to help or not?"

Vincent raised the bike while she worked the foot free. She slipped her arm under David's shoulders and tried to sit him up. "David," she whispered. "Tell me you're all right."

"Okay, okay," Vincent said, "I'll give him an eight."

She lowered David back down, dug her fingers into his hair and tapped his head against the ground. Then she did it again, harder. Finally his chest heaved as he began to breathe. His eyelids opened.

"I knew he was faking," Vincent said.

"You take the bike," she told him.

"Eric used to do it better, though."

"Shut up."

Vincent started to wheel the bike onto the sidewalk. He had to turn the handlebars so he did not run over a small mound on the grass.

"What the hell is that?" he said. "A dead raccoon?"

"Leave it."

"I hate those things." Vincent raised his foot, ready to kick it like a football.

"It's a possum. I said *leave it*."

She got up quickly, walked over, took hold of the animal by the fur and tapped it against the ground. Once was enough. The frightened creature sprang to life, wriggled free and scurried off.

"Faker!" said Vincent.

"Take the bike, I told you. We'll meet at his house."

She went back to David and held out her hand.

"Come on. I'll walk you home."

David blinked, trying to focus. "Is my dad there?"

"I didn't know you went out," said his grandmother from the porch.

"Sorry," said David.

"You should always tell someone."

"Do you know where my dad went?"

"To get some kind of tool."

"Oh."

"Come in the house. You don't look so good. Would your friends like a cold drink?"

"Not me," said Vincent.

"No, thank you," said the girl.

"Is he coming back?"

"Why, of course he is, Davey. Now come in before you get heat stroke."

"I have to put my bike away."

"Well, don't be long." She opened the screen door and went inside.

"I gotta go, anyway," Vincent said. He started out of the front yard. "Wanna come over to my place?"

"Not right now," said David.

"We can play anything you want."

David was not listening. His eyes moved nervously from the driveway to the end of the block and back again. The girl moved over and stood next to him.

"Maybe later," she said.

"Okay. Well, see ya."

She sat down on the porch as Vincent walked away.

"Are you sure you're all right?"

"Yeah."

"I thought you got hit by a car or something."

"Naw."

"What do you remember?"

"Nothing."

"You never do. But that's okay. We'll figure it out."

There was the rumbling of the muffler again, at the end of the block. David stood by the driveway until the pickup truck rounded the corner and turned in. His father got out, carrying a bag.

"Hey, champ," he said.

"Where were you?"

"At the Home Depot."

"Why didn't you take me?"

"Did you want to go?"

"I always do."

"Next time, I promise. Hello, there. Charlene, isn't it?"

"Sherron. Hi, Mr. Donohue."

"Of course. You're David's friend, from school. How have you been?"

"Fine."

"You knew Eric, didn't you? David's brother?"

"Yes," she said in a low voice.

"Dad . . ."

"I have an idea. Why don't you stay for lunch? Would you like that?"

Something moved in her chest, or at least in the pocket of her shirt, trying to get out. The cricket from the rosebush had come back to life. "I would. I mean, I do. But I sort of have to get home. My mom's expecting me. She's making something special."

"Another time, then."

"I was wondering," she said carefully. "Could David come, too? She said it was all right."

"Why, I think that's a fine invitation. Don't you, son?"

David considered. "Are you leaving again?"

"Not today. I've got plenty to do in the garage."

"Please?" she said to David. "I need you to help me with something."

"Well . . ."

"My science project. It's really cool."

"I'll bet it is," said the man. "You know, my wife was interested in science. Do you remember David's mother?"

"Yes," she said, looking at her shoes.

"Eileen was doing research when I met her, at college. We got married right after graduation . . . "

"Dad, please."

"She was a very nice lady," said the girl.

"Yes. She was." His father took a deep breath and closed his eyes for a second. "Anyway, you two have a great time. And don't be such a stranger, Sherron. You're always welcome here."

"Thanks, Mr. Donohue."

"Then—I'll see you later, Dad."

His father winked. "You can count on it."

"Are you going to tell my dad?"

"Not if you don't want me to."

They walked around the corner to the next street. The pavement smelled like melting asphalt. Somewhere a sprinkler hissed, beating steam into the air. Her house had trees that kept the sun away from the roof and the windows, so when they went inside it was hard to see for a minute. No one was home. She poured two glasses of sweet tea from the refrigerator and led him to her room.

As soon as she closed the door she took the cricket out of her pocket. Before it could hop away she put it in a Mason jar. A grasshopper and a beetle crawled along a leaf at the bottom. As soon as she touched the jar they stopped moving. She screwed the wire lid back on.

"Your folks let you keep those?"

"I told them it's for school."

"What do you need them for?"

"My project. If I get a fish tank, I can have frogs, too. And one of these." She opened a book to a picture of a small snake.

"Why?"

"I found it on the Internet."

"But *why*?"

She turned her computer on and showed him a page from a university website. There was an article called *Thanatosis: Nature's Way of Survival*, with close-ups of insects, a possum, a leopard shark and a hog-nosed snake. He read the first paragraph. It explained how some creatures protect themselves when afraid by pretending to be dead.

"You think I'm like them?"

"I don't know yet. But I'm going to find out."

"Well, you're wrong."

She noticed that his eyes were now focused on the bulletin board by the computer, and the headline of the newspaper clipping she had pinned there months ago: *LOCAL WOMAN, SON DIE IN FIERY CRASH*. She snatched it down and put it in the drawer.

"Oh, David. I'm really sorry."

"I better go."

"But I need you to help me."

"You think I'm faking it."

"No, I don't. I was there this time."

"Then you know I'm a freak," he said. "Like one of those animals. Like a bug."

"You're *not*."

"What's the difference?"

"They just—freeze up when they get scared. But you weren't even *breathing*. Your *heart* stopped."

"So what am I scared of?"

"It's okay to say it. David, I saw you chasing the truck. Every time he leaves—well, you're afraid he won't come back, either. Aren't you."

He made a sound like a laugh. "You don't know anything."

"Don't I?"

The laugh stopped. "If he doesn't, it means I got a second chance, and I blew it."

"What are you talking about?"

"Don't you get it? She was going to take me, but I was off playing that stupid game. She wasn't supposed to take Eric. It was supposed to be me."

Her mouth stayed open while she tried to find words.

"I have to go now," he said.

Once he was out from under the trees the sky was fierce again. Leaves curled, flowers turned away from the sun and the asphalt began to glisten. He heard footsteps on the sidewalk that were not his own.

"You're right. I don't know anything."

"Forget it, Sher."

They passed rosebushes, the yellow petals now almost white. It was half a block before she spoke again.

"Can I ask one question?"

"Go ahead."

"How does it feel?"

"I told you, I don't remember."

"Can you at least try?"

He kept walking, stepping over cracks. Mrs. Shaede's Rain Bird sprinkler came on and a silver mist rose into the air.

"Wilson's Market," he said under his breath.

"What?"

"Nothing."

"The one on Charter Way? What about it?"

"We used to go there, when I was little."

"We did, too."

"There was this one time," he said slowly, as they neared the end of the block. "I was four or five, I guess. Eric wasn't born yet. She was wearing her long coat."

"The gray one? I remember that."

"Anyway, we went like always, just the two of us. And we got a shopping cart and she let me push it, so I could help. You know, put the milk and the groceries in for her. I stopped to look at the cereal, and I was going to tell her what kind to get, but when I looked up she was way ahead. I could only see the back of her coat. And you know what? There was another cart behind her, and another little boy was pushing it, and she was handing *him* the cans. I didn't understand. I thought they were going to drive off and leave me there. So I started to cry. I yelled, 'Mama, that isn't me!' And when she turned around, it wasn't my mother. It was another lady with the same kind of coat. But before she turned, that was the feeling. If you want to know."

Her eyes were bright as diamonds and she had to look away.

And then she did something she had never done before. She hooked her arm through his and reached down and lifted his wrist and laced her fingers between his fingers and held his hand very tightly. He let her do that.

After a while she said, "You know, they have better nurses at middle school. Maybe they can give you pills to make it stop."

"I don't care."

"I do."

"Maybe I *was* dead. So what? Next time, I hope I don't wake up! What do you think of that? Huh?"

When she did not answer he looked around for her.

If she was not there she should have been.

The next school year was a crazy one, say like landing behind enemy lines and fighting your way out, and the next one was even worse, so he saw less of her, even before his father learned the truth and started driving him to the Institute for tests. By then it did not happen very often but at least David was with him. The only time he was not was when Dad's heart gave out suddenly during senior year. She broke up with Vincent when her family moved and people said she went away to college to study pre-med but no one knew exactly where. If you ever meet her, you might tell her this: Just that life goes on, and her project—say his name was David—finally figured out that there are so many small dyings along the way it hardly matters which one of them is Death.

*A hard-boiled used bookstore owner with a knack for finding things
has a murdered Chinaman, a unicorn's questionable gift,
and a pushy little sorceress to deal with . . .*

THE MALTESE UNICORN

Caitlín R. Kiernan

＊

New York City (May 1935)

It wasn't hard to find her. Sure, she had run. After Szabó let her walk like
that, I knew Ellen would get wise that something was rotten, and she'd
run like a scared rabbit with the dogs hot on its heels. She'd have it in her
head to skip town, and she'd probably keep right on skipping until she was
out of the country. Odds were pretty good she wouldn't stop until she was
altogether free and clear of this particular plane of existence. There are
plenty enough fetid little hidey holes in the universe, if you don't mind the
heat and the smell and the company you keep. You only have to know how
to find them, and the way I saw it, Ellen Andrews was good as Rand and
McNally when it came to knowing her way around. But first, she'd go back
to that apartment of hers, the whole eleventh floor of the Colosseum, with
its bleak westward view of the Hudson River and the New Jersey Palisades.
I figured there would be those two or three little things she couldn't leave
the city without, even if it meant risking her skin to collect them. Only
she hadn't expected me to get there before her. Word on the street was
Harpootlian still had me locked up tight, so Ellen hadn't expected me to
get there at all.

From the hall came the buzz of the elevator, then I heard her key in the
lock, the front door, and her footsteps as she hurried through the foyer and
the dining room. Then she came dashing into that French rococo nightmare
of a library, and stopped cold in her tracks when she saw me sitting at the
reading table with al-Jaldaki's grimoire open in front of me.

For a second, she didn't say anything. She just stood there, staring at
me. Then she managed a forced sort of laugh and said, "I knew they'd send
someone, Nat. I just didn't think it'd be you."

"After that gyp you pulled with the dingus, they didn't really leave me much choice," I told her, which was the truth, or all the truth I felt like sharing. "You shouldn't have come back here. It's the first place anyone would think to check."

Ellen sat down in the armchair by the door. She looked beat, like whatever comes after exhausted, and I could tell Szabó's gunsels had made sure all the fight was gone before they'd turned her loose. They weren't taking any chances, and we were just going through the motions now, me and her. All our lines had been written.

"You played me for a sucker," I said, and picked up the pistol that had been lying beside the grimoire. My hand was shaking, and I tried to steady it by bracing my elbow against the table. "You played me, then you tried to play Harpootlian and Szabó both. Then you got caught. It was a bonehead move all the way round, Ellen."

"So, how's it gonna be, Natalie? You gonna shoot me for being stupid?"

"No, I'm going to shoot you because it's the only way I can square things with Auntie H., and the only thing that's gonna keep Szabó from going on the warpath. And because you played me."

"In my shoes, you'd have done the same thing," she said. And the way she said it, I could tell she believed what she was saying. It's the sort of self-righteous bushwa so many grifters hide behind. They might stab their own mothers in the back if they see an angle in it, but that's jake, 'cause so would anyone else.

"Is that really all you have to say for yourself?" I asked, and pulled back the slide on the Colt, chambering the first round. She didn't even flinch . . . But, wait . . . I'm getting ahead of myself. Maybe I ought to begin nearer the beginning.

As it happens, I didn't go and name the place Yellow Dragon Books. It came with that moniker, and I just never saw any reason to change it. I'd only have had to pay for a new sign. Late in '28—right after Arnie "The Brain" Rothstein was shot to death during a poker game at the Park Central Hotel—I accidentally found myself on the sunny side of the proprietress of one of Manhattan's more infernal brothels. I say *accidentally* because I hadn't even heard of Madam Yeksabet Harpootlian when I began trying to dig up a buyer for an antique manuscript, a collection of necromantic erotica purportedly written by John Dee and Edward Kelley sometime in the sixteenth century. Turns out, Harpootlian had been looking to get her mitts on it for decades.

Now, just how I came into possession of said manuscript, that's another story entirely, one for some other time and place. One that, with luck, I'll never get around to putting down on paper. Let's just say a couple of years earlier, I'd been living in Paris. Truthfully, I'd been doing my best, in a sloppy, irresolute way, to *die* in Paris. I was holed up in a fleabag Montmartre boarding house, busy squandering the last of a dwindling inheritance. I had in mind how maybe I could drown myself in cheap wine, bad poetry, Pernod, and prostitutes before the money ran out. But somewhere along the way, I lost my nerve, failed at my slow suicide, and bought a ticket back to the States. And the manuscript in question was one of the many strange and unsavory things I brought back with me. I've always had a nose for the macabre, and had dabbled—on and off—in the black arts since college. At Radcliffe, I'd fallen in with a circle of lesbyterians who fancied themselves witches. Mostly, I was in it for the sex . . . But I'm digressing.

A friend of a friend heard I was busted, down and out and peddling a bunch of old books, schlepping them about Manhattan in search of a buyer. This same friend, he knew one of Harpootlian's clients. One of her *human* clients, which was a pretty exclusive set (not that I knew that at the time). This friend of mine, he was the client's lover, and said client brokered the sale for Harpootlian—for a fat ten percent finder's fee, of course. I promptly sold the Dee and Kelley manuscript to this supposedly notorious madam who, near as I could tell, no one much had ever heard of. She paid me what I asked, no questions, no haggling—never mind it was a fairly exorbitant sum. And on top of that, Harpootlian was so impressed I'd gotten ahold of the damned thing, she staked me to the bookshop on Bowery, there in the shadow of the Third Avenue El, just a little ways south of Delancey Street. Only one catch: she had first dibs on everything I ferreted out, and sometimes I'd be asked to make deliveries. I should like to note that way back then, during that long, lost November of 1928, I had no idea whatsoever that her sobriquet, "the Demon Madam of the Lower East Side," was anything more than colorful hyperbole.

Anyway, jump ahead to a rainy May afternoon, more than six years later, and that's when I first laid eyes on Ellen Andrews. Well, that's what she called herself, though later on I'd find out she'd borrowed the name from Claudette Colbert's character in *It Happened One Night*. I was just back from an estate sale in Connecticut, and was busy unpacking a large crate when I heard the bell mounted above the shop door jingle. I looked up, and there she was, carelessly shaking rainwater from her orange umbrella before folding it closed. Droplets sprayed across the welcome mat and the floor and onto the spines of several nearby books.

"Hey, be careful," I said, "unless you intend to pay for those." I jabbed a thumb at the books she'd spattered. She promptly stopped shaking the umbrella and dropped it into the stand beside the door. That umbrella stand has always been one of my favorite things about the Yellow Dragon. It's made from the taxidermied foot of a hippopotamus, and accommodates at least a dozen umbrellas, although I don't think I've ever seen even half that many people in the shop at one time.

"Are you Natalie Beaumont?" she asked, looking down at her wet shoes. Her overcoat was dripping, and a small puddle was forming about her feet.

"Usually."

"Usually," she repeated. "How about right now?"

"Depends whether or not I owe you money," I replied, and removed a battered copy of Blavatsky's *Isis Unveiled* from the crate. "Also, depends whether you happen to be *employed* by someone I owe money."

"I see," she said, as if that settled the matter, then proceeded to examine the complete twelve-volume set of *The Golden Bough* occupying a top shelf not far from the door. "Awful funny sort of neighborhood for a bookstore, if you ask me."

"You don't think bums and winos read?"

"You ask me, people down here," she said, "they panhandle a few cents, I don't imagine they spend it on books."

"I don't recall asking for your opinion," I told her.

"No," she said. "You didn't. Still, queer sort of a shop to come across in this part of town."

"If you must know," I said, "the rent's cheap," then reached for my spectacles, which were dangling from their silver chain about my neck. I set them on the bridge of my nose, and watched while she feigned interest in Frazerian anthropology. It would be an understatement to say Ellen Andrews was a pretty girl. She was, in fact, a certified knockout, and I didn't get too many beautiful women in the Yellow Dragon, even when the weather was good. She wouldn't have looked out of place in Flo Ziegfeld's follies; on the Bowery, she stuck out like a sore thumb.

"Looking for anything in particular?" I asked her, and she shrugged.

"Just you," she said.

"Then I suppose you're in luck."

"I suppose I am," she said, and turned toward me again. Her eyes glinted red, just for an instant, like the eyes of a Siamese cat. I figured it for a trick of the light. "I'm a friend of Auntie H. I run errands for her, now and then. She needs you to pick up a package and see it gets safely where it's going."

So, there it was. Madam Harpootlian, or Auntie H. to those few unfortunates she called her friends. And suddenly it made a lot more sense, this choice bit of calico walking into my place, strolling in off the street like maybe she did all her shopping down on Skid Row. I'd have to finish unpacking the crate later. I stood up and dusted my hands off on the seat of my slacks.

"Sorry about the confusion," I said, even if I wasn't actually sorry, even if I was actually kind of pissed the girl hadn't told me who she was right up front. "When Auntie H. wants something done, she doesn't usually bother sending her orders around in such an attractive envelope."

The girl laughed, then said, "Yeah, Auntie H. warned me about you, Miss Beaumont."

"Did she now. How so?"

"You know, your predilections. How you're not like other women."

"I'd say that depends on which other women we're discussing, don't you think?"

"*Most* other women," she said, glancing over her shoulder at the rain pelting the shop windows. It sounded like frying meat out there, the sizzle of the rain against asphalt, and concrete, and the roofs of passing automobiles.

"And what about you?" I asked her. "Are *you* like most other women?"

She looked away from the window, back at me, and she smiled what must have been the faintest smile possible.

"Are you always this charming?"

"Not that I'm aware of," I said. "Then again, I never took a poll."

"The job, it's nothing particularly complicated," she said, changing the subject. "There's a Chinese apothecary not too far from here."

"That doesn't exactly narrow it down," I said, and lit a cigarette.

"Sixty-five Mott Street. The joint's run by an elderly Cantonese fellow name of Fong."

"Yeah, I know Jimmy Fong."

"That's good. Then maybe you won't get lost. Mr. Fong will be expecting you, and he'll have the package ready at five thirty this evening. He's already been paid in full, so all you have to do is be there to receive it, right? And Miss Beaumont, please try to be on time. Auntie H. said you have a problem with punctuality."

"You believe everything you hear?"

"Only if I'm hearing it from Auntie H."

"Fair enough," I told her, then offered her a Pall Mall, but she declined.

"I need to be getting back," she said, reaching for the umbrella she'd only just deposited in the stuffed hippopotamus foot.

"What's the rush? What'd you come after, anyway, a ball of fire?"

She rolled her eyes. "I got places to be. You're not the only stop on my itinerary."

"Fine. Wouldn't want you getting in Dutch with Harpootlian on my account. Don't suppose you've got a name?"

"I might," she said.

"Don't suppose you'd share?" I asked her, and took a long drag on my cigarette, wondering why in blue blazes Harpootlian had sent this smart-mouthed skirt instead of one of her usual flunkies. Of course, Auntie H. always did have a sadistic streak to put de Sade to shame, and likely as not this was her idea of a joke.

"Ellen," the girl said. "Ellen Andrews."

"So, Ellen Andrews, how is it we've never met? I mean, I've been making deliveries for your boss lady now going on seven years, and if I'd seen you, I'd remember. You're not the sort I forget."

"You got the moxie, don't you?"

"I'm just good with faces is all."

She chewed at a thumbnail, as if considering carefully what she should or shouldn't divulge. Then she said, "I'm from out of town, mostly. Just passing through, and thought I'd lend a hand. That's why you've never seen me before, Miss Beaumont. Now, I'll let you get back to work. And remember, don't be late."

"I heard you the first time, sister."

And then she left, and the brass bell above the door jingled again. I finished my cigarette and went back to unpacking the big crate of books from Connecticut. If I hurried, I could finish the job before heading for Chinatown.

She was right, of course. I did have a well-deserved reputation for not being on time. But I knew that Auntie H. was of the opinion that my acumen in antiquarian and occult matters more than compensated for my not-infrequent tardiness. I've never much cared for personal mottos, but if I had one it might be, *You want it on time, or you want it done right?* Still, I honestly tried to be on time for the meeting with Fong. And still, through no fault of my own, I was more than twenty minutes late. I was lucky enough to find a cab, despite the rain, but then got stuck behind some sort of brouhaha after turning onto Canal, so there you go. It's not like old man Fong had any place more pressing to be, not like he was gonna get pissy and leave me high and dry.

When I got to 65 Mott, the Chinaman's apothecary was locked up tight, all the lights were off, and the "Sorry, We're Closed" sign was hung in the front window. No big surprise there. But then I went around back, to the alley, and found a door standing wide open and quite a lot of fresh blood on the cinderblock steps leading into the building. Now, maybe I was the only lady bookseller in Manhattan who carried a gun, and maybe I wasn't. But times like that, I was glad to have the Colt tucked snugly inside its shoulder holster, and happier still that I knew how to use it. I took a deep breath, drew the pistol, flipped off the safety catch, and stepped inside.

The door opened onto a stockroom, and the tiny nook Jimmy Fong used as his office was a little farther in, over on my left. There was some light from a banker's lamp, but not much of it. I lingered in the shadows a moment, waiting for my heart to stop pounding, for the adrenaline high to fade. The air was close, and stunk of angelica root and dust, ginger and frankincense and fuck only knows what else. Powdered rhino horn and the pickled gallbladders of panda bears. What the hell ever. I found the old man slumped over at his desk.

Whoever knifed him hadn't bothered to pull the shiv out of his spine, and I wondered if the poor SOB had even seen it coming. It didn't exactly add up, not after seeing all that blood drying on the steps, but I figured, hey, maybe the killer was the sort of klutz can't spread butter without cutting himself. I had a quick look-see around the cluttered office, hoping I might turn up the package Ellen Andrews had sent me there to retrieve. But no dice, and then it occurred to me: maybe whoever had murdered Fong had come looking for the same thing I was looking for. Maybe they'd found it, too, only Fong knew better than to just hand it over, and that had gotten him killed. Anyway, nobody was paying me to play junior shamus; hence the hows, whys, and wherefores of the Chinaman's death were not my problem. My problem would be showing up at Harpootlian's cathouse empty handed.

I returned the gun to its holster, then I started rifling through everything in sight—the great disarray of papers heaped upon the desk, Fong's accounting ledgers, sales invoices, catalogs, letters, and postcards written in English, Mandarin, Wu, Cantonese, French, Spanish, and Arabic. I still had my gloves on, so it's not like I had to worry over fingerprints. A few of the desk drawers were unlocked, and I'd just started in on those, when the phone perched atop the filing cabinet rang. I froze, whatever I was looking at clutched forgotten in my hands, and stared at the phone.

Sure, it wasn't every day I blundered into the immediate aftermath of this sort of foul play, but I was plenty savvy enough; I knew better than to answer that call. It didn't much matter who was on the other end of the line. If I answered, I could be placed at the scene of a murder only minutes after it had gone down. The phone rang a second time, and a third, and I glanced at the dead man in the chair. The crimson halo surrounding the switchblade's inlaid mother-of-pearl handle was still spreading, blossoming like some grim rose, and now there was blood dripping to the floor, as well. The phone rang a fourth time. A fifth. And then I was seized by an overwhelming compulsion to answer it, and answer it I did. I wasn't the least bit thrown that the voice coming through the receiver was Ellen Andrews's. All at once, the pieces were falling into place. You spend enough years doing the step-and-fetch-it routine for imps like Harpootlian, you find yourself ever more jaded at the inexplicable and the uncanny.

"Beaumont," she said, "I didn't think you were going to pick up."

"I wasn't. Funny thing how I did anyway."

"Funny thing," she said, and I heard her light a cigarette and realized my hands were shaking.

"See, I'm thinking maybe I had a little push," I said. "That about the size of it?"

"Wouldn't have been necessary if you'd have just answered the damn phone in the first place."

"You already know Fong's dead, don't you?" And, I swear to fuck, nothing makes me feel like more of a jackass than asking questions I know the answers to.

"Don't you worry about Fong. I'm sure he had all his ducks in a row and was right as rain with Buddha. I need you to pay attention—"

"Harpootlian had him killed, didn't she? And you *knew* he'd be dead when I showed up."

She didn't reply straight away, and I thought I could hear a radio playing in the background. "You knew," I said again, only this time it wasn't a query.

"Listen," she said. "You're a courier. I was told you're a courier we can trust, elsewise I never would have handed you this job."

"You didn't hand me the job. Your boss did."

"You're splitting hairs, Miss Beaumont."

"Yeah, well, there's a fucking dead celestial in the room with me. It's giving me the fidgets."

"So how about you shut up and listen, and I'll have you out of there in a jiffy." And that's what I did—I shut up, either because I knew it was the path of least resistance, or because whatever spell she'd used to persuade me to answer the phone was still working.

"On Fong's desk, there's a funny little porcelain statue of a cat."

"You mean the *maneki neko*?"

"If that's what it's called, that's what I mean. Now, break it open. There's a key inside."

I *tried* not to, just to see if I was being played as badly as I suspected I was being played. I gritted my teeth, dug in my heels, and tried *hard* not to break that damned cat.

"You're wasting time. Auntie H. didn't mention you were such a crybaby."

"Auntie H. and I have an agreement when it comes to free will. To *my* free will."

"*Break the goddamn cat*," Ellen Andrews growled, and that's exactly what I did. In fact, I slammed it down directly on top of Fong's head. Bits of brightly painted porcelain flew everywhere, and a rusty barrel key tumbled out and landed at my feet. "Now pick it up," she said. "The key fits the bottom left-hand drawer of Fong's desk. Open it."

This time, I didn't even try to resist her. I was getting a headache from the last futile attempt. I unlocked the drawer and pulled it open. Inside, there was nothing but the yellowed sheet of newspaper lining the drawer, three golf balls, a couple of old racing forms, and a finely carved wooden box lacquered almost the same shade of red as Jimmy Fong's blood. I didn't need to be told I'd been sent to retrieve the box—or, more specifically, whatever was *inside* the box.

"Yeah, I got it," I told Ellen Andrews.

"Good girl. Now, you have maybe twelve minutes before the cops show. Go out the same way you came in." Then she gave me a Riverside Drive address, and said there'd be a car waiting for me at the corner of Canal and Mulberry, a green Chevrolet coupe. "Just give the driver that address. He'll see you get where you're going."

"Yeah," I said, sliding the desk drawer shut again and locking it. I pocketed the key. "But, sister, you and me are gonna have a talk."

"Wouldn't miss it for the world, Nat," she said and hung up. I shut my eyes, wondering if I really had twelve minutes before the bulls arrived, and if they were even on their way, wondering what would happen if I endeavored *not* to make the rendezvous with the green coupe. I stood there, trying to decide whether Harpootlian would have gone back on her word and given this bitch permission to turn her hoodoo tricks on me, and if aspirin would do anything at all for the dull throb behind my eyes. Then I looked at Fong one last time, at the knife jutting out of his back, his thin gray hair powdered with porcelain dust from the shattered "lucky cat." And then I stopped asking questions and did as I'd been told.

The car was there, just like she'd told me it would be. There was a young colored man behind the wheel, and when I climbed in the back, he asked me where we were headed.

"I'm guessing Hell," I said, "sooner or later."

"Got that right," he laughed and winked at me from the rearview mirror. "But I was thinking more in terms of the immediate here and now."

So I recited the address I'd been given over the phone, 435 Riverside.

"That's the Colosseum," he said.

"It is if you say so," I replied. "Just get me there."

The driver nodded and pulled away from the curb. As he navigated the slick, wet streets, I sat listening to the rain against the Chevy's hardtop and the music coming from the Motorola. In particular, I can remember hearing the Dorsey Brothers, "Chasing Shadows." I suppose you'd call that a harbinger, if you go in for that sort of thing. Me, I do my best not to. In this business, you start jumping at everything that *might* be an omen or a portent, you end up doing nothing else. Ironically, rubbing shoulders with the supernatural has made me a great believer in coincidence.

Anyway, the driver drove, the radio played, and I sat staring at the red lacquered box I'd stolen from a dead man's locked desk drawer. I thought it might be mahogany, but it was impossible to be sure, what with all that cinnabar-tinted varnish. I know enough about Chinese mythology that I recognized the strange creature carved into the top—a *qilin*, a stout, antlered beast with cloven hooves, the scales of a dragon, and a long leonine tail. Much of its body was wreathed in flame, and its gaping jaws revealed teeth like daggers. For the Chinese, the *qilin* is a harbinger of good fortune, though it certainly hadn't worked out that way for Jimmy Fong. The box was heavier than it looked, most likely because of whatever was stashed inside. There was no latch, and as I examined it more closely, I realized there was no sign whatsoever of hinges or even a seam to indicate it actually had a lid.

"Unless I got it backwards," the driver said, "Miss Andrews didn't say nothing about trying to open that box, now did she?"

I looked up, startled, feeling like the proverbial kid caught with her hand in the cookie jar. He glanced at me in the mirror, then his eyes drifted back to the road.

"She didn't say one way or the other," I told him.

"Then how about we err on the side of caution?"

"So you didn't know where you're taking me, but you know I shouldn't open this box? How's that work?"

"Ain't the world just full of mysteries," he said.

For a minute or so, I silently watched the headlights of the oncoming traffic and the metronomic sweep of the windshield wipers. Then I asked the driver how long he'd worked for Ellen Andrews.

"Not very," he said. "Never laid eyes on the lady before this afternoon. Why you want to know?"

"No particular reason," I said, looking back down at the box and the *qilin* etched in the wood. I decided I was better off not asking any more questions, better off getting this over and done with, and never mind what did and didn't quite add up. "Just trying to make conversation; that's all."

Which got him to talking about the Chicago stockyards and Cleveland and how it was he'd eventually wound up in New York City. He never told me his name, and I didn't ask. The trip uptown seemed to take forever, and the longer I sat with that box in my lap, the heavier it felt. I finally moved it, putting it down on the seat beside me. By the time we reached our destination, the rain had stopped and the setting sun was showing through the clouds, glittering off the dripping trees in Riverside Park and the waters of the wide gray Hudson. He pulled over, and I reached for my wallet.

"No, ma'am," he said, shaking his head. "Miss Andrews, she's already seen to your fare."

"Then I hope you won't mind if I see to your tip," I said, and I gave him five dollars. He thanked me, and I took the wooden box and stepped out onto the wet sidewalk.

"She's up on the eleventh," he told me, nodding toward the apartments. Then he drove off, and I turned to face the imposing brick-and-limestone façade of the building the driver had called the Colosseum. I rarely find myself any farther north than the Upper West Side, so this was pretty much terra incognita for me.

The doorman gave me directions, *after* giving me and Fong's box the hairy eyeball, and I quickly made my way to the elevators, hurrying through that ritzy marble sepulcher passing itself off as a lobby. When the operator asked which floor I needed, I told him the eleventh, and he shook his head and muttered something under his breath. I almost asked him to speak up, but thought better of it. Didn't I already have plenty enough on my mind without entertaining the opinions of elevator boys? Sure, I did. I had a murdered Chinaman, a mysterious box, and this pushy little sorceress calling herself Ellen Andrews. I also had an especially disagreeable feeling about this job, and the sooner it was settled, the better. I kept my eyes on the brass needle as it haltingly swung from left to right, counting off the floors, and when the doors parted, she was there waiting for me. She slipped the boy a sawbuck, and he stuffed it into his jacket pocket and left us alone.

"So nice to see you again, Nat," she said, but she was looking at the lacquered box, not me. "Would you like to come in and have a drink? Auntie H. says you have a weakness for rye whiskey."

"Well, she's right about that. But just now, I'd be more fond of an explanation."

"How odd," she said, glancing up at me, still smiling. "Auntie said one thing she liked about you was how you didn't ask a lot of questions. Said you were real good at minding your own business."

"Sometimes I make exceptions."

"Let me get you that drink," she said, and I followed her the short distance from the elevator to the door of her apartment. Turns out, she had the whole floor to herself, each level of the Colosseum being a single apartment. Pretty ritzy accommodations, I thought, for someone who was *mostly* from out of town. But then, I've spent the last few years living in that one-bedroom cracker box above the Yellow Dragon—hot and cold running cockroaches and so forth. She locked the door behind us, then led me through the foyer to a parlor. The whole place was done up gaudy period French, Louis Quinze and the like, all floral brocade and orientalia. The walls were decorated with damask hangings, mostly of ample-bosomed women reclining in pastoral scenes, dogs and sheep and what have you lying at their feet. Ellen told me to have a seat, so I parked myself on a récamier near a window.

"Harpootlian spring for this place?" I asked.

"No," she replied. "It belonged to my mother."

"So, you come from money."

"Did I mention how you ask an awful lot of questions?"

"You might have," I said, and she inquired as to whether I liked my whiskey neat or on the rocks. I told her neat, and set the red box down on the sofa next to me.

"If you're not *too* thirsty, would you mind if I take a peek at that first," she said, pointing at the box.

"Be my guest," I said, and Ellen smiled again. She picked up the red lacquered box, then sat next to me. She cradled it in her lap, and there was this goofy expression on her face, a mix of awe, dread, and eager expectation.

"Must be something extra damn special," I said, and she laughed. It was a nervous kind of a laugh.

I've already mentioned how I couldn't discern any evidence the box had a lid, and I supposed there was some secret to getting it open, a gentle squeeze or nudge in just the right spot. Turns out, all it needed was someone to say the magic words.

"*Pain had no sting, and pleasure's wreath no flower,*" she said, speaking slowly and all but whispering the words. There was a sharp click and the top of the box suddenly slid back with enough force that it tumbled over her knees and fell to the carpet.

"Keats," I said.

"Keats," she echoed, but added nothing more. She was too busy gazing at what lay inside the box, nestled in a bed of velvet the color of poppies. She started to touch it, then hesitated, her fingertips hovering an inch or so above the object.

"You're fucking kidding me," I said, once I saw what was inside.

"Don't go jumping to conclusions, Nat."

"It's a dildo," I said, probably sounding as incredulous as I felt. "Exactly which conclusions am I not supposed to jump to? Sure, I enjoy a good rub-off as much as the next girl, but . . . you're telling me Harpootlian killed Fong over a dildo?"

"I never said Auntie H. killed Fong."

"Then I suppose he stuck that knife there himself."

And that's when she told me to shut the hell up for five minutes, if I knew how. She reached into the box and lifted out the phallus, handling it as gingerly as somebody might handle a stick of dynamite. But whatever made the thing special, it wasn't anything I could see.

"*Le godemiché maudit*," she murmured, her voice so filled with reverence you'd have thought she was holding the devil's own wang. Near as I could tell, it was cast from some sort of hard black ceramic. It glistened faintly in the light getting in through the drapes. "I'll tell you about it," she said, "if you really want to know. I don't see the harm."

"Just so long as you get to the part where it makes sense that Harpootlian bumped the Chinaman for this dingus of yours, then sure."

She took her eyes off the thing long enough to scowl at me. "Auntie H. didn't kill Fong. One of Szabó's goons did that, then panicked and ran before he figured out where the box was hidden."

(Now, as for Madam Magdalena Szabó, the biggest boil on Auntie H.'s fanny, we'll get back to her by and by.)

"Ellen, how can you *possibly* fucking know that? Better yet, how could you've known Szabó's man would have given up and cleared out by the time I arrived?"

"Why did you answer that phone, Nat?" she asked, and that shut me up, good and proper. "As for our prize here," she continued, "it's a long story, a long story with a lot of missing pieces. The dingus, as you put it, is usually called *le godemiché maudit*. Which doesn't necessarily mean it's actually cursed, mind you. Not literally. You do speak French, I assume?"

"Yeah," I told her. "I do speak French."

"That's ducky, Nat. Now, here's about as much as anyone could tell you. Though, frankly, I'd have thought a scholarly type like yourself would know all about it."

"Never said I was a scholar," I interrupted.

"But you went to college. Radcliffe, class of 1923, right? Graduated with honors."

"Lots of people go to college. Doesn't necessarily make them scholars. I just sell books."

"My mistake," she said, carefully returning the black dildo to its velvet case. "It won't happen again." Then she told me her tale, and I sat there on the récamier and listened to what she had to say. Yeah, it was long. There *were* certainly a whole lot of missing pieces. And as a wise man once said, this might not be schoolbook history, not Mr. Wells's history, but, near as I've been able to discover since that evening at her apartment, it's history, nevertheless. She asked me whether or not I'd ever heard of a fourteenth-century Persian alchemist named al-Jaldaki, Izz al-Din Aydamir al-Jaldaki, and I had, of course.

"He's sort of a hobby of mine," she said. "Came across his grimoire a few years back. Anyway, he's not where it begins, but that's where the written record starts. While studying in Anatolia, al-Jaldaki heard tales of a fabulous artifact that had been crafted from the horn of a unicorn at the behest of King Solomon."

"From a unicorn," I cut in. "So we believe in those now, do we?"

"Why not, Nat? I think it's safe to assume you've seen some peculiar shit in your time, that you've pierced the veil, so to speak. Surely a unicorn must be small potatoes for a worldly woman like yourself."

"So you'd think," I said.

"Anyhow," she went on, "the ivory horn was carved into the shape of a penis by the king's most skilled artisans. Supposedly, the result was so revered it was even placed in Solomon's temple, alongside the Ark of the Covenant and a slew of other sacred Hebrew relics. Records al-Jaldaki found in a mosque in the Taurus Mountains indicated that the horn had been removed from Solomon's temple when it was sacked in 587 BC by the Babylonians, and that eventually it had gone to Medina. But it was taken from Medina during or shortly after the siege of 627, when the Meccans invaded. And it's at this point that the horn is believed to have been given its ebony coating of porcelain enamel, possibly in an attempt to disguise it."

"Or," I said, "because someone in Medina preferred swarthy cock. You mind if I smoke?" I asked her, and she shook her head and pointed at an ashtray.

"A Medinan rabbi of the Banu Nadir tribe was entrusted with the horn's safety. He escaped, making his way west across the desert to Yanbu' al Bahr, then north along the al-Hejaz all the way to Jerusalem. But two years later, when the Sassanid army lost control of the city to the Byzantine emperor Heraclius, the horn was taken to a monastery in Malta, where it remained for centuries."

"That's quite a saga for a dildo. But you still haven't answered my question. What makes it so special? What the hell's it *do*?"

"Maybe you've heard enough," she said, and this whole time she hadn't taken her eyes off the thing in the box.

"Yeah, and maybe I haven't," I told her, tapping ash from my Pall Mall into the ashtray. "So, al-Jaldaki goes to Malta and finds the big black dingus."

She scowled again. No, it was more than a scowl; she *glowered*, and she looked away from the box just long enough to glower at me. "Yes," Ellen Andrews said. "At least, that's what he wrote. Al-Jaldaki found it buried in the ruins of a monastery in Malta, and then carried the horn with him to Cairo. It seems to have been in his possession until his death in 1342. After that it disappeared, and there's no word of it again until 1891."

I did the math in my head. "Five hundred and forty-nine years," I said. "So it must have gone to a good home. Must have lucked out and found itself a long-lived and appreciative keeper."

"The Freemasons might have had it," she went on, ignoring or oblivious to my sarcasm. "Maybe the Vatican. Doesn't make much difference."

"Okay. So what happened in 1891?"

"A party in Paris, in an old house not far from the Cimetière du Montparnasse. Not so much a party, really, as an out-and-out orgy, the way the story goes. This was back before Montparnasse became so fashionable with painters and poets and expatriate Americans. Verlaine was there, though. At the orgy, I mean. It's not clear what happened precisely, but three women died, and afterward there were rumors of black magic and ritual sacrifice, and tales surfaced of a cult that worshiped some sort of demonic objet d'art that had made its way to France from Egypt. There was an official investigation, naturally, but someone saw to it that *la préfecture de police* came up with zilch."

"Naturally," I said. I glanced at the window. It was getting dark, and I wondered if my ride back to the Bowery had been arranged. "So, where's Black Beauty here been for the past forty-four years?"

Ellen leaned forward, reaching for the lid to the red lacquered box. When she set it back in place, covering that brazen scrap of antiquity, I heard the *click* again as the lid melded seamlessly with the rest of the box. Now there was only the etching of the *qilin*, and I remembered that the beast had sometimes been referred to as the "Chinese unicorn." It seemed odd I'd not thought of that before.

"I think we've probably had enough of a history lesson for now," she said, and I didn't disagree. Truth be told, the whole subject was beginning to bore me. It hardly mattered whether or not I believed in unicorns or enchanted dildos. I'd done my job, so there'd be no complaints from Harpootlian. I admit I felt kind of shitty about poor old Fong, who wasn't such a bad sort. But when you're an errand girl for the wicked folk, that shit comes with the territory. People get killed, and worse.

"It's getting late," I said, crushing out my cigarette in the ashtray. "I should dangle."

"Wait. Please. I promised you a drink, Nat. Don't want you telling Auntie H. I was a bad hostess, now do I?" And Ellen Andrews stood up, the red box tucked snugly beneath her left arm.

"No worries, kiddo," I assured her. "If she ever asks, which I doubt, I'll say you were a regular Emily Post."

"I insist," she replied. "I really, truly do," and before I could say another word, she turned and rushed out of the parlor, leaving me alone with all that furniture and the buxom giantesses watching me from the walls. I wondered if there were any servants, or a live-in beau, or if possibly she had the place all to herself, that huge apartment overlooking the river. I pushed the drapes aside and stared out at twilight gathering in the park across the street. Then she was back (minus the red box) with a silver serving tray, two glasses, and a virgin bottle of Sazerac rye.

"Maybe just one," I said, and she smiled. I went back to watching Riverside Park while she poured the whiskey. No harm in a shot or two. It's not like I had some place to be, and there were still a couple of unanswered questions bugging me. Such as why Harpootlian had broken her promise, the one that was supposed to prevent her underlings from practicing their hocus-pocus on me. That is, assuming Ellen Andrews had even bothered to ask permission. Regardless, she didn't need magic or a spell book for her next dirty trick. The Mickey Finn she slipped me did the job just fine.

So, I came to, four, perhaps five hours later—sometime before midnight. By then, as I'd soon learn, the shit had already hit the fan. I woke up sick as a dog and my head pounding like there was an ape with a kettledrum loose inside my skull. I opened my eyes, but it wasn't Ellen Andrews's Baroque clutter and chintz that greeted me, and I immediately shut them again. I smelled the hookahs and the smoldering *bukhoor*, the opium smoke and sandarac and, somewhere underneath it all, that pervasive brimstone stink that no amount of incense can mask. Besides, I'd seen the spiny ginger-skinned thing crouching not far from me, the eunuch, and I knew I was somewhere in the rat's-maze labyrinth of Harpootlian's bordello. I started to sit up, but then my stomach lurched and I thought better of it. At least there were soft cushions beneath me, and the silk was cool against my feverish skin.

"You know where you are?" the eunuch asked; it had a woman's voice and a hint of a Russian accent, but I was pretty sure both were only affectations. First rule of demon brothels: Check your preconceptions of male and female at the door. Second rule: Appearances are fucking meant to be deceiving.

"Sure," I moaned and tried not to think about vomiting. "I might have a notion or three."

"Good. Then you lie still and take it easy, Miss Beaumont. We've got a few questions need answering." Which made it mutual, but I kept my mouth shut on that account. The voice was beginning to sound not so much feminine as what you might hear if you scraped frozen pork back and forth across a cheese grater. "This afternoon, you were contacted by an associate of Madam Harpootlian's, yes? She told you her name was Ellen Andrews. That's not her true name, of course. Just something she heard in a motion picture—"

"Of course," I replied. "You sort never bother with your real names. Anyway, what of it?"

"She asked you to go see Jimmy Fong and bring her something, yes? Something very precious. Something powerful and rare."

"The dingus," I said, rubbing at my aching head. "Right, but…hey…Fong was already dead when I got there, scout's honor. Andrews told me one of Szabó's people did him."

"The Chinese gentleman's fate is no concern of ours," the eunuch said. "But we need to talk about Ellen Andrews. She has caused this house serious inconvenience. She's troubled us, and troubles us still."

"You and me both, bub," I said. It was just starting to dawn on me how there were some sizable holes in my memory. I clearly recalled the taste of rye, and gazing down at the park, but then nothing. Nothing at all. I asked the ginger demon, "Where is she? And how'd I get here, anyway?"

"We seem to have many of the same questions," it replied, dispassionate as a corpse. "You answer ours, maybe we shall find the answers to yours along the way."

I knew damn well I didn't have much say in the matter. After all, I'd been down this road before. When Auntie H. wants answers, she doesn't usually bother with asking. Why waste your time wondering if someone's feeding you a load of baloney when all you gotta do is reach inside his brain and help yourself to whatever you need?

"Fine," I said, trying not to tense up, because tensing up only ever makes it worse. "How about let's cut the chitchat and get this over with."

"Very well, but you should know," it said, "Madam regrets the necessity of this imposition." And then there were the usual wet, squelching noises as the relevant appendages unfurled and slithered across the floor toward me.

"Sure, no problem. Ain't no secret Madam's got a heart of gold," and maybe I shouldn't have smarted off like that, because when the stingers hit me, they hit hard. Harder than I knew was necessary to make the connection. I might have screamed. I know I pissed myself. And then it was inside me, prowling about, roughly picking its way through my conscious and unconscious mind—through my soul, if that word suits you better. All the heady sounds and smells of the brothel faded away, along with my physical discomfort. For a while I drifted nowhere and nowhen in particular, and then, then I stopped drifting . . .

. . . Ellen asked me, "You ever think you've had enough? Of the life, I mean. Don't you sometimes contemplate just up and blowing town, not even stopping long enough to look back? Doesn't that ever cross your mind, Nat?"

I sipped my whiskey and watched her, undressing her with my eyes and not especially ashamed of myself for doing so. "Not too often," I said. "I've had it worse. This gig's not perfect, but I usually get a fair shake."

"Yeah, usually," she said, her words hardly more than a sigh. "Just, now and then, I feel like I'm missing out."

I laughed, and she glared at me.

"You'd cut a swell figure in a breadline," I said, and took another swallow of the rye.

"I hate when people laugh at me."

"Then don't say funny things," I told her.

And that's when she turned and took my glass. I thought she was about to tell me to get lost, and don't let the door hit me in the ass on the way out. Instead, she set the drink down on the silver serving tray, and she kissed me. Her mouth tasted like peaches. Peaches and cinnamon. Then she pulled back, and her eyes flashed red, the way they had in the Yellow Dragon, only now I knew it wasn't an illusion.

"You're a demon," I said, not all that surprised.

"Only a quarter. My grandmother . . . Well, I'd rather not get into that, if it's all the same to you. Is it a problem?"

"No, it's not a problem," I replied, and she kissed me again. Right about here, I started to feel the first twinges of whatever she'd put into the Sazerac, but, frankly, I was too horny to heed the warning signs.

"I've got a plan," she said, whispering, as if she were afraid someone was listening in. "I have it all worked out, but I wouldn't mind some company on the road."

"I have no . . . no idea . . . what you're talking about," and there was something else I wanted to say, but I'd begun slurring my words and decided against it. I put a hand on her left breast, and she didn't stop me.

"We'll talk about it later," she said, kissing me again, and right about then, that's when the curtain came crashing down, and the ginger-colored demon in my brain turned a page . . .

. . . I opened my eyes, and I was lying in a black room. I mean, a *perfectly* black room. Every wall had been painted matte black, and the ceiling, and the floor. If there were any windows, they'd also been painted over, or boarded up. I was cold, and a moment later I realized that was because I was naked. I was naked and lying at the center of a wide white pentagram that had been chalked onto that black floor. A white pentagram held within a white circle. There was a single white candle burning at each of the five points. I looked up, and Ellen Andrews was standing above me. Like me, she was naked. Except she was wearing that dingus from the lacquered box, fitted into a leather harness strapped about her hips. The phallus drooped obscenely and glimmered in the candlelight. There were dozens of runic and Enochian symbols painted on her skin in blood and shit and charcoal. Most of them I recognized. At her feet, there was a small iron cauldron, and a black-handled dagger, and something dead. It might have been a rabbit, or a small dog. I couldn't be sure which, because she'd skinned it.

Ellen looked down, and saw me looking up at her. She frowned, and tilted her head to one side. For just a second, there was something undeniably predatory in that expression, something murderous. All spite and not a jot of mercy. For that second, I was face to face with the one quarter of her bloodline that changed all the rules, the ancestor she hadn't wanted to talk about. But then that second passed, and she softly whispered, "I have a plan, Natalie Beaumont."

"What are you doing?" I asked her. But my mouth was so dry and numb, my throat so parched, it felt like I took forever to cajole my tongue into shaping those four simple words.

"No one will know," she said. "I promise. Not Harpootlian, not Szabó, not anyone. I've been over this a thousand times, worked all the angles." And she went down on one knee then, leaning over me. "But you're supposed to be asleep, Nat."

"Ellen, you don't cross Harpootlian," I croaked.

"Trust me," she said.

In that place, the two of us adrift on an island of light in an endless sea of blackness, she was the most beautiful woman I'd ever seen. Her hair was down now, and I reached up, brushing it back from her face. When my fingers moved across her scalp, I found two stubby horns, but it wasn't anything a girl couldn't hide with the right hairdo and a hat.

"Ellen, what are you doing?"

"I'm about to give you a gift, Nat. The most exquisite gift in all creation. A gift that even the angels might covet. You wanted to know what the unicorn does. Well, I'm not going to tell you; I'm going to *show* you."

She put a hand between my legs and found I was already wet.

I licked at my chapped lips, fumbling for words that wouldn't come. Maybe I didn't know what she was getting at, this *gift*, but I had a feeling I didn't want any part of it, no matter how exquisite it might be. I knew these things, clear as day, but I was lost in the beauty of her, and whatever protests I might have uttered, they were about as sincere as ol' Brer Rabbit begging Brer Fox not to throw him into that briar patch. I could say I was bewitched, but it would be a lie.

She mounted me then, and I didn't argue.

"What happens now?" I asked.

"Now I fuck you," she replied. "Then I'm going to talk to my grandmother." And, with that, the world fell out from beneath me again. And the ginger-skinned eunuch moved along to the next tableau, that next set of memories I couldn't recollect on my own . . .

. . . Stars were tumbling from the skies. Not a few stray shooting stars here and there. No, *all* the stars were falling. One by one, at first, and then the sky was raining pitchforks, only it *wasn't* rain, see. It was light. The whole sorry world was being born or was dying, and I saw it didn't much matter which. Go back far enough, or far enough forward, the past and future wind up holding hands, cozy as a couple of lovebirds. Ellen had thrown open a doorway, and she'd dragged me along for the ride. I was *so* cold. I couldn't understand how there could be that much fire in the sky, and me still be freezing my tits off like that. I lay there shivering as the brittle vault of heaven collapsed. I could feel her inside me. I could feel *it* inside me, and same as I'd been lost in Ellen's beauty, I was being smothered by that ecstasy. And then . . . then the eunuch showed me the gift, which I'd forgotten . . . and which I would immediately forget again.

How do you write about something, when all that remains of it is the faintest of impressions of glory? When all you can bring to mind is the empty place where a memory ought to be and isn't, and only that conspicuous absence is there to remind you of what cannot ever be recalled? Strain as you might, all that effort hardly adds up to a trip for biscuits. So, *how do you write it down?* You don't, *that's* how. You do your damnedest to think about what came next, instead, knowing your sanity hangs in the balance.

So, here's what came *after* the gift, since *le godemiché maudit* is a goddamn Indian giver if ever one was born. Here's the curse that rides shotgun on the gift, as impossible to obliterate from reminiscence as the other is to awaken.

There were falling stars, and that unendurable cold . . . and then the empty, aching socket to mark the countermanded gift . . . and *then* I saw the unicorn. I don't mean the dingus. I mean the *living creature*, standing in a glade of cedars, bathed in clean sunlight and radiating a light all its own. It didn't look much like what you see in storybooks or those medieval tapestries they got hanging in the Cloisters. It also didn't look much like the beast carved into the lid of Fong's wooden box. But I knew what it was, all the same.

A naked girl stood before it, and the unicorn kneeled at her feet. She sat down, and it rested its head on her lap. She whispered reassurances I couldn't hear, because they were spoken as softly as falling snow. And then she offered the unicorn one of her breasts, and I watched as it suckled. This scene of chastity and absolute peace lasted maybe a minute, maybe two, before the trap was sprung and the hunters stepped out from the shadows of the cedar boughs. They killed the unicorn, with cold iron lances and swords, but first the unicorn killed the virgin who'd betrayed it to its doom . . .

. . . And Harpootlian's ginger eunuch turned another page (a hamfisted analogy if ever there was one, but it works for me), and we were back in the black room. Ellen and me. Only two of the candles were still burning, two guttering, halfhearted counterpoints to all that darkness. The other three had been snuffed out by a sudden gust of wind that had smelled of rust, sulfur, and slaughterhouse floors. I could hear Ellen crying, weeping somewhere in the darkness beyond the candles and the periphery of her protective circle. I rolled over onto my right side, still shivering, still so cold I couldn't imagine being warm ever again. I stared into the black, blinking and dimly amazed that my eyelids hadn't frozen shut. Then something snapped into focus, and there she was, cowering on her hands and knees, a tattered rag of a woman lost in the gloom. I could see her stunted, twitching tail, hardly as long as my middle finger, and the thing from the box was still strapped to her crotch. Only now it had a twin, clutched tightly in her left hand.

I think I must have asked her what the hell she'd done, though I had a pretty good idea. She turned toward me, and her eyes . . . Well, you see that sort of pain, and you spend the rest of your life trying to forget you saw it.

"I didn't understand," she said, still sobbing. "I didn't understand she'd take so much of me away."

A bitter wave of conflicting, irreconcilable emotion surged and boiled about inside me. Yeah, I knew what she'd done to me, and I knew I'd been used for something unspeakable. I knew *violation* was too tame a word for it, and that I'd been marked forever by this gold-digging half-breed of a twist. And part of me was determined to drag her kicking and screaming to Harpootlian. Or fuck it, I could kill her myself, and take my own sweet time doing so. I could kill her the way the hunters had murdered the unicorn. But—on the other hand—the woman I saw lying there before me was shattered almost beyond recognition. There'd been a steep price for her trespass, and she'd paid it and then some. Besides, I was learning fast that when you've been to Hades's doorstep with someone, and the two of you make it back more or less alive, there's a bond, whether you want it or not. So, there we were, a cheap, latter-day parody of Orpheus and Eurydice, and all I could think about was holding her, tight as I could, until she stopped crying and I was warm again.

"She took so much," Ellen whispered. I didn't ask what her grandmother had taken. Maybe it was a slice of her soul, or maybe a scrap of her humanity. Maybe it was the memory of the happiest day of her life, or the ability to taste her favorite food. It didn't seem to matter. It was gone, and she'd never get it back. I reached for her, too cold and too sick to speak, but sharing her hurt and needing to offer my hollow consolation, stretching out to touch . . .

. . . And the eunuch said, "Madam wishes to speak with you now," and that's when I realized the parade down memory lane was over. I was back at Harpootlian's, and there was a clock somewhere chiming down to 3:00 a.m., the dead hour. I could feel the nasty welt the stingers had left at the base of my skull and underneath my jaw, and I still hadn't shaken off the hangover from that tainted shot of rye whiskey. But above and underneath and all about these mundane discomforts was a far more egregious pang, a portrait of that guileless white beast cut down and its blood spurting from gaping wounds. Still, I did manage to get myself upright without puking. Sure, I gagged once or twice, but I didn't puke. I pride myself on that. I sat with my head cradled in my hands, waiting for the room to stop tilting and sliding around like I'd gone for a spin on the Coney Island Wonder Wheel.

"Soon, you'll feel better, Miss Beaumont."

"Says you," I replied. "Anyway, give me a half a fucking minute, will you please? Surely your employer isn't gonna cast a kitten if you let me get my bearings first, not after the work over you just gave me. Not after—"

"I will remind you, her patience is not infinite," the ginger demon said firmly, and then it clicked its long claws together.

"Yeah?" I asked. "Well, who the hell's is?" But I'd gotten the message, plain and clear. The gloves were off, and whatever forbearance Auntie H. might have granted me in the past, it was spent, and now I was living on the installment plan. I took a deep breath and struggled to my feet. At least the eunuch didn't try to lend a hand.

I can't say for certain when Yeksabet Harpootlian set up shop in Manhattan, but I have it on good faith that Magdalena Szabó was here first. And anyone who knows her onions knows the two of them have been at each other's throats since the day Auntie H. decided to claim a slice of the action for herself. Now, you'd think there'd be plenty enough of the hellion cock-and-tail trade to go around, what with all the netherworlders who call the five boroughs their home away from home. And likely as not, you'd be right. Just don't try telling that to Szabó or Auntie H. Sure, they've each got their elite stable of "girls and boys," and they both have more customers than they know what to do with. Doesn't stop them from spending every waking hour looking for a way to banish the other once and for all—or at least find the unholy grail of competitive advantages.

Now, by the time the ginger-skinned eunuch led me through the chaos of Auntie H.'s stately pleasure dome, far below the subways and sewers and tenements of the Lower East Side, I already had a pretty good idea the dingus from Jimmy Fong's shiny box was meant to be Harpootlian's trump card. Only, here was Ellen Andrews, this mutt of a courier, gumming up the works, playing fast and loose with the loving cup. And here was me, stuck smack in the middle, the unwilling stooge in her double-cross.

As I followed the eunuch down the winding corridor that ended in Auntie H.'s grand salon, we passed doorway after doorway, all of them opening onto scenes of inhuman passion and madness, the most odious of perversions, and tortures that make short work of merely mortal flesh. It would be disingenuous to say I looked away. After all, this wasn't my first time. Here were the hinterlands of wanton physical delight and agony, where the two become indistinguishable in a rapturous *Totentanz*. Here were spectacles to remind me how Doré and Hieronymus Bosch never even came close, and all of it laid bare for the eyes of any passing voyeur. You see, there are no locked doors to be found at Madam Harpootlian's. There are no doors at all.

"It's a busy night," the eunuch said, though it looked like business as usual to me.

"Sure," I muttered. "You'd think the Shriners were in town. You'd think Mayor La Guardia himself had come down off his high horse to raise a little hell."

And then we reached the end of the hallway, and I was shown into the mirrored chamber where Auntie H. holds court. The eunuch told me to wait, then left me alone. I'd never seen the place so empty. There was no sign of the usual retinue of rogues, ghouls, and archfiends, only all those goddamn mirrors, because no one looks directly at Madam Harpootlian and lives to tell the tale. I chose a particularly fancy-looking glass, maybe ten feet high and held inside an elaborate gilded frame. When Harpootlian spoke up, the mirror rippled like it was only water, and my reflection rippled with it.

"Good evening, Natalie," she said. "I trust you've been treated well?"

"You won't hear any complaints outta me," I replied. "I always say, the Waldorf-Astoria's got nothing on you."

She laughed then, or something that we'll call laughter for the sake of convenience.

"A crying shame we're not meeting under more amicable circumstances. Were it not for this unpleasantness with Miss Andrews, I'd offer you something—on the house, of course."

"Maybe another time," I said.

"So, you *know* why you're here?"

"Sure," I said. "The dingus I took off the dead Chinaman. The salami with the fancy French name."

"It has many names, Natalie. Karkadann's Brow, *el consolador sangriento*, the Horn of Malta—"

"*Le godemiché maudit*," I said. "Ellen's cock."

Harpootlian grunted, and her reflection made an ugly, dismissive gesture. "It is nothing of Miss Andrews. It is mine, bought and paid for. With the sweat of my own brow did I track down the spoils of al-Jaldaki's long search. It's *my* investment, one purchased with so grievous a forfeiture this quadroon mongrel could not begin to appreciate the severity of her crime. But you, Natalie, you know, don't you? You've been privy to the wonders of Solomon's talisman, so I think, maybe, you are cognizant of my loss."

"I can't exactly say what I'm cognizant of," I told her, doing my best to stand up straight and not flinch or look away. "I saw the murder of a creature I didn't even believe in yesterday morning. That was sort of an eye opener, I'll grant you. And then there's the part I can't seem to conjure up, even after golden boy did that swell Roto-Rooter number on my head."

"Yes. Well, that's the catch," she said and smiled. There's no shame in saying I looked away then. Even in a mirror, the smile of Yeksabet Harpootlian isn't something you want to see straight on.

"Isn't there always a catch?" I asked, and she chuckled.

"True, it's a fleeting boon," she purred. "The gift comes, and then it goes, and no one may ever remember it. But always, *always* they will long for it again, even hobbled by that ignorance."

"You've lost me, Auntie," I said, and she grunted again. That's when I told her I wouldn't take it as an insult to my intelligence or expertise if she laid her cards on the table and spelled it out plain and simple, like she was talking to a woman who didn't regularly have tea and crumpets with the damned. She mumbled something to the effect that maybe she gave me too much credit, and I didn't disagree.

"Consider," she said, "what it *is*, a unicorn. It is the incarnation of purity, an avatar of innocence. And here is the *power* of the talisman, for that state of grace which soon passes from us, each and every one, is forever locked inside the horn—the horn become the phallus. And in the instant that it brought you, Natalie, to orgasm, you knew again that innocence, the bliss of a child before it suffers corruption."

I didn't interrupt her, but all at once I got the gist.

"Still, you are only a mortal woman, so what negligible, insignificant sins could you have possibly committed during your short life? Likewise, whatever calamities and wrongs have been visited upon your flesh or your soul, they are trifles. But if you survived the war in Paradise, if you refused the yoke and so are counted among the exiles, then you've persisted down all the long eons. You were already broken and despoiled billions of years before the coming of man. And your transgressions outnumber the stars.

"Now," she asked, "what would *you* pay, were you so cursed, to know even one fleeting moment of that stainless former existence?"

Starting to feel sick to my stomach all over again, I said, "More to the point, if I *always* forgot it, immediately, but it left this emptiness I feel—"

"You would come back," Auntie H. smirked. "You would come back again and again and again, because there would be no satiating that void, and always would you hope that maybe *this* time it would take and you might *keep* the memories of that immaculate condition."

"Which makes it priceless, no matter what you paid."

"Precisely. And now Miss Andrews has forged a copy—an *identical* copy, actually—meaning to sell one to me, and one to Magdalena Szabó. That's where Miss Andrews is now."

"Did you tell her she could hex me?"

"I would never do such a thing, Natalie. You're much too valuable to me."

"*But* you think I had something to do with Ellen's mystical little counterfeit scheme."

"Technically, you did. The ritual of division required a supplicant, someone to receive the gift granted by the unicorn, before the summoning of a succubus mighty enough to effect such a difficult twinning."

"So maybe, instead of sitting here bumping gums with me, you should send one of your torpedoes after her. And, while we're on the subject of how you pick your little henchmen, maybe—"

"*Natalie*," snarled Auntie H. from someplace not far behind me. "Have I failed to make myself *understood*? Might it be I need to raise my voice?" The floor rumbled, and tiny hairline cracks began to crisscross the surface of the looking glass. I shut my eyes.

"No," I told her. "I get it. It's a grift, and you're out for blood. But you *know* she used me. Your lackey, it had a good, long look around my upper story, right, and there's no way you can think I was trying to con you."

For a dozen or so heartbeats, she didn't answer me, and the mirrored room was still and silent, save all the moans and screaming leaking in through the walls. I could smell my own sour sweat, and it was making me sick to my stomach.

"There are some gray areas," she said finally. "Matters of sentiment and lust, a certain reluctant infatuation, even."

I opened my eyes and forced myself to gaze directly into that mirror, at the abomination crouched on its writhing throne. And all at once, I'd had enough, enough of Ellen Andrews and her dingus, enough of the cloak-and-dagger bullshit, and definitely enough kowtowing to the monsters.

"For fuck's sake," I said, "I only just met the woman this afternoon. She drugs and rapes me, and you think that means she's my sheba?"

"Like I told you, I think there are gray areas," Auntie H. replied. She grinned, and I looked away again.

"Fine. You tell me what it's gonna take to make this right with you, and I'll do it."

"Always so eager to please," Auntie H. laughed, and the mirror in front of me rippled. "But, since you've asked, and as I do not doubt your *present* sincerity, I will tell you. I want her dead, Natalie. Kill her, and all will be . . . forgiven."

"Sure," I said, because what the hell else was I going to say. "But if she's with Szabó—"

"I have spoken already with Magdalena Szabó, and we have agreed to set aside our differences long enough to deal with Miss Andrews. After all, she has attempted to cheat us both, in equal measure."

"How do I find her?"

"You're a resourceful young lady, Natalie," she said. "I have faith in you. Now . . . if you will excuse me," and, before I could get in another word, the mirrored room dissolved around me. There was a flash, not of light, but of the deepest abyssal darkness, and I found myself back at the Yellow Dragon, watching through the bookshop's grimy windows as the sun rose over the Bowery.

There you go, the dope on just how it was I found myself holding a gun on Ellen Andrews, and just how it was she found herself wondering if I was angry enough or scared enough or desperate enough to pull the trigger. And like I said, I chambered a round, but she just stood there. She didn't even flinch.

"I wanted to give you a gift, Nat," she said.

"Even if I believed that—and I don't—all I got to show for this *gift* of yours is a nagging yen for something I'm never going to get back. We lose our innocence, it stays lost. That's the way it works. So, all I got from you, Ellen, is a thirst can't ever be slaked. That and Harpootlian figuring me for a clip artist."

She looked hard at the gun, then looked harder at me.

"So what? You thought I was gonna plead for my life? You thought maybe I was gonna get down on my knees for you and beg? Is that how you like it? Maybe you're just steamed cause I was on top—"

"Shut up, Ellen. You don't get to talk yourself out of this mess. It's a done deal. You tried to give Auntie H. the high hat."

"And you honestly think she's on the level? You think you pop me and she lets you off the hook, like nothing happened?"

"I do," I said. And maybe it wasn't as simple as that, but I wasn't exactly lying, either. I needed to believe Harpootlian, the same way old women need to believe in the infinite compassion of the little baby Jesus and Mother Mary. Same way poor kids need to believe in the inexplicable generosity of Popeye the Sailor and Santa Claus.

"It didn't have to be this way," she said.

"I didn't dig your grave, Ellen. I'm just the sap left holding the shovel."

And she smiled that smug smile of hers and said, "I get it now, what Auntie H. sees in you. And it's not your knack for finding shit that doesn't want to be found. It's not that at all."

"Is this a guessing game," I asked, "or do you have something to say?"

"No, I think I'm finished," she replied. "In fact, I think I'm done for. So let's get this over with. By the way, how many women have you killed?"

"You played me," I said again.

"Takes two to make a sucker, Nat." She smiled.

Me, I don't even remember pulling the trigger. Just the sound of the gunshot, louder than thunder.

In a time when plague rules the land, a surviving rogue masquerades as Death itself, but discovers the extent of his rule and the power of his fright does not extend as far as he had thought . . .

KING DEATH

Paul Finch

The stately parade wound its way through the green shades of Cannock and Longforest.

A galaxy of radiant colors—blues, oranges, purples, pinks—shimmered from the heraldic flags and banners, from the gaudy canvases that roofed the carriages and carts, from the lavish, ermine-trimmed robes worn by the lords and ladies riding therein. The horses—for the most part strong, splendid beasts, hunters and palfreys, milk-white, roan, chestnut brown— walked resplendent in hooded coats emblazoned with baronial devices. Gilded spurs glinted in shafts of September sunlight; polished saddles gleamed; the tapestry curtains bedecking the elegant chaises were embossed with golden rays.

The handsome vehicles trundled in slow but steady cavalcade, their beasts moving at sedate pace, wending idly along the wooded trail. Yet there was no sound of merriment—just the creaking of wheels and woodwork, the gentle jingle of harness; no gay chatter, no laughter, no harmonious singing in chorals. Not a single jongleur—for gentlefolk rarely traveled these days without minstrels or songsters—plucked at his gittern or blew on his reed-pipes. There was no shouting of orders from the staller or the groom, no cracking of whips, no panting as liveried servants scampered back and forth with brimming wine-cups and ribald messages. And yet the retinue passed in regal fashion, the animals treading slowly, softly, nodding with contentment.

Because their masters and mistresses were dead.

All here were dead.

Save one.

A lone knight—dressed all in black, reined up by the roadside.

His name was Rodric, and he had witnessed many horrors over the last year, yet there was something especially odious about this. The combination, perhaps, of rich awning, elaborate fashion, opulent garb—with the caked blood and seeping pus of a thousand plague sores, with the drone of feeding bluebottles.

How long had these dead folk been on the move, he wondered? Hours? Days? Where were they traveling from, and where to? No one would ever know now. The stench was hideous—the stomach-turning fetor that hung over everything in these unhappy days, yet swam in waves from this grisly spectacle, this mobile feast for crows. Much good they'd drawn from the sachets they'd adorned their carriages with—the elf-wort, the honeysuckle, the lavender and thyme—the so-called "herbs of healing."

The cavalcade swung past, and, at length, Rodric spurred his horse forward. Despite all, there were rich pickings here. Forty or fifty corpses cluttered the carts and wagons—most huddled together, the dead eyes bulging in their raddled, rotted, pulp-apple faces. There would be treasures if one was prepared to look: strings of gems, brooches and clasps, jeweled drinking-vessels, ouches of solid gold. Many of the horses were riderless, the men-at-arms who'd accompanied their masters having fallen by the wayside; though at least one, his foot caught in a stirrup, dragged in the dust. However, their bolsters would be full—with inedible food and stagnant drink, but also purses. Even the pay of the common soldiery—a handful of copper coins, a rosary or a ring of service—was a haul in times like these.

Had Rodric the stomach for it, there was more than even he, with his team of pack-animals, could carry away. The clothing alone, an assortment of taffeta, satin, velvet, fox, and miniver, would bring dividends in due course. But, immune though he now fancied he was to this pestilence—for everyone he knew had died, even women he'd bedded and bosom friends he'd shared cups with, yet, somehow, he lived, unscathed by boil or tumor— even *he* would balk at rummaging among garb so stiff and sticky with the humors of corruption. But the jeweled vessels, the coin, the silver plate—in the absence of anyone else, they were now his.

It was the twenty-second year of Edward's reign—Edward, the third of that name—and England was a desolated wasteland.

From the high Cheviots to the Cornish moors, from the Fens to the Irish Sea, it was the same. The orchards and cornfields slipped into rack and ruin for want of someone to reap them, the highways lay deserted, the villages in dereliction, the wolds and cots in eerie, sepulchral silence. And then there were the bodies—always the bodies: thick as autumn leaves on the fields and roads, moldering in the ditches. Even Rodric, a veteran of Halidon Hill, where six-thousand Scots fell to English arrows in a single afternoon, and

Crecy, where twice that number of French were slain, had no memory of such carnage. And *all*, it seemed, were fair game. He'd seen peasants littering their roods, priests draped across altars, monks over half-finished manuscripts, merchants withering amid their produce. In the towns, rats ran riot across the husks of beggars and aldermen alike. The greatest magnates, he'd heard, had been struck: bishops and abbots, earls, dukes, even princes—cast like rubbish into the same stinking charnel-pits.

It was truly a scourge, a malediction of the worst kind.

Everything he saw, as he rode from one part of the kingdom to the next, bore the marks of cataclysm; not just death, but the wretchedness that went with it: the grief of loss, the agony of starvation, the wailing of hopeless prayers, the gasping of the cathedral flagellants, lashing themselves till they dropped insensible from blood-loss, the robbery, pillage, and chaos that resulted when sheriffs died in their castles, reeves in their jails, and justiciers in the very carriages that took them from one court to the next.

Yet, bewilderingly, he—Rodric—was spared.

He didn't have the faintest idea how. Even more puzzling, perhaps, was "why." He wasn't the most deserving specimen of humanity. Had he simply been overlooked? Was the obliteration of one worthless flyspeck deemed irrelevant after so many other, better ones, had gone before it? But these weren't his only questions. The disaster had become incomprehensible to him. When had it all started? He wasn't sure any more. How long had it dragged on for? Again, he couldn't calculate.

He knew only that it was here now. That it had arrived overnight, exploding across the realm with horrific speed. It rose to zeniths of destructiveness in the summer, but though it retreated again in the winter, it did so slowly, grudgingly, leaving waste and wreckage in its wake. The free-company of which Rodric had been part had died to a man during the plague's first few months, including its captain, Richard Warbeck, even though they had all remained ensconced in the Warbeck castle in Kent. After that, Rodric, the sole survivor, had made for the wild country, only to find that the wild country had come to him. One by one, the great estates, depopulated and collapsing under their own dead-weight, were reclaimed; tilled land disappearing beneath meadow and pasture, greenwood re-invading orchard and coppice.

Of course, it hadn't all been misery. Suddenly, Rodric had been able to take fish from the rivers, hare and squirrel from the hedgerows, even deer and boar from the chase, without fear of the verderer. On one occasion, a warden had shown himself, but Rodric had killed him, knowing there would be no retribution. Brief luxuries in the midst of catastrophe, but in truth, these were small consolation. Even Rodric—for all his military skills—was a stranger in this land that had once been his home. A power he might be, a force to be reckoned with—not just because he was alive, but because he actually made this calamity pay—but who knew what would follow in the ensuing months? Who knew what *could* follow? This wasn't just a changed world, but an *alien* one. There were times when even the most hardened outcasts yearned for things they found familiar.

He stood up beside his campfire on the ridge, stretched and gazed down onto the great plain. At first glance, it was glorious: unspoiled grasslands rolling from the Derbyshire hills to the wild Welsh borders. Directly below there was a narrow river-valley filled with ancient oak-woods. It was a great irony that only Man should be stricken by this torment; that the land remained verdant, that animals could wander freely.

Abruptly, Rodric's reverie was broken. He spotted movement, and dropped to a crouch. Below him, someone was making unsteady passage along the footpath beside the river. Rodric snaked to the edge of the ridge, and peered down. It was a boy, not yet begrimed by rough living, wearing quality clothes rather than scraps, which suggested he was attached to some great household, though walking drunkenly as he was, bowed by grief or sickness, or maybe both, that household was no more.

Rodric tarried a moment, to ensure nobody else was with the lad, then hurried down into the hollow where his horses were tethered. There were six of them, laden with sacks of loot. Some items were of outstanding value: goblets and crucifixes encrusted with gems; others—leather-bound books or reliquaries filled with bones—would be worth a tidy sum in due course. In addition, he had gold and silver—more than enough to set up his own house when the time was right. Under normal circumstances, to carry such wealth openly would invite attack. Not so now. Through a clever ruse, Rodric defended this hoard by the same means with which he had amassed it. He passed himself off as a knight, though in truth he had not been ordained into the equestrian order, having never been part of any noble or meritorious clique. He hadn't even served a squiredom, though for the knight whom Rodric masqueraded as no squiredom would have sufficed in any case.

The trickster chuckled as he readied himself. He was clad in a snug-fitting suit of black mail, but now donned his black plate as well, strapping rambraces, rerebraces and elbow-guards to his arms, greaves and knee-cops to his legs.

He was peasant-born, but had given up the rake and hoe in early youth to join a band of men-at-arms who, in times of war, served with the king's infantry, and, in peace, rented themselves out as mercenaries. His normal weapons were the dagger, the ax, the longbow, but after brutal years on the bloody fields of France and Scotland, he had collected all manner of arms and regalia. He pulled a studded leather brigandine over his hauberk, followed by a surcoat of black linen, and a massive, weather-stained cloak of heavy black wool. His gauntlets were of articulated iron, also black. His helmet was a visored bascinet fixed with a chain aventail. This too was black, and on the front of it he had painted the grinning visage of a skull. The same ghoulish device decked his wood and canvas shield.

Rodric slid a longsword into the scabbard by his waist, and selected the horse he always chose for these occasions; the pale one, Harefoot. Hanging by its flank was a huge scythe, which he'd found in a rotting hay-rig. Once mounted, Rodric put the scythe to his shoulder, hefted his shield, and spurred his animal over the ridge and down the slope.

The boy had made little ground. In the cover of the oak-woods, Rodric was able to overtake him unseen, and suddenly to emerge in front, stopping the lad dead in his tracks.

There was a tense, awesome silence. Rodric knew exactly what the boy was seeing, and how he would interpret it. He, himself, drew quick conclusions from what *he* was seeing. The boy was perhaps eight years old, and wore his fair hair in a fashionable bob, which suggested he had only recently come to destitution. He wore a tight, hooded tunic, which was parti-colored, one side green one side red. His hose, which extended into long spiked shoes, were of a similar pattern, one leg green, one red, creating a harlequin effect; a current fashion in the great country houses. Though the boy's hands were dirty, the rest of him was clean, which meant he hadn't come far. For all this, his face was drawn and waxy-white; his eyes were haunted holes of sorrow.

The duo stared at each other, Rodric sitting tall on his horse, shield-device fully displayed, scythe held outwards so that its full curve of razored steel was clearly on view. The boy held his ground, but wobbled back and forth, enfeebled by hunger.

"Don't you know me?" Rodric asked, his voice rasping and tinny through the visor.

"I think, sir . . . I think that you are Death."

"King Death!" Rodric asserted. "I am King Death! This realm belongs to *me*."

The boy clearly had no mind to disagree.

"Well?" Rodric demanded. "Do you not cower? Do you not quake in my presence?"

The boy worked dry, cracked lips together. He gazed at the nightmarish figure with vague wariness, yet such was his extreme of fatigue that he seemed almost indifferent.

"Good sire," he finally said, "it is an honor to make your acquaintance. But I can not fear you. For I have no fear left inside me."

"No fear?" Rodric was astounded. Whenever he'd presented this grim pantomime before, the least he usually received from the credulous fools still wandering the devastated land were shrieks of terror, or frantic flights to safety.

The boy rubbed a raw, red eye with the heel of his palm. "Everything I had is gone, my lord. My mother and father, my aunts and uncles, my brothers and sisters. There is nothing left for me." He sniffled. "No work to earn my keep, no roof for shelter. When the plague first came, I heard whispers that those who lived through it would come to envy those who did not. I understand that now."

"You haven't lived through it," Rodric reminded him. "Yet."

"And I would that I won't, sire. Might you strike me now? To end this pain?"

"First I have need of you."

The boy looked surprised, even puzzled.

"You say you have no lodgings," Rodric said. "Yet your garb tells a different tale. Aren't you enthralled to some master of note?"

"I was first-page to Sir Richard Bollinbeau, of Thorby."

"Thorby?"

"You must know it, sire. For you have been there. A fine manor, with many hides attached. Lord Richard held it as knight-vassal to the Abbott of Shrewsbury. Now it is a sorry place. Everyone who lived there has perished, my master and mistress included, the chamberlain and seneschal, the maids and porters . . . there was no reason for me to stay."

So the manor-house at Thorby stood empty.

It was difficult for Rodric to conceal his glee. "And you set out to make your fortune elsewhere?" he said.

The boy shook his head solemnly. "No, sire. As I say, I set out to find . . . *you*."

Rodric was briefly unnerved by such fatalism, but he kept his composure. "You have succeeded. And your wish will be granted, but not yet. First, you will be my servant."

If the lad felt this odd, he didn't question it. In fact, he made an effort to stand up straight, striving to adjust his clothes and wipe the tear-stains from his cheeks.

"Was Thorby a wealthy lordship?" Rodric asked.

"Middling to wealthy, sire. Many tithes and rents were attached, and a goodly herd of cattle. There was a wide acreage of plough-land too, fish-ponds, woods filled with game."

Rodric's appetite was whetted just to listen. "And is it far from here?"

"But you have been there, sire. Your mighty fist descended . . . "

The black knight exploded with suitably godlike wrath: *"Don't bandy words with me, boy! I have visited numberless places! Even a king cannot remember everything he sees!"*

Abashed, the boy hung his head. "It is half a day's march, my liege."

"You will lead me there. I am the conqueror of this land, and have booty to claim." As an afterthought, he added: "Your help will not go unrewarded."

"I seek only death, sire . . . to join my kin."

Rodric pondered this. "If death is what you seek . . . death you shall have."

It was late evening when they reached Thorby. The avenues of the forest, already turning russet and gold, were lit flame-red by the dying sun. Again, everything was pleasing to eye and ear. A pair of stags crossed the path; from somewhere in the spinney came the call of a nuthatch. A breeze blew from the west, rustling the ferns and thickets.

But then there was the stench.

Always these days, the stench. It lingered even in these fair woods. In fact, it grew denser, more cloying, until it didn't so much taint the air as saturate it.

Even Rodric, who'd known no other smell for twelve months or more, felt his eyes begin to water. Shortly afterwards, the trees parted and they found themselves on the outskirts of Sir Richard's holding. And what a sight greeted them.

The pestilence had come here like an army, first of all attacking the serfs in the outer villages, for here the victims had died without having a chance of burial. They strewed the fields and the narrow lanes between their hovels as though they had expired in the midst of their everyday chores. That most were little more than bones and tatters already indicated the length of time they had laid undisturbed.

Closer to the heart of the demesne, on the richer land where the sokemen dwelled, there had been more opportunity to prepare for the apocalypse. Again, the hamlets and their connecting roads were carpeted with corpses; nothing stirred save the rats and ravens, but red crosses were visible on cottage doors, grave-pits had been dug, and even carts—laden with limp, rag-bound figures—sat motionless, their horses cropping the cud, awaiting drivers who now would never come. In the center of one village there was a timber chapel with a thatched roof. Its front door stood open on blackness, from which came a monstrous buzzing of flies. Rodric didn't need to enter to know what he would find in there: bodies piled seven or eight deep; when all else failed, holy sanctuary would have been the only place left where the dying wretches could imagine they'd find solace or comfort, or—laughably, he now realized—refuge. Doubtless, the priest lay among them, maybe buried at the bottom of the putrefying mound.

The manor house had apparently been the last bastion to fall.

It was an imposing granite edifice, and it stood on a green hillock overlooking the surrounding weald. A low earthwork encircled it, and on the top of this a wooden palisade had been constructed. It would be difficult to assault such a structure, but this new enemy had made short work even of these defenses. Mailed serjeants still kept watch from the parapets, their gaze leveled across the landscape. They would shout no challenge, however, sound no alarum. When Rodric drew close, he saw that the faces under their wide-brimmed helms were clusters of black and purple boils; their staring eyes were glazed and lifeless.

"Every man held his ground 'til the last," the boy wept. "Sir Richard issued orders they should shoot at plague-carriers who came close." He indicated several husks of arrows half-buried in the grassy slope. "But still you came, overwhelming us in the heart of our stronghold." He trailed doggedly up the stony path to the outer gate.

This already stood open, presumably where he'd unbarred it, himself, and exited earlier that day. He passed through it, beckoning Rodric to follow. The knight glanced again at the ghoulish sentries, who would guard this place now until their flesh and muscle fell to carrion, then cast down his scythe, dismounted and followed.

Beyond the gate, the bailey, which might ordinarily be muddy and trampled and overrun with geese and pigs, was bare of life. More bodies lay here and there: servants—a couple beside the well, one in the entrance to the grain-house—and several men-at-arms who had tumbled from their gantries. The implacable silence was haunting. It was a *listening* silence, Rodric fancied, an eavesdropping silence—it made him feel that someone was watching him. He appraised the manor house warily. With its cruciform arrow-slits and high, castellated frontage, it was a brooding presence. Its great front door, a colossal slab of wood studded with iron nail-heads, was firmly closed, as though someone might still be inside, seeking to keep out marauders.

For long moments, Rodric was unnerved by this. Even in the Valley of Death it was a difficult thing for a low-born like he to overcome the age-old strictures that forbade him to approach the houses of the mighty, much less assault them. He knew it was nonsense to think that way—the old order no longer existed—but instincts, it seemed, died harder than men. He threw off his cloak—suddenly it felt hot and cumbersome. He was inclined to throw off his helm as well, to finally give up this charade. What was the point of it? He was here, he could sack his gold, finish off the witness, and flee—but some uncertainty, maybe the innate sixth sense that had kept him alive not just through war but now through plague, coaxed him continue the deception.

He strode to the manor house door, putting his shoulder to the wood and attempting to push his way in. There was no give; the door held fast even under Rodric's prodigious strength. He stood back. There was no ring-handle, only a large key-hole, which significantly had no key inserted. There'd be no other means of ingress, no tradesman's door or undercroft. The outbuildings in the bailey were adequate for those purposes, acting as servants' quarters and storerooms. This main building was purely the residence for the lord and his family, and, of course, for their trove.

He turned to the boy. "This place is locked, whey-face!"

The boy nodded. "Lord Richard's final instruction. Someday his heirs—for he felt certain they exist somewhere—will come and claim it."

"Lord Richard has no heir but me," Rodric replied. "You know that, for you have seen my power. Bring me a key. Unlock the door, so I may claim what is mine."

For the first time, the boy hesitated to obey. He glanced up at the house where he'd served for so long. Rodric lurched towards him, crouched and brought the full ghastly visage of his skullish helm to bear. "Do you refuse me?"

He made sure to sound shocked rather than angry, but the boy flinched backwards all the same. "No . . . sire," he stuttered. "The key is in the stable." He indicated a ramshackle structure, with two heavy wooden doors. "I put it there for safe-keeping, along with my own family. They too were servants here."

"You left your family in the stable?"

"To preserve them," the boy explained. "Laid them under straw to save them from scavengers. Though I worry the rats may still feast on them." He grimaced, new tears glimmering in his swollen eyes. "The rats own much of England that once was Man's."

"The rats own nothing," Rodric assured him, standing again. "England is mine. All of it. Now do as I command." He took the boy by his arm, turned him about-face and propelled him across the yard with a firm push.

The boy staggered off to do his new master's bidding. Rodric followed him part of the way, stopping once to survey his surroundings. The ember of the sun rested on the western parapet, and though long shadows now stole across the yard, it bathed the main building with a sultry, orange glow. Rodric had raided many houses and castles during his time in arms, and the scene here was depressingly familiar. There was ample evidence of last-minute preparations to withstand siege. Provisions had been brought from outside—logs and kindling, bushels of corn, sacks of nuts and fruit; all now stacked against walls, though many of these had been kicked and spilled in the chaos; the animals and fowls were noticeably absent—no doubt they had all been slaughtered, salted and put into stock. Elsewhere tools and weapons lay discarded, jobs were half-done, there'd been a general neglect of menial chores—the autumn leaves lay unswept, household rubbish cluttered every corner.

He glanced back at the house, wondering where the lord and his lady, themselves, were. Probably in their bedchamber. Often before, when he'd broken into plague-stricken houses, he'd found the master and mistress tucked up in bed. For all the gore and pus-clotted sheets, quite often they'd be clinging together in a final embrace. They might even be clasping a crucifix between them, seeking to sanctify their marriage in death, in a way they'd never managed to in life.

At first, when he'd seen such things, Rodric had felt—maybe not pity, but sympathy. It must have come as a terrible shock to these wealthy, commanding folk—the men often cold and ruthless, the women haughty, disdainful—that they could despair and die like the most downtrodden villeins. Little wonder, in the light of such revelation, they had shown a last a flicker of humanity, had made a final desperate gesture to win favor for their wretched souls. That was how Rodric *had* felt. Now, of course, he scoffed. He'd seen too much pain and sorrow. Why single the nobility out for sentiment? This callous, authoritarian breed; these overbearing braggarts; these cruel and arrogant sots who felt the world owed them position, who felt they were born to wealth and privilege while others must swim and wallow in cesspits of degradation.

"I don't care about you," he said, as he stared up at the house. Even louder, he added: "Do you understand . . . I don't care about any of you!"

"I know that, my lord," the boy said from the direction of the stables.

Rodric turned and saw that he had opened the two doors, revealing a dark and dusty interior, but also a hefty contraption of some sort, a great mechanism draped with a canvas awning.

"What's this?" Rodric asked impatiently. "Is the key under there? I need the key, damn you!"

The boy answered by tearing away the awning, sending plumes of dust into the air. Beneath it there was an infamous piece of battlefield ballistae: the dread *scorpion,* or archery-machine. In essence, it was an immense crossbow mounted on a wheeled base, but fitted with many springs and levers and two outspread arms of hugely-tensioned wood, so that it might hurl twenty cloth-yard bolts in a single volley.

Rodric's jaw dropped.

He'd seen these devilish devices cut swathes through lines of infantry, bring down entire companies of galloping knights. Even now, this one appeared to be fully primed. Maybe a dozen missiles were loaded into its central grooves, their needle-sharp bodkin tips glinting in the sunset.

By accident or design, he was standing directly in their line of flight.

"I know that," the boy said again. "It's why I must do this." Once again his eyes were sodden with tears, but his diminutive fist was clenched determinedly around the handle that served as the *scorpion*'s trigger.

"What do you mean?" Rodric tried not to show the dull fear creeping through him.

"I put my family here, in this stable . . . because this machine was here. I thought I could use it to protect them, should the wolves come. But now I have a better use for it." Then the boy bellowed—in a raw, hoarse voice: "*I will save my people!*"

Rodric hardly dared move. "Don't be foolish. You can't save them, you know that."

Tears streamed down the boy's hollow cheeks, cutting tracks through the encrusted dirt. "*You* took them away. *You* can give them back."

Rodric shook his head. "Who do you think I am, God?"

"I know who you are. You are . . . "

"Don't be a dolt! Whatever I told you is nonsense! You surely realize that?"

He slammed open his visor, to show that the lean bearded features beneath: pock-marked, criss-crossed with old scars—very human, very mortal. It was never pleasant to reveal that you were a fraud, but on this occasion he felt he could live with the shame.

The boy remained solemn; his grip tightened on the archery-machine's trigger. Many times in this blighted land, Rodric had encountered folk so deranged that they'd believe almost anything. Apparently, here was one more deranged than most.

"You cannot lie to me," the boy stated. "I remained here for days after everyone else died. But it was hopeless. You didn't come for me, so I went looking for you. I prayed that I might find you. And I did! At first I was going to plead, to beg for you to show pity . . . just a little pity. But I see now that begging and pleading falls silent on ears such as yours. So, instead . . . *I demand!*"

Rodric was now calculating the distance he'd have to run to put himself out of range. He was about twelve feet from the row of arrow-heads, which meant that scrambling backwards was out of the question. A quick dash sideways might suffice. Most of these heavy war-machines were mounted on a pivot so they could be swiveled, though he doubted this emaciated stripling would have the strength to do that. Even so, it would be a risk. Just for the moment, he opted to keep talking.

"Listen to me, boy . . . what I did to you was cruel, despicable. But it's . . . "

"You've got to give them back!" the boy shouted. *"All of them!"*

Rodric was stunned to silence. Frantic thoughts raced through his head. The *scorpion* looked old; almost certainly it was ill-maintained. Maybe it wouldn't work? But could he take that risk—wouldn't it be better to pre-empt the situation and try to hit the boy with his throwing-dagger? But no—these were gambles; wild, desperate gambles.

"You must know that I can't give them back," he said, in a firm but fatherly tone. "In your heart of hearts, you must know. No one can do that but Our Lord."

The boy chewed his pale lip. "If you can't return those you have already claimed . . . you must at least spare the rest."

"I cannot spare them."

"Cannot or *will* not?"

"I cannot." Rodric made a friendly gesture. "*We* cannot. Understand me when I say that . . . *we*. It's you and me now. We're practically all that's left. But at least we're together, and we should stay that way . . . "

The lad's youthful brow darkened; his tear-bright eyes narrowed to slivers. "It isn't *we!* It isn't we at all! You're not my friend, you're my enemy! And If I can't save or spare my people, I'll do the next best thing, and avenge them . . . "

"No!" Rodric shouted, seeing the muscles bunch in the small shoulder. He grabbed for the dagger at his belt. "You damned village-idiot, what good will it do you . . . ?"

The lever *clacked* backwards. There was *twang*, a violent recoil and a tumult of hissing air. Rodric was struck several times with battering-ram force.

He tottered where he stood, but managed to remain upright—just.

Seconds of dizziness passed. The air cooled as the sun slipped down over the top of the palisade. Through it all, the boy stayed in the doorway to the stable, the eyes wide in his white, ghost-like face. Rodric wanted to laugh at him, to nod and wink, to say: "You see . . . I told you this was pointless. That you and I should be companions . . . "

But it was difficult to concentrate on words when so many parts of his body felt as if they had all been caught between hammers and anvils. It was difficult even to hold the dagger, let alone throw it—not that throwing it would serve any purpose now. The weapon slid through his fingers and dropped to the floor. Rodric wanted to drop after it, but an inner voice told him not to, told him to stay on his feet and go and seek for help.

He nodded, as though receiving useful advice.

Help would be a good idea.

His armor was robust; it would have protected him to some extent, but several of the arrows had penetrated. He understood that without needing to glance down.

He stumbled back to the gate, and out through it. Beyond the palisade, Harefoot was grazing by the roadside. Far beyond the faithful brute, the last rays of blood-red sunlight were flooding across the land, the last spark of daytime about to wink out—and with it what remained of the late summer warmth, for a bone-numbing chill had come rushing in and wrapped itself around Rodric. He tried to ignore it, but it was a difficult task. Suddenly he was shivering. Even the hot fluid gurgling inside his armor failed to warm him.

He strode towards his horse, but when he got there found that his strength had drained to such an extent that he couldn't even mount up. His mailed foot was too heavy to lift to the stirrup. Then there were the feathered shafts; they got in the way, kept pushing him backwards from Harefoot's flank.

Rodric leaned sideways against the horse, exhausted. At first, he didn't notice the figure step up behind him. He only realized there was anyone there at all when a hand came to rest on his shoulder. He turned to look—and saw eyes that were rotted holes in green parchment, a curved mouth full of peg-teeth, and over the top of it all, a head-dress made from twisted iron barbs.

A crown, no less.

Rodric chuckled hoarsely.

King Death.

⟨⟩

What it's like to long for daylight, to be—in love *with daylight—and you can never see it for real, never feel the warmth, smell the scents of it or properly hear the sounds—never?*

WHY LIGHT?

Tanith Lee

PART ONE

My first memory is the fear of light.

The passage was dank and dark and water dripped, and my mother carried me, although by then I could walk. I was three, or a little younger. My mother was terrified. She was consumed by terror, and she shook, and her skin gave off a faint metallic smell I had never caught from her before. Her hands were cold as ice. I could feel that, even through the thick shawl in which she'd wrapped me. She said, over and over, "It's all right, baby. It's all right. It will be okay. You'll see. Just a minute, only one. It'll be all right."

By then of course I too was frightened. I was crying, and I think I wet myself, though I hadn't done anything like that since babyhood.

Then the passage turned, and there was a tall iron gate—I know it's iron, now. At the time it only looked like a burnt-out coal.

"Oh God," said my mother.

But she thrust out one hand and pushed at the gate and it grudged open with a rusty scraping, just wide enough to let us through.

I would have seen the vast garden outside the house, played there. But this wasn't the garden. It was a high place, held in only by a low stone wall and a curving break of poplar trees. They looked very black, not green the way the house lamps made trees in the garden. Something was happening to the sky; that was what made the poplars so black. I thought it was moonrise, but I knew the moon was quite new, and only a full moon could dilute the darkness so much. The stars were watery and blue, weak, like dying gas flames.

My mother stood there, just outside the iron gate, holding me, shaking. "It's all right . . . just a minute . . . only one . . . "

Suddenly something happened.

It was like a storm—a lightning flash maybe, but in slow-motion, that swelled up out of the dark. It was pale, then silver, and then like gold. It was like a high trumpet note, or the opening chords of some great concerto.

I sat bolt upright in my mother's arms, even as she shook ever more violently. I think her teeth were chattering.

But I could only open my eyes wide. Even my mouth opened, as if to drink the sudden light.

It was the color of a golden flower and it seemed to boil, and enormous clouds poured slowly upward out of it, brass and wine and rose. And a huge noise came from everywhere, rustling and rushing—and weird flutings and squeakings and trills—birdsong—only I didn't recognize it.

My mother now hoarsely wept. I don't know how she never dropped me.

Next they came out and drew us in again, and Tyfa scooped me quickly away as my mother collapsed on the ground. So I was frightened again, and screamed.

They closed the gate and shut us back in darkness. The one minute was over. But I had seen a dawn.

PART TWO

Fourteen and a half years later, and I stood on the drive, looking at the big black limousine. Marten was loading my bags into the boot. Musette and Kousu were crying quietly. One or two others lingered about; nobody seemed to grasp what exactly was the correct way to behave. My mother hadn't yet come out of the house.

By that evening my father was dead over a decade—he had died when I was six, my mother a hundred and seventy. They had lived together a century anyway, were already tired of each other and had taken other lovers from our community. But that made his death worse, apparently. Ever since, every seventh evening, she would go into the little shrine she had made to him, cut one of her fingers and let go a drop of blood in the vase below his photograph. Her name is Juno, my mother, after a Roman goddess, and I'd called her by her name since I was an adult.

"She should be here," snapped Tyfa, irritated. He too was Juno's occasional lover, but generally he seemed exasperated by her. "Locked in that damn room," he added sourly. He meant the shrine.

I said nothing, and Tyfa stalked off along the terrace, and started pacing about, a tall strong man of around two hundred or so, no one was sure—dark-haired as most of us were at Severin. His skin had a light brownness from a long summer of sun-exposure. He had always been able to take the sun, often for several hours in one day. I too have black hair, and my skin, even in winter, is pale brown. I can endure daylight all day long, day after day. I can *live* by day.

Marten had closed the boot. Casperon had got into the driver's seat, leaving the car door open, and was trying the engine. Its loud purring would no doubt penetrate the house's upper storey, and the end rooms which comprised Juno's apartment.

Abruptly she came sweeping out from the house.

June has dark red hair. Her skin is white. Her slanting eyes are the dark bleak blue of a northern sea, seen in a foreign movie with subtitles. When I was a child I adored her. She *was* my goddess. I'd have died for her, but that stopped. It stopped forever.

She walked straight past the others, as if no one else were there. She stood in front of me. She was still an inch or so taller than I, though I'm tall.

"Well," she said. She stared into my face, hers cold as marble, and all of her stone-still—this, the woman who trembled and clutched me to her, whispering that all would be well, when I was three years old.

"Yes, Juno," I said.

"Do you have everything you need?" she asked me indifferently, forced to be polite to some visitor now finally about to leave.

"Yes, thank you. Kousu helped me pack."

"You know you have only to call the house, and anything else can be sent on to you? Of course," she added, off-handedly, "you'll want for nothing, *there*."

I did not reply. What was there to say? I've 'wanted' for so much *here* and never got it—at least, my mother, from *you*.

"I wish you very well," she coldly said, "in your new home. I hope everything will be pleasant. The marriage is important, as you're aware, and they'll treat you fairly."

"Yes."

"We'll say goodbye then. At least for a while."

"Yes."

"Goodbye, Daisha." She drew out the *ay* sound: and foolishly through my mind skipped words that rhymed—fray, say . . . prey.

I said, "So long, Juno. Good luck making it up with Tyfa. Have a nice life."

Then I turned my back, crossed the terrace and the drive, and got into the car. I'd signed off with all the others before. They had loaded me with good wishes and sobbed, or tried to cheer me by mentioning images we had seen of my intended husband, and saying how handsome and talented he was, and I must write to them soon, email or call—not lose touch—come back next year—sooner—Probably they'd forget me in a couple of days or nights.

To me, they already seemed miles off.

The cream limousine of the full moon had parked over the estate as we drove away. In its blank blanched rays I could watch, during the hour it took to cross the whole place and reach the outer gates, all the nocturnal industry, in fields and orchards, in vegetable gardens, pens and horse-yards, garages and work-shops—a black horse cantering, lamps, and red sparks flying—and people coming out to see us go by, humans saluting the family car, appraising in curiosity, envy, pity or scorn, the girl driven off to become a Wife-of-Alliance.

In the distance the low mountains shone blue from the moon. The lake across the busy grasslands was like a gigantic vinyl disk dropped from the sky, an old record the moon had played, and played tonight on the spinning turn-table of the earth. This was the last I saw of my home.

The journey took just on four days.

Sometimes we passed through whitewashed towns, or cities whose tall concrete and glass fingers reached to scratch the clouds. Sometimes we were on motorways, wide and streaming with traffic in spate. Or there was open countryside, mountains coming or going, glowing under hard icing-sugar tops. In the afternoons we'd stop, for Casperon to rest, at hotels. About six or seven in the evening we drove on. I slept in the car by night. Or sat staring from the windows.

I was, inevitably, uneasy. I was resentful and bitter and full of a dull and hopeless rage.

I shall get free of it all—I had told myself this endlessly since midsummer, when first I had been informed that, to cement ties of friendship with the Duvalles, I was to marry their new heir. Naturally it was not only friendship that this match entailed. I had sun-born genes. And the Duvalle heir, it seemed, hadn't. My superior light-endurance would be necessary to breed a stronger line. A bad joke, to our kind—they needed my *blood*. I was *blood*stock. I was Daisha Severin, a young female life only seventeen years, and able to live day-long in sunlight. I was incredibly valuable. I would be, everyone had said, so *welcome*. And I was *lovely*, they said, with my brunette hair and dark eyes, my cinnamon skin. The heir—Zeev Duvalle—was very taken with the photos he had seen of me. And didn't I think *he* was fine—*cool*, Musette had said: "He's so *cool*—I wish it could have been me. You're so lucky, Daisha."

Zeev was blond, almost snow-blizzard white, though his eyebrows and lashes were dark. His eyes were like some pale shining metal. His skin was pale too, if not so colorless as with some of us, or so I'd thought when I watched him in the house movie I'd been sent. My pale-skinned mother had some light-tolerance, though far less than my dead father. I had inherited all *his* strength that way, and more. But Zeev Duvalle had none, or so it seemed. To me he looked like what he was, a man who lived only by night. In appearance he seemed nineteen or twenty, but he wasn't so much older in actual years. Like me, a new *young* life. So much in common. So very little.

And by now *I shall get free of it all*, which I'd repeated so often, had become my mantra, and also meaningless. How could I *ever* get free? Among my own kind I would be an outcast and criminal if I ran away from this marriage, now or ever, without a "valid" reason. While able to pass as human, I could hardly live safely among them. I can eat and drink a little in their way, but I need blood. Without blood I would die.

So, escape the families and their alliance, I would become not only traitor and thief—but a *murderer*. A human-slaughtering monster humanity doesn't believe in, or *does* believe in—something either way that, if discovered amongst them, they will kill.

That other house, my former home on the Severin estate, was long and quite low, two storeyed, but with high ceilings mostly on the ground floor. Its first architecture, gardens, and farm had been made in the early nineteenth century.

Their mansion—castle—whatever one has to call it—was colossal. Duvalle had built high.

It rose, this *pile*, like a cliff, with outcrops of slate-capped towers. Courtyards and enclosed gardens encircled it. Beyond and around lay deep pine woods with infiltrations of other trees, some maples, already flaming in the last of summer and the sunset. I spotted none of the usual workplaces, houses, or barns.

We had taken almost three hours to wend through their land, along the tree-rooted and stone-littered, upward-tending track. Once Casperon had to pull up, get out and examine a tire. But it was all right. On we went.

At one point, just before we reached the house, I saw a waterfall cascading from a tall rocky hill, plunging into a ravine below. In the ghostly dusk it looked beautiful, and melodramatic. Setting the tone?

When the car at last drew up, a few windows were burning amber in the house-cliff. Over the wide door itself glowed a single electric light inside a round pane like a worn-out planet.

No one had come to greet us.

We got out and stood at a loss. The car's headlamps fired the brickwork, but still nobody emerged. At the lit windows no silhouette appeared gazing down.

Casperon marched to the door and rang some sort of bell that hung there. All across the grounds crickets chirruped, hesitated, and went on.

The night was warm, and so empty; nothing seemed to be really alive anywhere, despite the crickets, the windows. Nothing, I mean, of *my* kind, our people. For a strange moment I wondered if something ominous had happened here, if everyone had died, and if so would that release me? But then one leaf of the door was opened. A man looked out. Casperon spoke to him, and the man nodded. A few minutes later I had to go up the steps and into the house.

There was a sort of vestibule, vaguely lighted by old ornate lanterns. Beyond that was a big paved court, with pruned trees and raised flowerbeds, and then more steps. Casperon had gone for my luggage. I followed the wretched sallow man who had let me in.

"What's your name?" I asked him as we reached the next portion of the house, a blank wall lined only with blank black windows.

"Anton."

"Where is the family?" I asked him.

"Above," was all he said.

I said, halting, "Why was there no one to welcome me?"

He didn't reply. Feeling a fool, angry now, I stalked after him.

There was another vast hall or vestibule. No lights, until he touched the switch and grayish weary side-lamps came on, giving little color to the stony towering space.

"Where," I said, in Juno's voice, "*is* he? He at least should be here. Zeev Duvalle, my husband-to-be." I spoke formally. "I am insulted. Go at once and tell him—"

"He does not rise yet," said Anton, as if to somebody invisible but tiresome. "He doesn't rise until eight o'clock."

Day in night. Night was Zeev's day, yet the sun had been gone over an hour now. Damn him, I thought. *Damn* him.

It was useless to protest further. And when Casperon returned with the bags, I could say nothing to him, because this wasn't his fault. And besides he would soon be gone. I was alone. As per usual.

I met Zeev Duvalle at dinner. It was definitely a dinner, not a breakfast, despite their day-for-night policy. It was served in an upstairs conservatory, the glass panes open to the air. A long table draped in white, tall old greenish glasses, plates of some red china, probably Victorian. Only five or six other people came to the meal, and each introduced themself in a formal, chilly way. Only one woman, who looked about fifty and so probably was into her several hundreds, said she regretted not being there at my arrival. No excuse was offered however. They made me feel like what I was to them, a new house computer that could talk. A doll that would be able to have babies . . . yes. Horrible.

By the time we sat down, in high-backed chairs, with huge orange trees standing around behind them like guards—a scene on a film set—I was boiling with cold anger. Part of me was afraid, too. I can't really explain the fear, or of what. It was like being washed up out of the night ocean on an unknown shore, and all you can see are stones and emptiness, and no light to show the way.

At Severin there were always types of ordinary food to be had—steaks, apples—we drank a little wine, took coffee or tea. But a lot of us were sun-born. Even Juno was. She hated daylight, but still tucked into the occasional croissant. Of course there was Proper Sustenance too. The blood of those animals we kept for that purpose, always collected with economy, care and gentleness from living beasts, which continued to live, well-fed and tended and never over-used, until their natural deaths. For special days there was special blood. This being drawn, also with respectful care, from among the human families who lived on the estate. They had no fear of giving blood, any more than the animals did. In return, their rewards were many and lavish. The same arrangement, so far as I knew, was similar among all the scattered families of our kind.

Here at Duvalle, we were served with a black pitcher of blood, a white pitcher of white wine. Fresh bread, still warm, lay on the red dishes.

That was all.

I had taken proper Sustenance at the last hotel, drinking from my flask. I'd drunk a Coke on the road, too.

Now I took a piece of bread, and filled my glass with an inch of wine.

They all looked at me. Then away. Every other glass by then gleamed scarlet. One of the men said, "But, young lady, this is the best, this is *human*. We always take it at dinner. Come now."

"No," I said, "thank you."

"Oh, but clearly you don't know your own mind—"

And then *he* spoke. From the doorway. He had only just come in, after his long rest or whatever else he had been doing for the past two and a half hours, as I was in my allotted apartment, showering, getting changed for this appalling night.

What I saw first about him, Zeev Duvalle, was inevitable. The blondness, the *whiteness* of him, almost incandescent against the candlelit room and the dark beyond the glass. His hair was like molten platinum, just sombering down a bit to a kind of white gold in the shadow. His eyes weren't gray, but green—gray-green like the crystal goblets. His skin after all wasn't that pale. It had a sort of tawny look to it—not in any way like a tan. More as if it fed on darkness and had drawn some into itself. He was handsome, but I knew that. He looked now about nineteen. He had a perfect body, slim and strong; most vampires do. We eat the perfect food and very few extra calories— nothing too much or too little. But he was tall. Taller than anyone I'd ever met. About six and a half feet, I thought.

Unlike the others, even me, he hadn't smartened up for dinner. He wore un-new black jeans and a scruffy T-shirt with long torn sleeves. I could smell the outdoors on him, pine needles, smoke and night. He had been out in the grounds. There was . . . there was a little brown-red stain on one sleeve. Was it *blood*? From *what*?

It came to me with a lurch what he really most resembled. A white wolf. And had this *bloody* wolf been out hunting in his vast forested park? What had he killed so mercilessly—some squirrel or hare—or a deer—that would be bad enough—or was it worse?

I knew *nothing* about these people I'd been given to. I'd been too offended and allergic to the whole idea to do any research, ask any real questions. I had frowned at the brief movie they sent of him, thought: so, he's cute and almost albino. I hadn't even got that right. He was a *wolf*. He was a feral animal that preyed in the old way, by night, on things defenseless and afraid.

This was when he said again, "Let her alone, Constantine." Then, "Let her eat what she wants. She knows what she likes." *Then*: "Hi, Daisha. I'm Zeev. If only you'd got here a little later, I'd have been here to welcome you."

I met his eyes, which was difficult. That glacial green, I slipped from its surface. I said quietly, "Don't worry. Who cares."

He sat down at the table's head. Though the youngest among them, he was the heir and therefore, supposedly, their leader now. His father died two years before, when his car left an upland road miles away. Luckily his companion, a woman from the Clays family, had called the house. The wreck of the car and his body had been retrieved by Duvalle before the sun could make a mess of both the living and the dead. All of us know, we survive largely through the wealth longevity enables us to gather, and the privacy it buys.

The others started to drink their dinner again, passing the black jug. Only one of them took any bread, and that was to sop up the last red elements from inside his glass. He wiped the bread round like a cloth then stuffed it in his mouth. I sipped my wine. Zeev, seen from the side of my left eye, seemed to touch nothing. He merely sat there. He didn't seem to look at me. I was glad of that.

Then the man called Constantine said loudly, "Better get on with your supper, Wolf, or she'll think you already found it in the woods. And among *her* clan that just *isn't* done."

And some of them sniggered a little, softly. I wanted to hurl my glass at the wall—or at all their individual heads.

But Zeev said, "What, you mean this on my T-shirt?" He too sounded amused.

I put down my unfinished bread and got up. I glanced around at them, at him last of all.

"I hope you'll excuse me, I've been traveling and I'm tired." Then I looked straight at him. Somehow it was shocking to do so. "And goodnight, *Zeev*. Now we've finally met."

He said nothing. None of them did.

I walked out of the conservatory, crossed the large room beyond and headed for the staircase.

Wolf. They even *called* him that.

Wolf.

"Wait," he said, just behind me.

I can move almost noiselessly and very fast, but not as noiseless and sudden as he apparently he could. Before I could prevent it I spun round wide-eyed. There he stood, less than three feet from me. He was expressionless, but when he spoke now his voice, actor-trained, I thought, was very musical. "Daisha Severin, I'm sorry. I've made a bad start with you."

"You noticed."

"Will you come with me—just upstairs—to the library. We can talk there without the rest of them making up an audience."

"Why do we want to? Talk, I mean."

"We should, I think. And maybe you'll be gracious enough to humor me."

"Maybe I'll just tell you to go to hell."

"Oh, *there*," he said. He smiled. "No. I'd never go there. Too bright, too hot."

"Fuck off," I said.

I was seven steps up the stairs when I found him beside me. I stopped again.

"Give me," he said, "one minute."

"I've been told I have to give you my entire *life*," I said. "And then I have to give you children, too, I nearly forgot. Kids who can survive in full daylight, just like me. I think that's enough, isn't it, Zeev Duvalle? You don't need a silly little *minute* from me when I have to give you all the rest."

He let me go then.

I ran up the stairs.

When I reached the upper landing I looked back down, between a kind of elation and a sort of horror. But he had vanished. The part-lit spaces of the house again seemed void of anything alive, except for me.

Juno. I dreamed about her that night. I dreamed she was in a jet-black cave where water dripped, and she held a dead child in her arms and wept.

The child was me, I suppose. What she had feared the most when they, my house of Severin, made her carry me out into the oncoming dawn, to see how much if anything I could stand. *Just one minute.* What he had asked for too, Zeev. I hadn't granted it to him. But she—and I—had had no choice.

When I survived sunrise, she was at first very glad. But then, when I began to keep asking, *When can I see the light again?* Then, oh then. Then she began to lose me, and I her, my tall, red-haired, blue-eyed mother.

She never told me, but it's simple to work out. The more I took to daylight, the more I proved I was a true sun-born, the *more* she lost me, and I lost her. She herself could stand two or three hours, every week or so. But she *hated* the light, the sun. They *terrified* her, and when I turned out so able to withstand them, even to like and—*want* them, then the doors of her heart shut fast against me.

Juno hated me just as she hated the light of the sun. She hated me, *loathed* me, *loathes* me, my mother.

Part Three

About three weeks went by. The pines darkened and the other trees turned to copper and bronze and shed like tall cats their fur of leaves. I went on walks about the estate. No one either encouraged or dissuaded me. They had then nothing they wanted to hide from me? But I don't drive, and so there was a limit to how far I could go and get back again in the increasingly chilly evenings. By day, anyway, there seemed little activity, in the house or outside it. I started sleeping later in the mornings so I could stay up at night fully alert, sometimes, until four or five. It was less I was checking on what went on in the house-castle of Duvalle, than that I was uncomfortable so many of them were around, and *active,* when I lay asleep. There was a lock on my door. I always used it. I put a chair against it too, with the back under the door-handle. It wasn't Zeev I was worried about. No one, in particular. Just the complete feel and atmosphere of that place. At Severin there had been several who were mostly or totally nocturnal—my mother, for one. But also quite a few like me who, even if they couldn't take much direct sunlight, as I could, still preferred to be about by day.

A couple of times during my outdoor excursions in daylight, I did find clearings in the woods, with small houses, vines, orchards, fields with a harvest already collected. I even once saw some men with a flock of sheep. Neither sheep nor men took any notice of me. No doubt they had been warned a new Wife-of-Alliance was here, and shown what she looked like.

The marriage had been set for the first night of the following month. The ceremony would be brief, unadorned, simply a legalization. Marriages in most of the houses were like this. Nothing especially celebratory, let alone religious, came into them.

I thought I'd resigned myself. But of course, I hadn't. As for him, Zeev Duvalle, I'd been "meeting" him generally only at dinner—those barren awful dinners where good manners seemed to demand I attend. Sometimes I was served meat—I alone. A crystal bowl of fruit had appeared—for me. I ate with difficulty amid their "fastidious" contempt. I began a habit of removing pieces of fruit to eat later in my rooms. He was only ever polite. He would unsmilingly and bleakly offer me bread and wine, water . . . Sometimes I did drink the blood. I needed to. To me it had a strange taste, which maybe I imagined.

During the night, now and then, I might see him about the house, playing chess with one of the others, listening to music or reading in the library, talking softly on a telephone. Three or four times I saw him from an upper window, outside and running in long wolf-like bounds between the trees, the paleness of his hair like a beam blown off the face of the moon.

Hunting?

I intended to get married in black. Like the girl in the Chekhov play, I too was in mourning for my life. That night I hung the dress outside the closet, and put the black pumps below, ready for tomorrow. No jewelry.

Also I made a resolve not to go down to their dire dinner. To the older woman who read novels at the table and laughed smugly, secretively at things in them; the vile man with his bread-cloth in the glass. The handful of others, some of whom never turned up regularly anyhow, their low voices murmuring to each other about past times and people known only to them. And him. Zeev. Him. He drank from his glass very couthly, unlike certain others. Sometimes a glass of water, or some wine—for him usually red, as if it must pretend to be blood. He had dressed more elegantly since the first night, but always his clothes were quiet. There was one dark white shirt, made of some sort of velvety material, with bone-color buttons . . . He looked beautiful. I could have killed him. We're easy to kill—car crashes, bullets—though we can live, Tyfa had once said, even a thousand years. But that's probably one more lie.

However, tonight I wouldn't go down there. I'd eat up here, the last apple and the dried cherries.

About ten thirty, a knock on my door.

I jumped, more because I expected it than because I was startled. I put down the book I'd been reading, the Chekhov plays, and said, "Who is it?" Knowing who it was.

"May I come in?" he asked, formal and musical, alien.

"I'd rather you left me alone," I said.

He said, without emphasis, "All right, Daisha. I'll go down to the library. No one else will be there. There'll be fresh coffee. I'll wait for you until midnight. Then I have things I have to do."

I'd got up and crossed to the door. I said through it with a crackling venom that surprised me, I'd thought I had it leashed, "*Things to do?* Oh, when you go out hunting animals and rip them apart in the woods for proper fresh blood, that kind of *thing* do you mean?"

There was silence. Then, "I'll wait till midnight," he flatly said.

Then he was gone, I knew, though I never heard him leave.

When I walked into the library it was after eleven, and I was wearing my wedding dress and shoes. I told him what they were.

"It's supposed to be unlucky, isn't it," I said, "for the groom to see the bride in her dress before the wedding. But there's no luck to spoil, is there?"

He was sitting in one of the chairs by the fire, his long legs stretched out. He'd put on jeans and sweater and boots for the excursion later. A leather jacket hung from the chair.

The coffee was still waiting but it would be cold by now. Even so he got up, poured me a cup, brought it to me. He managed—he always managed this—to hand it to me without touching me.

Then he moved away and stood by the hearth, gazing across at the high walls of books.

"Daisha," he said, "I think I understand how uncomfortable and angry you are—"

"*Do* you."

"—but I can ask that you listen. Without interrupting or storming out of the room—"

"Oh for God's—"

"*Daisha*." He turned his eyes on me. From glass-green they too had become almost white. He was flaming mad, anyone could see, but unlike me, he'd controlled it. He *used* it, like a cracking whip spattering electricity across the room. And at the same time—the *pain* in his face. The closed-in pain and—was it only frustration, or despair? That was what held me, or I'd have walked out, as he said. I stood there stunned, and thought, *He hurts as I do. Why? Who did this to him? God, he hates the idea of marrying me as much as I hate it. Or—he hates the way he—we—are being used.*

"Okay," I said. I sat down on a chair. I put the cold coffee on the floor. "Talk. I'll listen."

"Thank you," he said.

A huge old clock ticked on the mantlepiece above the fire. *Tock-tock-tock.* Each note a second. Sixty now. That minute he'd asked from me before. Or the minute when Juno held me in the sunrise, shaking.

"Daisha. I'm well aware you don't want to be here, let alone with me. I hoped you wouldn't feel that way, but I'm not amazed you do. You had to leave your own house, where you had familiar people, love, stability—" I had said I'd keep quiet, I didn't argue—"and move into this fucking monument to a castle, and be ready to become the partner of some guy you never saw except in a scrap of a movie. I'll be honest. The moment I saw the photos of you, I was drawn to you. I stupidly thought, this is a beautiful, strong woman that I'd like to know. Maybe we can make something of this pre-arranged mess. I meant make something for ourselves, you and me. Kids were—are—the last thing on my mind. We'd have a long time after all, to reach a decision on *that*. But you. I was—looking forward to meeting you. And I *would* have been there, to meet you. Only something happened. No. Not some compulsion I have to go out and tear animals apart and *drink* them in the forest. Daisha," he said, "have you been to look at the waterfall?"

I stared. "Only from the car . . ."

"There's one of our human families there. I had to go and—" he broke off. He said, "The people in this house have switched right off, like computers without any electric current. I grew up here. It was hell. Yeah, that place you wanted me to go to. Only not bright or fiery, just—*dead*. They're dead here. Living dead. *Undead*, just what they say in the legends, in that bloody book *Dracula*. But *I* am not dead. And nor are you. Did it ever occur to you," he said, "you name, *Daisha*—the way it sounds. *Day*—sha. Beautiful. Just as you are."

He had already invited me to speak, so perhaps I could offer another comment. I said, "But you can't stand the light."

"No, I can't. Which doesn't mean I don't *crave* the light. When I was two years old they took me out, my dad led me by the hand. *He* was fine with an hour or so of sunlight. I was so excited—looking forward to it. I remember the first colors—" He shut his eyes, opened them. "Then the sun came up. I never saw it after all. The first true light—I went blind. My skin . . . I don't remember properly. Just darkness and agony and terror. Just one minute. My body couldn't take even that. I was ill for ten months. Then I started to see again. After ten months. But I've seen daylight since, of course I have, on film, in photographs. I've read about it. And music—Ravel's *Sunrise* from that ballet. Can you guess what it's like to long for daylight, to be—*in love* with daylight—and you can never see it for real, never feel the warmth, smell the scents of it or properly hear the sounds, except on a screen, off a CD—*never*? When I saw you, you're like that, like a real daylight. Do you know what I said to my father when I started to recover, after those ten months, those thirty seconds of dawn? *Why*, I said to him, why is light my enemy, why does it want to kill me? *Why light?*"

Zeev turned away. He said to the sunny bright hearth, "And you're the daylight too, Daisha. And you've become my enemy. Daisha," he said, "I release you. We won't marry. I'll make it clear to all of them, Severin first, that any fault is all with me. There'll be no bad thing they can level at you. So, you're free. I regret so much the torment I've unwillingly, selfishly put you through. I'm sorry, Daisha. And now, God knows, it's late and I have to go out. It's not rudeness, I hope you'll accept that now. Please trust me. Go upstairs and sleep well. Tomorrow you can go home."

I sat like a block of concrete. Inside I felt shattered by what he had said. He pulled on his jacket and started towards the door, and only then I stood up. "*Wait.*"

"I can't." He didn't look at me. "I'm sorry. Someone—needs me. Please believe me. It's true."

And I heard myself say, "Some human girl?"

That checked him. He looked at me, face a blank. "*What?*"

"The human family you seem to have to be with—by the fall? Is that it? You want a human woman, not me."

Then he laughed. It was raw, and real, that laughter. He came back and caught my hands. "Daisha—my *Day*—you're insane. All right. Come with me and see. We'll have to race."

But my hands tingled, my heart was in a race already.

I looked up into his face, he down into mine. The night hesitated, shifted. He let go my hands and I flew out and up the stairs. Dragging off that dress I tore the sleeve at the shoulder, but I left it lying with the shoes. Inside fifteen more minutes we were sprinting, side by side, along the track. There was no excuse for this, no *rational* reason. But I had seen him, *seen*, as if sunlight had streamed through the black lid of the night and shown him to me for the first, light that was his enemy, and my mother's, *never* mine.

The moon was low by then, and stroked the edges of the waterfall. It was like liquid aluminum, and its roar packed the air full as a sort of deafness. The human house was about a mile off, tucked in among the dense black columns of the pines.

A youngish, fair-haired woman opened the door. Her face lit up the instant she saw him, no one could miss that. "Oh, Zeev," she said, "he's so much better. Our doctor says he's mending fantastically well. But come in."

It was a pleasing room, low-ceilinged, with a dancing fire. A smart black cat with a white vest and mittens, sat upright in an armchair, giving the visitors a thoughtful frowning scrutiny.

"Will you go up?" the woman asked.

"Yes," Zeev said. He smiled at her, and added, "This is Daisha Severin."

"Oh, are you Daisha? It's good of you to come out too," she told me. Zeev had already gone upstairs. The human woman returned to folding towels at a long table.

"Isn't it very late for you?" I questioned.

"We keep late hours. We like the nighttime."

I had been aware that this was often the case at Severin. But I'd hardly ever spoken much to humans, I wasn't sure now what I should say. But she continued to talk to me, and overhead I heard a floorboard creak; Zeev would not have caused that. The man was there, evidently, the one who was "mending."

"It happened just after sunset," the woman said, folding a blue towel over a green one. "Crazy accident—the chain broke. Oh God, when they brought him home, my poor Emil—" Her voice faltered and grew hushed. Above also a hushed voice was speaking, barely audible even to me. But she raised her face and it had stayed still rosy and glad, and her voice was fine again. "We telephoned up to the house and Zeev came out at once. He did the wonderful thing. It worked. It always works when he does it."

I stared at her. I was breathing quickly, frightened. "What," I said, "*what* did he do?"

"Oh, but he'll have told you," she strangely reminded me. "The same as he did for Joel—and poor Arresh when he was sick with meningitis—"

"*You* tell me," I said. She blinked. "Please."

"The blood," she said, gazing at me a little apologetically, regretful to have confused me in some way she couldn't fathom, "he gave them his blood to drink. It's the blood that heals, of course. I remember when Zeev said to Joel, it's all right, forget the stories—this won't change you, only make you well. Zeev was only sixteen then himself. He's saved five lives here. But no doubt he was too modest to tell you that. And with Emil, the same. It was shocking," now she didn't falter, "Zeev had to be here so quick—and he cut straight through his own sleeve to the vein, so it would be fast enough." *Blood on his sleeve,* I thought. *Vampires heal so rapidly . . . all done, only that little rusty mark . . .* "And my Emil, my lovely man, he's safe and alive, Daisha. Thanks to your husband."

His voice called to me out of the dim-roar of the water-falling firelight, "Daisha, come up a minute."

The woman folded an orange towel over a white one, and I numbly, speechlessly, climbed the stair, and Zeev said, "I have asked Emil, and he says, very kindly, he doesn't object if you see how this is done." So I stood in the doorway and watched as Zeev, with the help of a thin clean knife, decanted and poured out a measure of his life-blood into a mug, which had a picture on it of a cat, just like the smart black cat in the room below. And the smiling man, sitting on the bed in his dressing gown, raised the mug, and toasted Zeev, and drank the wild medicine down.

"We're young," he said to me, "we are both of us *genuinely* young. You're seventeen, aren't you. I'm twenty-seven. We are the only actual young *here*. And the rest of them, as I said, switched off. But we can do something, not only for ourselves, Day, but for our people. Or my people, if you prefer. Or *any* people. Humans. Don't you think that's fair, given what they do, knowingly or not, for us?"

We had walked back, slowly, along the upper terraces by the black abyss of the ravine, sure-footed, omnipotent. Then we sat together on the forest's edge, and watched the silver tumble of the fall. It had no choice. It *had* to fall, and go on falling forever, in love with the unknown darkness below, unable and not wanting to stop.

I kept thinking of the little blood-mark on his sleeve that night, what I'd guessed, and what instead was true. And I thought of Juno, with her obsessive wasted tiny blood-drop offerings in the "shrine," to a man she had no longer loved. As she no longer loved me.

She hates me because I have successful sun-born genes and can live in daylight. But Zeev, who can't take even thirty seconds of the sun, doesn't hate me for that. He . . . he doesn't *hate* me at all.

"So, will you go back to Severin tomorrow?" he said to me, as we sat at the brink of the night.

"No."

"Daisha, even when they've married us, please believe this: if you still want to go away, I won't put obstacles in your path. I will back you up."

"You care so little."

"So much."

His eyes glowed in the dark. They put the waterfall to shame.

When he touched me, touches me, I *know* him. From long ago, I remember this incredible joy, this heat and burning, this refinding *rightness*—and I fall down into the abyss forever, willing as the shining water. I never loved before. Except Juno, but she cured me of that.

He is a healer. His blood can heal, its vampiric vitality transmissible—but non-invasive. From his gift come no sub-standard replicants of our kind. They only—*live*.

Much, much later, when we parted just before the dawn inside the house—parted till the next night—our wedding day—it came to me that if *he* can heal by letting humans drink his blood, perhaps I might offer him some of my own. Because *my* blood might help him to survive the daylight, even if only for one unscathed and precious minute.

I'll wear green to be married. And a necklace of sea-green glass.

As the endless day trails by, unable to sleep, I've written this.

When he touched me, when he kissed me, Zeev, whose name actually *means* Wolf, became known to me. I don't believe he'll have to live all his long, long life without ever seeing the sun. For that was what he reminded me of. His warmth, his kiss, his arms about me—my first memory of that golden light which blew upwards through the dark. No longer any fear, which anyway was never mine, only that glorious *familiar* excitement and happiness, that *welcomed* danger. Perhaps I am wrong in this. Perhaps I shall pay heavily and cruelly for having been deceived. And for deceiving myself, too, because I realized what he was to me the moment I saw him—why else put up such barricades? Zeev is my sunrise out of the dark of the night of my so-far useless life. Yes, then. I love him.

We know only what our young narrator writes in his journal, so
there's a great deal we don't know, and some of what Josh tells
us may not be completely reliable . . .

JOSH

Gene Wolfe

10/2

Moving day for us. The movers came and took all our stuff. It is goodbye to
the old hometown. Dad was at work, mostly cleaning out his desk, he said.
Mom went nuts watching them pack her china and the glasses. I went up
to my room but they had cleaned it out. There was no place to sit down so
I walked down here. Nobody I know has come, only I keep thinking I do
not really know any of those guys any more. I never even started school last
month, like I said then.

Bill Bocanegra or however you spell that just came in. He said hi Josh
and wanted to know what I was doing, so I said I was making a list, what to
do in the new place. He is gone now, so maybe I should.

1. Remember not to e-mail any of them unless they e-mail me first. I will
let them forget me if that is what they want to do.

2. Get a dog. They say it is out in the country so why not? If Mom wants
it to stay outside I will build a dog house, only I am going to take it up to my
room at night sometimes.

3. Learn all the country stuff. Find out where the kids hang. What I
think is I cannot be an insider there so I will have to find out who the other
outsiders are and hang with them. Maybe there is a girl.

10/4

I did not write yesterday at all because what could I say? Besides I had to
split a room with Mom. I did not like it, but she said we could not waste the
money for me to have my own. So how could I write then with her looking
over my shoulder? Besides, she home-schooled, mostly geography. You do
not even bother with that stuff in a real school.

10/5

Here we are. Dad flew. Mom and I drove, mostly her but sometimes me. We had the camping stuff in back. Dad was waiting for us because today is Saturday. He had this rental car, but he is going to buy one here to replace the Dodge, only not yet. For now he will drive Mom's SUV to the station or she will drive him if she needs it. Only I said I would when she did not want to drive.

We got out the camping stuff, meaning I did it mostly. I set up all three cots, too. The electric is off, so no stove here. No freezer, either. No lights. No TV. None of that stuff. There is a gas pump at the well, so we can flush. There used to be an outhouse, I think. I can still see the path. I said, "When are they going to bring the furniture?" Mom said Dad will call from his office Monday, but it will probably be a week. We don't have a lot of stuff to eat. She will get more tomorrow.

10/6

They went into town. I was invited, but I could tell they did not want me, so I said I would stay here and figure out something to do. So I did, checking out the attic and basement. The attic is easier to get into than our old one and full of junk nobody wants, including me. The basement is practically empty except for dirt. There are some empty jars and tools, mostly for gardening. The tools are pretty rusty. One was an ax, so I thought I would go back into the woods and cut some wood and have a fire in the big fireplace. I went, but there was so much deadwood that I did not have to chop down anything. I carried in a bunch of sticks and wet them down with lamp fuel. That did it.

Now it is late and my fire is about out, but Mom and Dad have not come back. Maybe I should be worried, but if you ask me they got a motel room someplace. Probably they buzzed my phone while I was out getting wood. Now they are in the sack, because cots and sleeping bags are only good for sleeping. So I understand and it is fine with me, but if I had good-looking girl here I would spread a blanket on the floor and that would be plenty good enough. I have locked up (but no chain on the front door) and I am going to bed. It is still not really late and I could read this from last summer, what I did and what I thought, only I am pretty down already.

10/7

It is only about an hour after lunch, but there is nothing going on. So I might as well write this.

Either Mom and Dad came home and left again, or they have not come back at all. I am not sure which it is, and here is why. Last night I woke up.

It was really dark in my bedroom, no moon and no stars. Overcast over the whole sky, or that is what it seemed like.

And there was somebody else in my room. I have had that before, mostly when I was a little kid. Mom or Dad would come in to make sure I was OK. They would stand there as quiet as they could, then tiptoe back out when they saw I was in bed and not crying or anything.

So I thought that was what this was. I sat up and said, boy, you sure were out late. Or something like that.

Nobody answered. Whoever it was just stood there looking at me and not saying a word. Naturally I started to get out of my bag and felt around for my flashlight, only it was not there. I said, "What's the matter, why don't you talk?"

I knew just about where this person was standing, maybe four feet in from the door. I got out of the bag and stood up, and I went there, holding my arms out the way you do. Only whoever it was slipped out the door before I got there. I found the door and shut it, and felt around for my flashlight again, and finally I went back to bed. Only I did not sleep very much. I kept listening for the SUV to start or a door to close somewhere or something. Mostly I was listening for my door to open.

There was not anything for a long, long time. Then a little wind came up and I could hear the leaves outside whispering and whispering. By-and-by the overcast broke up just a little, and once I saw the moon, very thin, running fast through the clouds. Or that was what it looked like.

10/8

Today I went up to the attic and found a couple of old chairs. I will use them to block my door tonight.

After that I looked around for my flashlight. It was under my cot. I guess I kicked it when I got up, and it rolled under there. Tonight it is going in my bag with me. I fixed breakfast, which was not much, and went out here to write and think about things.

I dialed Mom's cell phone, and Dad's, over and over. Mine does not have many minutes left. There is an old-time phone in the house, but it is not hooked up.

Another thing I thought about was the tent, which is small but classy and nearly new. I unloaded it with the other camping stuff, so I had it if I needed it. OK, what about setting it up on the front lawn, and not sleeping in the house at all? That would be going pretty far, but if there is more trouble tonight I just might do it.

Now I am going to walk back into the woods and see what I can find.

The sun will be really low in about an hour, so I am going to write this now. It will not take long. I took a big hike in the woods, which are really beautiful, and got a little bit lost. Then I went over the top of a little hill and saw the house. I was really glad to see it and kept looking at it as I hiked along.

Only there was somebody looking at me from a second-floor window. At first I tried to tell myself it was Mom, but I knew it wasn't. She was very thin, with straight black hair and a white face. The funny thing is that I could see her really clearly when the house was almost out of sight. The closer I got, the harder she was to see, and pretty soon she was gone.

10/9

Last night I fixed my own supper, which was baked beans and bread. I ate it and drank a glass of water and went to bed.

Now I wish I knew what time it was so that I would know when I woke up, but my watch was on the windowsill and I did not look at it. The thing was that somebody was in the house playing the piano. I lay in bed and listened to it for quite a while. He was good, but I felt like there was something wrong with him just the same, something that I cannot explain. It seemed like he was playing to forget how bad things were, but sometimes he could not forget. That does not make sense but it is as close as I can come.

Finally it hit me that there was no furniture in the house except our camping stuff, so where was the piano? It had to be a CD or something. I got out of my sleeping bag and took down the chairs in front of my door. When I went out into the hallway I knew that the music was coming from downstairs, so I started down fast.

The music stopped, and then my flashlight went out. I stopped and shook it like you do, and then somebody passed me on the stairs. It is not what anybody would call a wide staircase, and I was holding the rail. She came down the other side where the wall is. The thing was, it was not somebody from downstairs coming up. This was somebody who had been upstairs with me coming down. She came up behind me and went on down, and I have never been so scared in my life.

My flashlight came back on, but I just stood there with my back pressing the rail, shaking and shaking. Will I think I was a wimp when I read this over later? Well, it is the truth. I never thought that anybody's teeth really chattered like you see on TV sometimes, but mine did then.

So I got out the pop-up tent and set it up on the front lawn in the dark, and staked it down, too. And I brought down my sleeping bag and slept in there until this morning.

This morning I decided I had been spending too much time in the house and too much behind the house, and the thing for me to do is hitch a ride into town and look for them. I mean the little town where the railroad station is. I can talk to the police there, and if there has been an accident and Mom and Dad are in the hospital or missing or something they will know. So I have watched the road a lot. Only one car has come by, an old one with an old man hunched up driving it. I tried to flag him down, but he pretended not to see me.

10/11

I did not write yesterday because Vikki was here. We did it in the tent, after. I was pretty bad, I think, but she was really good. She was hot, too. She showed me where to touch her and not hard, and how to keep from coming too soon. All the stuff.

I ought to write how I feel about it, but I am not sure yet. The thing is that she is gone. I am going to sleep in the house tonight. I just feel so lost.

It started yesterday afternoon when Mark and Vikki came. They had been hitchhiking since Arizona, Mark said, because it was where Mark's Harley got wrecked. I knew he was lying about something, only I did not let on. I told them my name, Josh, and they said Mark and Vikki. They were about starved, they said, and did I have anything? Only they could not pay.

So I said sure, and brought them inside the house and explained. Then we went out back, and I lit the camping stove and warmed up two cans of Irish stew. There was bread and stuff too. I had eaten my lunch already, so I did not eat much. Neither did Vikki, but Mark made up for both of us.

And all the time I kept thinking I had seen Vikki someplace before, but when it finally hit me I couldn't believe it. I had seen a girl who looked just like her hitching on TV, the leather jacket, the jeans and boots, the face and all that bushy black hair. Now here she was eating a cracker and smiling at me.

Then Mark wanted to use the john, so I told him where it was. As soon as he was gone, Vikki said she liked me better than Mark. I was nice and Mark had been mean to her. I was better looking, too, she said. So could she stay here with me and we would tell Mark to keep on going? I said yes. I knew there would be a showdown with Mark and it might get rough. Only I did not think it really would, just some yelling, and he was only a little bit bigger than me.

Only the main thing was that I could see she was worth it, and if I had said no I would be kicking myself for the rest of my life.

So when Mark came back, I said it was time for him to get back on the road and hitch. He said OK and come on Vikki like I expected, and I said no. She is staying here with me.

He pulled a knife. I had not expected that. So I said, OK take her. He kind of sneered and put the knife away. It went in a leather sheath on his belt. Vikki got up and went with him, but when they had started to go she looked back at me and I could not stand it. I jumped him from in back.

We fought and rolled around on the ground fighting, and then his knife was back. Vikki threw dirt in his eyes, and I got it and I stuck him with it deep three or four times. At first I did not think he was dead, but he was.

I said we had to bury him and she said she would help, so I went down in the basement and got an old shovel I had seen down there. When I got back where they were, Vikki was down beside him. She got up, and there was blood on her mouth. I said what were you doing, and she said saying goodbye.

We dragged him out into the woods and I dug a grave. There were rocks and roots, and it took so long that it was just about dark when we got back. We thought we ought to wash up, so she took the downstairs bathroom and me the upstairs one I had used before. When she came back outside where I was cooking she had taken off all her clothes and was wrapped up in a sheet she must have found in one of the closets. That was so cool I could not believe it. By the time we had finished my pasta and sauce it was dark. We went into the tent and zipped it up and everything. That was when we did it.

All that was yesterday.

This morning Vikki was all dressed again by the time I woke up. She said she had washed her underwear last night and hung it up in the bathroom, and it had been pretty dry now so she had put it on.

We ate breakfast bars and sort of made out together. I have never smelled another girl who smelled like she did or smelled as good, either. There was smoke in it, and that fresh smell you get after a storm. Most of all, rich dirt like you smell when you dig a flower bed or something. That does not sound so nice when I write it down, but she smelled wonderful. Just wonderful.

She looked wonderful, too. Those long legs and tits just big enough to fill my hands. No wonder Mark would have killed me for her.

Only I killed him.

I got to wondering if his grave was all right, so I told Vikki we would go out there and maybe take a little walk in the woods after.

So we did, and something had dug him up to eat and opened him up, too. A lot of the stuff from inside was gone. I got out the shovel again, and a mattock this time, too, and dug the grave a lot deeper. It took a long time, and a long time before I finished it Vikki was gone.

I thought she had just gone back to the house, maybe to fetch something. So I made a cross, which I had not done before, tying two sticks together.

Only when I got back here, she was gone. Somebody came by, probably, and she hitched, and I am all alone all over again.

Now I have struck the tent and carried it in. I am going to lock the doors and sleep inside tonight. There is something going on out back in the woods.

I can hear them.

There was nothing unusual about the day it happened,
nothing remarkable at all . . .

TIME AND TIDE

Alan Peter Ryan

Frank Parsons had to control the look of surprise and horror that came instantly to his face when his father asked him on Monday morning to help him move that old wardrobe out of the garage and up the stairs and into his room. He quickly turned his head away to hide the expression he knew would betray him. If there was anything in the world Frank didn't want in his room, even if it would only be there with him for the three nights he still had to spend in the house before going off to college on Thursday, it was that old wardrobe.

Families often acquire pieces of furniture in odd and offhand ways. A piece might have once belonged to a grandmother or a spinster aunt or a bachelor uncle, and when a house was emptied by death or marriage or a distant move, someone in the family supervising the move or the emptying of the house thought the piece too good or too useful or just too familiar to be sold to the local junk shop for a few dollars. It might serve well enough for a child's or teenager's room or a father's workshop where another few years of wear and tear would hardly leave it in worse shape and, while it still had some life in it, it would come in handy and cost nothing. Such a piece might survive in a family for decades, for generations, passing from room to room, house to house, eventually becoming so much a part of daily life that its rickety legs, squeaking doors, split wood veneer, and crackled varnish are no more perceived than the deepening wrinkles in a mother's or father's face.

So it was with the old wardrobe. It was mahogany, or at least mahogany veneer, dark brown with a hint of ancient reddishness in it, and it had a carved and curved wooden decoration across the top of the front, relic of an age that thought clean straight lines unattractive. It stood, only a little unsteadily, on thick curved legs with ball-and-claw feet. It was six feet high. Inside, at the bottom, there were two sets of three drawers. At the top there was a shelf and below the shelf a rod for hanging clothes. The two doors squeaked on old hinges and where wood rubbed against wood at top and bottom, but the latch still worked well and the doors still snapped together securely when closed. The doors had carved molding and set into each near the top was a mirror, about a foot high and rounded against the molding at the top. The mirrors had grown slightly dark and clouded with time.

Frank hated the wardrobe because it reminded him of Junior and Frank hated to be reminded of Junior. Frank had been named after his father's father but when Bill came along two years later he was named after their own father and was called Junior all his life. All fourteen years of it. He was the living image of his father. He looked like his father, moved and walked like him, held his head like him, and looked at you the exact same way. Even as a boy he sounded like his father, even talked like him, with the same rhythms and intonations. And when he got to be ten years old, and twelve, and then as a teenager, he even expressed himself and answered questions with the same ironic humor as their father. Everyone said he was the spitting image of Big Bill and, partly because of that and partly because he was the younger child, the baby, he was always the favorite of the family and openly acknowledged as such. Even Frank himself was in the habit of deferring to his younger brother.

When the Parsons moved from Englewood to Seashore Park, there was tangible proof of Junior's precedence in the family. Seashore Park was the southern extension of Seashore Heights, which was one of the liveliest and most popular vacation centers on the Jersey shore. Seashore Heights was filled with motels, boarding houses, and restaurants, and a mile and a half of its boardwalk was lined with games and arcades and food stands, and there were two amusement piers with rides. Fortunes were made there in pizza (some old signs still called it "tomato pie"), soft ice cream (still called "custard" by the oldest establishments), and saltwater taffy. Seashore Heights was busy and lively, with Central Avenue and the Boulevard and Ocean Avenue filled with impatient cars all day and late into the nights all summer long. Seashore Park, on the other hand, was residential and quiet. It had only three or four motels, all of them on Central Avenue, one very long block from the beach, and only a few restaurants, all offering "fine dining" and all concentrated at its southern end where Central Avenue ended at the entrance to Seashore Beach State Park, a twenty-five-mile stretch of sand dunes at the end of the peninsula, protected as a bird preserve. So between the summer noise and activity of Seashore Heights and the natural tranquility of the state park, Seashore Park kept its head down and minded its own business. For the most part, the only vacationers who came there were older people who preferred the less crowded beach and were willing to bring their own cold drinks with them. The quiet streets, prosaically named with letters of the alphabet, were lined with large old houses, many of whose owners rented rooms in the summer, and small cottages rented by the week or month.

The new Parsons home was on K Street. It had a "lawn" of white and golden stones, the common local substitute for grass that would not grow in the sand, and was bordered by large hydrangea bushes, thick with balls of pale blue and purplish petals. Downstairs there was a large screened porch that seemed to attract breezes, an enormous living room, and a large kitchen and bathroom at the back. Upstairs there was another bathroom and four bedrooms. There was a master bedroom, a guest room (they called it that although it had been used for that purpose only once, for a month, when Uncle Jack, Big Bill's brother, split up with his wife), and two rooms for the boys. Frank was fourteen when they moved in and Junior was twelve.

When the boys examined the house and the rooms, it was immediately obvious that one of the rooms designated for them was better than the other. It was larger, it had three windows instead of two, and it had a view of the beach at the end of the street. Junior said casually that he preferred that room. He didn't say it aggressively or challengingly, just with his usual easy assurance that his wish would be granted. And so it was. Frank did not object. He was used to giving in, he was happy with his own room, and the issue didn't really matter to him. Perhaps by way of compensation—Big Bill had merely laid a hand on Frank's shoulder one day and said he was glad he hadn't made "a thing" about the rooms—a handsome new wardrobe was bought for Frank's room and the old monstrosity that had been hauled all the way from Englewood was wrestled up the stairs and placed in Junior's room.

Big Bill was a construction supervisor and doing better and better all the time. He remodeled the kitchen and, when the porch was discovered to be sagging, he tore it down and built a new one that was larger and breezier. Once they had placed six rocking chairs and a couple of small tables on it, Frank's parents began to think about renting out rooms themselves, like their neighbors, when the boys were grown and gone off to college. It would be an easy job, Big Bill said, to wall off part of the huge living room to make a bedroom at the back for themselves. They could live downstairs and rent out the four bedrooms upstairs. Frank's mother, who enjoyed cooking and feeding people, said they could offer a full breakfast to their guests and make it a classy bed-and-breakfast, something that was unheard of in Seashore Heights or Seashore Park, and, with minimal cost, charge an even higher price for the rooms. They were excited at the idea of converting the house into a bed-and-breakfast. But of course that would have to wait until the boys got older.

But only one of the boys would grow older and go away to college.

The family had been in the house for two years and Junior was fourteen when he died. Ever since then, Frank did everything possible to avoid anything that would remind him of it, but he would never forget that day.

Frank was sixteen that summer and had his first job. Two of their neighbors on K Street were teachers at Toms River High School. In the summer, they had adjoining stands on the boardwalk in Seashore Heights where players placed money on numbers on a board and the operator spun a big wheel. If your number came up on the wheel, you won. It was a time-honored entertainment at Seashore Heights. At the back of each stand, right behind the operator, were shelves with a huge display of the prizes available. That year the hot items were digital cameras and iPods, but you could also win MP3 players and pendrives and, if you saved up enough winning coupons, maybe even a laptop. Other stands offered as prizes more traditional items: blankets and sets of towels, silverware, electrical appliances, candy, and huge stuffed animals in gaudy colors. The two stands, though they were side by side, were actually jointly owned and operated by the teachers, and customers whose luck failed them at one wheel would often just move next door and try again at the next one. Frank swept the boardwalk in front of the stands, emptied the garbage cans, went on food and drink runs, organized the stock of merchandise, fetched prizes down from the top shelves, and replaced items that were "won out." He worked six days a week and he was enjoying the summer. He was off on Mondays, the slow day on the boardwalk.

On Mondays, he went to the beach, usually with Junior. Mostly they played catch and swam, riding the waves. Sometimes Frank brought a book. He liked to read biographies of baseball players and he had recently discovered the books of Roger Angell. Those were good times. Frank and Junior could spend the day at the beach and it only took five minutes to walk home for lunch or to use the bathroom. They were both well tanned, although Junior, who had more beach time that summer, was darker.

There was nothing unusual about the day it happened, nothing remarkable at all. Big Bill had taken two weeks off from work to have a little summer vacation himself and to do some work around the house. That morning their parents had gone to the Ocean County Mall to buy something their mother had seen was on sale in the Sunday paper. They would be back by one o'clock and the boys could come home for lunch at one-thirty. At one-thirty the boys walked home for lunch, ate, and returned to the beach. Big Bill said he would meet them on the beach in half an hour or so.

The beach in Seashore Park, as usual on a weekday, especially a Monday, was sparsely populated. A few young mothers played with small children at the water's edge, lifting them up to jump the waves. The children were laughing. Two pairs of interesting-looking girls were sunbathing.

There was a tall, white wooden lifeguard stand nearby and the two guys there were chatting and looking bored. There were no more than fifteen or twenty swimmers in the water. An elderly couple, white-haired and with sagging bodies, strolled along the water's edge, holding hands. A little girl was knocked over by a wave and let out a howl before her mother could grab her. All these things, of which Frank was barely conscious at the time, lived vividly in his memory afterward.

He and Junior went into the water, jumping the swells and then riding the waves or the breakers rolling in toward the beach. Junior missed a swell and stayed behind in the water while Frank rode the wave in. When he felt the bottom under his feet he stood up and walked out of the water and up the slight slope of the beach. The two pairs of girls were still sunbathing. One of the girls smiled and waved to him. Frank raised his hand and gave her a half-wave, not sure in the glaring sunlight if he recognized her or not. He looked around for the blanket, spotted it, and saw his Roger Angell book and his and Junior's sunglasses and their suntan lotion on it. When he looked back toward the ocean and Junior, Junior wasn't there.

Frank put his hands on his hips and surveyed the water, checking out each of the dark heads he saw at the water's surface. Junior wasn't there. It was very strange. Where was Junior? Frank looked up toward the lifeguards. They were still chatting. One of them was rubbing the back of his neck with a white towel. Frank looked at the water again. There was no sign of Junior. He scanned the beach to his right and left, beyond the lifeguard stand. Of course Junior was not on the beach. Junior was in the water. But where? Frank surveyed the surface of the water again. He opened his mouth to shout. But to shout what? To whom? He walked down to the edge of the water, his eyes still surveying the surface. A glaring light came off the shifting surface and the rolling swells. There was no sign of Junior. I should do something, Frank thought. But what was there to do? He glanced sideways again at the lifeguards. They were talking and untroubled. He looked steadily out at the water. Junior had to be right out there. At any second, Junior's head would pop out of the water and he would wave an arm. Frank half-raised his right arm to wave back. But there was nobody to wave to. Junior did not appear.

Frank couldn't understand what was going on. He scanned the water again, left and right.

Suddenly he was aware of rapid motion and activity around him. The two lifeguards streaked past him and dove into the incoming waves. People on the beach were running down to stand at the edge of the water. Frank stepped down to the water with them, stood in it, felt a dying wave swirl around his legs, then stepped back and stood with the other people higher up the beach. They were all pointing to the lifeguards. Frank saw the elderly woman there with her hand raised to her mouth. The young woman with the little girl carried her away quickly up the beach in the direction of the boardwalk.

Then everything happened very quickly. The two lifeguards reached still water and bobbed for a moment on the swells. One of them dove and came up with a body. The other quickly took hold of it and started toward the shore. The first lifeguard stayed nearby until they reached the point where the swells were rising into waves, then dove into a wave himself and rode it almost onto the sand. He ran at once to the lifeguard stand and grabbed the emergency phone and talked into it, then ran back to help his partner as he emerged from the water with the person he had rescued. It was Junior.

Together they carried Junior out of the water and laid him on his back on the sand. The anxious crowds of onlookers gathered around and one of the lifeguards told them to move back. Frank moved back with them. Speculations were whispered. He must have had a cramp. He had a fainting spell. The hot sun made him faint. Frank said nothing.

Then Junior coughed, gagged, spat out water, and sat up. He was breathing hard but he said, even short of breath, "I'm okay, I'm okay." The lifeguards sat back on their heels. One of them asked Junior some questions. Frank could not hear the questions but he heard Junior say again, "I'm okay, I'm okay." Then he heard the wailing siren of Seashore's ambulance drawing near.

Now everything happened even more quickly. The ambulance drove onto the boardwalk and two attendants came running down the beach, one of them carrying a light stretcher. Junior struggled to his feet, tottered for a moment, and one of the lifeguards helped him to sit down again. The ambulance attendants, both of them volunteers wearing shorts and T-shirts, talked quickly with the lifeguards. Junior continued protesting that he was okay. They had to insist but they got him to lie down on the stretcher, then carried him quickly up the beach to the boardwalk, laid him on the collapsible gurney that stood waiting, and slid it briskly into the ambulance. In a moment the vehicle was driving away and the siren was starting up again.

And then Frank saw his father running down the beach toward where he still stood.

The little crowd had dispersed now, most of the people returning to their blankets, only a few going into the water. Frank stood alone in the glare of the sun.

He saw his father scanning the beach and the water as he hurried across the width of the sand. In a moment, breathing hard, he was in front of Frank, gripping both his arms at the elbows. His eyes looked straight into Frank's and pleaded for mercy.

"It was Junior," Frank told him.

Big Bill seemed to crumple inward. Then he turned and plodded heavily back up the beach, moving as quickly as he could across the sand. Frank saw him cross the boardwalk and then disappear in the direction of K Street. He remained standing where he was. A couple of minutes later, he heard the distant sound of tires screeching in the street.

The volunteer ambulance attendants, both well-meaning but inexperienced, reported later that Junior was a little shaken and out of breath, which seemed normal enough, but he seemed otherwise fine. He was talking and, like the lifeguards, they took him at his word that he was okay. And, like the lifeguards, they neglected to pump his chest. Junior, his lungs filled with water, drowned in the ambulance on the way to the hospital.

Frank and Big Bill never spoke about that day or about Junior again.

Three weeks later, Junior came back to haunt Frank. Or so Frank thought.

Frank had not been talking much with his parents about anything. They were easy to avoid. Big Bill was lost in a deep silence. Frank's mother kept herself busier than ever with cooking and laundry and taking care of the house, but Frank could sometimes hear her crying in their bedroom and his father's low voice talking to her. Dinner time, with only three of them at the table, was a terrible strain. Frank invented excuses to avoid it.

Even his father's nickname bothered him. It had come into use only after Junior was born and now, with no "little" Bill on the scene, it made no sense, but it stuck. Every time Frank heard somebody refer to his father as Big Bill, he had to hide a shiver.

Eventually, after some interminable weeks, Labor Day came and the terrible summer was over. Frank went back to school. Everybody at school knew what had happened and some of his friends and a number of his teachers tried to talk with him about Junior. Frank couldn't stand it. He nodded and mumbled something and then they left him alone. But he knew he was going to have to find a way to deal with Junior.

On the Thursday night of that first week of school, his parents went out to the supermarket and Frank was alone in the house. Get it over with, he told himself. He went up the stairs and stood for a long time in front of the closed door of Junior's room. He didn't think anybody had been in there since his mother had gone in to get clothes to dress Junior for burial. Frank took a deep breath and pulled the door open.

He didn't really know if he had been expecting something weird to happen but nothing did, weird or otherwise. It was just Junior's room and it looked pretty much the way it had always looked. His mother must have straightened up Junior's desk, which was usually covered with sports and music magazines. Now it was clear and clean and almost empty, but that was the only real difference in the room. Apart from the tidiness, everything was normal. The bed was neatly made. Junior's books stood neatly on their shelves. His plastic Mickey Mouse, a souvenir from Disney World, stood on top of the low bookcase. A blue windbreaker, a red flannel shirt, and a yellow slicker hung from the clothes tree in the corner. Frank looked at them for a long minute. Apparently his mother had not been able to make herself remove them or put them away.

Then he shook his shoulders, walked across the room, and sat down at the desk. Okay, he admitted to himself, it was kind of creepy being in here, with the way everything seemed so normal but so strangely still, as if Junior's things themselves knew he was gone forever. He opened the top drawer of the desk. An open package of looseleaf refill, a wooden ruler, three blue Bic pens and one red, a dozen large paperclips, a key ring without keys, an empty Pez dispenser with the head of Spider-Man, a crisp ten-dollar bill that looked like it just came from the bank, a plastic Skippy peanut butter jar with the label still on it, half-filled with quarters.

He closed the drawer, shifted on the chair, and looked around. The old wardrobe from Englewood stood where it had stood since they moved in. The doors were closed tight. It was filled with the rest of Junior's stuff but Frank had no desire to open the wardrobe and look inside.

Then a strange thing happened. Frank's eye caught some sort of movement where there could be no movement. He blinked and shook his head, hard, once. His eyes snapped sideways toward the wardrobe. Water was bobbing and sloshing against the inside of the mirrors on the wardrobe as if they were windows that looked into a swimming pool. Frank stared at it, then jumped and stood up.

The water swelled and rose against the inside of the glass and then subsided. Swelled and rose and subsided again. Frank stood frozen in the middle of the room. He knew it could not be so but suddenly he felt warm water moving all around him. His legs were light and only his toes were touching anything solid and he was floating and the water was holding him up. Then a swell came from behind him and caught him by surprise and his mouth and nose were filled with water and he was going under. Something was pulling at his legs and he tried to get his face out of the water to gulp air but he could not. For an instant he could see the line of the beach but the water pulled him downward. He needed help. He was afraid, for the first time in his life he was frightened, really frightened, in the water. He had to have help. Exerting all his strength and experience, he somehow raised himself in the water and got his nose and eyes above the surface for a moment. Junior! He could see Junior there on the beach, looking out toward the water, toward him. Couldn't Junior see him? Couldn't he see that he was in trouble?

Frank's knees wobbled and he nearly collapsed. He lurched over to the chair at the desk and clung to it, then carefully lowered himself and sat on the edge of the seat. If Junior had come back to haunt him, he had done a good job of it. For a minute or two there, for as long as he had stood there looking into those mirrors on the old wardrobe, if that was what they were, he had felt and seen what Junior had felt and seen that day at the beach weeks before. Felt the water pulling at his legs and body and arms and rushing into his nose and mouth. Felt his lungs straining for air. Felt his heart hammering heavily in panic. And he had seen his brother, himself, standing there on the beach and looking right at him, right there where he was struggling for his life, and doing nothing, nothing at all.

Frank, of course, had never spoken of this strange experience to anyone and he never went into Junior's room again and Junior never haunted him again.

But now, on this final Monday morning that he was going to spend in his childhood home, his father wanted to move that old wardrobe into his room.

Frank would be leaving on Thursday for the University of Iowa. After he applied and got a modest baseball scholarship and his parents had done the math and approved the decision, it occurred to Frank that, although it was not one of his reasons for applying to Iowa, Iowa was about as far as you could get in the United States of America from the ocean, any ocean. In fact, he thought, although he did not think about it a great deal, if he never saw the ocean again, he'd be just as happy. In high school he had read a novel called *The Sea of Grass* and he thought that a sea of grass or wheat or corn or whatever they had in Iowa would suit him just fine.

His imminent departure from the house did not seem to be troubling his parents a great deal. His mother was obviously worried about him and fussed about the clothes he was taking and the fierceness of winter weather in the Midwest. Big Bill was mostly silent with him, spoke briefly a couple of times about the cost of a college education these days and the importance of concentrating on studies instead of girls and beer, and let it go at that.

Frank knew that they were eager now to get on with their own lives. His departure from the house would make a complete break with the past. They had plans. They were already getting ready to go into the bed-and-breakfast business and they were excited about getting started.

The new business would only be opening at the Labor Day weekend, which was of course the official end of the summer vacation season, and a couple of their neighbors thought they were nuts and doomed to failure. But Big Bill and Frank's mother were confident. Big Bill had already put up the new wall downstairs and converted the living room, resplendent now with a large table where breakfast would be served to guests, a small reception desk in the corner, and a new large-screen HD TV on the wall. On the reception desk sat a box with a thousand new business cards. The baseboard heating had all been checked and found in good condition. The porch had been painted and the screens replaced, and three more rocking chairs had been purchased. Waiting in the garage were new double beds and a huge supply of bedclothes and towels and little bars of soap. The one bathroom upstairs was definitely going to be a problem but Big Bill had already made plans for redoing the bedrooms and adding another bathroom just as soon as the money started coming in. They didn't think it would be long. There was already a sign out on the gravel lawn announcing the place as "The Haven" and offering a/c in summer, heated rooms in winter, and breakfast every day and tea every afternoon. And the late start this year would actually be a good thing, they told themselves. They would almost certainly get some weekend business in September and maybe October too if the weather was good, maybe even some weekday business too for which The Haven would be pretty much the only game in town. And there were the added attractions of breakfast and afternoon tea, which were radical innovations at Seashore. Yes, it was going to be a great success.

Another week of final touch-ups on the paint, a few minor repairs, and moving the new furniture up from the garage, and they would be ready to welcome their first guests.

Big Bill only needed help with the old wardrobe because its size and weight made it hard to manage on the stairs and he was worried about snapping off the weak legs. It was going into Frank's room, he said, because "the other room" was bigger and would get the newer furnishings and they could then charge more for it. They would replace the old wardrobe later when there was money coming in.

Frank said nothing and just sweated and grunted along with his father as they wrestled the old wardrobe up the stairs and into his room. Frank's own wardrobe had already been moved into what had been the guest room and the clothes and things he was leaving at home were packed into cartons in a corner of the room.

That night Frank sat on the side of his bed and looked at the old wardrobe. It looked the same as it had always looked, the varnish still crackled and the mirrors still cloudy. Those mirrors, he thought, if that was what they really were. His heart thumped but he steadied his nerves and looked at them again. There was nothing unusual about them and what he had once seen in them seemed fantastic now. The wardrobe reminded him of Junior, of course, and he didn't like to think about Junior, but that was two years ago and it was all behind him now.

He stood up and stepped closer to the wardrobe. There was nothing in any way unusual about it. Apparently his parents had cleaned it out and gotten rid of Junior's things long ago because the wardrobe was obviously empty when he and Big Bill moved it. For a moment Frank thought he might open the doors and have a look inside. Maybe that would dispel once and for all that frightening vision of the ocean that still lingered at the edge of his memory.

He reached for the small wooden knob on the right-hand door, the one you had to pull open first. And almost instantly snatched his hand away. The knob was wet. But he was too late. His slight touch on the doorknob had released the catch on the doors that had seemed so firmly closed in place when he and his father had moved the wardrobe that morning. Now the two doors squealed and suddenly burst outward as if pushed by some mighty force from within. And from the quickly widening space between them welled a gushing cascade of sandy, salty water. Released now, the water, which seemed limitless, forced the doors back and a wall of it as tall as Frank himself, it seemed, and then taller still rushed out at him and covered the floor of the room, up to his ankles, almost instantly rising up to his knees, swirling around his waist, pulling at him, pulling him down into its currents and depths, cold against his throat, coming up to his mouth and his nose and making him gasp for air, stinging his wide-open, surprised eyes with its salt. He lost his balance and went over, his head beneath the water, his lungs laboring for breath, his arms spread in a struggle for balance, his neck stretching to lift his face above the seething surface. For an instant he got his face out of the water. He tried desperately to suck in air but got only more water. As he thrashed to keep himself upright and afloat, his vision cleared for a moment and he could see—so far away—the beach and people moving on it, an elderly couple, a woman carrying a small child, and one other figure, a boy, standing there and looking toward the water, looking right at him, Junior, it was Junior, back to haunt him again, standing there in that way of standing he had, but just looking, doing nothing to help him. Frank knew that shape and posture, that angle of the head. But why wasn't Junior coming to help him? Surely Junior could see that he was drowning, that any minute he would go under and not be able to come up again. It was Junior, wasn't it? Frank tried to cry out but only swallowed more water. But no, it wasn't Junior, it wasn't Junior at all. It was the shape of Junior, it was the unmistakable form and stance and posture of Junior, but it was not Junior at all. Junior was dead and buried and this was not him at all. Frank tried to wrench his body free of the silent current that gripped tightly and tugged downward on his legs. For one last instant he managed to get his face out of the water and he could see, far away there on the beach, Big Bill, his father, just standing there very still and looking straight at him and doing nothing, nothing, nothing at all.

Rakshasi are demon warriors, cursed to walk the earth as monsters,
wreaking havoc wherever they go. Disturbers. Defilers. Devourers.
But they can redeem themselves . . .

RAKSHASI

Kelley Armstrong

For two hundred years, I have done penance for my crimes as a human. After twenty, I had saved more lives than I had taken. After fifty, I had helped more people than I had wronged. I understand that my punishment should not end with an even accounting. Yet now, after two hundred years, that balance has long passed equilibrium. And I have come to realize that this life is no different than my old one. If I want something, I cannot rely on others to provide it.

I waited in the car while Jonathan checked the house. Jonathan. There is something ridiculous about calling your master by his given name. It's an affectation of the modern age. In the early years, I was to refer to them as *Master* or *Isha*. When the family moved West, it became *Sir*, then *Mr. Roy.*

My current master does not particularly care for this familiarity. He pretends otherwise, but the fact that I must refer to him by his full name, where his wife and others use "Jon," says much.

He called my cell phone.

"Amrita?" he said, as if someone else might be answering my phone. My name is not Amrita. My name is not important. Or, perhaps, too important. I have never given it to my masters. They call me Amrita, the eternal one.

"The coast is clear." He paused. "I mean—"

"I understand American idiom very well," I said. "I have been living here since before you were born."

He mumbled something unintelligible, then gave me my instructions, as if I hadn't been doing this, too, since before he was born.

I got out of the car and headed for the house.

As Jonathan promised, there was an open window on the second floor. I found a quiet place away from the road, then shifted to my secondary form: a raven. Fly to the bedroom window. Squeeze through. Shift back.

There wasn't even an alarm on the window to alert the occupant to my intrusion. Quite disappointing. These jobs always are. I long for the old days, when I would do bloody battle against power-mad English sahibs and crazed Kshatriyas. Then came the murderers and whore-masters, the Mob, the drug dealers. It was the last that made the Roys rethink their strategy. On the streets, drug dealers always came with well-armed friends. I may be immortal, but I can be injured, and while my personal comfort is not a concern, my income-earning potential is. They tried targeting the dealers at home, but there they were often surrounded by relative innocents. So, in this last decade, the Roys have concentrated on a new source of evil. A dull, weak, mewling source that bores me immeasurably. But my opinion, like my comfort, is of little consequence.

I took a moment to primp in the mirror. I am eternally young. Beautiful, too. More beautiful than when I was alive, which was not to say I was ugly then, but when I look in the mirror now, I imagine what my husband, Daman, would say. Imagine his smile. His laugh. His kiss. I have not seen him in two hundred years, yet when I primp for my target, it is still Daman I ready myself for.

I found the target—Morrison—in the study, talking on his speaker phone while working on his laptop. I moved into the doorway. Leaned against it. Smiled.

He stopped talking. Stopped typing. Stared.

Then, "Bill? I'll call you back."

He snapped his laptop shut. "How'd you get in here?"

"My name is Amrita. I am a surprise. From a very pleased client."

I slid forward, gaze fixed on his. For another moment he stared, before remembering himself.

"But how did you get—?"

"I would not be much of a surprise if I rang your front bell, would I?" I glanced back at the door. "I trust we are alone?" Jonathan said no one else was in the house, but I always checked.

"W-we are."

"Good."

I sidled over and rolled his chair away from the desk . . . and any alarms underneath or guns in the drawers.

I straddled Morrison's lap. Indecision wavered in his eyes. He was a smart man. He knew this was suspicious. And yet, as I said, I am a beautiful woman.

I put my arms around him, hands sliding down his arms, fingers entwining with his. I leaned over, lifting our hands . . . then wrenched his arms back so hard he screamed. I leapt from his lap, over the back of the chair, and bound his wrists with the cord I'd used as a belt.

I have subdued lapdogs that gave me more trouble than Morrison. He fought, but I have bound warriors. He was no warrior.

Next, I tortured him for information. It was a bloodless torture. Mental pain is the most effective of all, and with the power of illusion, I can make a man believe he is being rent limb from limb, and scream with the imagined agony.

As for the information I needed, it was a simple accounting of his misdeeds: details on the financial scam that paid for this mansion. I forced him to write out those details in a confession. Then I tortured him for the combination to his home safe.

With my help, the Roys kill—sorry, *eliminate*—the basest dregs of the criminal bucket. This is their divine mission, handed down to them millennia ago, when they were granted the ability to control my kind. They seek out evil. I eliminate it. A very noble profession, but one that does not pay the bills. Finding targets, researching them and preparing for my attack is a full-time job. So the Roys, like other isha families, also have divine permission to take what they require from their victims.

Once I had what I needed, I forced Morrison to take out his gun and shoot himself, leaving his confession on the desk and adequate compensation for his victims still in his safe.

Before he pulled the trigger, he looked at me. They always do. Seeking mercy, I suppose. But I know, better than anyone, that such sins cannot be pardoned in this life. If they are, mercy will be seen as a sign of weakness, and the perpetrator will revert to his former path once the initial scare passes.

Still, they always look at me, and they always ask the same thing.

"What are you?"

"Rakshasi," I replied, and pushed his finger on the trigger.

Rakshasi. Morrison didn't know what that meant. They never do. Even those of my own heritage rarely have more than a vague inkling of my kind, perhaps from a story told by a grandmother to frighten them into obedience.

The word means protector, which has always made me laugh. We are demon warriors, cursed to walk the earth as monsters, wreaking havoc wherever we go. Disturbers. Defilers. Devourers.

It is only after we accept the bargain of the isha that we become protectors. When we rise from our deathbed, we are met by a member of an isha family. He tells us our fate. Misery and guilt and pain, forever suffering everything that, in life, we visited upon others. Yet we can redeem ourselves. Submit to their bargain, work for them until we have repaid our debt, and we will be free.

I did not take that first offer. I doubt any rakshasi does. We are men and women of iron will and we do not cower at the first threat of adversity. I truly do not believe the isha expect agreement. Not then. They simply offer the deal, and when it is rejected they leave. Then, on every succeeding anniversary, they find us, and they offer again.

In the end, it was not the misery or guilt or pain that wore me down. It was loneliness. We are doomed to be alone as we walk the earth. I might have held out if the isha did not bring me a letter one year. A letter from Daman. He, too, had been doomed to this existence. Our crimes were shared, as had been every part of our lives from childhood.

Daman had accepted his isha's bargain, and he pleaded with me to do the same. Take the deal and we would be together again. So he had been promised. So I was promised. And so I accepted.

We returned to Jonathan's house. It is the same one I have lived in for sixty years, though Jonathan and Catherine only arrived two years ago, when he took over as isha from his uncle. I came with the house. Or, I should say, it came with me.

It was no modest home either. For size and grandeur, it was on a scale with Morrison's mansion. There were no vows of poverty in this family of crusaders. Like the Templar Knights, they lined their pockets extravagantly with the proceeds of their good deeds, which may explain part of the reason behind the switch to corporate sharks. We are in a recession. To some, that means tightening the purse-strings. To others, it means seeking richer sources of income. I cannot argue with that. I felt the same way when I walked the earth as a human. But it does bear noting that if the Roys free me, they will lose this income. Which gives them little incentive to agree that I have repaid my debt.

Jonathan took me to my apartment. As cages go, it is a well-gilded one. Sleeping quarters, living area, kitchen and bath, all lavishly furnished. The shelves are lined with books. A computer, stereo and television are provided for my amusement. Anything I wish is mine. Anything except freedom. The walls are imbued with magic that prevents me from leaving without my isha.

Beyond a recitation of events, Jonathan and I had not spoken on the four-hour drive from Morrison's house. Every isha is different. With some, I have found something akin to friendship. Most prefer a more businesslike relationship. Jonathan takes that to the extreme, talking to me only when necessary. To engage me in conversation might lead to asking about my thoughts or feelings, which would imply that I have such things. That I am a sentient being. Best to forget that.

In my apartment, I prepared dinner. A glass of human blood. A plate of human flesh. It is what I need to survive and my ishas provide it. At one time, they used their victims. Now, that is inconvenient. One of the isha families without a rakshasi saw a market and filled it. Jonathan orders my meals. They come in a refrigerated case, the blood in wine bottles and flesh neatly packaged and labeled as pork.

I fixed a plate of curry. I may be a cannibal, but I have retained some sense of taste. When I finished, I waited for Catherine. She gives me time after a job to eat, preferring not to visit while the scent of cooked flesh lingers in the air. As a courtesy, I cracked open the windows.

Catherine extended me a return courtesy by knocking before she entered. Most of my ishas do not—either they don't realize I may have a need for privacy or they wish to remind me of my place. Jonathan regularly "forgets" to knock, which is his way of asserting his position without challenging me. I would hold him in higher regard if he simply barged in.

"How did it go?" Catherine asked as she entered. One might presume she'd already spoken to her husband and was simply asking to be polite, but with this couple, such a level of communication was not a given.

As I told her it had been a success, I accompanied her to the living area, walking slowly to keep pace with her crutches. Catherine suffers from a crippling disease that today has a name—multiple sclerosis. In general, I'm not interested in the advances of science, but I have researched this particular ailment to help me better understand the first isha's wife who has sought my companionship.

Most wives have no knowledge of their husbands' otherworldly abilities, and thus no knowledge of me. For decades, I have been shunted in and out a side door and otherwise kept in my soundproof apartment.

Occasionally, though, the Roys take a wife from within the isha community. That is where Jonathan found Catherine. And if such a choice—not only an isha's daughter, but a cripple—helped him win his position over his brothers . . . It is not my concern.

As to what Catherine and I could possibly have in common, the answer is little, which gives us much to discuss. Catherine is endlessly fascinated with my life. To her, I am the star in some terrible yet endlessly thrilling adventure.

"Have you been doing better?" she asked as I fixed tea.

"I am surviving. We both know that I would prefer it wasn't so, but . . . " I smiled her way. "You have heard quite enough on that matter."

"I wish you could be happier, Amrita."

"I've been alive too long to be happy. I would prefer to be gone. At peace." I handed her a cup. "But, again, we've talked about this enough. It's a depressing way to spend your visits. I would prefer to talk about you and *your* happiness. Did you ask Jonathan about the trip?"

Her gaze dropped to her teacup. "He said it wasn't possible. He'd love to, but he can't take you and he can't leave his duties here."

"Oh. I had thought perhaps he would be able to take me. That the council would consider it acceptable to revisit my roots. I am sorry I mentioned it, then."

"Don't be. You know I want to see India. You make it sound so wonderful. I just hope . . . " She sipped her tea. "I hope by the time he's free of his obligation, I'm still in good enough health . . . "

Her voice trailed off. I didn't need to remind her that it was a fool's dream.

"He would like to take you," I said.

"I know."

"He would like to go himself."

"I know. But his obligation . . . "

Could be over anytime he chooses. Those were the words left unspoken. Also the words, "but he does not have the strength of will to do it, to defy his family by freeing me on his own, despite the fact it is his decision to make, and the council will support it."

"I would miss you," she blurted. "I'd miss our talks."

I smiled. "As would I. If you were free to travel, though, you would see these places for yourself, make new friends. Here, we are both prisoners."

Jonathan insists she stay in the house. He says it is for her own safety, so she can't be targeted in retaliation for our acts.

She suspects, I'm sure, that he keeps her here because it is convenient. She is as much his property as I am. Without his obligation as an excuse, she'd have more freedom, whether he liked it or not.

"Jonathan knows best," she said finally. "He will free you. I know he will. It just isn't the time."

It never would be. Not if I relied on Catherine.

There were many things Daman and I agreed on, as partners in life, in love, in ambition. One was that—despite the teachings of the Brahmins—all men are created equal. Each bears within him the capacity to achieve his heart's desire. He needs only the strength of will to see it through.

Daman's story was an old one. A boy from a family rich in respect and lineage, poor in wealth and power. His family wanted him to marry a merchant's daughter with a rich dowry. Instead he chose me, a scholar's daughter, his childhood playmate. I brought something more valuable than money—intelligence, ambition, and a shared vision for what could be.

A hundred years ago, when my ishas lived in England, one saw the play *Macbeth*, and forever after that he called me Lady Macbeth. I found the allusion insulting. Macbeth was a coward, his wife a harpy. Daman did not need me to push him. Every step we took, we took as one.

In our twenty years together, we recouped everything his family had lost over the centuries. Our supporters would say that we brought stability and prosperity to the region. Our detractors would point out the trail of bodies in our wake, and the growing piles of coin in our coffers. Neither is incorrect. We did good and we did evil. We left the lands better than we found them, but at a price that was, perhaps, too steep.

I do regret the path we took. Yet if given a second chance, I would not sit in a corner, content with my lot. My ambition would merely be checked by a better appreciation for the value of human life. That appreciation has stayed my hand in this matter. Which has gotten me nowhere.

My next assignment came nearly four months later. That is typical. While one might look at the world and see plenty of wrongdoers, it is a rare one that must be culled altogether. Jonathan needs to search for a target. Then he must compile a dossier and submit it to the council, who will return elimination approval or request more information. After that comes weeks of surveillance, at which point my participation is required, my talents for illusion and shape-shifting useful.

Jonathan is supposed to assist with the surveillance work. He claims he's conducting his own elsewhere, but when I've followed, I've found him in coffee shops, flirting with serving girls or working on his novel.

He is supposed to supervise me, in case I shirk my duties and find a coffee shop of my own. I've considered it. I even have an idea for a novel. While it amuses me to think of this, I cannot do it. I enjoy the unsupervised times too much to risk them, and I do not have the personality for lounging and storytelling.

However, this time when I did my surveillance I was . . . less than forthright about my findings.

The target was yet another financier. Unlike Morrison, this one had been the subject of death threats, so he employed a bodyguard—a young man he passed off as his personal assistant.

I learned about the death threats by eavesdropping. I left them out of the report. I discovered the assistant's true nature only by surveillance. I left that out of the report as well. My official conclusion was that this man—Garvey—was no more security conscious than the others, but that his assistant was rarely away from his side, so I would lure the young man away, then let Jonathan subdue him while I dealt with Garvey.

It went as one might expect. Separating the two had been easy enough. Such things are minor obstacles for one who has spent hundreds of years practicing the art of illusion.

I got the bodyguard upstairs, where Jonathan was waiting. Then I hurried back to Garvey.

Jonathan's cries for help came before I reached the bottom of the stairs. They alerted Garvey, as I knew they would. My job, then, was to subdue the financier before he could retrieve his gun. After that it would be safe for me to go to my isha's aid.

It took some time for me to subdue Garvey. He was unexpectedly strong. Or so I would later claim.

By the time I returned upstairs, the bodyguard had beaten Jonathan unconscious and was preparing the killing blow. I shot him with Garvey's gun. Then I left Jonathan where he lay, returned to Garvey and carried on. This was my mission, which superceded all else, even the life of my isha.

When I was finished with Garvey—after he confessed to killing his guard, then taking his own life—I drove Jonathan to the hospital. Then I called Catherine.

"I take responsibility for this," I said to Catherine as we stood beside Jonathan's hospital bed. "My job was to protect him. I failed."

"You didn't know about the bodyguard."

"I should have. That too is my job. We are both to conduct a proper survey—"

"If Jon didn't find out about him, there's no reason you would."

I fell silent. Stared down at Jonathan, still unconscious after surgery to staunch the internal bleeding. I snuck looks at Catherine, searching for some sign that she would secretly have been relieved by his death. I'd seen none.

She claimed to love him. She did love him. I could still work with this.

"It's becoming so much more dangerous," I murmured. "There have always been accidents, but it is so much harder to keep an isha safe these days."

"Accidents? This—this hasn't happened before, has it?"

I kept my gaze on Jonathan.

"*Amrita.*"

I looked up slowly, then hesitated before saying, "The council has assured me that the rate of injury on my missions is far below that of most."

"Rate of injury?" Her voice squeaked a little. "I've never heard of an isha being seriously injured. You mean things like sprained ankles and bruises, right?"

I said nothing.

"Amrita!"

Again, I looked up. Again I hesitated before speaking. "There have been . . . incidents. Jonathan's great-uncle's car accident, it was . . . not an accident. That was the story the council told the family. And there have been . . . others." I hurried on. "But the risk with me is negligible, compared to others."

Which didn't reassure her in the least.

I said nothing after that. I had planted the seed. It would take time to sprout.

A week later, Jonathan was still in the hospital, recovering from his injuries. I had not yet returned to my apartment—once I entered, I wouldn't be able to leave. Catherine had to retrieve my food and drink from the refrigerator. She didn't like that, but the alterative was to sentence her only helpmate to prison until Jonathan recovered.

The day before he was due to come home, Catherine visited me in the guest room.

She entered without a word. Sat without word. Stayed there for nearly thirty minutes without a word. Then she said, "Tell me how to release you."

We had to hurry. The only way to free me without Jonathan's consent was while he was unable to give consent.

We withheld his fever medication until his temperature rose. While befuddled by fever—and a few of my illusory tricks—he parted with the combination to his safe.

I retrieved what we needed, and fingered the stacks of hundred-dollar bills, but I took none. I had no need for them.

"Are you sure this is what you want?" Catherine asked as I prepared the ritual. "They say that when a rakshasi passes to the other side, there is no afterlife. This *is* your afterlife. There'll be nothing else."

"Peace," I said. "There will be peace."

She nodded. My death was, after all, to her benefit, meaning the council would not judge her or Jonathan as harshly as if they'd freed me.

I drew the ritual circle in sand around Jonathan's bed. I lit tiny fires in the appropriate locations. I placed a necklace bearing one half of an amulet around my neck, and the other around his. I recited the incantations. Endless details, etched into my brain, the memories of my kind, as accessible as any other aspect of my magic, but requiring Jonathan's assistance. Or the assistance of his bodily form—hair to be burned, fingernails to be ground into powder, saliva and blood to be mixed with that powder.

Finally, as Catherine waited anxiously, I injected myself with the mixture. The ritual calls for it to be rubbed into an open wound. I'd made this modernized alteration, and Catherine had readily agreed that it seemed far less barbaric.

Next I injected Jonathan. Then I began the incantations.

Jonathan shuddered in his sleep. His mouth opened and closed, as if gasping for air. Catherine grabbed his hand.

"What's happening?" she said.

"The bond is breaking."

Now *I* shuddered, feeling that hated bond tighten, as if in reflexive protest. Then slowly, blessedly, it loosened.

Catherine started to gibber that something was wrong. Jonathan wasn't breathing. Why wasn't he breathing? His heartbeat was slowing. Why was it slowing?

I kept my eyes closed, ignoring her cries, and her tugs on my arm, until at last, the bond slid away. One last deep shudder and I opened my eyes to see the world as I hadn't seen it in two hundred years. Bright and glimmering with promise.

Catherine was shrieking now. Shrieking that Jonathan's heart had stopped.

I turned toward the door. She lunged at me, crutches falling as she grabbed my shirt with both hands.

"He's dead!" she cried. "It's supposed to be you, not him. Something went wrong."

"No," I said. "Nothing went wrong."

She screamed then, an endless wail of rage and grief. I picked her up, ignoring her feeble blows and kicks, and set her gently in a chair, then leaned her crutches within reach.

She snatched them and pushed to her feet. When I tried to walk away, she managed to get in front of me.

"What have you done?" she said.

"Freed us. Both of us."

"You lied!"

"I told you what you needed to hear." I eased her aside. "I do not want annihilation. I want what I was promised—a free life. For that, I need his consent, and the council to provide the necessary tools. There is, however, a loophole. A final act of mercy from an isha to his rakshasi. On his deathbed, he may free me with his amulet and that ritual."

"I-I don't—"

"You will tell the council that is what happened here. The poison I injected is the one we've used many times on our targets, undetectable. The council will believe Jonathan unexpectedly succumbed to his injuries."

"I will not tell them—"

"Yes, you will. Otherwise, you will be complicit in his death. And even if you manage to convince them otherwise, you will forfeit this house and all that goes with it. It is yours only if he dies and I am freed. They may contest that, but even if they do, you will have already removed the contents of his safe. I left everything for you."

That was less generous than it seemed. For years, I'd been taking extra from our targets and hiding it in my room. I would not leave unprepared. I was never unprepared.

Now that the bond was broken, there was nothing to stop me from entering and exiting my apartment, and taking all I had collected. I passed Catherine and headed for the door.

She was silent until I reached it.

"What will I do now?" she said.

I glanced back at her. "Live. I intend to."

He does not know if what he is doing is right or wrong, mad or sane.
But he knows he cannot live with his wife's ghost any longer . . .

WHY DO YOU LINGER?

Sarah Monette

"Why do you linger?" he asks the empty room.

Dust motes fall through the dim shaft of sunlight from the window, and there is no answer.

When he goes downstairs, his wife is standing on the landing. The jingle sticks in his head—*standing on the landing, standing on the landing*—as he walks down the stairs toward her. Her eyes are dark, solemn; she watches him with neither reproach nor forgiveness.

He stops two steps up from the landing, unable to walk into the aura of cold that surrounds her. She looks at him, unsmiling, and turns to walk downstairs. Before she reaches the bottom, she fades into nothing.

She has been dead for three months.

She died suddenly, without warnings or omens or the sense of foreboding which he thought later he ought to have felt. Simply, one afternoon, he came home and found her lying dead in the foyer, her keys fallen like bones from her hand. She had been dead for three or four hours, the paramedics said. No cause of death was ever determined.

After the funeral, he drove home through the fog to the empty, dusty, desolate house. As he walked up the stairs to the door, he thought he saw his dead wife watching him through the front window. But when he opened the door, she was not there.

Some months before she died, lying in bed in the flat painted blackness of their bedroom, grown hostile with weeks of silence, as they lay not facing each other, each in their separate pocket of cold, she said, "Do you love her?" And after another silence, so hard and cold that it could have been used to preserve a beautiful, fragile corpse, like the death of love, he said, "No."

He thought she sighed, a tiny noise like a rose shedding its petals. But she did not ask the next question, the obvious question.

Do you love me?

Now that she is dead, she comes to him at night, her body naked, translucent, as cold and elusive as mist. She straddles him, her face twisted into an animal snarl of need, an expression he never saw on her face when she was alive. She cannot touch him; her fingers disappear into his body without the slightest effect. He is frightened at first, then repulsed, then aroused as he was never aroused by her in the sixteen years of their marriage. Night after night, she comes to him with her fierce, cold, insatiable need; night after night he couples with the frigid air, climaxing against nothing so that his semen spatters shockingly hot across his stomach.

When he opens his eyes, his wife is staring at him, her face as cold and unreadable as moonlight.

Knowing she will not answer, he asks, "Why do you linger?"

Her face does not change; she gets off him and walks to the window. As her hand reaches out toward the curtain, she dissolves into the darkness.

When he wakes in the mornings, the house is filled with a sourceless, wordless singing. He does not recognize the tune, but he knows his wife's voice. Some days he pretends to ignore it; other days he searches the house fruitlessly from top to bottom. Always the singing dies away just before noon.

He has not seen the young woman since the day before his wife's death. When the phone rings, he lets the machine pick up and erases the tape unheard.

A week after the funeral, he came in from shopping and found his wife's keys lying on the floor of the foyer, exactly where they had fallen from her hand when she died.

He wondered for a terrible moment if they had lain there all along, if he had been stepping over them without seeing them for more than a week. Carefully, he put down the grocery bag, as if it contained eggshells and wine glasses instead of frozen pizzas and a six-pack of beer. And then he remembered watching his wife's body being taken out of the house, her keys in his hand, his fingers clenching so tightly that the shapes of the keys imprinted themselves in his palm. And then, blindly, automatically, he had taken them into the kitchen, opened the drawer in which his wife kept her wooden spoons and serving utensils, and dropped the keys in as if they were a dead bird.

He knelt down beside his grocery bag. He reached out, slowly, as if the keys might startle and bite him. When he touched them, they were icy cold, so cold they hurt his fingers.

Before her death, he became accustomed to her watching him, her eyes shadowed and grave. She did not accuse him; only that once did she even question him. Merely, she watched, and in the silence that built up around them layer after layer, like lacquer concealing and preserving once-living wood, he heard the question she did not ask: *why are you still here?* If she had asked, he would not have been able to answer her, and thus he was angered by her refusal to ask, by her silent, passive watchfulness. He said nothing himself, feeling obscurely and angrily that it would be a sign of weakness, cowardice, to offer a defense when none had been asked for. He told himself that it was her responsibility to ask, that if she wanted to know, she would say something, and even came to believe, in a strange, inarticulate way, that the silent misery in the house was her fault, that because she would not ask, he could not answer, and his own guilt was lost in his resentment of her failure to be angry.

Sometimes now, waking in the thin early light to the sound of his wife singing, he wonders if it was the silence that killed her, if she drowned beneath its weight like a diver caught in the wreckage of a ship. Silence can kill; he knows that now. He can feel her silence killing him an inch at a time.

He got rid of all his wife's things less than a month after her death, abandoning them in an undifferentiated mass to a consignment store. He hired a cleaning service to go through the house from top to bottom, ridding it of her dust, imbuing the air with the scents of cleaning products she had never used. But when he came back to the house that night, after eating at a restaurant to which he had never taken his wife, her car keys were on the foyer floor again, in exactly the same place, strung on the key chain he had thrown out over a week previously. And they were cold.

He walks through the house as the sunlight turns to puddles of gold on the floor. He finds their wedding picture face down on the mantelpiece and takes it out of its frame. In the back of the bedroom closet, he finds one of her scarves, overlooked when he was frantically bagging her clothes. He takes a pillowcase that she had particularly liked, pale blue embroidered with garlands, and puts the scarf and the picture into it. Finally he goes back downstairs and picks up her keys from the corner of the foyer, where he had kicked them the last time they appeared.

He does not know if what he is doing is right or wrong, mad or sane. But he knows he cannot live with his wife's ghost any longer, and the mad dream-logic of the haunted tells him that he must get her to speak to him before he can be free of her. Her death and her silence and her ghost are entangled in his mind like strands of beads: beads of grief, beads of anger, of pity and fear and guilt.

The house cannot help him; the house is complicit in her silence. He walks out the back door, leaving it open.

The hill slopes down from the house toward a stand of birch trees. It has taken him longer than he realized to find the things he needs; the golden light is deepening to dusk, purple gloaming creeping out from the trees and the shadow of the house.

He builds a fire halfway down the hill, working quickly but carefully. It takes him three tries to light it because his hands are shaking. He kneels by the fire, choosing a position where he can see the house without turning his back on the birch trees. His wife loved the birches, and he feels them watching.

He gives the scarf to the fire first, then the photograph. They burn quickly; he watches his own face blacken and disappear. Then, although he knows they will not melt, he throws her keys in the fire. And he asks again, desperately, "Why do you linger?"

He sees movement and looks at the house. She comes out the back door and walks down the hill toward him and the fire. In the dusk she glows faintly, like moonlight.

He stands up as she approaches, curbing his desire to run from her, and asks again, "Why do you linger?"

She says nothing, and her face does not change.

"Damn you," he cries, "answer me!"

She stands and looks at him and does not speak.

He takes a step toward her before he remembers that she is dead and he cannot touch her. He says, "Please. You have to let me go."

He sees the anger flare in her eyes, sees the snarl she wears when she comes to him at night. She opens her mouth and cries in a terrible, thin, inhuman voice, "You were all that I had!"

He flinches back from her, from her black, boiling, dead pain. "You were all that I had, so how can I let you go? All that I had," she cries, "all that I had."

But she is fading; all her power was in her silence. He can see her beginning to tatter, her substance drifting away upward like smoke. She stretches out her hands toward him, but they are already dissolving. "All that I had," she cries, her voice faint and distant like the wind in the birch trees, and then she is gone. He can feel her absence like a throbbing pain in the bones of his skull and hands, and knows that he is free of her at last.

Numbly, methodically, he puts out the fire, using the garden hose to be sure the last lingering spark is extinguished. He gets the shovel and his work gloves from the shed and digs a hole; he puts his wife's keys in the pillowcase and drops the pillowcase in the hole. He shovels the ashes and earth back over the pillowcase and tamps the whole thing down carefully.

He replaces the shovel, gloves, hose. Full dark is almost here. He walks back into the empty, dusty, silent house, and shuts the door behind him.

Why do you linger?

There was power in those stories, in seeing them slide up against one another like cards in a poker hand you know will win the pot.

VAMPIRE LAKE

Norman Partridge

PART ONE: RUMSON'S SALOON

They heard the bounty killer an hour before they saw him. Out there in the desert night. Playing that harmonica of his, though the sounds that came out of it weren't anything you'd call music. But he kept at it, and the racket carved the desert sands like Lucifer trenching a brimstone field with his pitchfork. A man who could raise that kind of hell with a harmonica was a man who could unsettle a room full of other men.

And that's why the customers sitting in Rumson's saloon did the things they did. Some slapped coin to the bar and made their exits. Others ordered up and drank more deeply, which pleased the barkeep. Still others unbuckled their gunbelts as the man with the harmonica drew nearer. They rolled leather studded with sheathed bullets around holstered Colts, and they stowed those weapons far from reluctant hands.

Outside, the harmonica had grown silent. The creak of saddle-leather put a crease in the night. Then footsteps sounded across plank boards, and the bounty killer came through the batwings of Rumson's place.

He wore a patched coat the color of the desert, and he was dragging a man on a chain. One yank and the bounty killer bellied up to the bar. The gunman set his harmonica on the nicked pine surface. No one noticed the blood on the tarnished instrument, not with the poor skinny bastard trussed up in chains and padlocks crouching at the killer's feet. As far as the occupants of Rumson's saloon were concerned, that was the hunk of misery worth looking at, not a bloodstained Hohner that blew sour even on days that were sweet.

The bartender asked the bounty killer where he'd captured the man, and the gunman shook his head. Said the raw-boned Mex was a dynamite man who'd been locked up for years, and just tonight the bounty killer had broken him out of Yuma Territorial. "His name is Indio. If he put his mind to it, he could blow the gates off hell with a pissed-on fuse and a quarter-stick sweating nitro."

"The hell you say," Rumson said.

"The hell I do," said the bounty killer.

The bartender shrugged. "What can I get you?"

"Salt. Tequila. A guide."

"A guide? Where to?"

"Vampire Lake."

The bartender raised an eyebrow. "Most folks say there ain't no place like that in the world. It's just a legend, like the cave that's supposed to hold it. Of course, other folks say differently."

"That's what I hear. Same way I hear there's a kid in this town who's paid hell's own tab for a visit to that brimstone pit. Same way I hear there's a saloon-keeper who keeps that kid locked up in a cage and charges folks a double eagle to hear his story."

"Sounds to me like you're talking about a man who's got a piece of property and a piece of business. And that business would be the kid talking, not getting on a horse and riding to hell and gone out of here. A piece of business like you're talking about would be worth a good deal more than the freight you'd pay to hear an evening's worth of words."

"Let me talk to the boy about that."

"Let me see the color of your money."

"I think you've seen plenty enough money out of this deal already. My business is with the boy, not the half-shingled bastard who keeps him locked up like a circus chimp."

At the sound of those words, the bartender jerked in his boots. The two men stared at each other across the bar, nothing between them but dim quiet. Both of them watching and waiting for the thing that would happen next.

It was the dynamite man who broke the silence. "Amigo. If you're so soft on men in cages, what about me? I've been in a cage up in Yuma for three damn years. Why don't you crank a key in these locks and let me go, and we can call it square?"

"Shut up," the bounty killer said. "You're doing time for armed robbery and murder. Three years ago, you blew out a bank wall in Tucumcari and killed four men. I caught up to you in a whorehouse, stuck a pistol in your face, and the Territory of Arizona locked you in the poke. But I'm the one who put you in there, so I figure that gives me the right to take you out if I have the need. Once I'm done with you, maybe I'll take you back."

"You can get started on that little trip right now," Rumson said. "Get the hell out of my bar, and take that Mexican trash with you."

"Uh-uh. I don't move until you bring me that boy."

"You'll move. And directly—"

Rumson reached under the bar for a sawed-off shotgun. Before his hands could make the trip the barkeep lost the equipment to say anything. The stranger's pistol saw to that. It came out of its holster rattler-quick and sprayed Rumson's head across the barroom wall. In the brief moment after the bullet did its work, what was left of Rumson's skull looked like a diseased egg dropped by one sick chicken. By the time that bloody hunk of gristle hit the floor, the bounty killer's black rattler of a pistol was back in its holster.

Rumson's corpse followed his head, thudding against the bar, toppling bottles on its way to the floor. After that, the only sound was the barkeep's blood dripping off the wall and ceiling, making scarlet divots in a patch of sawdust behind the bar. Leastways, that was the only sound until the real commotion started. Chair legs scraped hardwood as men scrambled for the batwing doors, but it was the click of pistol hammers in the hands of fools with more guts than brains that brought the bounty killer's gun out of its holster again. When that happened there was more terror and tumult in Rumson's Saloon than there were shadows, and the gleam of that black Colt springing through the darkness sent a stampede scrambling for the doorway as the first shots were fired. As the crowd scrambled more men filled their hands with pistols of their own, but none of those pistols would put a man in mind of a snake.

The bounty killer's black rattler did its work. And when it was empty he ducked behind the bar and came up with Rumson's shotgun. And when that was empty, it was all over.

Or more properly: It had just begun.

Four men remained alive in the bar. The bounty killer. The dynamite man on a chain. A dark-eyed blacksmith roughly the size of a barn door. And a calculating preacher who kept a running ledger on the flyleaf pages of the prayer book tucked inside a pocket of his claw-hammer coat.

"Where's the boy?" the gunman asked.

"Probably out back eating a live chicken, feathers and all," the preacher said. "That child is crazy, mister. Apaches captured him in the desert. God knows what lies he told those red bastards, but it put them in a temper. A few days later some scalphunters found the boy tied to a wagon wheel, his head cooking over a Mescalaro fire along with a couple of scrawny prairie hens. The birds had gone to cinders, but the kid had it worse. Half his face was burned off, and his brain was boiling in his skull like a Christmas pudding.

Just because that misery scorched some nightmares in his head don't make them true."

"You talk but you don't tell me anything I need to know." The killer reloaded his pistol, slapped the cylinder closed, and gave it a spin for emphasis. "I asked one question. That question was: *Where?*"

"You don't need gun for answer." The blacksmith's voice was heavy with an accent born in a German forest he'd never see again. "Boy is out back—in cage in barn, behind horse stalls. No rivets in cage; all welds. Three locks on it. Hasps as strong as bars. Double-thick, like plates."

"How do you know all that?"

The blacksmith blinked. Words jumped from one tongue to another in his head, then made the trip through his lips. "I forge bars. I build locks and hasps. I make cage."

The bounty killer cocked his black rattler.

"Let's take a look," he said.

The barn doors swung open. Boots whispered over the dirty hay that covered the barn floor. A lantern swung on a creaky handle in the preacher's hand. It was close to midnight now, and the place was so dark it seemed the night had heaved in a dozen extra buckets of shadow.

The darkness lay heaviest in a patch transfixed by iron bars near the back corner of the barn. "Give me that lantern," the bounty killer said. Light played across the black bars as he took it from the preacher, and light painted the occupant along with the contents of the cage—a scuffed plate that didn't get used much and a few tattered books that did: *Idylls of the King*, *The Thousand and One Nights*, and a dime novel about Billy the Kid.

"Look at that damned animal," the preacher said. "Face like a scorched biscuit. The brain of a kicked chicken. Stinks like an Arizona outhouse in August."

Everyone squinted in the lantern's glow. Only the blacksmith knew better than to look. He stared down at his mule-eared boots. But the dynamite man didn't know better. He took a good long look. Then he turned his head and retched up his supper.

The bounty killer stared through the bars without saying a word. He fished the dead bartender's key ring from his pocket. A moment later he went to work with three of the keys, slipping padlocks from hasps, opening the door.

PART TWO: THE TOWN

"Come out of there," the bounty killer said.

"Yes, sir," I said.

I picked up my chicken. Henrietta flapped some, shedding a few of the feathers I hadn't plucked. I petted her and told her to hush, but she flapped her naked wings and squawked up a storm.

"Looks like we interrupted his supper," the preacher said.

I glared at him and didn't say a word, though there were plenty inside me I could have put to work. Instead I held Henrietta close, stretched myself in the lantern glow, and watched my shadow cast a path that led straight to the door.

We stood outside around an empty barrel, the lantern set on top of it. The bounty killer pulled a bank book from his pocket. "You get me to Vampire Lake, what's in this book is yours. It amounts to twenty years of killing and twenty years of bounties. The four of you get back alive, you can split it four ways." With that, he slapped the book on the barrelhead next to the lantern so we could get a look at it.

The blacksmith was confused. "This is book. Just paper."

"These days money is just paper, too, amigo," Indio said. "Banks are full of it, and one page from a book like this can bring many dollars. What our friend here collected for me and my gang alone would keep us in whores for a year."

"But I am blacksmith. Not killer."

"I take care of that job," the bounty killer said. "But there are other jobs that need doing. The kid here, he's our guide. He'll take us through the desert, find that cave, lead us down to the underground lake where those dead things roost. And Indio will take care of any trouble we run into along the way that can be handled with dynamite."

The big man said it again: "But I am blacksmith."

"Yeah. That's what you've got inside you, but it's bundled up in one hell of a package. Where we're going, I need a man who tops a couple hundred pounds and doesn't mind the scorch of hot coals. You're elected."

"Those three I understand." The preacher picked up the bank book and stared hard at the balance. "You need yourself a birddog, you've got a biscuit-faced geek uglier than Satan's own bitch. You think you're going to dynamite the gates of hell, you want the Mex along. The other one is a freight train on legs and too stupid to think for himself. But what about me? Why do you want a preacher along?"

"That's a lot of hard tongue for a man who carries a Bible," the bounty killer said.

"Fair enough . . . but right now I'm not behind a pulpit, friend. I'm doing business, and business calls for straight tongue. So what is it? What do you want from me? Is there something down in that devil's shithole that you want prayed to death?"

The gunslinger didn't blink.

"It's simple. I want words said over anything I kill tonight. The way I see it, you may not be the best man for the job, but you're the only one around tonight."

The preacher bit off a hard laugh. "Sometimes finding work is just a matter of being in the right place at the right time. And as far as words go, no one said a single damn one over those poor bastards you slaughtered back in the saloon."

"We're going to fix that right now."

"Well, we can talk about it. You killed a lot of men back there. Generally my fees for funeral services are one per customer. And since this piece of business doesn't have anything to do with going down in a cave, it's got to be a separate deal—"

"I already told you the deal." The bounty killer snatched the bank book out of the preacher's hand and grabbed him by the collar. The fuss the preacher put up did not last long, not after a couple hard slaps put the button to his lip.

We went back to the bar. Except for the dead men, it was empty. Even the whores were gone. God knows where the ladies had hustled off to, but they'd made themselves scarce after the gunfight.

The blacksmith and the bounty killer took a few doors off their hinges in the whores' rooms upstairs. They placed the doors flat, each one resting between a couple of chairs, and they laid the dead men on top of them. They crossed the corpses' arms over their chests—the ones who had two arms, anyway. One of the men who'd been sprayed with Rumson's sawed-off street howitzer was missing a wing. He lay there just as still as the others, the stiffening fingers of his remaining hand embracing the ruined socket just north of his heart. Rumson's headless corpse lay next to him; the leavings of his skull were in a canvas bag at his feet.

Once the dead were settled, the preacher said his piece. It was a short piece, and bereft of flowers. That was just fine with me. I was not much on flowers. As it turned out, the preacher was not much on words . . . especially when payday was a ways off.

When the praying was over, he sidled past the dynamite man.

A little blood trickled from the preacher's lip, and he wiped it away.

"He's one dirty bastard we're working for," he said. "But that was money in the bank."

The blacksmith did most of the grunt work. He harnessed a team of swaybacks to a wagon while Indio and the preacher looted the general store for supplies. I tipped a dude's beaver-skinned bowler out of a hatbox and nestled Henrietta inside it, then helped myself to a new set of clothes. It had been a while since I'd had one. I was almost seventeen, and had been wearing the set I had on for something like two years. They were tight and stiff with the sweat of misery. The preacher watched me as I stripped out of them.

"Jesus, you're ugly. You look worse than that half-plucked chicken."

"I don't have to speak to you," I said.

"Tell the truth. When we found you in that cage, you were ready to eat that chicken raw. You're probably still going to eat it as soon as you get a chance. Why else would you pluck the damn bird, anyway?"

"I keep Henrietta's wings plucked so she won't get away. She's not half-grown, even. She needs me to keep her warm. And that man with the gun is right. You don't talk like a preacher."

The man in black laughed. "Hell, I talk the way I please when there's not a collection plate around. And as for pets, you want one, get a dog. You want victuals, get a chicken. That's what god intended, son . . . unless you're a damn heathen Apache that'll eat both and follow the meal with a little skin jerky baked off a white boy's face for dessert."

I ignored him. After I had dressed, I helped myself to a wide-brimmed hat to shadow my scars. That was when I heard the others chattering over the events in Rumson's saloon. I closed my eyes and listened, saw everything happen in my head. It was just the way I pictured things when I read a book. When the men finished the story, the blacksmith and I loaded up the supplies in the wagon.

While I worked, I added pieces of the story to the things I'd already learned about the men. And I'll admit it. I thought about money while I did that. I thought about freedom, too. A place where I could be by myself, except for Henrietta and maybe some old tomcat. It'd be a place where I wouldn't have to tell that story about the cave, or have anyone look at me at all if I didn't want them to. Maybe it'd be a place where I could tell other stories, write them down and send them off to folks who would print them between hard covers. They'd send me money, and I'd write more when I wanted to. It seemed like that would be a square deal, and a lot better than the one I'd had at Rumson's place.

I thought about it long and hard.

Pretty soon I'd made a decision.

A smart person might risk just about anything for a setup like that.

Even a return trip to hell.

Soon the wagon was loaded, and that put the end to my thoughts. It was time to move on. The preacher and Indio went off somewhere and came back with a crate of dynamite. After the murders in Rumson's saloon, it was easy pickings in town tonight. We left the general store with the door wide open. It didn't matter. Sheriff Needham was nowhere in sight. I didn't know where the hard-eyed little lawdog and his deputy had got to, but whether they had made the trip out of luck or fear I figured they were smart to be clear of things this night.

We returned to the bar to get the bounty killer. He'd remained with the dead men, knowing there was no worry about any of us running off now that the numbers from his bank book were dancing in our heads. The desert night was cold, wind blowing down from the mountain. Dust devils swirled around us, erasing the footsteps of the men who lay dead in Rumson's bar. It was like the night wanted to clear off the last trace of them. The moon was full up by then, and it hung low in the sky, and light spilled from it like an Apache buck's knife had slit it straight across and turned all that bleeding white loose.

I sat in the wagon with the reins in my hands. Henrietta was asleep in the hatbox at my side. The other men were on horseback. We heard the bounty killer coughing inside Rumson's place as he walked from dead man to dead man, not getting too close to any of them, staring down at each one. Between coughs, he tried to work words through his lips. The batwings creaked in the wind, swinging in and out, and the gunman seemed to be strangling on those words, and through the gap I saw him go down on his knees as quick as if someone had clubbed him with an ax-handle.

He started to retch, and we heard a thick splatter slap the floorboards.

"The bastard gunned those men down like dogs," the preacher said. "You'd think he'd have the nerve to face them dead."

"Nerve ain't his problem," Indio said. "He's got plenty of nerve."

I wondered about that as I watched the bounty killer there in the shadows. His guts bucked him something awful. The sound was horrible, like something alive trying to eat its way out of him. We all looked away.

I closed my eyes. The night was black, but the only color in my head was red. It painted the barroom floor and the bounty killer's lips and the things I saw. They were things that had happened in the night, some that I'd seen and some that I hadn't, but all of them were broiling in my thoughts nonetheless. The bloodstained harmonica on the bar. The murders in the barroom. Rumson's head toppling off his shoulders, kicking up a sawdust cloud as it hit the floor. I saw all that like the blood on King Arthur's sword in the tales I read, and Aladdin's scimitar flashing through Arabian shadows, and Billy the Kid blasting a man's guts to ribbons with a shotgun. Everything I saw played to the sound of a harmonica scrabbling over the ribs of the night, and gunshots from a black rattler of a pistol, and whispered voices in a general store at midnight. All of it was red, and it went down my spine like a bucket of ice, and it made me sit up straight on that wagon box with my breath trapped in my throat.

And that was a long time ago. The night it happened, I mean. But I knew even then that there was power in those stories, in seeing them slide up against one another like cards in a poker hand you know will win the pot. That was like having a headful of magic, and a brain that could cast a thousand-league spell, and I let it spin awhile.

I didn't open my eyes until I heard the stiff creak of batwing doors. The bounty killer stepped out of Rumson's saloon. His pistol was in its holster, and his harmonica was in his hand.

He coughed a few times, then spit a mouthful of blood in the dirt.

"Let's ride," was all he said.

Part Three: The Desert

The morning wasn't bright. Not right off, anyway. It churned up out of the night slow and gray, like a dull reflection in an old mirror. I rode in the wagon behind the men. All I saw of them that morning was their backs and the dust raised by their horses. The gray light washed over them and the dust churned at their stirruped heels just as sure as the gray light, and when the light married up with the dirt it was like heaven and earth were stitching shrouds for the four men who'd walked out of Rumson's saloon alive the night before.

That was not an image born of fancy. I stared hard and saw straight through the men to things that lay ahead of them. Doing that was like reading a book, and seeing a scene bloom in my head before I so much as turned the page and sent my eyes across the black lines that told the same tale I'd imagined.

Some folks say that's a kind of witchcraft. They call it *second sight*. I say it's just paying attention. That's why I understood about Rumson and the rest of them in that town before they showed their true colors. I watched them and paid attention. In my mind's eye, I saw them do the things they'd do before they so much as thought about doing them. I understood which way they'd jump when push came to shove. I knew it the way I knew what Rumson did with his whores when the bar was closed and I was locked up tight in my cage, the same way I knew what he'd do if anyone ever challenged him the way the bounty killer did.

And I saw these men the same way. Bits of the night came back to me, that reverie in red glimpsed just hours before. Words blew at me through the wind, and the fisted nubs of my scorched ears caught them. They built the story that waited ahead of us. It sang in my head the way my memories sang, and with it came the crackle of fires that had warmed me and maimed me, and the red glow of the fire we'd build in the night that waited ahead. And in that night were other deeds and stories, some I saw clear and some I only felt like an October wind that promises the stark cold of November.

But everywhere I looked, the men were there. The preacher, with his ledger book Bible. The blacksmith, a man who found it easier to do what others told him than the things he might want to do for himself. And Indio, the dynamite man, whose mind was set on a life without shackles.

Those three were easy to know. But some men aren't so easy. You can't tell what they'll do until they do it. That's the way it was with the bounty killer. Men like that come straight at you, but you can't shear them of surprises. They have faces that show you nothing, and hearts that hold secrets maybe even they don't understand.

Of course, it took me a lifetime to learn that. I had good teachers. I learned the lesson from dead men with hearts built from shadows, who came out of a grave-hole in the desert and took me down to hell. I learned it from Apaches who tied me to a wagon wheel and roasted my face while their faces wore no expressions at all. I learned that lesson, and I learned it as well as the story I told in Rumson's saloon. Red or white, living or dead, sooner or later most men show you what they have inside . . . even if you can't see it coming.

I figured that's the way it would be with the bounty killer.

I figured it was only a matter of time.

Towards dusk, we camped in the middle of nothing. Just a playa of cracked earth that powdered an inch deep with every step so that it was like walking on pie crust. The preacher wrung the necks of a couple of hens he'd stolen from a coop behind the general store, and Indio cleaned them and set those birds on a spit over the fire. The blacksmith rigged a little crank on the end of the spit, turning it with a hand which had long ago befriended the lick of flame. The wind came at us and churned the white earth as I told my story, and the campfire kicked up spark and cinder that snapped at those dead birds like a hungry dog.

"We were part of a wagon train," I said, holding Henrietta close. "My family and me. One night we camped in a place like this. Big open space. White everywhere, too much white for the night to blanket. Just a little sliver of a moon above, but it lit up the whole place just as sure as that full moon is doing tonight. And I don't know—maybe this was the very same place where we camped. It could be, I guess. It seems just like it."

"Ain't that always the way it is." The preacher snorted a laugh. "Watch out, boys—there might be a booger-man behind you."

"Button it," the bounty killer said.

I went on with the story. "They came for us in the night. They didn't look like men. Looked more like shadows. Just patches of black moving with the wind, sliding over that desert with faces as white as smoke. They rose up out of a hole in the ground no bigger than a dug grave and did their business. Snatched blankets off folks so quick it was like they were tearing up the night, and they tossed those blankets to the wind and ripped folks open with clawed hands. Did it so fast it was like they'd popped the stitches on a goatskin canteen and spilled a fiesta's worth of Mexican wine.

"They gathered around drinking their fill before the earth soaked it up. There must have been fifty of those things, and they killed most everyone before we even knew what was happening. I woke up in a puddle of my older sister's blood with a leather strap tied around my ankles. I guess by then those bloodsuckers had chugged down their fill of blood, same way cowhands get their fill of whiskey when they're on a spree. But they weren't so full that they didn't want to rustle a bottle from behind the bar to see them through the next day and the night beyond.

"One yank of that strap and I dropped from the wagon bed. Another and I skidded across the sand. The dead man dragging me had no more trouble than if he was pulling a canteen behind him. He was just a shadow, but he was strong, with hands and arms like vined midnight. He turned that face built of smoke in my direction and smiled a butcher-shop smile. I screamed my head off, but there was no one to help me—every one of us who was still sucking wind was in the same fix. But those shadows didn't care. They just dragged us along, through the dirt and the patches of blood spilled by our kinfolks. And we set up a chorus of screams that sounded sure enough like a parade of souls headed straight for Satan's pit."

The wind rose just then, and the fire kicked up a crackle. The Mex crossed himself, and so did the blacksmith. Their eyes were trained on the campfire and the white smoke that rose from it, which swirled and twisted like it was trying to knot the darkness.

"Jesus, Mary, and Joseph," the blacksmith said.

Indio nodded. *"Madre de dios."*

"What a load of horseshit," the preacher said.

"I told you once to shut up," the bounty killer warned. And to me: "Go on."

"They dragged us into that coffin hole one by one, then through a burrow no wider than one a wolf would dig. That burrow widened into a tunnel, and then a cave. It was nothing but dark in there. Still, I heard things and nailed them up in my memory. The scrape of a key in a lock. A creaking iron door. Wind through a wall of bars. Then that door swinging shut on rusty hinges, and a key finding its notch. One turn and that door locked. The vampires put us on our feet on the other side of the gate and cut our bonds. Then they marched us down black tunnels, deep into the earth. A mole would have been lost in that darkness. Miles and miles we went, lower and deeper, with no sound but our footsteps, and folks crying, and walls that talked. Those walls told us, 'Welcome to hell, pilgrims,' laughing at us as we passed by. And if you reached out a hand in the darkness to steady yourself, you'd bring it back bit and bloody, because those walls were hungry for a taste of what the vampires had gorged on that night.

"The deeper we went, the lighter it got. Not any kind of light you'd find in the sky above you, but a kind that was just bright enough so you could keep your bearings. Mushrooms grew in patches on the wall, glowing the way fireflies do. So did smears of fungus that lay like a carpet at our feet. Air blew up the tunnel like it couldn't wait to escape through that grave hole up above in the piecrust earth, and the bite of that wind was as sharp as the bite of those things that lived in the walls behind us.

"And with that wind came the smell of Vampire Lake. It was waiting below. One whiff and I knew the water would be black. Suddenly I could see the shore in my mind's eye, the sand as white as bones. I knew there'd be dead men sitting there on coffin boxes. Waiting, just waiting, for us."

"I think you ate yourself a bellyful of those mushrooms down there in that hole," the preacher said. "And a couple bushels of loco weed, too."

I ignored him. "They kept me locked up down there for weeks. Months, maybe. I was never sure how much time had passed. We were corralled in a barred cave near a bridge that stretched out across the black water. The bridge was narrow, made of old planks that had nearly rotted through with time. It led to a small island in the middle of the lake. One of the guards told us that was where the vampire queen roosted, as solitary as a black widow spider. At least once a day the guards would come and get a prisoner. More often two. They'd march those folks across that bridge, and it was like watching someone mount the steps to a gallows. The shadow-faced guards marched them forward, and those old planks creaked under their tread, and that black water churned beneath them with every step. Something was down there, beneath the surface, waiting. Something just as hungry as those dead men and that wicked queen—"

"Save that part for later," the bounty killer said. "Tell us about that queen. What was her story?"

"I never saw her. Leastways, not face to face. That guard, he said she'd been down there since the days of the conquistadors. Made a trip into that cave with a captain and his men looking for Indian gold, found a lake that bubbled up out of hell. Of course, they didn't know that then. They camped down there in the dark while they searched for treasure. Drank from that lake. Swam in its waters. And one day those soldiers weren't men any more, and that señorita wasn't a woman. After that, they say she drank down a thousand men, and still she was always thirsty. Skinny as a rake she was, out there alone on that island with only a Navajo slave girl for company. She used that girl for a footstool. Made her sit still for hours, her cold bony feet on that girl's back, toenails digging in like tiny shovels. She'd sit there on a throne of bones with her feet up on that Navajo girl, her eyes so black they looked like giant ticks burrowed into her sockets. Staring across that dark water, never blinking, always watching. Waiting for a full belly she could never have no matter how many souls she drank down."

"And what made you so special?" the preacher asked, staring at the coals. "Why didn't that queen bee suck on you? You weren't as ugly then as you are now."

"She might have done the job . . . had I waited around. One night I managed to sneak out of there. The guards dragged off a couple of the younger girls. There was a big shivaree around the coffin boxes near the shore as the dead men took them down, and while that was going on I worked some rocks loose and made a gap near the end bar along the edge of the cave mouth. Soon enough, I wriggled my way out. I found a tunnel and followed those glowing mushrooms, and when the mushrooms started to thin out and the light began to dim I smeared myself all over with that fungus from the floor, made the rest of the trip glowing like a funeral candle with a short wick. I could hardly see at all, but I saw enough, and the things I saw set me running. I don't even remember what I did when I came to the gate at the end of the tunnel, but I figure I was so skinny and greased with sweat that I must have squeezed my way between the bars. I crawled out of that grave hole into another pocket of darkness. It was night, and the air was so fresh it seemed like ice poured straight into my lungs. I saw the stars above and they set me running again. I ran for miles, stumbling into the middle of an Apache camp. They grabbed me, and—"

"And you was out of the frying pan and into the fire." The preacher laughed heartily. "Then those red bastards took one look at you, thought you was some kind of devil, and cinched you to a wagon wheel. Cooked you up just like these here hens."

"I'm not going to tell you a third time," the bounty killer said.

"Yeah," said Indio. "Let the kid be."

The preacher cussed a blue streak. "You men are as weepy as a church choir. Let's all take up a collection plate for poor little biscuit-face, why don't we?" He turned to me, grinning. "Boy, I've got to say that bartender taught you one hell of a story to feed the rubes. Did he give you a live chicken to chew on when you finally learned to tell it right? I mean, I know telling whoppers is the only way a geek like you could make a living, but it's hell's own price for us to have to stare at the leavings of your face while you do the work."

With the sound of those words, Indio and the bounty killer started to move. The blacksmith was faster. He snatched the preacher by the scruff of the neck, lifted him off his feet like he was a sack of sugar. Then he spilled him across one knee as he crouched, and held his face just short of the fire.

"You like to talk. Maybe we fix your face now, and then you tell us story."

"Jesus!" the preacher shouted. "Get this bastard off me!"

Disgusted, the blacksmith chucked him backwards. The preacher flew a few feet, landing on his ass. A puff of desert playa rose up around him, and he scrambled around on all fours like a spider popping on a hot griddle before he gained his feet.

"I'll get even with you, you goddamn square-headed Heinie bastard," the preacher said. "And then you'll be a quarter-mile past *sorry*."

The blacksmith thought about that for a long moment.

"No," he said finally. "You can put bullet in me. You can put knife in me. You can open Bible and bring Jehovah down on white horse and have him twist me to a leper. You can do what you want. But I won't be sorry."

It was quiet after that. I stared at the fire. At the spit. I watched as the blacksmith turned his little homemade crank, and I watched the chickens go 'round and 'round. One was bigger than the other. The skin on that one started to crack and drip juice, while the little one's skin crisped up like a shell. Watching that, I started to sweat a little bit, and the scars on my face began to itch.

Finally, the bounty killer said, "Tell the rest of it, boy."

"No. I've said enough. Right now, you either believe me or you don't. Tomorrow, you can see for yourselves."

No one said anything for a while. The bounty killer tore a loaf of brown bread into four sections and gave one to everybody but the preacher. Soon, the first chicken was ready. Indio took a knife and carved up the scrawny bird. He passed hunks around on tin plates. He didn't give one to the preacher. By the time the Mexican was done with that knife, all that was left was the gizzard, and one black wing, and a knotted little lump of a head. The preacher helped himself to all that, swearing a little bit, and moved off from the fire to a spot behind the blacksmith.

Soon the other bird was done, but by then the men had eaten their fill . . . except the blacksmith, of course. The big German ate a couple of legs and half a breast, then left the rest of the chicken on his plate. I could tell that the preacher was eyeing the meal, but he didn't come into the blacksmith's range. Despite his hard tongue, he didn't dare.

But a little while later, the man in black passed me by. He bent low at my ear and shook that blackened chicken head like it was some big medicine.

Inside, the bird's dry brain rattled around like a pea in a whistle, and the preacher laughed. "That's all most folks have inside their skulls. You and me know that, don't we, boy?"

The other men rolled up in their blankets. All but the preacher and me. He sat ten feet distant, just short of the fire's glow, toting numbers in the back of his Bible. I stared into the fire's dying flames while Henrietta skirted the withering coals, her naked wings flapping against her fat little body. 'Round and 'round the fire she went, but in a different way than those birds we'd cooked. And all the while she pecked at the piecrust playa, her little beak burying itself in the white dirt time and time again. There was nothing much to eat there, but she kept at it. That's the way she was.

I guess I was, too. My brain kept pecking at the story churning in my head. The old and familiar parts had slipped over my tongue just an hour before, but it was the new parts that were on the boil and wouldn't let go of me. They tumbled around in my head along with the heartbeat of the day—the desert heat that had put all of us on edge, those pole-ax blows the preacher had landed with his tongue and not his fists, the greasy chicken I could barely choke down. I thought long and hard about all that, and the tale I'd told, and the way my heart had thundered when the blacksmith held the preacher's face to the fire.

And I remembered the way the men's eyes had flashed while they heard the different parts my story, the way some of them had looked away and some of them had tried to look deep inside me as the tale hit its peaks and valleys. But most of all I remember the one question the bounty killer had asked—that question about the vampire queen.

The bounty killer's voice was there in my head, and so was his question, and so was the sound of his bloodstained harmonica. Suddenly my gaze seemed to burrow into that dying fire circled with chicken tracks, and down through those glowing coals, and I found myself standing at the edge of Vampire Lake. The sandy shoreline gleamed like powdered bone, and the waves beyond were a dark whisper. Dead men sat on their coffin boxes, their faces bloody from a whipping they'd never expected. Funeral clothes hung in tatters from their cleaved skin. Others were history, dead straight through this time, their black blood spilled by blades and bullets coated with silver.

Beyond the carnage, that narrow bridge stretched across black water. In my vision I traveled across it like a bat on the wing, following an empty mile of hanging planks. I plunged headlong through a burrow of shadow, dropping to roost before the vampire queen.

She waited on a throne of bones, her tick eyes unblinking. She did not seem to notice me. Her black lace dress was tightly gathered around her narrow waist and the layered architecture of her collar bones and ribs. Her naked white feet rested hard on the bent back of the Navajo slave girl who served as her footstool. Now and then, the queen curled her toes and her sharp nails sliced into the girl's back, deep enough to raise a tiny scream. And even so the vampire did not smile. For she was waiting, staring across the water with no expression on her face, waiting with a cigarillo between her cold lips. Tobacco smoke traveled from her dead lungs through tight nostrils, whispering into the air on lifeless breaths.

And I turned away and saw why the vampire queen stared and didn't blink. I saw why she waited. The bounty killer was walking across the bridge, coming toward her. Black water gleamed through gaps in the rotten boards, churning beneath his every step. Albino alligators snapped against the water. Their great armored tails thrashed, casting guillotine ripples in waves that couldn't hold a shadow. Tired of a diet of dead carcasses discarded by the queen and her minions, the reptiles gnashed their teeth for a taste of something vital and alive. The bounty killer's scent drove them wild; it was as if they scented the dead men's shadows that dragged at his heels and thundered in his heart.

And that was something I felt in my gut as much as my head, for nothing in the bounty killer's expression conjured so much as a single word. He was a stone, and the expression he wore made the one on the face of the vampire queen seem as expressive as a Mexican carnival mask.

And then the vision was over, and just that fast. I blinked and I was back on the playa. Henrietta still circled the fire, pecking at the dirt. Shivering, I drew closer to the coals. The cold shadow of midnight had descended, so I wrapped up Henrietta in a Mexican sash one of Rumson's whores had given me and tucked her inside my coat. I put a little more wood on the fire. Suddenly I was hungry, and I slipped the leavings of the second chicken off the blacksmith's plate. I skewered the half-picked carcass and hung it over the fire to warm. Soon enough, the bird sizzled against the flame.

Just as before, the sound brought back memories. When memories came for you, you had to sit with them. I knew that much. If you were the kind who carried them with you, there was no way around it.

I was that kind, but that didn't mean I had to let those memories have their way with me.

I listened to the chicken crackle on the spit.

But I ate it all the same.

For now I was hungry, and the chicken tasted good.

I woke in the middle of the night and rose from my blankets. The moon still hung above, fat and full, and I moved easily beneath its light. I put the wagon between myself and the campfire, following a straight line behind my shadow for a couple hundred feet. Then I undid my drawers and waited for nature to make its call.

"Hey, pretty," the preacher said.

He was behind me, and I jerked as if slapped. Quickly, I buttoned my pants and turned to face him. There he was, maybe fifteen feet away. Laughing a little bit. Walking my way. His shadow spilling before him against the moonlight, that Bible in his hands. He held it up and gave it a tap. And then he started talking.

"I know something about stories, boy. This book is full of 'em. I know what they're good for and what they ain't. I know how to put them to work and which ones to use to get what you want. If you're straight with me, you and I can do that together. With a little training you'd make one hell of a preacher, and I've got the contacts to get you into the biggest churches from here to 'Frisco. The Apache business is a good start, but it's the trip to Vampire Lake that'll hook the suckers like fat trout. Anyway, we get that story fixed up for the holy-roller crowd and the sky is the limit. After that, it'll be champagne and oysters in any town where we want to shed starched collars and kick it up. Of course, I'll take a percentage of everything you make, but that's only fair with what I'd be teaching you and the business I'd push your way."

"It sounds like you've made lots of plans," I said. "You shouldn't."

"What do you mean?"

"You'd better worry about living through tomorrow, is what I think."

The preacher chuckled. "You want to drive a hard bargain, son, well step right up. But save the rest of it for the rubes. You and me both know that yarn of yours is a yard deep and a mile long, but it's the only divot you'll find on this playa. There's no cave out here, especially not one full up with dead men. And that means that bounty killer will never give us one red cent's worth of the loot in that bank book. Fact is, we'll be lucky if he doesn't get a little testy once he figures out he's been had. But we can avoid any ruckus. Hell, we can shake hands on a deal, get out of here tonight if you want."

"You want to partner up with me?"

"Yeah." The preacher smiled. "That's the idea."

"I tell the stories, and you take a percentage?"

"Now you've got it."

"Okay then. But I've got another story to tell you first."

I leaned forward and put a hand on the preacher's shoulder. My face twitched a little as my scarred lips twisted into an expression that passed for a smile. The preacher smiled back and reached out for my other hand.

"This story is kind of short," I said.

"Do tell," he said.

I bucked my knee into the soft spot between his legs. The preacher's breath shot by my ear, and he dropped to the ground like something that drops from the wrong end of a horse.

"You want to remember that one," I said as I turned my back on him. "And you want to remember this: You don't know anything about stories, or what they mean. But tomorrow, you're going to find out."

PART FOUR: THE CAVE

Indio lit a fuse and a minute later a dynamite blast ripped through the cave. Iron bars tore and twisted. Severed heads skewered on metal spikes exploded, and skull shrapnel shattered against the cave walls. Rivets from a lock forged in hell ricocheted up the tunnel like rounds from a Gatling gun, and flying metal tore at us in places that didn't much matter. We spilled blood in fat droplets on the ground while swirling smoke wrapped us like mummies, but we were none of us close to dying so we hurried down the tunnel and toward the wreckage, following the lead of the bounty killer's torch.

The flames tore a patch through the haze and the air cleared around the gunman. Smoke tumbleweeds rolled by us, low and slow, driven by a fetid wind from far below. I caught a familiar black scent on that gray stampede of nothing, and my throat seemed to blister at the taste of it, but I pushed on because the bounty killer was moving fast now, nearing the wrecked gate.

"Every devil in hell must have heard that noise," the Mexican said from behind. "And they'll be coming for us."

"Doesn't matter," the bounty killer said. "They'll hear a lot worse before we're done."

"But they know we're coming," the preacher said. "All that noise, there's no way they won't."

"I'm not here to throw them a surprise party," the gunman said. "I'm here to blaze a trail to hell."

No one said a word to that. It was the cave that did the talking now. The place was like a throat filled up with whispers, and they washed over the big stone gullet and hushed past us on their way to the narrow grave of a mouth above. Thanks to Indio's dynamite, the iron gate that corralled the vampires' corner of the world was now a twisted mess. That gate had once been a hell of a sight, scored with chains the blacksmith could never have cut, and spikes set with dead men's skulls and tattered human hides that flapped like scarecrow warnings in the subterranean breeze. But now the whole thing was so much scrap—just something to get on through, and get on past.

And that's what we did. The bounty killer hurried through the shorn hunk of darkness where the barred door had stood, past broken skulls and those tattered sheets of jerky flesh. Flames from his coal-oil torch licked the cold stone ceiling as we continued our descent. We followed, our torches blazing orange streaks where the bounty killer had passed.

The gunman had parceled out supplies before we entered the cave. He had come prepared and then some, and we all had our own stock. There were the torches, of course, and other things that gleamed in their light—and most everything that gleamed did the job with silver. The bounty killer had his black rattler tied down low, plus a pair of bandoleers crisscrossing his chest that held four other pistols charged with silver bullets. Indio carried a rucksack packed with dynamite, fuses, and a couple boxes of Lucifers, plus a Bowie knife with a silver-dipped blade sheathed on his hip in a rig not unlike the holster that held the gunman's black rattler. A steel can filled with coal oil was strapped to the blacksmith's back. He carried a branding iron in his big right hand, the brand-piece a silver cross cinched in place with a hard twist of barbed-wire. Me, I had Rumson's sawed-off shotgun and the pictures in my head. And the preacher didn't have anything but his Bible, which he held as if he wished it was a gun, or a knife, or a silver-plated pole ax.

But as fast as we were moving, there was no watching any of the men too closely. The air rippled against the flames from our torches, and the sound was like oars cutting water as we traveled lower. Our lungs pumped like bellows as we advanced down that black gullet, moving fast, and lower . . . and lower . . . and lower still. The bounty killer pulled ahead of us, his desert-colored coat like a hunk of the surface world misplaced in its belly. I was glad I'd left Henrietta on the surface, one leg tied to a wagon wheel. If she were here with me, wrapped up in that Mexican sash, she would have been wriggling as if she'd been sucked down and swallowed whole by the hungry earth itself.

But it was only the four of us who'd suffered that fate. Deeper we went, and lower, and deeper still. The tunnel grew narrower. Our torches began to flicker, flames licking low. We stopped to charge them—we had to stop. My heart thundered drumbeats, and the pulse filled my ears, and I could barely hear the talk that went back and forth in the darkness. The bounty killer tossed orders, telling the blacksmith to unstopper his coal-oil can and get busy charging those torches, and mind that oil around the flame because nary a one of us was bacon ready for the skillet and neither were those dynamite sticks Indio carried in his rucksack.

The blacksmith set about his work, slipping that steel tank off his back. Dying blue fire rippled over the torch heads. As darkness closed in, the patchy fungus carpet at our feet began to glow. Then the light from the torches grew dimmer still, and fat round blotches shimmered into view on the cave walls—those glowing mushrooms I remembered.

The preacher's torch went out. Suddenly the mushrooms glowed bigger . . . fuller . . . brighter. They put a filter to the rising wall of eternal night that loomed ahead of us, but it was light you couldn't trust, one that was only fit for ghosts. The walls seemed alive with it, rippling and pulsing in the growing darkness, and—

"Torches," the blacksmith said. "Put heads together."

And we did. Knotted lengths of oak gripped tightly in our hands, thick torch heads meeting between us. Dying flames danced as they joined, and the blacksmith poured coal oil over the top. Blue fire surged, then rose to a sunflower yellow, and soon the torch heads glowed between us like the fat moon that had hung in the desert sky the night before. Light swelled around us, finding the cave walls. The mushrooms seemed to turn their heads to it, and then some of them started moving—

A wind rose deep in the cavern. Just that fast, light filled the cave like whiskey brimming in a full bottle. It found the things that lived between those mushrooms, things that had been trapped alone in the darkness on my last trip to the cave. Since then a fresh crop of mushrooms had filled this corridor—growing along its walls, pillowing its ceiling as they spread—and now the unseen things that had once cursed a wagon party on their way to hell were wedged between them.

Splashes of whiskey light washed those creatures, and every one of them screamed with Satan's own fury. I saw them clearly now, nestling between thriving fungus on guano-caked walls. Some had faces like sick babies, and others looked like wretched old men with walnut skulls that begged to be cracked. I had no idea who they were or what they were. Maybe they were the lost souls of the vampires' victims, and they'd been trapped after death as they tried to make their journey to the surface and the heavens above. They sure enough screamed like creatures worthy of such a horror.

One other thing was sure—the tunnel was full of them. They roiled in their mushroom nests like maggots feeding on a rotting carcass, and their curses put the freeze to my bones and sent the preacher to his knees. He wasn't moving. I wasn't moving. Neither were Indio and the blacksmith. At first I thought the bounty killer was frozen, too. And maybe part of him was . . . but the part that pulled the black rattler wasn't.

The pistol fired six times. Mushrooms flew apart like dropped cakes, sending glowing spatters raining to the floor. Walnut skulls exploded, and dark blood slapped against stone. And then the gunman yanked another pistol from his bandoleer and put it to work. And another. And soon the bounty killer yelled: "Torches! Now!"

And in an instant we were all moving, raking our torches across the walls of the tunnel. Those mushrooms caught fire, caps burning as quickly as crumpled parchment. The screaming heads burrowed between them had no place to go. Fire licked the walls, and the mushrooms flaked to lumped coal and cindered off to smoke. And that smoke swirled around us and snaked deep into our lungs like a crawling thing, and I nearly hit the ground at the stink of it, and it busted off the cinches on everything I saw.

The bounty killer's pistol hissed past me in the haze. There were fangs set in its barrel, and reptile scales on the gunman's hand, and his eyes were yellow with black-pupil slits. The preacher screamed in one corner of the cavern, begging for mercy while walnut-faced devils roped him to a wagon wheel and set it turning over a brimstone spit. Then Indio carved through the smoke wearing armor like King Arthur of old, swinging his silver Bowie knife like Excalibur. And with him came Billy the Kid, loaded for bear, and Aladdin, and forty thieves ready to lay siege to hell.

And then the bounty killer grabbed me and shook me loose from my reverie. He pulled me out of there, into another tunnel. The subterranean wind whipped at me as the gunman sent me stumbling, and I caught that other scent on its breath . . . the scent of Vampire Lake.

We kept moving.

The mushroom smoke worked through me.

Pretty soon it was a bad memory, and we charged into an enormous cavern.

That's when all hell really broke loose.

Part Five: The Lake

I'd seen Apaches do their worst. I'd seen white men match them sin for sin and then go them one better. But I never saw anything like the horror I saw at Vampire Lake.

Indio and the blacksmith worked as a team, moving from coffin to coffin along the shore. One threw open the lid, and the other set to business. The Mexican slashing away like a wild butcher with that silver-bladed Bowie knife, carving until the throbbing pound of flesh in the vampire's chest came a cropper. The blacksmith roasting dead men's flesh with his silver branding-iron cross, planting his big hand over each squirming bloodsucker's heart while the poor devil bucked against the pain of unforgiving metal. And I did my part, too, taking care of any vampires who rushed Indio or the blacksmith. They came at any of us, they got a taste of Rumson's sawed-off shotgun.

I worked steady, blasting dead men with loads of silver and buckshot. I blew the fangs through the backs of their heads and reloaded as quickly as I could. But stack me up against the bounty killer and I was a full bucket of nothing at all. He was a clockwork reaping machine, working that black rattler and those four other pistols he kept holstered in his bandoleers, trading one for the other as the legion of shadowmen rushed him.

You can't truly believe something like that unless you've seen it. For the next few minutes, the shore of that lake was a flurry of black whispers and bloody fireworks. The bounty killer moved forward, dead men rushing him from all directions. Across the sand he went, and through the shadows, slaughtering the dead queen's minions as they tried to slow his progress toward that bridge.

He moved forward without a pause, pistols blazing, leaving nothing but gunsmoke where darkness had reigned. And the bridge was closer now. Behind the bounty killer lay a trail of paintbrush splatters and corpses that had hit the ground without so much as the rattle of a medicine man's spirit pouch. His narrowed lids squinted tight across cat-green eyes, as if the gunman were watching the whole blazing hell-riot from behind an iron mask. And when the killing was over you'd have thought he might have smiled, but he didn't have it in him. Instead he went down on his knees at the foot of the bridge, a litter of dead men behind him, surrounded by nothing except the pistols he dropped in the sand.

He started heaving again, and now it was his own blood that paintbrushed the shore. It was an awful sight—just as it had been back at the saloon. The bounty killer tried to get up, drove his fists down against the sand and pushed for all he was worth, but such was his misery he couldn't make the trip.

"Preacher," he said. "I'm out of steam. Say the words."

I looked around, because I'd lost track of the man in black. He was hiding behind a clutch of rocks further down the shore, crouching like a crab dreading a boiling pot.

"Preacher!" the gunman yelled. "Time to earn your money! Get over here now!"

The preacher hurried toward us, clutching his Bible, his face whiter than the faces of the devils we'd killed. His hands were shaking so badly he could barely open the book, but soon he managed to find the verse he was looking for, and he began to read.

"Louder!" the bounty killer said. "Make those damn words count!"

And the preacher tried. I really think he gave it his all, and maybe for the first time ever. His voice rang out over the bodies of men who'd died, and lived, and died again. It rang across the water. And it filled up the cavern, but at its heart it was a hollow echo. Soon enough, another sound eclipsed it.

It was the bounty killer. He was back on his knees, retching blood again. Red rushed from his mouth in a torrent. I'd never seen that much blood spill out of anything living in my life. It was as if the gullet that traveled from his mouth to his belly was his very own grave-hole of a cave, and men and monsters were doing battle in a cavern beneath his ribs, ripping him up from deep inside, filling every hollow space with blood.

This was the one time the preacher didn't twitch. In spite of the horror, he knelt at the bounty killer's side and kept on reading. His words charged harder now, and he spoke of Lazarus, and Jonah and the whale, and Noah and the flood. He put one hand on the gunman's shoulder and the words spilled out of his mouth as he begged for deliverance. But the bounty killer only cried out, his body bucking hard against the misery convulsing inside him. It looked like the devil had hold of his tongue and was going to yank him inside-out.

With one hand, the gunman pushed the preacher away.

He hawked another mouthful of blood on the ground.

"Damn," he said. "Damn."

Then he got to his feet. I saw it happen, but I still can't believe it. I don't know how the bounty man did it, but I do know it didn't have anything to do with any of the words the preacher had said. No. The gunman made the trip on his own, the same way a man climbs a gallows stairway. He made the journey deliberately, as if every inch of movement cost him more than he had inside, and once he was up he had the look of a man who wasn't going down again unless it was his own idea.

Spatters of blood were thick on his shirt and face. The preacher took one look at him and backed away. Other words rushed from the spindly man's mouth, and they were about money, and the deal he'd made with the bounty killer, and how there might be another bit of business he could try if the gunman cut him in for a bigger piece of the pie—

"I can't believe I spent a night and a day listening to you jabber like a damn parrot in a cage," the bounty killer said. "You're useless. It's time your feathers flew."

The black rattler filled the gunman's hand. None of us had even seen the bounty killer snatch it from the sand. One finger did all the work. Three quick tugs and three bullets hit the preacher square, and the man in black crumpled among the dead vampires.

Bank notes spilled from the preacher's prayer book as he hit the ground. That low subterranean wind caught them.

Some of the money blew into the black water.

Some clung to patches of spilled blood on the shore.

But there wasn't one of us wanted to touch any of it.

We left that money alone, and we did the same with the preacher.

The bounty killer went down to the water and washed his face in the lapping waves. I gathered up his pistols and walked to his side.

"Need any help?" I asked.

He smiled at me, red lines of blood filling the creased spaces between his teeth. "I've killed a lot of men," he said. "They're still inside me. That's why I'm here. I'm full up with dead men, and there ain't nothing that can turn them loose."

"That isn't so bad," I said. "I've got nothing but *alone* inside me. Sometimes I think it would be nice to have some company."

The bounty killer laughed at that, and then he stifled a cough. "You know, it's funny how life sets you on a trail. I first heard about you in a bar down in Tombstone. Brought in a dead horse-thief and collected the bounty from the marshal. After he handed over my bankroll, Virgil Earp told me your story over a beer. The marshal said he heard the tale from a prisoner who'd visited Rumson's place. That was the first I heard of Vampire Lake. First I'd heard of the vampire queen, too.

"Earp said she was a devil woman who could never drink her fill of blood. By then I'd been heaving red for three months, and the dead men trapped inside me were never far from my thoughts. They haunted me night and day. I knew I had to get shed of them. I figured that queen was the only woman who could see me clear of the hell I was living. I figured I'd track her down and let her drink her fill, and maybe if I managed to walk away I'd be a different man. That's when I busted Indio out of jail and came looking for you . . . and that's what brought us down in this hole tonight."

"But if you let her do that . . . If that queen sinks her fangs into you—"

"I let her do it. And I see where that trail takes me."

"But—"

The bounty killer held up a hand. "There's different kinds of death, boy. Different kinds of life, too. I don't want one spent down on my knees, strangling on my own blood. I don't want one that sidles up alongside me when my back is turned, wearing the face of some tinhorn who wants to prove he can gun down hell's worst. No. I want one I can stare square in the eye. One that'll stare right back and not blink so much as an eyelash. That queen sounds like the ticket to me."

"But what if she drinks you dry?"

"That's a chance I'll take. Whatever hand I draw out there on that island is the hand I'll play. A man can't do more than that."

The bounty killer splashed water on his face and wiped it clean with the back of his sleeve. He stood up. I stared at his face, but there was nothing else there. Not a single sign that could put the measure to his words. Just those cat-green eyes, slitted in his skin. He didn't even blink as he unbuckled his gunbelt and handed his sheathed black rattler over to me.

"You keep this for me," he said. "If you never see me again, you can call it yours."

"But what about you?"

The gunman patted the bandoleers crisscrossing his chest. "I still have four pistols here. Whatever's coming, they should see me through."

The bounty killer turned away from me then. Just that fast. Like he was done.

He motioned at the blacksmith. "You. Come here."

The big man came over, still sweating from exertion. The bounty killer pulled out his bank book. He asked us for our names, wrote them on the flyleaf, then scrawled a note and signed it.

"Ain't none of us lawyers, but this'll seal our bargain." He pressed the book into the German's hands. "I'm giving this to you, because I'm sure as hell not giving it to Indio. You'll see this job through for me, won't you?"

The blacksmith nodded. None of us knew what else to say. We stood there a moment, and it seemed it was as quiet as it had ever been in the world. And then the bounty killer turned toward the lake, and he took out his harmonica. He started playing, his eyes trained on that island, and the uneasy music that had raked over the desert two nights before seemed right at home down here in the earth's own belly.

Out there in the darkness, the bridge started to creak and sway as the Navajo slave girl started across it. She was just a slip of a thing, and the bounty killer watched her as she drew nearer.

He slipped his harmonica into his pocket. She walked up to him, barely making a sound.

The girl said a few words in Spanish, and that was it.

The bounty killer turned to Indio.

"What'd she say?" he asked.

"That dead queen wants you," Indio said. "She wants you now."

There was no reason for us to stay down there in the cavern after that, but we did. Even the Navajo slave girl stuck close to the shore. We watched the bounty killer walk over the half-planked bridge, heard the old wood moan beneath his tread. Those albino gators thrashed in the water beneath him, driven wild by the scent of the dead men's tide rushing through his veins.

Once the bounty killer hit the shore of the island, that queen didn't parley long. She rose from her throne of bones, tossed her cigarillo into the water. Next came a couple minutes of jaw, and one long stare between them that said more than any words could. Maybe that was the thing that did the trick. Whatever it was, a second later she attacked the bounty killer like a ravenous spider.

That was what he wanted, after all. Her skinny arms scrabbled over his big shoulders. That black dress hiked up around the shanks of her white legs as she wrapped herself around his hips like a harlot flying the eagle. But it was those teeth of hers that did the work no words could. Her fangs trenched the bounty killer's neck, digging in like coffin nails. We heard him grunt even though we were far across the water, and we watched blood geyser from his wounds. The red shower caught the shadows and matched their darkness inch for inch, and it flowed over the shrouded island and seeped into the ebony water beyond.

They say that queen had drank down a thousand men, but it was a fact she'd never met one like the bounty killer. He was a gusher, filled up with life and filled up with death, and too much of both had spent years stoppered up inside him. He was more than that queen could handle. The wet sound of her feasting sent a horrible echo rippling through the cavern, and soon she began to swell like some monstrous babe that had nursed too long at the devil's own teat. The back of her dress ripped apart, black lace shredding like cobwebs. Still, the queen didn't cut loose of the gunman's pumping artery. She hung on and burrowed in deeper, and still she drank.

Another vein let loose, spewing blood from the bounty killer's neck. Red mist sprayed across the island, and dead men rose in its wake. We'd had no hint that the queen had companions out there, but there must have been one last pack of shadowmen that served as bodyguards. They hurried to her side, fanged maws spreading for bad business, teeth latching onto the bounty killer as if he were a lone steer turned loose in an empty butcher shop.

But he did not fall, and he did not go to his knees. The killer stood there with those things roiling over him. Every bite was like another hole burrowed into a dam. The bounty man's blood was everywhere now. It was a red mist driven by underground winds, spreading over the water. It ran in thick rivulets over his shirt and down his boots and across the island shore, sending scarlet veins rushing into the lapping tide. That was when the gators went crazy. They swam toward the island, thick tails cutting steely wakes, thrashing in the blood-charged water as if the lake itself were on the boil.

And soon that lake wasn't black anymore. It was as red as everything else. On the island, a few of the vampires burst like ticks. Others drank furiously. Still others tried to stopper the bounty killer's wounds with clawed hands, but there was no plugging the dike. Everything on the island was the color of blood, and the red lake was rising all around it.

At last, the queen and her shadowmen broke away from that wild gusher of a man. They started across the bridge, coming our way. The queen was sow-fat now, her tattered lace dress a rag on the shore. She ran naked and white and round like the moon, the bridge swaying under her weight. It was her and her followers above the lake, and those rotten planks between, and a riptide of white gators below. And the whole pack of them were coming our way, with nothing behind them but the bounty killer, dancing alone on that island like a man trapped in a scarlet hurricane.

And the lake was rising higher, blood lapping the bone-colored beach at our feet. The gators and vampires were closer now. One of the albino reptiles charged between a couple rocks and latched onto the blacksmith. The big German went over like a falling redwood, and two more gators hit him like bait on a hook. I saw the bounty killer's bank book tumble from his shorn pocket, watched it disappear into a gator's mouth. Then the blacksmith screamed as the same beast came after him, and he caught a pair of snapping jawbones between his big hands.

I yanked the bounty killer's black rattler, but by the time I got it out of the holster the blacksmith's head was already gone. I fired at the gator anyway. The bullets drilled it straight through. Three of the other beasts set on the dead monster and slaked their hunger. By the time I reloaded the bounty killer's Colt, Indio had shoved me backward. He had his rucksack open, and dynamite sticks filled his hand.

He scratched a Lucifer alive and put those sticks to work.

The bridge exploded in a million toothpicks.

The queen and her men did just about the same.

Blood was everywhere, but the gators didn't mind.

They were hungry.

They ate.

PART SIX: RUMSON'S SALOON

We came up out of that empty grave hole in the desert. Indio and I did, plus the Navajo girl. Double-quick, we grabbed that crate of dynamite out of the wagon and took it into the cave. Indio set a couple charges near the twisted iron gate, set another couple further down the tunnel, then ran fuses through the burrow that led to the surface. He put a match to them and we slapped leather for safety, Indio on horseback and me with the Navajo girl in the wagon.

Henrietta was with us, too. In the ruckus I almost forgot to untie the rawhide cord that held her to the wagon wheel, but I remembered at the last moment. We were less than a mile away when thunder exploded in the earth's belly. A huge cloud coughed out of the ground like the wave of blood that had risen from the lake. Only this wave caught us, then overtook us, then set us riding even faster with bandanas wrapped around our faces. Me in the wagon slapping the ribbons while Henrietta squawked from her hatbox nest beneath the seat, and the Navajo girl holding on for dear life at my side, and Indio in front of us giving his horse plenty of spur.

In other words, we didn't look back. What was behind us had been blown to hell and gone, and we knew it. The deal was finished, and in more ways than one. Without the bounty killer's bank book there was nothing between Indio and me at all anymore. That book was in some dead gator's belly down there in hell, and we'd never touch it in this lifetime. So there was nothing to fight over, and nothing to celebrate. We parted ways without much more than a handshake, and Indio headed south for Mexico.

The Navajo girl and I camped in the desert that night. When I awoke the next morning, she was gone. So I came back to town. There really wasn't anywhere else to go. After a few weeks I discovered Rumson had written a will, leaving his saloon to the whores. They decided to go into another business—or the same business, but minus the beds upstairs—and they hired me. So here I am, standing behind the bar where Rumson used to stand.

Still minus half a face, of course.

But plus another story.

Besides the whiskey, that's what we sell around here. I tend this bar night after night and tell it, and then I sleep the wee hours through and get up in the morning and do it all over again.

And some nights, even as the words spill out of my mouth, I think about the bounty killer. A man like that, you want to imagine there was something else in him. Something that could excuse the killing, and his hard ways, and the things that brought him to the point where he'd ride into a town and do the horrible things he did, then go down in a hole in the ground and do worse. And maybe there was something, and maybe there wasn't. Maybe there was only a kind of desire. The kind you can't really know until death starts to push the door closed behind you. The kind that pushes at you when you put the spurs to a horse and ride it hard toward a place you've never been.

Some nights I think it was one way, and some nights I think it might have been another. And maybe that's what keeps me here, night after night, telling the story. The wondering, I mean. Maybe that's why I do what I do. I don't rightly know. I can't rightly say.

But that's my story, stranger. You can believe it or not. If you want to know more, come back tomorrow morning. We've got a little museum out back. You can see the bounty killer's black rattler of a pistol. You can look at Rumson's sawed-off shotgun, too. There's a glass case with Indio's shackles, and a letter from the warden up at Yuma which testifies to the fact that they're real. In one corner there's the hatbox I took from the general store on the night Rumson died, and most afternoons you'll find Henrietta sleeping in it. She's old now, doesn't get around much. You can even buy a book I wrote where I set down the story straight. It's illustrated by a fellow from Philadelphia who does drawings for all the Eastern magazines. I'll even sign it for you if you want.

But the story you heard tonight, that one's cash on the barrelhead.

Now pay up and hit the trail, amigo.

We're closed for the night.

*Whatever lived in the teapot, it was not more difficult to believe in
than the blighted landscape above their trenches. Something bright
and shining ought not be more impossible than that . . .*

LORD DUNSANY'S TEAPOT

Naomi Novik

The accidental harmony of the trenches during the war produced,
sometimes, odd acquaintances. It was impossible not to feel a certain
kinship with a man having lain huddled and nameless in the dirt beside
him for hours, sharing the dubious comfort of a woolen scarf pressed over
the mouth and nose while eyes streamed, stinging, and gunpowder bursts
from time to time illuminated the crawling smoke in colors: did it have a
greenish cast? And between the moments of fireworks, whispering to one
another too low and too hoarsely to hear even unconsciously the accents of
the barn or the gutter or the halls of the public school.

What became remarkable about Russell, in the trenches, was his smile: or
rather that he smiled, with death walking overhead like the tread of heavy
boots on a wooden floor above a cellar. Not a wild or wandering smile, reckless
and ready to meet the end, or a trembling rictus; an ordinary smile to go with
the whispered, "Another one coming, I think," as if speaking of a cricket ball
instead of an incendiary; only friendly, with nothing to remark upon.

The trench had scarcely been dug. Dirt shook loose down upon them,
until they might have been part of the earth, and when the all-clear sounded
at last out of a long silence, they stood up still equals under a coat of mud,
until Russell bent down and picked up the shovel, discarded, and they were
again officer and man.

But this came too late: Edward trudged back with him, side by side, to
the more populated regions of the labyrinth, still talking, and when they
had reached Russell's bivouac he looked at Edward and said, "Would you
have a cup of tea?"

The taste of the smoke was still thick on Edward's tongue, in his throat,
and the night had curled up like a tiger and gone to sleep around them. They
sat on Russell's cot while the kettle boiled, and he poured the hot water into

a fat old teapot made of iron, knobby, over the cheap and bitter tea leaves from the ration. Then he set it on the little campstool and watched it steep, a thin thread of steam climbing out of the spout and dancing around itself in the cold air.

The rest of his company were sleeping, but Edward noticed their cots were placed away, as much as they could be in such a confined space; Russell had a little room around his. He looked at Russell: under the smudges and dirt, weathering; not a young face. The nose was a little crooked and so was the mouth, and the hair brushed over the forehead was sandy-brown and wispy in a vicarish way, with several years of thinning gone.

"A kindness to the old-timer, I suppose," Russell said. "Been here—five years now, or near enough. So they don't ask me to shift around."

"They haven't made you lance-jack," Edward said, the words coming out before he could consider all the reasons a man might not have received promotion, of which he would not care to speak.

"I couldn't," Russell said, apologetic. "Who am I, to be sending off other fellows, and treating them sharp if they don't?"

"Their corporal, or their sergeant," Edward said, a little impatient with the objection, "going in with them, not hanging back."

"O, well," Russell said, still looking at the teapot. "It's not the same for me to go."

He poured out the tea, and offered some shavings off a small brown block of sugar. Edward drank: strong and bittersweet, somehow better than the usual. The teapot was homely and common. Russell laid a hand on its side as if it were precious, and said it had come to him from an old sailor, coming home at last to rest from traveling.

"Do you ever wonder, are there wars under the sea?" Russell said. His eyes were gone distant. "If all those serpents and the kraken down there, or some other things we haven't names for, go to battle over the ships that have sunk, and all their treasure?"

"And mer-men dive down among them, to be counted brave," Edward said, softly, not to disturb the image that had built clear in his mind: the great writhing beasts, tangled masses striving against one another in the endless cold dark depths, over broken ships and golden hoards, spilled upon the sand, trying to catch the faintest gleam of light. "To snatch some jewel to carry back, for a courting-gift or an heirloom of their house."

Russell nodded, as if to a commonplace remark. "I suppose it's how they choose their lords," he said, "the ones that go down and come back: and their king came up from the dark once with a crown—beautiful thing, rubies and pearls like eggs, in gold."

The tea grew cold before they finished building the undersea court, turn and turn about, in low voices barely above the nasal breathing of the men around them.

It skirted the lines of fraternization, certainly; but it could not have been called deliberate. There was always some duty or excuse which brought them into one another's company to begin with, and at no regular interval. Of course, even granting this, there was no denying it would have been more appropriate for Edward to refuse the invitation, or for Russell not to have made it in the first place. Yet somehow each time tea was offered, and accepted.

The hour was always late, and if Russell's fellows had doubts about his company, they never raised their heads from their cots to express it either by word or look. Russell made the tea, and began the storytelling, and Edward cobbled together castles with him shaped of steam and fancy, drifting upwards and away from the trenches.

He would walk back to his own cot afterwards still warm through and lightened. He had come to do his duty, and he would do it, but there was something so much *vaster* and more dreadful than he had expected in the wanton waste upon the fields, in the smothered silence of the trenches: all of them already in the grave and merely awaiting a final confirmation. But Russell was still alive, so Edward might be as well. It was worth a little skirting of regulations.

He only half-heard Russell's battalion mentioned in the staff meeting, with one corner of his preoccupied mind; afterwards he looked at the assignment: a push to try and open a new trench, advancing the line.

It was no more than might be and would be asked of any man, eventually; it was no excuse to go by the bivouac that night with a tin of his own tea, all the more precious because Beatrice somehow managed to arrange for it to win through to him, through some perhaps questionable back channel. Russell said nothing of the assignment, though Edward could read the knowledge of it around them: for once not all the other men were sleeping, a few curled protectively around their scratching hands, writing letters in their cots.

"Well, that's a proper cup," Russell said softly, as the smell climbed out of the teapot, fragrant and fragile. The brew when he poured it was clear amber-gold, and made Edward think of peaches hanging in a garden of shining fruit-heavy trees, a great sighing breath of wind stirring all the branches to a shake.

For once Russell did not speak as they drank the tea. One after another the men around them put down their pens and went to sleep. The peaches swung from the branches, very clear and golden in Edward's mind. He kept his hands close around his cup.

"That's stirred him a bit, it has," Russell said, peering under the lid of the teapot; he poured in some more water. For a moment, Edward thought he saw mountains, too, beyond the orchard-garden: green-furred peaks with clouds clinging to their sides like loose eiderdown. A great wave of homesickness struck him very nearly like a blow, though he had never seen such mountains. He looked at Russell, wondering.

"It'll be all right, you know," Russell said.

"Of course," Edward said: the only thing that could be said, prosaic and untruthful; the words tasted sour in his mouth after the clean taste of the tea.

"No, what I mean is, it'll be all right," Russell said. He rubbed a hand over the teapot. "I don't like to say, because the fellows don't understand, but you see him too; or at least as much of him as I do."

"Him," Edward repeated.

"I don't know his name," Russell said thoughtfully. "I've never managed to find out; I don't know that he hears us at all, or thinks of us. I suppose if he ever woke up, he might be right annoyed with us, sitting here drinking up his dreams. But he never has."

It was not their usual storytelling, but something with the uncomfortable savor of truth. Edward felt as though he had caught a glimpse from the corner of his eye of something too vast to be looked at directly or all at once: a tail shining silver-green sliding through the trees, a great green eye like oceans peering back with drowsy curiosity. "But he's not *in* there," he said involuntarily.

Russell shrugged expressively. He lifted off the lid and showed Edward: a lump fixed to the bottom of the pot, smooth white glimmering like pearl, irregular yet beautiful even with the swollen tea-leaves like kelp strewn over and around it.

He put the lid back on, and poured out the rest of the pot. "So it's all right," he said. "I'll be all right, while I have him. But you see why I couldn't send other fellows out. Not while I'm safe from all this, and they aren't."

An old and battered teapot made talisman of safety, inhabited by some mystical guardian: it ought to have provoked the same awkward sensation as speaking to an earnest Spiritualist, or an excessively devoted missionary; it called for polite agreement and withdrawal. "Thank you," Edward said instead; he was comforted, and glad to be so.

Whatever virtue lived there in the pitted iron, it was not more difficult to believe in than the blighted landscape above their trenches, the coils of hungry barbed black wire snaking upon the ground, and the creeping poisonous smoke that covered the endless bodies of the dead. Something bright and shining ought not be more impossible than that; and even if it was not strong enough to stand against all devastation, there was pleasure in thinking one life might be spared by its power.

They brought him the teapot three days later: Russell had no next of kin with a greater claim. Edward thanked them and left the teapot in a corner of his bag, and did not take it out again. Many men he knew had died, comrades in arms, friends; but Russell lying on the spiked and poisoned ground, breath seared and blood draining, hurt the worse for seeming wrong.

Edward dreamed of sitting with Russell: the dead man's skin clammy gray, blood streaking the earthenware where his fingers cupped it, where his lips touched the rim, and floating over the surface of the tea. "Well, and I was safe, like I said," Russell said. Edward shuddered out of the dream, and washed his face in the cold water in his jug; there were flakes of ice on the surface.

He went forward himself, twice, and was not killed; he shot several men, and sent others to die. There was a commendation at one point. He accepted it without any sense of pride. In the evenings, he played at cards with a handful of other officers, where they talked desultorily of plans, and the weather, and a few of the more crude of conquests either real or hoped-for in the French villages behind the lines. His letters to Beatrice grew shorter. His supply of words seemed to have leached away into the dirt.

His own teapot was on his small burner to keep warm when the air-raid sounded; an hour later after the all-clear it was a smoking cinder, the smell so very much like the acrid bite of gas that he flung it as far up over the edge of the trench as he could manage, to get it away, and took out the other teapot to make a fresh cup and wash away the taste.

And it was only a teapot: squat and unlovely except for the smooth pearlescent lump inside, some accident of its casting. He put in the leaves and poured the water from the kettle. He was no longer angry with himself for believing, only distantly amused, remembering; and sorry with that same distance for Russell, who had swallowed illusions for comfort.

He poured his cup and raised it and drank without stopping to inhale the scent or to think of home; and the pain startled him for being so vivid. He worked his mouth as though he had only burned his tongue and not some unprepared and numbed corner of his self. He found himself staring blindly at the small friendly blue flame beneath the teapot. The color was the same as a flower that grew only on the slopes of a valley on the other side of the world where no man had ever walked, which a bird with white feathers picked to line its nest, so the young when they were born were soft gray and tinted blue, with pale yellow beaks held wide to call for food in voices that chimed like bells.

The ringing in his ears from the sirens went quiet. He understood Russell then finally; and wept a little, without putting down the cup. He held it between his hands while the heat but not the scent faded, and sipped peace as long as it lasted.

He was always excited on days the days he saw it—unhealthily excited, he was sure—but terrified of the phenomenon only once. A single time he was deeply terrified, and fled as if devils were after him . . .

THE DUNE

Stephen King

As the judge climbs into the kayak beneath a bright morning sky, a slow and clumsy process that takes him almost five minutes, he reflects that an old man's body is nothing but a sack filled with aches and indignities. Eighty years ago, when he was ten, he jumped into a wooden canoe and cast off, with no bulky life jacket, no worries, and certainly with no pee dribbling into his underwear. Every trip out to the little unnamed island began with a great and uneasy excitement. Now there is only unease. And pain that seems centered deep in his guts and radiates everywhere. But he still makes the trip. Many things have lost their allure in these shadowy later years—most things, really—but not the dune on the far side of the island. Never the dune.

In the early days of his exploration, he expected the dune to be gone after every big storm, and following the 1944 hurricane that sank the USS *Raleigh* off Siesta Key, he was sure it would be. But when the skies cleared, the island was still there. So was the dune, although the hundred-mile-an-hour winds should have blown all the sand away, leaving only the bare rocks. Over the years he has debated back and forth about whether the magic is in him or in the dune. Perhaps it's both, but surely most of it is in the dune.

Since 1932, he has crossed this short stretch of water thousands of times. Usually there's nothing but rocks and bushes and sand; sometimes there is something else.

Settled in the kayak at last, he paddles slowly from the beach to the island, his frizz of white hair blowing around his mostly bald skull. A few turkey buzzards wheel overhead, making their ugly conversation. Once he was the son of the richest man on the Florida Gulf coast, then he was a lawyer, then he was a judge on the Pinellas County Circuit, then he was appointed to the State Supreme Court. There was talk, during the Reagan years, of a nomination to the United States Supreme Court, but that never happened, and a week after the idiot Clinton became president, Judge Harvey Beecher—just Judge to his many acquaintances (he has no real friends) in Sarasota, Osprey, Nokomis, and Venice—retired. Hell, he never liked Tallahassee, anyway. It's cold up there.

Also, it's too far from the island, and its peculiar dune. On these early-morning kayak trips, paddling the short distance on smooth water, he's willing to admit that he's addicted to it. But who wouldn't be addicted to a thing like this?

On the rocky east side, a gnarled bush juts from the split in a guano-splattered rock. This is where he ties up, and he's always careful with the knot. It wouldn't do to be stranded out here. His father's estate (that's how he still thinks of it, although the elder Beecher has been gone for forty years now) covers almost two miles of prime Gulf-front property, the main house is far inland, on the Sarasota Bayside, and there would be no one to hear him yelling. Tommy Curtis, the caretaker, might notice him gone and come looking; more likely, he would just assume the judge was locked up in his study, where he often spends whole days, supposedly working on his memoirs.

Once upon a time Mrs. Riley might have become nervous if he didn't come out of the study for lunch, but now he hardly ever eats at noon (she calls him "nothing but a stuffed string," but never to his face). There's no other staff, and both Curtis and Riley know he can be cross when he's interrupted. Not that there's really much to interrupt; he hasn't added so much as a line to the memoirs in two years, and in his heart he knows they will never be finished. The unfinished recollections of a Florida judge? No great loss there. The one story he could write is the one he never will. The judge wants no talk at his funeral about how, in his last years, a previously fine intellect was corrupted by senility.

He's even slower getting out of the kayak than he was getting in, and turns turtle once, wetting his shirt and trousers in the little waves that run up the gravelly shingle. Beecher is not discommoded. It isn't the first time he's fallen, and there's no one to see him. He supposes it's unwise to continue these trips at his age, even though the island is so close to the mainland, but stopping isn't an option. An addict is an addict is an addict.

Beecher struggles to his feet and clutches his belly until the last of the pain subsides. He brushes sand and shells from his trousers, double-checks his mooring rope, then spots one of the turkey buzzards perched on the island's largest rock, peering down at him.

"Hi!" he shouts in the voice he now hates—cracked and wavering, the voice of a fishwife. "Hi, you bugger! Get on about your business."

After a brief rustle of its raggedy wings, the turkey buzzard sits right where it is. Its beady eyes seem to say, *But, Judge—today you are my business.*

Beecher stoops, picks up a larger shell and shies it at the bird. This time it does fly away, the sound of its wings like rippling cloth. It soars across the short stretch of water and lands on his dock. *Still,* the judge thinks, *a bad omen.* He remembers a fellow on the Florida State Patrol telling him once that turkey buzzards didn't just know where carrion was; they also knew where carrion would be.

"I can't tell you," the patrolman said, "how many times I've seen those ugly bastards circling a spot on the Tamiami where there's a fatal wreck a day or two later. Sounds crazy, I know, but just about any Florida road cop will tell you the same."

There are almost always turkey buzzards out here on the little no-name island. He supposes it smells like death to them, and why not? What else?

The judge sets off on the little path he has beaten over the years. He will check the dune on the other side, where the sand is beach-fine instead of stony and shelly, and then he will return to the kayak and drink his little jug of cold tea. He may doze awhile in the morning sun (he dozes often these days, supposes most nonagenarians do), and when he wakes (if he wakes), he'll make the return trip. He tells himself that the dune will be just a smooth blank upslope of sand, as it is most days, but he knows better.

That damned buzzard knew better, too.

He spends a long time on the sandy side, with his age-warped fingers clasped in a knot behind him. His back aches, his shoulders ache, his hips ache, his knees ache; most of all, his gut aches. But he pays these things no mind. Perhaps later, but not now.

He looks at the dune, and what is written there.

Anthony Wayland arrives at Belcher's Pelican Point estate bang on 7:00 p.m., just as promised. One thing the Judge has always appreciated—both in the courtroom and out of it—is punctuality, and the boy is punctual. He reminds himself never to call Wayland *boy* to his face (although, this being the South, *son* is okay). Wayland wouldn't understand that, when you're ninety, any fellow under the age of forty looks like a boy.

"Thank you for coming," the judge says, ushering Wayland into his study. It's just the two of them; Curtis and Mrs. Riley have long since gone to their homes in Nokomis Village. "You brought the necessary document?"

"Yes, indeed, Judge," Wayland says. He opens his attorney's briefcase and removes a thick document bound by a large steel clip. The pages aren't vellum, as they would have been in the old days, but they are rich and heavy just the same. At the top of the first, in forbidding Gothic type (what the judge has always thought of as graveyard type), are the words 𝕷𝖆𝖘𝖙 𝖂𝖎𝖑𝖑 𝖆𝖓𝖉 𝕿𝖊𝖘𝖙𝖆𝖒𝖊𝖓𝖙 𝖔𝖋 𝕳𝖆𝖗𝖛𝖊𝖞 𝕷. 𝕭𝖊𝖊𝖈𝖍𝖊𝖗.

"You know, I'm kind of surprised you didn't draft this document yourself. You've probably forgotten more Florida probate law than I've ever learned."

"That might be true," the judge says in his driest tone. "At my age, folks tend to forget a great deal."

Wayland flushes to the roots of his hair. "I didn't mean—"

"I know what you mean, son," the judge says. "No offense taken. Not a mite. But since you ask . . . you know that old saying about how a man who serves as his own lawyer has a fool for a client?"

Wayland grins. "Heard it and used it plenty of times when I'm wearing my public defender hat and some sad-sack wife-abuser or hit-and-runner tells me he's going to go the DIY route in court."

"I'm sure you have, but here's the other half: a lawyer who serves as his own lawyer has a *great* fool for a client. Goes for criminal, civil, and probate law. So, shall we get down to business? Time is short." This is something he means in more ways than one.

They get down to business. Mrs. Riley has left decaf coffee, which Wayland rejects in favor of a Co'-Cola. He makes copious notes as the Judge dictates the changes in his dry courtroom voice, adjusting old bequests and adding new ones. The major new one—four million dollars—is to the Sarasota County Beach and Wildlife Preservation Society. In order to qualify, they must successfully petition the State Legislature to have a certain island just off the coast of Pelican Point declared forever wild.

"They won't have a problem getting that done," the Judge says. "You can handle the legal for them yourself. I'd prefer pro bono, but of course that's up to you. One trip to Tallahassee should do it. It's a little spit of a thing, nothing growing there but a few bushes. Governor Scott and his Tea Party cronies will be delighted."

"Why's that, Judge?"

"Because the next time Beach and Preservation comes to them, begging money, they can say, 'Didn't old Judge Beecher just give you four million? Get out of here, and don't let the door hit you in the ass on your way out!'"

Wayland agrees that this is probably just how it will go—Scott and his friends are all for giving if they're not the ones doing it—and the two men move on to the smaller bequests.

"Once I get a clean draft, we'll need two witnesses and a notary," Wayland says when they've finished.

"I'll get all that done with this draft here, just to be safe," the Judge says. "If anything happens to me in the interim, it should stand up. There's no one to contest it; I've outlived them all."

"A wise precaution, judge. It would be good to take care of it tonight. I don't suppose your caretaker and housekeeper—"

"Won't be back until eight tomorrow," Beecher says. "But I'll make it the first order of business. Harry Staines on Vamo Road's a notary and he'll be glad to come over before he goes in to his office. He owes me a favor or six. You give that document to me, son. I'll lock it in my safe."

"I ought to at least make a . . . " Wayland looks at the gnarled, outstretched hand and trails off. When a State Supreme Court judge (even a retired one) holds out his hand, demurrals must cease. What the hell, it's only an annotated draft, anyway, soon to be replaced by a clean version. He passes the unsigned will over and watches as Beecher rises (painfully) and swings a picture of the Florida Everglades out on a hidden hinge. The judge enters the correct combination, making no attempt to hide the touchpad from view, and deposits the will on top of what looks to Wayland like a large and untidy heap of cash. Yikes.

"There!" Beecher says. "All done and buttoned up! Except for the signing part, that is. How about a drink to celebrate? I have some fine single malt Scotch."

"Well . . . I guess one wouldn't hurt."

"It never hurt me when I was your age, although it does now, so you'll have to pardon me for not joining you. Decaf coffee and a little sweet tea are the strongest drinks I take these days. Ice?"

Wayland holds up two fingers, and Beecher adds two cubes to the drink with the slow ceremony of old age. Wayland takes a sip and high color immediately dashes into his cheeks. It is the flush, Judge Beecher thinks, of a man who enjoys his tipple. As Wayland sets his glass down he says, "Do you mind if I ask what the hurry is? You're all right, I take it?"

The judge doubts if young Wayland takes it that way at all. He's not blind.

"A-country fair," he says, see-sawing one hand in the air and sitting down with a grunt and a wince. Then, after consideration, he says, "Do you really want to know what the hurry is?"

Wayland considers the question, and Beecher likes him for that. Then he nods.

"It has to do with that island we took care of just now. Probably never even noticed it, have you?"

"Can't say that I have."

"Most people don't. It barely sticks out of the water. The sea turtles don't even bother with that old island. Yet it's special. Did you know my grandfather fought in the Spanish-American War?"

"No, sir, I did not." Wayland speaks with exaggerated respect, and Beecher knows the boy believes his mind is wandering. The boy is wrong. Beecher's mind has never been clearer, and now that he's begun, he finds that he wants to tell this story at least once, before . . .

Well, before.

"Yes. There's a photograph of him standing on top of San Juan Hill. It's around here someplace. Grampy claimed to have fought in the Civil War as well, but my research—for my memoirs, you understand—proved conclusively that he couldn't have. He would have been a mere child, if born at all. But he was quite the fanciful gentleman, and he had a way of making me believe the wildest tales. Why would I not? I was only a child, not long from believing in Kris Kringle and the tooth fairy."

"Was he a lawyer, like you and your father?"

"No, son, he was a thief. The original Light-Finger Harry. Anything that wasn't nailed down. Only like most thieves who don't get caught—our current governor might be a case in point—he called himself a businessman. His chief business—and chief thievery—was land. He bought bug- and gator-infested Florida acreage cheap and sold it dear to folks who must have been as gullible as I was as a child. Balzac once said, 'Behind every great fortune there is a great crime.' That's certainly true of the Beecher family, and please remember that you're my lawyer. Anything I say to you must be held in confidence."

"Yes, Judge." Wayland takes another sip of his drink. It is by far the finest Scotch he has ever drunk.

"Grampy Beecher was the one who pointed that island out to me. I was ten. He had care of me for the day, and I suppose he wanted some peace and quiet. Or maybe what he wanted was a bit noisier. There was a pretty housemaid, and he may have been in hopes of investigating beneath her petticoats. So he told me that Edward Teach—better known as Blackbeard—had supposedly buried a great treasure out there. 'Nobody's ever found it, Havie,' he said— Havie's what he called me—'but you might be the one. A fortune in jewels and gold doubloons.' You'll know what I did next."

"I suppose you went out there and left your grandfather to cheer up the maid."

The judge nods, smiling. "I took the old wooden canoe we had tied up to the dock. Went like my hair was on fire and my tail feathers were catching. Didn't take but five minutes to paddle out there. Takes me three times as long these days, and that's if the water's smooth. The island's all rock and brush on the landward side, but there's a dune of fine beach sand on the Gulf side. It never goes away. In the eighty years I've been going out there, it never seems to change. At least not geographically."

"Didn't find any treasure, I suppose?"

"I did, in a way, but it wasn't jewels and gold. It was a name, written in the sand of that dune. As if with a stick, you know, only I didn't see any stick. The letters were drawn deep, and the sun struck shadows into them, making them stand out. Almost as if they were floating."

"What was the name, Judge?"

"I think you have to see it written to understand."

The judge takes a sheet of paper from the top drawer of his desk, prints carefully, then turns the paper around so Wayland can read it: ROBIE LADOOSH.

"All right ! . . . " Wayland says cautiously.

"On any other day, I would have gone treasure-hunting with this very boy, because he was my best friend, and you know how boys are when they're best friends."

"Joined at the hip," Wayland says, smiling.

"Tight as a new key in a new lock," Wayland agrees. "But it was summer and he'd gone off with his parents to visit his mama's people in Virginia or Maryland or some such northern clime. So I was on my own. But attend me closely, counselor. The boy's *actual* name was Robert LaDoucette."

Again Wayland says, "All right . . . " The judge thinks that sort of leading drawl could become annoying over time, but it isn't a thing he'll ever have to actually find out, so he lets it go.

"He was my best friend and I was his, but there was a whole gang of boys we ran around with, and everyone called him Robbie LaDoosh. You follow?"

"I guess," Wayland says, but the Judge can see he doesn't. That's understandable; Beecher has had a lot more time to think about these things. Often on sleepless nights.

"Remember that I was ten. If I had been asked to spell my friend's nickname, I would have done it just this way." He taps ROBIE LADOOSH.

Speaking almost to himself, he adds: "So some of the magic comes from me. It *must* come from me. The question is, how much?"

"You're saying you didn't write that name in the sand?"

"No. I thought I made that clear."

"One of your other friends, then?"

"They were all from Nokomis Village, and didn't even know about that island. We never would have paddled out to such an uninteresting little rock on our own. Robbie knew it was there, he was also from the Point, but he was hundreds of miles north."

"All right . . . "

"My chum Robbie never came back from that vacation. We got word a week or so later that he'd taken a fall while out horseback riding. He broke his neck. Killed instantly. His parents were heartbroken. So was I, of course."

There is silence while Wayland considers this. While they both consider it. Somewhere far off, a helicopter beats at the sky over the Gulf. The DEA looking for drug runners, the judge supposes. He hears them every night. It's the modern age, and in some ways—in many—he'll be glad to be shed of it.

At last Wayland says, "Are you saying what I think you're saying?"

"Well, I don't know," the judge says. "What do you think I'm saying?"

But Anthony Wayland is a lawyer, and refusing to be drawn in is an ingrained habit with him. "Did you tell your grandfather?"

"On the day the telegram about Robbie came, he wasn't there to tell. He never stayed in one place for long. We didn't see him again for six months or more. No, I kept it to myself. And like Mary after she gave birth to Jesus, I considered these things in my heart."

"And what conclusion did you draw?"

"I kept canoeing out to that island to look at the dune, and that should answer your question. There was nothing . . . and nothing . . . and nothing. I guess I was on the verge of forgetting all about it, but then I went out one afternoon after school and there was another name written in the sand. *Printed* in the sand, to be courtroom-exact. No sign of a stick that time, either, although I suppose a stick could have been thrown into the water. This time the name was Peter Alderson. It meant nothing to me until a few days later. It was my chore to go out to the end of the road and get the paper, and it was my habit to scan the front page while I walked back up the drive—which, as you know from driving it yourself, is a good quarter-mile long. In the summer I'd also check on how the Washington Senators had done, because back then they were as close to a Southern team as we had.

"This particular day, a headline on the bottom of the front page caught my eye: WINDOW WASHER KILLED IN TRAGIC FALL. The poor guy was doing the third-floor windows of the Sarasota Public Library when the scaffolding he was standing on gave way. His name was Peter Alderson."

The judge can see from Wayland's face that he believes this is either a prank or some sort of elaborate fantasy the Judge is spinning out. He can also see that Wayland is enjoying his drink, and when the Judge moves to top it up, Wayland doesn't say no. And, really, the young man's belief or disbelief is beside the point. It's just such a luxury to tell it.

"Maybe you see why I go back and forth in my mind about where the magic lies," Beecher says. "I *knew* Robbie, and the misspelling of his name was my misspelling. But I didn't know this window washer from Adam. In any case, that's when the dune really started to get a hold on me. I began going out every day when I was here, a habit that's continued into my very old age. I respect the place, I fear the place, but most of all, I'm addicted to the place.

"Over the years, many names have appeared on that dune, and the people the names belong to always die. Sometimes it's within the week, sometimes it's two, but it's never more than a month. Some have been people I knew, and if it's by a nickname I knew them, it's the nickname I see. One day in 1940 I paddled out there and saw GRAMPY BEECHER drawn into the sand. He died in Key West three days later. Heart attack."

With the air of someone humoring a man who is mentally unbalanced but not actually dangerous, Wayland asks, "Did you never try to interfere with this . . . this process? Call your grandfather, for instance, and tell him to see a doctor?"

Beecher shakes his head. "I didn't know it was a heart attack until we got word from the Monroe County medical examiner, did I? It could have been an accident, or even a murder. Certainly there were people who had reasons to hate my grandfather; his dealings were not of the purest sort."

"Still . . . he was your grandfather and all . . . "

"The truth, counselor, is that I was afraid. I felt—I still feel—as if there on that island, there's a hatch that's come ajar. On this side is what we're pleased to call 'the real world.' On the other is all the machinery of the universe, running at top speed. Only a fool would stick his hand into such machinery in an attempt to stop it."

"Judge Beecher, if you want your paperwork to sail through probate, I'd keep quiet about all this. You might think there's no one to contest your will, but when large amounts of money are at stake, third and fourth cousins have a way of coming out of the woodwork. And you know the criterion: 'Being of sound mind and body.'"

"I've kept it to myself for eighty years," Beecher says, and in his voice Wayland can hear *objection overruled*. "Never a word until now. And I'm sure you won't talk."

"Of course not," Wayland says.

"I was always excited on days when names appeared in the sand—unhealthily excited, I'm sure—but terrified of the phenomenon only once.

That single time I was deeply terrified, and fled back to the Point in my canoe as if devils were after me. Shall I tell you?"

"Please." Wayland lifts his drink and sips. Why not? Billable hours are, after all, billable hours.

"It was 1959. I was still on the Point. I've always lived here except for the years in Tallahassee, and it's better not to speak of them although I now think part of the hate I felt for that provincial backwater of a town, perhaps even most of it, was simply a masked longing for the island, and the dune. I kept wondering what I was missing, you see. *Who* I was missing. Being able to read obituaries in advance gives a man an extraordinary sense of power. Perhaps you find that unlovely. The truth often is.

"So. 1959. Harvey Beecher lawyering in Sarasota and living at Pelican Point. If it wasn't pouring down rain when I got home, I'd always change into old clothes and paddle out to the island for a look-see before supper. On this particular day I'd been kept at the office late, and by the time I'd gotten out to the island, tied up, and walked over to the dune side, the sun was going down big and red, as it so often does over the Gulf. What I saw stunned me. I literally could not move.

"There wasn't just one name written in the sand that evening but many, and in that red sunset light they looked as if they had been written in blood. They were crammed together, they wove in and out, they were written over and above and up and down. The whole length and breadth of the dune was covered with a tapestry of names. The ones down by the water had been half erased."

Wayland looks awed in spite of his core disbelief.

"I think I screamed. I can't remember for sure, but yes, I think so. What I *do* remember is breaking the paralysis and running away as fast as I could, down the path to where my canoe was tied up. It seemed to take me forever to unpluck the knot, and when I did, I pushed the canoe out into the water before I climbed in. I was soaked from head to toe, and it's a wonder I didn't tip over. Although in those days I could have easily swum to shore, pushing the canoe ahead of me. Not these days; if I tipped my kayak over now, that would be all she wrote."

"Then I suggest you stay onshore, at least until your will is signed, witnessed, and notarized."

Judge Beecher gives the young man a wintry smile. "You needn't worry about that, son," he says. He looks toward the window, and the Gulf beyond. His face is long and thoughtful. "Those names . . . I can see them yet, jostling each other for place on that blood-red dune. Two days later, a TWA plane on its way to Miami crashed in the Glades. All one hundred and nineteen souls on board were killed. The passenger list was in the paper. I recognized some of the names. I recognized many of them."

"You saw this. You saw those names."

"Yes. For several months after that I stayed away from the island, and I promised myself I would stay away for good. I suppose drug addicts make the same promises to themselves about their dope, don't they? And like them, I eventually weakened and resumed my old habit. Now, counselor: do you understand why I called you out here to finish the work on my will, and why it had to be tonight?"

Wayland doesn't believe a word of it, but like many fantasies, this one has its own internal logic. It's easy enough to follow. The judge is ninety, his once ruddy complexion has gone the color of clay, his formerly firm step has become shuffling and tentative. He's clearly in pain, and he's lost weight he can't afford to lose.

"I suppose that today you saw your name in the sand," Wayland says.

Judge Beecher looks momentarily startled, and then he smiles. It is a terrible smile, transforming his narrow, pallid face into a death's-head grin.

"Oh no," he says. "Not *mine*."

The music was stopped by the tolling of the bell.
A sound not belonging to the dead of night.
A signal to take flight.

THE FOX MAIDEN

Priya Sharma

⬦

Owens never told a soul, not even his wife in later life, but he could have sworn the girl scrambled out of the blackness on all fours. The cave's interior was dark. Animal bones crunched underfoot. He blinked away the caul of sunshine and shadows from his eyes.

There was a disembodied snuffling. Owens watched, rifle ready, as sound took shape. He had the impression of a pointed face.

He'd survived mutinies and dysentery. He didn't want to die, ravaged by some beast, so far from home. As the shadow became clearer, he saw it was small. Some sort of dog, perhaps. He lowered his rifle. The shape now walked on hind legs. He must have been mistaken.

She tried to scamper past. Poor mite. There was no doubt it was the captain's child. A sight to break the heart. Dirty with a mass of matted hair. Crusted blood beneath her fingernails. Too old to be naked as the day she'd come upon the earth. Too young to be so unhinged by grief.

Owens crossed himself.

Early morning, late in autumn. The meet gathered. Strutted in their black and scarlet. Drank Madeira from crystal glasses. The horses stamped and pranced, unhappy in Lily's company. Steam poured from their nostrils, as though her inclusion made them fume. Lord Lacey had found for Lily the most docile mare, fit for novices and children.

"I'll be a liability," Lily protested.

"You'll come. You'll be my luck."

The dappled pony clattered about the yard, spooked by Lily's approach. When she finally managed to mount the animal, it skittered under her as though she wore a set of spurs. Lily's rivals smirked. Thin, ravenous things in glossy skirts, bound together by their loathing of her.

The whipper in brought the hounds, a seething mass of white and tan. They liked Lily even less.

"Pity anything so hunted."

Lily hadn't meant to speak aloud. She was shocked they'd heard above the din. If they were waiting for her error, here it was. The ladies, huntswomen to their fingertips, scoffed at this display. The men, politely outraged, turned away. Lily's true affinities had been betrayed.

Lord Lacey's laugh showed he didn't give a hoot.

"Better hunter than hunted."

Lily's aunt watched from the manor steps with eyes like shiny beads. They reflected all she wanted from the world. Everything she felt she was entitled to that she'd been denied. Her thwarted avarice festered inside.

Lily could still feel the brush raking her scalp. Her aunt complained. A tiresome task. The russet mass would not be tamed.

"You will accept him."

"He's not asked."

"He will and you'll say yes. Accept him or I'll put you out."

Her aunt had managed to pull her hair into some semblance of a coil. She drove the pins to fix it, drawing blood. A demonstration of her resolve.

Lily was no equestrian. Whenever she approached a horse, it shied away. No matter. Riding wasn't a luxury she could afford. She walked instead, her pace more like a trot. Her aunt bemoaned this orphaned niece from distant lands. She didn't like her wayward shock of hair. Surely from the girl's mother's side. No such color belonged among the Hastings stock.

The aunt's redbrick terrace was at Botheringstile. Built for economy and function. A spinster's existence reflected in the polished aspidistra and glazed tiles. She'd been resigned to a middle-class and single life.

The girl disrupted everything. She traipsed dirt in on her boots. She shed the leaves caught up in her hair. The house couldn't contain her.

"You've been seen. Running on the common. Really, Lily, it's too much."

Lily, behaving like an urchin, not a young lady with slender limbs and neck.

"Are you listening? Keep off there. And for heaven's sake, stay away from Grissleymire. The tenant's mad. Gypsies loiter in the grounds. Dirty fellows. They steal children."

"Really?" Lily's ears pricked up. Her teacup was at the saucer's edge, threatening to spill. Then, "I'm not a child."

"Your interest is inappropriate and morbid. You shouldn't be wandering so far. You're not to go out alone again. Now, we must discuss your future."

The conversation was a dismal failure. Lily, freedom curtailed, became obstinate and obtuse. Cornered, she took on a shifty look that her aunt disliked. She berated Lily for chances squandered and ambition lacked. It soon became a tirade against Lily's father and a lament in his foolish choice of wife.

"You'll join Lord Lacey for the hunt. There's an end to it."

"I don't want to."

"As you said, you're not a child. We can't do as we want. We do as we must."

"Why?"

"You suppose that you'll live off me forever? I took you in. I'd hoped for some sensitivity in return."

"You talk as if I were some stranger, not your own family."

"How dare you!"

The fire spat as they sat in silence.

"I'm sorry, Aunt."

"We'll never mention it again. We'll forget it."

She set her mouth into a line that meant, on the contrary, it wouldn't be forgotten for some time. Once Lily had been excused, her aunt chastised the maid instead, until the girl wept over some imaginary stains upon the nets.

By "Lily's future," her aunt had meant her suitor. Lily often saw him riding in the distance as she roamed her days away. She asked who he was, and it seemed Lord Lacey of Marshcombe had been inquiring about her, too, and learned her family was of a minor pedigree and her father was an army man who'd left his sister and daughter impoverished.

They received an invitation to a ball at Marshcombe Hall. Lily's aunt fussed, dressing her in an unfashionable gown cut for a child. Lacking family jewels, Lily's hair would have to be her only embellishment.

Lord Lacey's mistresses encircled her, wearing banal diamonds and silks the colors of the night. Reflected alongside them in the mirror, Lily could see she was handsome in a feral way but nothing like the classical beauties of the day. She was relieved. A man like him would have no use for freshness. Lacey could inspect her at close quarters and once rejected, she'd be free to go on as before.

Lily didn't try to ensnare him. She didn't smile or flutter her eyelashes. As he bent to kiss her hand, she could feel the fluttering of her heart, the beat at the base of her throat, as if it were desperate to escape. She couldn't help but notice he was staring at the telltale pulse at her neck, licking his lips, as if fear was what attracted him the most.

Lord Lacey's thighs tensed across his hunter's back as he wheeled about Lily.

"Try and keep up." His unconcealed pleasure at her discomfort made her bristle. Nor did she like the way he ordered her about. "Pike will stay close but should he lose you, don't stray. If you see smoke, turn back. That's the gypsy campfires on Grissleymire."

The word made Lily shiver.

"The tenant, Victor Mallory, is deranged. A circus performer or something equally vulgar. He refuses to let us hunt there. He's let loose all kinds of dangerous animals on the land."

A woman trotted alongside of them, eager to join in.

"His bear," she said, "has ravished a village girl."

Lily wasn't listening. Victor Mallory. The name was a stone dropped down a well into the past. It landed on her father's lips. She knew this man.

Victor Mallory. Seek him out if you're ever in need. He's one of us.

Her father's dying lips.

Lily was unprepared for the anarchy of the hunt. The howling, scrambling of the pack. The tally-ho. The hue and cry. The thunder of the ride. Hooves churned the earth, great clods thrown into the air. Pike goaded her mare with his crop. He didn't want to miss the fun.

She caught the flash of red upon the hill and wished it Godspeed, but it wasn't to be. They chased the vixen to exhaustion. Lily didn't see the kill. Unfortunately, with Pike's help, she arrived in time to see the trophies taken. The mask, the pads, the glorious brush. Lily appalled them with her squeamishness. This fox, this monarch of the field and copse, had been a stunner. Now she was tossed and torn apart at the frothy jaws of mere dogs.

Lily flinched when Lord Lacey came close. She swayed and swooned, only to be caught. Faces filled her vision as it narrowed to the long corridor of a faint. Her eyelids fluttered as she clung to consciousness. Lord Lacey knelt beside her, gripping her foot. She felt his hand slide up to caress her calf.

"She's turned her ankle," he announced. Lily tried to protest but he hushed her, adding, "She may have hit her head. Pike and I will take her to Mother Biddie's cottage where she can rest a while."

Lily didn't like Pike's sly smile.

"You," Lacey beckoned a groom, "ride back and tell her aunt not to be alarmed. I'll ride back later with news and arrange a carriage when she's well enough to travel."

The rest rode away. None of the women saw fit to stay, even to act as chaperone for another lady in distress. She wouldn't be a lady for much longer. They mistook her for a toy, not a contender for the role of Lady Lacey. They could not help but smirk. Let him have his way. They were only happy to leave Lily to her fate.

Lily awoke in Pike's arms. She struggled against his grip, the pain of his digging fingertips. She didn't want a voyeur to her humiliation. She didn't want Pike to enjoy her shame.

Lacey lifted her veil as though she were a bride. He daubed her face with the fox's brush. Cold and clotted brush across her cheeks. The bedsprings creaked as she tried to jerk away. She heard Mother Biddie lock the door.

"Your first time," he turned her head to admire his work, "I've bloodied you."

Lily bared her teeth. An involuntary response. It earned her a slap, which excited Lacey even more. Now other blood sports were on his mind. He'd hunted her to the edge of ecstasy. Her creeping skirt was creased between her thighs. It ignited his more violent desires. He would spoil her if it was the only way to possess her. She wasn't so defiant now. A wild thing cowed.

Lily knew she'd need guile. She was resourceful.

She'd run away after her father died. She was still a child. His regiment searched for a full eight weeks. She'd been hiding in a cave. A scrawny thing that screamed and bit, who struggled and raved. As if she'd forgotten how to behave. Lily denied this time when she'd been wild with sorrow. This merciful amnesia didn't obliterate the trauma that followed. She could never forget the terrors of the cabin. The tipping of the sea. Homesickness replaced seasickness. Her aunt's embraces were devoid of any comfort. The odors of England were baffling. She longed for the fragrances of India and her father's hair pomade.

"Wait." Her mind seized on Victor Mallory. She must have cleverness and courage.

Lacey paused in pawing her.

"I can give you something better."

"What's better than this?"

"Riches."

"I *am* rich."

"Women."

Her audacity made Lacey gasp. That he'd misjudged her delighted him. It appealed to his corruption. This new-Lily was delicious.

"I don't lack for those either. I plan on having you. Now and whenever I want once you're my wife."

It was worse than she had feared. She thought that afterwards she'd be free.

"Hunting." There. She had struck him. That she knew him so well already made him tremble. "The best day's hunting you've ever had."

Now Lord Lacey had a different sort of quarry. If he caught Lily, he could have her on the spot, if he wanted. Then there'd be a wedding without delay. He agreed to give her a head start by sending for fresh horses and a different type of dog.

"You have twenty-four hours to find me. After that, you relinquish your claim. You'll make no proposal. I go free."

Lily suggested the terms with an encouraging smile, as if truly game. *It'll be much better this way.* All he had to do was catch her. She responded to his query about her virginity with quiet dignity.

Lacey tore off her drawers.

"For the dogs," he explained.

She was just a girl on foot but her endless roaming had kept her fit and given her the geography for miles around. She thanked her stars for her stout boots.

She took care when she set her pace. The ground was uneven. Too fast and she'd be at risk of flagging or falling, too slow and they'd soon catch her up. She didn't strike out randomly. She had a destination. A source of possible salvation. Grissleymire and Victor Mallory.

The bog was the safest route. If she showed respect it would let her pass. She'd learnt its tricks and treachery, the secrets of its sucking love. Its foulness might help to mask her smell. If she was fortunate, it might even claim Lacey, Pike, and all their hounds.

Lily was a sight. Mud on her skirt, blood-smeared face, her veil torn remnants of lace. The bodice that had been laced to make her waist narrow now only served to make her breaths come fast and shallow.

It was in this state that she reached Grissleymire. She limped along in dappled shade. A bird flew down the tree-darkened lane. Darting and swooping, it showed her the way. The estate was overgrown. Ivy smothered shut the gates. She would have to find another way.

The wind had swept up the fallen leaves. Lily paused as they stirred and a snout, followed by a pair of eyes and pointed ears emerged from its hiding place within the pile. The fox shook off this crackling autumn robe. A male of the species, in his prime. Sleek coat. A brawler. Torn lip. A wound that had long since healed. He sniffed the fox blood on her and then flowed away.

Lily climbed over a broken wall. The hall was before her, once elegant, now in decay. There was a lion on what was once the lawn. He came out of the long grass to inspect her with amber eyes. Prowling back and forth, tail twitching, lip licking. Tawny skin taut. Immense paws. Testicles and teeth.

Lily backed towards the hall's doors. Her hand found the knocker. The bronze was cool in her clammy palm. She rapped slowly so as not to startle her stalker.

The door fell open. Lily fell in.

The servant was not the sort of man she'd ever encountered in service. That he was hare lipped made her pause. His livery was old and in disarray, buttons missing and ragged braid. There was an oak leaf, stained yellow by the season, caught in his hair. Lily was accustomed to servants who stood to attention. This one didn't show her a jot of deference or respect. He didn't even help her from the floor. That he was too busy saluting the lion annoyed her even more.

"What do you want?"

"To see your master."

An inauspicious start. A well-trained servant would have taken a bloodied, muddied lady in his stride.

"It's imperative that I see him."

The haughty tilt of her head had no effect.

"Please. It's important. I've come all the way from," she was about to say Marshcombe but thought better of it, "Botheringstile."

"So far?" he mocked.

He was handsome. Or, at least, Lily found him so. His auburn hair much darker than her own. Lively eyes. A smile that danced around his damaged mouth.

"What's it about?"

Brazen, too.

"That's for his ears alone."

He didn't show her to the parlor but left her standing in the hall. A grandfather clock was several hours astray in its estimation of the time. The stained glass, stained rugs and stained flags all needed a good scrub. The medieval tapestries were fantastical. A lion in armor skewering a man. A ring of wolves dancing around a fire and the coronation of a fox. This whimsical court was well beyond repair. Shabby relics of glories past.

The servant returned.

The library. Books languished on the shelves, pages crumbling between moldy covers. A dying fire smoldered in the grate. Lily went to the long windows. A spider's web spanned an entire pane. It was a striking creature, plump body marked in paler shades. It picked at its web's threads as a harpist plucks her strings. The flies quivered as they listened to her tune.

Lily gasped. Figures were reflected in the glass. Gods filled the library's alcoves. Mallory was an idolater. His deities had trunks and tusks and fangs. They demanded the fiercest of devotions.

"Do you like them?"

"You startled me."

Mallory had crept close despite his size, sniffing at her hair. Satisfied, he hobbled to the fire and sank into a chair.

"What's your name?"

"Lily Hastings."

"Are we acquainted?"

Lily had been prepared to be outrageous in her lies but now she saw he would spot a ruse.

"I come here in desperation. I come here to throw myself upon your mercy." She flung herself at his feet and grasped his folded hands. The ebbing firelight caught her hair and set it alight. Burnished copper winked amid the red. It made the white flash of her throat seem more exposed.

"Sir, I implore you."

Victor smirked.

"You mock me," Lily cried, "you are cruel."

"Hush now. What books you girls must read nowadays! Such lurid melodrama. It might work on the page and younger men but I'm neither."

"You're not so old." Her wet eyes and sudden smile were a charming combination.

"Such a lovely little trickster."

Victor was immune to womanly wiles. She would have to try a different way.

"You're a magician."

"A long time ago. I learnt my craft in Africa and China. I've performed for prime ministers and kings."

He'd sunk into his reminisces. A vacant stare. Lily wondered if she was in error but his face was unmistakable despite the burden of age.

"The things I've seen. I've walked on the roof of the world and been where the canopy's so dense that it's perpetual night."

"You're The Theologist," she prompted.

"The Theologist of Transformation," he sounded surprised by his own stage name.

"I need your help to make me disappear."

"I don't do tricks upon request."

"I've nowhere else to go. No benefactor sympathetic to my cause. I have a suitor . . . "

"I should imagine you have many."

"He's a beast."

"We're all beasts, my dear."

"Not just a beast. A brute."

"Refuse him then."

"I can't. I rely on my aunt's charity. She'll turn me out."

Victor picked up the bowl beside him. He raked his fingers through the jumble of gems. A discarded fortune, their luster dulled by dust. He pulled out a tiara and threw it on her lap. It was encrusted with diamonds and grime.

"Have that. The means to leave. Not enough? Have more."

A rain of jewels. They lay where they fell, scattered on the floor.

"It's not just the money," Lily was unsure why she was dithering, "it's something else."

Now her tears were real.

"Don't waste my time!" Victor roared.

Lily thrust her fists against her eyes. She was undone, lacking in the words. Now, when she had to explain to someone else, she realized that she didn't understand herself.

"I saw you when I was a child. In India. After my mother died. My father said you'd help if I was ever in need."

"Who was your father?"

"Captain Harry Hastings."

"I don't know him."

"I saw you. At the palace. I sat on your knee during the performance. Afterwards my father was angry at me for being so bold."

Victor's face froze.

"So angry that he frightened me."

"You don't remember why?" Victor asked.

Lily shook her head.

"Later he said he was sorry that he'd lost his temper. I'd stopped speaking when my mother died. Everyone thought I'd lost my wits. He said it was because of you that I recovered them."

"Where's your father now?"

"He died. A hunting accident."

"Who was hunting him?"

"I'm sorry?" Lily thought that she'd misheard.

The Theologist stared at her.

"No, I am," he sounded weary, "unhappy is the one who doesn't know themselves."

"I came for magic," Lily blurted out, hardly sure what she was asking for. Unsure if Lacey was far behind.

"There's none left. It's all spent. Now leave me be."

"Please."

"Robert, make her go away. Give her a room if she needs a place to stay."

Robert, the hare-lipped servant, grasped her elbow and pulled her to her feet. She wondered how long he'd been standing there.

"He's tired. He needs to sleep."

She turned back but Victor's chin was on his chest, eyelids moving as if already in a dream.

"Run, dear," Victor muttered from his sudden slumber. "Run."

The walls were lined with portraits, eyes flat and blank. They held no regard for Lily. She was just another girl. At the stair's turn there was a line of brass urns, each brimming with gold coins. They lay there, uncoveted. The smell of the house was stronger here. Pungent, like a lair.

There was a rocking horse on the minstrel's gallery. Someone had thought to groom it. The tail combed out and the wood polished until it shone, yet it had been attacked. Something had clawed at its wooden flanks. Three parallel lines bit deep.

I'm among lunatics, she thought.

Lily followed Robert to the upper floors. Here were Victor's strange family, with all its inbreeding, its bastards, whelps and wards. Fathered at Grissleymire or found on travels abroad. They turned to see Lily trying to catch a glimpse. One man kicked the door shut with his heel. Through a gap she saw a man writing in a ledger, the boy at his feet batting a ball of yarn between his palms. In the next room a woman loosened her dress to suckle her young, one at each breast. Straw matted the floor. The room was rank with urine, milk, and regurgitated meat.

"Who's this?" she barked at them. Her accent was Russian. "Put her out. She stinks of lies. Tell Victor I said so."

"Tell him yourself, Vivien."

Lily followed Robert to the end of the corridor. He shoved the door open and leant against the frame. Lily squeezed past him. He was unwashed. Musky and provocative.

"You can bed down here."

"I need a fire. A bath."

The room was filthy. Full of dander and dirt. The furniture and the mirror were coated with the stuff.

"The jug's there. You'll get water from the kitchen pump. Logs are by the back door."

Stood so close, his smell was stronger. It made her nose twitch. It made her itch.

"Of course, there's other ways of keeping warm," he said, straight faced, "if you should want me, I'll be just along the hall."

Not the proper place for a servant at all.

Lily stepped from her clothes, layer by layer. Just garments, not the essence of herself. She used them to make a nest beneath the bed. This was how her father used to find her. In a den of her own design.

Lily hadn't planned to sleep so long. She only meant to ease her aching legs. When she woke the sky had already darkened. A fire laid and lit. Hot water steamed from the ewer and the mirror had been polished. A plain twill dress was laid out on the bed, a shawl folded at its head.

She cleaned off the sweat and mud. The blood. Then went back along the corridor and down the stairs. From the higher windows she could see the maze, its geometry wracked and ruined. When she turned a corner she saw Robert was outside. She went to him.

"Thank you for the fire and the water. You're not a footman at all, are you?"

"No."

Robert had changed too. His shirt was darned but clean. They walked together in the equality of these new clothes.

"I'm Lily."

They turned onto the avenue of oaks, once the fine approach to Grissleymire from the road. One of the giants had been felled in a lightning storm. Its charred corpse blocked their way. Something sluggish and sinuous slithered along the broken boughs.

"One of Victor's," Robert explained. "It was part of his performance."

The dappled python was lost in the English undergrowth.

"Like the lion?"

Robert looked at her from the corner of his eye.

"He wasn't in the show. Victor just wanted him to have a home."

"My aunt says hunters and poachers are run off Grissleymire."

"We don't want strangers here. And killing for food is one thing but sport is quite another."

Lily imagined a democracy of carnivores. The otters floated downstream. The badger lay quiet in his set. The fox and the lion went unmolested.

"So it's safe here?"

"Safer. For now. For a certain sort."

"What sort?"

"The hunted. The cursed. The damned."

Hunted. Cursed. Where was Lacey now? Lily wished him to the very bottom of the bog. She'd already decided that she'd never be his wife. She'd rather take her own life.

Past the diseased limes and through the kissing gate, rusted on its broken hinge. They reached the devastated water gardens. The fountains, unrefreshed with spilling water, stagnated. There was only one pond that remained clean being fed by an overflowing stream. Robert knelt and trailed his fingers along the surface to draw the monstrous carp lurking in its depths. Ghostly creatures, flecked in blues and golds. They nibbled at his fingertips and then drifted into darkness, unsatisfied.

"What do you dream about?"

"My dreams?"

"Yes," he coaxed.

"I dream of running."

"Yes," as if he understood, "but what's your most vivid dream?"

"I can't say."

"You have to." She writhed in his sudden grip. "This is why you're here, isn't it? You want to know about your dreams. You want to know what they mean."

"No!" Lily tried to twist away. His smell was maddening. It enraged her in the most disturbing way.

"Tell me. Or do I have to tell you? You dream you're dead . . . "

"I dream I'm dead . . . " Lily repeated. "No, I dream I'm playing dead. I'm lying on the ground. My eyes are shut. My tongue hangs out. Crows caw at me. I wait for them to come too close. I let them peck at me. I wait until one is far too close."

"Then, snap! You have them!"

Feigning death. A foxy trick to lure scavengers. Lily would gorge on those who would devour her.

"And you steal from the coop," Robert prompted.

It was too much. The poultry yard raids and eggs for burying carried in her jaws. Both she and Robert were scatter hoarders who hid their treasures in the ground.

"You've come too late for Victor's help. He's dying."

So many years wasted, when he'd been here all along. Indignation rose like bile in her throat, her cry stalled by the sadness on Robert's face.

"I'm sorry."

"Victor found me at a circus."

"You were an acrobat?" She tried to make him smile. "A clown?"

Robert shook his head.

"My father sold me when I was a boy. My face wasn't always so."

Not hare lipped then but scarred. In his eyes, Lily saw the whip, the chain, incarceration in a cage.

"Victor bought and freed me. He taught me what it meant to be myself."

Lily touched his lip where it had been too damaged to reunite. A vulnerable flaw that she found seductive and of which Robert was ashamed. She put her mouth to it. To kiss it better. As if to fuse their flesh together and make it whole. She'd bargained for her virtue only hours ago. Now she wanted to throw it away. Once gone, Lord Lacey could hardly take it from her.

She shed her dress, the shift, the torn stockings made of silk. Robert undressed for her in turn. They stood before each other as their natures intended. Not nude but naked. Revealed as they were, not as others saw them.

They leapt at one another. Moonlight struck their backs. It made them dance with joy. A pair of foxes, rolling in the grass. The chill of the coming winter did not sting. They had pelts to keep them warm.

"Lily, stop!"

Harry Hastings was too late. His daughter had slipped away and run onstage. For months she'd been a silent, fading shade, refusing all but the most babyish of foods. She'd pined away, day by day. By night she refused to sleep anywhere but under his bed.

Being fast, she'd got away from him, burrowing under the velvet covers of the cage. Being so small, she slid between the bars.

The women, even the royal ones, let out a scream. The men were on their feet with swords and pistols drawn. They'd come to see The Theologist perform a miracle, not the slaughter of a child. Hastings barged past the stagehands who tried to pull him back. He snatched a heavy swathe of velvet and pulled the curtain to the floor.

Victor Mallory had been perched upon the stool as they secured the cage. The Raja himself had checked the locks. Now, the Theologist wasn't there. It was his famous bear. The animal didn't rear up and bare his teeth as it normally did to impress the crowds. It was perched upon the stool, a fox cub curled up on its knee. Bear and fox gazed at each other in awe.

Afterwards, Lily rolled away from Robert. She surprised herself. There was no surge of shame, just relief. It had been urgent. Essential, even. She'd been unburdened. The reality of dreaming set her free. To kill, to feast, to copulate, to bathe in moonlight if she choose.

"Your dreams are your own," he stroked her back, "Victor can't give them to you."

"Nor can you," she turned to face him. "This doesn't mean I'm yours. Or any man's. I am my own."

"Of course you are." Then more softly, "None of us here at Grissleymire hold with ownership."

It was the gentlest of reproaches.

He pulled their clothes over them. It was colder in their human skins. Lily could smell smoke. Music carried on the breeze. The strains of a jig played on a distant fiddle.

"Gypsies. Is it them that keep hunters off the land?"

"Warn them off. No more. They wouldn't break the law for us."

"They don't work for Victor?"

Robert considered this.

"No, but Grissleymire's a haven for them too. They'll help if we need to leave here in a hurry."

She sat up, shawl clutched to her breasts. "Leave?"

"Our sort doesn't die peacefully in our beds. Someone will come for us eventually. Someone will always want our skins."

The music was stopped by the tolling of the bell. A sound not belonging to the dead of night. A signal to take flight.

Grissleymire had once had its own chapel, but now all that remained was the tower and the bell. Someone had raised the alarm. The Romany camped around the grounds answered the call, having empathy for the displaced. Sympathy for the damned. They came with carriages and carts. Blinkers and nosebags filled with lavender quieted the horses.

Lily and Robert came upon an evacuation. Parents had shaken children from their beds. Those that roamed at night returned on all fours. Chests and carpetbags spilled clothes and pots and pans. The man with the ledger was at the door, ordering the chaos, doling out diamonds and gold. Everyone would have a share.

"What happened?" Robert asked.

"In there." He didn't pause in counting coins.

There'd been carnage. Lacey's mastiffs lay where they'd been struck down. They'd been picked up and shaken by a snarling snout. Their throats ripped out.

"Arthur! Arthur!" Robert called. He'd seized Lily's hand so as not to lose her in the crowd.

Arthur was a sad-faced man with amber eyes and a cloud of golden hair. He clapped Robert on the arm.

"Where have you been? I've been looking for you everywhere. Two men came with dogs. They wanted the girl."

"You did that?" Robert meant the hounds spread across the hall.

"Yes," Arthur looked ashamed.

"You'd better get going."

"Will I see you again, my friend?"

"Of course."

Lily turned away, unable to bear the final goodbyes in their eyes.

Vivien came jostling down the stairs, a cub under each arm. She spat at Lily and gnashed her teeth, angry to have to take her babies on the road so young.

"I believe this is yours."

Vivien unknotted her apron and the head within rolled across the floor. She could spot ruffians like Pike at a mile. He'd received a savaging for her lifetime of ill use. Woe the man who threatened her brood. Lily noted that in Pike's last moments, he'd had the grace to be surprised.

"Victor's in the library with the other one. He says he's staying here." Then to Lily, "This is your fault."

Victor and Lacey were alone. Lacey lay upon the floor. Lily could tell him from his clothes. His face lay separated, torn off by a single swipe from Victor's paw. Lily stepped over him.

Blood-stained Victor didn't get up.

"Victor. It's me. Lily." She knelt beside him.

"We were gods once." He was looking at statues in the niches, the papyrus of the jackal headed man.

"Victor, we must leave," Robert pleaded. "More men will come."

Victor put a hand on Lily's head. The weight of it was immense. A single strike would send her reeling across the room. Instead, there was only a gentle pat.

"They always come, eventually."

"It's my fault," Lily confessed, "they followed me."

She waited for the killing blow.

"I dare say I've done much worse in my time. You really don't remember that day at the palace?"

"Yes, I do now. Papa was so angry. He said I was showing off."

"He was frightened for you."

"He made me promise never to do it again. I thought I hadn't. Then, when he died, the dreams started. What I thought were dreams."

"It's time for you to go."

"Not without you," Robert said. "Come with me. I'll take care of you."

Victor tutted.

"You've gone soft. You shouldn't make such offers. You've forgotten how to survive. She knows," he pointed at Lily, "you should learn from her."

Nature had deemed that Victor had outlived his usefulness but he'd not outlived Robert's love. The fierceness of his feeling for another was what moved Lily the most. Robert clung to Victor, who pried him off. Lily dragged him from the room. He raised his head and howled. It took all her strength to calm his down.

"Come away, he's tired. He needs to sleep, my love."

Late morning, early in winter. The meet gathered, strutted in their scarlet. Drank Madeira from crystal glasses. The horses stamped and pranced, steam streamed from their nostrils. The hounds were brought. A seething mass.

They did not smell the vixen or her mate. They'd rolled in juniper bushes to mask their scent. They watched the hunt move off from their vantage point upon the outhouse roof. No one was left to see them slide off and run along the wall. Streaks of brown and white and red, then gone.

*In which we learn why having a zombie play baseball is
not a good idea . . . even if you put him in left field.*

ROCKET MAN

Stephen Graham Jones

The dead aren't exactly known for their baseball skills, but still, if you're a
player short some afternoon, just need a body to prop up out in left field—it
all comes down to how bad you want to play, really. Or, in our case—where
you can understand that by "our" I mean "my," in that I promised off four
of my dad's cigarettes, one of my big brother's magazines, and one sleepover
lie—how bad you want to impress Amber Watson, on the walk back from the
community pool, her lifeguard eyes already focused on everything at once.

Last week, I'd actually smacked the ball so hard that Rory at shortstop
called time, to show how the cover'd rolled half back, the red stitching
popped.

"You scalped it," he said, kind of curling his lip in awe.

I should mention I'm Indian, except everybody's always doing that for
me.

The plan that day we pulled a zombie in (it had used to be Michael T from
over on Oak Circle, but you're not supposed to call zombies by their people
names), my plan was to hit that same ball—I'd been saving it—even harder,
so that there'd just be a cork center twirling up over our diamond, trailing
leather and thread. Amber Watson would track back from that cracking
sound to me, still holding my follow-through like I was posing for a trophy.
And then of course I'd look through the chain link, kind of nod to her that
this was me, yeah, this was who I really am, she's just never seen it, and she'd
smile and look away, and things in the halls at school would be different
between us then. More awkward. She might even start timing her walks to
coincide with some guess at my spot in the batting order.

Anyway, it wasn't like there was anything else I could ever possibly do
that might have a chance of impressing her.

But first, of course, we needed that body to prop up out in left field.
Which, I know you're thinking "right, *right* field," these are sixth graders,

they never wait, they always step out, slap the ball early, and, I mean, maybe the kids from Chesterton or Memphis City do, I don't know. But around here, we've been taught to wait, to time it out, to let that ball kind of hover in the pocket before we launch it into orbit. Kids from Chesterton? None of them are ever going pro. Not like us.

It's why we fail the spelling test each Friday, why we blow the math quiz if we're not sitting by somebody smart. You don't need to know how to spell "homerun" to hit one. You don't have to add up runners in your head, so long as you knock them all in. Easy as that.

As for Michael T, none of us had had much to do with him since he got bit, started playing for the other team. There were the lunges from behind the fence on the way to school, there was that shape kind of scuffling around when you took the trash out some nights, but that could have been any zombie. It didn't have to be Michael T. And, pulling him in that day to just stand there, let the flies buzz in and out of his mouth—it's not like that's not what he did *before* he was dead. You only picked Michael T if he was the only one to pick, I'm saying. You wouldn't think that either, him being a year older than us and all, but he'd always just been our size, too. Most kids like that, a grade up but not taller, they'd at least be fast, or be able to fling the ball home all the way from the center fence. Not Michael T. Michael T—the best way to explain him, I guess, it's that his big brother used to pin him down to the ground at recess, drop a line of spit down almost to his face, the rest of us looking but not looking. Glad just not to be him.

That day, though, with Amber Watson approaching on my radar, barefoot the way she usually was, her shoes hooked over her shoulder like a rich lady's purse, that day, it was either Michael T or nobody. Or, at first it *was* nobody, but then, just joking around, Theodore said he'd seen Michael T shuffling around down by the rocket park anyway.

"Michael *T*?" I asked.

"He still can't catch," Theodore said.

"That was all the way before lunch, though, yeah?" Rory said, socking the ball into his glove for punctuation.

It was nearly three, now.

"Can you track him?" Les said, falling in as we rounded the backstop.

"Your nose not work?" I asked him back.

Just another perfect summer afternoon.

We kicked a lopsided rock nearly all the way to where Michael T was supposed to have been, and then we turned to Theodore. He shrugged, was ready to fight any of us, even tried some of the words he'd learned from spying on his uncles in the garage. He wasn't lying, though. Splatted all over the bench were the crab apples him and Jefferson Banks had been zinging Michael T with.

"Jefferson," I said, "what about him?"

"Said he had to go home," Theodore shrugged, half-embarrassed for Jefferson. "His mom."

Figured. The one time I can impress Amber Watson and Jefferson's cleaning out all the ashtrays in the house then reading romance novels to his mom while she tans in the backyard.

"Who then?" Les asked, shading his eyes from the sun, squinting across all the glinty metal of the old playground.

None of us came to this one anymore. It was for kids.

"He's got to be around," Theodore said. "My dad said they like beef jerky."

I seconded this, had heard it as well.

You could lure a zombie anywhere if you had a twist of dried meat on a long string. It was supposed to be getting bad enough with the high schoolers that the stores in town had put a limit on beef jerky, two per customer.

I kicked at another rock that was there by the bench. It wasn't our lopsided one, was probably one Jefferson and Theodore had tried on Michael T. There was still a little bit of blood on it. All the ants were loving the crab apple leftovers, but, for them, there was a force field around where that rock had been. Until the next rain, anyway.

"She's never going to see me," I said, just out loud.

"Who?" Theodore asked, studying the park like Amber Watson could possibly be walking through it.

I shook my head no, never mind, and, turning away, half-planning to set a mirror up in right field, let Gerald just stand kind of by it, so it would seem like we had a full team, I caught a flash of cloth all the way in the top of the rocket.

"It's not over yet," I said, pointing up there with my chin.

Somebody was up there, right at the top where the astronauts would sit if it were a real rocket. The capsule part. And they were moving.

"Jefferson?" Theodore asked, looking to us for support.

Like monkeys, Les and Rory crawled up the outside of the rocket, high enough that their moms had to be having heart attacks in their kitchens.

When they got there, Rory had to turn to the side to throw up. It took that loogey of puke forever to make it to the ground. We laughed because it was throw-up, then tracked back up to the top of the rocket.

"It's Michael T!" Les called down, waving his hand like there was anywhere else in the whole world we might be looking.

"What's he doing?" I asked, not really loud enough, my eyes kind of pre-squinted, because this might be going to mess our game up.

"It's Jefferson," Theodore filled in, standing right beside me, and he was right.

Instead of going home like his mom wanted, Jefferson had spiraled up into the top of the rocket, probably to check if his name was still there, and never guessed Michael T might still be lurking around. Even a first grader can outrun or outsmart a zombie, but, in a tight place like that, and especially if you're in a panic, are freaking out, then it's a different kind of game altogether.

"Shouldn't have thrown those horse apples at him," Gerald said, shaking his head.

"Shouldn't have been stupid, more like," I said, and slapped my glove into Gerald's chest, for him to hold.

Ten minutes later, Les and Rory using cigarettes from the outside of the rocket to herd him away from his meal, Johnny T. lumbered down onto the playground, stood in that crooked, hurt way zombies do.

"Hunh," Theodore said.

He was right.

In the year since Michael T had been bitten, he hadn't grown any. He was shorter than all us now. Rotted away, Jefferson's gore all drooled down his frontside, some bones showing through the back of his hand, but still, that we'd outgrown him this past year. It felt like we'd cheated.

It was exhilarating.

One of us laughed and the rest fell in, and, using a piece of a sandwich Les finally volunteered to open his elbow scab on—we didn't have any beef jerky—we were able to lure Michael T back to the baseball diamond.

After everybody'd crossed the road, I studied up and down it, to be sure Amber Watson hadn't passed yet.

I didn't think so.

Not on an afternoon this perfect.

So then it was the big vote: whose glove was Michael T going to wear, probably try to gnaw on? When I got tired of it all, I just threw mine into his chest, glared all around.

"Warpath, chief," Les said, picking the glove up gingerly, watching Michael T the whole time.

"Scalp *your* dumb ass," I said, and turned around, didn't watch the complicated maneuver of getting the glove on Michael T's left hand, and only casually kept track of the stupid way he kept breaking position. Finally Timmy found a dead squirrel in the weeds, stuffed it into the school backpack that had kind of become part of Michael T's back. The smell kept him in place better than a spike through his foot. He kept kind of spinning around in his zombie way, tasting the air, but he wasn't going anywhere.

And then—this because my whole body was tuned into it, because the whole summer had been pointing at it—the adult swim whistle went off down at the community pool. Or maybe I was tuned into the groan from all the swimmers. Either way, this was always when the lifeguards would change chairs, was always when, if somebody was going off-shift, they would go.

"Amber," I said to myself, tossing my ragged, lucky ball to Les then tapping my bat across home plate, waiting for him to wind up.

"Am-*what*?" Theodore asked from behind the catcher's mask his mom insisted on.

I shook my head no, nothing, and, because I was looking down the street, down that tunnel of trees, Les slipped the first pitch by me.

"That one's free," I called out to him, tapping my bat again. Licking my lips.

Les wound up, leaned back, and I stepped up like I was already going to swing. He cued into it, that I was ahead of him here, and it threw him off enough that he flung the ball over Theodore's mitt, rattled the backstop with it.

"That one's free too," he called out to me, and I smiled, took it.

Just wait, I was saying inside, sneaking a look up the road again, and, just like in the movies, the whole afternoon slowed almost to a stop right there.

It was her. I smiled, nodded, my own breath loud in my ears, and slit my eyes back to Les.

He drove one right into the pocket, and if I'd wanted I could have shoveled it over all of their heads, dropped it out past the fence, into no man's land.

Except it was too early.

After it slapped home, I spun out of the box, spit into the dirt, hammered my bat into the fence two times.

And it was definitely her. Shoes over her shoulder, gum going in her mouth, nose still zinced, jean shorts over her one-piece, the whole deal.

I timed it perfect, getting back to the box, was wound up to *launch* this ball just at the point when she'd be closest to me.

So of course Les threw it high.

I could see it coming a mile away, how he'd tried to knuckle it, had lost it on the downsling like he always did, so there was maybe even a little arc to the ball's path. Not that it mattered, it was too high to swing at, but still—now or never, right? This is what all my planning had come down to.

I stepped back, crowding Theodore, who was already leaned forward to catch the ball when it dropped, and I swung at a ball that was higher than my shoulders, a ball my dad would have already been turning away from in disgust, and knew the instant my bat cracked into it that there wasn't going to be any lift, that it was a line drive, an arrow I was shooting out, blind. One I was going to have to run faster than, somehow.

Still, even though I didn't scoop under it like I would have liked, and even though I was making contact with it earlier than I would have wanted, I gave it every last thing I had, gave it everything I'd learned, everything I had to gamble.

And it worked. The cover flapping behind it just like a comet tail, it was a thing of beauty.

Les being Les, of course he bit the dirt to get out of the way, and Gerald and Rory—second and short—nearly hit each other, diving for what they knew was a two-run hit. A ball that wasn't even going to skip grass until—

Until left field, yeah.

Until Michael T.

And, if you're thinking he raised his glove here, that some long-forgotten reflex surfaced in his zombie brain for an instant, then guess again.

Dead or alive, he would have done the same thing: just stood there like the dunce he was.

Only, now, his face was kind of spongy, I guess.

The ball splatted into his left eye socket, sucked into place, stayed there, some kind of dark juice burping from his ears, trickling down along his jaw, the cover of the ball pasted to his cheek.

For a long moment we were all quiet, all holding our breaths—this was like hitting a pigeon with a pop-fly—and then, of everybody, I was the only one to hear Amber Watson stop on the sidewalk, look from the ball back to me, exactly like I'd planned.

I smiled, kind of shrugged, and then Gerald called it in his best umpire voice: "*Out!*"

I turned to him, my face going cold, and everybody in the infield was kind of shrugging that, yeah, the ball definitely hadn't hit the ground. No need to burn up the baseline.

"But, but," I said, pointing out to Michael T with my bat, to show how obvious it was that that wasn't a catch, that it didn't really count, and then Rory and Theodore and Les all started nodding that Gerald was right. Worse, now the outfield was chanting: "Mi-chael, Mi-cheal, Mi-chael." And then my own dugout fell in, clapping some Indian whoops from their mouth to memorialize what had happened here, today. How I was the only one who could have done it.

But I wasn't out.

Michael T wasn't even a real player, was just a body we'd propped up out there.

I looked back to Amber Watson and could tell she was just waiting to see what I was going to do here, waiting to see what was going to happen.

So I showed her.

I charged the mound, and, when Les sidestepped, holding his hands up and out like a bullfighter, I kept going, bat in hand, held low behind me, Rory and Gerald each giving me room as well, so that by the time I got out to left field I was running.

"*You didn't catch it!*" I yelled to Michael T, singlehandedly trying to ruin my whole summer, wreck my love life, trash my reputation—"Even a zombie can get him out"—and I swung for the ball a second time.

Instead of driving it off the T his head was supposed to be, I thunked it deeper, into his brain, I think, so that the rest of him kind of spasmed in a brainstemmy way, the bat shivering out of my hands so I had to let it go. And, because I hadn't planned ahead—charging out of the box isn't exactly about thinking everything through, even my dad would cop to this—the follow-through of my swing, it wrapped me up into Michael T's dead arms, and we fell together, me first.

And, like everything else since Les's failed knuckle ball, it took forever to happen. Long enough for me to hear that little lopsided plastic ball rattling in Amber Watson's whistle right before she set her feet and blew it. Long enough for me to see the legs of a single fly, following us down. Long enough for me to hear my chanted name stop in the middle.

This wasn't just a freak thing happening, anymore.

We were stepping over into legend, now.

Because the town was always on alert these days, Amber Watson's whistle was going to line the fence with people in under five minutes, and now everybody on the field and in the dugout, they were going to be witness to this, were each going to have their own better vantage point to tell the story from.

Meaning, instead of me being the star, everybody else would be.

And, Amber Watson.

It hurt to even think about.

We were going to have a special bond, now, sure, but not the kind where I was ever going to get to buy her a spirit ribbon. Not the kind where she'd ever tell me to quit smoking, because it was bad for me.

If I even got to live that long, I mean. If the yearbook staff wasn't already working my class photo onto the casualties page.

I wasn't there yet, though.

This wasn't the top of a rocket, I mean.

Sure, I was on my back in left field, and Michael T was over me, pinning me down by accident, the slobber and blood and brain juice stringing down from his lips, swinging right in front of my face so that I wanted to scream, but I could still kick him away, right? Lock my arms against his chest, keep my mouth closed so nothing dripped in it.

All of which would have happened, too.

Except for Les.

He'd picked up the bat that I guess I'd dragged through the chalk between second and third, so that, when he slapped it into the side of Michael T's head, a puff of white kind of breathed up. At first I thought it was bone, powdered skull—the whole top of Michael T's rotted-out head *was* coming off—but then there was sunlight above me again, and Les was hauling me up, and, on the sidewalk, Amber Watson was just staring at me, her whistle still in her mouth, her hair still wet enough to have left a dark patch on the canvas of the sneakers looped over her shoulder.

I put two of my fingers to my eyebrow like I'd seen my dad do, launched them off in salute to her, and in return she shook her head in disappointment. At the kid I still obviously was. So, yeah, if you want to know what it's like living with zombies, this is it, pretty much: they mess everything up. And if you want to know why I never went pro, it's because I got in the habit of charging the mound too much, like I had all this momentum from that day, all this unfairness built up inside. And if you want to know about Amber Watson, ask Les Moore—that's his real, stupid name, yeah. After that day he saved my life, after Les became the real Indian because *he'd* been the one to scalp Michael T, he stopped coming to the diamond so much, started spending more time at the pool, his hair bleaching in the sun, his reflexes gone, always thirty-five cents in his trunks to buy a lifeguard a lemonade if she wanted.

And she did, she does.

And, me? Some nights I still go to the old park, spiral up to the top of the rocket with a "Bury the Tomahawk" or "Circle the Wagons" spirit ribbon, and I let it flutter a bit through the grimy bars before letting it go, down through space, down to the planet I used to know, miles and miles from here.

⎯⟨⎯⟩⎯

Her words were from Lewis Carroll's "The Walrus and the Carpenter"—spoken by the Walrus just before he and the Carpenter began devouring the gullible oysters . . .

A JOURNEY OF ONLY TWO PACES

Tim Powers

She had ordered steak tartare and Hennessey XO brandy, which would, he reflected, look extravagant when he submitted his expenses to the court. And God knew what parking would cost here.

He took another frugal sip of his beer and said, trying not to sound sour, "I could have mailed you a check."

They were at one of the glass-topped tables on the outdoor veranda at the Beverly Wilshire Hotel, just a couple of feet above the sidewalk beyond the railing, looking out from under the table's umbrella down the sunlit lanes of Rodeo Drive. The diesel-scented air was hot even in the shade.

"But you were his old friend," she said. "He always told me that you're entertaining." She smiled at him expectantly.

She had been a widow for about ten years, Kohler recalled—and she must have married young. In her sunglasses and broad Panama hat she only seemed to be about twenty now.

Kohler, though, felt far older than his thirty-five years.

"He was easily entertained, Mrs. Halloway," he said slowly. "I'm pretty . . . lackluster, really." A young man on the other side of the railing overheard him and glanced his way in amusement as he strode past on the sidewalk.

"Call me Campion. But a dealer in rare books must have some fascinating stories."

Her full name was Elizabeth St. Campion Halloway. She signed her paintings "Campion." Kohler had looked her up online before driving out here to deliver the thousand dollars, and had decided that all her artwork was morbid and clumsy.

"He found you attractive," she went on, tapping the ash off her cigarette into the scraped remains of her steak tartare. He noticed that the filter was smeared with her red lipstick. "Did he ever tell you?"

"Really. No." For all Kohler knew, Jack Ranald might have been gay. The two of them had only got together about once a year since college, and then only when Kohler had already begged off on two or three e-mail invitations. Kohler's wife had always thought Jack was inwardly mocking her—*He forgets me when he's not looking right at me,* she'd said—and she wouldn't have been pleased with these involvements in the dead man's estate.

Kohler's wife had looked nothing like Campion.

Campion was staring at him now over the coal of her cigarette—he couldn't see her eyes behind the dark lenses, but her pale, narrow face swung carefully down and left and right. "I can already see him in you. You have the Letters Testamentary?"

"Uh." The shift in conversational gear left him momentarily blank. "Oh, yes—would you like to see them? and I'll want a receipt—"

"Not the one from the court clerk. The one Jack arranged."

Kohler bent down to get his black vinyl briefcase, and he pushed his chair back from the table to unzip it on his lap. Inside were all the records of terminating the water and electric utilities at the house Jack had owned in Echo Park and paying off Jack's credit cards, and, in a manila envelope along with the death certificate—which discreetly didn't mention suicide—the letters he had been given by the probate court.

One of them was the apparently standard sort, signed by the Clerk and the Deputy Clerk, but the other had been prepared by Jack himself.

Kohler tugged that one out and leaned forward to hand it across the table to Campion, and while she bent her head over it he mentally recalled its phrases: . . . *having been appointed and qualified as enactor of the will of John Carpenter Ranald, departed, who expired on or about 28 February 2009, Arthur Lewis Kohler is hereby authorized to function as enactor and to consummate possession* . . . In effect it was a suicide note. It had been signed in advance by Jack, and Kohler had recently been required to sign it too.

"Kabbalah," she said, without looking up, and for a moment Kohler thought he had somehow put one of his own business invoices into the briefcase by mistake and handed it to her. She looked up and smiled at him. "Are you afraid to get drunk with me? I'm sure one beer won't release any pent-up emotions, you can safely finish it. What *is* the most valuable book you have in stock?"

Kohler was frowning, but he went along with her change of subject. Jack must have told her what sort of books he specialized in.

"I guess that would be a manuscript codex of a thing called the *Gallei Razayya*, written in about 1550. It, uh, differs from the copy at Oxford." He shrugged. "I've got it priced high—it'll probably just go to my," he hesitated, then sighed and completed the habitual sentence, "my heirs."

"Rhymes with prayers, and you don't have any, do you? Heirs? Anymore? I was so sorry to hear about that."

Kohler stared at her, wondering if he wanted to make the effort of taking offense at her flippancy.

"No," he said instead, carefully.

"But it's about transmigration of souls, isn't it? Your codex book? Maybe you could . . . bequeath it to yourself."

She pushed her own chair back and stood up, brushing out her white linen skirt. "Have you tried to find the apartment building he owned in Silver Lake?"

Kohler began hastily to zip up his briefcase, and he was about to ask her how she knew about the manuscript when he remembered that she was still holding the peculiar Letter Testamentary.

"Uh . . . ?" he said, reaching for it.

"I'll keep for a while," she said gaily, tucking it into her purse. "I bet you couldn't find the place."

"That's true." He lowered his hand and finished zipping the case; the letter signed by the clerks was the legally important one. "I need to get the building assessed for the inventory of the estate. The address on the tax records seems to be wrong." Finally he asked, "You . . . know a lot about Kabbalah?"

"I can take you there. The address is wrong, as you say. Do you like cats? Jack told me about your book, your *codex*."

Kohler got to his feet and drank off half of the remaining beer in his glass. It wasn't very cold by this time. Jack had always wanted to hear about Kohler's business—Kohler must have acquired the manuscript shortly before they had last met for dinner, and told Jack about it.

"Sure," he said distractedly. She raised one penciled eyebrow, and he added, "I like cats fine."

"I'll drive," she said. "I have no head for directions, I couldn't guide you." She started toward the steps down to the Wilshire Boulevard sidewalk, then turned back and frowned at his briefcase. "You've followed all the directions he left in his will?"

Kohler guessed what she was thinking of. "The urn is in the trunk of my car," he said.

"You can drive. Your car is smaller, better for the tight turns."

Kohler followed her down out of the hotel's shadow onto the glaring Wilshire sidewalk, wondering how she knew what sort of car he drove, and when he had agreed to go right now to look at the apartment building.

———

She directed him east to the Hollywood freeway and then up into the hills above the Silver Lake Reservoir. The roads were narrow and twisting and overhung with carob and jacaranda trees.

Eventually, after Kohler had lost all sense of direction, Campion said, "Turn left at that street there."

"That? That's a driveway," Kohler objected, braking to a halt.

"It's the street," she said. "Well, lane. Alley. Anyway, it's where the apartment building is. Where are you living these days?"

In an apartment building, Kohler thought, probably not as nice as the one we're trying to find here. The old house was just too unbearably familiar. "Culver City."

"Did you like him? Jack?"

Kohler turned the wheel sharply and then steered by inches up onto the narrow strip of pavement, which curled away out of sight to the right behind a hedge of white-blooming oleander only a few yards ahead. Dry palm-fronds scattered across the cracked asphalt crunched under the tires. The needle of the temperature gauge was still comfortably on the left side of the dial, but he kept an eye on it.

"I liked him well enough," he said, squinting through the alternating sun-glare and palm-trunk shadows on the windshield. He exhaled. "Actually I didn't, no. I liked him in college, but after his father died, he—he just wasn't the same guy anymore."

"It was a shock," she said, nodding. "A trauma. He had heartworms."

Kohler just shook his head. "And Jack was sick, he said. What was wrong with him?"

She shrugged. "What does it matter? Something he didn't want to wait for. But—" And then she sang, "We're young and heal*thy*, so let's be *bold*." She giggled. "Do you remember that song?"

"No."

"No, it would have been before your time."

The steep little road did seem to be something more than a driveway— Kohler kept the Saturn to about five miles an hour, and they slowly rumbled past several old Spanish-style houses with white stucco walls and red roof-tiles and tiny garages with green-painted doors, the whole landscape as apparently empty of people as a street in a de Chirico painting. Campion had lit another cigarette, and Kohler cranked down the driver's-side window, and even though it was hot he was grateful for the sage and honeysuckle breeze.

"It's on the right," she said, tapping the windshield with a fingernail. "The arch there leads into the parking court."

Kohler steered in through the chipped white arch between tall trees, and he was surprised to see five or six cars parked in the unpaved yard and a big Honda Gold Wing motorcycle leaning on its stand up by the porch, in the shade of a vast lantana bush that crawled up the side of the two-story old building.

"Tenants?" he said, rocking the Saturn into a gap beside a battered old Volkswagen. "I hope . . . what's-his-name, the guy who inherited the place, wants to keep it running." A haze of dust raised by their passage across the yard swirled over the car.

"Mister Bump. He will, he lives here." She pointed at the motorcycle. "Jack's bike—running boards, a windshield, stereo, passenger seat—it's as if his RV had pups."

Kohler hadn't turned off the engine. "I could do this through the mail, if I could get a valid address."

"They get mail here, sort of informally. Somebody will tell you how to address it." She had opened her door and was stepping out onto the dry dirt, so he sighed and twisted the ignition key back and pulled it out. Now he could hear a violin playing behind one of the upstairs balconies—some intricate phrase from *Scheherazade*, rendered with such gliding expertise that he thought it must be a recording.

With the wall around it, and the still air under the old pepper trees, this compound seemed disconnected from the surrounding streets and freeways of Los Angeles.

"These were Jack's friends," Campion said. "Bring the urn."

Kohler was already sweating in the harsh sunlight, but he walked to the trunk and bent down to open it. He lifted out the heavy cardboard box and slammed the trunk shut.

"Jack is who we all have in common," said Campion, smiling and taking his free arm.

She led Kohler across the yard and up the worn stone steps to the porch, and the French doors stood open onto a dim, high-ceilinged lobby.

The air was cooler inside, and Kohler could hear an air-conditioner rattling away somewhere behind the painted screens and tapestries and potted plants that hid the walls. Narrow beams of sunlight slanted in and gleamed on the polished wooden floor.

Then Kohler noticed the cats. First two on an old Victorian sofa, then several more between vases on high shelves, and after a moment he decided that there must be at least a dozen cats in the room, lazily staring at the newcomers from heavy-lidded topaz eyes.

The cats were all identical—long-haired orange and white creatures with long fluffy tails.

"Campion!"

A tanned young man in a Polo shirt and khaki shorts had walked into the lobby through the French doors on the far side, and Kohler glimpsed an atrium behind him—huge shiny green leaves and orchid blossoms motionless in the still air.

"You *bitch*," the man said cheerfully, "did you lose your phone? Couldn't at least *honk* while you were driving up? " 'Tis just like a summer birdcage in a garden.' "

"Mr. Bump," said Campion, "I've brought James Kohler for the, the *wake*."

"No," said Kohler hastily, "I can't stay—"

"Can I call you Jimmy?" interrupted Mr. Bump. He held out his hand. "Mentally I'm spelling it J-I-M-I, like Hendrix."

Kohler shook the man's brown hand, then after several seconds flexed his own hand to separate them.

"No time to go a-waking, eh?" said Mr. Bump with a smile.

"I'm afraid not. I'll just—"

"Is that Jack?"

Kohler blinked, then realized that the man must be referring to the box he carried in his left hand.

"Oh. Yes."

"Let's walk him out to the atrium, shall we? We can disperse his ashes in the garden there."

Over Mr. Bump's shoulder, one of the orange cats on a high shelf flattened its ears.

"I'm supposed to—" Kohler paused to take a breath before explaining Jack Ranald's eccentric instructions. "I'm supposed to give him—his ashes—to somebody who quotes a certain poem to me. And I think it would be illegal to . . . pour out the ashes in a, a residence."

Behind him Campion laughed. "It's not a *poem*."

"Jimi isn't literary, is all," said Mr. Bump to her reprovingly. He crouched to pick up a kitten that seemed to be an exact miniature copy of all the other cats.

I'm a rare-books dealer! thought Kohler, but he just turned to her and said, "What is it?"

"I quoted a bit of it just now," said Mr. Bump, holding the kitten now and stroking it. " 'Tis just like a summer birdcage in a garden; the birds that are without despair to get in, and the birds that are within despair and are in a consumption for fear they shall never get out.' "

Kohler nodded—that was it. The will had specified the phrase,

Consumption for fear they shall never get out, and he had assumed it was a line of anapestic quatrameter.

"What's it from?" he asked, setting the box on a table and lifting out of it the black ceramic urn.

"A play," said Campion, taking his free arm again, apparently in anticipation of walking out to the atrium. "Webster's *The White Devil*."

"It's a filthy play," put in Mr. Bump.

The cats were bounding down from their perches and scurrying out the far doors into the atrium, their tails waving like a field of orange ferns in a wind.

The three people followed the cats out into the small, tiled courtyard that lay below second-floor balconies on all four sides. The atrium was crowded with tropical-looking plants, and leafy branches and vines hid some corners of the balconies—but Kohler noted uneasily that more than a dozen young men and women were leaning on the iron railings and silently looking down on them. The air smelled of jasmine and cat-boxes.

"The character who says the birdcage business," remarked Campion, "rises from the dead, at the end."

"And then gets killed again," noted Mr. Bump.

Campion shrugged. "Still." She looked up at the audience on the balconies. "Jack's back!" she called. "This nice man has been kind enough to carry him."

The men and women on the balconies all began snapping their fingers, apparently by way of applause. Kohler was nervously tempted to bow.

They didn't stop, and the shrill clacking began to take on a choppy rhythm.

The cats had all sat down in a ring in the center of the atrium floor—no, Kohler saw, it wasn't a ring, it was a triangle, and then he saw that they were all sitting on three lines of red tile set into the pavement. The space inside the triangle was empty.

Campion had stepped away to close the French doors to the lobby, and Mr. Bump leaned close to Kohler and spoke loudly to be heard over the shaking rattle from above. "This is the last part of your duty as executor," he said. The kitten he was holding seemed to have gone to sleep, in spite of the noise.

"It's not the last, by any means," said Kohler, who was sweating again. "There's the taxes, and selling the house, and—and I don't think this *is* part of my duties." He squinted up at the finger-snapping people—they were all dressed in slacks and shirts that were black or white, and the faces he could make out were expressionless. *Something's happening here*, he thought, *and you don't know what it is.* The sweat was suddenly cold on his forehead, and he pushed the urn into Mr. Bump's hands.

"I have to leave," Kohler said, turning back toward the lobby. "Now."

Campion stood in front of the closed doors, and she was pointing a small black automatic pistol at him—it looked like .22 or .25 caliber. "It was so kind of you to come!" she cried merrily. "And you are very nice!"

Kohler was peripherally aware that what she had said was a quote from something, but all his attention was focused on the gun muzzle. Campion's finger was inside the trigger guard. He stopped moving, then slowly extended his empty hands out to the side, his fingers twitching in time to his heartbeat.

Mr. Bump shook his head and smiled ruefully at Kohler. "Campion is so *theatrical!* We just, we'd be very grateful if you'd participate in a—memorial service."

The people on the balconies must have been able to see the situation, but the counterpoint racket never faltered—clearly there would be no help from them, whoever they were. "Then," said Kohler hoarsely, "I can go?"

"You might very well prefer to stay," said Campion. "It's a leisurely life."

Stay? Kohler thought.

"What," he asked, "do I do?"

"You were his closest friend," said Mr. Bump, "so you should—"

"I hardly knew him! Since college, at least. Maybe once or twice a year—"

"You're who he nominated. You should step over the cats, into the open space there, and after everybody has recited Jack's Letter Testamentary, you simply break the urn. At your feet."

Mr. Bump pressed the urn into Kohler's right hand, and Kohler closed his fingers around the glassy neck of it.

"And then I—can leave."

Campion nodded brightly. "Yours will be a journey only of two paces into view of the stars again," she said.

Kohler recognized what she had said as lines from a Walter de la Mare poem, and he recalled how the sentence in the poem ended—*but you will not make it.*

And belatedly he recognized what she had said a few moments ago: *It was so kind of you to come! And you are very nice!*—that was from Lewis Carroll's "The Walrus and the Carpenter," spoken by the Walrus just before he and the Carpenter began devouring the gullible oysters.

Kohler was grasping the urn in both hands, and now he had to force his arms not to shake in time to the percussive rhythm of all the rattling hands.

He glanced at Campion, but she was still holding the gun pointed directly at the middle of him.

"You really should have had more to drink," she called.

God only knew who these people were, or what weird ritual this was, and Kohler was considering causing some kind of diversion and just diving over some plants and rolling through one of the ground-floor French doors, and then just running. Out of this building, over the wall, and away.

It seemed unrealistic.

He obediently stepped over the cats into the clear triangle of pavement.

"Now wait till they've recited it all," said Mr. Bump loudly.

With her free hand Campion dug the peculiar Letter Testamentary out of her purse and flapped it in the still air to unfold it.

And then a young woman on one of the balconies whispered, "*Having . . .*" and a man on a balcony on the other side of the atrium whispered, " *. . . been . . .* " and another followed with " *. . . appointed . . .* "

The hoarse whispers undercut the shrill finger-snapping and echoed clearly around the walled space. They were reciting the text of Jack's letter, and each was enunciating only one word of it, letting a pause fall between each word.

The glassy bulge of the urn was slippery in Kohler's sweating hands, and he assembled some of the disjointed phrases in his mind: *enactor of the will of John Carpenter Ranald . . . Arthur Lewis Kohler . . . to consummate possession . . .*

And he recognized this technique—in first century Kabbalistic mysticism, certain truths could be spoken only in whispers, and the writing of certain magical texts required that a different scribe write each separate word.

As clearly as if she were speaking now, Campion's words at lunch came back to him: *But it's about transmigration of souls, isn't it?* and *I can already see him in you.*

And he recalled saying, *After his father died, he just wasn't the same guy anymore.*

Jack Ranald had been executor of his father's will.

"*To,*" whispered one of the black-or-white-clad people on the balconies. "*Consummate,*" whispered another. "*Possession,*" breathed one more, and then they stopped, and the finger-snapping stopped too. The silence that followed seemed to spring up from the paving stones, and the cats sitting in a triangle around Kohler shifted in place.

Mr. Bump nodded to Kohler and raised the kitten in both hands.

"Where do you want to go, from here?" whispered Campion. "Is there anything *you* want to wait for?"

Kohler sighed, a long exhalation that relaxed all his muscles and seemed to empty him. Go? he thought. Back to my studio apartment in Culver City . . . Wait for? No. I *could* do this—I *could* stay here, hidden from everything, even from myself, it seems.

He could hear the cats around the triangle purring. It's a leisurely life, Campion had said.

"What have you got to lose?" whispered Campion.

Lose? he thought. Nothing—nothing but memories I don't seem to have room for anymore.

And he remembered again what his wife had said about Jack—*He forgets me when he's not looking right at me.* Kohler couldn't look at her anymore—

—but to do this, whatever it was, would pretty clearly be to join Jack.

Kohler took a deep breath, and he felt as if he were stepping back out of a warm doorway, back into the useless tensions of a cold night.

And he flung the urn as hard as he could straight up. Everyone's eyes followed it, and Kohler stepped out of the triangle and, in a sudden moment of inspiration, picked up one of the cats and leaned forward to set it down in the clear triangular patch before hurrying toward a door away from Campion.

The urn shattered on the pavement behind him with a noise like a gunshot as Kohler was grabbing the doorknob, but two sounds stopped him—the cat yowled two syllables and, in perfect synchronization, a voice in his head said, in anguish, *Jimmy.*

It was Jack's voice. Even the cat's cry had seemed to be Jack's voice.

Helplessly Kohler let go of the doorknob and turned around.

The rest of the cats had scattered. Campion had had hurried into the triangular space, the gun falling from her fingers and skittering across the paving stones, and she was cradling the cat Kohler had put there. Mr. Bump had let the kitten jump down from his arms now and was just staring open-mouthed, and the people on the balconies were leaning forward and whispering in agitation—but their whispers now weren't audible.

"Jack!" Campion said hitchingly through tears, "Jack, darling, what has he done, what has he done?"

The cat was staring over Campion's shoulder directly at Kohler, and Kohler shivered at its intense amber glare.

But he nodded and said softly, "So long, Jack." Then he recalled that it was probably Jack's father, and looked away.

He took two steps forward across the tiles and picked up the little automatic pistol that Campion had dropped. There seemed to be no reason now not to leave by the way he'd come in.

Mr. Bump was shaking his head in evident amazement. "It was supposed to be you," he said, standing well back as he held the lobby door open, "into the kitten, to make room for Jack. That cat's already got somebody—I don't know how that'll work out." He stepped quickly to keep up with Kohler's stride across the dim lobby toward the front doors. "No use, anyway, they can't even write. Just not enough brain in their heads!" He laughed nervously, watching the gun in Kohler's hand. "You're—actually going to *leave* then?"

At the front doors, with his hand on one of the old iron handles, Kohler stopped. "I don't think anybody would want me to stay."

Mr. Bump shrugged. "I think Campion likes you. Likes *you*, I mean, too." He smiled. "'Despair to get in,' and I think you've paid the entry fee. Stay for dinner, at least? I'm making a huge cioppino, plenty for everybody, even the cats."

Kohler found that he was not sure enough about what had happened, not *quite* sure enough, to make the impossible denunciations that he wanted to make. It might help to read some of the books in his stock, but at this moment he was resolved never to open one again except to catalogue it.

"Give Jack mine," was all he said, as he pulled the door open; and then he hurried down the steps into the sunlight, reaching into his pocket for his car keys and bleakly eyeing the lane that would lead him back down to the old, old, terribly familiar freeway.

⇐⟩⇒

Some say it is still a good idea to avoid the moors near Zennor . . .

NEAR ZENNOR

Elizabeth Hand

He found the letters inside a round metal candy tin, at the bottom of a plastic storage box in the garage, alongside strings of outdoor Christmas lights and various oddments his wife had saved for the yard sale she'd never managed to organize in almost thirty years of marriage. She'd died suddenly, shockingly, of a brain aneurysm, while planting daffodil bulbs the previous September.

Now everything was going to Goodwill. The house in New Canaan had been listed with a realtor; despite the terrible market, she'd reassured Jeffrey that it should sell relatively quickly, and for something close to his asking price.

"It's a beautiful house, Jeffrey," she said, "not that I'm surprised." Jeffrey was a noted architect: she glanced at him as she stepped carefully along a flagstone path in her Louboutin heels. "And these gardens are incredible."

"That was all Anthea." He paused beside a stone wall, surveying an emerald swathe of new grass, small exposed hillocks of black earth, piles of neatly raked leaves left by the crew he'd hired to do the work that Anthea had always done on her own. In the distance, birch trees glowed spectral white against a leaden February sky that gave a twilit cast to midday. "She always said that if I'd had to pay her for all this, I wouldn't have been able to afford her. She was right."

He signed off on the final sheaf of contracts and returned them to the realtor. "You're in Brooklyn now?" she asked, turning back toward the house.

"Yes. Green Park. A colleague of mine is in Singapore for a few months, he's letting me stay there till I get my bearings."

"Well, good luck. I'll be in touch soon." She opened the door of her Prius and hesitated. "I know how hard this is for you. I lost my father two years ago. Nothing helps, really."

Jeffrey nodded. "Thanks. I know."

He'd spent the last five months cycling through wordless, imageless night terrors from which he awoke gasping; dreams in which Anthea lay beside him, breathing softly then smiling as he touched her face; nightmares in which the neuroelectrical storm that had killed her raged inside his own head, a flaring nova that engulfed the world around him and left him floating in an endless black space, the stars expiring one by one as he drifted past them.

He knew that grief had no target demographic, that all around him versions of this cosmic reshuffling took place every day. He and Anthea had their own shared experience years before, when they had lost their first and only daughter to sudden infant death syndrome. They were both in their late thirties at the time. They never tried to have another child, on their own or through adoption. It was as though some psychic house fire had consumed them both: it was a year before Jeffrey could enter the room that had been Julia's, and for months after her death neither he nor Anthea could bear to sit at the dining table and finish a meal together, or sleep in the same bed. The thought of being that close to another human being, of having one's hand or foot graze another's and wake however fleetingly to the realization that this too could be lost—it left both of them with a terror that they had never been able to articulate, even to each other.

Now as then, he kept busy with work at his office in the city, and dutifully accepted invitations for lunch and dinner there and in New Canaan. Nights were a prolonged torment: he was haunted by the realization that Anthea had been extinguished, a spent match pinched between one's fingers. He thought of Houdini, arch-rationalist of another century, who desired proof of a spirit world he desperately wanted to believe in. Jeffrey believed in nothing, yet if there had been a drug to twist his neurons into some synaptic impersonation of faith, he would have taken it.

For the past month he'd devoted most of his time to packing up the house, donating Anthea's clothes to various charity shops, deciding what to store and what to sell, what to divvy up among nieces and nephews, Anthea's sister, a few close friends. Throughout he experienced grief as a sort of low-grade flu, a persistent, inescapable ache that suffused not just his thoughts but his bones and tendons: a throbbing in his temples, black sparks that distorted his vision; an acrid chemical taste in the back of his throat, as though he'd bitten into one of the pills his doctor had given him to help him sleep.

He watched as the realtor drove off soundlessly, returned to the garage and transferred the plastic bin of Christmas lights into his own car, to drop off at a neighbor's the following weekend. He put the tin box with the letters on the seat beside him. As he pulled out of the driveway, it began to snow.

That night, he sat at the dining table in the Brooklyn loft and opened the candy tin. Inside were five letters, each bearing the same stamp: RETURN TO SENDER. At the bottom of the tin was a locket on a chain, cheap gold-colored metal and chipped red enamel circled by tiny fake pearls. He opened it: it was empty. He examined it for an engraved inscription, initials, a name, but there was nothing. He set it aside and turned to the letters.

All were postmarked 1971—February, March, April, July, end of August—all addressed to the same person at the same address, carefully spelled out in Anthea's swooping, schoolgirl's hand.

Mr. Robert Bennington,
Golovenna Farm,
Padwithiel,
Cornwall

Love letters? He didn't recognize the name Robert Bennington. Anthea would have been thirteen in February; her birthday was in May. He moved the envelopes across the table, as though performing a card trick. His heart pounded, which was ridiculous. He and Anthea had told each other about everything—three-ways at university, coke-fueled orgies during the 1980s, affairs and flirtations throughout their marriage.

None of that mattered now; little of it had mattered then. Still, his hands shook as he opened the first envelope. A single sheet of onionskin was inside. He unfolded it gingerly and smoothed it on the table.

His wife's handwriting hadn't changed much in forty years. The same cramped cursive, each *i* so heavily dotted in black ink that the pen had almost poked through the thin paper. Anthea had been English, born and raised in North London. They'd met at the University of London, where they were both studying, and moved to New Canaan after they'd married. It was an area that Anthea had often said reminded her of the English countryside, though Jeffrey had never ventured outside London, other than a few excursions to Kent and Brighton. Where was Padwithiel?

21 February, 1971

Dear Mr. Bennington,
My name is Anthea Ryson . . .

And would a thirteen-year-old girl address her boyfriend as "Mr.," even forty years ago?

. . . I am thirteen-years-old and live in London. Last year my friend Evelyn let me read Still the Seasons *for the first time and since then I have read it two more times, also* Black Clouds Over Bragmoor *and* The Second Sun. *They are my favorite books! I keep looking for more but the library here doesn't have them. I have asked and they said I should try the shops but that is expensive. My teacher said that sometimes you come to schools and speak, I hope some day you'll come to Islington Day School. Are you writing more books about Tisha and the great Battle? I hope so, please write back! My address is 42 Highbury Fields, London NW1.*

Very truly yours,
Anthea Ryson

Jeffrey set aside the letter and gazed at the remaining four envelopes. *What a prick*, he thought. He never even wrote her back. He turned to his laptop and googled Robert Bennington.

Robert Bennington (1932-), British author of a popular series of children's fantasy novels published during the 1960s known as "The Sun Battles." Bennington's books rode the literary tidal wave generated by J.R.R. Tolkien's work, but his commercial and critical standing were irrevocably shaken in the late 1990s, when he became the center of a drawn-out court case involving charges of pedophilia and sexual assault, with accusations lodged against him by several girl fans, now adults. One of the alleged victims later changed her account, and the case was eventually dismissed amidst much controversy by child advocates and women's rights groups. Bennington's reputation never recovered: school libraries refused to keep his books on their shelves. All of his novels are now out of print, although digital editions (illegal) can be found, along with used copies of the four books in the "Battles" sequence . . .

Jeffrey's neck prickled. The court case didn't ring a bell, but the books did. Anthea had thrust one upon him shortly after they first met.

"These were my *favorites*." She rolled over in bed and pulled a yellowed paperback from a shelf crowded with textbooks and Penguin editions of the mystery novels she loved. "I must have read this twenty times."

"Twenty?" Jeffrey raised an eyebrow.

"Well, maybe seven. A *lot*. Did you ever read them?"

"I never even heard of them."

"You have to read it. Right now." She nudged him with her bare foot. "You can't leave here till you do."

"Who says I want to leave?" He tried to kiss her but she pushed him away.

"Uh uh. Not till you read it. I'm serious!"

So he'd read it, staying up till 3:00 a.m., intermittently dozing off before waking with a start to pick up the book again.

"It gave me bad dreams," he said as gray morning light leaked through the narrow window of Anthea's flat. "I don't like it."

"I know." Anthea laughed. "That's what I liked about them—they always made me feel sort of sick."

Jeffrey shook his head adamantly. "I don't like it," he repeated.

Anthea frowned, finally shrugged, picked up the book and dropped it onto the floor. "Well, nobody's perfect," she said, and rolled on top of him.

A year or so later he did read *Still the Seasons,* when a virus kept him in bed for several days and Anthea was caught up with research at the British Library. The book unsettled him deeply. There were no monsters *per se*, no dragons or Nazgûl or witches. Just two sets of cousins, two boys and two girls, trapped in a portal between one of those grim post-war English cities, Manchester or Birmingham, and a magical land that wasn't really magical at all but even bleaker and more threatening than the council flats where the children lived.

Jeffrey remembered unseen hands tapping at a window, and one of the boys fighting off something invisible that crawled under the bedcovers and attacked in a flapping wave of sheets and blankets. Worst of all was the last chapter, which he read late one night and could never recall clearly, save for the vague, enveloping dread it engendered, something he had never encountered before or since.

Anthea had been right—the book had a weirdly visceral power, more like the effect of a low-budget, black-and-white horror movie than a children's fantasy novel. How many of those grown-up kids now knew their hero had been a pedophile?

Jeffrey spent a half-hour scanning articles on Bennington's trial, none of them very informative. It had happened over a decade ago; since then there'd been a few dozen blog posts, pretty equally divided between *Whatever happened to . . . ?* and excoriations by women who themselves had been sexually abused, though not by Bennington.

He couldn't imagine that had happened to Anthea. She'd certainly never mentioned it, and she'd always been dismissive, even slightly callous, about friends who underwent counseling or psychotherapy for childhood traumas. As for the books themselves, he didn't recall seeing them when he'd sorted through their shelves to pack everything up. Probably they'd been donated to a library book sale years ago, if they'd even made the crossing from London.

He picked up the second envelope. It was postmarked "March 18, 1971." He opened it and withdrew a sheet of lined paper torn from a school notebook.

Dear Rob,

Well, we all got back on the train, Evelyn was in a lot of trouble for being out all night and of course we couldn't tell her aunt why, her mother said she can't talk to me on the phone but I see her at school anyway so it doesn't matter. I still can't believe it all happened. Evelyn's mother said she was going to call my mother and Moira's but so far she didn't. Thank you so much for talking to us. You signed Evelyn's book but you forgot to sign mine. Next time!!!

Yours sincerely your friend,
Anthea

Jeffrey felt a flash of cold through his chest. *Dear Rob, I still can't believe it all happened.* He quickly opened the remaining envelopes, read first one then the next and finally the last.

12 April 1971

Dear Rob,

Maybe I wrote down your address wrong because the last letter I sent was returned. But I asked Moira and she had the same address and she said her letter wasn't returned. Evelyn didn't write yet but says she will. It was such a really, really great time to see you! Thank you again for the books, I thanked you in the last letter but thank you again. I hope you'll write back this time, we still want to come again on holiday in July! I can't believe it was exactly one month ago we were there.

Your friend,
Anthea Ryson

July 20, 1971

Dear Rob,

Well, I still haven't heard from you so I guess you're mad maybe or just forgot about me, ha ha. School is out now and I was wondering if you still wanted us to come and stay? Evelyn says we never could and her aunt would tell her mother but we could hitch-hike, also Evelyn's brother Martin has a caravan and he and his girlfriend are going to Wales for a festival and we thought they might give us a ride partway, he said maybe they would. Then we could hitch-hike the rest. The big news is Moira ran away from home and they called the POLICE. Evelyn said she went without us to see you and she's really mad. Moira's boyfriend Peter is mad too.

If she is there with you is it okay if I come too? I could come alone without Evelyn, her mother is a BITCH.

Please please write!
Anthea (Ryson)

Dear Rob,
I hate you. I wrote FIVE LETTERS including this one and I know it is the RIGHT address. I think Moira went to your house without us. FUCK YOU Tell her I hate her too and so does Evelyn. We never told anyone if she says we did she is a LIAR.
FUCK YOU FUCK YOU FUCK YOU

Where a signature should have been, the page was ripped and blotched with blue ink—Anthea had scribbled something so many times the pen tore through the lined paper. Unlike the other four, this sheet was badly crumpled, as though she'd thrown it away then retrieved it. Jeffrey glanced at the envelope. The postmark read "August 28." She'd gone back to school for the fall term, and presumably that had been the end of it.

Except, perhaps, for Moira, whoever she was. Evelyn would be Evelyn Thurlow, Anthea's closest friend from her school days in Islington. Jeffrey had met her several times while at university, and Evelyn had stayed with them for a weekend in the early 1990s, when she was attending a conference in Manhattan. She was a flight-test engineer for a British defense contractor, living outside Cheltenham; she and Anthea would have hour-long conversations on their birthdays, planning a dream vacation together to someplace warm—Greece or Turkey or the Caribbean.

Jeffrey had e-mailed her about Anthea's death, and they had spoken on the phone—Evelyn wanted to fly over for the funeral but was on deadline for a major government contract and couldn't take the time off.

"I so wish I could be there," she'd said, her voice breaking. "Everything's just so crazed at the moment. I hope you understand . . . "

"It's okay. She knew how much you loved her. She was always so happy to hear from you."

"I know," Evelyn choked. "I just wish—I just wish I'd been able to see her again."

Now he sat and stared at the five letters. The sight made him feel light-headed and slightly queasy: as though he'd opened his closet door and found himself at the edge of a precipice, gazing down some impossible distance to a world made tiny and unreal. Why had she never mentioned any of this? Had she hidden the letters for all these years, or simply forgotten she had them? He knew it wasn't rational; knew his response derived from his compulsive sense of order, what Anthea had always called his architect's left brain.

"Jeffrey would never even try to put a square peg into a round hole," she'd said once at a dinner party. "He'd just design a new hole to fit it."

He could think of no place he could fit the five letters written to Robert Bennington. After a few minutes, he replaced each in its proper envelope and stacked them atop each other. Then he turned back to his laptop, and wrote an e-mail to Evelyn.

He arrived in Cheltenham two weeks later. Evelyn picked him up at the train station early Monday afternoon. He'd told her he was in London on business, spent the preceding weekend at a hotel in Bloomsbury and wandered the city, walking past the building where he and Anthea had lived right after university, before they moved to the US.

It was a relief to board the train and stare out the window at an unfamiliar landscape, suburbs giving way to farms and the gently rolling outskirts of the Cotswolds.

Evelyn's husband, Chris, worked for one of the high-tech corporations in Cheltenham; their house was a rambling, expensively renovated cottage twenty minutes from the congested city center.

"Anthea would have loved these gardens," Jeffrey said, surveying swathes of narcissus already in bloom, alongside yellow primroses and a carpet of bluebells beneath an ancient beech. "Everything at home is still brown. We had snow a few weeks ago."

"It must be very hard, giving up the house." Evelyn poured him a glass of Medoc and sat across from him in the slate-floored sunroom.

"Not as hard as staying would have been," Jeffrey raised his glass. "To old friends and old times."

"To Anthea," said Evelyn.

They talked into the evening, polishing off the Medoc and starting on a second bottle long before Chris arrived home from work. Evelyn was florid and heavy-set, her unruly raven hair long as ever and braided into a single plait, thick and gray-streaked. She'd met her contract deadline just days ago, and her dark eyes still looked hollowed from lack of sleep. Chris prepared dinner, lamb with fresh mint and new peas; their children were both off at university, so Jeffrey and Chris and Evelyn lingered over the table until almost midnight.

"Leave the dishes," Chris said, rising. "I'll get them in the morning." He bent to kiss the top of his wife's head, then nodded at Jeffrey. "Good to see you, Jeffrey."

"Come on." Evelyn grabbed a bottle of Armagnac and headed for the sunroom. "Get those glasses, Jeffrey. I'm not going in till noon. Project's done, and the mice will play."

Jeffrey followed her, settling onto the worn sofa and placing two glasses on the side-table. Evelyn filled both, flopped into an armchair and smiled. "It *is* good to see you."

"And you."

He sipped his Armagnac. For several minutes they sat in silence, staring out the window at the garden, narcissus and primroses faint gleams in the darkness. Jeffrey finished his glass, poured another, and asked, "Do you remember someone named Robert Bennington?"

Evelyn cradled her glass against her chest. She gazed at Jeffrey for a long moment before answering. "The writer? Yes. I read his books when I was a girl. Both of us did—me and Anthea."

"But—you knew him. You met him, when you were thirteen. On vacation or something."

Evelyn turned, her profile silhouetted against the window. "We did," she said at last, and turned back to him. "Why are you asking?"

"I found some letters that Anthea wrote to him. Back in 1971, after you and her and a girl named Moira saw him in Cornwall. Did you know he was a pedophile? He was arrested about fifteen years ago."

"Yes, I read about that. It was a big scandal." Evelyn finished her Armagnac and set her glass on the table. "Well, a medium-sized scandal. I don't think many people even remembered who he was by then. He was a cult writer, really. The books were rather dark for children's books."

She hesitated. "Anthea wasn't molested by him, if that's what you're asking about. None of us were. He invited us to tea—we invited ourselves, actually, he was very nice and let us come in and gave us Nutella sandwiches and tangerines."

"Three little teenyboppers show up at his door, I bet he was very nice," said Jeffrey. "What about Moira? What happened to her?"

"I don't know." Evelyn sighed. "No one ever knew. She ran away from home that summer. We never heard from her again."

"Did they question him? Was he even taken into custody?"

"Of course they did!" Evelyn said, exasperated. "I mean, I don't know for sure, but I'm certain they did. Moira had a difficult home life, her parents were Irish and the father drank. And a lot of kids ran away back then, you know that—all us little hippies. What did the letters say, Jeffrey?"

He removed then from his pocket and handed them to her. "You can read them. He never did—they all came back to Anthea. Where's Padwithiel?"

"Near Zennor. My aunt and uncle lived there, we went and stayed with them during our school holidays one spring." She sorted through the envelopes, pulled out one and opened it, unfolding the letter with care. "February twenty-first. This was right before we knew we'd be going there for the holidays. It was my idea. I remember when she wrote this—she got the address somehow, and that's how we realized he lived near my uncle's farm. Padwithiel."

She leaned into the lamp and read the first letter, set it down and continued to read each of the others. When she was finished, she placed the last one on the table, sank back into her chair and gazed at Jeffrey.

"She never told you about what happened."

"You just said that nothing happened."

"I don't mean with Robert. She called me every year on the anniversary. March 12." She looked away. "Next week, that is. I never told Chris. It wasn't a secret, we just—well, I'll just tell you.

"We went to school together, the three of us, and after Anthea sent that letter to Robert Bennington, she and I cooked up the idea of going to see him. Moira never read his books—she wasn't much of a reader. But she heard us talking about his books all the time, and we'd all play these games where we'd be the ones who fought the Sun Battles. She just did whatever we told her to, though for some reason she always wanted prisoners to be boiled in oil. She must've seen it in a movie.

"Even though we were older now, we still wanted to believe that magic could happen like in those books—probably we wanted to believe it even more. And all that New Agey, hippie stuff, Tarot cards and Biba and 'Ride a White Swan'—it all just seemed like it could be real. My aunt and uncle had a farm near Zennor, my mother asked if we three could stay there for the holidays and Aunt Becca said that would be fine. My cousins are older, and they were already off at university. So we took the train and Aunt Becca got us in Penzance.

"They were turning one of the outbuildings into a pottery studio for her, and that's where we stayed. There was no electricity yet, but we had a kerosene heater and we could stay up as late as we wanted. I think we got maybe five hours sleep the whole time we were there." She laughed. "We'd be up all night, but then Uncle Ray would start in with the tractors at dawn. We'd end up going into the house and napping in one of my cousin's beds for half the afternoon whenever we could. We were very grumpy houseguests.

"It rained the first few days we were there, just pissing down. Finally one morning we got up and the sun was shining. It was cold, but we didn't care—we were just so happy we could get outside for a while. At first we just walked along the road, but it was so muddy from all the rain that we ended up heading across the moor. Technically it's not really open moorland—there are old stone walls criss-crossing everything, ancient field systems. Some of them are thousands of years old, and farmers still keep them up and use them. These had not been kept up. The land was completely overgrown, though you could still see the walls and climb them. Which is what we did.

"We weren't that far from the house—we could still see it, and I'm pretty sure we were still on my uncle's land. We found a place where the walls were higher than elsewhere, more like proper hedgerows. There was no break in the wall like there usually is, no gate or old entryway. So we found a spot that was relatively untangled and we all climbed up and then jumped to the other side. The walls were completely overgrown with blackthorn and all these viney things. It was like Sleeping Beauty's castle—the thorns hurt like shit. I remember I was wearing new boots and they got ruined, just scratched everywhere. And Moira tore her jacket and we knew she'd catch grief for that. But we thought there must be something wonderful on the other side—that was the game we were playing, that we'd find some amazing place. Do you know *The Secret Garden*? We thought it might be like that. At least I did."

"And was it?"

Evelyn shook her head. "It wasn't a garden. It was just this big overgrown field. Dead grass and stones. But it was rather beautiful in a bleak way. Ant laughed and started yelling 'Heathcliff, Heathcliff!' And it was warmer—the walls were high enough to keep out the wind, and there were some trees that had grown up on top of the walls as well. They weren't in leaf yet, but they formed a bit of a windbreak.

"We ended up staying there all day. Completely lost track of the time. I thought only an hour had gone by, but Ant had a watch, at one point she said it was past three and I was shocked—I mean, really shocked. It was like we'd gone to sleep and woken up, only we weren't asleep at all."

"What were you doing?"

Evelyn shrugged. "Playing. The sort of let's-pretend game we always did when we were younger and hadn't done for a while. Moira had a boyfriend, Ant and I really *wanted* boyfriends—mostly that's what we talked about whenever we got together. But for some reason, that day Ant said 'Let's do Sun Battles,' and we all agreed. So that's what we did. Now of course I can see why—I've seen it with my own kids when they were that age, you're on the cusp of everything, and you just want to hold on to being young for as long as you can.

"I don't remember much of what we did that day, except how strange it all felt. As though something was about to happen. I felt like that a lot, it was all tied in with being a teenager; but this was different. It was like being high, or tripping, only none of us had ever done any drugs at that stage. And we were stone-cold sober. Really all we did was wander around the moor and clamber up and down the walls and hedgerows and among the trees, pretending we were in Gearnzath. That was the world in *The Sun Battles*— like Narnia, only much scarier. We were mostly just wandering around and making things up, until Ant told us it was after three o'clock.

"I think it was her idea that we should do some kind of ritual. I know it wouldn't have been Moira's, and I don't think it was mine. But I knew there was going to be a full moon that night—I'd heard my uncle mention it—and so we decided that we would each sacrifice a sacred thing, and then retrieved them all before moonrise. We turned our pockets inside-out looking for what we could use. I had a comb, so that was mine—just a red plastic thing, I think it cost ten pence. Ant had a locket on a chain from Woolworths, cheap but the locket part opened.

"And Moira had a pencil. It said RAVENWOOD on the side, so we called the field Ravenwood. We climbed up on the wall and stood facing the sun, and made up some sort of chant. I don't remember what we said. Then we tossed our things onto the moor. None of us threw them far, and Ant barely tossed hers—she didn't want to lose the locket. I didn't care about the comb, but it was so light it just fell a few yards from where we stood. Same with the pencil. We all marked where they fell—I remember mine very clearly, it came down right on top of this big flat stone.

"Then we left. It was getting late, and cold, and we were all starving—we'd had nothing to eat since breakfast. We went back to the house and hung out in the barn for a while, and then we had dinner. We didn't talk much. Moira hid her jacket so they couldn't see she'd torn it, and I took my boots off so no one would see how I'd got them all mauled by the thorns. I remember my aunt wondering if we were up to something, and my uncle saying what the hell could we possibly be up to in Zennor? After dinner we sat in the living room and waited for the sun to go down, and when we saw the moon start to rise above the hills, we went back outside.

"It was bright enough that we could find our way without a torch—a flashlight. I think that must have been one of the rules, that we had to retrieve our things by moonlight. It was cold out, and none of us had dressed very warmly, so we ran. It didn't take long. We climbed back over the wall and then down onto the field, at the exact spot where we'd thrown our things.

"They weren't there. I knew exactly where the rock was where my comb had landed—the rock was there, but not the comb. Ant's locket had landed only a few feet past it, and it wasn't there either. And Moira's pencil was gone, too."

"The wind could have moved them," said Jeffrey. "Or an animal."

"Maybe the wind," said Evelyn. "Though the whole reason we'd stayed there all day was that there was no wind—it was protected, and warm."

"Maybe a bird took it? Don't some birds like shiny things?"

"What would a bird do with a pencil? Or a plastic comb?"

Jeffrey made a face. "Probably you just didn't see where they fell. You thought you did, in daylight, but everything looks different at night. Especially in moonlight."

"I knew where they were." Evelyn shook her head and reached for the bottle of Armagnac. "Especially my comb. I have that engineer's eye, I can look at things and keep a very precise picture in my mind. The comb wasn't where it should have been. And there was no reason for it to be gone, unless . . . "

"Unless some other kids had seen you and found everything after you left," said Jeffrey.

"No." Evelyn sipped her drink. "We started looking. The moon was coming up—it rose above the hill, and it was very bright. Because it was so cold there was hoarfrost on the grass, and ice in places where the rain had frozen. So all that reflected the moonlight. Everything glittered. It was beautiful, but it was no longer fun—it was scary. None of us was even talking; we just split up and criss-crossed the field, looking for our things.

"And then Moira said, 'There's someone there,' and pointed. I thought it was someone on the track that led back to the farmhouse—it's not a proper road, just a rutted path that runs alongside one edge of that old field system. I looked up and yes, there were three people there—three torches, anyway. Flashlights. You couldn't see who was carrying them, but they were walking slowly along the path. I thought maybe it was my uncle and two of the men who worked with him, coming to tell us it was time to go home. They were walking from the wrong direction, across the moor, but I thought maybe they'd gone out to work on something. So I ran to the left edge of the field and climbed up on the wall."

She stopped, glancing out the window at the black garden, and finally turned back. "I could see the three lights from there," she said. "But the angle was all wrong. They weren't on the road at all—they were in the next field, up above Ravenwood. And they weren't flashlights. They were high up in the air, like this—"

She set down her glass and got to her feet, a bit unsteadily, extended both her arms and mimed holding something in her hands. "Like someone was carrying a pole eight or ten feet high, and there was a light on top of it. Not a flame. Like a ball of light . . . "

She cupped her hands around an invisible globe the size of a soccer ball. "Like that. White light, sort of foggy. The lights bobbed as they were walking."

"Did you see who it was?"

"No. We couldn't see anything. And, this is the part that I can't explain—it just felt bad. Like, horrible. Terrifying."

"You thought you'd summoned up whatever it was you'd been playing at." Jeffrey nodded sympathetically and finished his drink. "It was just marsh gas, Ev. You know that. Will o' the wisp, or whatever you call it here. They must get it all the time out there in the country. Or fog. Or someone just out walking in the moonlight."

Evelyn settled back into her armchair. "It wasn't," she said. "I've seen marsh gas. There was no fog. The moon was so bright you could see every single rock in that field. Whatever it was, we all saw it. And you couldn't hear anything—there were no voices, no footsteps, nothing. They were just there, moving closer to us—slowly," she repeated, and moved her hand up and down, as though calming a cranky child. "That was the creepiest thing, how slowly they just kept coming."

"Why didn't you just run?"

"Because we couldn't. You know how kids will all know about something horrible, but they'll never tell a grown-up? It was like that. We knew we had to find our things before we could go.

"I found my comb first. It was way over—maybe twenty feet from where I'd seen it fall. I grabbed it and began to run across the turf, looking for the locket and Moira's pencil. The whole time the moon was rising, and that was horrible too—it was a beautiful clear night, no clouds at all. And the moon was so beautiful, but it just terrified me. I can't explain it."

Jeffrey smiled wryly. "Yeah? How about this: three thirteen-year-old girls in the dark under a full moon, with a very active imagination?"

"Hush. A few minutes later Moira yelled: she'd found her pencil. She turned and started running back toward the wall, I screamed after her that she had to help us find the locket. She wouldn't come back. She didn't go over the wall without us, but she wouldn't help. I ran over to Ant but she yelled at me to keep searching where I was. I did, I even started heading for the far end of the field, toward the other wall—where the lights were.

"They were very close now, close to the far wall I mean. You could see how high up they were, taller than a person. I could hear Moira crying, I looked back and suddenly I saw Ant dive to the ground. She screamed 'I found it!' and I could see the chain shining in her hand.

"And we just turned and hightailed it. I've never run so fast in my life. I grabbed Ant's arm, by the time we got to the wall Moira was already on top and jumping down the other side. I fell and Ant had to help me up, Moira grabbed her and we ran all the way back to the farm and locked the door when we got inside.

"We looked out the window and the lights were still there. They were there for hours. My uncle had a Border collie, we cracked the door to see if she'd hear something and bark but she didn't. She wouldn't go outside—we tried to get her to look and she wouldn't budge."

"Did you tell your aunt and uncle?"

Evelyn shook her head. "No. We stayed in the house that night, in my cousin's room. It overlooked the moor, so we could watch the lights. After about two hours they began to move back the way they'd come—slowly, it was about another hour before they were gone completely. We went out next morning to see if there was anything there—we took the dog to protect us."

"And?"

"There was nothing. The grass was all beat down, as though someone had been walking over it, but probably that was just us."

She fell silent. "Well," Jeffrey said after a long moment. "It's certainly a good story."

"It's a true story. Here, wait."

She stood and went into the other room, and Jeffrey heard her go upstairs. He crossed to the window and stared out into the night, the dark garden occluded by shadow and runnels of mist, blueish in the dim light cast from the solarium.

"Look. I still have it."

He turned to see Evelyn holding a small round tin. She withdrew a small object and stared at it, placed it back inside and handed him the tin. "My comb. There's some pictures here too."

"That tin." He stared at the lid, blue enamel with the words St. Austell Sweets: Fudge from Real Cornish Cream stamped in gold above the silhouette of what looked like a lighthouse beacon. "It's just like the one I found, with Anthea's letters in it."

Evelyn nodded. "That's right. Becca gave one to each of us the day we arrived. The fudge was supposed to last the entire two weeks, and I think we ate it all that first night."

He opened the tin and gazed at a bright-red plastic comb sitting atop several snapshots; dug into his pocket and pulled out Anthea's locket.

"There it is," said Evelyn wonderingly. She took the locket and dangled it in front of her, clicked it open and shut then returned it to Jeffrey. "She never had anything in it that I knew. Here, look at these."

She took back the tin. He sat, waiting as she sorted through the snapshots then passed him six small black-and-white photos, each time-stamped October 1971.

"That was my camera. A Brownie." Evelyn sank back into the armchair. "I didn't finish shooting the roll till we went back to school."

There were two girls in most of the photos. One was Anthea, apple-cheeked, her face still rounded with puppy fat and her brown hair longer than he'd ever seen it; eyebrows unplucked, wearing baggy bell-bottom jeans and a white peasant shirt. The other girl was taller, sturdy but long-limbed, with long straight blond hair and a broad smooth forehead, elongated eyes and a wide mouth bared in a grin.

"That's Moira," said Evelyn.

"She's beautiful."

"She was. We were the ugly ducklings, Ant and me. Fortunately I was taking most of the photos, so you don't see me except in the ones Aunt Becca took."

"You were adorable." Jeffrey flipped to a photo of all three girls laughing and feeding each other something with their hands, Evelyn still in braces, her hair cut in a severe black bob. "You were all adorable. She's just—"

He scrutinized a photo of Moira by herself, slightly out of focus so all you saw was a blurred wave of blonde hair and her smile, a flash of narrowed eyes. "She's beautiful. Photogenic."

Evelyn laughed. "Is that what you call it? No, Moira was very pretty, all the boys liked her. But she was a tomboy like us. Ant was the one who was boy-crazy. Me and Moira, not so much."

"What about when you saw Robert Bennington? When was that?"

"The next day. Nothing happened—I mean, he was very nice, but there was nothing strange like that night. Nothing *untoward*," she added, lips pursed. "My aunt knew who he was—she didn't know him except to say hello to at the post office, and she'd never read his books. But she knew he was the children's writer, and she knew which house was supposed to be his. We told her we were going to see him, she told us to be polite and not be a nuisance and not stay long.

"So we were polite and not nuisances, and we stayed for two hours. Maybe three. We trekked over to his house, and that took almost an hour. A big old stone house. There was a standing stone and an old barrow nearby, it looked like a hayrick. A fogou. He was very proud that there was a fogou on his land—like a cave, but man-made. He said it was three thousand years old. He took us out to see it, and then we walked back to his house and he made us Nutella sandwiches and tangerines and Orange Squash. We just walked up to his door and knocked—*I* knocked, Ant was too nervous and Moira was just embarrassed. Ant and I had our copies of *The Second Sun*, and he was very sweet and invited us in and said he'd sign them before we left."

"Oh, sure—'Come up and see my fogou, girls.'"

"No—he wanted us to see it because it gave him an idea for his book. It was like a portal, he said. He wasn't a dirty old man, Jeffrey! He wasn't even that old—maybe forty? He had long hair, longish, anyway—to his shoulders—and he had cool clothes, an embroidered shirt and corduroy flares. And pointy-toed boots—blue boot, bright sky-blue, very pointy toes. That was the only thing about him I thought was odd. I wondered how his toes fit into them—if he had long pointy toes to go along with the shoes." She laughed. "Really, he was very charming, talked to us about the books but wouldn't reveal any secrets—he said there would be another in the series but it never appeared. He signed our books—well, he signed mine, Moira didn't have one and for some reason he forgot Ant's. And eventually we left."

"Did you tell him about the lights?"

"We did. He said he'd heard of things like that happening before. That part of Cornwall is ancient, there are all kinds of stone circles and menhirs, cromlechs, things like that."

"What's a cromlech?"

"You know—a dolmen." At Jeffrey's frown she picked up several of the snapshots and arranged them on the side table, a simple house of cards: three photos supporting a fourth laid atop them. "Like that. It's a kind of prehistoric grave, made of big flat stones. Stonehenge, only small. The fogou was a bit like that. They're all over West Penwith—that's where Zennor is. Aleister Crowley lived there, and D.H. Lawrence and his wife. That was years before Robert's time, but he said there were always stories about odd things happening. I don't know what kind of things—it was always pretty boring when I visited as a girl, except for that one time."

Jeffrey made a face. "He was out there with a flashlight, Ev, leading you girls on."

"He didn't even know we were there!" protested Evelyn, so vehemently that the makeshift house of photos collapsed. "He looked genuinely startled when we knocked on his door—I was afraid he'd yell at us to leave. Or, I don't know, have us arrested. He said that field had a name. It was a funny word, Cornish. It meant something, though of course I don't remember what."

She stopped and leaned toward Jeffrey. "Why do you care about this, Jeffrey? *Did* Anthea say something?"

"No. I just found those letters, and . . ."

He lay his hands atop his knees, turned to stare past Evelyn into the darkness, so that she wouldn't see his eyes welling. "I just wanted to know. And I can't ask her."

Evelyn sighed. "Well, there's nothing to know, except what I told you. We went back once more—we took torches this time, and walking sticks and the dog. We stayed out till 3:00 a.m. Nothing happened except we caught hell from my aunt and uncle because they heard the dog barking and looked in the barn and we were gone.

"And that was the end of it. I still have the book he signed for me. Ant must have kept her copy—she was always mad he didn't sign it."

"I don't know. Maybe. I couldn't find it. Your friend Moira, you're not in touch with her?"

Evelyn shook her head. "I told you, she disappeared—she ran away that summer. There were problems at home, the father was a drunk and maybe the mother, too. We never went over there—it wasn't a welcoming place. She had an older sister but I never knew her. Look, if you're thinking Robert Bennington killed her, that's ridiculous. I'm sure her name came up during the trial, if anything had happened we would have heard about it. An investigation."

"Did you tell them about Moira?"

"Of course not. Look, Jeffrey—I think you should forget about all that. It's nothing to do with you, and it was all a long time ago. Ant never cared about it—I told her about the trial, I'd read about it in *The Guardian*, but she was even less curious about it than I was. I don't even know if Robert Bennington is still alive. He'd be an old man now."

She leaned over to take his hand. "I can see you're tired, Jeffrey. This has all been so awful for you, you must be totally exhausted. Do you want to just stay here for a few days? Or come back after your meeting in London?"

"No—I mean, probably not. Probably I need to get back to Brooklyn. I have some projects I backburnered, I need to get to them in the next few weeks. I'm sorry, Ev."

He rubbed his eyes and stood. "I didn't mean to hammer you about this stuff. You're right—I'm just beat. All this—" He sorted the snapshots into a small stack, and asked, "Could I have one of these? It doesn't matter which one."

"Of course. Whichever, take your pick."

He chose a photo of the three girls, Moira and Evelyn doubled over laughing as Anthea stared at them, smiling and slightly puzzled.

"Thank you, Ev," he said. He replaced each of Anthea's letters into its envelope, slid the photo into the last one, then stared at the sheaf in his hand, as though wondering how it got there. "It's just, I dunno. Meaningless, I guess; but I want it to mean something. I want *something* to mean something."

"Anthea meant something." Evelyn stood and put her arms around him. "Your life together meant something. And your life now means something."

"I know." He kissed the top of her head. "I keep telling myself that."

Evelyn dropped him off at the station next morning. He felt guilty, lying that he had meetings back in London, but he sensed both her relief and regret that he was leaving.

"I'm sorry about last night," he said as Evelyn turned into the parking lot. "I feel like the Bad Fairy at the christening, bringing up all that stuff."

"No, it was interesting." Evelyn squinted into the sun. "I hadn't thought about any of that for awhile. Not since Ant called me last March."

Jeffrey hesitated, then asked, "What do you think happened? I mean, you're the one with the advanced degree in structural engineering."

Evelyn laughed. "Yeah. And see where it's got me. I have no idea, Jeffrey. If you ask me, logically, what do I think? Well, I think it's just one of those things that we'll never know what happened. Maybe two different dimensions overlapped—in superstring theory, something like that is theoretically possible, a sort of duality."

She shook her head. "I know it's crazy. Probably it's just one of those things that don't make any sense and never will. Like how did Bush stay in office for so long?"

"That I could explain." Jeffrey smiled. "But it's depressing and would take too long. Thanks again, Ev."

They hopped out of the car and hugged on the curb. "You should come back soon," said Ev, wiping her eyes. "This is stupid, that it took so long for us all to get together again."

"I know. I will—soon, I promise. And you and Chris, come to New York. Once I have a place, it would be great."

He watched her drive off, waving as she turned back onto the main road; went into the station and walked to a ticket window.

"Can I get to Penzance from here?"

"What time?"

"Now."

The station agent looked at her computer. "There's a train in about half-an-hour. Change trains in Plymouth, arrive at Penzance a little before four."

He bought a first-class, one-way ticket to Penzance, found a seat in the waiting area, took out his phone and looked online for a place to stay near Zennor. There wasn't much—a few farmhouses designed for summer rentals, all still closed for the winter. An inn that had in recent years been turned into a popular gastropub was open; but even now, the first week of March, they were fully booked. Finally he came upon a B&B called Cliff Cottage. There were only two rooms, and the official opening date was not until the following weekend, but he called anyway.

"A room?" The woman who answered sounded tired but friendly. "We're not really ready yet, we've been doing some renovations and—"

"All I need is a bed," Jeffrey broke in. He took a deep breath. "The truth is, my wife died recently. I just need some time to be away from the rest of the world and . . . "

His voice trailed off. He felt a pang of self-loathing, playing the pity card; listened to a long silence on the line before the woman said, "Oh, dear, I'm so sorry. Well, yes, if you don't mind that we're really not up and running. The grout's not even dry yet in the new bath. Do you have a good head for heights?"

"Heights?"

"Yes. Vertigo? Some people have a very hard time with the driveway. There's a two-night minimum for a stay."

Jeffrey assured her he'd never had any issues with vertigo. He gave her his credit card info, rang off and called to reserve a car in Penzance.

He slept most of the way to Plymouth, exhausted and faintly hungover. The train from Plymouth to Penzance was nearly empty. He bought a beer and a sandwich in the buffet car, and went to his seat. He'd bought a novel in London at Waterstones, but instead of reading gazed out at a landscape that was a dream of books he'd read as a child—granite farmhouses, woolly-coated ponies in stone paddocks; fields improbably green against lowering gray sky, graphite clouds broken by blades of golden sun, a rainbow that pierced a thunderhead then faded as though erased by some unseen hand. Ringnecked pheasants, a running fox. More fields planted with something that shone a startling goldfinch-yellow. A silvery coastline hemmed by arches of russet stone. Children wrestling in the middle of an empty road. A woman walking with head bowed against the wind, hands extended before her like a diviner.

Abandoned mineshafts and slagheaps; ruins glimpsed in an eyeflash before the train dove into a tunnel; black birds wheeling above a dun-colored tor surrounded by scorched heath.

And, again and again, groves of gnarled oaks that underscored the absence of great forests in a landscape that had been scoured of trees thousands of years ago. It was beautiful yet also slightly disturbing, like watching an underpopulated, narratively fractured silent movie that played across the train window.

The trees were what most unsettled Jeffrey: the thought that men had so thoroughly occupied this countryside for so long that they had flensed it of everything—rocks, trees, shrubs all put to some human use so that only the abraded land remained. He felt relieved when the train at last reached Penzance, with the beachfront promenade to one side, glassy waves breaking on the sand and the dark towers of St. Michael's Mount suspended between aquamarine water and pearly sky.

He grabbed his bag and walked through the station, outside to where people waited on the curb with luggage or headed to the parking lot. The clouds had lifted: a chill steady wind blew from off the water, bringing the smell of salt and sea wrack. He shivered and pulled on his wool overcoat, looking around for the vehicle from the rental car company that was supposed to meet him.

He finally spotted it, a small white sedan parked along the sidewalk. A man in a dark blazer leaned against the car, smoking and talking to a teenage boy with dreadlocks and rainbow-knit cap and a woman with matted dark-blond hair.

"You my ride?" Jeffrey said, smiling.

The man took a drag from his cigarette and passed it to the woman. She was older than Jeffrey had first thought, in her early thirties, face seamed and sun-weathered and her eyes bloodshot. She wore tight flared jeans and a fuzzy sky-blue sweater beneath a stained Arsenal windbreaker.

"Spare anything?" she said as he stopped alongside the car. She reeked of sweat and marijuana smoke.

"Go on now, Erthy," the man said, scowling. He turned to Jeffrey. "Mr. Kearin?"

"That's me," said Jeffrey.

"Gotta 'nother rollie, Evan?" the woman prodded.

"Come on, Erthy," said the rainbow-hatted boy. He spun and began walking toward the station. "Peace, Evan."

"I apologize for that," Evan said as he opened the passenger door for Jeffrey. "I know the boy, his family's neighbors of my sister's."

"Bit old for him, isn't she?" Jeffrey glanced to where the two huddled against the station wall, smoke welling from their cupped hands.

"Yeah, Erthy's a tough nut. She used to sleep rough by the St. Erth train station. Only this last winter she's taken up in Penzance. Every summer we get the smackhead hippies here, there's always some poor souls who stay and take up on the street. Not that you want to hear about that," he added, laughing as he swung into the driver's seat. "On vacation?"

Jeffrey nodded. "Just a few days."

"Staying here in Penzance?"

"Cardu. Near Zennor."

"Might see some sun, but probably not till the weekend."

He ended up with the same small white sedan. "Only one we have, this last minute," Evan said, tapping at the computer in the rental office. "But it's better really for driving out there in the countryside. Roads are extremely narrow. Have you driven around here before? No? I would strongly recommend the extra damages policy . . . "

It had been decades since Jeffrey had been behind the wheel of a car in the U.K. He began to sweat as soon as he left the rental car lot, eyes darting between the map Evan had given him and the GPS on his iPhone. In minutes the busy roundabout was behind him; the car crept up a narrow, winding hillside, with high stone walls to either side that swiftly gave way to hedgerows bordering open farmland. A brilliant yellow field proved to be planted with daffodils, their constricted yellow throats not yet in bloom. After several more minutes, he came to a crossroads.

Almost immediately he got lost. The distances between villages and roads were deceptive: what appeared on the map to be a mile or more instead contracted into a few hundred yards, or else expanded into a series of zigzags and switchbacks that appeared to point him back toward Penzance. The GPS directions made no sense, advising him to turn directly into stone walls or gated driveways or fields where cows grazed on young spring grass. The roads were only wide enough for one car to pass, with tiny turnouts every fifty feet or so where one could pull over, but the high hedgerows and labyrinthine turns made it difficult to spot oncoming vehicles.

His destination, a village called Cardu, was roughly seven miles from Penzance; after half-an-hour, the odometer registered that he'd gone fifteen miles, and he had no idea where he was. There was no cell phone reception. The sun dangled a hand's-span above the western horizon, staining ragged stone outcroppings and a bleak expanse of moor an ominous reddish-bronze, and throwing the black fretwork of stone walls into stark relief. He finally parked in one of the narrow turnouts, sat for a few minutes staring into the sullen blood-red eye of the sun, and at last got out.

The hedgerows offered little protection from the harsh wind that raked across the moor. Jeffrey pulled at the collar of his wool coat, turning his back to the wind, and noticed a small sign that read PUBLIC FOOTPATH. He walked over and saw a narrow gap in the hedgerow, three steps formed of wide flat stones. He took the three in one long stride and found himself at the edge of an overgrown field, similar to what Evelyn had described in her account of the lights near Zennor. An ancient-looking stone wall bounded the far edge of the field, with a wider gap that opened to the next field and what looked like another sign. He squinted, but couldn't make out what it read, and began to pick his way across the turf.

It was treacherous going—the countless hummocks hid deep holes, and more than once he barely kept himself from wrenching his ankle. The air smelled strongly of raw earth and cow manure. As the sun dipped lower, a wedge of shadow was driven between him and the swiftly darkening sky, making it still more difficult to see his way. But after a few minutes he reached the far wall, and bent to read the sign beside the gap into the next field.

CAS CIRCLE

He glanced back, saw a glint of white where the rental car was parked, straightened and walked on.

There was a footpath here. Hardly a path, really; just a trail where turf and bracken had been flattened by the passage of not-many feet. He followed it, stopping when he came to a large upright stone that came up his waist. He looked to one side then the other and saw more stones, forming a group more ovoid than circular, perhaps thirty feet in diameter. He ran his hand across the first stone—rough granite, ridged with lichen and friable bits of moss that crumbled at his touch.

The reek of manure was fainter here: he could smell something fresh and sweet, like rain, and when he looked down saw a silvery gleam at the base of the rock. He crouched and dipped his fingers into a tiny pool, no bigger than his shoe. The water was icy cold, and even after he withdrew his hand, the surface trembled.

A spring. He dipped his cupped palm into it and sniffed warily, expecting a fetid whiff of cow muck.

But the water smelled clean, of rock and rain. Without thinking he drew his hand to his mouth and sipped, immediately flicked his fingers to send glinting droplets into the night.

That was stupid, he thought, hastily wiping his hand on his trousers. *Now I'll get dysentery. Or whatever one gets from cows.*

He stood there for another minute, then turned and retraced his steps to the rental car. He saw a pair of headlights approaching and flagged down a white delivery van.

"I'm lost," he said, and showed the driver the map that Evan had given him.

"Not too lost." The driver perused the map, then gave him directions. "Once you see the inn you're almost there."

Jeffrey thanked him, got back into the car and started to drive. In ten minutes he reached the inn, a rambling stucco structure with a half-dozen cars out front. There was no sign identifying Cardu, and no indication that there was anything more to the village than the inn and a deeply rutted road flanked by a handful of granite cottages in varying states of disrepair. He eased the rental car by the mottled gray buildings, to where what passed for a road ended; bore right and headed down a cobblestoned, hairpin drive that zigzagged along the cliff-edge.

He could hear but could not see the ocean, waves crashing against rocks hundreds of feet below. Now and then he got a skin-crawling glimpse of immense cliffs like congealed flames—ruddy stone, apricot-yellow gorse, lurid flares of orange lichen all burned to ash as afterglow faded from the western sky.

He wrenched his gaze back to the narrow strip of road immediately in front of him. Gorse and brambles tore at the doors; once he bottomed out, then nosed the car across a water-filled gulley that widened into a stream that cascaded down the cliff to the sea below.

"Holy fucking Christ," he said, and kept the car in first gear. In another five minutes he was safely parked beside the cottage, alongside a small sedan.

"We thought maybe you weren't coming," someone called as Jeffrey stepped shakily out onto a cobblestone drive. Straggly rosebushes grew between a row of granite slabs that resembled headstones. These were presumably to keep cars from veering down an incline that led to a ruined outbuilding, a few faint stars already framed in its gaping windows. "Some people, they start down here and just give up and turn back."

Jeffrey looked around, finally spotted a slight man in his early sixties standing in the doorway of a gray stone cottage tucked into the lee of the cliff. "Oh, hi. No, I made it."

Jeffrey ducked back into the car, grabbed his bag and headed for the cottage.

"Harry," the man said, and held the door for him.

"Jeffrey. I spoke to your wife this afternoon."

The man's brow furrowed. "Wife?" He was a head shorter than Jeffrey, clean-shaven, with a sun-weathered face and sleek gray-flecked dark brown hair to his shoulders. A ropey old cable knit sweater hung from his lank frame.

"Well, someone. A woman."

"Oh. That was Thomsa. My sister." The man nodded, as though this confusion had never occurred before. "We're still trying to get unpacked. We don't really open till this weekend, but . . . "

He held the door so Jeffrey could pass inside. "Thomsa told me of your loss. My condolences."

Inside was a small room with slate floors and plastered walls, sparely furnished with a plain deal table and four chairs intricately carved with Celtic knots; a sideboard holding books and maps and artfully mismatched crockery; large gas cooking stove and a side table covered with notepads and pens, unopened bills, and a laptop. A modern cast-iron wood-stove had been fitted into a wide, old-fashioned hearth. The stove radiated warmth and an acrid, not unpleasant scent, redolent of coal-smoke and burning sage. Peat, Jeffrey realized with surprise. There was a closed door on the other side of the room, and from behind this came the sound of a television.

Harry looked at Jeffrey, cocking an eyebrow.

"It's beautiful," said Jeffrey.

Harry nodded. "I'll take you to your room," he said.

Jeffrey followed him up a narrow stair beneath the eaves, into a short hallway flanked by two doors. "Your room's here. Bath's down there, you'll have it all to yourself. What time would you like breakfast?"

"Seven, maybe?"

"How about seven-thirty?"

Jeffrey smiled wanly. "Sure."

The room was small, white plaster walls and a window-seat overlooking the sea, a big bed heaped with a white duvet and myriad pillows, corner wardrobe carved with the same Celtic knots as the chairs below. No TV or radio or telephone, not even a clock. Jeffrey unpacked his bag and checked his phone for service: none.

He closed the wardrobe, looked in his backpack and swore. He'd left his book on the train. He ran a hand through his hair, stepped to the window-seat and stared out.

It was too dark now to see much, though light from windows on the floor below illuminated a small, winding patch of garden, bound at the cliff-side by a stone wall. Beyond that there was only rock and, far below, the sea. Waves thundered against the unseen shore, a muted roar like a jet turbine. He could feel the house around him shake.

And not just the house, he thought; it felt as though the ground and everything around him trembled without ceasing. He paced to the other window, overlooking the drive, and stared at his rental car and the sedan beside it through a frieze of branches, a tree so contorted by wind and salt that its limbs only grew in one direction. He turned off the room's single light, waited for his eyes to adjust; stared back out through one window, and then the other.

For as far as he could see, there was only night. Ghostly light seeped from a room downstairs onto the sliver of lawn. Starlight touched on the endless sweep of moor, like another sea unrolling from the line of cliffs brooding above black waves and distant headlands. There was no sign of human habitation: no distant lights, no street-lamps, no cars, no ships or lighthouse beacons: nothing.

He sank onto the window seat, dread knotting his chest. He had never seen anything like this—even hiking in the Mojave Desert with Anthea ten years earlier, there had been a scattering of lights sifted across the horizon and satellites moving slowly through the constellations. He grabbed his phone, fighting a cold black solitary horror. There was still no reception.

He put the phone aside and stared at a framed sepia-tinted photograph on the wall: a three-masted schooner wrecked on the rocks beneath a cliff he suspected was the same one where the cottage stood. Why was he even here? He felt as he had once in college, waking in a strange room after a night of heavy drinking, surrounded by people he didn't know in a squalid flat used as a shooting gallery. The same sense that he'd been engaged in some kind of psychic somnambulism, walking perilously close to a precipice.

Here, of course he actually *was* perched on the edge of a precipice. He stood and went into the hall, switching on the light; walked into the bathroom and turned on all the lights there as well.

It was almost as large as his bedroom, cheerfully appointed with yellow and blue towels piled atop a wooden chair, a massive porcelain tub, hand-woven yellow rugs and a fistful of daffodils in a cobalt glass vase on a wide windowsill. He moved the towels and sat on the chair for a few minutes, then crossed to pick up the vase and drew it to his face.

The daffodils smelled sweetly, of overturned earth warming in the sunlight. Anthea had loved daffodils, planting a hundred new bulbs every autumn; daffodils and jonquil and narcissus and crocuses, all the harbingers of spring. He inhaled again, deeply, and replaced the flowers on the sill. He left a light on beside the sink, returned to his room and went to bed.

He woke before 7:00. Thin sunlight filtered through the white curtains he'd drawn the night before, and for several minutes he lay in bed, listening to the rhythmic boom of surf on the rocks. He finally got up, pulled aside the curtain and looked out.

A line of clouds hung above the western horizon, but over the headland the sky was pale blue, shot with gold where the sun rose above the moor. Hundreds of feet below Jeffrey's bedroom, aquamarine swells crashed against the base of the cliffs and swirled around ragged granite pinnacles that rose from the sea, surrounded by clouds of white seabirds. There was a crescent of white sand, and a black cavern-mouth gouged into one of the cliffs where a vortex rose and subsided with the waves.

The memory of last night's horror faded: sunlight and wheeling birds, the vast expanse of air and sea and all but treeless moor made him feel exhilarated. For the first time since Anthea's death, he had a premonition not of dread but of the sort of exultation he felt as a teenager, waking in his boyhood room in early spring.

He dressed and shaved—there was no shower, only that dinghy-sized tub, so he'd forgo bathing till later. He waited until he was certain he heard movement in the kitchen, and went downstairs.

"Good morning." A woman who might have been Harry's twin leaned against the slate sink. Slender, small-boned, with straight dark hair held back with two combs from a narrow face, brown-eyed and weathered as her brother's. "I'm Thomsa."

He shook her hand, glanced around for signs of coffee then peered out the window. "This is an amazing place."

"Yes, it is," Thomsa said evenly. She spooned coffee into a glass cafetière, picked up a steaming kettle and poured hot water over the grounds. "Coffee, right? I have tea if you prefer. Would you like eggs? Some people have all sorts of food allergies. Vegans, how do you feed them?" She stared at him in consternation, turned back to the sink, glancing at a bowl of eggs. "How many?"

The cottage was silent, save for the drone of a television behind the closed door and the thunder of waves beating against the cliffs. Jeffrey sat at a table set for one, poured himself coffee and stared out to where the moor rose behind them. "Does the sound of the ocean ever bother you?" he asked.

Thomsa laughed. "No. We've been here thirty-five years, we're used to that. But we're building a house in Greece, in Hydra, that's where we just returned from. There's a church in the village and every afternoon the bells ring, I don't know why. At first I thought, isn't that lovely, church bells! Now I'm sick of them and just wish they'd just shut up."

She set a plate of fried eggs and thick-cut bacon in front of him, along with slabs of toasted brown bread and glass bowls of preserves, picked up a mug and settled at the table. "So are you here on holiday?"

"Mmm, yes." Jeffrey nodded, his mouth full. "My wife died last fall. I just needed to get away for a bit."

"Yes, of course. I'm very sorry."

"She visited here once when she was a girl—not here, but at a farm nearby, in Zennor. I don't know the last name of the family, but the woman was named Becca."

"Becca? Mmmm, no, I don't think so. Maybe Harry will know."

"This would have been 1971."

"Ah—no, we didn't move here till '75. Summer, us and all the other hippie types from back then." She sipped her tea. "No tourists around this time of year. Usually we don't open till the second week in March. But we don't have anyone scheduled yet, so." She shrugged, pushing back a wisp of dark hair. "It's quiet this time of year. No German tour buses. Do you paint?"

"Paint?" Jeffrey blinked. "No. I'm an architect, so I draw, but mostly just for work. I sketch sometimes."

"We get a lot of artists. There's the Tate in St. Ives, if you like modern architecture. And of course there are all the prehistoric ruins—standing stones, and Zennor Quoit. There are all sorts of legends about them, fairy tales. People disappearing. They're very interesting if you don't mind the walk."

"Are there places to eat?"

"The inn here, though you might want to stop in and make a booking. There's the pub in Zennor, and St. Ives of course, though it can be hard to park. And Penzance."

Jeffrey winced. "Not sure I want to get back on the road again immediately."

"Yes, the drive here's a bit tricky, isn't it? But Zennor's only two miles, if you don't mind walking—lots of people do, we get hikers from all over on the coastal footpath. And Harry might be going out later, he could drop you off in Zennor if you like."

"Thanks. Not sure what I'll do yet. But thank you."

He ate his breakfast, making small talk with Thomsa and nodding at Harry when he emerged and darted through the kitchen, raising a hand as he slipped outside. Minutes later, Jeffrey glimpsed him pushing a wheelbarrow full of gardening equipment.

"I think the rain's supposed to hold off," Thomsa said, staring out the window. "I hope so. We want to finish that wall. Would you like me to make more coffee?"

"If you don't mind."

Jeffrey dabbed a crust into the blackcurrant preserves. He wanted to ask if Thomsa or her brother knew Robert Bennington, but was afraid he might be stirring up memories of some local scandal, or that he'd be taken for a journalist or some other busybody. He finished the toast, thanked Thomsa when she poured him more coffee, then reached for one of the brochures on the sideboard.

"So does this show where those ruins are?"

"Yes. You'll want the Ordnance map. Here—"

She cleared the dishes, gathered a map and unfolded it. She tapped the outline of a tiny cove between two spurs of land. "We're here."

She traced one of the spurs, lifted her head to stare out the window to a gray-green spine of rock stretching directly to the south. "That's Gurnard's Head. And there's Zennor Head—"

She turned and pointed in the opposite direction, to a looming promontory a few miles distant, and looked back down at the map. "You can see where everything's marked."

Jeffrey squinted to make out words printed in a tiny, Gothic font. Tumuli, Standing Stone, Hut Circle, Cairn. "Is there a fogou around here?"

"A fogou?" She frowned slightly. "Yes, there is—out toward Zennor, across the moor. It's a bit of a walk."

"Could you give me directions? Just sort of point the way? I might try and find it—give me something to do."

Thomsa stepped to the window. "The coastal path is there—see? If you follow it up to the ridge, you'll see a trail veer off. There's an old road there, the farmers use it sometimes. All those old fields run alongside it. The fogou's on the Golovenna Farm, I don't know how many fields back that is. It would be faster if you drove toward Zennor then hiked over the moor, but you could probably do it from here. You'll have to find an opening in the stone walls or climb over—do you have hiking shoes?" She looked dubiously at his sneakers. "Well, they'll probably be all right."

"I'll give it a shot. Can I take that map?"

"Yes, of course. It's not the best map—the Ordnance Survey has a more detailed one, I think."

He thanked her and downed the rest of his coffee, went upstairs and pulled a heavy woolen sweater over his flannel shirt, grabbed his cell phone and returned downstairs. He retrieved the map and stuck it in his coat pocket, said goodbye to Thomsa rinsing dishes in the sink, and walked outside.

The air was warmer, almost balmy despite a stiff wind that had torn the line of clouds into gray shreds. Harry knelt beside a stone wall, poking at the ground with a small spade. Jeffrey paused to watch him, then turned to survey clusters of daffodils and jonquils, scores of them scattered across the terraced slopes among rocks and apple trees. The flowers were not yet in bloom, but he could glimpse sunlit yellow and orange and saffron petals swelling within the green buds atop each slender stalk.

"Going out?" Harry called.

"Yes." Jeffrey stooped to brush his fingers across one of the flowers. "My wife loved daffodils. She must have planted thousands of them."

Harry nodded. "Should open in the next few days. If we get some sun."

Jeffrey waved farewell and turned to walk up the drive.

In a few minutes, the cottage was lost to sight. The cobblestones briefly gave way to cracked concrete, then a deep rut that marked a makeshift path that led uphill, toward the half-dozen buildings that made up the village. He stayed on the driveway, and after another hundred feet reached a spot where a narrow footpath meandered off to the left, marked by a sign. This would be the path that Thomsa had pointed out.

He shaded his eyes and looked back. He could just make out Cliff Cottage, its windows a flare of gold in the sun. He stepped onto the trail, walking with care across loose stones and channels where water raced downhill, fed by the early spring rains. To one side, the land sheared away to cliffs and crashing waves; he could see where the coastal path wound along the headland, fading into the emerald crown of Zennor Head. Above him, the ground rose steeply, overgrown with coiled ferns, newly sprung grass, thickets of gorse in brilliant sun-yellow bloom where bees and tiny orange butterflies fed. At the top of the incline, he could see the dark rim of a line of stone walls. He stayed on the footpath until it began to bear toward the cliffs, then looked for a place where he could break away and make for the ancient fields. He saw what looked like a path left by some kind of animal and scrambled up, dodging gorse, his sneakers sliding on loose scree, until he reached the top of the headland.

The wind here was so strong he nearly lost his balance as he hopped down into a grassy lane. The lane ran parallel to a long ridge of stone walls perhaps four feet high, braided with strands of rusted barbed wire. On the other side, endless intersections of yet more walls divided the moor into a dizzyingly ragged patchwork: jade-green, beryl, creamy yellow; ochre and golden amber. Here and there, twisted trees grew within sheltered corners, or rose from atop the walls themselves, gnarled branches scraping at the sky. High overhead, a bird arrowed toward the sea, and its plaintive cry rose above the roar of wind in his ears.

He pulled out the map, struggling to open it in the wind, finally gave up and shoved it back into his pocket. He tried to count back four fields, but it was hopeless—he couldn't make out where one field ended and another began.

And he had no idea what field to start with. He walked alongside the lane, away from the cottage and the village of Cardu, hoping he might find a gate or opening. He finally settled on a spot where the barbed wire had become engulfed by a protective thatch of dead vegetation. He clambered over the rocks, clutching desperately at dried leaves as the wall gave way beneath his feet and nearly falling onto a lethal-looking knot of barbed wire. Gasping, he reached the top of the wall, flailed as wind buffeted him then crouched until he could catch his breath.

The top of the wall was covered with vines, gray and leafless, as thick as his fingers and unpleasantly reminiscent of veins and arteries. This serpentine mass seemed to hold the stones together, though when he tried to step down the other side, the rocks once again gave way and he fell into a patch of whip-like vines studded with thorns the length of his thumbnail. Cursing, he extricated himself, his chinos torn and hands gouged and bloody, and staggered into the field.

Here at least there was some protection from the wind. The field sloped slightly uphill, to the next wall. There was so sign of a gate or breach. He shoved his hands into his pockets and strode through knee-high grass, pale green and starred with minute yellow flowers. He reached the wall and walked alongside it. In one corner several large rocks had fallen. He hoisted himself up until he could see into the next field. It was no different from the one he'd just traversed, save for a single massive evergreen in its center.

Other than the tree, the field seemed devoid of any vegetation larger than a tussock. He tried to peer into the field beyond, and the ones after that, but the countryside dissolved into a glitter of green and topaz beneath the morning sun, with a few stone pinnacles stark against the horizon where moor gave way to sky.

He turned and walked back, head down against the wind; climbed into the first field and crossed it, searching until he spied what looked like a safe place to gain access to the lane once more. Another tangle of blackthorn snagged him as he jumped down and landed hard, grimacing as a thorn tore at his neck. He glared at the wall, then headed back to the cottage, picking thorns from his overcoat and jeans.

He was starving by the time he arrived at the cottage, also filthy. It had grown too warm for his coat; he slung it over his shoulder, wiping sweat from his cheeks. Thomsa was outside, removing a shovel from the trunk of the sedan.

"Oh, hello! You're back quickly!"

He stopped, grateful for the wind on his overheated face. "Quickly?"

"I thought you'd be off till lunchtime. A few hours, anyway?"

"I thought it *was* lunchtime." He looked at his watch and frowned. "That can't be right. It's not even ten."

Thomsa nodded, setting the shovel beside the car. "I thought maybe you forgot something." She glanced at him, startled. "Oh my. You're bleeding—did you fall?"

He shook his head. "No, well, yes," he said sheepishly. "I tried to find that fogou. Didn't get very far. Are you sure it's just ten? I thought I was out there for hours—I figured it must be noon, at least. What time did I leave?"

"Half-past nine, I think."

He started to argue, instead shrugged. "I might try again. You said there's a better map from the Ordnance Survey? Something with more details?"

"Yes. You could probably get it in Penzance—call the bookstore there if you like, phone book's on the table."

He found the phone book in the kitchen and rang the bookshop. They had a copy of the Ordnance map and would hold it for him. He rummaged on the table for a brochure with a map of Penzance, went upstairs to spend a few minutes washing up from his trek, and hurried outside. Thomsa and Harry were lugging stones across the grass to repair the wall. Jeffrey waved, ducked into the rental car and crept back up the drive toward Cardu.

In broad daylight it still took almost ten minutes. He glanced out to where the coastal footpath wound across the top of the cliffs, could barely discern a darker trail leading to the old field systems, and, beyond that, the erratic cross-stitch of stone walls fading into the eastern sky. Even if he'd only gone as far as the second field, it seemed impossible that he could have hiked all the way there and back to the cottage in half-an-hour.

The drive to Penzance took less time than that; barely long enough for Jeffrey to reflect how unusual it was for him to act like this, impulsively, without a plan. Everything an architect did was according to plan. Out on the moor and gorse-grown cliffs, the strangeness of the immense, dour landscape had temporarily banished the near-constant presence of his dead wife. Now, in the confines of the cramped rental car, images of other vehicles and other trips returned, all with Anthea beside him. He pushed them away, tried to focus on the fact that here at last was a place where he'd managed to escape her; and remembered that was not true at all.

Anthea had been here, too. Not the Anthea he had loved but her mayfly self, the girl he'd never known; the Anthea who'd contained an entire secret world he'd never known existed. It seemed absurd, but he desperately wished she had confided in him about her visit to Bennington's house, and the strange night that had preceded it. Evelyn's talk of superstring theory was silly—he found himself sympathizing with Moira, content to let someone else read the creepy books and tell her what to do. He believed in none of it, of course. Yet it didn't matter what he believed, but whether Anthea had, and why.

Penzance was surprisingly crowded for a weekday morning in early March. He circled the town's winding streets twice before he found a parking space, several blocks from the bookstore. He walked past shops and restaurants featuring variations on themes involving pirates, fish, pixies, sailing ships. As he passed a tattoo parlor, he glanced into the adjoining alley and saw the same rainbow-hatted boy from the train station, holding a skateboard and standing with several other teenagers who were passing around a joint. The boy looked up, saw Jeffrey and smiled. Jeffrey lifted his hand and smiled back. The boy called out to him, his words garbled by the wind, put down his skateboard and did a headstand alongside it. Jeffrey laughed and kept going.

There was only one other customer in the shop when he arrived, a man in a business suit talking to two women behind the register.

"Can I help you?" The older of the two women smiled. She had close-cropped red hair and fashionable eyeglasses, and set aside an iPad as Jeffrey approached.

"I called about an Ordnance map?"

"Yes. It's right here."

She handed it to him, and he unfolded it enough to see that it showed the same area of West Penwith as the other map, enlarged and far more detailed.

The woman with the glasses cocked her head. "Shall I ring that up?"

Jeffrey closed the map and set it onto the counter. "Sure, in a minute. I'm going to look around a bit first."

She returned to chatting. Jeffrey wandered the shop. It was small but crowded with neatly-stacked shelves and tables, racks of maps and postcards, with an extensive section of books about Cornwall—guidebooks, tributes to Daphne du Maurier and Barbara Hepworth, DVDs of *The Pirates of Penzance* and *Rebecca*, histories of the mines and glossy photo volumes about surfing Newquay. He spent a few minutes flipping through one of these, and continued to the back of the store. There was an entire wall of children's books, picture books near the floor, chapter books for older children arranged alphabetically above them. He scanned the Bs, and looked aside as the younger woman approached, carrying an armful of calendars.

"Are you looking for something in particular?"

He glanced back at the shelves. "Do you have anything by Robert Bennington?"

The young woman set the calendars down, ran a hand along the shelf housing the Bs; frowned and looked back to the counter. "Rose, do we have anything by Robert Bennington? It rings a bell but I don't see anything here. Children's writer, is he?" she added, turning to Jeffrey.

"Yes. *The Sun Battles*, I think that's one of them."

The other customer nodded goodbye as Rose joined the others in the back.

"Robert Bennington?" She halted, straightening a stack of coffee table books, tapped her lower lip then quickly nodded. "Oh yes! The fantasy writer. We did have his books—he's fallen out of favor." She cast a knowing look at the younger clerk. "He was the child molester."

"Oh, right." The younger woman made a face. "I don't think his books are even in print now, are they?"

"I don't think so," said Rose. "I'll check. We could order something for you, if they are."

"That's okay—I'm only here for a few days."

Jeffrey followed her to the counter and waited as she searched online.

"No, nothing's available." Rose shook her head. "Sad bit of business, wasn't it? I heard something recently, he had a stroke I think. He might even have died, I can't recall now who told me. He must be quite elderly, if he's still alive."

"He lived around here, didn't he?" said Jeffrey.

"Out near Zennor, I think. He bought the old Golovenna Farm, years ago. We used to sell quite a lot of his books—he was very popular. Like the *Harry Potter* books now. Well, not that popular." She smiled. "But he did very well. He came in here once or twice, it must be twenty years at least. A very handsome man. Theatrical. He wore a long scarf, like Doctor Who. I'm sure you could find used copies online, or there's a second-hand bookstore just round the corner—they might well have something."

"That's all right. But thank you for checking."

He paid for the map and went back out onto the sidewalk. It was getting on to noon. He wandered the streets for several minutes looking for a place to eat, settled on a small, airy Italian restaurant where he had grilled sardines and spaghetti and a glass of wine. Not very Cornish, perhaps, but he promised himself to check on the pub in Zennor later.

The Ordnance map was too large and unwieldy to open at his little table, so he stared out the window, watching tourists and women with small children in tow as they popped in and out of the shops across the street. The rainbow-hatted boy and his cronies loped by, skateboards in hand. Dropouts or burnouts, Jeffrey thought; the local constabulary must spend half its time chasing them from place to place. He finished his wine and ordered a cup of coffee, gulped it down, paid the check, and left.

A few high white clouds scudded high overhead, borne on a steady wind that sent up flurries of grit and petals blown from ornamental cherry trees. Here in the heart of Penzance, the midday sun was almost hot: Jeffrey hooked his coat over his shoulder and ambled back to his car. He paused to glance at postcards and souvenirs in a shop window, but could think of no one to send a card to. Evelyn? She'd rather have something from Zennor, another reason to visit the pub.

He turned the corner, had almost reached the tattoo parlor when a plaintive cry rang out.

"Have you seen him?"

Jeffrey halted. In the same alley where he'd glimpsed the boys earlier, a forlorn figure sat on the broken asphalt, twitchy fingers toying with an unlit cigarette. Erthy, the thirty-ish woman who'd been at the station the day before. As Jeffrey hesitated she lifted her head, swiped a fringe of dirty hair from her eyes and stumbled to her feet. His heart sank as she hurried toward him, but before he could flee she was already in his face, her breath warm and beery. "Gotta light?"

"No, sorry," he said, and began to step away.

"Wait—you're London, right?"

"No, I'm just visiting."

"No—I saw you."

He paused, thrown off-balance by a ridiculous jolt of unease. Her eyes were bloodshot, the irises a peculiar marbled blue like flawed bottle-glass, and there was a vivid crimson splotch in one eye, as though a capillary had burst. It made it seem as though she looked at him sideways, even though she was staring at him straight on.

"You're on the London train!" She nodded in excitement. "I need to get back."

"I'm sorry." He spun and walked off as quickly as he could without breaking into a run. Behind him he heard footsteps, and again the same wrenching cry.

"*Have you seen him?*"

He did run then, as the woman screamed expletives and a shower of gravel pelted his back.

He reached his rental car, his heart pounding. He looked over his shoulder, jumped inside and locked the doors before pulling out into the street. As he drove off, he caught a flash in the rear-view mirror of the woman sidling in the other direction, unlit cigarette still twitching between her fingers.

When he arrived back at the cottage, he found Thomsa and Harry sitting at the kitchen table, surrounded by the remains of lunch, sandwich crusts and apple cores.

"Oh, hello." Thomsa looked up, smiling, and patted the chair beside her. "Did you go to The Tinners for lunch?"

"Penzance." Jeffrey sat and dropped his map onto the table. "I think I'll head out again, then maybe have dinner at the pub."

"He wants to see the fogou," said Thomsa. "He went earlier but couldn't find it. There is a fogou, isn't there, Harry? Out by Zennor Hill?"

Jeffrey hesitated, then said, "A friend of mine told me about it—she and my wife saw it when they were girls."

"Yes," said Harry after a moment. "Where the children's writer lived. Some sort of ruins there, anyway."

Jeffrey kept his tone casual. "A writer?"

"I believe so," said Thomsa. "We didn't know him. Someone who stayed here once went looking for him, but he wasn't home—this was years ago. The old Golovenna Farm."

Jeffrey pointed to the seemingly random network of lines that covered the map, like crazing on a piece of old pottery. "What's all this mean?"

Harry pulled his chair closer and traced the boundaries of Cardu with a dirt-stained finger. "Those are the field systems—the stone walls."

"You're kidding." Jeffrey laughed. "That must've driven someone nuts, getting all that down."

"Oh, it's all GPS and satellite photos now," said Thomsa. "I'm sorry I didn't have this map earlier, before you went for your walk. "

"It'll be on this survey." Harry angled the map so the sunlight illuminated the area surrounding Cardu. "This is our cove, here . . . "

They pored over the Ordnance Survey. Jeffrey pointed at markers for hut circles and cairns, standing stones and tumuli, all within a hands-span of Cardu, as Harry continued to shake his head.

"It's this one, I think," Harry said at last, and glanced at his sister. He scored a square half-inch of the page with a blackened fingernail, minute Gothic letters trapped within the web of field systems.

CHAMBERED CAIRN

"That looks right," said Thomsa. "But it's a ways off the road. I'm not certain where the house is—the woman who went looking for it said she roamed the moor for hours before she came on it."

Jeffrey ran his finger along the line marking the main road. "It looks like I can drive to here. If there's a place to park, I can just hike in. It doesn't look that far. As long as I don't get towed."

"You shouldn't get towed," said Thomsa. "All that land's part of Golovenna, and no one's there. He never farmed it, just let it all go back to the moor. You'd only be a mile or so from Zennor if you left your car. They have musicians on Thursday nights, some of the locals come in and play after dinner."

Jeffrey refolded the map. When he looked up, Harry was gone. Thomsa handed him an apple.

"Watch for the bogs," she said. "Marsh grass, it looks sturdy but when you put your foot down it gives way and you can sink under. Like quicksand. They found a girl's body ten years back. Horses and sheep, too." Jeffrey grimaced and she laughed. "You'll be all right—just stay on the footpaths."

He thanked her, went upstairs to exchange his overcoat for a windbreaker, and returned to his car. The clouds were gone: the sun shone high in a sky the summer blue of gentians. He felt the same surge of exultation he'd experienced that morning, the sea-fresh wind tangling the stems of daffodils and iris, white gulls crying overhead. He kept the window down as he drove up the twisting way to Cardu, and the honeyed scent of gorse filled the car.

The road to Zennor coiled between hedgerows misted green with new growth and emerald fields where brown-and-white cattle grazed. In the distance a single tractor moved so slowly across a black furrow that Jeffrey could track its progress only by the skein of crows that followed it, the birds dipping then rising like a black thread drawn through blue cloth.

Twice he pulled over to consult the map. His phone didn't work here—he couldn't even get the time, let alone directions. The car's clock read 14:21. He saw no other roads, only deeply-rutted tracks protected by stiles, some metal, most of weathered wood. He tried counting stone walls to determine which marked the fields Harry had said belonged to Golovenna Farm, and stopped a third time before deciding the map was all but useless. He drove another hundred feet, until he found a swathe of gravel between two tumbledown stone walls, a rusted gate sagging between them. Beyond it stretched an overgrown field bisected by a stone-strewn path.

He was less than a mile from Zennor. He folded the map and jammed it into his windbreaker pocket along with the apple, and stepped out of the car.

The dark height before him would be Zennor Hill. Golovenna Farm was somewhere between there and where he stood. He turned slowly, scanning everything around him to fix it in his memory: the winding road, intermittently visible between walls and hedgerows; the ridge of cliffs falling down to the sea, book-ended by the dark bulk of Gurnards Head in the south-west and Zennor Head to the north-east. On the horizon were scattered outcroppings that might have been tors or ruins or even buildings. He locked the car, checked that he had his phone, climbed over the metal gate and began to walk.

The afternoon sun beat down fiercely. He wished he'd brought a hat, or sunglasses. He crossed the first field in a few minutes, and was relieved to find a break in the next wall, an opening formed by a pair of tall, broad stones. The path narrowed here, but was still clearly discernible where it bore straight in front of him, an arrow of new green grass flashing through ankle-high turf overgrown with daisies and fronds of young bracken.

The ground felt springy beneath his feet. He remembered Thomsa's warning about the bogs, and glanced around for something he might use as a walking stick. There were no trees in sight, only wicked-looking thickets of blackthorn clustered along the perimeter of the field.

He found another gap in the next wall, guarded like the first by two broad stones nearly as tall as he was. He clambered onto the wall, fighting to open his map in the brisk wind, and examined the survey, trying to find some affinity between the fields around him and the crazed pattern on the page. At last he shoved the map back into his pocket, set his back to the wind and shaded his eyes with his hand.

It was hard to see—he was staring due west, into the sun—but he thought he glimpsed a black bulge some three or four fields off, a dark blister within the haze of green and yellow. It might be a ruin, or just as likely a farm or outbuildings. He clambered down into the next field, crushing dead bracken and shoots of heather; picked his way through a breach where stones had fallen and hurried until he reached yet another wall.

There were the remnants of a gate here, a rusted latch and iron pins protruding from the granite. Jeffrey crouched beside the wall to catch his breath. After a few minutes he scrambled to his feet and walked through the gap, letting one hand rest for an instant upon the stone. Despite the hot afternoon sun it felt cold beneath his palm, more like metal than granite. He glanced aside to make sure he hadn't touched a bit of rusted hardware, but saw only a boulder seamed with moss.

The fields he'd already passed through had seemed rank and overgrown, as though claimed by the wilderness decades ago. Yet there was no mistaking what stretched before him as anything but open moor. Clumps of gorse sprang everywhere, starbursts of yellow blossom shadowing pale-green ferns and tufts of dogtooth violets. He walked cautiously—he couldn't see the earth underfoot for all the new growth—but the ground felt solid beneath mats of dead bracken that gave off a spicy October scent. He was so intent on watching his step that he nearly walked into a standing stone.

He sucked his breath in sharply and stumbled backward. For a fraction of a second he'd perceived a figure there, but it was only a stone, twice his height and leaning at a forty-five degree angle, so that it pointed toward the sea. He circled it, then ran his hand across its granite flank, sun-warmed and furred with lichen and dried moss. He kicked at the thatch of ferns and ivy that surrounded its base, stooped and dug his hand through the vegetation, until his fingers dug into raw earth.

He withdrew his hand and backed away, staring at the ancient monument, at once minatory and banal. He could recall no indication of a standing stone between Cardu and Zennor, and when he checked the map he saw nothing there.

But something else loomed up from the moor a short distance away—a house. He headed toward it, slowing his steps in case someone saw him, so that they might have time to come outside.

No one appeared. After five minutes he stood in a rutted drive beside a long, one-storey building of gray stone similar to those he'd passed on the main road; slate-roofed, with deep small windows and a wizened tree beside the door, its branches rattling in the wind. A worn hand-lettered sign hung beneath the low eaves: GOLOVENNA FARM.

Jeffrey looked around. He saw no car, only a large plastic trash bin that had blown over. He rapped at the door, waited then knocked again, calling out a greeting. When no one answered he tried the knob, but the door was locked.

He stepped away to peer in through the window. There were no curtains. Inside looked dark and empty, no furniture or signs that someone lived here, or indeed if anyone had for years. He walked round the house, stopping to look inside each window and half-heartedly trying to open them, without success. When he'd completed this circuit, he wandered over to the trash bin and looked inside. It too was empty.

He righted it, then stood and surveyed the land around him. The rutted path joined a narrow, rock-strewn drive that led off into the moor to the west. He saw what looked like another structure not far from where the two tracks joined, a collapsed building of some sort.

He headed towards it. A flock of little birds flittered from a gorse bush, making a sweet high-pitched song as they soared past him, close enough that he could see their rosy breasts and hear their wings beat against the wind. They settled on the ruined building, twittering companionably as he approached, then took flight once more.

It wasn't a building but a mound. Roughly rectangular but with rounded corners, maybe twenty feet long and half again as wide; as tall as he was, and so overgrown with ferns and blackthorn that he might have mistaken it for a hillock. He kicked through brambles and clinging thorns until he reached one end, where the mound's curve had been sheared off.

Erosion, he thought at first; then realized that he was gazing into an entryway. He glanced behind him before drawing closer, until he stood knee-deep in dried bracken and whip-like blackthorn.

In front of him was a simple doorway of upright stones, man-high, with a larger stone laid across the tops to form a lintel. Three more stones were set into the ground as steps, descending to a passage choked with young ferns and ivy mottled black and green as malachite.

Jeffrey ducked his head beneath the lintel and peered down into the tunnel. He could see nothing but vague outlines of more stones and straggling vines. He reached to thump the ceiling to see if anything moved.

Nothing did. He checked his phone—still no signal—turned to stare up into the sky, trying to guess what time it was. He'd left the car around 2:30, and he couldn't have been walking for more than an hour. Say it was four o'clock, to be safe. He still had a good hour-and-a-half to get back to the road before dark.

He took out the apple Thomsa had given him and ate it, dropped the core beside the top step; zipped his windbreaker and descended into the passage.

He couldn't see how long it was, but he counted thirty paces, pausing every few steps to look back at the entrance, before the light faded enough that he needed to use his cell phone for illumination. The walls glittered faintly where broken crystals were embedded in the granite, and there was a moist, earthy smell, like a damp cellar. He could stand upright with his arms outstretched, his fingertips grazing the walls to either side. The vegetation disappeared after the first ten paces, except for moss, and after a few more steps there was nothing beneath his feet but bare earth. The walls were of stone, dirt packed between them and hardened by the centuries so that it was almost indistinguishable from the granite.

He kept going, glancing back as the entryway diminished to a bright mouth, then a glowing eye, and finally a hole no larger than that left by a finger thrust through a piece of black cloth.

A few steps more and even that was gone. He stopped, his breath coming faster, then walked another five paces, the glow from his cell phone a blue moth flickering in his hand. Once again he stopped to look back.

He could see nothing behind him. He shut off the cell phone's light, experimentally moved his hand swiftly up and down before his face; closed his eyes then opened them. There was no difference.

His mouth went dry. He turned his phone on, took a few more steps deeper into the passage before halting again. The phone's periwinkle glow was insubstantial as a breath of vapor: he could see neither the ground beneath him nor the walls to either side. He raised his arms and extended them, expecting to feel cold stone beneath his fingertips.

The walls were gone. He stepped backward, counting five paces, and again extended his arms. Still nothing. He dropped his hands and began to walk forward, counting each step—five, six, seven, ten, thirteen—stopped and slowly turned in a circle, holding the phone at arm's-length as he strove to discern some feature in the encroaching darkness. The pallid blue gleam flared then went out.

He swore furiously, fighting panic. He turned the phone on and off, to no avail; finally shoved it into his pocket and stood, trying to calm himself.

It was impossible that he could be lost. The mound above him wasn't that large, and even if the fogou's passage continued for some distance underground, he would eventually reach the end, at which point he could turn around and painstakingly wend his way back out again. He tried to recall something he'd read once, about navigating the maze at Hampton Court—always keep your hand on the left-hand side of the hedge. All he had to do was locate a wall, and walk back into daylight.

He was fairly certain that he was still facing the same way as when he had first entered. He turned, so that he was now facing where the doorway should be, and walked, counting aloud as he did. When he reached one hundred he stopped.

There was no way he had walked more than a hundred paces into the tunnel. Somehow, he had gotten turned around. He wiped his face, slick and chill with sweat, and breathed deeply, trying to slow his racing heart. He heard nothing, saw nothing save that impenetrable darkness. Everything he had ever read about getting lost advised staying put and waiting for help;

but that involved being lost above ground, where someone would eventually find you. At some point Thomsa and Harry would notice he hadn't returned, but that might not be till morning.

And who knew how long it might be before they located him? The thought of spending another twelve hours or more here, motionless, unable to see or hear, or touch anything save the ground beneath his feet, filled Jeffrey with such overwhelming horror that he felt dizzy.

And that was worst of all: if he fell, would he even touch the ground? He crouched, felt an absurd wash of relief as he pressed his palms against the floor. He straightened, took another deep breath and began to walk.

He tried counting his steps, as a means to keep track of time, but before long a preternatural stillness came over him, a sense that he was no longer awake but dreaming. He pinched the back of his hand, hard enough that he gasped. Yet still the feeling remained, that he'd somehow fallen into a recurring dream, the horror deadened somewhat by a strange familiarity. As though he'd stepped into an icy pool, he stopped, shivering, and realized the source of his apprehension.

It had been in the last chapter of Robert Bennington's book, *Still the Seasons*; the chapter that he'd never been able to recall clearly. Even now it was like remembering something that had happened *to* him, not something he'd read: the last of the novel's four children passing through a portal between one world and another, surrounded by utter darkness and the growing realization that with each step the world around her was disintegrating and that she herself was disintegrating as well, until the book ended with her isolated consciousness fragmented into incalculable motes within an endless, starless void.

The terror of that memory jarred him. He jammed his hands into his pockets and felt his cell phone and the map, his car keys, some change. He walked more quickly, gazing straight ahead, focused on finding the spark within the passage that would resolve into the entrance.

After some time his heart jumped—it was there, so small he might have imagined it, a wink of light faint as a clouded star.

But when he ran a few paces he realized it was his mind playing tricks on him. A phantom light floated in the air, like the luminous blobs behind one's knuckled eyelids. He blinked and rubbed his eyes: the light remained.

"Hello?" he called, hesitating. There was no reply.

He started to walk, but slowly, calling out several times into the silence. The light gradually grew brighter. A few more minutes and a second light appeared, and then a third. They cast no glow upon the tunnel, nor shadows: he could see neither walls nor ceiling, nor any sign of those who carried the lights. All three seemed suspended in the air, perhaps ten feet above the floor, and all bobbed slowly up and down, as though each was borne upon a pole.

Jeffrey froze. The lights were closer now, perhaps thirty feet from where he stood.

"Who is it?" he whispered.

He heard the slightest of sounds, a susurrus as of escaping air. With a cry he turned and fled, his footsteps echoing through the passage. He heard no sounds of pursuit, but when he looked back, the lights were still there, moving slowly toward him. With a gasp he ran harder, his chest aching, until one foot skidded on something and he fell. As he scrambled back up, his hand touched a flat smooth object; he grabbed it and without thinking jammed it into his pocket, and raced on down the tunnel.

And now, impossibly, in the vast darkness before him he saw a jot of light that might have been reflected from a spider's eye. He kept going. Whenever he glanced back, he saw the trio of lights behind him.

They seemed to be more distant now. And there was no doubt that the light in front of him spilled from the fogou's entrance—he could see the outlines of the doorway, and the dim glister of quartz and mica in the walls to either side. With a gasp he reached the steps, stumbled up them and back out into the blinding light of afternoon. He stopped, coughing and covering his eyes until he could see, then staggered back across first one field and then the next, hoisting himself over rocks heedless of blackthorns tearing his palms and clothing, until at last he reached the final overgrown tract of heather and bracken, and saw the white roof of his rental car shining in the sun.

He ran up to it, jammed the key into the lock and with a gasp fell into the driver's seat. He locked the doors, flinching as another car drove past, and finally looked out the window.

To one side was the gate he'd scaled, with field after field beyond; to the other side the silhouettes of Gurnard's Head and its sister promontory. Beyond the fields, the sun hung well above the lowering mass of Zennor Hill. The car's clock read 15:23.

He shook his head in disbelief: it was impossible he'd been gone for scarcely an hour. He reached for his cell phone and felt something in the pocket beside it—the object he'd skidded on inside the fogou.

He pulled it out. A blue metal disc, slightly flattened where he'd stepped on it, with gold-stamped words above a beacon.

St. Austell Sweets: Fudge from Real Cornish Cream

He turned it over in his hands and ran a finger across the raised lettering.

Becca gave one to each of us the day we arrived. The fudge was supposed to last the entire two weeks, and I think we ate it all that first night.

The same kind of candy tin where Evelyn had kept her comb and Anthea her locket and chain. He stared at it, the tin bright and enamel glossy-blue as though it had been painted yesterday. Anyone could have a candy tin, especially one from a local company that catered to tourists.

After a minute he set it down, took out his wallet and removed the photo Evelyn had given him: Evelyn and Moira doubled-up with laughter as Anthea stared at them, slightly puzzled, a half-smile on her face as though trying to determine if they were laughing at her.

He gazed at the photo for a long time, returned it to his wallet, then slid the candy lid back into his pocket. He still had no service on his phone.

He drove very slowly back to Cardu, nauseated from sunstroke and his terror at being underground. He knew he'd never been seriously lost—a backwards glance as he fled the mound reassured him that it hadn't been large enough for that.

Yet he was profoundly unnerved by his reaction to the darkness, the way his sight had betrayed him and his imagination reflexively dredged up the images from Evelyn's story. He was purged of any desire to remain another night at the cottage, or even in England, and considered checking to see if there was an evening train back to London.

But by the time he edged the car down the long drive to the cottage, his disquiet had ebbed somewhat. Thomsa and Harry's car was gone. A stretch of wall had been newly repaired, and many more daffodils and narcissus had opened, their sweet fragrance following him as he trudged to the front door.

Inside he found a plate with a loaf of freshly baked bread and some local blue cheese, beside it several pamphlets with a yellow Sticky note.

Jeffrey—
   Gone to see a play in Penzance. Please turn off lights downstairs. I found these books today and thought you might be interested in them.
                                                                Thomsa

He glanced at the pamphlets—another map, a flyer about a music night at the pub in Zennor, a small paperback with a green cover—crossed to the refrigerator and foraged until he found two bottles of ale. Probably not proper B&B etiquette, but he'd apologize in the morning.

He grabbed the plate and book and went upstairs to his room. He kicked off his shoes, groaning with exhaustion, removed his torn windbreaker and regarded himself in the mirror, his face scratched and flecked with bits of greenery.

"What a mess," he murmured, and collapsed onto the bed.

He downed one of the bottles of ale and most of the bread and cheese. Outside, light leaked from a sky deepening to ultramarine. He heard the boom and sigh of waves, and for a long while he reclined in the window-seat and stared out at the cliffs, watching as shadows slipped down them like black paint. At last he stood and got some clean clothes from his bag. He hooked a finger around the remaining bottle of ale, picked up the book Thomsa had left for him, and retired to the bathroom.

The immense tub took ages to fill, but there seemed to be unlimited hot water. He put all the lights on and undressed, sank into the tub and gave himself over to the mindless luxury of hot water and steam and the scent of daffodils on the windowsill.

Finally he turned the water off. He reached for the bottle he'd set on the floor and opened it, dried his hands and picked up the book. A worn paperback, its creased cover showing a sweep of green hills topped by a massive tor, with a glimpse of sea in the distance.

OLD TALES FOR NEW DAYS
BY ROBERT BENNINGTON

Jeffrey whistled softly, took a long swallow of ale and opened the book. It was not a novel but a collection of stories, published in 1970—Cornish folktales, according to a brief preface, "told anew for today's generation." He scanned the table of contents—"Pisky-Led," "Tregeagle and the Devil," "Jack the Giant Killer"—then sat up quickly in the tub, spilling water as he gazed at a title underlined with red ink: "Cherry of Zennor." He flipped through the pages until he found it.

Sixteen-year-old Cherry was the prettiest girl in Zennor, not that she knew it. One day while walking on the moor she met a young man as handsome as she was lovely.

"Will you come with me?" he asked, and held out a beautiful lace handkerchief to entice her. "I'm a widower with an infant son who needs tending. I'll pay you better wages than any man or woman earns from here to Kenidjack Castle, and give your dresses that will be the envy of every girl at Morvah Fair."

Now, Cherry had never had a penny in her pocket in her entire young life, so she let the young man take her arm and lead her across the moor . . .

There were no echoes here of *The Sun Battles*, no vertiginous terrors of darkness and the abyss; just a folk tale that reminded Jeffrey a bit of "Rip Van Winkle," with Cherry caring for the young son and, as the weeks passed, falling in love with the mysterious man.

Each day she put ointment on the boy's eyes, warned by his father never to let a drop fall upon her own. Until of course one day she couldn't resist doing so, and saw an entire host of gorgeously dressed men and women moving through the house around her, including her mysterious employer and a beautiful woman who was obviously his wife. Bereft and betrayed, Cherry fled; her lover caught up with her on the moor and pressed some coins into her hand.

"You must go now and forget what you have seen," he said sadly, and *touched the corner of her eye. When she returned home she found her parents dead and gone, along with everyone she knew, and her cottage a ruin open to the sky. Some say it is still a good idea to avoid the moors near Zennor.*

Jeffrey closed the book and dropped it on the floor beside the tub. When he at last headed back down the corridor, he heard voices from the kitchen, and Thomsa's voice raised in laughter. He didn't go downstairs; only returned to his room and locked the door behind him.

He left early the next morning, after sharing breakfast with Thomsa at the kitchen table.

"Harry's had to go to St. Ives to pick up some tools he had repaired." She poured Jeffrey more coffee and pushed the cream across the table toward him. "Did you have a nice ramble yesterday and go to the Tinners?"

Jeffrey smiled but said nothing. He was halfway up the winding driveway back to Cardu before he realized he'd forgotten to mention the two bottles of ale.

He returned the rental car then got a ride to the station from Evan, the same man who'd picked him up two days earlier.

"Have a good time in Zennor?"

"Very nice," said Jeffrey.

"Quiet this time of year." Evan pulled the car to the curb. "Looks like your train's here already."

Jeffrey got out, slung his bag over his shoulder and started for the station entrance. His heart sank when he saw two figures arguing on the sidewalk a few yards away, one a policeman.

"Come on now, Erthy," he said, glancing as Jeffrey drew closer. "You know better than this."

"Fuck you!" she shouted, and kicked at him. "Not my fucking name!"

"That's it."

The policeman grabbed her wrist and bent his head to speak into a walkie-talkie. Jeffrey began to hurry past. The woman screamed after him, shaking her clenched fist. Her eye with its bloody starburst glowed crimson in the morning sun.

"London!" Her voice rose desperately as she fought to pull away from the cop. "London, please, take me—"

Jeffrey shook his head. As he did, the woman raised her fist and flung something at him. He gasped as it stung his cheek, clapping a hand to his face as the policeman shouted and began to drag the woman away from the station.

"London! *London!*"

As her shrieks echoed across the plaza, Jeffrey stared at a speck of blood on his finger. Then he stooped to pick up what she'd thrown at him: a yellow pencil worn with toothmarks, its graphite tip blunted but the tiny, embossed black letters still clearly readable above the ferrule.

RAVENWOOD.

The story of the goddess Inanna's journey to the underworld has been retold for at least five thousand years. Here, the ancient is combined with the science fictional for a powerful and poetic tale.

CONSERVATION OF SHADOWS

Yoon Ha Lee

There is no such thing as conservation of shadows. When light destroys shadows, darkness does not gain in density elsewhere. When shadows steal over earth and across the sky, darkness is not diluted.

Hello, Inanna. You have seven inventory slots, all full. The seventh contains your heart, which cannot be removed. We will do our best to remedy this.

A feast awaits you at the end, sister. I am keeping it warm for you. You will be cold by the time you reach my hall beneath the floors of the world. Meadow honey on barley cakes, cheese, and the tender flesh of goats; plums and pears brighter than the jewels in your hair; wine less sweet than birdsong and more bitter than tears. Taken together they form a nutritionally complete diet.

You think that all we eat in the underworld is dust and all we drink is the dregs of rain, but that is not the case. Come and share the feast.

You hesitate over the shadow-gun at your waist. Notice the holster, leather stamped with a lioness on each side. The leather comes from a lioness's hide. She is dead, sister. She cannot aid you here.

I can't tell you how to pass through the first gate. More accurately, I could, but I won't. We live by different laws in the underworld, we who live at all. Now you must respect those laws as well.

The gate lies there. Your fingers move toward it, then draw back. How wise of you. Gates are hungry. They demand propitiation. Once a woman put her hand in a gate and it ate her fingers. A five-legged spider with red eyes crawled out. That woman put in three fingers from her other hand, so that the spider might be complete. Do you have that integrity of purpose, sister?

No, what you feed the gate is other. It is easy for gates to be dark, maws opening to the earth's own secrets. They wonder what light is like. So you tempt it with the jewels in your hair. Poor gate: it knows nothing about symbolism. It knows only that the tinted diamonds and emeralds and lapis lazuli glint with the evening star's passion. Down you draw the golden pins from your dark hair and let that torrent free.

Eagerly, the gate lips at the diamonds' fire, the emeralds' intimation of bounty, the lapis lazuli's memory of the sky that cannot be seen. The color leaches from the diamonds, leaving them ashen. The other stones, less hardy, crumble into dust, their virtue vanished.

Sated, the gate eats no more of you as you pass through, divested of glory yet more beautiful than ever.

The fires won't hurt you unless you let them, sister. Hungry already? You'll be hungrier still. Don't roast the flesh off your bones. It's not time yet.

Did you think the underworld moved in ignorance of summer? The season that scours the earth and fills the stomachs of those above ground while leaving us below-ground with the rotting chaff? At least we know that we are the chaff of days, the dust of time.

It is summer because you've scarcely left the world above. Just think, sister: the longer you linger here, the more the leaves shrivel gold and brown on the branches; the more the last grapes wither on the vines.

Now you are hungry again, and thirsty as well. I know. I know you so well that you could flense yourself bare of face and fingerprints and still I would recognize you. After all, I recognized you the first seventy-four times you came my way.

Does it surprise you that your inventory comes up in the shape of an eight-pointed star? Blink once and it appears; twice, and it folds out of your field of vision. It reports nothing you can't find upon you.

One slot is empty now, black as a gate, as the absence of day; black as your hair. Pick up something else if you like. Yes, that pencil will do. The graphite's luster is dark. It grows darker yet in your grasp.

I don't recognize the words you are writing on my walls, sister: graffiti, in scratchy bird-claw marks. Maybe you mean it to be illegible. That would be unkind.

Consider this. The seventy-four earlier iterations of you left no guide-star tags upon the walls, no cheat sheets, no maps tattooed upon their skins. Underneath your armor there is skin, the organ on which your boundaries are written. You'll know the instant it dissolves and opens your secrets to the air.

Nothing's left of your pencil but a stub. One point of the eight-pointed star flares diamond-bright as the inventory slot empties itself in response.

Did I speak to you of skin? The walls are my skin, the gold-painted pillars my bones. Do what you will with them. You always did.

You are silent. I don't know whether this is an improvement or not. Do you think your words will inscribe themselves upon the air like the coming frost upon fallen leaves? Twenty degrees Celsius, room temperature. You are in a room.

There is no way out of the room, except now there is. Like a hundred mutilated lips the letters—are they letters or logograms?—crack wide, wider. Gap to gap, they gape until they dissolve into a single opening.

A wind rushes through the gate. The wind chill factor is 14 degrees Celsius. You may feel that is excessive. From that number you can calculate the speed of the wind. Unfortunately, your pencil's stub will write no more for you. Perhaps you can do the figures in your head.

If you came to the feast, you would soon sate yourself with warm food. You would watch as dancers clad in feathers reenacted the descent of your first self, or the eighth, or the forty-ninth. How many gates do you think your sad, brave clones survived? Do not worry. You are different, you are special, more clever and greater of heart. I will make sure you reach the barley cakes brimming with dark honey.

Now you are singing. Your formants are rich with despair. Some languages can be recorded without stylus or pencil.

The gate swallows the holy sweetness of your voice. It cancels the waveform, replacing it with silence beyond imagining. Sister, you have not known silence until you have sat in the dark among the dead for generations.

You don't know, yet you do. These are the things you sing of: the embryos of mice, stillborn, albinos that have never known light; the needle's prick drawing blood directly from the betrayed artery; curling strands of fossil DNA, a language more legible than yours. Memory is not inherited, memory is no mirror to times past, yet you divine the experiments that I oversee here.

The gate is as still as matter ever is. Even you cannot cancel that lowest level of vibration, absolute zero thrumming. It will have to do.

Assured of the gate's momentary toothlessness, you step through, and it lets you. Silence drifts in your wake like leaves and petals, like all things ephemeral.

This time it's not so easy to ignore the fire, is it? Go deep enough and you'll meet the mantle's heat. You think of the underworld as cold and dank, inhabited by pale, eyeless creatures whose circulatory systems are written within them with ink redder than spinels. That is not the whole of us. We can kill you by fire, too.

Are you worried about dying? You shy from the fires, watch your balance on the narrow walkways. It helps to have good reflexes in death as well as life. It's good that you practice. Of course I support your efforts.

Traverse the spiraling maze and who do you find at the center? Imagine peeling the layers of yourself away. What's left when you reach your hallowed heart, when the hollows admit no shadows but what you carry with you? I forgot: with no voice, you can't answer me.

Walk and walk as you may, you only knot yourself further into the maze's pattern. Isn't this the way of the world? From the moment you first draw breath, you're woven into the world's overbearing warp.

Look: the necklace at your throat responds to the fire, capturing and releasing that warm light with its own golden gleam. In this surfeit of light I can read the inscription on your eight-pointed pendant, spider-scratch marks deep in the metal. No cipher hides you from me. I have mapped you down to your mitochondria. I can read your rate of respiration, the flush of your skin. Surely the heat isn't unbearable yet.

You unclasp the bright unknot from around your neck. Which lover gave you that necklace? Was it before or after he pressed you against the flowering earth, the leafing tree? Through the floor of the earth, I heard your demands. You were never easy to please, no matter how many lovers you dragged from bars, drugged by the honey of your voice and the heat of your mouth. Nevertheless the mares and does swelled, and the boughs curved under the weight of tender fruit.

Did the lionesses nuzzle each other, wondering over cubs to come?

Like a sleepy snake the necklace ripples over your hands, throwing bright glints across knuckles and prominent bones. I will listen when you explain to your beloved that his gift was worth nothing except as a talisman against one more nexus of shadow and insatiable envy. That's the problem, surely: not that you discarded the gift, but that it was discarded in such small cause.

There are people who would kill for fire: fire to stoke youth in the furnace beneath their skins, fire to brighten the faded cloth of their lives. Better to die burning than chilled by slow moments into the silvered dark. No? Tell that to all those whose bones embrace beneath the worm-furrowed loam.

A narrow opal flares open in the air at the maze's heart, narrow like a woman before she grows great with child. Were this gate a woman you could dance with her, span her with your hands—no. Instead, you fasten the necklace around the gate, adorning it as you once adorned yourself.

The gold shines with the warmth of the surrounding fires. The gate does not drain away the reflected light. Instead, darkness seeps into the inscription. You can't turn away from the words, sister, the seething shapes of *summer*, *hope*, *health* inverted.

The gate offers you its embrace. Without hesitation or tenderness, you accept, ducking your head so that you are briefly crowned in gold.

Do you know how deep in the earth you are, sister? You squint in the near-dark. There is only a single lantern to comfort you. Imagine: maybe that lantern is the only thing between you and utter darkness. Shall I snuff it out? Don't shiver so; it doesn't become you.

The stalactites and stalagmites grip the light in their jaws, returning only washed-out, variegated colors: poor exchange for that faint gold.

You shouldn't have sold your voice so cheaply. It makes conversation difficult. Would you like to borrow the voices that whisper in the underworld for your own? You never know who might wander here. They might remember the world's oldest hymns. They might be praising the serpentine coils of your hair, the silent cunning of your hands. They might not know who you are at all, now that you're stripped of your war-chariot, far from the morning star. For all the storms you dragged in your wake, all the rain-tossed days and nights, you craved light as your nourishment: star or moon, lightning scarring the shrouded sky. You always were one for fanfare.

Here are no drums to shake the stone columns and threaten you with the slow death of suffocation. Don't worry about the air, dear sister. You breathe as darkness does, without need of oxygen or any element but your very self. Light travels through the void without a mediating æther; why should darkness be any different?

Come to my halls, sister, and there will be no more talk of light or dark or the permutations in between. We will sit side by side on our thrones, drinking young wine and old rather than the dark, dank water that trickles just beneath the world's skin. We will bestow treasures upon those who please us, luminous cabochons and spiral emblems of gold, chains sometimes of silver and sometimes of bronze.

In the earth's hidden hoards you can taste treasure as though it were a nectar beyond price. Underground, so deep that even fungi find no nourishment, the earth fruits metal and precious stones. It is of no concern to us that living creatures starve contemplating such fruit.

You unfasten your belt, such a short, blunt length to encircle your waist. Jewels of varying cuts are set in the leather, all polished to the brilliance of river water beneath a fecund moon. They fling colored sparks across the floor and walls. Did you ever spare a thought for the underground spirits that had to be disturbed by the digging for your treasures?

With the belt you whip the largest geode in the wall, already cracked half-open to reveal its jagged amethyst heart. The jewels fall out of your belt and scatter to the floor, uncracked yet dimmer, duller. You should be more patient, sister. After all, when you reach the final gate there will be no returning. Doesn't the thought distress you even a little?

Heedless, you bunch up the belt in your fist, then thrust it into the gate that is growing from the crack in the geode. Is that how you regard the underworld's gleaming treasures? Obstacles to be destroyed?

I suppose I haven't learned anything that I didn't already know. You are all the same, all of you.

The geode's teeth scratch your skin as you enter, even through the stiff curves of your armor.

This deep in the earth, you can't hear the seasons breathing even in your dreams. Tell me true: when you close your eyes, can you smell the earthy sweetness of rotting leaves, or taste the last fruits of fall? If I set before you a feast of the finest wines and hearty porridge and roast boar, would it taste like the dust that surrounds you?

Come to me before it's too late, before you lose all ability to see color or to taste salt or sweet.

You tilt your head, listening to the laments of the dead. Their voices sound very like your own, don't they? Maybe they always have. There is no use for fertility without death, you know.

All your faces are mine. You can verify that with a mirror when we meet, except that mirrors are liars when there is no light, claiming that everything is equal to everything. Perhaps that's the sort of lie you like to tell yourself.

Here's the thing about shadows. Even at their most distorted, shadows are mathematically precise. They show you what is given to them to show. If a shadow portrays you as larger as you are, it's no fault of the shadow's. It's all a matter of light, of angles and intensity and color.

If I loom so large in your experience here, sister, you might consider what it is about you that has made me who I am.

Don't worry about the candles here, or the supply of oxygen. The ventilation is quite adequate for our purposes.

Your shadows flicker and jump in perfect time to the candles' flames, like dancers yearning after each other. Which one most truly represents your face? Or mine?

When you close your eyes, just before sleep bears you beneath the surface of the world, do you have a face at all? Can you differentiate yourself from the shadows at all?

Furiously, you pull open your jacket, unfasten your tunic. I know all the scars you bear, sister. The abrupt cuneiform shapes of scars embellish your skin. Scars from battle or love or all the jagged shapes in between, cicatrices and burn scars, round and pale and lightning-shaped.

Of course: no shadow living ever bore a scar.

You feed the shadows your scars, erasing all record of those past triumphs and defeats. As the scars smooth out, becoming invisible against the brown canvas of your body, the shadows gain in depth and form, braiding themselves together until they are a cold, tangible presence on the floor.

Unhesitating, you refasten your tunic and step through, falling without falling.

You're shielding your eyes. Surprised at how bright it is? I thought you could use a reminder. The spectrum produced by each lamp imitates that of a sun you or one of your clone-sisters has visited. Sadly, no matter how faithful a lamp is, it can never rival the real thing.

Don't look for their remnants here. Seasons in human time are one thing, but seasons in the lives of starfarers—what is a human winter to people like you or me? You've been breathing their dust, treading on their fossilized despair.

Nevertheless, you crouch, heedless of the gray grit that clings to your clothes, and draw figures on the cave's floor. If you think your calculus will save you, you are sorely mistaken. In your formula the infinitesimals come to a positive sum. Here, the sum of iterated emptiness will only be more emptiness.

Let me tell you a story to distract you from the useless fable you are telling yourself. Long ago, the people of a great and fertile land resolved to explore worlds that circled the god-stars that they had watched and worshiped since their people first set brick upon brick to build cities. But for all their ambitions, they were loyal, and did not forget their gods. They knew they would need their gods to guard them from the dangers that lie deep in space.

So they made sure that their gods would follow them into that shining darkness, a pantheon of gods for each world. They made you, all of you, and they made me.

If you must console yourself over your journey here, tell yourself that those who made you achieved their purpose, and that you are perfectly recapitulating that old story so that your world will pass into its winter rest. You will not live to see your world's renewal, but another of you will.

Don't bother scratching out a message to her. She won't read the same languages you do, won't take the same twisting path. I will tell her the same things that I have told you. You may be sure of it.

You've removed the shadow-gun from its holster and are cradling it in your hands. You knew it would come to this. We both did.

It's a beautiful weapon. It has the same coiled intensity that you do when you are intent on war, sister. And it has killed people in your hands. You are not the kind to beg forgiveness; you were made for bloodshed. I don't understand why you regard the gun with such loathing, then.

Steadily, you raise the shadow-gun and squeeze the trigger. The room explodes into utter darkness, the kind of darkness that swallows sound and stifles thought. Even the spangled otherspace behind your eyelids is brighter than this.

A moment later, your fingers close around empty air as the gun dissolves. It has served its purpose. All but one of your inventory slots is empty as well.

The entire room is a gate now. It remains only for you to take a step. It speaks well of you that you listen for a long, careful moment before moving in the direction leading downward, toward me.

Your heart thuds one-two, one-two, one-two like a march without an army. There is only you, alone before the last gate. What did you hope to accomplish when you set out, sister? Did you have some brave notion of unseating me from my dark throne, or tearing asunder all the underworld gates so the dead would roam free and outnumber the living?

I have always admired your purity of purpose, mistaken as it is. We are not so different, you and I. We play the roles that are given to us. Yours is to die, and mine is to kill you. Don't spoil the symmetry of the story.

The only reason you can see anything here, where the darkness is thicker than honey, is that you still have a heart. It shines red-bright in the final inventory slot, last remaining illumination. If I cared to, I could grow you a new, more compliant heart. But that is not my duty. Would you deny Number Seventy-Six her chance at this journey?

There is a small, angular object in your hand like a dead star. Your inventory system needs to be debugged. Why was I not informed?

You kneel again. I can hear the painful harshness of your breathing. More important is what you are scratching into the dust on the floor with your pointed fingernail. This time it is in a language I understand:

I have always known I am not the only one. You are not the only one of your kind, either. My clone-sisters and I have planned for this moment, a coordinated strike. It is the only way we can be free. I am s—

How can it be that I feel the touch of rain so deep beneath the earth, blotting out the last word you would have written?

You timed it to your traitor heart. And now that I know to look, I see it: a mass inside your heart, tangled inextricably into it.

In the end you give up your heart after all, but I am the one who loses everything, in a springtime effusion of light.

Other survivors often talked about the cold, about the deep bone chill they
felt after a few days. More than one of them said that
a long gray man had visited them . . .

ALL YOU CAN DO IS BREATHE

Kaaron Warren

Stuart lay trapped underground for five days before the tall man appeared and stared into his eyes.

He thought he sensed movement. Flicked on his caplamp. "Barry? Did you make it through the wall?" But there was no one.

There was something though, in his face so close he pulled back and banged his head on the rock behind. He shouted, mouth open, squeezed his eyes shut. He'd never felt such terror, not even when his daughter had fallen into the pool and they didn't notice for god knows how long.

This was a man. Something like a man. Tall, elongated, the thing looked deep into his eyes. It reached out and almost took his chin with its bony fingers, keeping his head still, paralyzing him even though it wasn't actually touching him.

Stuart could smell sour cherries, something like that. It made him hungry, and that hunger somehow beat out the terror.

He pulled his head backwards. The man nodded, stepped back, and was gone.

Within a minute or two, Stuart was sure he'd imagined it. Though he had words in his ear. "See you soon, Stuart." He was sure he'd heard those words.

It felt like the walls were getting closer, but he kept testing by stretching his arms and the distance was the same. The part of the mine he was working had collapsed so quickly, it seemed like time stopped and froze and when it started up again, he was surrounded on all sides by rock

Barry, his workmate, was on the other side, but he'd heard nothing from him for twelve hours now.

Thank god for the luminous hand on his watch. The kid gave it to him for Father's Day years ago and even at the time he'd been thrilled. You don't always get that with Father's Day presents.

It wasn't what you'd call a worker's watch. It was full of gadgets, like the watches of the office men who drove to work each day, passing him as he stood, cold in the dark, at the bus stop with the other miners. Their cars blinked with gadgets.

This watch kept perfect time, and followed the date, and the hand provided a warm green glow in the pitch black. At home he had to keep it in his bedside drawer at night because the light kept his wife awake. But he could still see the thin green line across the top of the drawer where the light escaped.

Since the walls came down, he'd slept sporadically, waking a couple of times thinking he was home in bed, because of the glow. He'd covered it up with his lunchbox and only a small line escaped.

He had his caplamp but he really didn't want to use that. There'd been mine rescues lasting two weeks and he wanted to know he could have bright light if he needed to. He knew they wouldn't give up. They never left a body underground, mostly because they didn't want it found much later.

He had his GPS so they knew where he was. He could see Barry's blip, too, but that didn't mean he was still going. Just his GPS.

Stuart stretched his legs and arms out and in, counting to a hundred. His wife was always on at him to do more exercise, so she'd be pleased to see him do this. His water and food had run out on the third day. He knew there was no sense keeping the food. It'd just go off and make him sick. Some gritty water dripped down the wall. Licking it made his tongue ache it was so cold and there wasn't enough of it. He pissed into his water bottle and knew that drinking it wouldn't kill him. He pretended it was lime cordial, the sour stuff, not the sweet.

Foodwise he knew he could last without for a while but it didn't help the hunger pains. Lucky his wife packed him heaps and there was Barry's lunch as well, on Stuart's side of the wall where Barry couldn't get to it.

He'd tried moving the rocks but it just caused more of a tumble no matter where he took the rocks from. He wanted to keep trying but his instincts told him just to leave it.

Bugs skittered about and he could eat them. The strap of his lunch box was leather and he chewed on that, making jokes that it was about as good as his sister-in-law's roast dinner. If he got out, he'd make that joke and people would write it up and his sister-in-law would be famous for her bad cooking.

Stuart tried to sleep when he figured it was night time outside, to keep a routine going. It was hard without a change of light and with an empty stomach, and he hadn't done anything to wear himself out. Usually he'd drop into bed after a shift and a feed exhausted. On a Saturday, if he hadn't been in the mine, he and his wife might have sex, but it wasn't something he thought about much.

He thought about it now.

He spent a lot of the time with his eyes closed but he tried not to think about the dark. Instead, he went through football matches he remembered.

It was seven days before they found him. Nowhere near the record, but enough to have a media frenzy going on. As they were getting close they'd managed to get a tube through to him, and sent him notes from his wife and daughter and bags of glucose. They dropped some biscuits down, too. "I was hoping for a meat pie," he called up the tube. He could talk with his mouth close to the tube, tell them shit he wanted his family to know. Tell them all the jokes he'd thought up while he was down there. Nothing worse than a joke without an audience. They called questions down, like, "Are you scared?"

"Naah, I'm not scared. I'm fearless! Nothing scares me!"

He asked them about Barry and they said they were working on it. Ever since the long man had visited him, Stuart had had a bad feeling about Barry. He thought perhaps that was Barry's ghost and he felt bad about screaming. He wished he'd said, "G'day, mate," whatever.

It was overcast when they pulled him out, but still far warmer than inside the mine. It meant he didn't have to squint because of the sun. His wife Cheryl was there, and his daughter Sarah, and for a long time he couldn't talk, just held them and cried. He'd never actually cried before, not since he was a little kid, anyway, but this he couldn't help. He thought he'd never see them again and he loved them, loved them hard. Sarah looked so beautiful, so grown up for her thirteen years. Underground he'd imagined her future. In his darkest times, like the hours after the long man disappeared and he felt like giving up, he imagined her future. Who she'd be, what she'd do, who she'd marry. What her kids would look like. He dreamed it all in case he didn't get to see it, and now, there she was.

His rescuers were there, too. None of them keen to go home. Dirty faced, exhausted, he couldn't believe how happy they were to see him. He knew he'd have to live well, every day of his life, to justify what they'd done.

"Where's Barry? Did you get him out yet?" he asked once he'd had a warm drink. They loaded him into an ambulance although he said he felt fine.

"They haven't got Barry yet," Cheryl said, but her eyes were downcast and he knew she was fibbing. She didn't do it very often and he thought only to protect him. Like the time half the mine was shut down and the wives knew about it first. And the time Sarah had broken her arm because of the kid next door. Cheryl didn't want to tell him that because she knew how angry he'd be, but he didn't do anything about it. The kid was never allowed in their front door again, but that was it.

"I'd rather know than not know," he said.

There were news cameras, people with microphones and others with notepads.

"Why do you think you survived?" they shouted at him. "Why you and not Barry?"

The tears took again at that and Cheryl squeezed his hand hard. The ambulance crew shut the door and then it was a week in hospital before he had to face the questions again.

They told him about Barry once they thought he was all good. Barry'd been trapped, his leg under the rocks. Stuart could imagine how bad that must have felt. So Barry tried to cut his way through, Jesus, cut his way through his own leg.

They said he bled to death.

"He wrote you something while he was down there," Cheryl said.

"He was always scribbling, that Barry. He'd write a letter to the Pope if he could get the address," Stuart said. It was an old joke which made him tear up, thinking that Barry would have laughed at this one.

"He was hallucinating, they reckon. But still. You should read it."

I thought you'd got through the wall, Stu. I didn't hear you but heard a rock shift so thought you must be to my left. You wouldn't answer me so I cracked the shits. I couldn't turn my body but turned my face as far as I could, twisted my caplamp around to catch you. I figured you wanted to kill and eat me, that's how stupid I was.

Wasn't you.

My light went right through this thing. I could see it, though. Looked almost like a man, but stretched out like a piece of bubble gum or something. Or when you press Blu-Tack onto newspaper and get some print and stretch it out. Like that. He had long fingers, twice as long as mine. Dunno if you heard me scream but this thing freaked me out. It came at me and I would have pissed myself if I wasn't already sitting in my own wet pants. It leaned forward and put its eyes real close to mine. Stared into me. I screamed my head off, no reason, just scared shitless. It came at me, touched my nose with its long finger, then it shook its head and drifted back.

I thought, shit, it's going to Stu, and I screamed louder. I wanted to warn you. But what do you do? I didn't know what to tell you.

I don't know if I'll last until they find me. Tell my mates they did me proud and if you can find my mother tell her I'm sorry.

"Do you know anything about this long man, Stuart? Did you hear anything, see anything?" his wife asked him.

Stuart nodded. He spoke quietly. "I saw a man like that. I thought I must have imagined it. But maybe it was a ghost. Maybe someone died in there and he was looking at us, going, *you're not going to make it. No way. You're going to die.* Because he made me feel so bad I almost wanted to die."

"That's awful, Stuart. We're so lucky to have you back." He kissed her, as he did any chance he got. "Maybe keep it just between us for now. About this long man. Other people won't understand it. Don't tell the media types. Okay?"

"You think I'm crazy."

"No, I don't. But I know you and they don't. Just keep it to the simple stuff, hey? Shouldn't be hard for you!"

He discovered he was good at talking. Cheryl thought it was funny. "You're a gabber now, Stuart. Couldn't get ten words a day out of you beforehand!" She fixed his hair, getting him ready for the next press conference.

"Yeah, well, they're always asking me for answers," he said. He didn't mind. It was always the same thing, so he didn't have to think too hard. This one, the room was packed. They knew he was fully recovered and had some others to talk, too. The mine owner, who Stuart had never met. One of his rescuers. And some doctor, a psychologist.

They had a good go at the mine owner for a while about responsibilities and compensation, then they turned to Stuart.

"Did you always think you'd be found?"

"I always expected to be found. I'm a bit like that. I expect I'm gonna get good luck. Just that kind of person. All credit to the rescuers, though. I can't believe those guys, still can't believe what they did. We'll be friends for life because of it."

The rescuer next to him clapped a hand on his shoulder.

"Was there any time you wanted to give up?"

He thought of the long gray man and the feelings of despair he'd left behind. They wouldn't believe him if he talked about that, think he was mad.

"Nah. I just thought of my wife's pot roast and that got me through."

"What is it you've got? Why did you survive and not Barry?"

"I can't answer that."

The psychologist stepped in. "There are many reasons why people survive. For Stuart, he had thoughts of his family to sustain him. Barry didn't have that and studies have shown it makes a difference. Also, Stuart was less dramatic in his actions. Maybe he thought ahead a bit more, and maybe Barry thought he could get out of it."

"You're saying it's Barry's fault he was trapped? His own fault he died?"

"No. Not at all. But the fact is that Stuart thought it through and trusted the rescuers."

"Do you think yourself lucky, Stuart?"

"Couldn't be luckier," Stuart said. "Luckiest man left alive."

"I'm sure your rescuers will be happy to hear that. Do you feel any sense of obligation to them? Do you owe them anything?"

"Yeah, look they're all spread out around the place, but they can come to my place for a feed any time they like. And you know what I really owe them? I owe them a good life."

He and the rescuer shook hands, and the cheering of the audience went on for two minutes.

"What do you say to the idea that some people don't survive because they may have died helping others?"

"Yeah, well, if I coulda helped Barry survive I would have."

"What about his food? Is it true you ate his food?"

"Yeah, I ate his food. He couldn't get to it and it was only going off. That's not what killed him."

The psychologist said, "It is true that often it is the survivors don't help others. Especially in times of famine. Survivors are the ones who will take food from a child's mouth."

Stuart felt stunned. He wasn't sure how the conversation had turned against him and what a hero he was, but it seemed it had.

"All I did was survive," he said. "No one had to die for me to survive. I did it because I love my family, I love my life, and I wanted to get here on TV for the free beer I've heard about."

With that, he had the audience back.

Afterwards, there was plenty of beer drunk. The crew took him out to the local pub and he was there long after they left. People had watched the interview and they all wanted to talk to him about it.

"If only we could bottle what you've got, there'd be no little kiddies dying of cancer," people said to him more often than he wanted to hear.

"If only we could bottle it, you'd be a rich man."

"If only we could bottle it, we'd save the world."

They thought he had some magic power, that it wasn't a willingness to drink your own piss and a great desire to have proper sex with your wife again, it was something else. Something they couldn't have.

He took a drink well but even he was feeling a bit woozy by around midnight. By 3:00 a.m., the pub was almost empty. He could no longer remember who he'd spoken to, so when a sad-faced man said hello, he nodded and went back to his beer.

"Hello, Stuart," the man said again. His voice was soft. It had an amused tone, as if he knew more than other people, found something amusing. Stuart no longer wondered how people knew his name. Plenty of them did. He rather liked the celebrity. He'd always enjoyed making connections with people all over.

Stuart looked at him this time. "Do I know you?" he asked.

His teeth were bright, white and even. Clearly false. His hair, pale blond, sat flat on his head. He smelt strongly of aftershave, the kind Stuart used to smell wafting out of the cars while he waited for the bus. His mouth drooped. *Sad man*, Stuart thought.

"How are you holding up?"

"I'm okay. Bit tired."

The man moved so that he looked directly into Stuart's eyes. Stuart froze. This is how the apparition in the cave had looked at him. With this intensity. He was used to people staring at him greedily but this was different. The sad face, the long arms. Long, long fingers.

It was the apparition from the mine.

The man's hand went out and grabbed Stuart by the wrist with a powerful grip.

"Hold still, Stuart. This won't take long."

Stuart shivered, feeling as cold as he had underground. Chilled to the bone and dreaming of snow.

"Leggo, mate, wouldya?" he said. He tried to pull back but he felt deep lethargy, as if he'd been injected with golden syrup and his limbs couldn't move.

The man raised his other arm and brought it up to pinch the bridge of Stuart's nose. Stuart was paralyzed. He wanted one of the other drinkers to intervene, to hit the man, knock him away, but no one did. It was so quiet Stuart felt as if he was back in the mine and the idea of it made him choke.

No. It wasn't that. He had a nose bleed, blood pouring backwards down his throat because the man held his sinuses so tight.

He let go and Stuart slumped forward, spitting blood. He felt movement return.

Turned his head away from the man.

The man bent and helped him up. "Nose bleed, nose bleed, make a bit of room, I'll take him and clean him up. Nose bleed, he'll be fine."

Stuart tried to pull his arm away. His mouth was full of blood.

"Come on, Stuart, it'll be all right."

He led Stuart into the men's toilets. Propped him against the wall.

Stuart heard a skittering sound, like cockroaches across the kitchen bench at midnight. He thought he caught a whiff of them, that slightly plasticy smell. A smell of sour cherries.

"It won't hurt," the man said.

Stuart felt the creatures and, by straining his eyes, could watch them walking up his arm. The scream in his head deafened him.

Up his forearm, his biceps, over his shoulders and onto his neck, where he could feel them latching on.

"It's not your blood they're taking," the man said. His voice was soft and almost too broad to listen to. "It's something else. You won't miss it. It'll be like it was never there. You won't know."

He clicked his tongue and Stuart thought the sucking stopped. He felt light-headed and nauseous. The man plucked a beetle off Stuart's shoulder and ate it. Crunched it like it was a nut and took the next. Two more and he was smacking his lips. Stuart couldn't move. He felt so cold he felt like he'd been buried in snow. Or was back in the cave. But it was light in here. Very bright.

"Look at me." The man's cheeks were pink, his eyes bright. He looked younger. Happy.

"Thank you, Stuart. Have a good life."

He tapped Stuart on the head and Stuart slept.

He awoke on the filthy toilet floor. Someone had dropped a wad of shitty toilet paper and he could smell that.

He felt little compunction to rise, to lift himself. It was like this was the only moment and there was nothing beyond.

Another man came in and helped him up. "Home time for you, mate? Wait here while I take a piss and I'll get you to a taxi."

"Do I know you?" Stuart said. Things seemed blurred and he couldn't remember much.

"Nah, but you'll always help someone in trouble, right? Specially a survivor like you."

I am a survivor, Stuart thought as the stranger helped him to a taxi. *That's what I did.*

But he felt as if he could never do it again.

He woke up on his lounge room floor, his shirt stiff with dried blood.

"Big night was it?" Cheryl said, poking him with her toe.

Sarah, stood over him, ready for school, her shoes all shined, her white socks folded neatly.

He shivered, feeling cold. "The long man pinched my nose." His face felt swollen and he knew he must look awful.

"Get off the floor," Sarah said. "You're shivering."

"I will soon." He felt a deep sense of pure lethargy.

Cheryl helped him up onto the couch and brought him a cup of tea. "You're too old to drink like that anymore."

"Wasn't the drink. Well, I did give it a bit of a hiding, but it was this guy. This long gray guy who gave me a bloody nose and then did something to me. I'm tired. I'm so tired. And cold."

She brought him a fluffy pink blanket and covered his knees with it. "The TV producers sent over a copy of your interview. Sarah and I have already watched it twice! Want to have a look? You come across really well."

She didn't wait for his answer but played the DVD anyway.

He watched the interview over and over that day, wondering at the person talking. "Jeez, I'm a smart-arse, aren't I?" he said, smiling at his Cheryl. She kissed his forehead.

"You always were." The lightness of her tone warmed him slightly. She had suffered postnatal depression and he was terrified every day it would come on again. He saw it behind her eyes sometimes, in the droop of her mouth. A wash of sadness. Those were the times he tried harder lift her up. Out of the corner of his eye he thought he saw a bug climbing the wall and he curled up, pulling his blanket up over his eyes. "We need to get the rent-a-kill guys in here. Get rid of the cockroaches," he said.

She nodded. "Ants, too. All over the kitchen, rotten little things." She sat beside him, laying her head on his shoulder. "I still can't believe you're back," she said. His little bird, his sparrow, but a tower of strength at the same time.

Usually sitting beside her he felt something. Irritation, often, when she went on about small domestic details, none of which interested him. Boredom, talking about her family. Affection, when they sat together watching TV. Love, when they laughed together at a joke he'd made, when her eyes crinkled up and little tears formed. He loved those little tears.

She held his hand. He let it lie loose.

"Are you okay?" she said.

"I just can't really feel anything. It's all gone numb."

She stared at him. "We have to tell the doctor. Something's wrong. You shouldn't feel like that."

"I don't feel anything, love. That's the thing. Nothing at all. Just cold. Like I've got an ice block inside my stomach." He didn't tell her he meant emotionally as well, that looking at her left him cold.

To cover it up, he kissed her. Usually they'd do this stuff at night, with the door closed, but he kissed her with passion and moved his hands around her body, touching all his favorite bits.

The weeks passed. He ate meals he had no real desire to eat, had conversations and many, many interviews. Sponsorships brought money in. Newspaper reports listed everything he'd eaten underground and those people approached him. It was Vegemite, Tip Top bread, Milo chocolate bars, apples (the local fruit shop took on that one), and the local butcher had a go, too. The watch company put him on TV, talking about how he'd never need another watch, that one was so good. So at least he didn't have to work. People kept asking him if he was going back underground and he'd bluff at them, give them the real man answer, the hero stuff, but he wasn't going back.

He spent a lot of time reading the paper. He started cutting out stories of other survivors, especially the ones who talked about the cold, about the deep bone chill they felt after a few days.

"Dad, let me hook you up with an online forum. You can meet other survivors. Talk to them. Most of them are probably feeling what you're feeling," Sarah said. He sat at the computer for a while but it only made sense when she talked him through it and he didn't want her to know it all.

She asked him about the long man. "The one you said pinched your nose. We should try to track him down and make sure he doesn't do it again. People can't go round pinching my dad's nose like that."

"Willy nilly," he said. It was an old joke. "I don't know if we'll find him. I don't think he's at the pub much, or if he's got a job. I saw him when I was buried, you know. He sent his ghost in to find me."

Others had talked about seeing visions. Buried in the snow, or caught in a car for two days on a country road. They said, more than one of them, that a long man had visited them. "It's not just me," he told Sarah. "No one knows why he doesn't help. He just looks."

"Did he pinch their noses? This is the stuff we can find online, Dad."

"Yeah, maybe. Maybe. What about stuff about cockroaches? How to get rid of them? I saw a huge one in the bathroom. They say they'll survive nuclear war. That's what they reckon." He shivered. "I hate them."

He felt like a fraud. Life exhausted him, all the people wanting what he had. And Cheryl and Sarah got nothing but harassment. *Lucky your dad's alive, your husband*, people said to them. *Imagine what life would have been like without him, how sad, how hard.* Making them think about it. All those people wanting to talk to him, but they paid him at least and it kept them in beer and roast beef. Always the same questions.

"What is it you think you were kept alive for?" they asked, putting the onus on him to make something of his life. As if he'd been given a second chance and he'd be a fool to waste it.

"Dunno what I was kept alive for, but mostly I'm enjoying every extra minute with my daughter and my wife," was his stock answer.

But he no longer really cared.

They asked him, "Are you scared of anything? Seems like you're not." It was a stupid question, he thought. Who wasn't scared?

"Cockroaches. I really hate cockroaches." The interviewer sighed in agreement.

Another question they always asked him was, "Put in the same situation, would or could you do it again?"

"Well, I won't mate, will I? Just not going to happen."

They always ended with, "If only you could bottle it." His standard joke was to hold out his wrists.

"Ya wanna take a liter or two? Go for it! I can spare it!"

It was all an act and he was good at it.

He was waiting in the queue to buy fish and chips ("Aren't you that guy? That miner guy?") when he smelt sour cherries. It took him straight back to the cave and the smell of the long man. He felt cold through his layers of clothing and did not want to turn around. He felt someone behind him, close, but people did that. They seemed to think if they got physically close to him they could absorb some of him, that they could be like him.

He took his package of food and left the shop, eyes down. Climbed into the car some sponsor had given him, sat there to eat it.

The long man opened the passenger door and climbed in.

Stuart dropped the food on his lap where it sat, greasy and hot. He barely felt it. He scrabbled for the door handle but the long man took his wrist. Pressed hard and Stuart couldn't move. Just like last time.

"You seem to be enjoying that fish, Stuart. You know what that tells me? That I didn't take it all. The fact that you want to eat tells me that."

Stuart tried to shake his head, to say, "I'm faking it, it's all fake, I can't feel a fucking thing," but the cockroaches were out, skittering and sucking and

346   KAARON WARREN

if he thought he was cold before, *that* was nothing. His eyelids felt frozen open, his nostrils frozen shut, breathing was so painful he wanted to stop doing it.

"That's it now," the long man said, picking cockroach feelers out of his teeth. "You're done."

Stuart sat slumped in the seat for a while, then started the car. A tape was playing; one of his interviews. He liked listening to himself, hearing his own voice.

"I'll do anything to stay alive, anything to keep my family alive," he heard himself say. "You know I got stuck in a pipe once when I was a kid. Fat kid, I was. I sang songs from TV shows to keep me occupied." Listening from his car, chilled to the bone and tired, Stuart wondered if he'd seen the long man then. If the long man had waited, and waited, until he was good and strong.

He pulled out of the car park. It was only his sense of duty making him do it, long-instilled. He had to go to a school visit someone had organized for him. Some school where there was a survivor kid, a young girl recently rescued. It took him a while to get there; wrong turns, bad traffic. Angry traffic. He thought there was more road rage than usual but then wondered if it was his driving? If all that stuff about driving carefully did make sense, because he didn't care now, didn't care how he drove or what he hit.

"We'd like to welcome Stuart Parker to the school. He's taken time out of his busy day to talk to us and to talk to Claire, our own hero."

The children clapped quietly. Stuart guessed they were tired of hearing about Claire.

She'd been trapped in the basement of a building. A game of hide and seek gone wrong; no one knew she was playing. No one knew where she was. It took six days for them to find her.

"Tell us how you coped, Claire," the teacher said.

"I pretended I was at school doing boring work and that's why it was so boring. Sometimes I thought about this nice man from the mine. He said he kept thinking of nice things and that's what I did too."

The children shuffled, started to talk, bored. Claire looked at them wide-eyed. "I ate bugs. Lots of bugs. Like he did. And I had some chips I took from the cupboard but I didn't want to tell Mum and Dad cos I didn't want to get in trouble."

She had their attention, but not completely. "And then there was the creepy guy."

"You were alone in the basement, Claire, weren't you?" the teacher said, passive-aggressive. "No one there."

"Who did you see?" Stuart said. He hadn't had a chance to speak before then. "What did he look like?"

The audience were rapt. They didn't often get to see adults this way, all het up and loud.

"I was all by myself but then this creepy long guy was there. I never seen him before but I thought he might help me to get out. But he didn't, he just stared at me. I told him he should go away but the only thing I think he said was, 'See you soon, Claire.' That's why I'm scared. I really don't want to see him again."

Stuart wanted to care. He wanted to save her but there was nothing left in him. Only the memory of the man who would have killed to save that girl. Would have ripped the arms off any man who tried to hurt her.

Just a memory though.

"Stuart, we haven't heard from you. What can you tell the children?"

"That there is no purpose in life. We all die and rot and none of it is worth anything. You're only taking up space. And that the long man is real. You need to keep her safe from him because he'll destroy her."

The principal, stunned and speechless, took a moment to answer. The children were silent and he wondered if he'd laid seeds of sadness and emptiness in them all. He didn't mean to. But he was too tired and cold to lie anymore.

"But . . . but Mr. Parker, you're a role model. We asked you here to lift the children. Inspire them."

"I'm nothing. Nothing at all," he said.

Claire. Claire was in the news and so was he, with his awful statements, his cruelty to the children. He had the media at his door again but they hated him now for turning on the children, you don't do that to the kiddies, do you? He watched Claire; she didn't look chilled to the bone, so he thought perhaps the long man hadn't come to her yet.

His house was full of his sponsors' food and friends came over to eat it because he wouldn't. Some of the rescuers too, looking at him as if they'd wasted their time. Sitting there in front of the television, warm rug, warm slippers, all skinny and pale.

He couldn't even fake a smile anymore. His famous watch had slipped off his wrist and sat in the dust under the couch.

"We shoulda bottled it. We could give him a taste of his own self," one of the rescuers said. He knew they were disappointed in him, that he wasn't doing what they wanted him to do.

"Three days of my life, I gave to save him," he heard one say in the kitchen. "Now look at him."

They left him alone.

And he didn't care.

*Is it possible that we are haunted in dreams by our beloved dead,
not just in metaphor but in actual fact? If so, is it impossible to
imagine a plane or space where they might commune?*

MYSTERIES OF THE OLD QUARTER

Paul Park

⟡

*(Newly excerpted and translated from the journals and correspondence
of Dr. Philippe Delorme, among other sources)*

1. "THE RAIN AGAINST THE CASEMENT . . . "

. . . I write this from my hotel room, which constitutes the majority of what
I have seen so far, here in what was once the greatest city of New France.
Outside, the narrow road is full of water, fog, and sodden filth. I have heard
rumors of another, more modern metropolis on the other side of Canal Street,
broad boulevards and large houses that contain actual Americans in their
natural surroundings, as well as poorer but more vibrant neighborhoods of
Germans and Italians. Though I could walk to that metropolis in half an
hour, I gather that would be to break some sort of secret code. The indigenous
culture of the city has curled in upon itself because it knows it is dying, even
though it is in itself quite new, by European standards. But these sequences
run quicker here, partly because of a mania for destroying and rebuilding,
and partly because the land itself, a bend of miasmic and mephitic swamp
between the river and the lake, appears to me a sink of dissolution, which
has accelerated all natural processes of corruption and decay.

So far I have kept this opinion to myself. At least I am attempting to do so.
But perhaps some of my prejudices have already leaked out. This evening, for
example, I addressed a local scientific society on the subject of an experiment
into the nature of electricity, and in particular the electrical impulses in
the brains of rats and monkeys. Afterwards I answered questions from the
audience. It is an infuriating and pervasive characteristic of this tour that
these questions by no means have confined themselves to the subject of

my demonstrations. A few days ago, a gentleman in Chicago asked me my opinion of the weather in the coming week—I might have predicted it would rain forever! And tonight I answered several questions about the theories of Mr. Charles Darwin.

The religiousness of these people does not cease to astound. After my second attempt at reconciling what cannot, after all, be reconciled, I allowed myself a joke, although I did not smile. "Perhaps," I suggested, "it was our simian ancestors that inhabited the Garden of Eden, as none of the activities described as taking place there would have required a brain much larger than an ordinary potato. It was in the land of Canaan, surely, that we began our inexorable descent, guided by the process of natural selection." The most foolish beasts, I meant to imply, have the wit to copulate, and our development as a species, and as individual moral beings, could only commence at the moment we had turned our back on God.

I was speaking in response to an enquiry about "reverse evolution," an absurd and backward theory that has nevertheless found nourishment here in the superstitions of the inhabitants. During the ensuing silence I was tempted to mention your own observation that since God is reputed to have created man in his own image, then perhaps the early migration of Africans to Europe is evidence of man's fall. Contrasting your and my complexions, you once observed how Lucifer's supposed "brightness" might be more properly translated to emphasize the pallor of his skin, at least in comparison with God himself. But that would be a joke too painful to express in this crude nation. As you know, I am sometimes irritated by how the Continental newspapers can scarcely mention my work without including a line or phrase that concerns my "Moorish grandmother," a lady whom I never had the privilege to meet. In Paris, a small amount of African or even Hebrew blood is considered a mark of distinction, perhaps of genius, at least in intellectual or artistic circles. That is not so here. If my history were well-known, my lectures would attract a different audience entirely, such as might buy tickets to observe a chimpanzee solve quadratic equations in the zoo.

Ah, my love, the hour is late. The rain against the casement rattles like escaping steam. Soon I will close the humid curtains, climb onto the lumpy bed. If you were here in my exile I would embrace you, and you would no longer complain that I was diffident or shy. I would run my fingers down the buttons of your back, and lower still. Doubtless we would converse, if at all, in the language of the angels in paradise, at least if our current scientific thinking is correct . . .

(Addressed to Mme. Solange Baziat, May 23, 1888—unsent)

2. LATER THAT NIGHT: "I DO NOT DWELL UPON MY FAILURES . . . "

. . . Why do I persist in seeking some relief in these attempts at correspondence? Why do I expect to find comfort in the act of sharing my thoughts and actions with my friends, with you, for instance? No, it is more pertinent to ask why I am so often disappointed, why at these moments of attempted intimacy my loneliness attacks me with renewed ferociousness. I know already the attempt at connection will be in vain. And yet it is natural to try again and again. Surely this is the foundation of the sexual urge. And surely this is part of the religious urge as well, the faith that at one time we understood each other, and the hope that after death we will again, once we have lost the illusion of our separateness.

My friend, I have already abandoned my first letter of the evening. It was to a woman of our mutual acquaintance. Always with her I am obliged to hide something of myself, in order to preserve her good opinion. In this case there was a name I must not mention for the sake of her jealousy—I understand that. But even so the details and events that I described—some trivial, some essential—had split so sharply from reality by the end of the first page, that I threw down my pen. And then no sooner did I lie down in darkness than I found myself fumbling for the lamp, gasping for breath, with an elevated heart rate. There is no sleep for me tonight.

Now I will try again. Perhaps what I am about to say, I can share with none but you.

The purpose of my previous letter was to allow me to distract myself with nocturnal fantasies, so that I might forget my anxiousness. Perhaps you will be relieved to hear I have given up hope of that. My current missive has a different cause, though I will begin with the same base of fact, the root of every possible narrative—it has not stopped raining since my arrival. I am staying at the house of a Creole gentleman, a narrow, three-storey mansion in the Rue Dauphine. He is the sponsor of my lectures, a tall, thin, dignified, and upright person, who is also, as it happens, quite insane. His name is Maubusson, and he owns an indigo plantation outside of the city, an enterprise that he himself must know is doomed to fail, because of a recent artificial synthesis.

Despite the weather, this evening I was well disposed. My host was generous enough to buy me supper at a restaurant that might not have offended even you. I observed during the meal that he seemed distracted and glum, but he showed no obvious lunacy—my dear, he was just lying in wait! After coffee we proceeded to the ballroom of a nearby hotel. Three-quarters of an hour afterwards, I had finished my lecture and then rapidly disposed of several infuriating and irrelevant questions about the origin of species. My friend, I thought I could perceive the finish line, when I espied his outstretched hand. "Sir," he said, "I would like to ask you news of some earlier experiments, in which you corresponded with the spirits of the dead."

I grimaced, then cut him off. "I do not like to dwell upon my failures. You understand—"

Alas, he understood nothing. He was not satisfied, and so obliged me to persist: "You speak of a line of inquiry that is several years old, during the course of which I must admit that I allowed my personal desires to dominate my scientific objectivity. It is true that through the use of electrical stimulation, I was able to prolong consciousness in a small number of recently expired subjects. But the accounts of these experiments were distorted by a sensationalist press, and I am now convinced that I was wrong in my conclusions. The boundary between living and dying is not as firm, perhaps, as we imagine, or at least as I imagined at that time."

While I was speaking, still he had not lowered his hand. His smile was skull-like, and exposed his yellow teeth. Because he was my host and benefactor, I was compelled to let him speak. "But I recall a description of a scene at the bedside of a Parisian lady—I forget her name—when she was reconciled to her niece and nephews, and was even able to explain to them the terms of her estate . . . "

"I recall the exact words of Mlle. de Noailles," I said, as coldly as I could. (But inside I was burning, you must imagine.) "I'm afraid I cannot repeat them in a public place. If her sister's children could find reconciliation in anything that occurred that day, they are more imaginative than I, who witnessed the entire event. As for the will, I believe it is in litigation. Now, if you please . . . "

But he would not be silenced! "Perhaps at that moment she was speaking to other emanations in the room," he said. "Perhaps in the hours since her death, these souls were as real to her as you are to me. Perhaps at that moment, you yourself were insubstantial as a ghost."

These words, indeed, reminded me of long-dismissed hypotheses. But I felt I could not display any uncertainty, perhaps out of a sense of foreboding. "If she were speaking to these other emanations, it is clear she was not pleased with them," I concluded in a tone that ended the debate. And in fact the meeting broke up shortly afterwards. Imagine my displeasure, subsequently, walking home with my host and even sharing his umbrella, when I heard him explain how the entire reason for my presence in this city, the entire reason he had found the money to invite me to address his miserable society—all that was a blind, a trick. He had no interest in my recent work, but had fixed instead on the death of Sophie de Noailles, which in my own terrible grief I had allowed myself to desecrate with criminal absurdities and humiliations. In other words, he begged me to revisit the worst moments of my life, because he also (as I might have guessed!) had lost someone who was dear to him. His only daughter, a young lady not yet twenty years old, was recently deceased under painful and mysterious circumstances.

"If I could speak to her once more," said Monsieur Maubusson. "Only to ask her what occurred. If I could hear from her lips who was responsible, no matter how veiled and shrouded her speech—you see it is a matter of justice! And I think it was not true what you said in the hotel, even according to your own description. That woman you mentioned, was it possible she spoke in code? You imply the words themselves were meaningless. But I think it likely that these spirits would employ a code."

I considered this. But Maubusson was wrong to say there was no meaning in the words that Sophie de Noailles spoke on her deathbed. It is that the words themselves were barnyard epithets I could not believe she knew.

Could one imagine a code made up of three or four of the most obscene vulgarities, repeated over and over? The street was very dark, very wet. The water swirled around my boots. We were passing a line of wooden cottages with wide porches and long shuttered windows. Light gleamed between the slats.

I stopped, and made him return with his umbrella. For several moments I had known what he was asking. "No," I said. "I cannot do this. I refuse."

His face was close to mine. But he would not look me in the eyes. "Please," he said. "If I could just . . . "

But at that moment something new occurred to me. It had been more than a month since I'd received his invitation. "When did your daughter die?"

"Six weeks ago." When he saw my look of horror, he put up his hand. "You needn't worry. I have taken all precautions."

He would not look me in the eye. But as he spoke I could perceive, as if vaguely through the fog, the lineaments of his insanity. For six weeks he had packed the girl in ice, which he had transported in box-cars to a city where every courtyard and alleyway is lined with banana trees and bottlebrush palms.

"Monsieur, I'm begging you," he said. "And you must forgive me for not telling you what I intended. But I guessed that if I asked you in a letter, you would have refused."

In addition, he had bought or reconstructed what he imagined were the instruments from my laboratory, as he had seen them represented or described, powered by a coal-fired dynamo of his own invention. "I also am a man of science," he protested. "Nor am I ignorant of medicine. Before the war my father would attend to all our laborers, as was the custom at that time."

I shuddered, and looked away from him. A negress floundered toward us down the middle of the street, carrying a lantern. Her old-fashioned dress and her wide hat were drenched. She stood behind my host, so that he couldn't see her—I had heard this district of the city, or nearby, was notorious for prostitution, either in large palaces or else small, individual residences. She was a pretty girl, of a type that I admire, and I studied the silent movement of her lips. "*Vous cherchez quelque chose?*"

"Sir," I said, "you must abandon this."

By the light of the lantern flame, I could see my host was weeping. "I cannot. Monsieur, you are my final hope. If you won't help me . . . "

I made a signal with my hand. The woman turned away, and we came here. Perhaps now you can guess why I lie sleepless in my room. I am on the third floor, but elsewhere, somewhere, I can hear the steam-powered generator, throbbing faintly in the walls. Tomorrow I will ask for the first train to Jackson. In the meantime, the rain hisses like escaping steam . . .

(Addressed to M. Joachim Valdor, May 23rd—unsent)

3. Early Morning: " . . . a gesture I recognized . . . "

. . . I ask myself if I should finish or amend this second letter now, at a remove of many hours. But when I re-read it I can see it is as misleading as the first, in mood, in fact, in everything. No doubt it is useful to descend through layers, saying adieu at every step, first to the man I ought or else imagine myself to be. Second, perhaps, I could take leave of all my thoughts, feelings, and intentions. Then finally I am reduced to describing what I have done, or I will do. I only hope I am bold enough to admit them to myself.

After midnight, then, I closed my letter to Joachim and lay down for the second time. I was mistaken to say I would not sleep, for how else to describe what happened? Perhaps I was experiencing the first effects of the fever that that this morning has registered on my thermometer, and which is at the stage now that it sharpens my awareness, rather than diminishing it.

But I anticipate—I was asleep in bed. This is what I must conclude, even though according to my own perception I lay awake, braiding my heartbeat with the throbbing in the walls. There was some disturbance in the street, a man shouting. Someone spoke, a different kind of voice, well-remembered, close to my ear. I started up, and then I saw her in a corner of the wall beside the curtain, her hand on the tasseled cord. "Solange," I said, because Solange Baziat was in my mind. Dressed in black, she turned toward me, smiled and touched her hair in a gesture I recognized. "*Mon Dieu*," I murmured, because my interest in Mme. Baziat has always been measured by how much, at any given moment, she resembles someone else, someone who now approached me dressed in the same black, beaded dress that I remembered from the night I had attempted to take her in my arms, in her father's apartment in the Place Vendôme. Then I had been cruelly, even violently rebuffed, but this time I expected something different, I don't know why. "Sophie," I cried, reaching out my hand to hide her face, and she moved under it and laid her cheek against my breast. Then I felt her fingers on my lips, while at the same time her other hand grasped me lower down, to such effect that I felt myself let go, as in a dream. I bent to kiss her, and she seized my lip between her teeth, and at that moment I knew I'd been mistaken, fooled by my regrets— Sophie was dead. This woman in my arms was someone else, younger and smaller, someone I didn't know at all, an actual woman who had slipped into my room, perhaps the same one I had seen that evening in the street outside. "*Vous cherchez quelque chose?*"

No, it was impossible, absurd. How could she have gotten in? And by the time I was fully awake, she had disappeared, although the door remained closed. She left me to wipe myself with my nightshirt, and attend to my bleeding lip. A smell lingered in the air, a mixture of perfume and decay.

Now convinced I'd been asleep, I tried immediately to remember. But as so often happens, my dream faded, and the woman in it also faded from my mind. As she did so, her complexion changed, and lost its color, so that I was no longer sure I was remembering the negress of the Rue Dauphine. In fact I was convinced it was not she. And yet the doctors say it is impossible to invent a new face in a dream, the face of someone we have never met.

Then the generator stopped, and the silence in the house was enormous, baffling. Over the course of the night I'd become accustomed to the sound, until I felt rather than heard it. I stood over the basin washing my face, and now I raised my head to look into the dark mirror. In the sudden quiet, I thought I heard the sound of my host's surrender, of his submission to his grief, at the moment (I thought—irrationally) of his success. How else could I explain the experience I'd just had? Subsequently I discovered several ways, but at that moment I was convinced. At the same time I imagined a new sympathy with my host, because in my own thoughts I had merged my unhappiness with his. And though the emotions of a father might seem different from those of a lover (if I could aspire to calling myself that—I speak only of my feelings, not of her response), still I could understand his grief in the death of a beautiful woman in her prime.

I wiped my face, threw on my clothes. I needed to confirm that the person from my dream, the small, delicate, cat-like woman who had bit me on the lip, was indeed Mademoiselle Maubusson. In my febrile state, it was imperative for me to verify this fact, and at the same time I felt some vestige of my excitement when I first attacked the problem of re-animation in the year prior to Mlle. de Noailles's death, little knowing that before long I would have such a personal interest in my success.

I opened the door of my bedroom, and followed the new silence down the stairs. As I descended step by step, my candle in my hand, I reconsidered momentarily the contempt with which I had rejected my host's theory of ghosts, or spirits, or "emanations," in the light of my own recent experience. Was it possible that we are haunted in dreams by our beloved dead, not just in metaphor but in actual fact? If so, was it impossible to imagine a plane or space where they might commune, or even share each other's bodies, as I had conceived in that transitional moment between sleep and wakefulness?

The wallpaper was heavily patterned, pink and cream. Yet there was a dirty stripe opposite the banister, where many hands had slid. It was not hard for me to find, on the second storey, the room I sought. I heard low voices beyond the door.

I knocked, then entered. How can I describe the scene? I stood in a lady's bedroom, furnished with the dark, mahogany, over-embellished chests and cabinets that are habitual in rich Creole households. There was a four-poster bed—unoccupied. The wallpaper was pink and green, hand-painted with scenes along the river. The gas was lit, and by its spectral flame I saw my host, dressed in shirt-sleeves, the electrodes still in his hand. The dynamo was in the courtyard outside, and the wires snaked in the open window, together with a number of black rubber tubes, which led to a zinc bathtub in the middle of the room.

There was another man also, a young, curly-headed fellow, and when he spoke I could tell by his accent that French was not his native language: "Who the devil are you?"

I scarcely heard him. In the bathtub, packed in ice, was the woman from my dream.

She was dressed in a pink nightgown, and her rich black hair was loose around her shoulders. She had high cheekbones, a small, sharp nose, and a soft line of hair along her upper lip. Her skin was pale, but whether because of the constant refrigeration or else from the effect of the electrical stimulation, it still retained a rosy glow. Astonished by this, immediately I perceived that one of the tubes that ran to her must have maintained the circulation of her blood, while another, perhaps, pumped air into her lungs—I could see the harness and the plugs for her nostrils, which her father had just now cleared away.

"How have you fed her?" I enquired.

My host came toward me. "By means of a tube right through to her stomach. And a protein solution, which I saw described in—"

"Who the devil are you, sir?" repeated the curly-headed gentleman. But I was studying the electrodes in Maubusson's hands, and didn't answer. Besides, I thought, it was up to my host to explain my presence, which he did. "Henry, this is Professor Delorme, from Paris. I spoke to you—"

"Did you now? Well perhaps he would be good enough to wait outside, until we are finished here. Under the circumstances—"

I looked at him now, a young man with a mottled complexion and side-whiskers. "Monsieur," said my host, "may I present my daughter's fiancé, Mr. Henry Lockett?"

"*Enchanté*," I said. "But am I right in thinking it was to the young lady's temples that you attached the posts? I can see the marks—"

"It was unclear in your description," confessed Monsieur Maubusson. Then he paused. "Professor, I can tell from your face that I have blundered—please, if you could help us now. It's not been five minutes since—"

"No, it's enough," cried Mr. Lockett, in English. He moved to confront me, a menacing, muscular figure, though he was not my height. "It is finished. Make an end, sir. Make an end."

He was talking to Maubusson, but he was staring at me. As for my host, he continued without stopping. "I had thought I could duplicate your results by following your descriptions. Forgive me. If that had been possible, I never would have thought to involve you . . . "

I had turned away from Mr. Lockett, and was examining instead the face of Mlle. Maubusson in her zinc bathtub. I examined her long eyelashes and dark lips. Already, though, there was a yellowish pallor to her cheeks, which suggested we had not much time. "The electrodes must be divided, and fastened to several places on the cranium," I said. "Other places also."

I only said this because she resembled so completely the woman in my dream. Mr. Lockett threw up his hands. "By God, that's enough," he said. "Maubusson, I can't tolerate this—I won't have this fellow touch her with his black hands. I will not stay here. If you persist, I will inform the authorities the first thing in the morning—no, by God, sir, stand aside."

It occurred to me that Henry Lockett might have heard some chance rumor of my dear grandmama. In short, he might not have been so ignorant of me and of my reputation as he had claimed. Wishing to confound him, as he was speaking I had reached for the young lady's wrist.

A wet gust of wind pushed into the room, disturbing the curtains by the open sash, where a braided cable of wires and rubber tubes ran down into the courtyard. Reflected there, I could see indirectly the evil, red glow of the generator. Monsieur Maubusson crossed the room as if to shut the window. But he turned back before he reached it, revealing a pistol in his hand. "Stand away, sir," he cried. "No, you—Henry. Please, my boy, you must understand. There is no time to be lost."

"Sir, you must be drunk or else insane," began the outraged fiancé, a diagnosis that coincided with my own, although I saw no reason why the two possibilities had to exclude each other. In fact, I wondered if Lockett himself had been excessively fortified with liquor, as I could smell it on his breath and clothes the moment he'd approached me, where I stood by Mlle. Maubusson's tub, testing the rigidity of her arm and elbow—her skin was very cold. Her father made a sudden gesture, and Lockett backed away from me all the way to the door, where he stood impotently, his eyes wet, his face red.

Another gesture, and he was gone. My host followed him to the open door. "I'll see him out," he said, putting the pistol aside. "Besides, I must restart the engine."

I was happy they were gone. I wanted Mlle. Maubusson to myself. No sooner had her father left the room, than I went to work. Along one wall, incongruous against the painted wallpaper, there was a wheeled metal bed of a type that is used in hospitals. I brought it over, and, neglecting my clothes, I lifted Mlle. Maubusson onto the enamel surface. During my dream I had had such a strong impression of her weight in my arms, I felt I must confirm it at the expense of my waistcoat.

As my host had said, there was no time to be lost. But I had another reason to hurry. The electrodes must be divided, and at least one placed under her clothes, between her *labia minora*. I had not wanted to perform this operation under her father's scrutiny, although without it, or the equivalent procedure on my male subjects, I had had no success in the past—so strong in the dead are these bestial urges.

And as I fumbled under the young lady's drenched nightgown, I could not but remember the horrifying moment when I had discovered, in the underclothes of Sophie de Noailles, the pearl and sapphire ring I had given her in a past moment of happiness. Anticipating everything I did, she had secreted it there before her death, to mock me and torment me. She knew I would do everything in my power to resuscitate her, if only so that I could beg for her forgiveness.

An enamel tray hung from the bed-rail, containing an assortment of medical implements. I had pulled apart the second skein of electrodes and was attaching them to Mlle. Maubusson's cranium, when I heard the roar of the dynamo, outside in the courtyard. I felt the electric thrill in my fingertips, as I was able to manipulate a cage of stimulation over the cerebral hemispheres. This is what Maubusson had already attempted. But at the same time I affixed the posts so as to enclose and affect the hypothalamus and the medulla oblongata, the most primitive portions of the brain. The effect was instantaneous; I felt her body shudder and convulse. Her spine curved like a bow, and her eyes snapped open as I bent over her. Because of the electricity, her lips pulled away from her teeth, and her mottled tongue protruded next to my ear. And she started in at once, in a harsh, breathy whisper—"Oh, I have waited for this moment—do not touch me. You have forfeited the right."

"Forgive me," I murmured next to her ear.

"I cannot. Instead, I must remember that night when you revealed yourself to me. Monsieur, perhaps it is not possible to know another person, to trust that you have seen into the bottom of his soul. But then at certain moments we reveal ourselves. That night I saw an animal, a creature whose only impulse was violence and desire. What is it that separates men from beasts, can you answer that? And how is it that a woman is expected to continue, once she has finally understood a man she trusted, or might have trusted with her soul? What shall a woman do, once she has seen the truth? For shame, monsieur. Must I remind you of that night, when you would have taken me by force in my father's house? And I felt I could say nothing, because of your friendship with him, and the money that he owed. Can you blame me for my response, which was to discover an extract of conium—you know where I found it! Ah, how cold I was!"

Her voice had risen to a shriek. I tried to restrain her, press her down to the enamel surface, but she struggled against me. With one hand, from the enamel tray she grabbed up a pair of scissors, which I had been using to cut pieces of surgical tape. Fearing for my life, I let her go and stumbled away, as she clambered off the bed and stood brandishing the scissors, her eyes wide and staring. But she was held from attacking me by the wires in her hair, connected to the electrical cable that was stretched to its entire length across the room, and which by its weight was pulling her head back, so that the sinews stood out from her neck. Furious, she jabbed at me with the scissors, and when she realized that she couldn't reach me, with her other hand she ripped the net of wires from her head, and immediately fell lifeless to the floor.

"Brute," said Monsieur Maubusson, standing by the door. I had not heard him come in.

"Animal," he repeated. "To think I welcomed him into my house. Now I see why he wanted to impede us. Why he ran from us. He was afraid we would discover—"

"No," I murmured.

"And this apothecary," he continued as he came into the room and collapsed over his daughter's corpse. "I will hunt him down. I will have him arrested. He must be in a shop near here."

"You will not find him," I murmured.

"Besides," I pleaded, after a moment. "You must not trust the literal accuracy of these words. You say yourself they speak in code . . . "

"Does this sound like a code to you, monsieur? She told us straight out what has happened. Ah God, ever since her death, this has been my fear. I could have predicted this. And yet I saw no trace of poison, no discarded vial."

"These women are devious," I said. "You cannot trust them. *Conium maculatum* leaves no trace."

No matter what we undertook, we could not rouse her again. Instead, after another hour, we shut down the dynamo for the last time, and then deposed Mlle. Maubusson upon the table. My host picked up the scissors from the floor. "She must have mistaken you for him," he said. "I can only apologize on her behalf."

"She was evidently blind," I concurred.

I write this at dawn. Perhaps I can claim a few hours' sleep, before my train. As I climbed the stairs, I saw my host descend to the front hall, an umbrella in his hand. I hate to think what he intends.

*(From the private diary of Philippe Delorme, May 24*th*)*

4. " . . . A CONGENITAL DEFECT . . . "

Q: You understand what I am saying to you?

A: Yes, monsieur. Although I cannot speak English to my satisfaction, I can understand perfectly well.

Q: Good. How long have you worked for Mr. Maubusson?

A: Seven years.

Q: Good. Will you explain in your own words what happened on the morning of the 24th of May—that is, on Tuesday of last week?

A: What happened?

Q: I'm talking about Dr. Delorme.

A: Well, I brought him coffee in the morning. There was a break in the weather, and my master had already gone out. This was perhaps at eight o'clock. Professor Delorme was agitated, and complained of a small fever. He told me he must take a carriage to the station, and so then I must inform him that the tracks were somewhat underwater between here and Jackson. You remember that morning—there was no steamship also, because the river was so high. Beyond St. Claude Avenue, the streets were all in flood.

Q: Delorme was a white man? What did he say?

A: Well, he was agitated, as I tell you. He said he would verify this information as he could.

Q: And Mr. Maubusson?

A: He was already gone, as I have said. I had no idea, yet, of the tragedy. And I must tell you, it was unnecessary. Mlle. Maubusson, she had a heart defect, it was well known. There was no mystery—she had a congenital defect, like her mother. But my master couldn't accept it. He was so distracted in his grief. He could not see what was before his face. He must persuade himself of something different, or else make himself to be persuaded. It was Delorme that must have accomplished this, I don't know why. But I must blame him. Monsieur Lockett and my master, until that night they were together in all things.

Q: A heart defect. You're a doctor, are you?

A: No, sir.

Q: No medical training?

A: No.

Q: No. Where were you born? Santo Domingo, isn't it? Tell me what Delorme did then.

A. He left his luggage and went out. It is still upstairs. He inquired from me after a girl, whom he had seen in the street the night before. A local girl, whom I recognized from his description. But he did not understand. He thought she was a woman of the town. But this was not the place, so close to St. Roch's church—it was not possible. I gave him the address. I told him, "Oh, so you will get your fortune read?" But he did not understand. He was a bad man, I think. He looked for another meaning, because he was desperate for this woman, even so early in the morning . . .

(From the police deposition of Prosper Charrière, May 30th)

5. "Vous cherchez quelque chose?"

LADIES AND GENTLEMEN, ARE YOU LOOKING FOR SOMETHING OR SOMEONE WHO IS LOST AND CANNOT BE FOUND? ARE YOU LOOKING

FOR THE ANSWERS TO YOUR SECRET QUESTIONS? IS THERE A MAN
OR WOMAN, WHOSE HEART YOU MUST UNLOCK? PERHAPS THERE IS
A MAN WHO LANGUISHES IN PRISON, FALSELY OR ELSE RIGHTFULLY
ACCUSED. MADAME SEMIRAMIS WILL HELP, EMPLOYING ALL THE
LATEST SCIENTIFIC INSTRUMENTS. FOLLOW THESE SIGNS TO HER
ADDRESS . . .

(Posted in the Rue Royale, earlier that week)

6. POST-SCRIPT.

. . . And one more thing, my God. An hour's sleep without rest, buffeted by
dreams. You stand before me in your same black beaded dress, bloodless
and pale. When you touch me I can measure in your body's temperature
the effect of the conium, which you discovered in my laboratory. And when
you kneel down to unbutton me, where I once might have joyfully supposed
you had been taught by nature alone, now I can perceive the course of your
instruction in a brothel of dead souls, and a malign efficiency which gives
me no pleasure or relaxation, but rather the reverse. I left France to avoid
these dreams, but they have followed me. Where can I go to find relief?

(From the private diary of Philippe Delorme, May 24ᵗʰ, eight o'clock)

7. OF POSSIBLE SIGNIFICANCE: AN INTERVIEW WITH MARIE LOUISE GLASPION, IN THE INFIRMARY OF THE URSULINE CONVENT, CHARTERS STREET, AUGUST 10ᵀᴴ, 1936.

. . . I understand why you have come. You want to ask me about Madame
Semiramis, how I left her house. Isn't that right?

Even last year I would have told you nothing. But now you see me lying
here too weak to raise my head, connected by this tube to this machine.

For some weeks now I have understood that I am dying. I have treated
many others through this same infection of the lung, especially this summer,
because of my work here with the sisters. But that is not the only reason.

Many years I have denied this, though by now I am too tired to continue:
I still have the gift, which I inherited from my mother and have tried to turn
to God's purposes. When it refers to that night, my gift is where it starts,
because of those two men that I saw arguing in the Rue Dauphine, when
I was late returning to my mother's house. The older one, he stood at the
abyss. The snake was out upon his temple, as we used to say, and of course
in the next days his name was in the papers, because he had been shot by
some American.

Always one pauses, wondering to intervene, but how could I? What intervention could be made? I was only a girl, not yet fifteen years old. Besides, it was the younger man who stared at me with such hostility, because he thought I was a prostitute selling my body in an alleyway. In those days I was full of pride, not like now.

That was the night of a big storm. In the morning the streets were flooded in the Third District, not yet where I was, but toward the Rue Claibourne. So long ago! But I was soaked when I got home, and my mother scolded me. She was with some customers around the fire, although it was almost midnight. The rain fell though the roof into some pots. She had killed the cock.

What came to disgust me finally were the images of saints around the altar, St. Roch and St. John especially, together with the devil's images from Saint Domingue. But in those days I saw this as normal. Maman told me to dry myself beside the fire, and I hated that also, because of the eyes of the customers, even though I knew full well that this was part of why they came, part of the devil's net, part of that nonsense with Damboolah and Bamboolah and these things, my mother knew it too. It was she who stripped the wet scarf from my throat.

Will you give me some water, please? Thank you. You see I am too weak to pour a glass. Oh, you must not spill water on your microphone. Bring it close. I will speak to it as if it were a priest—I was astonished to see that same man the next morning, the one who had watched me in the Rue Dauphine, a gentleman of color, but light-skinned. Gray eyes. The rain had stopped for a moment. A humid wind chased the clouds over the rooftops, away toward the river. He came in drunk out of the street, stinking of tafia. I was sweeping with the wet broom, my sleeves rolled up. I thought my mother was still asleep behind the curtain. But this fellow scarcely spoke a greeting. He took me by surprise. He backed me up against the wall before I could resist. He was begging for pity. I'd heard that from a man before! I screamed, and then my mother was there, and he released me. She was a tall woman with a powerful eye, dressed in her robe, and with her long hair bound up. "Forgive me," he protested.

She saw from his fine clothes that he had money. "I am Semiramis, Queen of Babylon," she said, which was her usual nonsense in those days. I was breathless in a corner, and monsieur was in tears. Maman could see immediately that he was ill, because she began to assemble from her shelf of jars one of her nostrums. I see now, after years of training in this infirmary, how harmful this was. I believe now that she might have poisoned many customers over the years, but in those days I thought it only foolishness, as I saw her prepare a sachet of goufre dust and pepper, because of the man's fever. His eyes shone. My mother lit the altar candles, and then closed the shutters and the door into the yard.

"Monsieur," she said, "someone is haunting you."

"Yes."

"And this person is a woman."

"Yes."

"And she disturbs your rest."

"Yes."

She said this to every man, and it was always so. She had placed him in an armchair, and put a stool under his boots. Then she sat down beside him to take his pulse, and put a damp cloth over his brow. Nor did he pull away from her, because he was desperate to be comforted, and in spite of my past fear I looked at him, a gentleman not yet thirty-five, with good teeth and hair.

"Shall we ask her what she wants? But monsieur, please tell me. Must we search for her among the living or the dead?"

His expression was desolate. Maman gave a signal, and I went to the altar to light a pyramid of incense and then wash my hands.

Will you hand me my rosary, there from the table? Thank you. It is not a serpent! It won't bite you! I can see you are a skeptical person, as I was in my naiveté. But this Voodoo conjuring was not a matter of an error, or harmless tricks, or the waste that comes from believing something that is not so. But it is an opposing force. Not to believe, it is a kind of innocence. Now I think my faith commenced that day, the faith that brings me to this white bed. Before I was unable to distinguish, because I loved my mother, who jumbled them together, good and bad, sin and love. But this is our work on earth, to separate these things.

Now it began raining again, first gently, and then making spots on the dirt floor. I heard the thunder in the direction of St. Roch. Superstitious, I touched the crucifix around my neck, while my mother began to croon her language, most of it entirely invented out of nonsense words. Though I had heard these things before, and though they could not fail to embarrass me, still I was impressed to see her in her blue, flowered robe tied with a crimson sash, her thick hair knotted up. She was a tall woman, taller than I. She stood with her hand on monsieur's forehead, while he stared up at her. An educated man, doubtless he was not convinced by her mumbo-jumbo, and at the same time he might have realized he was in a dangerous position, closed up in a poor woman's cottage. I saw him glance toward the door. At the same time I was fumbling through my mother's wooden chest, and laying out on the altar her scientific implements, as she called them, her beakers and alembics for distilling her love potions, her hypodermic syringes, her fortune cards and tablets for automatic writing. If these things reassured monsieur, he gave no sign. "She is very near," my mother said. "I feel her wanting to come in," words I had heard before.

Often on these occasions she would contort her face, and the voice of the spirit would slip between her clenched lips in a whisper, easy to misunderstand. That morning I was surprised all this had progressed so quickly. Usually my mother would sit to ask some questions, gaining confidences that she then would give back, though nothing that might shock someone, for her purpose was always to console or reassure. These phrases that she used were very bland. But now monsieur had not yet been a quarter of an hour in the house. And it really was as if something was desperate to get in. I could hear the shutters rattle in the wind. My mother's transformation was so violent and abrupt I was astonished. I dropped the vial in my hand and watched it shatter on the hearth, between the enormous bags of charcoal that my father sometimes brought. She did not stop to scold me. Her eyes were turned back in her head. When she spoke, it was in a type of language different from the patois I had always heard from her, a woman who could not write her name. In a moment she had the accent of the Creoles sent to Paris for their education. "Oh, monsieur, I felt I could say anything, show you my secret self. Perhaps it even gave me pleasure to think of you as a more natural man, less civilized than others I had met, because of your heritage. But civilization has its uses, of which self-restraint is the most prominent—too late I see that now. When I stumbled back and collapsed on the settee, at that moment you mistook my hesitation for surrender! I can never forgive you for misjudging me. And even if it took me less than a minute to recover my strength, so that I was able to strike you in that area, the source of all your urges, still it was enough. A second would have been enough! It is in our impulses that we betray each other and ourselves. Our actions are pale shadows, chasing afterward. Besides, did you think it was impossible for me to have found out, that you had come that evening from Mme. Baziat's house? Did you think I would not smell her perfume on your breath, while you were kissing me?"

"I had had a . . . glass of wine," faltered monsieur. His cravat had come undone. My mother stood over him with his hand on his forehead, pushing him back into his chair.

Even when she beat me, I had never seen her in a rage like this, a mixture of ice and flame. "Do you think I am interested in your excuses? You betrayed me."

"But I never—"

"Fool, do you think I am still speaking of that night? You were to visit me the next afternoon, at two o'clock. I specifically told you. Did you forget? One month before, when you gave my father and me a tour of your laboratory, you spoke of the death of Socrates, and the poison you were using for you experiments—I stole it. I wanted to provide my own experiment, perhaps with a kitten or a mouse. But then at one o'clock, because of my despair, I thought I'd use a larger animal. How would I know you would not come? Can you be so stupid as to think I wished to die? No, I wished to punish you as you deserved. I imagined you'd have all the time to make the antidote. I'd read the book. Socrates—the fellow talked for hours. But how could you think that I was serious, when I said I never wished to see your face again?"

There was thunder over the river, and rain upon the roof of our little house. Monsieur was quiet. I think he must have guessed what was to happen. He had a fever, after all, and his skin was yellow, streaked with sweat. He could not look my mother in the face. Instead, he glanced at me. But in place of helping him, perhaps I gave him the last shock to his system, for at that moment I felt something beside my ear. When I looked up I saw my mother's serpent, which she used sometimes in her ceremonies. It lived in a wicker basket underneath the altar, but was forever getting out, a harmless creature from the swamp. So it was reaching toward me from one of the shelves, a long, green creature that was like this tube that runs to the cylinder of compressed oxygen, right by my nose, like this.

I brushed it away. Because I have the gift, I was afraid. But at the same time I was thinking how terrible this woman was, so cruel and such a liar. Innocent as I was, even I could see that if you reject this man one day, and kick him in the place she mentioned, perhaps you can't expect for him to visit you the next day as if nothing had happened. Who would swallow deadly poison, unless she wanted to destroy herself? And these mice and these kittens—at fourteen, I could not bear to think about them. I'd had enough. I stepped toward him, and monsieur followed me with his eyes. I don't know what I was going to do. But I was finished with something. My mother turned toward me also, and I could see it mixed together in her face, something that knew that I was going to challenge her, and reject her, and run away from her, not only that morning, but forever in the years to come. Her face twisted with rage. She had her fingers locked in monsieur's hair, and she forced his head back and forth, and turned his neck one way and another. When I came toward her, she turned his head so that he watched me, twisting his neck with her right hand. She was a strong woman, but what she used was not her strength. It was the strength of the devil that was inside of her, a devil in league with many others, and many other names. But always it requires a human agency. Another drink of water, please. You see I offer a confession at long last, but not just for myself . . .

(Recorded and transcribed as part of the research into a book, Mysteries of the Old Quarter, *by Ernest Butler Smith [Grossett & Dunlap, 1938], an interview never quoted or otherwise mentioned in the published text.)*

8. THREE YEARS PREVIOUS: " . . . THE MORNING HAS COME AFTER THE STORM."

September 10, 1885

My dear Monsieur,

I thank you for the flowers you have sent. I will be so happy to see you when I have returned from the sanatorium, which Papa tells me we have you to thank for the arrangements, due to your friendship with the director, a kind gentleman, even though he is a Swiss with a long beard. It is hard to remember how I must have behaved to be so desperate in that place. But now the morning has come after the storm, because of your generosity. Oh, I am so ashamed. But now Papa tells me there is no reason to concern myself, that these attacks of nerves are quite common and can be easily forgotten. To be a woman is to have these moods. Oh, I am happy to think so! I am quite sure you will be proud of me, and of the progress I have made. I wish it were tomorrow. But what will come, will come quickly, after all.

Fondly,
S. N.

(From a letter discovered in the inside waistcoat pocket of a corpse, otherwise unidentified, found in a coal sack in a flooded alley off the Rue Dumaine, May 26, 1888.)

Sometimes it's not what you hear, or think you hear, that unsettles you. It's what you don't.

STILL

Tia V. Travis

I.

Jodi stands still as air and envisions the field as it might have been then: the same sky or close to it, edges with a brittle luster observed only at particular times of day, under certain conditions of light, at the close of winter. Clouds scud on the back of the Chinook, beads of ice in the slow white melt of spring.

A child died on an afternoon like this.

Jodi thinks: *I know this place . . . or somewhere like it.*

A car heads north on the highway, a passing reflection: there, then gone. Geese return home in arrowhead formation with a metallic green sheen on their wings. Then . . . stillness. So quiet she hears ice dissolving.

It's the turning point in the weather that's brought her here, a disturbance in the air. But it's different this time. In the smallest of ways, perhaps: the temperature and relative humidity, the brightness of light. *Different.* She surveys the landscape: field, highway. Nothing more.

It's not that I've moved, Jodi decides. *It's the world that's moved.*

And: *You should have come before this.*

It rained hard last summer, same as forty years ago. Big storms with lightning slashes, as if something had slit the sky with a silver knife. That winter was warm and wet snow piled deep across the prairies. Now, only the top tier of fence is visible above the half-frozen slough. The wind picks up, carrying with it the decay of a bird thawing in the grass. Jodi thinks about a child with hair the same shade as that grass: faded sunshine beneath a veneer of ice as perfect and fragile as glass.

Little girl died out there by that fence.

That's what they say sometimes when they drive by, nodding towards an invisible point in the passing landscape.

Little girl, you say? When was that?

Long time back. Before you were born.

Jodi's footprints break evenly across the white field. Her progress to this time and place is, like points on a map or barbs on wire, visible in all directions. Her shadow clings to the snow like smoke. It could belong to anything, that shadow. Fence post, car exhaust. Sheet snapping on a line. Anything. She imagines the dead sparrow perched on the rim of her footprint, poised for departure in any direction: this world, the next. Jodi shades her eyes, waits. But no bird takes flight from her runway of footprints to the sky.

Rumors scatter like seeds. Used to be you'd hear them anywhere along this section of highway. It's a long, straight drive with little to divert your attention but the radio, and soon you're thinking about nothing more momentous than the flyspeck on the windshield that's been there the last twenty miles . . . sunlight bouncing off the mirror that makes it hard to see anyone who might decide to pass.

You think about how late it's getting.

About the sun dipping beneath the mountains to the west.

About how you wanted to be home by now.

See that fence runs alongside the road?

Barbed wire coils like ball lightning, a glint of silver in the rearview mirror.

I see it.

See that rise, the crest of the hill? There's a field on the other side, slopes down to a slough with another fence running through it. An old trailer out there someplace, where the Ghost Woman lives.

Ghost Woman?

No one goes out there now.

Jodi's shadow has lengthened during the time she's stood here in the Ghost Woman's field. The sunlight filling the hollows of her footprints has the same bluish tinge as a crocus. Harbinger of spring. You can't pick a crocus, Jodi knows. Not without mangling the fuzzy violet stems in your fingers as if they were the throats of newborn birds. She looks at the trailer set a half mile off the highway. The trailer's siding is the same bruised purple as a crocus, the same dull white of bone . . . curved wing of a bird.

Crocus and bird.

Bones and snow.

———

No one goes out there now. No call to. Except kids, sometimes, looking for trouble.

Anyone ever see anything?

Oh, sure. You hear things from time to time.

What about the Ghost Woman?

They say she's looking for her little girl who drowned in the slough. Say you can still see her nights, walking the fields, calling to her.

Some folks don't like the prairie. They don't like the sky pressing down on them. In summer, wind combs the fields like a hand passing through hair. In winter, snowdrifts layer down the highway and the wind sounds like someone's quiet weeping a long way away.

Jodi understands why people might feel anxious out here. Why they might jump at any sound. Or get the feeling something's hidden in the grass, attending their every movement. But sometimes . . . it's not what you hear, or *think* you hear, that unsettles you.

It's what you don't.

And sometimes there's nothing more lonesome than an empty field under an empty sky, when the only sound is your own breathing and your own boots punching through a blanket of spring snow. Because that's when you know that not only are you alone . . . you always have been.

The Ghost Woman's husband is gone.

Looking for work

looking for

looking . . .

The little girl watches him leave early one morning while her mother sleeps. She stands at the window, her breath frosting the glass. Her father sets out across the field in the golden haze as if something draws him onward. And the girl remembers, long afterwards, that he'd glowed in that sunlight . . . glittering in the distance like a lost coin.

There, then gone.

After the crystalline brightness outside it takes a minute for Jodi's eyes to adjust to the dim trailer. The carpet remnants covering parts of the flooring are islands in a swamp of buckled plywood. An armchair swollen as a mushroom seats a radio with a broken dial. An ancient space heater shelters a family of mice. Next to the heater sits a cardboard box of musty clothes and a child's pair of gumboots crusted with mud.

Jodi moves through shadows.

It's best not to think too much about who lived here. Who left here. Who died here.

So she closes her mind to the past.

Next to the kitchen sink, a bowl lies tipped on its side. Petrified cornflakes stick to the rim. Wedged inside a half-open drawer is a shoebox crammed with yellowed receipts and government checks. Through a smudge in the window, Jodi sees the smooth stretch of sky and field. Telephone poles disappearing down the highway. Shimmer of ice. The slough doesn't look far, though it must have seemed the end of the world to an eight-year-old girl who'd lived every one of her years in a trailer parked in the middle of nowhere.

What's on the other side of the fence, Mama?

Fields and more fields. Same as this side.

The girl runs through the field with empty jars in each hand, trying to catch the wind. If she captures enough, its invisible power will buoy her above the earth where, looking down, she will see—

What?

Everything.

Field, fence . . . her father's footprints in the snow. What God sees when he looks down from heaven.

Everything.

An old *Farmer's Almanac* calendar hangs on a nail beside the kitchen window. Jodi pages through phases of the moon. Sees that favorable dates for picking Saskatoon berries, putting in preserves, cutting hair, have been marked in faded pencil. *When the breastbone of a fresh-cooked turkey is dark purple it will be a cold winter.* The perception of bones foretells the future . . . knowledge deepens the marrow.

Jodi wonders what color the turkey's breastbone had been forty years ago. She wonders if it would have made a difference, whether the little girl might have lived had that breastbone been dark as a ripe plum.

She turns over February's frozen lake, sees March's field of crocuses.

When the crocus opens, warm weather is in store.

Except for the January cold snap it hasn't been a bitter winter, not for a prairie province west of the Canadian Shield and east of the Rocky Mountains. And yet, when Jodi steps out of the trailer into the mild afternoon her hands are chilled to the bone, her skin tough as the meat of a fresh-cooked turkey too long in the freezer.

Using even pressure as you walk across the icy slough, you can test the physical properties of frozen hydrogen and oxygen: the universal law of cause and effect. With experience you will soon determine, with a reasonable degree of accuracy, whether or not the ice possesses sufficient density to sustain your weight.

The moment that air pocket jumps like a bubble in a spirit level or the last breath of air you'll ever take, you are faced with a decision: that is, whether or not you should place the balance of your life and faith in Mother Nature's hands, in the same way you know to bake bread on the seventeenth and twenty-fourth of this month, or to can fruit from the third to the fifth.

Jodi considers whether the ability to walk on water would have made a difference. Eyes closed, she raises one foot several inches above the frozen slough. Her boot hovers over the ice.

If you look down, you'll see there's nothing there.

The secret, then, is not to look down. Then you can walk forever.

But when Jodi opens her eyes, she sees that she has not walked on water. That she has not, in point of fact, gone anywhere at all.

Skates, the little girl knows, are remarkable things. Sparkling blades and shining leather as white and unobtainable as a cottontail rabbit. So she sits on the edge of the slough and pulls on the next best thing: gumboots dug out of the Sally Ann with worn soles ideal for sliding. Her mother wears a beaver coat that might have belonged to a movie star but has seen more glamorous days, and a pair of Daddy's tightly laced work boots.

Mother and daughter hold hands and wobble onto the ice like a couple of ducks. Before long they're practicing figure eights on the slick surface. It seems too soon when a warm wind gusts out of nowhere and Mama looks up at the changing sky.

Time to be getting home, *she says.*

The girl reaches round to brush a circle of snow from her coat. Her Christmas coat, red as cranberries.

Just a few more minutes!

We can't, the ice is thawing. We've already been out too long.

But the girl is eyeing the barbed-wire fence that runs through the center of the slough . . . white-stubbled fields, telephone poles on the horizon, voices whispering in the sky.

What's on the other side of the fence, Mama?

Fields and more fields. Let's go home and we'll make molasses cookies.

The girl clasps her mittened hand in her mother's bare red one. Then they glide across layers of water gleaming on the ice. The girl slides backwards, staring at the mysterious expanse of fence and sky that makes up their backyard. Mama nudges her homeward like a wayward calf at sunset.

It's the same as this side, honey.

Fields and more fields, *the girl whispers.*

So quiet not even the birds hear.

The dead child gazes up at Jodi from beneath the ice. Her face is pale as the last afternoon of sunlight. Snails leave glistening trails across her ribs. Smooth round stones weight the pockets of her coat. Grains of sand settle beneath her fingernails, sedimentary layers recording the passage of time, seasonal variations.

Nothing ever happens here, nothing ever changes but the wind.

Sunlight breaks through the bank of clouds. Suddenly the sky seems too exposed.

Jodi thinks about the little girl setting out across the field. She sees her glance anxiously at the trailer, hoping her mother won't notice how far she's come. But she needs to see what lies beyond that fence. Needs to see why her father left them for a chimera of field, the lure of an empty sky.

The wirecutters in the girl's pocket are heavy, and she doesn't know how to use them. But she'll find a way. Red mittens dangle on strings through the sleeves of her coat; it's warm enough and she doesn't need them. The Chinook is blowing today and everything is clean and white, the melting snowdrifts so wet they're translucent.

Translucent, Jodi tells the girl. *That's what your dreams are. I see through them like I see through air.* For a moment she expects a small hand to break through the ice.

But no. Nothing lives in this slough but hibernating frogs, sleeping tadpoles. Fear, thick as mud. Heavy and still as water trapped beneath ice.

It's *time* that changes everything, Jodi realizes. The passage of time—a drop of water, a grain of sand. Memories sifting to the bottom like silt.

And here I am, looking down.

The girl's world had ended here. Her last moments of awareness preserved like a bird beneath the snow. But Jodi can't let herself think about those last seconds of life, the last spirit bubble of breath the girl took before water closed over her.

So she examines the barbed-wire fence.

The posts have rotted, the wire rusted to the Indian-red of a grain elevator. It's so predictable, this cycle of sun and rain, thaw and freeze, she could mark it in on the almanac. But predictability isn't something that little girl had understood.

Jodi applies her boot heel to the slough, as much slush and snow as it is ice. Soon it begins to give. A few more kicks and she's broken through. She heaves a slab of ice loose and water sloshes through the opening she's made.

All it takes, Jodi knows, is a moment of inattention. Of childish defiance. The stubborn refusal to listen to that still small voice inside yourself that will tell you what to do if only you'd let it, will show you how to keep yourself from harm's way. *But can we ever really keep ourselves from harm's way?*

The sun is setting, the deepening sky soon to be drowned in a river of night. Jodi lies flat on the ice and plunges her arm deep as she can into the frigid water.

The little girl's gumboots slip out from under her and she cracks through the ice too fast to let out much more than a startled hiccup. The wirecutters anchor her straight down to the bottom. Barbed wire jabs to the bone, snags the soft skin of her wrists. She wriggles like a minnow on a pin. Her hair tangles in the reeds. Blood ribbons from her punctured wrists like mitten-strings. She kicks the submerged fencepost, catches her sodden coat on the wire, struggles for that air bubble inches above her mouth—

Jodi rolls onto her back, breathing hard, and holds her half-frozen arm to her chest. Water pools beside her on the ice. She pictures a turkey's breastbone, arterial purple in the cold.

It would be so easy to stay here. To never leave.

She blinks hard.

Once, twice.

Then she repositions herself beside the ice-hole and thrusts her arm back into the water. This time she doesn't stop until her hand grazes the sludgy bottom. Leaves stick to her arm like leeches. Something solid—dead fish, maybe. Bird with a broken wing, lying in a footprint filled with snowmelt. Jodi's hand closes around something cold and metal. She pulls the wire cutters free of the water and they thud beside her on the ice. She drags herself to her knees. Standing now, her hands numb, she pries open the wirecutters and positions them on the barbed wire that runs between the fenceposts.

When she cuts through the steel line it recoils like a springing deer.

She cuts the next wire, and the next, until nothing separates her from the other side. It takes all her strength to do the job. She knows now that the little girl never stood a chance, that she never could have cut her way through this wire, no matter how desperately she'd wanted to follow her father into the sunlit morning.

On the other side of the open fence she sees an old woman in the field. Her head is bowed before a stone that might be a shadow. Something inside Jodi breaks, splinters like ice, slivers her heart like falling glass. *How old you've become*, she thinks. And: *Has it been so long?*

She steps into the indigo twilight.

II.

It's colder now that the sun's gone down.

The Ghost Woman glances at the plum-colored sky, cracks her arthritic knuckles. Crocus-purple veins twist across the backs of them, road maps to places she's never been. These can't be the hands she remembers from her youth. Someone else must have buried her little girl. Someone else must have broken the shovel blade on that hard ground because she couldn't have done it with these ruined claws.

It was on an afternoon in March, just like today.

The sun reflecting on the slough. The shadow of a bird on the snow.

A sudden departure, from this world to the next . . .

The Ghost Woman turns over her hands in the fading light. *Seems I can see right through them*, she thinks. But that's what comes from being alone. No one sees you, eventually you stop seeing yourself.

She must have passed on. That's what they say.

Passed on, eh? When was that?

Oh, must be years now. Least, I haven't heard anything.

They never sold that property, did they?

Couldn't say.

Sometimes people see the Ghost Woman's flashlight dancing in the night sky. Will-o'-the-wisp of the prairies. But no one comes near. Not in daylight, not at night. Because it's only fields and fence, and frozen water. Someone else's sorrows.

The Ghost Woman collects checks the government still sends once a month to the rail route box. Sometimes she walks five miles into town to cash them when she remembers, like an afterthought, that she needs bread or cornflakes or milk. No one pays her any mind as she shuffles down the highway in a beaver coat that smells of decaying birds. She still wears the workboots her husband left on the doorstep. Shoelaces trail behind like earthworms curled on the sidewalk after a rain. In springtime, grass sprouts from soles that never seem to dry out and still hold forty summers of mud from the field.

The sun has fallen behind the windbreak and the bare trees look like hands. An old woman's hands. Crippled and useless, but still holding on by bare roots. *But what's left to hold on to after all these years?* the Ghost Woman wonders. Old bones crumbling in the earth . . . the remains of love. If she waits long enough perhaps those bones will return to her someday, the way a broken saucer or a plough handle works through the soil in the direction of sunlight.

It's in the waiting that you pass on, the Ghost Woman knows. Waiting for the change of seasons. Waiting for the right time to pick berries or cook turkey or cut your daughter's hair. Waiting for your husband to return home, for the little girl who slipped through your hands as easily as a ray of light. Enough time passes and there's nowhere you belong. Even stones don't last forever. Wind and rain wear them down. Glaciers retreat and scatter them in a field miles from home. People move the stones and move on themselves. They don't remember you're lying under them and if they do . . . well, the world goes on, always does.

How could she have left her child lying under a piece of prairie, swallowed by grass in summer, buried beneath a mountain of snow in winter? The pickup jolting down to the highway while she watched her little girl's stone recede in the mirror? It would be as if she had never lived at all.

The stone itself has no name carved on it. Sand yellow, faded tan, blackberry preserve; a bruise when the hurt's begun to mend or the grass has died but not quite, no—there's still a little green down deep. The stone hadn't been so big the Ghost Woman couldn't lift it. She was a strong woman then and she'd estimated its heaviness, weighed it in her mind the way some do footsteps across an empty field.

A voice whispers, deep in the earth. The Ghost Woman strains her eyes in the gathering darkness. *Nothing there*, she tells herself. *Just bones settling. They sleep through winter.*

Bones, or the wind in the grass . . .

This has always been a restless place.

But the Ghost Woman knows she's alone out here.

There's nothing beyond the fence that stretches clear to the horizon, where field and sky melt into purple twilight, where this world ends and another begins.

You were right, Mama, Jodi tells the bundled figure kneeling by the stone. *It is the same on the other side.*

The Ghost Woman shivers, pulls up the threadbare collar of her beaver coat.

How cold it is. Just now.

Snow falls from her knees as she hauls herself up. A bird perches on the stone as if listening to a voice beyond the limits of human perception. Its eyes are trained on something just outside the old woman's line of sight.

How still, the Ghost Woman thinks. *How still it is.*

We are there, then not there—

The bird stares at her a moment, then is gone in a blur of wings.

Crossroads are bad places. Magicians and devils are bad news. Dusk and dawn and noon overhead are bad times. Every child knows this . . .

CROSSROADS

Laura Anne Gilman

John came to the crossroads at just shy of noon, where a man dressed all in black stared up at another man hanging from a gallows-tree. No, not hanging; he was being hung, the loop still slack around his neck, his body dangling in mid-air. That, John thought, his pack heavy on his shoulder and his hat pulled low, was not something a wise man would get involved in. And yet, he could not resist asking, "What did he do?"

The man in black turned around and glared at John. "He asked too many impertinent questions."

The man with the rope around his neck laughed at that, a rueful, amused sound, and John decided he liked the dead man.

"You might want to move on," the man in black continued in a voice that wasn't a suggestion. "This is a bad place to be for a lone traveler."

"Looks like he might agree," John said, but slung his pack off his shoulder, resting it on the ground, and looked up at the hanging man. "You okay with this?"

"It's not my first choice for nuncheon," the man admitted, but did not try to explain or ask for help.

John stepped forward and around, circling the man in black and coming up alongside the gallows-tree, carefully out of reach of the hanging man's potential to kick. You met a stranger out here, miles from the nearest town or farm, it paid to suss him out. They were both long, lean men, their boots spit-shined where John's were dusty and worn, but he did not mistake either for city-folk. The man in black still stared at the hanging man, who seemed to be watching something far over the horizon, unconcerned by his predicament.

John studied them both, casually, the way a catamount watches a man. No, not city-folk, nor farm-folk, either. Didn't take a college boy to figure it out. Crossroads were bad places. Magicians and devils were bad news. Dusk and dawn and noon overhead were bad times. Every child knew that.

John rocked back on his heels, considering. Magician or devil, this wasn't his place, this wasn't his business. It wasn't his responsibility. He should just move on, and not get involved. Let them do what they would do, and be done.

A prickling against his chest reminded him it wasn't all that simple, for him. He slipped the pack down from his shoulder, feeling the smooth leather, the shape of his belongings below. He breathed in through his nose, out through his mouth. The air was warm already, and filled with the dust of the road.

Sunrise and sunset, and high noon overhead. The crossroads. Places and times of transit, of coming upon and slipping away. Power ebbed and flowed and could be taken from another, if you knew how.

John knew what he was about, as another might not. He had sworn an oath.

These two were no business of his, by the letter of that oath. The spirit, though . . .

Every step of the road was a choice.

"Some things, there's no real choice at all," he said softly, and slid his hand under the flap of the pack, his fingers touching cool metal.

"Stay out of this, boy," the man in black said, misinterpreting his action.

John hadn't been a boy in decades. The slip made the edge of his mouth curl slightly, even as he tilted his head to look at the man in black from under the brim of his hat. Magician or devil, it made no difference to John. Immortals were always trouble. Two immortals meant twice as much trouble.

The silver flask under his fingers seemed to almost shiver, and John drew it out slowly, not allowing his actions to be misinterpreted. "Was just planning to drink to your health," he said to the hanging man, raising the flask in salute. "Might I know your name afore you aren't using it no more?"

"Benjamin," the hanging man said. "Benjamin West."

Magician, then. Magicians took their names from one of the four weatherly winds. Devils took their names from their masters.

"Your memory, master Benjamin West," John said, and took a swig. Cool, fresh water washed down his throat. Others might think he carried rotgut or whiskey; water was safer. Water couldn't be magicked. Silver and water, and the dead man's name; that should cover all possibilities. . . .

"So what question did he ask?" Folly, to query a magician, but every detail could help.

The man in black had turned back to the hanging man, his hands raised as though to cast the final spell. John's question arrested the movement, although the man's back and shoulders did not betray any emotion.

"Why do you care?"

John shrugged, letting the silver flask hang from his hand, casually. "Naturally curious?"

"I wanted to know where he got that lovely walking stick." The hanging man's voice was filled with laughter. Laughing at himself, laughing at John. He knew. He knew what John intended to do.

John didn't look around for a stick, but kept his gaze on the man in black. He wasn't so easily caught, him: The dead man was as dangerous as the man in black, and only a fool lost sight of that. "Is that so?"

"What do you think?" The man in black's voice was gritty and hard now, and although he lowered his arms, he didn't turn around.

"Must have been a hell of a question you didn't want to answer." John took another swig from the flask, his body loose and gangly, just passin' time, three strangers on the road. He could play the fool, when it suited him.

Casually, he made a tip of the flask, here, and a step and a step and a third step away, then another tip of the flask. Bare splutters in the dust, a dark splatter left behind. Step and a step and a step, all the way around the gallows-tree, all the way around the man in black and the hanging man: locking all three within. Locking any innocents out.

Damn magicians never gave a thought to the innocent.

"If you're to kill him, don't let my bein' here pause you," John said conversationally as he walked, taking another sip when he was done. "I've no mule in this pull."

A hesitation in the breath of the world. John's fingers sweated against the cool silver, his pack abandoned outside the circle, the leather shape casting a low shadow on the dirt. The dead man's gaze sharpened like he saw something coming over that horizon, and the man in black growled. John felt the sharp knife of risk scratch against his spine, but merely let his fingers rest on the flask, and studied the sun overhead.

"Mighty warm out, once the sun hits directly. Be a mercy to finish him off by then. Or not, if'n that's what you're aiming for."

The flask was near-empty now, and it shimmered again under his hand, like a warning. Sun directly overhead. The man in black had no choice but to choose, and now, or the dead man's power died with him.

John's heart beat too hard, his chest tight until he felt the first whisper of enchantment like the roll of thunder in the distance, barely recognizable until it swept down over the plains and knocked you out of the saddle or off your feet.

The dead man didn't move, not resigned so much as simply waiting. They had forgotten John now, dismissed him in the greater business of their battle.

Taking advantage of their concentration, he tilted the silver flask in the four directions, making an offering of spirit if not flesh, and then tilted it in towards the center of his water-bound circle, to where the two magicians posed, gathering their will.

After that first warning rumble, the wind was still, the air silent, the sun too hot for a spring afternoon. A normal man, a man set about his own business, would think it odd; suspect a storm rising, or a predator in the woods. He would not be wrong. John let his breath exhale, and waited.

The sun shifted, barely a twitch in the shadows, and the man in black set himself hard against the ground and raised his arms until his hands cupped the sun, settling into position directly above.

"Hang or fly," the hanging man said, lifting his hands to the mid of his chest, palms pressed together, fingers likewise pointing toward the sky.

Magician duels were iffy things. To chance upon one was rare and risky, and it could easily all go wrong. John moved his arm slow, taking that last drink of water. Silver and fresh water, and a dead man's name. If he was wrong . . .

Dying at the crossroads meant being trapped there, forever.

When it happened, it happened all at once.

The man in black did not move but his shadow did, the first direct shaft of sunlight dancing it forward, reaching up and yanking the rope tight. The hanging man jerked, legs kicking high and arms falling low, and the shadow swarmed but John moved faster, the water in his mouth spitting high and clear.

Shadow and water spluttered and sparked like an old campfire, and the man in black swore but did not turn. A battle of nerves, now, as the hanging man danced and stilled, water dripping down shadow, shadow sizzling-dry water, and the dead man's power hanging between them.

John had no sweat, no moisture for his breath, everything he had gone to tie him into the battle raging around him. The silver flask fell to the ground and water spilled into the dirt, his throat cracking and swelling like the fever had taken him, but he did not relent.

Magicians named themselves for one of the four winds, drifting across the surface of the Earth, unstoppable, mostly unseen. And they killed each other; only each other, never anyone else, and so nobody cared, because one less magician in the world did nobody any harm. But John knew better. One magician dead meant one less magician, not one less bit of magic.

Crossroad rules: Killer had claim, killer took the power, and made it his own. Master Benjamin West had been caught and killed fair by his rules.

But their rules didn't allow for someone like John, with clean water and pure silver, and the strength of his oath to drive him on.

The man in black whispered one single word, sweet and ragged, too strange for John to hear, but it hit the air like a rock into water. The rope turned bronze, then black under the direct noon light, and the hanging man's skin seemed to ripple, like wheat under wind, and tightened around his bones.

"Give over," the man in black ordered. "Fair caught, fair bound, under the midday sun. Give over. It is mine."

"Take it," the dead man said, but meant "if you can."

Thunder cracked. The air smelt burnt, the dry dust at their feet swirling faintly. Magic filled the air, an ugly black-blue hiss. John felt his skin crawl, sweat now running under his clothing like a summer's blast, but he held steady, bending to pick up the silver flask, holding it with its mouth angled out and up toward the two magicians. The water he had dripped into the soil sizzled, and the magic curled back around, turning like eddies in a stream, like souls in a devil's hand.

"I will," the man in black said, and clenched his fingers together. The dead man's skin burst into flames, the rope squeezing tight, and his heels kicked up, drumming at the air. The man in black sucked in his breath, and the magic, thick and strong, streamed toward him.

Magic went to the strongest, the quickest, the most determined to win. But that did not mean it always went to the magician.

"Benjamin West," John whispered. The flask shimmered, the flask filling; clear water resisting the magic's pull, holding it still and safe.

The man in black, cheated, snarled in rage, and the dead man danced at the end of his rope; John screwed the cap on tight. A dead man's name bound the magic he once held while breath still warmed his lungs, if not one beat longer. More fool them, if they did not guard such knowledge from men such as him.

The man in black turned, clenching his hands in anger, even as afternoon light filled the spaces and painted the hanging man's shadow with long strokes on the ground behind him.

"Damn you."

"No doubt," John said, not meeting the magician's eyes.

"You cannot use it," the man in black said, his voice gritty and soft, the voice of a man who already knows more than he can exploit, and yet always wants more. "You have not the skill."

"It went to the man quick enough to catch it," John replied, feeling the menace in the man's voice. He slipped a hand under his coat, and let the silver star pinned beneath shine. "Usin' it's not my intention."

Magicians were none of his business, but he was likewise none of theirs—unless the man in black chose to make it so. If he did . . .

Then all hell might break loose, for certain.

They stared at each other, deadly and calm, and then John turned, stepping across the circle to where his pack waited. Silver and pure water, and sigil-cut rounds for his gun hung low and ready at his hip. A wise man was prepared. A smart man was ready. A lawman in these territories needed to be both, and more.

He slid the flask back under the flap, closing the lacing tight. "What's done is done, and done square and fair." It was not a threat, merely an observation of fact. When he turned around again, the man in black was gone.

John tilted his head back, the brim of his hat still shading his eyes. The sun would be past-direct in a matter of moments. The crossroads was safe for travelers; he could move on.

"A good day, sirs," he said to the afternoon air, for it never harmed a man to be polite, and walked out of the crossroads, the hanging man slack and sunlit behind him.

You wouldn't know it to look at the place, but a demon lived there ...

THE BREAD WE EAT IN DREAMS

Catherynne M. Valente

In a sea of long grass and tiny yellow blueberry flowers some ways off of Route 1, just about halfway between Cobscook Bay and Passamaquoddy Bay, the town of Sauve-Majeure puts up its back against the Bald Moose Mountains. It's not a big place—looks a little like some big, old cannon shot a load of houses and half-finished streets at the foothills and left them where they fell. The sun gets here first out of just about anywhere in the country, turning all the windows bloody-orange and filling up a thousand lobster cages with shadows.

Further up into the hills, outside the village but not so far that the post doesn't come regular as rain, you'll find a house all by itself in the middle of a tangly field of good red potatoes and green oats. The house is a snug little hall-and-parlor number with a moss-clotted roof and a couple of hundred years of whitewash on the stones. Sweet William and vervain and crimson beebalm wend out of the window-jambs, the door-hinges, the chimney blocks. There's carrots in the kitchen garden, some onions, a basil plant that may or may not come back next year.

You wouldn't know it to look at the place, but a demon lives here.

The rusted-out mailbox hangs on a couple of splinters and a single valiant, ancient bolt, its red flag at perpetual half-mast. Maybe there's mail to go out, and maybe there isn't. The demon's name is Gemegishkirihallat, but the mailbox reads: Agnes G. and that seems respectable enough to the mailman, who always has to check to see if that red flag means business, even though in all his considerable experience working for the postal service, it never has. The demon is neither male nor female—that's not how things work where it came from. But when it passed through the black door it came out Agnes on the other side. She's stuck with she now, and after five hundred years, give or take, she's just about used to it.

The demon arrived before the town. She fell out of a red oak in the primeval forest that would eventually turn into Schism Street and Memorial Square into a white howl of snow and frozen sea-spray. She was naked, her body branded with four-spoked seals, wheels of banishment, and the seven psalms of hell. Her hair burnt off and she had no fingernails or toenails. The hair grew back—black, naturally—and the sixteenth century offered a range of options for completely covering female skin from chin to heel, black-burnt with the diamond trident-brand of Amdusias or not.

The fingernails never came in. It's not something many people ever had occasion to notice.

The ice and lightning lasted for a month after she came; the moon got big and small again while the demon walked around the coves. Her footsteps marked the boundaries of the town to come, her heels boiling the snow, her breath full of thunder. When she hungered, which she did, often, for her appetites had never been small, she put her head back in the frigid, whipping storm and howled the primordial syllable that signified stag. Even through the squall and scream of the white air, one would always come, his delicate legs picking through the drifts, his antlers dripping icicles.

She ate her stags whole in the dark, crunching the antlers in her teeth.

Once, she called a pod of seals up out of the sea and slept on the frozen beach, their gray mottled bodies all around her. The heat of her warmed them, and they warmed her. In the morning the sand beneath them ran liquid and hot, the seals cooked and smoking.

The demon built that house with her own hands. Still naked come spring, as she saw no particular reason not to be, she put her ear to the mud and listened for echoes. The sizzling blood of the earth moved beneath her in crosshatch patterns, and on her hands and knees she followed them until she found what she wanted. Hell is a lot like a bad neighbor: it occupies the space just next to earth, not quite on top of it or underneath it, just to the side, on the margins. And Hell drops its chestnuts over the fence with relish. Agnes was looking for the place on earth that shared a cherry tree and a water line with the house of Gemegishkirihallat in Hell. When she found it, she spoke to the trees in proto-Akkadian and they understood her; they fell and sheared themselves of needles and branches. Grasses dried in a moment and thatched themselves, eager to please her. With the heat of her hands she blanched sand into glass for her windows; she demanded the hills give her iron and clay for her oven, she growled at the ground to give her snap peas and onions.

Some years later, a little Penobscot girl got lost in the woods while her tribe was making their long return from the warmer south. She did not know how to tell her father what she'd seen when she found him again, having never seen a house like the place the demon had built, with a patch of absurd English garden and a stone well and roses coming in bloody and thick. She only knew it was wrong somehow, that it belonged to someone, that it made her feel like digging a hole in the dirt and hiding in it forever.

The demon looked out of the window when the child came. Her hair had grown so long by then it brushed her ankles. She put out a lump of raw, red, bleeding meat for the girl. Gemegishkirihallat had always been an excellent host. Before he marked her flesh with his trident, Amdusias had loved to eat her salted bread, dipping his great long unicorn's horn into her black honey to drink.

The child didn't want it, but that didn't bother Agnes. Everybody has a choice. That's the whole point.

Sauve-Majeure belongs to its demon. She called the town to herself, on account of being a creature of profound order. A demon cannot function alone. If they could, banishment would be no hurt. A demon craves company, their own peculiar camaraderie. Agnes was a wolf abandoned by her pack. She could not help how she sniffed and howled for her litter-mates, nor how that howl became a magnetic pull for the sort of human who also loves order, everything in its place, all souls accounted for, everyone blessed and punished according to strict and immutable laws.

The first settlers were mostly French, banded together with whatever stray Puritans they'd picked up along the way north. Those Puritans would spice the Gallic stew of upper Maine for years, causing no end of trouble to Agnes, who, to be fair, was a witch and a succubus and everything else they ever called her, but that's no excuse for being such poor neighbors, when you think about it.

The demon waited. She waited for Martin le Clerq and Melchior Pelerin to raise their barns and houses, for Remy Mommacque to breed his dainty little cow to William Chudderley's barrel of a bull, for John Cabot to hear disputes in his rough parlor. She waited for Hubert Sazarin to send for both money and a pair of smooth brown stones from Sauve-Majeure Abbey back home in Gironde, and use them to lay out the foundations of what he dreamed would be the Cathedral of St. Geraud and St. Adelard, the grandest edifice north of Boston. She waited for Thomas Dryland to get drunk on Magdeleine Loliot's first and darkest beer, then march over to the Sazarin manse and knock him round the ears for flaunting his Papist devilry in the face of good honest folk. She waited for Dryland to take up a collection amongst the Protestant minority and, along with John Cabot and Quentin

Pole, raised the frame of the Free Meeting House just across what would eventually be called Schism Street, glaring down the infant Cathedral, and pressed Quentin's serious young son Lamentation into service as pastor. She waited, most importantly, for little Crespine Moutonnet to be born, the first child of Sauve-Majeure. (Named by Sazarin, stubbornly called Help-on-High by the congregation at the Free Meeting House up until Renewal Pole was shot over the whole business by Henri Sazarin in 1890, at which point it was generally agreed to let the matter drop and the county take the naming of the place—which they did, once Sazarin had quietly and handsomely paid the registrar the weight of his eldest daughter in coin, wool, beef, and blueberries.) She waited for the Dryland twins, Reformation and Revelation, for Madame le Clerq to bear her five boys, for Goodwife Wadham to deliver her redoubtable seven daughters and single stillborn son. She waited for Mathelin Minouflet to bring his gentle wife over the sea from Cluny—she arrived already, and embarrassingly, pregnant, since she had by then been separated from her good husband for five years. Mathelin would have beaten her soundly, but upon discovering that his brother had the fault of it, having assumed Mathelin dead and the responsibility of poor Charlotte his own, tightened his belt and hoped it would be a son. The demon waited for enough children to be born and grow up, for enough village to spring up, for enough order to assert itself she that could walk among them and be merely one of the growing, noisy lot of new young folk fighting over Schism Street and trading gray, damp wool for hard, new potatoes.

The demon appeared in Adelard-in-the-Garden Square, the general marketplace ruled wholly by an elderly, hunched Hubert Sazarin and his son Augustine. Adjoining it, Faith-My-Joy Square hosted the Protestant market, but as one could not get decent wine nor good Virginia pipe tobacco in Faith-My-Joy nor Margery Cabot's sweet butter and linen cloth in Adelard, a great deal of furtive passage went on between the two. The demon chose Adelard, and laid out her wares among the tallow candles and roasting fowl and pale bluish honey sold by the other men. A woman selling in the market caused a certain amount of consternation among the husbands of Sauve-Majeure. Young Wrestling Dryland, though recently bereaved of his father Thomas, whose heart had quite simply burst with rage when Father Simon Charpentier arrived from France to give Mass and govern the souls of St. Geraud and Adelard, had no business at all sneaking across the divide to snatch up a flask of Sazarin's Spanish Madeira. Wrestling worked himself up into a positively Thomas-like fury over the tall figure in a black bonnet, and screwed in his courage to confront the devil-woman. He took in her severe dress, her covered hair, her table groaning with breads he had only heard of from his father's tales of a boyhood in London—braided rounds and glossy cross-buns studded with raisins (where had she got raisins in this forsaken land?), sweet French egg bread and cakes dusted with sugar, (what act of God or His Opposite granted this brazen even the smallest measure of sugar?), dark jams and butter-plaits stuffed with cream. He fixed to shame the slattern of Adelard, as he already thought of her, his gaze meant to cut down—but when he looked into the pits of her eyes he quieted, and said nothing at all, but meekly purchased a round of her bread even though his mother Anne made a perfectly fine loaf of her own.

Gemegishkirihallat had been the baker of Hell.

It had been her peculiar position, her specialty among all the diverse amusements and professions of Hades, which performs as perfectly and smoothly in its industries as the best human city can imagine, but never accomplish. Everything in its place, all souls accounted for, everyone blessed and punished according to strict and immutable laws. She baked bread to be seen but ultimately withheld, sweetcakes to be devoured until the skin split and the stomach protruded like the head of a child through the flesh, black pastry to haunt the starved mind. The ovens of Gemegishkirihallat were cathedral towers of fire and onyx, her under-bakers Akalamdug and Ekur pulling out soft and perfect loaves with bone paddles. But also she baked for her own table, where her comrades Amdusias, King of Thunder and Trumpets, Agares, Duke of Runaways and his loyal pet crocodile, Samagina, Marquis of the Drowned, Countess Gremory Who-Rides-Upon-a-Camel, and the Magician-King Barbatos gathered to drink the wines crushed beneath the toes of rich and heartless men and share between them the bread of Gemegishkirihallat. She prepared the bloodloaf of the great Emperor's own infinite table, where, on occasion, she was permitted to sit and keep Count Andromalius from stealing the slabs of meat beloved of Celestial Marquis Oryax.

And in her long nights, in her long house of smoke and miller's stones, she baked the bread we eat in dreams, strangest loaves, her pies full of anguish and days long dead, her fairy-haunted gingerbread, her cakes wet with tears. The Great Duke Gusion, the Baboon-Lord of Nightmares, came to her each eve and took up her goods into his hairy arms and bore them off to the Pool of Sleep.

Those were the days the demon longed for in her lonely house with only one miserable oven that did not even come up to her waist, with her empty table and not even Shagshag, the weaver of Hell, to make her the Tea of Separation-from-God and ravage her in the dark like a good neighbor should. Those were the days she longed for in her awful heart—for a demon has no heart as we do, a little red fist in our chest. A demon's body is nothing but heart, its whole interior beating and pulsing and thundering in time to the clocks of Pandemonium.

Those were the days that floated in the demon's vast and lightless mind when she brought, at long last, her most perfect breads to Adelard-in-the-Garden. She would have her pack again, here between the mountains and the fish-clotted bay. She would build her ovens high and feed them all, feed them all and their children until no other bread would sate them. They would love her abjectly, for no other manner of loving had worth.

They burned her as a witch some forty years later.

As you might expect, it was a Dryland's hand at work in it, though the fingers of Sébastienne Sazarin as well as Father Simon's successor, Father Audrien, made their places in the pyre.

The demon felt it best, when asked, to claim membership in a convent on the other side of Bald Moose Mountain, traveling down into the bay-country to sell the sisters' productions of bread. She herself was a hermit, of course, consecrated to the wilderness in the manner of St. Viridiana or St. Julian, two venerated ladies of whom the poor country priest Father Simon had never heard. This relieved everyone a great deal, since a woman alone is a kind of unpredictable inferno that might at any moment light the hems of the innocent young. Sister Agnes had such a fine hand at pies and preserves, it couldn't hurt to let little Piety and Thankful go and learn a bit from her—even if she was a Papist demoness, her shortbread would make you take Communion just to get a piece. She's a right modest handmaiden, let Marie and Heloise and Isabelle learn their letters from her. She sings so beautifully at Christmas Mass, poor Christophe Minouflet fell into a swoon when she sang the Ave—why not let our girl Beatrice learn her scales and her octaves at her side?

And then there was the matter of Sister Agnes's garden. Not a soul in Sauve-Majeure did not burn to know the secret of the seemingly inexhaustible earth upon which their local hermit made her little house. How she made her pumpkins swell and her potatoes glow with red health, how her peas came up almost before the snow could melt, how her blueberry bushes groaned by June with the weight of their dark fruit. Let Annabelle and Elisabeth and Jeanne and Martha go straight away and study her methods, and if a seed or two of those hardy crops should find its way into the pockets of the girls' aprons, well, such was God's Will.

Thus did the demon find herself with a little coven of village girls, all bright and skinny and eager to grow up, more eager still to learn everything Sister Agnes could teach. The demon might have wept with relief and the peculiar joy of devils. She took them in, poor and rich, Papist and Puritan, gathered them round her black hearth like a wreath of still-closed flowers—and she opened them up. The clever girls spun wool that became silk in their hands. They baked bread so sweet the body lost all taste for humble mother's loaf. They read their Scriptures, though Sister Agnes's Bible seemed rather larger and heavier than either Father Audrien's or Pastor Pole's, full of books the girls had never heard of—the Gospel of St. Thomas, of Mary Magdalen, the Apocryphon of James, the Pistis Sophia, the Trimortic Protennoia, the Descent of Mary, and stranger ones still: the Book of the Two Thieves, the Book of Glass, the Book of the Evening Star. When they had tired of these, they read decadent and thrilling novels that Sister Agnes just happened to have on hand.

You might say the demon got careless. You could say that—but a demon has no large measure of care to begin with. The girls seated around her table like Grand Dukes, like seals on a frozen beach, made her feel like her old self again, and who among us can resist a feeling like that? Not many, and a demon hasn't even got a human's meager talent for resisting temptation.

Sébastienne Sazarin did not like Sister Agnes one bit. Oh, she sent her daughter Basile to learn lace from her, because she'd be damned if Marguerite le Clerq's brats would outshine a Sazarin at anything, and if Reformation Dryland's plain, sow-faced granddaughter made a better marriage than her own girl, she'd just have to lie down dead in the street from the shame of it. But she didn't like it. Basile came home smiling in a secretive sort of way, her cheeks flushed, her breath quick and delighted. She did her work so quickly and well that there was hardly anything left of the household industries for Sébastienne to do. She conceived her fourth child, she would always say, out of sheer boredom.

"Well, isn't that what you sent her for?" her husband Hierosme said. "Be glad for ease, for it comes but seldom."

"It's unwholesome, a woman living alone out there. I wish Father Audrien would put a stop to it."

But Father Simon had confided to his successor before he passed into a peaceful death that he felt Sauve-Majeure harbored a saint. When she died, and the inevitable writ of veneration arrived from Rome, the Cathedral of St. Geraud and Adelard might finally have the funds it needed—and if perhaps St. Geraud, who didn't have much to recommend him and wasn't patron of anything in particular, had to be replaced with St. Agnes in order to secure financing from Paris, such was the Will of God. Hubert Sazarin's long dream would come to pass, and Sauve-Majeure would become the

Avignon of the New World. A cathedral required more in the way of coin and time than even the Sazarins could manage on their own, and charged with this celestial municipal destiny, Father Audrien could not bring himself to censure the hermit woman on which it all depended.

Pastor Pole had no such hesitation. Though the left side of Schism Street thought it unsavory to hold the pastorship in one family, Lamentation Pole had raised his only son Troth to know only discipline and abstinence, and no other boy could begin to compete with him in devotion or self-denial. Pastor Pole's sermons in the Free Meeting House (which he would rename the Free Gathered Church) bore such force down on his congregation that certain young girls had been known to faint away at his roaring words. He condemned with equal fervor harvest feasting, sexual congress outside the bonds of marriage, woman's essential nature, and the ridiculous names the Sazarins and other Papist decadents saddled themselves with as they were certainly not fooling God with that nonsense.

Yet, still, the grumbling might have stayed just that, if not for the sopping-wet summer of '09 and the endless, bestial winter that followed. If it had not been bad enough that the crops rotted on the vine and sagged on the stalk, cows and sheep froze where they stood come December, and in February, Martha Chedderley discovered frantic mice invading her thin, precious stores of flour.

Yet the demon's garden thrived. In May her tomatoes were already showing bright green in the rain, in June she had bushels of rhubarb and knuckle-sized cherries, and in that miserable, gray August she sent each of her students home with a sack of onions, cabbages, apples, squash, and beans. When Basile Sazarin showed her mother her treasure, her mother's gaze could have set fire to a block of ice. When Weep-Not Dryland showed her father, Wrestling's eldest and meanest child, Elected Dryland, her winter's store, his bile could have soured a barrel of honey.

Schism Street was broached. Sébastienne Sazarin, prodding her husband and her priest before her, walked out halfway across the muddy, contested earth. Pastor Pole met her, joined by Elected Dryland and his mother, Martha and Makepeace Chedderley, and James Cabot, grandson of the great judge John Cabot may God rest his soul. On the one side of them stood the perpetually unfinished Cathedral of St. Geraud and St. Adelard, its ancient clerestory, window pane, and foundation stones standing lonely beside the humble chapel that everyone called the Cathedral anyhow. On the other, the clean steeple and whitewash of the Free Gathered Church.

She's a witch. She's a succubus. Why should we starve when she has the devil's own plenty?

You know this song. It's a classic, with an old workhorse of a chorus.

My girl Basile says she waters her oats with menstrual blood and reads over them from some Gospel I've never heard of. My maid Weep-Not says her cows give milk three times a day. Our Lizzie says she hasn't got any fingernails. She holds Sabbats up there and the girls all dance naked in a circle of pine. My Bess says on the full moon they're to fornicate with a stag up on the mountain while Sister Agnes sings the Black Vespers. If I ask my poor child, what will I hear then?

The demon heard them down in the valley. She heard the heat of their whispers, and knew they would come for her. She waited, as she had always waited. It wasn't long. James Cabot made out a writ of arrest and Makepeace Chedderley got burly young Robert Mommacque and Charles Loliot to come with him up the hill to drag the witch out of her house and install her in the new jail, which was the Dryland barn, quite recently outfitted with chains forged in Denis Minouflet's shop and a stout hickory chair donated out of the Sazarin parlor.

The demon didn't fight when they bound her and gagged her mouth—to keep her from bewitching them with her devil's psalms. It did not actually occur to her to use her devil's psalms. She was curious. She did not yet know if she could die. The men of Sauve-Majeure carried Gemegishkirihallat in their wagon down through the slushy March snow to stand trial. She only looked at them, her gaze mild and interested. Their guts twisted under those hollow eyes, and this was further proof.

It took much longer than anticipated. The two Sauve-Majeures had never agreed on much, and they sure as spring couldn't agree on the proper execution of a witch's trial. Hanging, said Dryland and Pole. Burning, insisted Sazarin and le Clerq. One judge or a whole bench, testimony from the children or a just simple quiet judgment once the charges were read? A water test or a needle test? Who would question her and what questions would they ask? Would Dr. Pelerin examine her, who had been sent down for schooling in Massachusetts, where they knew about such dark medicine, or the midwife Sarah Wadham? Who would have the credit of ferreting out the devil in their midst, the Church in Rome or their own stalwart Pastor Pole? What name would the town bear on the warrants, Sauve-Majeure (nest of snakes and Papistry) or Help-on-High (den of jackals and schismatics)? Most importantly, who would have the caring of her garden now and when she was gone? Who would have her house?

The demon waited. She waited for her girls to come to her—and they did. First the slower students who craved her approval, then finally Basile and Weep-Not and Lizzie Wadham and Bess Chedderley and the other names listed on the writ though no one had asked them much about it. The demon slipped her chains easily and put her hands to their little heads.

"Go and do as I have done," Sister Agnes said. "Go and make your gardens grow, make your men double over with desire, go and dance until you are full up of the moon."

"Are you really a witch?" ventured Basile Sazarin, who would be the most beautiful woman Sauve-Majeure would ever reap, all the way up till now and further still.

"No," said the demon. "A witch is just a girl who knows her mind. I am better than a witch. But look at the great orgy coming up like a rose around me. No night in Hell could be as bright."

And Sister Agnes took off her black wool gown before the young maids. They saw her four-spoked seals and her wheels of banishment and the seven burnt psalms on her skin. They saw that she had no sex. They saw her long name writ upon her thighs. They knew awe in that barn, and they danced with their teacher in the starlight sifting through the moldering hay.

A certain minister came to visit the demon while she waited for her trial. Pastor Pole managed not to wholly prostrate himself before the famous man, but took him immediately to speak with the condemned woman, whom that illustrious soul had heard of all the way down in Salem: a confirmed demoness, beyond any doubt.

Pastor Pole's own wife Mary-in-the-Manger brought a chair to seat the honored minister upon, and what cider and cheese they had to spare (in truth the Poles had used up the demon's apples to make it, and the demon's milk besides). The great man looked upon the black-clad woman chained in her barn-prison. Her gaze sounded upon his soul and boomed there, deafening.

"Art thee a witch, then?" he whispered.

"No," said the demon.

"But not a Christian lady, either," said he.

"No," said the demon.

"How came you to grow such bounty on your land without the help of God?"

The demon closed her hands in her lap. Her long hair hung around her like an animal's skin.

"My dear Goodman Mather, there is not a demon in Hell who was not once something quite other, and more interesting. In the land where the Euphrates runs green and sweet, I was a grain-god with the head of a bull. In the rough valley of the Tyne I was a god of fertility and war, with the head of a crow. I was a fish-headed lord of plenty in the depths of the Tigris. Before language I was she-who-makes-the-harvest-come, and I rode a red boar. The earth answers when I call it by name. I know its name because we are family."

"You admit your demonic nature?"

"I would have admitted it before now if anyone had asked. They ask only if I am a witch, and a witch is small pennies to me. I am what I am, as you are what you are. I want to live, as all creatures do. I cannot sin, so I have done no wrong."

The minister wet his throat with the demon's cider. His hand shook upon the tankard. When he had mastered himself he spoke quickly and softly, in the most wretched tones. He poured out onto the ground between him all his doubt and misery, all his grief and guilt. He gave her those things because she proved his whole heart, his invisible world, she proved him a good man, despite the hanging hill in his heart.

"Tell me," he rasped finally, as the dawn came on white and pitiless, "tell me that I will know the Kingdom of God in my lifetime. Tell me the end of days is near—for you must be the harbinger of it, you must be its messenger and its handmaiden. Tell me the dead will rise and we will shed out bodies like the shells of beautiful snails, that I will leave behind this horror that is flesh and become as light. Tell me I need never again be a man, that I need never err more, nor dwell in the curse of this life. Tell me you have come to murder this world, so that the new one might swallow us all."

The demon looked on him with infernal pity, which is, in the end, not worth the tears it sheds. Demons may pity men every hour of the day, but that pity never moves.

"No," the demon said.

And, slipping her chains, Gemegishkirihallat shed her gown once more before the famous man, showing the black obliteration of her skin. She folded her arms around him like wings and brought down the scythe of her mouth on his. Straddling his doubt, the demon made plain the reality of his flesh, and the arrow of his need.

They burned her at sunrise, before the Free Gathered Church could say anything about it. Bad enough they had brought that man to their town, the better people of Sauve-Majeure would not stand to let a Protestant nobody pass judgment on her. There were few witnesses: Father Audrien, who made his apologies to Father Simon in Heaven, Sébastienne and Hierosme Sazarin with young Basile clutched between them, Marguerite le Clerq and her husband Isaac. The Church would handle their witch, and the schismatics, to be bold, could lump it. They had all those girls down south—Rome had to have its due in the virtuous north.

Father Audrien tied the demon to a pine trunk and read her the last rites. She did not spit or howl, but only stared down the priest with a gaze like dying. She said one word before the end, and no one understood it. Each of the witnesses lit the flames so that none alone would have to bear the weight of the sin. A year later, Sébastienne Sazarin would insist, drunk and half-toothless, hiding sores on her breast and losing her voice, would rasp to her daughter, insisting that as Sister Agnes burned she saw a bull's head glowing through the pyre, its horns molten gold, and garlanded in black wheat. Marguerite le Clerq, half-mad with syphilis her husband brought home from Virginia, would weep to her priest that she had seen a red boar in the flames, its tusks made of diamond, its head crowned with millet and barley. Hierosme Sazarin, shipwrecked three years hence in Nova Scotia, his cargo of Madeira spilling out into the icy sea, would tell his blue-mouthed, doomed sailors that once he had seen a saint burn, and in the conflagration a white crow, its beak wet with blood, had flown up to Heaven, its wings seared black.

Father Audrien dreamed of the demon's burning body every night until he died, and the moment her bones shattered into a thousand fiery fish, he woke up reaching for his Bible and finding nothing in the dark.

The demon's house stood empty for a long while. Daisies grew in her stove. Moss thickened her great Bible. The girls she had drawn close around her grew up—Basile Sazarin so lovely men winced to look at her, so lovely she married a Parisian banker and never returned to Sauve-Majeure. Weep-Not Dryland bore eight daughters without pain or even much blood, and every autumn took them up to the top of the Bald Moose while her husband slept in his comfort. Lizzie Wadham's cloth wove so fine she could sell it in Boston and even New York for enough money to build a school, where she insisted on teaching the young ladies' lessons, the content of which no male was ever able to spy out.

And whenever Basile and Weep-Not went up to Sister Agnes's house to shoo out the foxes and raccoons and keep the garden weeded, they saw a crow perched on the chimney or pecking at an old apple, or a boney old cow peering at them with a rheumy eye, or a fat piglet with black spots scampering off into the forest as soon as they called after it.

The cod went scarce in the bays. The textile men came up from Portland and Augusta, with bolts of linen and money to build a mill on the river, finding ready buyers in Remembrance Dryland and Walter Chedderley. The few Penobscot and Passamaquoddy left found themselves corralled into bare land not far from where a little girl had once run crying from a strange doorstep in the snow. The Free Gathered Church declined into Presbyterianism and the Cathedral of St. Geraud and St. Adelard remained a chapel, despite obtaining a door and its own relic—the kneecap of St. Geraud himself—before the Sazarin fortune wrecked on the New York market and scattered like so much seafoam. And the demon waited.

She had found burning to be much less painful than expulsion from Hell, and somewhat fortifying, given the sudden warmth in the March chill. When they buried the charred stumps of her bones, she was grateful, to be in the earth, to be closed up and safe. She thought of Prince Sitri, Lord of Naked Need, and how his leopard-skin and griffin-wings had burnt up every night, leaving his bare black bones to dance before the supper table of the upper Kings. His flesh always returned, so that it could burn again. When she thought about it, he looked a little like Thomas Dryland, with his stern golden face. And Countess Gremory—she'd had a body like Basile Sazarin had hid under those dingy aprons—riding her camel naked through the boiling fields to her door, when she'd had a door. When the shards of the demon dreamed, she dreamed of them all eating her bread together, in one house or another, Agares and Lamentation Pole and Amdusias and Sebastienne Sazarin and lovely old Akalamdug and Ekur serving them.

Gemegishkirihallat slowly fell apart into the dirt of Sauve-Majeure.

Sometimes a crow or a dog would dig up a bone and dash off with it, or a cow would drag a knuckle up with her cud. They would slip their pens or wing north suddenly, as if possessed, and before being coaxed home, would drop their prize in a certain garden, near a certain dark, empty house.

The lobster trade picked up, and every household had their pots. Schism Street got its first cobblestones, and cherry trees planted along its route. Something rumbled down south and the Minouflet boys were all killed in some lonely field in Pennsylvania, ending their name. In the name of the war dead, Pastor Veritas Pole and Father Jude dug up the strip of grass and holly hedges between Faith-My-Joy Square and Adelard-in-the-Garden Square and joined them into Memorial Square. The Dryland girls married French boys and buried whatever hatchet they still had biting at the tree. Raulguin Sazarin and his Bangor business partner Lucas Battersby found tourmaline up in Bald Moose, brilliant pink and green and for a moment it seemed Sauve-Majeure really would be something, would present a pretty little ring to the state of Maine and become its best bride, hoping for better days, for bigger stones sometime down the way—but no. The seam was shallow, the mine closed down as quickly as it had sprung up, and that was all the town would ever have of boom and bustle.

One day Constance Chedderley and Catherine le Clerq came home from gathering blackberries in the hills and told their mother that they'd seen chimney smoke up there. Wasn't that funny? Deliverance Dryland and Restitue Sazarin, best friends from the moment one had stolen a black-gowned, black-haired doll from the other, started sneaking up past the town line, coming home with muffins and shortbread in their school satchels. When questioned, they said they'd found a nunnery in the mountains, and one of the sisters had given them the treats as presents, admonishing them not to tell.

The mill went bust before most of the others, a canary singing in the textile mine of New England. The fisherman trade picked up, though, and soon enough even Peter Mommacque had a scallop boat going, despite having the work ethic of a fat housecat. A statue of Minerva made an honest woman of Memorial Square, with a single bright tourmaline set into her shield, which was promptly stolen by Bernard and Richie Loliot. First Presbyterian Church crumpled up into Second Methodist, and the first Pastor not named Pole, though rather predictably called Dryland instead, spoke on Sundays about the dangers of drink. And you know, old Agnes has just always lived up there, making her pies and candies and muffins. A nicer old lady you couldn't hope to meet. Right modest, always wearing her buttoned-up old-fashioned frocks even in summer. Why, Marie Pelerin spends every Sunday up there digging in the potatoes and learning to spin wool like the wives in Sauve-Majeure did before the mill. Janette Loliot got her cider recipe but she won't share it round. We're thinking of sending Maude and Harriet along as well. Young ladies these days can never learn too much when it comes to the quiet industries of home.

Far up into the hills above the stretch of land between Cobscook and Passamaquoddy Bay, if you go looking for it, you'll find a house all by itself in the middle of a brambly field of good straight corn and green garlic. It's an old place, but kept up, the whitewash fresh and the windows clean. The roof needs mending, it groans under the weight of hensbane and mustard and rue. There's tomatoes coming in under the kitchen sill in the kitchen, a basil plant that may or may not come back next year.

Jenny Sazarin comes by Sunday afternoons for Latin lessons and to trade a basket of cranberries from her uncle's bog down in Lincolnville for a loaf of bread with a sugar-crust that makes her heart beat faster when she eats it. She looks forward to it all week. It's quiet up there. You can hear the potatoes growing down in the dark earth. When October acorns drop down into the old lady's soot-colored wheelbarrow, they make a sound like guns firing. Agnes starts the preserves right away, boiling the bright, sour berries in her great huge pot until they pop.

"D'you know they used to burn witches here? I read about it last week," she says while she munches on a trifle piled up with cream.

"No," the demon says. "I've never heard that."

"They did. It must have been awful. I wonder if there really are witches? Pastor Dryland says there's demons, but that seems wrong to me. Demons live in Hell. Why would they leave and come here? Surely there's work enough for them to do with all the damned souls and pagans and gluttons and such."

"Perhaps they get punished, from time to time, and have to come into this world," the demon says, and stirs the wrinkling cranberries. The house smells of red fruit.

"What would a demon have to do to get kicked out of Hell?" wonders little Jenny, her schoolbooks at her feet, the warm autumn sun lighting up her face so that she looks so much like Hubert Sazarin and Thomas Dryland, both of whom can claim a fair portion of this bookish, gentle girl, that Gemegishkirihallat tightens her grip on her wooden spoon, stained crimson by the bloody sugar it tends.

The demon shuts her eyes. The orange coal of the sun lights up the skin and the bones of her skull show through. "Perhaps, for one moment, only one, so quick it might pass between two beats of a sparrow's wings, she had all her folk around her, and they ate of her table, and called her by her own name, and did not vie against the other, and for that one moment, she was joyful, and did not mourn her separation from a God she had never seen."

Cranberries pop and steam in the iron pot; Jenny swallows her achingly sweet bread. The sun goes down over Bald Moose Mountain, and the lights come on down in the soft black valley of Sauve-Majeure.

━◆━

He remembered, oddly, a tale from childhood: "Where is my heart, dear wife? Here it is, dear husband: I am keeping it wrapped up in my hair."

HAIR

Joan Aiken

Tom Orford stood leaning over the rail and watching the flat hazy shores of the Red Sea slide past. A month ago he had been watching them slide in the other direction. Sarah had been with him then, leaning and looking after the ship's wake, whispering ridiculous jokes into his ear.

They had been overflowingly happy, playing endless deck games with the other passengers, going to the ship's dances in Sarah's mad, rakish conception of fancy dress, even helping to organize the appalling concerts of amateur talent, out of their gratitude to the world.

"You'll tire yourself out!" somebody said to Sarah as she plunged from deck-tennis to swimming in the ship's pool, from swimming to dancing, from dancing to Ping-Pong.

"As if I could," she said to Tom. "I've done so little all my life, I have twenty-one years of accumulated energy to work off."

But just the same, that was what she had done. She had died, vanished, gone out, as completely as a forgotten day, or a drift of the scent of musk. Gone, lost to the world. Matter can neither be created nor destroyed, he thought. Not matter, no. The network of bones and tendons, the dandelion clock of fair hair, the brilliantly blue eyes that had once belonged to Sarah, and had so riotously obeyed her will for a small portion of her life—a forty-second part of it, perhaps—was now quietly returning to earth in a Christian cemetery in Ceylon. But her spirit, the fiery intention which had coordinated that machine of flesh and bone and driven it through her life—the spirit, he knew, existed neither in air nor earth. It had gone out, like a candle.

He did not leave the ship at Port Said. It was there that he had met Sarah. She had been staying with friends, the Acres. Orford had gone on a trip up the Nile with her. Then they had started for China. This was after they had been married, which happened almost immediately. And now he was coming back with an address, and a bundle of hair to give to her mother. For she had once laughingly asked him to go and visit her mother, if she were to die first.

"Not that she'd enjoy your visit," said Sarah drily. "But she'd be highly offended if she didn't get a lock of hair, and she might as well have the lot, now I've cut it off. And you could hardly send it to her in a registered envelope."

He had laughed, because then death seemed a faraway and irrelevant threat, a speck on the distant horizon.

"Why are we talking about it, anyway?" he said.

"Death always leaps to mind when I think of Mother," she answered, her eyes dancing. "Due to her I've lived in an atmosphere of continuous death for twenty-one years."

She had told him her brief story. When she reached twenty-one, and came into an uncle's legacy, she had packed her brush and comb and two books and a toothbrush ("All my other possessions, if they could be called mine, were too ugly to take."), and, pausing only at a hairdressers' to have her bun cut off (he had seen a photograph of her at nineteen, a quiet, dull-looking girl, weighed down by her mass of hair), she had set off for Egypt to visit her only friend, Mrs. Acres. She wrote to her mother from Cairo. She had had one letter in return.

"My dear Sarah, as you are now of age I cannot claim to have any further control over you, for you are, I trust, perfectly healthy in mind and body. I have confidence in the upbringing you received, which furnished you with principles to guide you through life's vicissitudes. I know that in the end you will come back to me."

"She seems to have taken your departure quite lightly," Orford said, reading it over her shoulder.

"Oh, she never shows when she's angry," Sarah said. She studied the letter again. "Little does she know," was her final comment, as she put it away. "Hey, I don't want to think about her. Quick, let's go out and see something—a pyramid or a cataract or a sphinx. Do you realize that I've seen absolutely nothing—nothing—nothing all my life? Now I've got to make up for lost time. I want to see Rome and Normandy and Illyria and London—I've never been there, except Heath Row—and Norwegian fjords and the Taj Mahal."

Tomorrow, Orford thought, he would have to put on winter clothes. He remembered how the weather had become hotter and hotter on the voyage out. Winter to summer, summer to winter again.

London, when he reached it, was cold and foggy. He shrank into himself, sitting in the taxi which squeaked and rattled its way from station to station, like a moving tomb. At Charing Cross he ran into an acquaintance who exclaimed, "Why, Tom old man, I didn't expect to see you for another month. Thought you were on your honeymoon or something?"

Orford slid away into the crowd.

"And can you tell me where Marl End is?" he was presently asking at a tiny, ill-lit station which felt as if it were in the middle of the steppes.

"Yes, sir," said the man, after some thought. "You'd best phone for a taxi. It's a fair way. Right through the village and on over the sheepdowns."

An aged Ford, lurching through the early winter dusk, which was partly mist, brought him to a large red-brick house, set baldly in the middle of a field.

"Come back and call for me at seven," he said, resolving to take no chances with the house, and the driver nodded, shifting his gears, and drove away into the fog as Orford knocked at the door.

The first thing that struck him was her expression of relentless, dogged intention. Such, he thought, might be the look on the face of a coral mite, setting out to build up an atoll from the depths of the Pacific.

He could not imagine her ever desisting from any task she had set her hand to.

Her grief seemed to be not for herself but for Sarah.

"Poor girl. Poor girl. She would have wanted to come home again before she died. Tired herself out, you say? It was to be expected. Ah well."

Ah well, her tone said, it isn't my fault. I did what I could. I could have prophesied what would happen; in fact I did; but she was out of my control, it was her fault, not mine.

"Come close to the fire," she said. "You must be cold after that long journey."

Her tone implied he had come that very night from Sarah's cold un-Christian deathbed, battling through frozen seas, over Himalayas, across a dead world.

"No, I'm fine," he said. "I'll stay where I am. This is a very warm room." The stifling, hothouse air pressed on his face, solid as sand. He wiped his forehead.

"My family, unfortunately, are all extremely delicate," she said, eyeing him. "Poor things, they need a warm house. Sarah—my husband—my sister—I daresay Sarah told you about them?"

"I've never seen my father," he remembered Sarah saying. "I don't know what happened to him—whether he's alive or dead. Mother always talks about him as if he were just outside in the garden."

But there had been no mention of an aunt. He shook his head.

"Very delicate," she said. She smoothed back her white hair, which curved over her head like a cap, into its neat bun at the back. "Deficient in thyroid—thyroxin, do they call it? She needs constant care."

Her smile was like a swift light passing across a darkened room.

"My sister disliked poor Sarah—for some queer reason of her own—so all the care of her fell on me. Forty years."

"Terrible for you," he answered mechanically.

The smile passed over her face again.

"Oh, but it is really quite a happy life for her, you know. She draws, and plays with clay, and of course she is very fond of flowers and bright colors. And nowadays she very seldom loses her temper, though at one time I had a great deal of trouble with her."

I manage all, her eyes said, I am the strong one, I keep the house warm, the floors polished, the garden dug, I have cared for the invalid and reared my child, the weight of the house has rested on my shoulders and in these hands.

He looked at her hands as they lay in her black silk lap, fat and white with dimpled knuckles.

"Would you care to see over the house?" she said.

He would not, but could think of no polite way to decline. The stairs were dark and hot, with a great shaft of light creeping round the corner at the top.

"Is anybody there?" a quavering voice called through a half-closed door. It was gentle, frail, and unspeakably old.

"Go to sleep, Miss Whiteoak, go to sleep," she called back. "You should have swallowed your dose long ago."

"My companion," she said to Orford, "is very ill."

He had not heard of any companion from Sarah.

"This is my husband's study," she told him, following him into a large, hot room.

Papers were stacked in orderly piles on the desk. The bottle of ink was half full. A half-written letter lay on the blotter. But who occupied this room? "Mother always talks as if he were just outside."

On the wall hung several exquisite Japanese prints. Orford exclaimed in pleasure.

"My husband is fond of those prints," she said, following his glance. "I can't see anything in them myself. Why don't they make objects the right size, instead of either too big or too small? I like something I can recognize, I tell him."

Men are childish, her eyes said, and it is the part of women to see that they do nothing foolish, to look after them.

They moved along the corridor.

"This was Sarah's room," she said.

Stifling, stifling, the bed, chair, table, chest all covered in white sheets. Like an airless graveyard waiting for her, he thought.

"I can't get to sleep," Miss Whiteoak called through her door. "Can't I come downstairs?"

"No, no, I shall tell you when you may come down," the old lady called back. "You are not nearly well enough yet!"

Orford heard a sigh.

"Miss Whiteoak is wonderfully devoted," she said as they slowly descended the stairs. "I have nursed her through so many illnesses. She would do anything for me. Only, of course, there isn't anything that she can do now, poor thing."

At the foot of the stairs an old, old woman in a white apron was lifting a decanter from a sideboard.

"That's right, Drewett," she said. "This gentleman will be staying to supper. You had better make some broth. I hope you are able to stay the night?" she said to Orford.

But when he explained that he could not even stay to supper, she took the news calmly.

"Never mind about the broth, then, Drewett. Just bring in the sherry."

The old woman hobbled away, and they returned to the drawing room. He gave her the tissue-paper full of Sarah's hair.

She received the bundle absently, then examined it with a sharp look. "Was this cut before or after she died?"

"Oh—before—before I married her." He wondered what she was thinking.

She gave a long, strange sigh, and presently remarked, "That accounts for everything."

Watching the clutch of her fat, tight little hands on the hair, he began to be aware of a very uneasy feeling, as if he had surrendered something that only now, when it was too late, he realized had been of desperate importance to Sarah. He remembered, oddly, a tale from childhood: "Where is my heart, dear wife? Here it is, dear husband: I am keeping it wrapped up in my hair."

But Sarah had said, "She might as well have the lot, now I've cut it off."

He almost put out his hand to take it back; wondered if, without her noticing, he could slip the packet back into his pocket.

Drewett brought in the sherry in the graceful decanter with a long, fine glass spout at one side. He commented on it.

"My husband bought it in Spain," she said. "Twenty years ago. I have always taken great care of it."

The look on her face gave him again that chilly feeling of uneasiness. "Another glass?" she asked him.

"No, I really have to go." He looked at his watch and said with relief, "My taxi will be coming back for me in five minutes."

There came a sudden curious mumbling sound from a dim corner of the room. It made him start so violently that he spilt some of his sherry. He had supposed the place empty, apart from themselves.

"Ah, feeling better, dear?" the old lady said.

She walked slowly over to the corner and held out a hand, saying, "Come and see poor Sarah's husband. Just think—she had a husband—isn't that a queer thing?"

Orford gazed aghast at the stumbling slobbering creature that came reluctantly forward, tugging away from the insistent white hand.

His repulsion was the greater because in its vacant, puffy-eyed stare he could detect a shadowy resemblance to Sarah.

"She's just like a child, of course," said the old lady indulgently. "Quite dependent on me, but wonderfully affectionate, in her way." She gave the cretin a fond glance. "Here, Louisa, here's something pretty for you! Look, dear—lovely hair."

Dumbly, Orford wondered what other helpless, infirm pieces of humanity might be found in this house, all dependent on the silver-haired old lady who brooded over them, sucking them dry like a gentle spider. What might he trip over in the darkness of the hall? Who else had escaped?

The conscious part of his mind was fixed in horror as he watched Louisa rapaciously knotting and tearing and plucking at the silver-gold mass of hair.

"I think I hear your taxi," the old lady said. "Say goodnight, Louisa!"

Louisa said goodnight in her fashion, the door shut behind him—and he was in the car, in the train, in a cold hotel bedroom, with nothing but the letter her mother had written her to remind him that Sarah had ever existed.

*No one warned her about the dangers of swimming in the
lake—especially without clothing. In retrospect, she
was foolish. But how could she have known?*

THE LAKE

Tananarive Due

◄══►

*The new English instructor at Graceville Prep was chosen with the greatest
care, highly recommended by the Board of Directors at Blake Academy in
Boston, where she had an exemplary career for twelve years. There was no
history of irregular behavior to presage the summer's unthinkable events.*

—Excerpt from an internal memo,
Graceville Preparatory School Graceville, Florida

Abbie LaFleur was an outsider, a third-generation Bostonian, so no one
warned her about summers in Graceville. She noticed a few significant
glances, a hitched eyebrow or two, when she first mentioned to locals that
she planned to relocate in June to work a summer term before the start of
the school year, but she'd assumed it was because they thought no one in her
right mind would move to Florida, even northern Florida, in the wet heat
of summer.

In fairness, Abbie LaFleur would have scoffed at their stories as hysteria.
Delusion. This was Graceville's typical experience with newcomers and
outsiders, so Graceville had learned to keep its stories to itself.

Abbie thought she had found her dream job in Graceville. A fresh start.
Her glasses had fogged up with steam from the rain-drenched tarmac as
soon as she stepped off the plane at Tallahassee Airport; her confirmation
that she'd embarked on a true adventure, an exploration worthy of Ponce de
León's storied landing at St. Augustine.

Her parents and her best friend, Mary Kay, had warned her not to jump
into a real estate purchase until she'd worked in Graceville for at least a
year—The whole thing's so hasty, what if the school's not a good fit? Who
wants to be stuck with a house in the sticks in a depressed market?—but

Abbie fell in love with the white lakeside colonial she found listed at
one-fifty, for sale by owner. She bought it after a hasty tour—too hasty, it
turned out—but at nearly three-thousand square feet, this was the biggest
house she had ever lived in, with more room than she had furniture for. A
place with potential, despite its myriad flaws.

A place, she thought, very much like her.

The built-in bookshelves in the Florida room sagged. (She'd never known
that a den could be called a Florida room, but so it was, and so she did.) The
floorboards creaked and trembled on the back porch, sodden from summer
rainfall. And she would need to lay down new tiles in the kitchen right away,
because the brooding mud-brown flooring put her in a bad mood from the
time she first fixed her morning coffee.

But there would be boys at the school, strong and tireless boys, who could
help her mend whatever needed fixing. In her experience, there were always
willing boys.

And then there was the lake! The house was her excuse to buy her piece
of the lake and the thin strip of red-brown sand that was a beach in her
mind, although it was nearly too narrow for the beach lounger she'd planted
like a flag. The water looked murky where it met her little beach, the color
of the soil, but in the distance she could see that its heart of rich green-
blue, like the ocean. The surface bobbed with rings and bubbles from the
hidden catfish and brim that occasionally leaped above the surface, damn
near daring her to cast a line.

If not for the hordes of mosquitoes that feasted on her legs and whined
with urgent grievances, Abbie could have stood with her bare feet in the
warm lake water for hours, the house forgotten behind her. The water's
gentle lapping was the meditation her parents and Mary Kay were always
prescribing for her, a soothing song.

And the isolation! A gift to be treasured. Her property was bracketed by
woods of thin pine, with no other homes within shouting distance. Any spies
would need binoculars and a reason to spy, since the nearest homes were far
across the lake, harmless little dollhouses in the anonymous subdivision
where some of her students no doubt lived. Her lake might as well be as wide
as the Nile, protection from any envious whispers.

As if to prove her newfound freedom, Abbie suddenly climbed out of the
tattered jeans she'd been wearing as she unpacked her boxes, whipped off
her T-shirt and draped her clothing neatly across the lounger's arm rails.
Imagine! She was naked in her own backyard. If her neighbors could see her,
they would be scandalized already, and she had yet to commence teaching
at Graceville Prep.

Abbie wasn't much of a swimmer—she preferred solid ground beneath her feet even when she was in the water—but with her flip-flops to protect her from unseen rocks, Abbie felt brave enough to wade into the water, inviting its embrace above her knees, her thighs. She felt the water's gentle kiss between her legs, the massage across her belly, and, finally, a liquid cloak upon her shoulders. The grade was gradual, with no sudden drop-offs to startle her, and for the first time in years Abbie felt truly safe and happy.

That was all Graceville was supposed to be for Abbie LeFleur: new job, new house, new lake, new beginning. For the week before summer school began, Abbie took to swimming behind her house daily, at dusk, safe from the mosquitoes, sinking into her sanctuary.

No one had told her—not the realtor, not the elderly widow she'd only met once when they signed the paperwork at the lawyer's office downtown, not Graceville Prep's cheerful headmistress. Even a random first-grader at the grocery store could have told her that one must never, ever go swimming in Graceville's lakes during the summer. The man-made lakes were fine, but the natural lakes that had once been swampland were to be avoided by children in particular. And women of childbearing age—which Abbie LaFleur still was at thirty-six, albeit barely. And men who were prone to quick tempers or alcohol binges.

Further, one must never, *ever* swim in Graceville's lakes in summer without clothing, when crevices and weaknesses were most exposed.

In retrospect, she was foolish. But in all fairness, how could she have known?

Abbie's ex-husband had accused her of irreparable timidity, criticizing her for refusing to go snorkeling or even swimming with dolphins, never mind the scuba diving he'd loved since he was sixteen. The world was populated by water people and land people, and Abbie was firmly attached to terra firma. Until Graceville. And the lake.

Soon after she began her nightly wading, which gradually turned to dog-paddling and then awkward strokes across the dark surface, she began to dream about the water. Her dreams were far removed from her nightly dipping—which actually *was* somewhat timid, if she was honest. In sleep, she glided effortlessly far beneath the murky surface, untroubled by the nuisance of lungs and breathing. The water was a muddy green-brown, nearly black, but spears of light from above gave her tents of vision to see floating plankton, algae, tadpoles and squirming tiny creatures she could not name . . . and yet knew. Her underwater dreams were a wonderland of tangled mangrove roots coated with algae, and forests of gently waving lily-pads and swamp grass. Once, she saw an alligator's checkered, pale belly above her, until the reptile hurried away, its powerful tail lashing to give it speed. In her dream, she wasn't afraid of the alligator; she'd sensed instead (smelled instead?) that the alligator was afraid of *her.*

Abbie's dreams had never been so vivid. She awoke one morning drenched from head to toe, and her heart hammered her breathless until she realized that her mattress was damp with perspiration, not swamp water. At least . . . she *thought* it must be perspiration. Her fear felt silly, and she was blanketed by sadness as deep as she'd felt the first months after her divorce.

Abbie was so struck by her dreams that she called Mary Kay, who kept dream diaries and took such matters far too seriously.

"You sure that water's safe?" Mary Kay said. "No chemicals being dumped out there?"

"The water's fine," Abbie said, defensive. "I'm not worried about the water. It's just the dreams. They're so . . . " Abbie rarely ran out of words, which Mary Kay knew full well.

"What's scaring you about the dreams?"

"The dreams don't scare me," Abbie said. "It's the opposite. I'm sad to wake up. As if I belong there, in the water, and my bedroom is the dream."

Mary Kay had nothing to offer except a warning to have the local Health Department come out and check for chemicals in any water she was swimming in, and Abbie felt the weight of her distance from her friend. There had been a time when she and Mary Kay understood each other better than anyone, when they could see past each other's silences straight to their thoughts, and now Mary Kay had no idea of the shape and texture of Abbie's life. No one did.

All liberation is loneliness, she thought sadly.

Abbie dressed sensibly, conservatively, for her first day at her new school.

She had driven the two miles to the school, a red-brick converted bank building in the center of downtown Graceville, before she noticed the itching between her toes.

"LaFleur," the headmistress said, keeping pace with Abbie as they walked toward her assigned classroom for the course she'd named Creativity & Literature. The woman's easy, Southern-bred tang seemed to add a syllable to every word. "Where is that name from?"

Abbie wasn't fooled by the veiled attempt to guess at her ethnicity, since it didn't take an etymologist to guess at her name's French derivation. What

Loretta Millhouse really wanted to know was whether Abbie had ancestry in Haiti or Martinique to explain her sun-kissed complexion and the curly brown hair Abbie kept locked tight in a bun.

Abbie's itching feet had grown so unbearable that she wished she could pull off her pumps. The itching pushed irritation into her voice. "My grandmother married a Frenchman in Paris after World War II," she explained. "LaFleur was his family name."

The rest was none of her business. Most of her life was none of anyone's business.

"Oh, I see," Millhouse said, voice filled with delight, but Abbie saw her disappointment that her prying had yielded nothing. "Well, as I said, we're so tickled to have you with us. Only one letter in your file wasn't completely glowing . . . "

Abbie's heart went cold, and she forgot her feet. She'd assumed that her detractors had remained silent, or she never would have been offered the job.

Millhouse patted her arm. "But don't you worry: Swimming upstream is an asset here." The word *swimming* made Abbie flinch, feeling exposed. "We welcome independent thinking at Graceville Prep. That's the main reason I wanted to hire you. Between you and me, how can anyone criticize a . . . creative mind?"

She said the last words conspiratorially, leaning close to Abbie's ear as if a creative mind was a disease. Abbie's mind raced: The criticism must have come from Johanssen, the vice-principal at Blake who had labeled her argumentative—*a bitch*, Mary Kay had overheard him call her privately, but he wouldn't have put that in writing. What did Millhouse's disclosure mean? Was Millhouse someone who pretended to compliment you while subtly putting you down, or was a shared secret hidden beneath the twinkle in her aqua-green eyes?

"Don't go easy on this group," Millhouse said as when they reached Room 113. "Every jock trying to make up a credit to stay on the roster is in your class. Let them work for it."

Sure enough, when Abbie walked into the room, she faced desks filled with athletic young men. Graceville was a co-ed school, but only five of her twenty students were female.

Abbie smiled.

Her house would be fixed up sooner than she'd expected.

Abbie liked to begin with Thomas Hardy. *Jude the Obscure*. That one always blew their young minds, with its frankness and unconventionality. Their other instructors would cram conformity down their throats, and she would teach rebellion.

No rows of desks would mar her classroom, she informed them. They would sit in a circle. She would not lecture; they would have conversations. They would discuss the readings, read pages from their journals, and share poems. Some days, she told them, she would surprise them by playing music and they would write whatever came to mind.

Half the class looked relieved, the other half petrified.

During her orientation, Abbie studied her students' faces and tried to guess which ones would be most useful over the summer. She dismissed the girls, as she usually did; most were too wispy and pampered, or far too large to be accustomed to physical labor.

But the boys. The boys were a different matter.

Of the fifteen boys, only three were unsuitable at a glance—bird-chested and reedy, or faces riddled with acne. She could barely stand to look at them.

That left twelve to ponder. She listened carefully as they raised their hands and described their hopes and dreams, watching their eyes for the spark of maturity she needed. Five or six couldn't hold her gaze, casting their eyes shyly at their desks. No good at all.

Down to six, then. Several were basketball players, one a quarterback. Millhouse hadn't been kidding when she'd said that her class was a haven for desperate athletes. The quarterback, Derek, was dark-haired with a crater-sized dimple in his chin; he sat at his desk with his body angled, leg crossed at the knee, as if the desk were already too small. He didn't say "uhm" or pause between his sentences. His future was at the tip of his tongue.

"I'm sorry," she said, interrupting him. "How old did you say you are, Derek?"

He didn't blink. His dark eyes were at home on hers. "Sixteen, ma'am."

Sixteen was a good age. A mature age.

A female teacher could not be too careful about which students she invited to her home. Locker-room exaggerations held grave consequences that could literally steal years from a young woman's life. Abbie had seen it before; entire careers up in flames. But this Derek . . .

Derek was full of possibilities. Abbie suddenly found herself playing Millhouse's game, noting his olive complexion and dark features, trying to guess if his jet-black hair whispered Native American or Hispanic heritage. Throughout the ninety-minute class, her eyes came to Derek again and again.

The young man wasn't flustered. He was used to being stared at.

Abbie had made up her mind before the final bell, but she didn't say a word to Derek. Not yet. She had plenty of time. The summer had just begun.

As she was climbing out of the shower, Abbie realized her feet had stopped their terrible itching. For three days, she'd slathered the spaces between her toes with creams from Walgreens, none helping, some only stinging her in punishment.

But the pain was gone.

Naked, Abbie raised her foot to her mattress, pulling her toes apart to examine them . . . and realized right away why she'd been itching so badly. Thin webs of pale skin had grown between each of her toes. Her toes, in fact, had changed shape entirely, pulling away from each other to make room for webbing. And weren't her toes longer than she remembered?

No *wonder* her shoes felt so tight! She wore a size eight, but her feet looked like they'd grown two sizes. She was startled to see her feet so altered, but not alarmed, as she might have been when she was still in Boston, tied to her old life. New job, new house, new feet. There was a logical symmetry to her new feet that superseded questions or worries.

Abbie almost picked up her phone to call Mary Kay, but she thought better of it. What else would Mary Kay say, except that she should have had her water tested?

Instead, still naked, Abbie went to her kitchen, her feet slapping against her ugly kitchen flooring with unusual traction. When she brushed her upper arm carelessly across her ribs, new pain made her hiss. The itching had migrated, she realized.

She paused in the bright fluorescent lighting to peer down at her rib-cage, and found her skin bright red, besieged by some kind of rash. *Great*, she thought. *Life is an endless series of challenges.* She inhaled a deep breath, and the air felt hot and thin. The skin across her ribs pulled more tautly, constricting. She longed for the lake.

Abbie slipped out of her rear kitchen door and scurried across her back yard toward the black shimmer of the water. She'd forgotten her flip-flops, but the soles of her feet were less tender, like leather slippers.

She did not hesitate. She did not wade. She dove like an eel, swimming with an eel's ease. *Am I truly awake, or is this a dream?*

Her eyes adjusted to the lack of light, bringing instant focus. She had never seen the true murky depths of her lake, so much like the swamp of her dreams. Were they one and the same? Her ribs' itching turned to a welcome massage, and she felt long slits yawn open across her skin, beneath each rib. Warm water flooded her, nursing her; her nose, throat and mouth were a useless, distant memory. Why hadn't it ever occurred to her to breathe the water before?

An alligator's curiosity brought the beast close enough to study her, but it recognized its mistake and tried to thrash away. But too late. Too late. Nourished by the water, Abbie's instincts gave her enough speed and strength to glide behind the beast, its shadow. One hand grasped the slick ridges of its tail, and the other hugged its wriggling girth the way she might a lover. She didn't remember biting or clawing the alligator, but she must have done one or the other, because the water flowed red with blood.

The blood startled Abbie awake in her bed, her sheets heavy with dampness. Her lungs heaved and gasped, shocked by the reality of breathing, and at first she seemed to take in no air. She examined her fingers, nails and naked skin for blood, but found none. The absence of blood helped her breathe more easily, her lungs freed from their confusion.

Another dream. Of course. How could she mistake it for anything else?

She was annoyed to realize that her ribs still bore their painful rash and long lines like raw, infected incisions.

But her feet, thank goodness, were unchanged. She still had the delightful webbing and impressive new size, longer than in her dream. Abbie knew she would have to dress in a hurry. Before school, she would swing by Payless and pick up a few new pairs of shoes.

Derek lingered after class. He'd written a poem based on a news story that had made a deep impression on him; a boy in Naples had died on the football practice field. *Before he could be tested by life,* Derek had written in his eloquent final line. One of the girls, Riley Bowen, had wiped a tear from her eye. Riley Bowen always gazed at Derek like the answer to her life's prayers, but he never looked at her.

And now here was Derek standing over Abbie's desk, on his way to six feet tall, his face bowed with shyness for the first time all week.

"I lied before," he said, when she waited for him so to speak. "About my age."

Abbie already knew. She'd checked his records and found out for herself, but she decided to torture him. "Then how old are you?"

"Fifteen." His face soured. "'Til March."

"Why would you lie about that?"

He shrugged, an adolescent gesture that annoyed Abbie no end.

"Of course you know," she said. "I heard your poem. I've seen your thoughtfulness. You wouldn't lie on the first day of school without a reason."

He found his confidence again, raising his eyes. "Fine. I skipped second grade, so I'm a year younger than everyone in my class. I always say I'm sixteen. It wasn't special for you."

The fight in Derek intrigued her. He wouldn't be the type of man who would be pushed around. "But you're here now, bearing your soul. Who's that for?"

His face softened to half a grin. "Like you said, when we're in this room, we tell the truth. So here I am. Telling the truth."

There he was. She decided to tell him the truth too.

"I bought a big house out by the lake," she said. "Against my better judgment, maybe."

"That old one on McCormack Road?"

"You know it?"

He shrugged, that loathsome gesture again. "Everybody knows the McCormacks. She taught Sunday school at Christ the Redeemer. Guess she moved out, huh?"

"To her sister's in . . . Quincy?" The town shared a name with the city south of Boston, the only reason she remembered it. Her mind was filled with distraction to mask strange flurries of her heart. Was she so cowed by authority that she would leave her house in a mess?

"Yeah, Quincy's about an hour, hour and a half, down the 10 . . . " Derek was saying in a flat voice that bored even him.

They were talking about nothing. Waiting. They both knew it.

Abbie clapped her hands once, snapping their conversation from its trance. "Well, an old house brings lots of problems. The porch needs fixing. New kitchen tiles. I don't have the budget to hire a real handyman, so I'm looking for people with skills . . . "

Derek's cheeks brightened, pink. "My dad and I built a cabin last summer. I'm pretty good with wood. New planks and stuff. For the porch."

"Really?" She chided herself for the girlish rise in her pitch, as if he'd announced he had scaled Mt. Everest during his two weeks off from school.

"I could help you out, if . . . you know, if you buy the supplies."

"I can't pay much. Come take a look after school, see if you think you can help." She made a show of glancing toward the open doorway, watching the stream of students passing by. "But you know, Derek, it's easy for people to get the wrong idea if you say you're going to a teacher's house . . . "

His face was bright red now. "Oh, I wouldn't say nothing. I mean . . . anything. Besides, we go fishing with Coach Reed all the time. It's no big deal around here. Not like in Boston, maybe." The longer he spoke, the more he regained his poise. His last sentence had come with an implied wink of his eye.

"No, you're right about that," she said, and she smiled, remembering her new feet. "Nothing here is like it was in Boston."

That was how Derek Voorhoven came to spend several days a week after class helping Abbie fix her ailing house, whenever he could spare time after football practice in the last daylight. Abbie made it clear that he couldn't expect any special treatment in class, so he would need to work hard on his atrocious spelling, but Derek was thorough and uncomplaining. No task seemed too big or small, and he was happy to scrub, sand, and tile in exchange for a few dollars, conversation about the assigned reading, and fishing rights to the lake, since he said the catfish favored the north side, where it was quiet.

As he'd promised, he told no one at Graceville Prep, but one day he asked if his cousin Jack could help from time to time, and after he'd brought the stocky, freckled youth by to introduce him, she agreed. Jack was only fourteen, but he was strong and didn't argue. He also attended the public school, which made him far less a risk. Although the boys joked together, Jack's presence never slowed Derek's progress much, so Derek and Jack became fixtures in her home well into July. Abbie looked forward to fixing them lemonade and white chocolate macadamia nut cookies from ready-made dough, and with each passing day she knew she'd been right to leave Boston behind.

Still, Abbie never told Mary Kay about her visits with the boys and the work she asked them to do. Her friend wouldn't judge her, but Abbie wanted to hold her new life close, a secret she would share only when she was ready, when she could say: *You'll never guess the clever way I got my improvements done,* an experience long behind her. Mary Kay would be envious, wishing she'd thought of it first, rather than spending a fortune on a gardener and a pool boy.

But there were other reasons Abbie began erecting a wall between herself and the people who knew her best. Derek and Jack, bright as they were, weren't prone to notice the small changes, or even the large ones, that would have leaped out to her mother and Mary Kay—and even her distracted father.

Her mother would have spotted the new size of her feet right away, of course. And the odd new pallor of her face, fishbelly pale. And the growing strength in her arms and legs that made it so easy to hand the boys boxes, heavy tools or stacks of wooden planks. Mary Kay would have asked about the flaky skin on the back of her neck and her sudden appetite for all things rare, or raw. Abbie had given up most red meat two years ago in an effort to remake herself after the divorce tore her self-esteem to pieces, but that summer she stocked up on thin-cut steaks, salmon, and fish she could practically eat straight from the packaging. Her hunger was also *voracious,* her mouth watering from the moment she woke, her growling stomach keeping her awake at night.

She was hungriest when Derek and Jack were there, but she hid that from herself.

Her dusk swims had grown to evening swims, and some nights she lost track of time so completely that the sky was blooming pink by the time she waded from the healing waters to begin another day of waiting to swim. She resisted inviting the boys to swim with her.

The last Friday in July, with only a week left in the summer term, Abbie lost her patience.

She was especially hungry that day, dissatisfied with her kitchen stockpile. Graceville was suffering a record heat wave with temperatures hovering near 110 degrees, so she was sweaty and irritable by the time the boys arrived at five-thirty. And itching terribly. Unlike her feet, the gills hiding beneath the ridges of her ribs never stopped bothering her until she was in her lake. She was so miserable, she almost asked the boys to forget about painting the refurbished back porch and come back another day.

If she'd only done that, she would have avoided the scandal.

Abbie strode behind the porch to watch the strokes of the boys' rollers and paintbrushes as they transformed her porch from an eyesore to a snapshot of the quaint Old South. Because of the heat, both boys had taken their shirts off, their shoulders ruddy as the muscles in their sun-broiled backs flexed in the Magic Hour's furious, gasping light. They put Norman Rockwell to shame; Derek with his disciplined football player's physique, and Jack with his awkward baby fat, sprayed with endless freckles.

"Why do you come here?" she asked them.

They both stopped working, startled by her voice.

"Huh?" Jack said. His scowl was deep, comical. "You're paying us, right?"

Ten dollars a day each was hardly pay. Derek generously shared half of his twenty dollars with his cousin for a couple hours' work, although Jack talked more than he worked, running his mouth about summer superhero blockbusters and dancers in music videos. Abbie regretted that she'd encouraged Derek to invite his cousin along, and that day she wished she had a reason to send Jack home. Her mind raced to come up with an excuse, but she couldn't think of one. A sudden surge of frustration pricked her eyes with tears.

"I'm not paying much," she said.

"Got *that* right," Derek said. Had his voice deepened in only a few weeks? Was Derek undergoing changes too? "I'm here for the catfish. Can we quit in twenty minutes? I've got my rod in the truck. And some chicken livers I've been saving."

"Quit now if you want," she said. She pretended to study their work, but she couldn't focus her eyes on the whorls of painted wood. "Go on and fish, but I'm going swimming. Good way to wash off a hot day."

She turned and walked away, following the familiar trail her feet had beaten across her back yard's scraggly patch of grass to the strip of sand. She'd planned to lay sod with the boys closer to fall, but that might not happen now.

Abbie pulled off her T-shirt, draping it nonchalantly across her beach lounger, taking her time. She didn't turn, but she could feel the boys' eyes on her bare back. She didn't wear a bra most days; her breasts were modest, so what was the point? One more thing Johanssen had tried to hold against her. Her feet curled into the sand, searching for dampness.

"It's all right if you don't have trunks," she said. "My back yard is private, and there's no harm in friends taking a swim."

She thought she heard them breathing, or maybe the harsh breaths were hers as her lungs prepared to give up their reign. The sun was unbearable on Abbie's bare skin. Her sides burned like fire as the flaps beneath her ribs opened, swollen rose petals.

The boys didn't answer; probably hadn't moved. She hadn't expected them to, at first.

One after the other, she pulled her long legs out of her jeans, standing at a discreet angle to hide most of her nakedness, like the Venus de Medici. She didn't want them to see her gills, or the rougher patches on her scaly skin. She didn't want to answer questions. She and the boys had spent too much time talking all summer. She wondered why she'd never invited them swimming before.

She dove, knowing just where the lake was deep enough not to scrape her at the rocky floor. The water parted as startled catfish dashed out of her way. Fresh fish was best. That was another thing Abbie had learned that summer.

When her head popped back up above the surface, the boys were looking at each other, weighing the matter. Derek left the porch first, tugging on his tattered denim shorts, hopping on one leg in his hurry. Jack followed, but left his clothes on, arms folded across his chest.

Derek splashed into the water, one polite hand concealing his privates until he was submerged. He did not swim near her, leaving a good ten yards between them. After a tentative silence, he whooped so loudly that his voice might have carried across the lake.

"Whooo-HOOOOO!" Derek's face and eyes were bright, as if he'd never glimpsed the world in color before. "Awesome!"

Abbie's stomach growled. She might have to go after those catfish. She couldn't remember being so hungry. She felt faint.

Jack only made it as far as the shoreline, still wearing his Bermuda shorts. "Not supposed to swim in the lake in summer," he said sullenly, his voice barely loud enough to hear. He slapped at his neck. He stood in a cloud of mosquitoes.

Derek spat, treading water. "That's little *kids,* dumb-ass."

"Nobody's supposed to," Jack said.

"How old are you, six? You don't want to swim—fine. Don't stand staring. It's rude."

Abbie felt invisible during their exchange. She almost told Jack he should follow his best judgment without pressure, but she dove into the silent brown water instead. Young adults had to make decisions for themselves, especially boys, or how would they learn to be men? That was what she and Mary Kay had always believed. Anyone who thought differently was just being politically correct. In ancient times, or in other cultures, a boy Jack's age would already have a wife, a child of his own.

Just look at Mary Kay. Everyone had said her marriage would never work, that he'd been too young when they met. She'd been vilified and punished, and still they survived. The memory of her friend's trial broke Abbie's heart.

As the water massaged her gills, Abbie released her thoughts and concerns about the frivolous world beyond the water. She needed to feed, that was all. She planned to leave the boys to their bickering and swim farther out, where the fish were hiding.

But something large and pale caught her eye above her.

Jack, she realized dimly. Jack had changed his mind, swimming near the surface, his ample belly like a full moon, jiggling with his breaststroke.

That was the first moment Abbie felt a surge of fear, because she finally understood what she'd been up to—what her new body had been preparing her for. Her feet betrayed her, their webs giving her speed as she propelled toward her giant meal. Water slid across her scales.

The beautiful fireball of light above the swimmer gave her pause, a reminder of a different time, another way. The tears that had stung her in her back yard tried to burn her eyes blind, because she saw how it would happen, exactly like a dream: She would claw the boy's belly open, and his scream would sound muffled and far away to her ears. Derek would come to investigate, to try to rescue him from what he would be sure was a gator, but she would overpower Derek next. Her new body would even if she could not.

As Abbie swam directly beneath the swimmer, bathed in the magical light fighting to shield him, she tried to resist the overpowering scent of a meal and remember that he was a boy. Someone's dear son. As Derek (was that the other one's name?) had put it so memorably some time ago—perhaps while he was painting the porch, perhaps in one of her dreams—neither of them yet had been tested by life.

But it was summertime. In Graceville.

In the lake.

Ars Lacuna is a strange city. In this brief tale, we find the daily lives of its citizens revolve around paper, printing, binding, and books. There's also a market for parchment . . .

WALLS OF PAPER, SOFT AS SKIN

Adam Callaway

━━◆━━

Tomai awoke to whispers. Hundreds of whispers. All whispering at once. A whirlwind of soft sound. Whispers in a dozen different languages. On a thousand subjects. Whispers of dark demands. Of heady passions. Of dread and hope. Whispers of anguish and of ecstasy. Whispers so inconsequential as to be forgotten the moment they were whispered. Tomai rolled over and went back to sleep.

He awoke to silence. Silence, and the sound of Ars Lacuna waking up. Autocarriages growled. Book vendors hawked hardcovers. The city was as it always was, and so was he.

Tomai sat on the edge of his bed. His apartment was small. Ten feet on a side. No windows. Layers of parchment enclosed the room. Walls yellowed and tearing. Ceiling shedding like a lizard. Floor worn through.

Opposite his bed was a door. Next to the door was a washbasin. Above the washbasin was a cracked mirror.

A photo hung from one corner. The photo held a girl. Skin the color of hazelnuts. Purple birthmark staining her left cheek. A circle of dark rouge. She was smiling. Tomai stared.

The sun moved, and he grunted. A tall pile of blank pages served as a bed stand. Tomai grabbed a cigarette from the bed stand. He put the paper roll in his mouth. He used his tongue to roll it around. Across his upper lip. From one side of his mouth to the other. Tomai would do this until the cigarette disintegrated. It was what he did every day.

He opened the door. A small pail of water sat in front of him. Small pails of water sat in front of every door. In every hallway. On every level. He grabbed the pail and washed himself in the basin. Spat out the bitter tobacco grit.

He only had one shirt. One pair of pants. No shoes. He brushed his hand along one wall. The parchment was soft with age. He closed the door, walked down the hall, down the stairs, and into the street.

Parchment Run was four blocks away. Nothing to see in between but beggars. Nothing to hear but rapids running. And logs thunking. And blades screeching.

The pole workers shared a common room, a tent, outside of the pulping section of the Run. Poles twenty feet long. Made of a variety of trees. They took up one wall. Misshaped boxes for valuables took up another. They were always empty.

Tomai walked in through a flap.

"Tomai. Did you hear, Tomai? An entire debarking team swam into the termite's jaws. On purpose, Tomai!" Kork said pulling at Tomai's frayed shirt. Kork stood waist high on his tiptoes.

"I can believe it," Tomai said. He looked for a pine or birch pole.

"Really, Tomai? I can't. Debarkers have sickle bone arms. They can swim better than any trout, Tomai! Who'd want to kill themselves with features like that, Tomai?" Kork made wild hand gestures.

"I can believe it."

"Even if they decided, 'Okay, let's do this, girls,' they could have come up with a better way. The autoblades would have made short work of them. The paper sizers down the way too. But being hacked up and digested by a bug the size of a city block though! Really, Tomai? Can you believe it, Tomai?"

Tomai spotted a curved pine pole under a stack of oak. He grabbed it.

"I can believe it."

Kork squinted. "I'm not talking to you anymore today."

Tomai dragged his pole through the inside flap. Into Parchment Run. Where the river exchanged a canopy of sky for corrugated tin. Dozens of pole workers were straightening sawn, debarked logs to enter the jaws of the bug. He took an open spot.

"I can't believe it. I just can't believe it," Kork muttered next to him. Kork's pole was special. The only reserved pole. It was thin. Very thin.

Hours passed. Tomai didn't miss a log. Kork didn't miss a log. Kork didn't miss a moment to speak. Tomai didn't miss his mind.

Above the corrugated tin that enclosed the Run, the day fled. Darkness replaced the light that trickled through holes in the tin. Tomai hardly noticed. The lamps were working tonight.

A woman approached Tomai with a dozen loaves of stale brown bread. She stood between him and Kork, tearing the loaves into chunks and throwing them at the debarkers.

"Tonight," she said. "Behind Xerro's. Bring coin."

The woman walked back the way she came. Further down the Run. Tomai sighed.

Hours passed. Tomai and Kork dragged their poles into the common room.

"Want to go get a drink? Bleeding Antons are only a brass a'piece tonight."

"No."

Kork left without another word. Tomai was thankful. He walked back into the Run.

Xerro's was downriver. After the pulpers and shapers and cutters. Before the printers and binders and dealers. It sold stationary.

Tomai saw the woman from earlier. He knew this woman. She had helped him before. Every time, a different disguise. Always the same smell of resin.

Ms. Resin was dressed as a secretary. A Brothers Publishing House secretary. Floor-length gray skirt. White blouse. Auburn hair loose to the shoulder.

"Coin?" she asked, holding out her hand.

"Parchment?" he asked, holding out his hand.

They exchanged items. Tomai gave her two square copper pieces. A month's wages for a pole worker. She gave him a dozen blank pages.

"I'm running out of people parchment. There needs to be a new plague. Don't you miss the brittle pink skinflakes?" Resin disappeared through a tear in the Run's tin.

It was dark. Staring down, Tomai couldn't even make out his bare feet. He tucked the pages under his arm and left.

The way home was similar to the way there, but different. Two moonbeams instead of two sunbeams. A dead cat. Someone eating it.

He opened his door with a key he kept on twine around his neck, and bolted it once inside.

Tomai grabbed a candle and a metal pan from under his mattress. He placed one on the other. With the pages still under his arm, he sat down on the wooden floor, lit the candle, and set it in front of him.

The pages were blank, and they weren't. Color gradients shifted across each page, from cream to tarnished gold. Small lines, like paper veins, crossed and re-crossed. A watermark stained the third page.

The watermark was a light purple. Shaped not entirely unlike a circle.

Tomai shook. "My girl," he said. "My beautiful girl."

◆━◆

An old woman and a junkie form an unusual alliance in order to do what needs to get done—including dealing with the spell of the Last Triangle

THE LAST TRIANGLE

Jeffrey Ford

I was on the street with nowhere to go, broke, with a habit. It was around Halloween, cold as a motherfucker in Fishmere—part suburb, part crumbling city that never happened. I was getting by, roaming the neighborhoods after dark, looking for unlocked cars to see what I could snatch. Sometimes I stole shit out of people's yards and pawned it or sold it on the street. One night I didn't have enough to cop, and I was in a bad way. There was nobody on the street to even beg from. It was freezing. Eventually I found this house on a corner and noticed an open garage out back. I got in there where it was warmer, lay down on the concrete, and went into withdrawal.

You can't understand what that's like unless you've done it. Remember that *Twilight Zone* where you make your own hell? Like that. I eventually passed out or fell asleep, and woke, shivering, to daylight, unable to get off the floor. Standing in the entrance to the garage was this little old woman with her arms folded, staring down through her bifocals at me. The second she saw I was awake, she turned and walked away. I felt like I'd frozen straight through to my spine during the night and couldn't get up. A splitting headache, and the nausea was pretty intense too. My first thought was to take off, but too much of me just didn't give a shit. The old woman reappeared, but now she was carrying a pistol in her left hand.

"What's wrong with you?" she said.

I told her I was sick.

"I've seen you around town," she said. "You're an addict." She didn't seem freaked out by the situation, even though I was. I managed to get up on one elbow. I shrugged and said, "True."

And then she left again, and a few minutes later came back, toting an electric space heater. She set it down next to me, stepped away and said, "You missed it last night, but there's a cot in the back of the garage. Look," she said, "I'm going to give you some money. Go buy clothes. You can stay here and I'll feed you. If I know you're using, though, I'll call the police. I hope you realize that if you do anything I don't like I'll shoot you." She said it like it was a foregone conclusion, and, yeah, I could actually picture her pulling the trigger.

What could I say? I took the money, and she went back into her house. My first reaction to the whole thing was to laugh. I could score. I struggled up all dizzy and bleary, smelling like the devil's own shit, and stumbled away.

I didn't cop that day, only a small bag of weed. Why? I'm not sure, but there was something about the way the old woman talked to me, her unafraid, straight-up approach. That, maybe, and I was so tired of the cycle of falling hard out of a drug dream onto the street and scrabbling like a three-legged dog for the next fix. By noon, I was pot high, downtown, still feeling shitty, when I passed this old clothing store. It was one of those places like you can't fucking believe is still in operation. The mannequin in the window had on a tan leisure suit. Something about the way the sunlight hit that window display, though, made me remember the old woman's voice, and I had this feeling like I was on an errand for my mother.

I got the clothes. I went back and lived in her garage. The jitters, the chills, the scratching my scalp and forearms were bad, but when I could finally get to sleep, that cot was as comfortable as a bed in a fairy tale. She brought food a couple times a day. She never said much to me, and the gun was always around. The big problem was going to the bathroom. When you get off the junk, your insides really open up. I knew if I went near the house, she'd shoot me. Let's just say I marked the surrounding territory. About two weeks in, she wondered herself and asked me, "Where are you evacuating?"

At first I wasn't sure what she was saying. "Evacuating?" Eventually, I caught on and told her, "Around." She said that I could come in the house to use the downstairs bathroom. It was tough, 'cause every other second I wanted to just bop her on the head, take everything she had, and score like there was no tomorrow. I kept a tight lid on it till one day, when I was sure I was going to blow, a delivery truck pulled up to the side of the house and delivered, to the garage, a set of barbells and a bench. Later when she brought me out some food, she nodded to the weights and said, "Use them before you jump out of your skin. I insist."

Ms. Berkley was her name. She never told me her first name, but I saw it on her mail, "Ifanel." What kind of name is that? She had iron-gray hair, pulled back tight into a bun, and strong green eyes behind the big glasses.

Baggy corduroy pants and a zip-up sweater was her wardrobe. There was a yellow one with flowers around the collar. She was a busy old woman. Quick and low to the ground.

Her house was beautiful inside. The floors were polished and covered with those Persian rugs. Wallpaper and stained-glass windows. But there was none of that goofy shit I remembered my grandmother going in for: suffering Christs, knitted hats on the toilet paper. Every room was in perfect order and there were books everywhere. Once she let me move in from the garage to the basement, I'd see her reading at night, sitting at her desk in what she called her "office." All the lights were out except for this one brass lamp shining right over the book that lay on her desk. She moved her lips when she read. "Good night, Ms. Berkley," I'd say to her and head for the basement door. From down the hall I'd hear her voice come like out of a dream, "Good night." She told me she'd been a history teacher at a college. You could tell she was really smart. It didn't exactly take a genius, but she saw straight through my bullshit.

One morning we were sitting at her kitchen table having coffee, and I asked her why she'd helped me out. I was feeling pretty good then. She said, "That's what you're supposed to do. Didn't anyone ever teach you that?"

"Weren't you afraid?"

"Of you?" she said. She took the pistol out of her bathrobe pocket and put it on the table between us. "There's no bullets in it," she told me. "I went with a fellow who died and he left that behind. I wouldn't know how to load it."

Normally I would have laughed, but her expression made me think she was trying to tell me something. "I'll pay you back," I said. "I'm gonna get a job this week and start paying you back."

"No, I've got a way for you to pay me back," she said and smiled for the first time. I was 99 percent sure she wasn't going to tell me to fuck her, but, you know, it crossed my mind.

Instead, she asked me to take a walk with her downtown. By then it was winter, cold as a witch's tit. Snow was coming. We must have been a sight on the street. Ms. Berkley, marching along in her puffy ski parka and wool hat, blue with gold stars and a tassel. I don't think she was even five foot. I walked a couple of steps behind her. I'm six foot four inches, I hadn't shaved or had a haircut in a long while, and I was wearing this brown suit jacket that she'd found in her closet. I couldn't button it if you had a gun to my head and my arms stuck out the sleeves almost to the elbow. She told me, "It belonged to the dead man."

Just past the library, we cut down an alley, crossed a vacant lot, snow still on the ground, and then hit a dirt road that led back to this abandoned factory. One story, white stucco, all the windows empty, glass on the ground, part of the roof caved in. She led me through a stand of trees around to the left side of the old building.

From where we stood, I could see a lake through the woods. She pointed at the wall and said, "Do you see that symbol in red there?" I looked but all I saw was a couple of *Fucks*.

"I don't see it," I told her.

"Pay attention," she said and took a step closer to the wall. Then I saw it. About the size of two fists. It was like a capital *E* tipped over on its three points, and sitting on its back, right in the middle, was an *o*. "Take a good look at it," she told me. "I want you to remember it."

I stared for a few seconds and told her, "Okay, I got it."

"I walk to the lake almost every day," she said. "This wasn't here a couple of days ago." She looked at me like that was supposed to mean something to me. I shrugged; she scowled. As we walked home, it started to snow.

Before I could even take off the dead man's jacket, she called me into her office. She was sitting at her desk, still in her coat and hat, with a book open in front of her. I came over to the desk, and she pointed at the book. "What do you see there?" she asked. And there it was, the red, knocked-over *E* with the *o* on top.

I said, "Yeah, the thing from before. What is it?"

"The Last Triangle," she said.

"Where's the triangle come in?" I asked.

"The three points of the capital *E* stand for the three points of a triangle."

"So what?"

"Don't worry about it," she said. "Here's what I want you to do. Tomorrow, after breakfast, I want you to take a pad and a pen, and I want you to walk all around the town, everywhere you can think of, and look to see if that symbol appears on any other walls. If you find one, write down the address for it—street and number. Look for places that are abandoned, rundown, burned out."

I didn't want to believe she was crazy, but . . .

I said to her, "Don't you have any real work for me to do—heavy lifting, digging, painting, you know?"

"Just do what I ask you to do."

Ms. Berkley gave me a few bucks and sent me on my way. First things first, I went downtown, scored a couple of joints, bought a forty of Colt. Then I did the grand tour. It was fucking freezing, of course. The sky was brown, and the dead man's jacket wasn't cutting it. I found the first of the symbols on the wall of a closed-down bar. The place had a pink plastic sign that said *Here It Is*, with a silhouette of a woman with an Afro sitting in a martini glass. The *E* was there in red on the plywood of a boarded front window. I had to walk a block each way to figure out the address, but I got it. After that I kept looking. I walked myself sober and then some and didn't get back to the house till nightfall.

When I told Ms. Berkley that I'd found one, she smiled and clapped her hands together. She asked for the address, and I delivered. She set me up with spaghetti and meatballs at the kitchen table. I was tired, but seriously, I felt like a prince. She went down the hall to her office. A few minutes later, she came back with a piece of paper in her hand. As I pushed the plate away, she set the paper down in front of me and then took a seat.

"That's a map of town," she said. I looked it over. There were two dots in red pen and a straight line connecting them. "You see the dots?" she asked.

"Yeah."

"Those are two points of the Last Triangle."

"Okay," I said and thought, "Here we go . . . "

"The Last Triangle is an equilateral triangle; all the sides are equal," she said.

I failed math every year in high school, so I just nodded.

"Since we know these two points, we know that the last point is in one of two places on the map, either east or west." She reached across the table and slid the map toward her. With the red pen, she made two dots and then made two triangles sharing a line down the center. She pushed the map toward me again. "Tomorrow you have to look either here or here," she said, pointing with the tip of the pen.

The next day I found the third one, to the east, just before it got dark. A tall old house, on the edge of an abandoned industrial park. It looked like there'd been a fire. There was an old rusted Chevy up on blocks in the driveway. The *E*-and-*o* thing was spray-painted on the trunk.

When I brought her that info, she gave me the lowdown on the triangle. "I read a lot of books about history," she said, "and I have this ability to remember things I've seen or read. If I saw a phone number once, I'd remember it correctly. It's not a photographic memory; it doesn't work automatically or with everything. Maybe five years ago I read this book on ancient magic, *The Spells of Abriel the Magus*, and I remembered the symbol from that book when I saw it on the wall of the old factory last week. I came home, found the book, and reread the part about the Last Triangle. It's also known as Abriel's Escape or Abriel's Prison.

"Abriel was a thirteenth-century magus . . . magician. He wandered around

Europe and created six powerful spells. The triangle, once marked out, denotes a protective zone in which its creator cannot be harmed. There's a limitation to the size it can be, each leg no more than a mile. At the same time that zone is a sanctuary, it's a trap. The magus can't leave its boundary, ever. To cross it is certain death. For this reason, the spell was used only once, by Abriel, in Dresden, to escape a number of people he'd harmed with his dark arts who had sent their own wizards to kill him. He lived out the rest of his life there, within the Last Triangle, and died at one hundred years of age."

"That's a doozy."

"Pay attention," she said. "For the Last Triangle to be activated, the creator of the triangle must take a life at its geographical center between the time of the three symbols being marked in the world and the next full moon. Legend has it, Abriel killed the baker Ellot Haber to induce the spell."

It took me almost a minute and a half to grasp what she was saying. "You mean, someone's gonna get iced?" I said.

"Maybe."

"Come on, a kid just happened to make that symbol. Coincidence."

"No, remember, a perfect equilateral triangle, each one of the symbols exactly where it should be." She laughed, and, for a second, looked a lot younger.

"I don't believe in magic," I told her. "There's no magic out there."

"You don't have to believe it," she said. "But maybe someone out there does. Someone desperate for protection, willing to believe even in magic."

"That's pretty far fetched," I said, "but if you think there's a chance, call the cops. Just leave me out of it."

"The cops," she said and shook her head. "They'd lock me up with that story."

"Glad we agree on that."

"The center of the triangle on my map," she said, "is the train-station parking lot. And in five nights there'll be a full moon. No one's gotten killed at the station yet, not that I've heard of."

After breakfast she called a cab and went out, leaving me to fix the garbage disposal and wonder about the craziness. I tried to see it her way. She'd told me it was our civic duty to do something, but I wasn't buying any of it. Later that afternoon, I saw her sitting at the computer in her office. Her glasses near the end of her nose, she was reading off the Internet and loading bullets into the magazine clip of the pistol. Eventually she looked up and saw me. "You can find just about anything on the Internet," she said.

"What are you doing with that gun?"

"We're going out tonight."

"Not with that."

She stopped loading. "Don't tell me what to do," she said.

After dinner, around dusk, we set out for the train station. Before we left, she handed me the gun. I made sure the safety was on and stuck it in the side pocket of the brown jacket. While she was out getting the bullets she'd bought two chairs that folded down and fit in small plastic tubes. I carried them. Ms. Berkley held a flashlight and in her ski parka had stashed a pint of blackberry brandy. The night was clear and cold, and a big waxing moon hung over town.

We turned off the main street into an alley next to the hardware store and followed it a long way before it came out on the south side of the train station. There was a rundown one-story building there in the corner of the parking lot. I ripped off the plywood planks that covered the door, and we went in. The place was empty but for some busted-up office furniture, and all the windows were shattered, letting the breeze in. We moved through the darkness, Ms. Berkley leading the way with the flashlight, to a back room with a view of the parking lot and station just beyond it. We set up the chairs and took our seats at the empty window. She killed the light.

"Tell me this is the strangest thing you've ever done," I whispered to her.

She brought out the pint of brandy, unscrewed the top, and took a tug on it. "Life's about doing what needs to get done," she said. "The sooner you figure that out, the better for everyone." She passed me the bottle.

After an hour and a half, my eyes had adjusted to the moonlight and I'd scanned every inch of that cracked, potholed parking lot. Two trains a half-hour apart rolled into the station's elevated platform, and from what I could see, no one got on or off. Ms. Berkley was doing what needed to be done—namely, snoring. I took out a joint and lit up. I'd already polished off the brandy. I kept an eye on the old lady, ready to flick the joint out the window if I saw her eyelids flutter. The shivering breeze did a good job of clearing out the smoke.

At around 3:00 a.m., I'd just about nodded off, when the sound of a train pulling into the station brought me back. I sat up and leaned toward the window. It took me a second to clear my eyes and focus. When I did, I saw the silhouette of a person descending the stairs of the raised platform. The figure passed beneath the light at the front of the station, and I could see it was a young woman, carrying a briefcase. I wasn't quite sure what the fuck I was supposed to be doing, so I tapped Ms. Berkley. She came awake with a splutter and looked a little sheepish for having corked off. I said, "There's a woman heading to her car. Should I shoot her?"

"Very funny," she said and got up to stand closer to the window.

I'd figured out which of the few cars in the parking lot belonged to the young woman. She looked like the white-Honda type. Sure enough, she made a beeline for it.

"There's someone else," said Ms. Berkley. "Coming out from under the trestle."

"Where?"

"Left," she said, and I saw him, a guy with a long coat and hat. He was moving fast, heading for the young woman. Ms. Berkley grabbed my arm and squeezed it. "Go," she said. I lunged up out of the chair, took two steps, and got dizzy from having sat for so long. I fumbled in my pocket for the pistol as I groped my way out of the building. Once I hit the air, I was fine, and I took off running for the parking lot. Even as jumped up as I was, I thought, "I'm not gonna shoot anyone," and left the gun's safety on.

The young woman saw me coming before she noticed the guy behind her. I scared her, and she ran the last few yards to her car. I watched her messing around with her keys and didn't notice the other guy was also on a flat-out run. As I passed the white Honda, the stranger met me and cracked me in the jaw like a pro. I went down hard but held onto the gun. As soon as I came to, I sat up. The guy—I couldn't get a good look at his face—drew a blade from his left sleeve. By then the woman was in the car, though, and it screeched off across the parking lot.

He turned, brandishing the long knife, and started for me.

You better believe the safety came off then. That instant, I heard Ms. Berkley's voice behind me. "What's the meaning of this?" she said in a stern voice. The stranger looked up, and then turned and ran off, back into the shadows beneath the trestle.

"We've got to get out of here," she said and helped me to my feet. "If that girl's got any brains, she'll call the cops." Ms. Berkley could run pretty fast. We made it back to the building, got the chairs, the empty bottle, and as many cigarette butts as I could find, and split for home. We stayed off the main street and wound our way back through the residential blocks. We didn't see a soul.

I couldn't feel how cold I was till I got back in the house. Ms. Berkley made tea. Her hands shook a little. We sat at the kitchen table in silence for a long time.

Finally, I said, "Well, you were right."

"The gun was a mistake, but if you didn't have it, you'd be dead now," she said.

"Not to muddy the waters here, but that's closer to dead than I want to get. We're gonna have to go to the police, but if we do, that'll be it for me."

"You tried to save her," said Ms. Berkley. "Very valiant, by the way."

I laughed. "Tell that to the judge when he's looking over my record."

She didn't say anything else, but left and went to her office. I fell asleep on the cot in the basement with my clothes on. It was warm down there by the furnace. I had terrible dreams of the young woman getting her throat cut but was too tired to wake from them. Eventually, I came to with a hand on my shoulder and Ms. Berkley saying, "Thomas." I sat up quickly, sure I'd forgotten to do something. She said, "Relax," and rested her hand for a second on my chest. She sat on the edge of the cot with her hat and coat on.

"Did you sleep?" I asked.

"I went back to the parking lot after the sun came up. There were no police around. Under the trestle, where the man with the knife had come from, I found these." She took a handful of cigarette butts out of her coat pocket and held them up.

"Anybody could have left them there at any time," I said. "You read too many books."

"Maybe, maybe not," she said.

"He must have stood there waiting for quite a while, judging from how many butts you've got there."

She nodded. "This is a serious man," she said. "Say he's not just a lunatic, but an actual magician?"

"Magician," I said and snorted. "More like a creep who believes his own bullshit."

"Watch the language," she said.

"Do we go back to the parking lot tonight?" I asked.

"No, there'll be police there tonight. I'm sure that girl reported the incident. I have something for you to do. These cigarettes are a Spanish brand, Ducados. I used to know someone who smoked them. The only store in town that sells them is over by the park. Do you know Maya's Newsstand?"

I nodded.

"I think he buys his cigarettes there."

"You want me to scope it? How am I supposed to know whether it's him or not? I never got a good look at him."

"Maybe by the imprint of your face on his knuckles?" she said.

I couldn't believe she was breaking my balls, but when she laughed, I had to.

"Take my little camera with you," she said.

"Why?

"I want to see what you see," she said. She got up then and left the basement. I got dressed. While I ate, she showed me how to use the camera. It was a little electronic job, but amazing, with telephoto capability and a little window you could see your pictures in. I don't think I'd held a camera in ten years.

I sat on a bench in the park, next to a giant pine tree, and watched the newsstand across the street. I had my forty in a brown paper bag and a five-dollar joint in my jacket. The day was clear and cold, and people came and went on the street, some of them stopping to buy a paper or cigs from Maya. One thing I noticed was that nobody came to the park, the one nice place in crumbling Fishmere.

All afternoon and nothing criminal, except for one girl's miniskirt. She was my first photo—exhibit A. After that I took a break and went back into the park, where there was a gazebo looking out across a small lake. I fired up the joint and took another pic of some geese. Mostly I watched the sun on the water and wondered what I'd do once the Last Triangle hoodoo played itself out. Part of me wanted to stay with Ms. Berkley, and the other part knew it wouldn't be right. I'd been on the scag for fifteen years, and now somebody's making breakfast and dinner every day. Things like the camera, a revelation to me. She even had me reading a book, *The Professor's House* by Willa Cather—slow as shit, but somehow I needed to know what happened next to old Godfrey St. Peter. The food, the weights, and staying off the hard stuff made me strong.

Late in the afternoon, he came to the newsstand. I'd been in such a daze, the sight of him there, like he just materialized, made me jump. My hands shook a little as I telephotoed in on him. He paid for two packs of cigs, and I snapped the picture. I wasn't sure if I'd caught his mug. He was pretty well hidden by the long coat's collar and the hat. There was no time to check the shot. As he moved away down the sidewalk, I stowed the camera in my pocket and followed him, hanging back fifty yards or so.

He didn't seem suspicious. Never looked around or stopped, but just kept moving at the same brisk pace. Only when it came to me that he was walking us in a circle did I get that he was on to me. At that point, he made a quick left into an alley. I followed. The alley was a short one with a brick wall at the end. He'd vanished. I walked cautiously into the shadows and looked around behind the dumpsters. There was nothing there. A gust of wind lifted the old newspapers and litter into the air, and I'll admit I was scared. On the way back to the house, I looked over my shoulder about a hundred times.

I handed Ms. Berkley the camera in her office. She took a wire out of her desk drawer and plugged one end into the camera and one into the computer. She typed some shit, and then the first picture appeared. It was the legs.

"Finding the focus with that shot?" she asked.

"Everyone's a suspect," I said.

"Foolishness," she murmured. She liked the geese, said it was a nice composition. Then the one of the guy at the newsstand came up, and, yeah, I nailed it. A really clear profile of his face. Eyes like a hawk and a sharp nose. He had white hair and a thick white mustache.

"Not bad," I said, but Ms. Berkley didn't respond. She was staring hard at the picture and her mouth was slightly open. She reached out and touched the screen.

"You know him?" I asked.

"You're wearing his jacket," she said. Then she turned away, put her face in her hands.

I left her alone and went into the kitchen. I made spaghetti the way she'd showed me. While stirring the sauce, I said to my reflection in the stove hood, "Now the dead man's back, and he's the evil magician?" Man, I really wanted to laugh the whole thing off, but I couldn't forget the guy's disappearing act.

I put two plates of spaghetti down on the kitchen table and then went to fetch Ms. Berkley. She told me to go away. Instead I put my hands on her shoulders and said, "Come on, you should eat something." Then, applying as little pressure as possible, I sort of lifted her as she stood. In the kitchen, I held her chair for her and gave her a cup of tea. My spaghetti was undercooked and the sauce was cold, but still, not bad. She used her napkin to dry her eyes.

"The dead man looks pretty good for a dead man," I said.

"It was easier to explain by telling you he was dead. Who wants the embarrassment of saying someone left them?"

"I get it," I said.

"I think most people would, but still . . . "

"This clears something up for me," I told her. "I always thought it was pretty strange that two people in the same town would know about Abriel and the Last Triangle. I mean, what's the chances?"

"The book is his," she said. "Years after he left, it just became part of my library, and eventually I read it. Now that I think of it, he read a lot of books about the occult."

"Who is he?"

"His name is Lionel Brund. I met him years ago, when I was in my thirties. I was already teaching at the college, and I owned this house. We both were at a party hosted by a colleague. He was just passing through and knew someone who knew someone at the party. We hit it off. He had great stories about his travels. He liked to laugh. It was fun just going to the grocery store with him. My first real romance. A very gentle man."

The look on her face made me say, "But?"

She nodded. "But he owned a gun, and I had no idea what kind of work he did, although he always had plenty of money. Parts of his life were a secret. He'd go away for a week or two at a time on some 'business' trip. I didn't mind that, because there were parts of my life I wanted to keep to myself as well. We were together, living in this house, for over two years, and then, one day, he was gone. I waited for him to come back for a long time and then moved on, made my own life."

"Now you do what needs to get done," I said.

She laughed. "Exactly."

"Lionel knows we're onto him. He played me this afternoon, took me in a circle and then was gone with the wind. It creeped me."

"I want to see him," she said. "I want to talk to him."

"He's out to kill somebody to protect himself," I said.

"I don't care," she said.

"Forget it," I told her and then asked for the gun. She pushed it across the table to me.

"He could come after us," I said. "You've got to be careful." She got up to go into her office, and I drew the butcher knife out of its wooden holder on the counter and handed it to her. I wanted her to get how serious things were. She took it but said nothing. I could tell she was lost in the past.

I put the gun, safety off, on the stand next to my cot and lay back with a head full of questions. I stayed awake for a long while before I eventually gave in. A little bit after I dozed off, I was half wakened by the sound of the phone ringing upstairs. I heard Ms. Berkley walk down the hall and pick up. Her voice was a distant mumble. Then I fell asleep for a few minutes, and the first thing I heard when I came to again was the sound of the back door closing. It took me a minute to put together that he'd called and she'd gone to meet him.

I got dressed in a flash, but put on three T-shirts instead of wearing Lionel's jacket. I thought he might have the power to spook it since it belonged to him. It took me a couple of seconds to decide whether to leave the gun behind as well. But I was shit scared so I shoved it in the waist of my jeans and took off. I ran dead out to the train-station parking lot. Luckily there were no cops there, but there wasn't anybody else either. I went in the station, searched beneath the trestles, and went back to the rundown building we'd sat in. Nothing.

As I walked back to the house, I tried to think of where he would have asked to meet her. I pictured all the places I'd been to in the past few weeks. An image of Ms. Berkley's map came to mind, the one of town with the red dots and the triangles, east and west. I'd not found a triangle point to the west, and as I considered that, I recalled the point I had found in the east, the symbol spray-painted on the trunk of an old car up on blocks. It came to me—say that one didn't count because it wasn't on a building, connected to the ground. That was a fake. Maybe he knew somehow Ms. Berkley would notice the symbols and he wanted to throw her off.

Then it struck me: what if there was a third symbol in the west I just didn't see? I tried to picture the map as the actual streets it represented and figure where the center of a western triangle would be. At first it seemed way too complicated, just a jumble of frustration, but I took a few deep breaths, and, recalling the streets I'd walked before, realized the spot must be somewhere in the park across the street from Maya's Newsstand. It was a hike, and I knew I had to pace myself, but the fact that I'd figured out Lionel's twists and turns gave me a burst of energy. What I really wanted was to tell Ms. Berkley how I'd thought it through. Then I realized she might already be dead.

Something instinctively drew me toward the gazebo. It was a perfect center for a magician's prison. The moonlight was on the lake. I thought I heard them talking, saw their shadows sitting on the bench, smelled the smoke of Ducados, but when I took the steps and leaned over to catch my breath, I realized it was all in my mind. The place was empty and still. The geese called from out on the lake. I sat down on the bench and lit a cigarette. Only when I resigned myself to just returning to the house, it came to me I had one more option: to find the last point of the western triangle.

I knew it was a long shot at night, looking without a flashlight for something I couldn't find during the day. My only consolation was that since Lionel hadn't taken Ms. Berkley to the center of his triangle, he might not intend to use her as his victim.

I was exhausted, and although I set out from the gazebo jogging toward my best guess as to where the last point was, I was soon walking. The street map of town with the red triangles would flash momentarily in my memory and then disappear. I went up a street that was utterly dark, and the wind followed me. From there, I turned and passed a row of closed factory buildings.

The symbol could have been anywhere, hiding in the dark. Finally, there was a cross street, and I walked down a block of row homes, some boarded, some with bars on the windows. That path led to an industrial park. Beneath a dim streetlight, I stopped and tried to picture the map, but it was no use.

I was totally lost. I gave up and turned back in the direction I thought Ms. Berkley's house would be.

One block outside the industrial park, I hit a street of old four-story apartment buildings. The doors were off the hinges, and the moonlight showed no reflection in the shattered windows. A neighborhood of vacant lots and dead brick giants. Halfway down the block, hoping to find a left turn, I just happened to look up and see an unbroken window, yellow lamplight streaming out. From where I stood, I could only see the ceiling of the room, but faint silhouettes moved across it. I took out the gun. There was no decent reason why I thought it was them, but I felt drawn to the place as if under a spell.

I took the stone steps of the building, and when I tried the door, it pushed open. I thought this was strange, but I figured he might have left it ajar for Ms. Berkley. Inside, the foyer was so dark and there was no light on the first landing. I found the first step by inching forward and feeling around with my foot. The last thing I needed was three flights of stairs. I tried to climb without a sound, but the planks creaked unmercifully. "If they don't hear me coming," I thought, "they're both dead."

As I reached the fourth floor, I could hear noises coming from the room. It sounded like two people were arguing and wrestling around. Then I distinctly heard Ms. Berkley cry out. I lunged at the door, cracked it on the first pounce and busted it in with the second. Splinters flew, and the chain lock ripped out with a pop. I stumbled into the room, the gun pointing forward, completely out of breath. It took me a second to see what was going on.

There they were, in a bed beneath the window in the opposite corner of the room, naked, frozen by my intrusion, her legs around his back. Ms. Berkley scooted up and quickly wrapped the blanket around herself, leaving old Lionel out in the cold. He jumped up quick, dick flopping, and got into his boxers.

"What the hell," I whispered.

"Go home, Thomas," she said.

"You're coming with me," I said.

"I can handle this," she said.

"Who's after you?" I said to Lionel. "For what?"

He took a deep breath. "Phantoms more cruel than you can imagine, my boy. I lived my young life recklessly, like you, and its mistakes have multiplied and hounded me ever since."

"You're a loser," I said and it sounded so stupid. Especially when it struck me that Lionel might have been old, but he looked pretty strong.

"Sorry, son," he said and drew that long knife from a scabbard on the nightstand next to the bed. "It's time to sever ties."

"Run," said Ms. Berkley.

I thought, "Fuck this guy," and pulled out the gun.

Ms. Berkley jumped on Lionel, but he shrugged her off with a sharp push that landed her back on the bed. "This one's not running," he said. "I can tell."

I was stunned for a moment by Ms. Berkley's nakedness. But as he advanced a step, I raised the gun and told him, "Drop the knife."

He said, "Be careful; you're hurting it."

At first his words didn't register, but then, in my hand, instead of a gun, I felt a frail wriggling thing with a heartbeat. I released my grasp, and a bat flew up to circle around the ceiling. In the same moment, I heard the gun hit the wooden floor and knew he'd tricked me with magic.

He came toward me slowly, and I whipped off two of my T-shirts and wrapped them around my right forearm. He sliced the air with the blade a few times as I crouched down and circled away from him. He lunged fast as a snake, and I got caught against a dresser. He cut me on the stomach and the right shoulder. The next time he came at me, I kicked a footstool in front of him and managed a punch to the side of his head. Lionel came back with a half dozen more slices, each marking me. The T-shirts on my arm were in shreds, as was the one I wore.

I kept watching that knife, and that's how he got me, another punch to the jaw worse than the one in the station parking lot. I stumbled backward and he followed with the blade aimed at my throat. What saved me was that Ms. Berkley grabbed him from behind. He stopped to push her off again, and I caught my balance and took my best shot to the right side of his face. The punch scored, he fell backward into the wall, and the knife flew in the air. I tried to catch it as it fell but only managed to slice my fingers. I picked it up by the handle and when I looked, Lionel was steam-rolling toward me again.

"Thomas," yelled Ms. Berkley from where she'd landed. I was stunned, and automatically pushed the weapon forward into the bulk of the charging magician. He stopped in his tracks, teetered for a second, and fell back onto his ass. He sat there on the rug, legs splayed, with that big knife sticking out of his stomach. Blood seeped around the blade and puddled in front of him.

Ms. Berkley was next to me, leaning on my shoulder. "Pay attention," she said.

I snapped out of it and looked down at Lionel. He was sighing more than breathing and staring at the floor.

"If he dies," said Ms. Berkley, "you inherit the spell of the Last Triangle."

"That's right," Lionel said. Blood came from his mouth with the words. "Wherever you are at dawn, that will be the center of your world." He laughed. "For the rest of your life you will live in a triangle within the rancid town of Fishmere."

Ms. Berkley found the gun and picked it up. She went to the bed and grabbed one of the pillows.

"Is that true?" I said and started to panic.

Lionel nodded, laughing. Ms. Berkley took up the gun again and then wrapped the pillow around it. She walked over next to Lionel, crouched down, and touched the pillow to the side of his head.

"What are you doing?" I asked.

Ms. Berkley squinted one eye and steadied her left arm with her right hand while keeping the pillow in place.

"What else?" said Lionel, spluttering blood bubbles. "What needs to be done."

The pillow muffled the sound of the shot somewhat as feathers flew everywhere. Lionel dropped onto his side without magic, the hole in his head smoking. I wasn't afraid anyone would hear. There wasn't another soul for three blocks. Ms. Berkley checked his pulse. "The Last Triangle is mine now," she said. "I have to get home by dawn." She got dressed while I stood in the hallway.

I don't remember leaving Lionel's building, or passing the park or Maya's Newsstand. We were running through the night, across town, as the sky lightened in the distance. Four blocks from home, Ms. Berkley gave out and started limping. I picked her up and, still running, carried her the rest of the way. We were in the kitchen, the tea whistle blowing, when the birds started to sing and the sun came up.

She poured the tea for us and said, "I thought I could talk Lionel out of his plan, but he wasn't the same person anymore. I could see the magic's like a drug; the more you use it, the more it pushes you out of yourself and takes over."

"Was he out to kill me or you?" I asked.

"He was out to get himself killed. I'd promised to do the job for him before you showed up. He knew we were onto him and he tried to fool us with the train-station scam, but once he heard my voice that night, he said he knew he couldn't go through with it. He just wanted to see me once more, and then I was supposed to cut his throat."

"You would have killed him?" I said.

"I did."

"You know, before I knifed him?"

"He told me the phantoms and fetches that were after him knew where he was, and it was only a matter of days before they caught up with him."

"What was it exactly he did?"

"He wouldn't say, but he implied that it had to do with loving me. And I really think he thought he did."

"What do you think?" I asked.

Ms. Berkley interrupted me. "You've got to get out of town," she said. "When they find Lionel's body, you'll be one of the usual suspects, what with your wandering around drinking beer and smoking pot in public."

"Who told you that?" I said.

"Did I just fall off the turnip truck yesterday?"

Ms. Berkley went to her office and returned with a roll of cash for me. I didn't even have time to think about leaving, to miss my cot and the weights, and the meals. The cab showed up and we left. She had her map of town with the triangles on it and had already drawn a new one—its center, her kitchen. We drove for a little ways and then she told the cab driver to pull over and wait. We were in front of a closed-down gas station on the edge of town. She got out and I followed her.

"I paid the driver to take you two towns over to Willmuth. There's a bus station there. Get a ticket and disappear," she said.

"What about you? You're stuck in the triangle."

"I'm bounded in a nutshell," she said.

"Why'd you take the spell?"

"You don't need it. You just woke up. I have every confidence that I'll be able to figure a way out of it. It's amazing what you can find on the Internet."

"A magic spell?" I said.

"Understand this," she said. "Spells are made to be broken." She stepped closer and reached her hands to my shoulders. I leaned down. She kissed me on the forehead. "Not promises, though," she said and turned away, heading home.

"Ms. Berkley," I called after her.

"Stay clean," she yelled without looking.

Back in the cab, I said, "Willmuth," and leaned against the window. The driver started the car, and we sailed through an invisible boundary, into the world.

Booklovers can be fanatical in their devotion to books and books can be very dangerous things . . .

AFTER-WORDS

Glen Hirshberg

⟹

Prologue

The first bombing occurred on a fogbound summer Saturday night, on the just-vacated premises of Harbor Lights Books, in the midst of the 7th Annual Naked Bike Ride. The damage proved minimal: a few blown-out windows; a foot-long splinter of wood driven through the windshield of a parked police car; an elderly upstairs neighbor rumbled out of bed and sent shrieking down the stairwell in her nightfrock, convinced of an earthquake, just as the first bikers swarmed past in their goose-pimpled, genital-beribboned glory. Days elapsed before anyone realized there'd actually *been* an explosion.

The second bomb went off near Fisherman's Wharf in the middle of the night, in the exact spot where that half-senile bookwagon man tried to open a Left Bank-style antiquarian stall in the shadows of the shuttered Barnes and Noble. It was during the next day's investigation that someone finally realized that the old card-catalogue notecards scattered amid the refuse in both locations weren't debris. Were, in fact, messages. From the bombers.

The notecards really had come from some long-extinct branch of the San Francisco Public Library. The book titles on the fronts of the cards seemed random, at first—*Insects Do the Strangest Things,* Ferlinghetti's *Love in the Days of Rage*—until police found the one marked *Tom "the Bomb" Tracy and the Play that Shook San Francisco.* Only then did some bright young sergeant think to flip the cards over, take another look at that seemingly innocuous stamp on the back: *Property of the Library.*

We'd heard about the Library before then, of course. Seen their self-proclaimed leader standing on his milk-crate under the Clocktower on weekday evenings. With his goatee and his stick-figure legs and his bleat of a voice, he reminded some of Satan, and some of Pan. We'd seen his followers, too. Most were dropouts from the gutted comp-lit program at San Francisco State, plus some runaways and junkies, all of them sallow, lurking around the Book Depots near Hunter's Point and Potrero Hill. It was their uniform appearance that first marked them: tan overcoats, the pockets stuffed with moldy hardbacks scavenged from the Depots; black, rubber sandals; gaunt faces; most of all, that paper-white skin tone, those eyes blinking fast even against the lights from street-lamps, which drove some online wag to name them Morlocks.

And yet, somehow, it hadn't occurred to us to fear them until that moment. Within hours of the bright young sergeant's discovery, a SWAT team and the entire Homeland Security unit of the Bay Area Police descended upon Library headquarters en masse, arresting everyone in sight and dragging Erick Kinney, who'd taken to calling himself the Librarian, out of the group's warehouse headquarters before rapt television cameras in handcuffs and ankle-chains.

"Do you have any comment?" one reporter yelled as Kinney was hustled past.

And Kinney had somehow dragged himself to a stop. One hand lifted against the glare of the lights, narrow eyes stutter-blinking, satyr-goatee wagging in the misting rain, Manson-smile dancing across his face. "Book 'em, Danno," he'd said. Then he was shoved forward into a squad car.

But despite a furious three-day search involving several dozen officers, the police found nothing more incriminating than a few small baggies of hash scattered amid the dust and food scraps and sleeping-mats and piles of reclaimed, moldering books in the warehouse. Late on a Sunday evening, to none of the fanfare with which he had been arrested, Erick Kinney was returned to his cavernous home and his adoring disciples.

The next bombing, of the rug store that had once housed the legendary Allen Ginsberg/Gary Snyder Six Gallery reading, was bigger. It blew out windows more than a block away and maimed a security guard who'd unexpectedly returned to his post to get his coffee thermos. This time, bomb crews confiscated every mat and scavenged book, testing repeatedly for explosive residue while BATF officials on loan from Washington grilled the whole group. That investigation, too, turned up nothing. There was talk of holding Erick Kinney as an enemy combatant, and also of condemning the so-called Library and driving all of Kinney's followers onto the streets.

Gradually, though, over a period of weeks, the investigation lost momentum. And with virtually all of San Francisco's bookstores now closed, and the libraries long-since eliminated or reduced to weekend hours, the bombings ceased, and the city and Erick Kinney seemed to reach an uneasy peace. Police still kept the building under surveillance. And Kinney still showed up from time to time on his street-corner at dusk, looking more pathetically thin and less threatening with each appearance. He bleated away, regaling tourists and passers-by with his agitprom poems about rotting fruit and dead brain cells. Sometimes people tossed coins at his feet.

Meanwhile, the Depots swelled with unwanted books, and the Morlocks from the Library took them over, combing the rows and rows of paperbacks, occasionally spiriting away volumes to their warehouse. And Erick Kinney joined the Naked Bike Paraders and the Beatniks and Emperor Norton on the roll-call of San Francisco's legendary utopian cranks, forever hearkening back to an age few of them actually believed had existed, or else heralding a new dawn even fewer thought would ever come.

AFTER-WORDS
THE SECOND BOOK DEPOSITORY STORY

" . . . whilst evil is expected, we fear; but when it is certain, we despair."
—Robert Burton, *The Anatomy of Melancholy*

Aaron came back on a damp, foggy night in early June. I'd just shown Mrs. Morton out the clinic's front door. She'd cursed my name, spit on the linoleum in the waiting room, and rebuffed my offer to walk her to the bus. I stood under the dripping overhang anyway and watched her edge down the block, through the swarms of homeless people already emerging out of the mist to perch against the shuttered windows of the shelter next door, even though dinner wasn't for over an hour yet. She didn't actually need the motorized wheelchair I'd offered to make Medicaid provide for her yet. And the drugs she'd begged me for, weeping, gripping my lab-coat in her clawed hands, might actually have helped, if only temporarily.

But she wouldn't have been able to take the drugs anyway. Her dealer-grandson would have ripped them from her hands the second she got back to her one-room apartment. Maybe he wouldn't kill her for not coming home with them. Some of my patient's grandsons let them live.

Retreating inside, I locked the door, making straight for my sanctuary in the back. I did notice, as I turned the knob, that the lights were already on, reprimanded myself for the waste and in the same moment realized I *hadn't* left them on, and the shadow separated from the shelves along the back wall and lurched toward me.

Gasping, I stumbled back, tripping toward the nearest examination room so I could lock myself in. Hands grabbed me around both shoulders and spun me around.

"Aunt A., it's me," he said.

I recognized the voice instantly, of course. But he was backlit by the lamp in my sanctuary. And his presence was so unexpected, and I'd dreamed of it for so hopelessly long, that it still took me a moment to understand what was happening.

"*Aaron?*"

My hands flew up automatically to hug him, pull his face to my shoulder, but he flinched back. I stared at him, silhouetted against my bookcases. There were flakes of what looked like sawdust in his hair, and the grit on his hands and throat had thickened and coagulated into little black spider-shapes. I imagined them scurrying up his sleeves, down his collarbone into the drooping neck of his threadbare sweatshirt. Tears welled in my eyes.

"You look filthy," I said. "Happy birthday."

He flinched again, ran a shaky hand through his mess of dark curls.

"Aaron, my god, are you all right?"

"You still remember my birthday?"

The fury that had also been massing these last four years, ever since he'd walked out of his father's life and mine, erupted from me. "If you were dead a hundred years, I'd remember your birthday, you stupid, selfish—"

"You're not my mother, Aunt A."

"I'm not your aunt, either. So just A. Okay?"

Squinting his eyes, he looked at me, in that wondrous way he'd had even when I'd first met him, when he was three years old. A gaze so quiet it could lure mice from their hiding places, baby oak trees from their acorns. That's how I'd put in the bedtime stories I used to tell him when he was four and five, during the years I'd lived with and almost won the love of his recently widowed, lost, marvelous father. The saddest, best years of my life.

"Go wash your face," I said, and felt myself smile. "Your hands, too. No touching my books with those hands."

I got just a ghost of a smile. He moved off toward the bathroom, limping visibly, and twice he had to put his hands out to steady himself against the wall. *What had they done to him in the goddamn Library?* The home he'd traded his life and my love and his father's love for.

Out of habit, I went to the shelves, trailed my fingers along the spines. The sagas-and-wonders section, Norse gods and *Kwaidan* and Pu Songling. Because they'd always been Aaron's favorites, back when he'd still stopped here on his way home from school and let me read to him. And because this was clearly a night for fox spirits and changelings: fog in summer; my patients spitting curses; Aaron coming back.

Through a fresh swell of tears, I realized I'd better call Oliver, let him know his son was alive. I took a step toward my desk and Aaron reappeared in the doorway.

"Well?" he said.

In truth, he looked better than I'd worried he would. He was gaunt, all right, still grit-encrusted everywhere but his face and hands, pasty in that trademark Library way. But his hair, though filthy, shone its familiar, lustrous black, and his dark eyes still flashed with mischief-specks of hazel and green. Fox-spirit eyes, all right.

"I'm calling your dad."

"What for?"

"To tell him you're all right, what do you think?"

"What makes you think he gives a shit?"

"Aaron, you can't really think—"

"More to the point, what makes you think he wants to hear it from you? God, I've never understood it. Why are you still friends with him. Why did you let him treat you like that?"

"What? Aaron, you don't know anything about it. And it was a long time ago. I still care—"

"I need your help," he said, and one of his legs quivered visibly, and he almost fell down.

Dropping the phone, I moved fast around my desk, put my hand to his cheek, then pulled him against me. "You've got a fever."

He pushed me away, steadied himself. "Not me," he murmured. Then he looked me up and down. "You're looking pretty undernourished yourself, Aunt A." Another ghost-smile.

I couldn't tell if he was concerned or teasing, and I didn't care. "Then let's go eat. Saigon Sandwich Shop. When's the last time? I'll get my coat."

"I need you to come to the Library," he said, and the hope I'd almost allowed myself froze in my chest.

"Aaron," I started, after a few silent moments, "I can't—"

"Oh, don't start, Aunt A. Christ, sometimes you really are like him." The contempt in his voice hit me like spittle. "I'm not asking you to join. Or to do anything that might help the cause. It's not like either you or my father understand about why saving books from extinction might be worth fighting for or anything, how could you?" He flung a single, ironic wave toward my shelves.

"So why are we going there?" I said.

"Because he's sick."

"Who's sick?"

"Erick Kinney."

Whatever else I'd meant to say evaporated from my lips. "The *Librarian*, Erick Kinney?"

"Yes, The Librarian Erick Kinney. He's really sick. I mean, a lot of us are sick. Bad flu bug or something. But he's all twisted up. I think he's going to die."

For a long moment, I just looked at him. My long-ago almost-stepson. The closest I was ever likely to get, now, to an actual son. Once upon a time—not so long ago—when he'd still wanted me in his life, that had seemed very nearly enough.

"I'll get my coat and my keys," I said.

"You can't take your car down there. To the Library. It's not safe."

"My Saturn? Too yellow, you think?"

"Jesus Christ, that's still your car? What is it, twenty years old? Aren't you a doctor?"

"Probably still got the dirt from our Sequoia trip."

"The one we took when I was twelve?"

"You'll find it under the dirt from the decade since then."

"We can take that car," Aaron said. This time, his smile was bright and unexpected and gentle. I was so grateful that I almost cried out, but controlled myself.

He leaned his head back, rolled it very slowly around his shoulders, stopped halfway with a wince.

"Are you all right, Aaron?"

"Get your keys."

"I'm getting you antibiotics, too."

"Later."

The homeless had already gone in to dinner, and the smell of burnt tomatoes and chicken grease wafted from the doors of the shelter. From somewhere not far, metal clanged, but we were the only things moving on the entire block. All around us, forever leaning and tilting on its hills, San Francisco rode the waves of marine layer like a fishing trawler.

"Isn't it a little bright yet for Morlocks?" I teased. "Moon might still peek through."

"Funny, Aunt A."

He kept putting his hands in the small of his back, stretching. Once, stumbling on a raised square of sidewalk, he unleashed a violent, unintentional grunt.

"Aaron, what's wrong? Come on, seriously. Are you really sick? Let me help." We'd reached my car, and I watched him ease in, tilting sideways to keep his back straight.

Once settled, he glanced up. "It's just from crawling. You know, around the Book Depots. Occupational hazard."

And badge of distinction, apparently. "Bay Bridge Base, right? Somewhere down there?"

Traffic proved predictably dismal. Wisps of fog drifted through the dead ducts of my Saturn's fan, floating between and around us. I couldn't decide whether I was warm or cold, and didn't care. We didn't speak. It felt as though we'd cast ourselves adrift, floated into the bay. I kept my eyes on the road and hoped we'd never arrive.

But all too soon, as we reached the empty warehouses and glass-strewn lots of the wasteland under the Bay Bridge, Aaron began pointing me to the right. Then to the left. I saw the building before he told me to stop, recognizing it from newspaper photographs.

"That's it, isn't it?" I cut the engine, let the car drift to a stop against a curb that in classic Frisco fashion wasn't long enough even for my Saturn. Somehow, I suspected the parking patrol wouldn't be by. I pointed toward the mottled, rectangular gray and green warehouse, hunched between two much larger derelict structures on either side. "That's the Library."

"There's no place like home," Aaron said quietly. Lovingly. "There's no place like home. There's no place like home."

"Stop it," I told him. "You sound—"

"Brainwashed? Isn't that what you think I am? What we all are? SLA'd? Jonestowned?"

"Well? Are you?"

Aaron just pushed open his door, grimacing as he pulled himself from the car. "Come and see."

The fog felt warmer, here, almost fetid. It had been such a strange, damp summer. The street was devoid not only of people but other cars. A few blocks to the right, just visible through the mist, the glassy towers of the latest Rincon Hill revitalization project blazed like great, blue lighthouses. They were mostly empty, too, I knew. Prospective renters had vanished with the housing bust.

"I'm going to have to blindfold you so you don't see the secret knock," Aaron said.

"You try it, I'm gone," I told him.

"Kidding, Aunt A. Gullible as ever, I see." He put an arm around my shoulder, squeezed me. "I've missed you," he said.

Through new tears, I watched him scoop a handful of pebbles off the curb and pitch them at the lowered, metal door of the Library. The clatter they made seemed farther away than it should have, like children's footsteps racing around a corner.

Nothing moved or changed. The fog had a stench, here, to go with its disconcerting warmth: cat urine, old tar, mold.

"Maybe they didn't teach *you* the secret knock," I said.

The Library door hoisted itself slowly open.

It was like a cave. No overhead lights. Just a few glimmers floating in what appeared to be a single, cavernous room. No one moving. Fingers of fog began to walk up my back.

"Aaron, why did you bring me here?"

He looked genuinely surprised. "I told you why."

"I just want to make this clear. Whatever rejection you're imagining, it was all on your side, at least as far as I'm concerned. I can't speak for your dad. You hear me? I love you."

"I know you love me, Aunt A. I love you, too."

"But I reject this."

"You don't know anything about this."

"I reject brilliant young people living in rank poverty as some transcendent, subversive statement against the status-quo. I reject malnourishment-by-choice. I reject wasted time. I reject bombing."

"Not one person has been hurt. Not one, except that guard, and he wasn't supposed to be there, and even he only lost a couple fingers."

I turned, mouth agape. He looked away.

"Someone has to fight, Aunt A. Someone has to stand up and say, you can't just take it all. We want it back. We'll *take* it back."

He moved off, shoulders rigid, head rolling again around his neck. The shadows swallowed him. I hurried and caught up.

As I soon as I was through the door, I realized it wasn't actually dark in there. Every twenty feet or so, all the way to the back where some towering red curtains had been suspended from the ceiling, kerosene lanterns balanced precariously on old camera tripods. At the foot of each tripod, arrayed in a sort of daisy-petal shape, lay four or five blue tumbling mats, the kind one finds in elementary school gyms. Stuffing bulged from rents in their vinyl covering, and they seemed to be sagging into the cement. Most were unoccupied.

But not all. As we continued forward, I saw occasional, curled shapes draped in shabby overcoats or humped up under some other improvised covering. I even glimpsed a few faces. Most of those were young. Late teens.

Twenty-somethings. The great majority male, almost all of them prostrate. Some were sleeping or staring blank-eyed into the shadows spread like spider webs across the length of the ceiling, their heads sinking into moldy mounds of paperback books, their legs curled up underneath or folded over each other, as if they'd been frozen in the midst of a long-form yoga exercise.

The ones who weren't sleeping were reading, tilting books toward the nearest kerosene lantern. No one spoke. No one looked up at Aaron or accosted me. Shuddering, I realized the place really did feel like a library. Kind of. Certainly, it was nowhere to raise one's voice or shout hello.

"How many of you did you say there were?" I whispered.

"I didn't. I don't even know for sure. People come and go."

I was relieved to hear that, anyway. Also glad that as yet, no one had hoisted himself off his or her mattress and pulled the door down behind us.

"Not a single one of you knows how to dust? Wield a mop? You lie down in this? It's not sanitary."

"Aunt A., have you seen your car?"

Not quite like a library, I thought. All the way back to the curtains, I tried to place the sensation, and then I had it: it was like a Natural History Museum diorama. Something you'd see between the Cro-Magnon room and the Animals of North America hallway. The Reading Chamber. "*Look now, children. See those things in their hands? They called those 'books.' See how still they all are? This is what it was like . . .* "

Glancing behind me, I was startled to find that the outside door had been drawn down after all. And yet, the only thing moving in the whole expanse was lantern-light dancing down wicks, spinning shadows through the dust. A few mats away from where I now stood, someone coughed. Someone else whimpered.

The curtains hung in a circular ring suspended fully fifteen feet off the ground. Not until we were right in front of them did I hear the voice.

There really was something goat-like about its quaver, its nagging, monotonous bleat. It wasn't soothing, and it wasn't friendly. And it almost yanked me through the curtains.

"*Then the butterfly stamped . . .* "

"Aaron, don't," I said suddenly, but too late. He'd already pulled back the curtain.

I don't know what I was expecting. A throne, maybe. A white orgy-couch straight out of *Caligula*. The Wizard, working levers.

The first startling thing was how many of them there were. Twenty, at least, maybe more, all seated in a rude semi-circle, tilting against one another or else stretched lengthwise on the filthy floor mats. None of these people was sleeping, and not a one so much as glanced around. Except the Librarian.

He was hunched almost double on top of a stool. The lantern at his feet cast a reddish glow up the side of his face, which made him look less Satanic than molten. His eyes were small, yellowish-brown, and after lingering on mine for an uncomfortable few seconds, they drifted to Aaron.

"I told you, no doctors," he said, in the same bleat he'd used for reading.

"I brought one anyway," said Aaron. "This is—"

"Your not-Aunt Ariel. Yes."

"You're going to like her, Erick. She's not much for taking shit. Even from people she likes. And I doubt she'll like you much."

There it was again. The ghost of Aaron's smile. I grabbed for his hand, squeezed it, and felt him suck in a sharp breath.

"Sorry," I murmured.

Erick Kinney stared me up and down. Everything about him, from the blades of his shoulders to his drawn-up knees to his hawk's beak of a nose, looked pointy. If he'd had antennae, he could have passed for a grasshopper.

"Aaron, maybe we should go," I said.

Abruptly, the Librarian smiled. Except for the lantern light in his teeth, it was just an ordinary smile. A lopsided and tired one.

"You think you can help? Doctor? Solve the mystery?"

"You mean, How the Morlocks got their limp?"

The Librarian's smile widened. Which made it look more lopsided, something sketched with a crayon by a six year-old. "Well. All right, then. Make way, boys and girls. The doctor's come to tell us a story."

I shook my head. "Not here."

That gave him pause, briefly, and I wondered when he'd last left the Library. Certainly, there hadn't been any news footage of him recently. His bony fingers trailed over the pages of the chipped, cracked Kipling from which he'd been reading, probing into the crease of the binding and scratching softly at the words on the page, as though he were petting a cat.

"Then Brother Aaron will finish tonight's reading," he said, and held up the book. "Make sure each of you gives it a goodnight kiss."

He didn't so much stand as slump forward off the stool. Very slowly, clearly in pain, he straightened. His right arm dangled, and he dragged his right leg behind him as though he were some Dickens character with a club foot. His ailment was exaggerated, I was certain. Also clearly real.

"Aaron, please tell me you'll come again," I said. "Tomorrow. The next day. Please."

He turned, and in that one moment I forgot where I was, forgot the light and the bombings and everything else except the love I was never going to lose for this boy.

"Soon, Aunt A. You owe me a birthday sandwich."

I don't know why it seemed so important to keep Erick Kinney from seeing me cry. Spinning away fast, I walked straight across the warehouse and out of the Library. Once back in my car, I sat in the driver's seat with the door open to the fetid fog, waiting for the Librarian to make his slow way out of the world he'd created and into mine.

Seated on my examination table in a backless paper gown in the ruthless fluorescent light, Erick Kinney looked no less pointy. His sallow skin seemed stretched too thin, and his dirty blond hair fell in scraggles to his shoulders. His satyr-goatee dangled listlessly off his chin. Except for the angry red rash spreading up his back and curling into his ribs, the man was almost entirely bones and hair. A talking owl-pellet.

Or, not talking, as had been the case since the moment we'd reached the clinic. "Are you in pain?" I asked, arranging implements on my little pushcart next to the table.

As I moved about the room, I could feel his gaze, but every time I looked up, his eyes were aimed past me, out the door and across the hall. At my bookshelves, I realized.

"You're not answering," I said.

"You're not actually asking," said the Librarian. No smile creased his face, but something flickered in his eyes. Whatever it was, it was hard to look away from.

"Hold still," I told him. "Say aah." I stuck a swab in his throat.

He had his knees open, so I had to stand between them. Up close, he appeared even more grizzled, with little hairs sprouting from virtually every pore. He was also looking right at me, now. There was a *draw* to him, all right. I could feel it in my knees and under the soles of my feet, like an undertow. I held the swab in place a split second longer than I usually do. I think I wanted to see him gag.

He just sat there. Shoulders hunched, eyes dancing.

As soon as I removed the swab, he asked, "Can I look at your books?"

I held up the blood-pressure sleeve. Sighing, he extended his bony arm. In the end, I had to get the child-sleeve to fit him. I was squeezing the bulb, pressing the bell of my stethoscope into the crook of his elbow, when he said, "Is he really that stupid?"

I kept my attention on the pressure gauge as it nudged up, plunged down. "Which 'he' would that be?"

"Aaron's father. For not marrying you."

When I just ripped the Velcro open and removed the sleeve, he laughed. "No mock outrage? No *how-dare-me*? No *how-much-has-Aaron-told-you*? Oh, you're one of mine, all right."

"Hold out your hand," I said, separating the tiny needle from its sterilizing bag. "I'll try to get enough from your finger. I don't need much."

"Blood from a stone."

"A suddenly talkative stone." I jabbed the needle down, watched the blood well vibrant red in the yellow light. He stayed silent as I collected droplets. Somehow, his silence made me more nervous than his chatter did, so I asked, "What else has Aaron said?"

"That you're my kind of doctor."

"Meaning?"

"You serve the people who need serving, not the people who can pay. You read every spare second of your life. You don't judge anyone, except sometimes Aaron."

"I don't judge Aaron. Except about bombing. Want to talk about involving idealistic young people who damn near worship you in bombing, since we're talking?"

"That you keep yourself to yourself, because deep down you know that's not only for the best, it's better."

It was his voice as much as his words, that grated in my ears and all over my skin. That bleat, sharp and quavery, too raw, like notes struck on a ruined piano with the lid thrown open. Or vocal cords with no sheath of skin. I had a momentary but powerful impulse to strap this Morlock, or faux-Weather Undergrounder, or whatever he was, to the examination table, rush back to the warehouse, roust the rest of them, and light the whole place on fire. Bring Aaron home.

"You can look at the books, now," I said, pushing a hard breath through my teeth. "I'll just be a minute. A couple more tests, and I'll run you back."

"So you're going to discover what's wrong with us?" he said, sliding off the table, the gown slipping up his thighs as he landed, too close to me. He wasn't attractive. Just . . . *present*. In a way I'd almost forgotten people could be.

"I'm concerned that I already know," I said, making myself look away, but not before I saw him startle. "You're going to need a spinal tap to confirm. It's going to hurt."

"What do you know?" he said quietly.

"Your joints hurt, yes?"

"All the time."

"Your back?"

"All the time."

"That rash been there long?"

"A while."

"Fever?"

"It comes and goes. Or, it came and it went."

"Diarrhea?"

"Some. Yes."

"Tired a lot?"

He didn't answer that.

"I'll need a stool sample before you go. Bad luck living where you live. By the water, I mean. Especially this particular summer. With all the mosquitoes. This isn't just about you, by the way, and I'm not giving you a choice. I think you've got West Nile, and I'm going to contact the CDC, and they're going to make good and damn sure you get checked."

I was in the process of turning away, and almost missed his grin. My limbs had become heavy, as though Erick Kinney had poured concrete into them in the seconds we'd been standing there.

"West Nile Virus," he said. "Imagine that."

"Bound to happen here sooner or later. And given where you live, and the filthy way you keep yourselves . . . "

Without bothering with his pants or his socks, he lurched out of the examination room and across the hall into my office.

"There's no cure yet," I called after him, wanting him to turn around. Wanting him not to touch my books. I didn't trust him in there. Which wasn't rational, wasn't like me. I closed my eyes and ground my teeth and held on to the cool metal of my pushcart and opened my eyes again. "But there's plenty that can be done to ease the symptoms. Unless it turns into encephalitis or meningitis or something more serious, it's not going to kill you."

"That's what they told my father," Erick Kinney said dreamily, one long finger trailing across the decaying spines of my Hawthornes. Coming to rest for a moment on the fat, green bulk of my Robert Burton. My favorite books. He'd gone right to them. *Contaminated them.*

Which was ridiculous. Juvenile. Stupid.

"Your father had West Nile? What are you talking about? We just discovered it, and by the way, It's not inheritable, and—"

"No, no," he said. "I know. Just chatting. It's rare I find someone worth having a chat with."

"I have to tell you something else, I'm afraid."

"Anything," he bleated. "Lay it on me, Doc."

"The rest of them. Your . . . whatever you call them. Followers."

"Friends?"

"They're not your friends," I snapped.

He swung his head around. There was that grin again. "No? I suppose not."

"They're going to have be tested, too. Immediately, do you hear? Their lives could depend on it. And this could spread fast."

"Not inheritable, you say," he half-sang, to himself. "In a way, I suppose you're right."

"Hello? Mr. Kinney? I'm telling you you need to help me. You've got to get your people help. This is serious."

He shrugged. "One already died."

I almost dropped the materials I'd been bagging. Stepping into the hall, I felt that new heaviness again in my limbs. On my tongue, It was hard to speak.

"Died? Died how?"

"Couldn't breathe. Clenched up. As far as we could tell."

"You didn't send him for help? You didn't do anything for him?"

"Her. And you seem to have a mistaken impression of the way the Library works, my dear doctor. My personal physician, from here on out. I'm not their emperor. I'm not Jim Jones. I'm certainly not their prison guard. She could have strolled out the front door anytime she liked." For a moment, he stood still, hunched over my desk, the fingers of his right hand straying up and down the spine of *The Anatomy of Melancholy*.

Then he grinned again. "Lurched out, I mean."

My mouth opened. Closed. I wanted to run. Couldn't remember how to move.

"You don't love them," I whispered.

"Good god, of course I don't love them. What's to love? I love the *idea* of them, though. The Avenging Booklovers' Army. An all new branch of the ABA. Isn't that what we do, after all? You and me? We always love the idea of them."

I couldn't speak. Didn't need to. He might as well have been back on his milk crate under the Clocktower, now, except that he was talking only to me. That was part of the secret, I realized. Part of his power. He always seemed to be talking only to the person right in front of him.

"Take an achievement like this," he said, and lifted *The Anatomy of Melancholy* off my shelf, gently, with his crooked hands. It was a 1920s one-volume edition, gilt-lettered, heavy. If it dropped on him, I thought, it would crush him like a cockroach.

"Be careful with that," I said pointlessly.

"Perhaps the greatest act of understanding—no, more than that, of creative insight—no, more than that, too . . . of *empathy* ever attempted. A complete parsing of the weight every single human being feels, no matter where they're from or what they achieve or whose love they attain, from the moment they draw breath until the moment they cease to do so." He had the book open now, turning his hands this way and that so that every square inch of his skin brushed the pages, as though he were performing an ablution in holy water.

"Books like this. The greatest tools the supposedly magnificent human animal has ever come up with for transcending its own skin and inhabiting another's . . . but they can only be used, appreciated, or created when one is alone. There is no literary irony greater than that of the medium itself."

"I'll take that stool sample, now," I said.

He sighed. And then he actually *tsked*. But his fingers lifted away from my book.

"I'll put it back," I told him. *Because I didn't want him touching it anymore.*

"Too late. You've already opened it. Already shown it to your precious . . . stepson? Ward? Anyway, once that's done, you've left him wide open." He was out of my office now, passing uncomfortably close (*because I couldn't seem to step back*) as he took the collection kit from my limp hands and made for the bathroom.

"Open to what?" I asked. Not wanting to know, helpless to keep quiet.

His smile was different, now. Slow. Self-satisfied. "To every little germ of an idea. Everything we decide we are going to refuse to burn or bury as instructed."

The moment he was out of sight, I forced myself to walk. I went into the examination room, labeled vials, bound everything together, entered notations on the computer. Then I grabbed my keys, shut out the lights, and made for the front door.

"Just leave the kit on the exam table," I called into the silence. "I'll be out front. I'll drive you home."

He wasn't long. And I was relieved to find that on the sidewalk, in the night air, my limbs felt lighter, and they moved when I told them to. Erick Kinney stopped talking until long after we were in the car, down the hill, almost all the way back to the Library. If the radio had worked, I would have turned it up as loud as it would go. I was practically pressed up against the driver's-side door by the time we reached the street of warehouses. He just sat, hunched, pallid, breathing in quick pants like a coyote.

"You know, my father didn't particularly like Hawthorne," he murmured as I pulled my Saturn to the curb. From the pensive way he stared into the fog, he almost seemed to be reading it. "It's just what they sent him. That summer."

"I like Hawthorne," I said.

"Me, too."

"His Veiled Lady."

"His men 'of shabby appearance, met in an obscure part of the street.'" He plucked at his own shabby jeans, turned to me, and through the goatee, under the corpse-like pallor, I glimpsed something. Thought I did. "You should really come in," he said. "Veiled Lady."

And I felt myself stir. Start to unlock my door. For Aaron, I was thinking. Just to get Aaron. Then I was gripping the door handle. Holding on.

"Get them to doctors, Mr. Kinney," I said. "Tomorrow. I'll be back with the police to check."

I wanted him to grin again. His grin scared me. And his shrug made me furious. Fear and fury would keep me nailed where I was. Instead, of course, he sat there reading my face, the way he had the fog. The way he did the whole world. "Goodnight, Personal Physician," he said.

Then he was out of my car, lurching across the street, and Aaron was emerging from the doorway where he'd clearly been waiting, throwing an arm around his mentor's shoulders to help him back to his Library. And I was all but gunning the engine as I turned around, floored the accelerator, and got the hell out of there.

I should have gone home. I didn't generally spend much time in my apartment, passed my after-clinic hours eating out or walking the Castro or over to Haight, sometimes seeing concerts or movies but often just haunting the blocks where the used bookshops used to be, and which still retained their traces. I should have done that then.

Instead, I went back to the clinic, figuring I needed to work. Get my brain clear. Get the reek of Erick Kinney out of it. I put *The Anatomy of Melancholy* back in the gaping space it had left on my shelf. I did data entry and paperwork for a while. I ordered out for Pad Thai and turned on the radio. Eventually, I lay back in my reclining armchair and turned out the lights and let the sounds of my street seep into the room. That far-off clanging, as though something were always being built nearby, just around the next corner, but I could never find it. Occasional stumbling footsteps or slurred shouts from a homeless person or a drunk. That faint echo passing cars leave in fog. My nighttime companions for so long.

Is he really that stupid, the bastard had asked? Damn right, too. Why had Oliver let me go? I'd never understood. Aaron hadn't either, he'd been furious even at five. The last thing I'd ever wanted, to come between the two of them. And I'd never quite gotten past it all either, apparently.

Very early—too early—I'd settled on this image of myself. The creature in the clinic. The Veiled Lady. Alone with her spells, her private regrets. Why had I done that?

I closed my eyes and tried to sleep. But what I saw was the Librarian's wagging beard, his satyr-grin. And what I heard was that bleat, reverberating inside my head. *Burn or bury. That summer.* His panting breath, his crooked hands. *That's what they told my father. That summer.* His followers arrayed around him in the Library, like broken pieces of a model. Kissing the decrepit book he read them. *How the Morlocks got their limp. The germ of an idea. That summer.*

I sat bolt upright, mouth open, grabbing so hard at the chain for the lamp beside my chair that I knocked the whole lamp over, heard the bulb smash on the floor. I stood, the fragments grinding to dust under my soles.

"Jesus Christ," I said aloud. The words small and useless in my useless little room.

Hurrying into the hall, I flipped on every light in the Clinic, as though that would help. As though light would make any difference. *It's crazy*, I was thinking. *A night terror. A fog phantom.* I grabbed Erick Kinney's kit out of my drawer anyway, removed the throat swab from its vial, took it upstairs to the little lab I'd built myself, as a hobby, mostly, over the lonely years.

But it would take weeks—and a much more sophisticated lab, and an expert—to prove what I already knew. What couldn't be happening, and clearly was. There wasn't even anyone for me to call. No one who'd believe me enough to run the tests right away. Even if they did, by the time the tests provided results, it would be too late. Because the Scourge of Summer had already risen from the dead.

All the way down the hill toward the Bay, I worked it over in my head. Tried to convince myself it was impossible. Then I gave that up and worked on figuring out how it had happened, instead. *How had I even known?*

But I had the answer to that one. I'd figured it out the same way I'd figured out virtually everything I knew: I'd read it somewhere. God knows where. Retained, it somehow. Those summers. Those damp, terrifying Julys and Augusts, when families fled the beaches. When parents kept their children indoors, away from their friends, and prayed the killer in the streets would sweep past them. When kindhearted librarians assembled bundles of books from the shelves and sent them in pouches to the already-afflicted, the ones who'd been quarantined, so they'd have something to do to pass the hours while their muscles withered and their lungs froze and they slowly, slowly strangled. The pouches all came with little candies, a card full of get-well wishes, and a letter of instruction asking that the books not be returned. That they be burned, or buried, just in case polio really could linger on the pages.

Erick Kinney was seated by himself on the sidewalk outside the Library. The door had been yanked shut. I moved straight past him, kicked repeatedly at the metal. The sound boomed and rolled like thunder. No one came.

"They're gone," the Librarian said, after the echoes from my volley of kicks finally subsided.

I looked down. "Gone?"

That grin. Horrible. Lopsided. "Every. Last. One."

My mouth fell open, and I sank to my knees. I would have grabbed the door if there'd been anywhere to grab. I stared straight into the flicker in his eyes. "You *know*," I said.

"Well of course I know."

"How did you know? Weren't you vaccinated?"

"I was indeed. Alarming, no? And that's not even the most fascinating part."

His words, in that goat-voice, buzzed in my ears, seemed to set my brain vibrating so that I couldn't answer, couldn't even remember how to speak.

"The fascinating part—the real poetry, if you'll forgive me—is where I think it came from." And from his lap, he lifted the Kipling book. Held it out to me.

"Your father's," I mumbled.

He nodded. "They thought they were going to have to put him in an iron lung, but they didn't, quite. He just lost the use of his arms. And one leg. He really should have burned this, don't you think? And yet, how wonderful that he didn't."

"It's . . . " My brain cleared. I sucked fog deep into my lungs. "That's absurd. Impossible. A virus can't live on a page. Not for fifty seconds, let alone fifty years."

"Impossible. Sure. But what other explanation could there be? And just think, Veiled Lady. Personal Physician to the Library. What if it's true? What was our virus doing, all these long years, with no one to hold it, no one to play with? All curled up in a book? What sort of bedtime stories do you think a virus tells itself?"

He was rambling again, off on one of his milk-crate rants. I just sagged against the metal doors, momentarily stunned to helplessness.

"I've been imagining one," he said. "Want to hear it? It's not so different than any of the stories any living thing tells: '*Once upon a time, I got out. I*

got free. I sailed the summer wind. I met others, and fell in love. I leapt from
island to island. I confronted my enemies, and laid them waste. I made more
of me. I made more of me. I made more of me.'"

"Gone," I said. "Meaning, you sent them out?"

He stopped talking, smiled that smile. "Sharing the good word. Like all proper Librarians before me."

My hands flashed out, grabbed his, yanked him sideways toward me. His squeal of pain was awful, pig-like, and satisfying.

"Did you tell them? You murdering, fucked-up son-of-a-bitch, did you tell them what they have?"

"The ones who wanted to hear. Mostly, I just said it was time to go see old friends. Go to the parks and teach the children."

"Jesus. Oh my God."

"Much better than bombing, don't you think? The ironies abound."

Tears blurred my eyes, ran in rivulets down my face. I kept his wrists clutched in mind. "Aaron. He's got it, too. What did you tell Aaron?"

"Well, Aaron's pretty special. As you know."

Absurdly, I felt myself nodding. My breath catching.

"A loving young man. And brave. And very angry. Mostly about what's happened to you."

I jerked his wrists. "Does he know?"

"He knows."

"And he went to 'spread the word'? To kill children? I don't believe it."

"Not at all," said Erick Kinney. And he smiled once more. "He said to tell you you were right. That it's long past time he went home to tell his idiot father exactly where he's been."

⸻◆⸻

Greek theatre is like magic. There are specific rules you must follow,
or the spell is broken.

FOUR LEGS IN THE MORNING

Norman Prentiss

Fresh air lured him from the musty interior of Dr. Sibley's cabin, and Leonard's bare feet tested the dry half-circle of dirt outside the porchless doorway. "There's plumbing and electricity," Sibley had told him, "but you'll have to bring your own comforts, I'm afraid." Leonard interpreted comfort as a coffee maker and a stockpile of vacuum-sealed bricks of caffeine—food supplies and warm clothing were almost an afterthought, so naturally he hadn't bothered to pack bedroom slippers. If he was lucky, heat from the metal carafe in his hand might eventually work its way down; in the meantime, he curled his toes and favored the outside arch of his feet to minimize contact with cold, hard ground.

This would be an academic's idea of "roughing it": no distractions from television or telephone. He brought his laptop, but would do most of his work the old-fashioned way, with notes on index cards, and chapters scratched in longhand on stacks of legal pads. Sibley approved: that was how he'd written his textbook on Greek tragedy. A single book, not one that would merit tenure in the current market, but with good, close readings of Sophocles' plays. Critics at the time praised Sibley's depiction of classical performance: outdoor amphitheaters, choric dancers, stone masks over the actors' faces. Pretty standard historical background, actually, but influential enough in 1956 to establish Sibley's reputation. Even today, you couldn't write about the Oedipus trilogy and not cite Bennet Sibley.

Dr. Sibley. Leonard's department chair at Graysonville University. As a mentor, Sibley couldn't really provide helpful advice: he was too out-of-touch with recent scholarly trends. But he had the cabin, and generously offered it to Leonard for the full month between semesters. Enough time, Leonard hoped, to kick start ideas for his second book. As a new member to the Graysonville faculty, he needed to make a strong impression.

He sipped his coffee, bracing against the January wind. Caffeine was his muse. He would linger with her a while in the chill outdoors, then retreat to the warm cabin, to his boxes of books and notecards, to pages of half-formed ideas he'd spread last night over a folding card table. Although he briefly considered driving into town for more supplies—surely there was *some*thing vital he'd forgotten?—Leonard resisted. He had to focus on his project. That's why he was here. And that's why he'd stepped outside without shoes, without his down-filled jacket: so he wouldn't be tempted to wander away from the cabin on a lengthy mission that was nine parts avoidance to one part exploration.

He didn't *need* to explore the area around the cabin. He needed to work.

Look at the text, Sibley had advised. *All the answers you need are in the text.* Easy for him to say. In 1956, critics didn't have to worry about new historicism, feminist or queer theory, structuralism and post-structuralism, and all the backlash against (and redefinition of) these same critical approaches.

Unconsciously, either from irritation or to keep warm, Leonard started to pace. He stayed next to the cabin, avoiding the stone-step path to the carport, and the line of grass and rocks and sticks that beckoned to surrounding woods. The cool dirt beneath his feet was packed tight, smooth as asphalt but with occasional bumps of buried stone or tree root. When he stopped pacing, Leonard backed one heel against a broken branch that was thick as a roll of pennies.

He barely brushed over it, expecting to roll the branch with his heel. Instead, he crushed the segment flat.

Startled, Leonard nearly lost his balance. Was it hollow? Rotted through? A sliver of bark stuck to his bare heel; without looking, he scratched it out with his fingernail.

He set his empty carafe on the ground and kneeled to examine the flattened branch. The bark was as thin as paper. The patterns along the segment seemed more fauna than flora. Hard to trace after he'd crushed the hollow cylinder, but it seemed like a repeating geometric design of dark lines and inscribed ovals. Beneath the design were faint ridges, like the whorl of fingerprints.

Probably, this was a segment of snakeskin. How did that work, exactly? The snake wriggled out of the sleeve of its old skin, emerged shiny and fresh—didn't it? Well, he was no expert on reptiles, wasn't certain what species were common to this region. Venomous or non-venomous? Either way, he hoped the skin's former resident had slithered far away by now.

Leonard peeled up the empty skin—brittle, like a piece of overcooked bacon—and brought it inside. He shut the door behind him, checked the seal between the door and the frame. Then he made a nervous sweep of the cabin's four rooms, looking under furniture, behind appliances, inside closets.

The cabin offered no resources to help alleviate his uneasiness as the day progressed. No Internet access, no phone, and no books on Sibley's shelf titled *Deadly Snakes of Northeast Alabama*. As he sat in the main room of the cabin, several times he caught himself peering beneath the table to check his feet—now in socks and shoes, thank you, although he wished his pants were more snug at the cuffs. He considered fastening them closed above his ankles with rubber bands.

Again, the temptation to ride into town. He could stop at the General Store, maybe find some out-of-work locals huddled in a warm booth at the Gas 'n' Dine. He'd show them his strip of bacon, get advice from old coots who'd survived wars and the depression, had hiked through years of Alabama woods, dodging snakes along dark paths. But, for all Leonard knew, his skin sample really was bacon—and how silly he'd feel, then.

The worst thing for an academic was to look like a fool. He'd take the risk of his silence.

Better to concentrate on his book. He'd chosen a creative deconstructionist approach—a mode of criticism mostly out-of-favor since the early nineties (and thus, Leonard gambled, due for a trendy come-back). At the very least, a deconstructionist approach would help him make original claims about an ancient, over-examined play. The idea was to take *Oedipus Rex* apart, ask questions that tore at the perfect fabric critics had admired since Aristotle's day.

Sacrilege! Bennet Sibley exclaimed when Leonard first mentioned the project. *You don't need fancy critical approaches. Sophocles will teach you how to read Sophocles.*

Sibley had too much respect for the text. It limited him.

The play was based on a riddle. Why not treat the play itself as if it needed a new solution?

He'd transcribed the famous Riddle of the Sphinx on the first sheet of a fresh legal pad: *What walks on four legs in the morning, two legs in the afternoon, and three legs in the evening?* The equally famous solution is "Man," since he crawls on all fours as a baby, walks upright as an adult, and needs the assistance of a cane in later years. But Leonard had scribbled notes over the page to ridicule the accepted answer. *Two arms aren't two legs! A cane is not a leg!*

Sophocles didn't invent the riddle, doesn't quote it within his play. But it's crucial back-story, the reason Oedipus fills the newly vacant seat as King of Thebes. And yet, why praise a man for solving an unfair riddle? Rather, grieve for the guiltless heroes before him, who stood their turn before a feather-breasted monster, half eagle and half lion, and tried to shape an honest answer to the Sphinx's trickery. What might these men have guessed, in days when such she-monsters could besiege a town? Did some say "Chimera," their voices rising in a fearful squeak? Perhaps some others made up an animal, in Seuss- or Swift-like fashion: "A bumble-glumph," or "Hurgle-whynn." Others, soiling themselves with fear, could have blurted out a desperate, hopelessly wrong answer: "A frog?" "A donkey?" Or maybe a few of them proposed the only reasonable response: "There's no creature in this world that fits your description."

The answers don't matter. The Sphinx kills them all.

When Oedipus offers his solution, it's over-elegant: an analogy of life-span to time-of-day, tucked inside other substitutions of *crawl* for *walk*, *cane* for *leg*. Legend asks us to believe the Sphinx is so upset by Oedipus's attack on her riddle—her monstrous sense of self so tied to that impossible one-question quiz show—that she immediately commits suicide.

Would that all monsters were this sensitive to criticism.

These were Leonard's whimsical musings, yet they supported his thesis about the classical unities of time, place, and action. In his argument, these rules actually weakened our ability to appreciate Sophocles' play. All those important moments from the past, all those bits of violence banished tastefully off-stage and reported by a weeping messenger—if these scenes were represented somehow, in a radical re-staging of *Oedipus Rex*, the audience would have an entirely new understanding of the central character. The usual interpretation presented Oedipus as an intelligent, well-meaning king (he saved the city from the Sphinx!), undermined by his tragic flaw (pride and impulsiveness . . . and that unfortunate accidentally-killing-his-father-and-sleeping-with-his-mother scandal). In Leonard's view, Oedipus's tragic flaw is not an exception to an otherwise noble life. Oedipus *is* his tragic flaw.

Abandon the classical unities. Imagine a production of *Oedipus Rex* where the Sphinx towers over the stage of Thebes, appearing in gruesome flashback when summoned by the Chorus. Or, as Oedipus recollects possibly the world's first instance of "road rage," show onstage his disproportionate reaction as he beats a man to death at a crossroads, simply because the apparent stranger (his father) refused to grant him right-of-way.

Perhaps such a staging would be impossible: too costly, too violent or inappropriate, a logistical nightmare. But his book could do the same work. A chapter for each of the unrepresented scenes, envisioned in a creative section, followed by serious critical commentary. The book would be controversial and attention-getting. Did it matter if the interpretations were "correct"?

Blasphemy! Sibley would say. *Greek theatre is like magic. There are specific rules you must follow, or the spell is broken.*

Well, he was planning to break a lot of spells. By the time Leonard was finished, Sibley would likely regret allowing him use of the cabin.

Leonard worked through the day, mostly brainstorming and outlining, and the ideas came almost faster than he could write. The shift to handwriting rather than typing seemed to open new floodgates. He devoted a separate legal pad to each chapter; in different ink colors, he drew arrows from one idea to the next, spread new thoughts into margins or pinched them in tiny print between previously written lines. It was a strange and welcome reverie, his vague fear of snakes easily forgotten.

He nearly forgot lunch, too. At three o'clock he fixed a quick sandwich, smearing peanut butter on bread using a thick handled steak knife he discovered in a kitchen drawer. Then he worked past the winter day's early sundown, his pen scratches accompanied by the steady rumble of the generator that kept the cabin warm and lighted.

The generator sat in the utility closet on the other side of the small kitchen. Propane-fueled, it produced a noise similar to the rhythmic rattle of an old-fashioned film projector. Leonard fancied himself in a movie: the scholar, hunched over a table, frenzied in the formative stages of his most brilliant work.

Then the film jumped out of the sprockets. At least, that's what it sounded like: a metallic screech from the generator, like something got jammed in the mechanism. Leonard rushed to the utility closet out of instinct. The generator was his life-line, and if it broke down he'd have to return home— just as he was getting started, after his most-productive day in recent memory.

He threw open the closet door, and the generator rumbled even louder. This close, the sound was overwhelming. The machine shuddered as if trying to shake itself into pieces. Not that he understood the equipment, but Leonard studied the beige and copper engine, and all the screws and bolts and belts seemed in their proper places. The rumble was loud and steady, with no trace of the scrape and screech he'd heard from the main room.

Or, perhaps a slight screech, like an undercurrent. Maybe in the mechanism—maybe more distant, outside the cabin, an animal's awful cry of pain.

Leonard had slept well the previous night, exhausted after the drive up I-20, then side-turns down country roads into twisting, barely marked, gravel and dirt lanes to Sibley's cabin. He'd thrown fresh linens over the cot's thin mattress, fluffed his own pillow over the lumpy one Sibley had left behind, and then dropped into calm slumber.

Tonight was different. The day's mental activity refused to abate; ideas tumbled through his head in time with the spinning gears and belts of the straining generator. The two bedrooms were each equipped with a working fireplace, but they were too much trouble to get started. He'd pulled the cot into the main room, where he could huddle close to the wall-mounted electric heater. As a result, he literally couldn't get away from the day's work: it loomed near his bedside, spread overtop the card table.

Now that the glow of inspiration had faded, Leonard began to worry that his day's work wasn't as good as he'd thought. Was he a victim of that dreaded malady Sibley called "Scholar's Delusion"? Even in Leonard's young career, he'd seen his share of the afflicted. Most recently, a colleague had grown so wrapped up in study of a minor nineteenth-century poet, that he convinced himself she was the greatest writer who ever lived. *Honestly*, Don had said to him in all seriousness, *I prefer Felicia Hemans's poetry to Wordsworth's.*

Had Leonard fallen into a similar trap of self-deception? His department chair would probably agree. Bennet Sibley's skeptical countenance floated before him in the dark, a bearded Tiresias eager to express the most awful prophesy of failure. *You're welcome to use my cabin, but . . . Why would you want to write that kind of criticism? Why would anyone want to read it?*

No, no, he had to remind himself. Forget Sibley and his outdated, reverent respect for the text. He wasn't writing to please Sibley. Indeed, he'd spent too much of his life trying to please people whom he didn't respect. The same problem plagued his romantic and family entanglements—which largely explained why he was free to spend an entire month alone in a secluded cabin.

Leonard wrote for a more sophisticated audience, one fully aware that drama was a living organism, no longer the author's property. You can't appreciate a text by ignoring its flaws. Oedipus's story relies on ridiculous coincidence: that a man should flee his adopted father, only to cross paths with the father of his blood; that a she-Sphinx kills each challenger, until one man twists out a solution to her torturous riddle; that a land should need a king, and one walks in. The drama finds its convenience in uncanny chance.

These were the kinds of observations liable to give Sibley a heart attack. But that's what the play was all about, wasn't it—the younger generation taking the place of the old? Harold Bloom said the same thing about writers in *Anxiety of Influence*: to make their reputations, authors had to reshape the works of their predecessors—kill the fathers of literary tradition, so to speak. The theory should hold equally true in the cutthroat world of academic tenure and promotion. Someday, stodgy old Sibley would have to retire as Chair of the English Department; in his place, Leonard would encourage the inventive scholarship and teaching Sibley hoped to suppress.

The film projector continued to rattle from the utility closet. Leonard's thoughts threaded through the sprockets: some projected a grandiose, satisfying future; others cast "Father" Sibley's vision of doom. He pictured the man's rich, fuzzy beard, with its neat convex shape—as if half a gray tennis ball were glued over Sibley's chin. And Leonard knew his thoughts had gone loopy now, from the day's excitement and subsequent lack of sleep. Sibley typically would rub his bearded chin with one fingertip as he conjured phrases—no insult intended, nothing more than observations, really—but phrases that might undermine a young teacher's confidence. If the old man had magical powers, they were centered in that weird tuft of beard. Push aside those stiff, overcombed hairs, and from behind would wink his third eye, the source of his prophetic insight.

These were Leonard's last semi-lucid thoughts before sleep finally overtook him. He was unable to rouse himself from bed in early morning, when faint cries again seemed to rise above steady mechanical thrums. He was on a train that passed between strange villages. The shades were drawn against the sunrise. In the fields, small animals lifted their heads in a shrill chorus, high-pitched yet also guttural, as if they gargled food, or they were being strangled.

Slightly after noon, Leonard staggered outside with his coffee. Thick clouds masked the sun, a diffuse gray light breaking through. Another abandoned fragment of skin lay, hollow and fragile, on the patch of ground fronting the cabin door. It was not a snake skin.

He kneeled on the ground to get a closer look. The same repeating design of lines and ovals around the circumference, the same ridges faint beneath, the texture of fingerprints. He hadn't crushed this specimen with his heel, so the cylindrical shape was preserved. It swelled thicker on one end, and bent at a right angle directly in the middle of the hollow tube. In size and shape, with a brown-bark dead-leaf color, it looked like a broken cigar.

The smaller opening was frayed in tiny strips; they curled like paper at the end of an exploded firecracker. Leonard brushed the side of his forefinger against the frayed edge, then pulled his hand away in surprise. The tiny strips were sharp, like pincers.

Without thinking, he pressed his finger to his lips, then bit down slightly where he'd been scratched.

Maybe he really should drive into town, find somebody who could tell him what the heck this thing was.

Then that animal cry again, familiar from last night, and from this morning's hypnogogic daze. He had trouble judging direction, here in new surroundings and with sound waves echoing off the perimeter of trees. But the noise seemed to come from the other side of the cabin.

This morning, his exit from bed had been more leisurely. He'd put on shoes and dressed for the day. The air was brisk, but not as chilly as yesterday. He could walk for a short while. Go exploring.

He didn't find any strange animals. But he found something equally strange.

Some evergreens grew close to the back of the cabin, giving the building year-long shade on that side. Past the edge of the woods, most of the trees were bare. Leonard found the obvious foot path, and followed it. A few yards in, the path sloped into a steep drop. Through thin, leafless branches, Leonard could easily distinguish a clearing far, far below.

At the center of the clearing sat an impossible, full-scale replica of a Greek amphitheatre.

Hidden out here? In the middle of nowhere?

Leonard had to see it up close. He followed the path, keeping the outdoor theatre in sight. He felt dizzy after a moment, and soon realized the cause. It was a trick of perspective. The clearing wasn't as far below as it seemed, and the amphitheatre wasn't a full-sized model.

Once he corrected his erroneous impression, it took little time to reach the small clearing. He stood with his hands on his hips, an unlikely Gulliver. The amphitheatre was made out of stone blocks, as the originals had been, but they were set in a round cement foundation—about the size of a large dinner table. A rectangular stage occupied one ground-level section, with all the appropriate elements: the *parados*, aisles where choric singers entered from the sides; the flat orchestra area where dancers would perform between scenes; and the *skene*, the building that formed the backdrop to the stage, with three doors in place for the main actors' entrances and exits. The *theatron* itself, where the audience sat, fanned out from the orchestra area in rising cement steps, forming the main bulk of the structure.

Some people might lay down cement to build a barbeque area next to their wooded cabin. But Sibley, he built himself a miniature amphitheatre. From the looks of it, the model was old—showing some chipped decay, to echo the modern-day ruins of the real theatres in Greece. Leonard guessed it dated back to the fifties, from when Sibley was writing his one and only book.

He wondered if Sibley's wife ever accompanied him to the cabin. She might have sat there and watched him, knitting while her husband envisioned a miniature Oedipus or Creon or Iocaste pacing the puppet-sized stage; or pictured the *deus ex machina* contraption lowered from the top of the *skene* replica, like a tiny God from a tiny heaven.

Nothing currently perched on the roof of this *skene*—no serpent-drawn chariot for Medea to ride, no cut-outs of the sun for Apollo, the lightning bolt for Zeus. But the detail on the small building was remarkable. Faded paint over the rough concrete simulated the brick-pattern of a royal palace. Thin rectangular panels along the top border glowed with faint gold inlays. The three doors along the front of the *skene* looked like weather-worn wood, rather than concrete. They each had a small hook-latch on the front, as if they were actually functional doors.

Were they? Leonard bent toward the left-most door and tapped it with a knuckle. The answering sound was a wooden thunk.

He tried the latch. The rusty hook was stuck in the eyelet, and needed to be forced before it would lift. The door itself, in contrast, swung outward with little protest. Inside, the model *skene* was hollow and mostly dark.

Leonard put his mouth near the opening, shouted "Hello" to amuse himself.

No answer, which was just as well. He remembered the shrill cry he'd tried to follow, and cautioned himself not to upset some animal's nest.

Even the day's dim light was enough to reveal, luckily, that the inside of this tiny bunker was uninhabited. The building's floor was a continuation of the cement base, with a faint layer of undisturbed dirt overtop.

Maybe it was okay to try another door. Number two, in the center. He placed one foot inside the model, planting it on the flat circle of the orchestra stage. He rested his elbow on his knee while he reached toward the second hinge. This latch flipped up easily, and he pulled the door open.

A shape of lumped fabric lay inside the middle doorway. A dark-blue, flannel rag. It didn't seem like an article of clothing—there was no pattern to the cloth, no seams or pockets or buttons. Leonard brought his other leg into the dipped center of the amphitheatre, then lowered his Gulliver-giant rear onto the jagged slope of the theatron seats. Holding his hands to each side for leverage, he eased the tip of his right shoe into the doorway, giving the cloth lump a gentle nudge.

No animal growl or hiss, thank goodness. Only a slight clacking sound. It seemed safe enough to investigate further.

It turned out to be a small cloth sack, cinched at the top with a threaded rope of yellow yarn. In earlier days, the yarn might have appeared golden.

He lifted it from underneath with one hand. The sack rattled, as if it were filled with tiny bones. He tugged at the yarn, and the soft flannel opened at the mouth of the sack. Again, a clacking rattle as the contents shifted over his supporting hand.

Leonard was disappointed by the contents. Empty walnut shells. Roughly two dozen, at first glance.

Then he looked more closely. The split shells had tiny markings on the surface. Colors. Carved furrows. Threads and faded tinsel.

They were masks. Half-masks for the chorus, full-face ovals for the main characters. Leonard picked up one of them: a miniature comic mask, the smile painted in a delicate red curl, pin-hole eyes drilled in careful symmetry above a natural nose-like ridge in the shell. The craftsmanship was amazing.

He lifted another from the sack. This one was clearly a tragic mask, mouth twisted in an agonized black line, a spiked tin-foil crown attached askew atop the head. Wisps of red thread were glued beneath blinded eye sockets, simulating blood. The shell had a thin elastic band looped around the back, as if to hold the mask on a tiny head.

On a whim, Leonard set down the bag and slid the Oedipus mask over his right thumb. He wiggled the thumb, and the small face shook on its new perch; from the motion, red threads waved faintly in the air, fresh blood streaming from the doomed king's empty eyes.

After the strange discovery, Leonard accomplished little else that day. He'd spent some time admiring the skill that produced those small masks, many with painstaking details that helped him easily identify the characters: Antigone, her expression firm in quiet defiance of the king's law; Creon, face ablaze with self-righteous anger. Although the masks obviously had been designed to fit dolls or marionettes, Leonard found no such puppets in the hollow *skene* replica; a cursory search of the cabin also turned up nothing.

As much as he appreciated the meticulous artistry of those masks, the oddness of the project unsettled him. Similarly skilled fingers assembled ridiculous "ship in a bottle" models, popular with old men in a previous generation. Those ship models eventually became so common that they lost much of their charm. Something dusty and pointless, earning a curious glance then low bids (if any) at an estate auction. The people who built these ships were eccentric retired men with too much time on their hands.

Sibley had invented his own peculiar pastime, without the calming association of shared practitioners. A twisted version of an old man's hobby—but Sibley, obsessed with classical texts, would have been an old soul before his time. This state of mind surely explained his life-long resistance to new ideas.

The man's headstrong resistance had seemed annoying to Leonard, maybe slightly affected or quaint. But now he wondered if his former teacher hadn't long ago left quaint behind, and crossed into more disturbing territory. Mrs. Sibley had passed on in the early nineties, yet the doctor still spent summer months in his isolated cabin. Supposedly he was working on his second book, but that was decades overdue; when asked, he declined to state a title or clarify the topic. Looking for the marionettes earlier, Leonard had uncovered no evidence of scholarly work: no textbooks or journals or scribbled notes.

What did he do all summer: act out the plays with his walnut-shell masks, recreating his own festival of Dionysus at his miniature amphitheatre? Leonard considered the building where he'd found the masks, the roof of the *skene* from which a god could descend to resolve the play. In *Herakles*, the spirit of madness scratches at the roof, breaks through and forces its way into the hero's mind. Perhaps something similar had happened to Sibley.

Phrases from Sibley's book gained new meaning. (But were they from his book? Or simply those expressions he repeated in class, in the faculty room? The sources tended to blur.) *Greek theater is like magic. The unities cast a kind of spell.*

And all that emphasis on masks. *The actors wore masks. They conveyed no emotion through their faces—it was all in the words themselves.* Sibley's face was expressionless whenever he said this.

Leonard tried to push these troubling thoughts away and work on his book, but ended up doing little more than pushing his notepads in new arrangements across the card table. Doubts overshadowed the productivity of his first day at the cabin: doubts about his own project, and doubts about the sanity of Bennet Sibley.

Which affected his sleep again that night. How frustrating to waste the day, then lie awake knowing that, without rest, the next day could follow the same frustrated pattern. A mechanical screech from the generator closet compounded the problem. Leonard was too exhausted to investigate, and the worrisome machine seemed to wail loudest when he teetered on the edge of sleep, startling him awake.

Sometime in the night, he must have gotten up to turn off the generator. The wailing mostly stopped, but the room grew cold. Leonard huddled under borrowed blankets, and another sound circled the dry dirt outside the cabin—a sound the generator's hum must have obscured the other two nights. It was something like footsteps. *Two small feet have a predictable rhythm*, he thought. *Three is two with an extra sound. Click click thump. Click click thump.*

He'd kicked the blankets away during the night, and the sweatshirt and sweatpants weren't enough to keep him warm. He lay in the fetal position, his arms hugged tight to his chest. Leonard wasn't sure he'd gotten any sleep. Certainly, he was awake earlier than he should be: only a faint morning light, and his battery clock indicating twenty minutes after six.

And that howl. That howl that was *not* the generator. A gargling, choking sound, like a human infant needing to vomit, but too young to know how.

Outside the cabin.

Leonard unfolded himself from the bed, stumbled in stocking feet to the door, then opened it in a quick motion to catch whatever was making that awful sound.

When he saw it, Leonard was unable to step closer. He held onto the door frame for support, clenched the wood for a reminder of something solid and familiar.

The creature stood near the far edge of the dirt porch. It was about a foot tall, covered with scales like a lizard, but with a hard insect back. Its head was the size of a walnut; wire-like bristles sprouted out the top, approximating the appearance of human hair. Impossibly, the creature stood upright. A third leg, thicker than the other two, looked as if it had burst through the creature's neck, distorting its guttural growls. Flaps of skin, like the suckers of a lamprey, twisted and agitated against the throat-end of the leg. The howling sound whistled over these flaps, a wet and frantic wail.

As Leonard watched in horror, the third leg began to swing back and forth. The lamprey-flaps pushed and scraped until the skin of this thick digit began to slough off. The leg bent and wiggled, and the casing of skin slipped to the ground. The creature howled again through the opening in its throat, a faint hiss from its mouth joining the awful cry. As it screamed, the raw limb began to tear itself down the middle. Two newly formed legs stretched in opposite directions, then the creature's body shifted, and the new legs lowered to the ground. It walked on four legs in the morning.

What was it?

Bumble-glumph, Leonard thought. *Hurgle-whynn*.

No.

The creature studied him, its eyes black in a pruned and scaled face that expressed a terrible malice.

Leonard backed into the cabin and slammed the door. He flicked the latch to hold it closed, noticing now that it was a similar hook-and-eyelet contraption to the three doors at Sibley's miniature amphitheatre. Next he heard a gallop of four legs, two of them untested and shuffling in the dirt. A hard crack hit the bottom of the door, as if a golf ball had been rolled into it. The wood shook beneath his hand. He heard a quick chittering sound, then the creature scrambled away.

Thank God. The thing was some weird hybrid, a chimera. Leonard's late-night musings seemed less preposterous after such evidence. Perhaps Sibley was some kind of magician after all, his studies of ancient texts uncovering dark secrets other scholars overlooked or avoided out of fear. Sibley had summoned this creature somehow—or he'd had some hand in its making, as surely as he'd crafted those bizarre, tiny masks that would fit perfectly over the creature's head. Leonard imagined this had been Sibley's real project all these years: not a second book, but a quest for new, literal truth in the Riddle of the Sphinx. A creature that transformed each day, its two front legs withering away to an upright noon, then a new thick leg tearing through the throat as evening fell. At night the throat would swell around a leg that choked each awkward step. By early morning this leg would itch and wriggle itself into agony: Leonard thought of his own hand, if the webbing between the middle and ring fingers were stretched until it split, then the palm ripped raw, the whole arm torn up the middle. And cursed to suffer this same metamorphosis each day? No wonder the creature howled. No wonder it looked so angry.

As if it blamed Leonard for its pain.

He heard the howl again: the throat gurgle and the hiss combined. A similar cry answered from the right side of the cabin. Then two distinct calls from the left.

Leonard slid to a seated position, his back supporting the door. Tiny feet scuffed in the dirt, the leader's gallop more steady. A patter joined from the sides, like rain, then a series of hail-stone cracks battered against the bottom of the door. Leonard's lower back jolted with each strike.

He couldn't hold this door forever. He wondered about other entrances. In the kitchen, the window was up high, over the sink; but in the main room of the cabin, the sill was a scant two feet above the floor. Those legs—the two back legs, constant through all the transformations, their muscles strengthened over time . . . How high might these creatures be able to jump?

A weapon would help ease his mind, and Leonard recalled the steak knife he'd used for yesterday's meals. He saw the wooden handle along the edge of the kitchen counter, knew he could retrieve the weapon in a few quick seconds. But he was too afraid to leave the front door unguarded.

The chittering noise grew louder, then the scuffle of retreat before a renewed assault. In that instant, Leonard realized he'd neglected the early part of Oedipus's story. King Laius learns that his son will grow up to murder him. To circumvent the prophesy, he instructs a servant to abandon the infant in an isolated place, where he would surely die.

In this formulation, Sibley hadn't loaned the cabin to Leonard out of kindness, but to remove a threat from the new generation of scholars. He struggled to remember Sibley's exact phrasing. *You're welcome to use my cabin. But I'm afraid no one will ever read that book.*

More patter of small feet in distant dirt, getting louder.

The words of these plays are like magic. They cast a spell.

Leonard concentrated, even as the feet grew closer, the steps more numerous. A word appeared to him, in Greek letters, but somehow beyond pronunciation. The letters enveloped him, out of focus. If he could grasp the letters, speak the word . . .

The creatures' heads battered against the lower door. The latch rattled with each hit, and he knew that soon either the wood would splinter, or the hook would jiggle out of the eyelet. To drown out the fearful sound Leonard covered his ears and shouted that strange word.

The spell. The name. The true answer to the riddle.

The door ceased to move against his back. Leonard dropped his hands from his ears, and heard nothing. The creatures were silent. No chittering. No shuffles in the dirt as they moved away.

He stood up, then rushed to retrieve the steak knife from the kitchen counter. Dry clumps of peanut butter stuck to parts of the serrated edge, but the tip was sharp and the heavy wooden handle offered some comfort as Leonard returned to the windowless door. He wasn't ready to open it, yet he was certain the creatures had disappeared. They were banished once their name was spoken, the Riddle of the Sphinx solved after all these centuries. Leonard had accomplished something where Sibley, where even the mighty Oedipus, had failed.

Beneath that pride, Leonard worried he might have seen too much. The mask of his face must have held its expression, the curious look he'd worn all weekend, brow furrowed in the perpetual pose of a scholar's inquiry.

A rush of wind blasted through the silence, like the flap of large wings over the cabin. A hideous shriek sent tremors through the walls; the floor shook beneath his feet.

The old story was wrong. She wasn't suicidal: she was angry.

He clutched the knife's handle, certain that the Sphinx was ready to pose a new riddle, one he'd never be able to answer. Heavy talons scraped along the roof. Leonard felt the temptation of an itch behind each eye.

═══◆═══

Bordertown can be a harsh mistress to the unwary.

A TANGLE OF GREEN MEN

Charles de Lint

1.

When Tía Luba talks everybody listens. That's just the way it is for us kids, on or off the rez.

I'm getting my release from the Kikimi County Young Offenders Correction Facility, which is just a fancy way of saying juvie. I've been on good behavior, done my time. Studied for my classes—even got my grade 9. Didn't mouth off to the guards or psychologists or counselors. Moved rocks and dirt around on the weekends to build character and amuse the guards. Basically, I kept my head down and my nose clean.

The guard accompanies me from the buildings to the outer gate. As we walk toward it, I get a good look at the twelve-foot-high chain-link fence with the barbed wire on top that makes a big loop around the facility. I've stared at it for the past eight months but the last time I was up this close, I was on the outside being bused in from the city.

The guard talks into his walkie-talkie and the gate swings open. I step through and taste freedom.

"There's two buses a day," the guard says. "You missed the first one but another comes by at five."

It's noon. The sun's high, beating down on the desert. It's got to be 110 out here on the pavement. The road stretches for as far as I can see in either direction. There's only scrub and cacti.

The guard spits on the ground as the gate closes.

"Should have brought some water with you," he says.

I hear him chuckle as he makes his way back to the main building.

I start walking. I've got two choices: the city or the mountains. The city's what got me in trouble the last time, so I walk northeast to where the Hierro Maderas rise tall and graying in the distance.

My baseball cap helps against the sun but there's only so much it can do. I can feel the moisture leaving my body. A couple of hours of this and I'll be as parched as the dirt on either side of the blacktop. A couple hours more and I'll be dry enough for the wind to pick me up and blow me away.

When I hear the pickup slowing down behind me, I don't turn around. I just keep walking. Being around people's another thing that got me in trouble. I either buy into their crap—which is how I found myself in Kikimi—or I end up taking a swing at them. I don't seem to have a whole lot of middle ground, but I'm working on it.

The pickup pulls up beside me and a familiar voice says, "You want a ride?"

I sigh. When the truck stops, I pop the passenger door and get in. I look at my aunt. She looks back at me, those dark brown eyes seeing everything. Her skin's brown but still smooth. Her black hair's tied back in a braid. She's wearing jeans and a man's flannel shirt with the sleeves rolled up.

"Hey, Tía," I say as she puts the pickup in gear and pulls away. "What brings you out here?"

Like I don't already know.

"I was interested in seeing which direction you'd choose."

"I'm guessing since you stopped, I got that part right."

Her lip twitches, which is about as much of a smile as I've ever gotten out of her. She pulls a pack of smokes out of her pocket and tosses them onto my lap. I take one out and light it with one of the matches stuck into the empty half of the pack. When I offer it to her, she shakes her head. I close up the pack and put it on the console between the bucket seats.

"So now let's see how you do with the second part," she says. "I've got a ticket to Baltimore for you. If you're interested, Herbert's got a job for you and you can stay with him."

What she doesn't say is I'm turning eighteen next month. The next time I get busted I won't be going into juvie. Instead I'll be going into the adult prison system, which for my people is pretty much the biggest rez in the country.

"What's the job?" I ask.

"Well, you won't be stealing cars."

I nod. "I'd like that."

"If you screw this up . . . "

"I won't," I tell her.

I probably will. So far it's been the story of my life. I can see in her eyes she's thinking the same thing. But I'm willing to give it a try and she sees that, too.

Her lip twitches again.

"We'll make a man out of you yet," she says.

It's a ways to the rez. I reach over and turn on the radio, moving through the bands till I get the tribal station. Her lip twitches a third time. She must be in a really good mood.

Uncle Herbert lives like he's still in the shadows of the Hierro Maderas. He's got a basement apartment that smells of piñon, sweetgrass and cedar. He's eating Indian tacos and beans and flatbread that I have to admit taste as good as anything I ever had back home. And he still makes his coffee the way we do on the rez, water and coffee all mixed up in the same pot. Doesn't matter how well you strain it, you're still picking grounds from between your teeth, but seriously? I can't think of a better way to start the day.

He was a medicine man back on the rez, but he left when the war of words between the traditionalists and the casino crowd got too heated.

"If we were supposed to fight over possessions like white men," he told me, "the Creator would have made us white men."

Except now he lives here in Baltimore and works as a foreman for a company that provides the set-up gear for conventions and shows. Go figure. I feel like telling him he's living like the casino crowd, except he's poorer, but keeping my mouth shut's been working pretty good these days so I keep it to myself.

The work's easy. It's hard, sweaty work, but you don't have to think—that's the easy part. We just follow the floor plan that the organizers give us. We haul in all the tables, chairs, and podiums, set up the bare bones of the booths, build stages—whatever they need.

Uncle Herbert's got a solid team. They're mostly Mexican and black. They aren't afraid to work and they love Uncle Herbert to a man. It was like that back on the rez, too, which is why he left. People were ready to go to war if he just said the word. He knew if he stayed any longer, he'd ending up doing that and he didn't want anybody's blood on his hands.

"Do you miss it?" I asked as we drove home from a job one night.

He's got this old Ford pickup that's held together with rust and body filler, but it runs like a charm. Me, I'm still saving for a ride.

"I miss the quiet," he said, then he looked at me and grinned. "And I miss living on Indian time."

Having spent the eight months before I came up here following an institutional schedule, I'm used to getting up early and being on time. But I gave him a smile and nodded.

"I hear you," I said.

Uncle Herbert goes to bed early—pretty much after dinner. I'd maybe get bored, but I fill my time. I'm trying to teach myself wood carving. I don't have any tools except my jackknife, but wood's cheap and I've got all the time in the world to learn. Uncle Herbert doesn't have a TV, but he's got an old radio that someone left on the curb. He tinkered with it until he got it working again, so I listen to Public Radio while I work on my carvings. Little bears and lizards and birds like Hopi fetishes except they're made of wood. Sometimes I go to the corner bar and nurse a couple of ginger ales while I watch a game on their big screen.

We get all kinds of gigs but the ones that give me the biggest kick are where the people all play dress-up. Since I got here we've done two sci-fi conventions. The set-up's no different than it is for any other kind of convention, but if you hang around the back halls of the hotel you can watch them walking around like spacemen and barbarians and everything in between.

Some people really put a lot of work into their costumes and seeing grown men and women dressed up like their favorite characters just puts a smile on my face. It reminds me of the powwows where everybody trades in their jeans and Ts for ribbon shirts and jingle dresses. For a couple of days they get to step out of their lives and be the people they wish they were.

But the sci-fi conventions have nothing on our current job. With the sci-fi crowd the regular folks outnumber the ones in costume. At this FaerieCon pretty much *everybody's* in costume, from the organizers to the people working the tables in the dealers' room. There are a lot more girls, too—pretty girls with sparkles in their hair and faerie wings on their backs. The guys are working the faerie theme, too, but some of them look like walking shrubs in cloaks with leaves sewn all over their shirts and pants and masks that look they're made of leaves and tree bark.

"Man," Luther says, "I'd like me a piece of that."

I nod like I do when anybody says something to me. I find when you do, people pick the response they want so you don't have to actually say anything.

He's checking out an Asian girl who wouldn't have been out of place at one of the sci-fi conventions. She's wearing leather with lots of buckles, high boots and a short skirt. Her top hat's got brass buttons all over it and what looks like a weird pair of binoculars resting on the brim. And of course she's got wings.

"She looks good," Luther says, "and she knows it. Wonder what she wears when she's not playing dress-up?"

I shrug.

"Yeah," he says. "Doesn't make much difference. Girl like that, she doesn't even see a guy like you or me. But she sure is hot."

I go get another table from the dolly.

I'm outside on a smoke break later when I see one of those guys wearing a costume all made of leaves. I quit smoking since I moved to Baltimore, but I'll take the break. This guy's pretty old—in his fifties, I'd guess—and not in the best of shape. I watch him for a moment as he wrestles with some big box in the back of his van, so I go over and ask him if he wants a hand.

"Hey, thanks," he says as I take one end of the box.

We put it on his dolly and get another box from the van.

"Can I ask you something?" I say.

"Sure."

"No offense, but what makes a guy your age dress up the way you do?"

He laughs. "What do you think I'm supposed to be?"

"I don't know. A tree?"

"Close. I'm a Green Man."

"I still don't get it."

He straightens up and launches into his spiel. As he talks I'm still not sure I get it, but I like his enthusiasm.

"The Green Men are the messengers of spring," he says. "We're the ones who carry the seeds of rebirth. We're always looking for a good resting place because we have to sleep away the winter, dreaming the promise of renewal."

"And that's a Baltimore thing?"

"No, it goes back to England. Have you ever been over there?"

I shake my head.

"You see the image of the Green Man all over the place," he says. "On pub signs and on carvings in churches. They're literally everywhere. On some buildings you see them in place of gargoyles, the water draining from their open mouths. The funny thing is, people don't really notice them anymore. And if they do, most of them don't understand their significance."

"That they're messengers of spring," I say.

"Exactly. We're symbols of hope, but it's more than just a promise. The Green Man brings in the spring. Without us, all you get is winter."

"So the people coming to this convention—it's like a spiritual thing for them?"

"Partly. For some of us. But it's also fun to just dress up and fill a hotel with a gathering of faeries and goblins and all."

We're done loading his dolly and he locks up his van.

"So how come it's all European faeries?" I ask. "I've never heard of Green Men before, but I've seen faeries in kids' books and the people here look like they do in the pictures, or in a Disney movie. How come there aren't any native faeries?"

"You mean Native American?"

"Sure, but I was talking more about North America in general."

He gives me a curious look and I realize that since I moved here, this is the longest conversation I've had with anyone except for Uncle Herbert.

"I've got to get this stuff inside and set up," he says, "but you should come by my booth when the Market closes. We can talk some more then."

I shake my head. "I don't think I'd fit in with your crowd."

"You'd be surprised," he says. "We come in all shapes and sizes." He offers me his hand. "I'm Tom Hill. If you change your mind, I'm in booth forty-eight."

I take his hand. "I'm Joey Green," I say, then I laugh. "Maybe I *would* fit in."

"What's the story behind your surname?" he asks.

"As in what does it mean?"

He nods.

I shrug. "It just means one of my ancestors liked the sound of it. We never used surnames until the government forced us, so people just made up whatever they felt like calling themselves."

"I still think this is an auspicious meeting," he says.

I'm not sure what the word means so I just give him another shrug.

"Thanks again for your help," he adds. "Think about dropping by later."

"Sure," I tell him, because it's easier than coming up with excuses.

I don't realize I'm going to take him up on it until later in the day when this part of the job's all done. Uncle Herbert comes over to where I'm sitting with the rest of the crew, listening to them talk.

"You ready to go, Joey?" he asks.

I shake my head. "One of the guys in the show asked me to stick around so I thought I might."

He checks me out with a look that would do Tía Luba proud, then he just nods.

"I'll see you later, then," he says.

I like the fact that he trusts me enough to not feel like he's got to give me any advice.

"You got your eye on one of those girls?" Luther asks.

I don't bother answering.

Luther laughs. "See if she's got a friend for me," he says as he heads off with Uncle Herbert and the others.

I have second thoughts when I go back into the hotel. What do I really think is going to happen here? Hill's probably going to just give me a blank look when I show up at his booth.

I hesitate in the doorway of the Market. The place is transformed. It looks more like some old-fashioned market set up in a forest glade than a dealers' room in a hotel. Somebody comes up and starts to tell me that the room's closed, but I tell him I'm part of the set-up crew.

"I'm supposed to meet Tom Hill," I add.

The man nods. "Do you know where his booth is?"

"Number forty-eight."

But when I get to the booth, he's not there. There's only a pretty girl about my age in a silky green dress with flowers and leaves sewn onto it. Her long red-gold hair hangs in a braid halfway to her waist and she'd got the little points on the tips of her ears that everybody here seems to have. I walked by a booth that was selling them on my way to Hill's. The girl has a closed book on her lap—a big old book with a tooled leather binding—and she's playing with a beaded bracelet of some kind. The only thing that seems out of place are the cat's-eye sunglasses she's wearing.

I stand at the booth, unsure again, so I check out what's for sale. Hill specializes in tooled leather masks. His work's incredible. I've got a cousin who does this kind of thing with boots, so I know how much artistry and skill is involved. Most of the masks are intricate collections of leaves with eyeholes. Some are simple, little more than leafy Zorro masks. Others are so complicated I can't imagine how many hours it took to complete them.

I look at the price tag on one of them. If people are buying these, he's making a good profit.

I'm about to turn away when the girl suddenly lifts her head. She looks in my direction but her gaze doesn't quite find me.

"Is someone there?" she asks.

I feel like telling her that she'll see a lot better without the shades on but all I say is, "I'm looking for Tom Hill."

"He's my dad. He just stepped out for a couple of minutes to talk to the rest of his hedge, but he should be back soon."

"His what?"

She laughs and it sounds like delicate bells.

"Are you new to the con?" she asks.

"Pretty much.

"Do you know what a Green Man is?"

I nod, but she doesn't go on, so I add, "Yeah, your dad was explaining them to me."

"Well, a hedge is what they call a line of Green Men. I think they're working out a welcome for one of the Guests of Honor."

"Okay."

She laughs again and I find myself wishing I had a recording of it so that I could play it whenever I wanted.

"Why don't you come into the booth?" she says. "You can keep me company while you wait for him. I promise I don't bite."

"You should be careful about who you talk to. I could be anybody."

"But that's one of the cool things about life," she says.

"What? That strangers can be dangerous?"

"No, silly. That we can be anybody we choose."

"It doesn't really work that way in my world," I tell her.

"Now you really have to come sit with me and tell me all about this world of yours."

Why not? I think. Maybe I can get her to laugh some more for me.

As I come around the table to where she's sitting, the bracelet she's been playing with drops from her hand.

"Crap," she says. "Would you get that for me?"

She doesn't even look at where it fell.

Why don't you get it yourself, princess? I want to say, but then I suddenly realize something and I feel like a heel.

"You can't see, can you?" I say.

"Well, I can see light and dark shapes to some degree, but I'm pretty much legally blind."

She just says it like a fact with no hint of bitterness or self-pity.

I don't know what to say so I settle for, "Bummer."

"Yeah, I miss colors most of all, especially with all the costumes here at FaerieCon."

"So you weren't always blind."

She shakes her head. "I like to say that I strayed into Faerieland and it was such an intense experience that I went blind—you know, like the stories say some people go mad when they come back."

"Faerieland," I repeat.

"Work with me," she says.

"Okay. You lost your sight going into Faerieland. Got it."

"And so," she goes on, "the only way I can get my sight back is if I return there. Or maybe I can find my way to Bordertown and some faerie mage can cure me."

"Bordertown?" I repeat. "The only border towns I know are places like Nogales and I don't think you're going to find any faeries there."

"No, I mean the capital 'B' Bordertown that sits between Faerieland and our world."

"Right."

"I thought you were working with me," she says.

I grin, but she can't see it.

"Well, let me know if you need someone to take you there," I say.

That earns me another hit of that intoxicating laugh of hers.

"Are you volunteering?" she asks.

"Isn't that how it works in faerie tales? You're supposed to help people out as you wander around trying to make your fortune."

"Is that what you're doing?"

"No, I'm just trying to save up enough to buy myself a pick-up."

I sit on her extra chair and lean down to pick up the bracelet for her.

"Here," I say.

She takes my hand in one of her own and plucks the bracelet out with the other. Then she lifts her free hand toward my face.

"May I?" she asks.

It's like butterfly wings on my skin as explores the contours of my face.

"You've got a strong nose," she says.

"Yeah, that's why they called me Big Nose back on the rez when I was growing up."

I don't add that they stopped because I went after whoever used the nickname. If you don't nip something like that in the bud, you're stuck with it for life. Just ask Six-Toes George, Uncle Herbert's brother.

"You're Native American?" she asks.

I nod, then add, "Yeah," because I'm not sure how much she can see with her limited sight. "I belong to the desert tribes. Kikimi on my mother's side and my dad was a Yaqui."

"Not exactly faerie tale country."

"Not so much."

"So what brings you to FaerieCon?"

"I'm with the crew that set up the booths," I tell her. "I ran into your dad this afternoon. He said I should come by so we could talk some more."

I figure that'll be the end of any interest she might have in me. Girls like her don't hang out with the behind-the-scenes joes who are supposed to stay invisible. But she only smiles.

"I should warn you," she says, "when Dad says 'talk' he usually means he talks and everybody else listens."

"He seemed okay to me."

"Oh, he's awesome. He's just not a good listener. The good thing is that he's full of all sorts of interesting information so he's rarely boring."

"That's not a problem," I tell her. "I'm more of a listener myself anyway."

"Really? You've got such a compelling voice."

Is she flirting with me? Time to shut that down. The last thing I need is to have some nice middle-class white girl flirting with me, even if her dad does think he's a tree.

"I just find things work out better when I don't talk too much," I tell her. "I can have a big mouth and it gets me into trouble. Or at least it did back when I was still drinking."

That should do it.

"How old are you?" she asks.

"Seventeen."

With the sunglasses on, it's hard to tell what she's thinking.

"Me, too," she says. "But I'm thinking I've still had a way easier life than you did."

"I don't think of it like that," I tell her. "Growing up the way I did—that's just the way it is down in Kikimi County. I could beat myself up about it, but I'd rather look at it as learning experiences that shaped who I am today. I'll be the first to admit I've messed up a lot, but I'm getting better at doing the right thing."

Speaking of which, I add to myself.

"I should go," I tell her.

I don't know what it is about this girl and her father that have me yakking away like girls on the rez.

"Don't," she says as I stand up.

I hesitate. I know I shouldn't stay but I can't help feeling flattered by her interest. I can't remember the last time that happened. Maybe never, unless I was paying for the drinks.

"What's your name?" she asks.

"Joey."

"I'm Juliana."

She puts out her hand and I automatically shake. As soon as her fingers close around mine, she pulls me back down onto the chair.

"I'm enjoying your company," she says. "Because of my disability, people can feel a little awkward around me. It's easier for them to just give me a friendly hello, then go off to carry on with whatever else they're doing. They don't actually want to sit with me."

"That's got to be hard."

She shrugs. "It's what it is. But it can make me feel a little lonely sometimes." She pauses before she adds, "You don't seem to focus on it at all."

"I guess I can stay awhile longer."

She beams. Then she lifts the book from her lap.

"If you don't want to talk," she says, "maybe you could read to me."

"I'm not that good a reader."

"Oh, I'm sorry. I didn't mean to—"

"I can read," I tell her. "I'm just slow at it."

"Then maybe you could tell me a story."

"You mean like a Kikimi faerie tale?"

"Do you know any?"

"Not really." Though right now I wish I did. "All I know are Jimmy Littlecreek stories."

"Who's Jimmy Littlecreek?"

"He was kind of a legend back on the rez—always getting into these complicated situations and then making even more of a mess of things than they already were. But at the same time he had these desert rat smarts that always made things work out in the end. Back home, everybody knows a story or two about him."

"He sounds like a trickster."

"I guess he is. Sort of a little cousin to Coyote."

"I'd love to hear one."

So I tell her about how he and Bobby Morago stole a train in Linden and drove it backwards all the way from the mountains down to Santo del Vado Viejo just so they could have a date with a couple of Mexican girls they'd met the previous weekend. It's a good choice, because I get the reward of her laughter over and over again. Truth is, I stretch it into an even taller tale just to keep her laughing.

I'm just finishing up when her dad shows up. He stands there smiling as I tell the end of the story.

"Sorry I didn't get back sooner," he says. "Green Man business always seems to take longer than I think it will."

"That's okay. Juliana's been keeping me entertained."

She laughs. "It's more like the other way around."

Tom's still smiling, but I can see he's studying me. Probably regretting that he asked me to come around to his booth. But then he surprises me.

"I was wondering if you could do me a favor," he says.

"What do you need?"

"My friend Sam drove the van you helped me unload this afternoon but I just found him in the bar and he's had far too much to drink. Now I'm stuck with having to get both the van and my station wagon home. What makes it more complicated is that I also have drive out to the airport to pick up Juliana's mother. Her plane's coming in around nine and it's already eight."

I nod to show I'm listening, but I don't know where he's going with this.

"So I was wondering," he says, "if you'd mind dropping Sam off at his place and then taking Juliana home. She hates the drive out to the airport at night."

"Hate it," she puts in.

You don't know anything about me, but you're going to entrust your daughter to my care? But then I remember the way he was studying me a moment ago. He had that look in his eyes that Tía Luba gets when she's taking somebody's measure. Maybe he's got her gift for reading character. If that's the case he knows he can trust me.

"I can do that," I tell him.

"Yay," Juliana says.

"I really appreciate it," Tom says. "I'll go round up Sam and meet you in the parking lot."

After he leaves, I help Juliana gather her things. She slips her hand into the crook of my arm. I don't think I've ever walked arm-in-arm with a girl before. Back on the rez I wouldn't be caught dead doing this. But I like it. At least I like it with this girl.

We get to the station wagon around the same time that Tom and Sam do. Tom's half-carrying his friend. I remember how that feels. It looks even less pretty.

Sam's geared up like a male version of that girl Luther was lusting after earlier today. He's wearing a mix of pointed ears and wings with some tooled-leather clothes and boots. The jacket has odd little clockwork accessories sewn onto the shoulders and lapels and he's wearing a top hat that has something that looks like a combination of a monocle and a short telescope attached to the brim.

Tom takes off the hat, unhooks his wings and steers Sam into the backseat. He puts the hat and wings beside him. When he straightens up he looks at me.

"Did you drive here?" he asks.

I shake my head. "I'm taking the bus home."

"I'll give you a lift when I get back."

"Or he could just stay the night," Juliana says.

Tom laughs. "Or you could stay the night." He gives Juliana a gentle poke in the shoulder. "But not in your room, young missy."

I've never been around people like this before. Is this how the rest of the world lives?

"Thanks again, Joey," he says. "I'll see you kids later."

I walk Juliana around to the passenger's side, then get in the car myself. I adjust the rear-view mirror and see that Sam's already passed out.

"So what's he supposed to be dressed as?" I ask.

"What's he wearing?" When I describe his outfit, she says, "He's a steampunk faerie."

"Should I ask?"

"It's a faerie look inspired by a mash-up of—oh, I don't know. Jules Verne and *A Midsummer Night's Dream* with maybe a dash of Tim Powers and some pirates."

"I've no idea what that means."

She smiles. "It's just another look. It hasn't been around long but Dad likes it because they're really into the tooled leather."

I start up the car.

"I forgot to ask your dad for directions," I say.

"There's a GPS in the glove compartment, but I can tell you where to go. I won't be able to tell if you make a wrong turn, but we should be fine."

"I'm in your hands."

For some reason that makes her giggle, which is just as endearing as her laugh, and I realize I'm in trouble.

When it comes to girls, I'm not the most experienced guy in the world. I've never fallen for one before; I've just hooked up. Stoned or drunk at a party, maybe in one of the bars in VV that will look the other way for a minor who's got the cash. The longest "relationship" I've had lasted a weekend.

And I'm not saying I had a lot of hook-ups, though to be honest, I can't really remember. Those days just blur into each other. I remember my times in juvie, but I was sober then. Juvie's like jail: rehab for poor people, and it doesn't usually take. But I'm good right now. Ten months and seven days, counting jail time. That's the longest I've been straight since I was twelve.

I remember how scared I was, the first few times I got locked up. But this is scarier. Maybe Juliana's just slumming, having some fun as she flirts with me. But if she's not, if she's feeling anything like what I'm feeling, I've got to step up to a world of responsibility. I've got to do right by her. And for damn sure I can't start something I can't finish.

I'm getting way ahead of myself. Who knows what she's thinking? But that's the funny thing about hope.

I opt to use the GPS so we don't get lost. We drop Sam off at his apartment. I take him upstairs and get him laid out on top of his bed.

"You're on your own now," I tell him.

He pushes his face into his pillow and I doubt he hears me leave. When he wakes up he probably won't even know that I was here in the first place or that I drove him home.

Back in the car, I set the GPS to "home" and read out the address it gives me.

"That's us," she says.

It's not far to the Hills' house and I'm feeling nervous right up until when we pull into the driveway. I was expecting something fancy, all modern lines and expensive. I see old buses and cars parked along one side of the property. The house itself is a bungalow that's been added onto a few times so that it does this zigzag walk into the backyard. A couple of lanky dogs get up off the porch to greet us and I feel right at home because none of this would be out of place back on the rez.

"That's Lucky and Bud," Juliana says as the dogs push their noses into my crotch.

I move them away.

"I would have thought they'd have faerie names," I say as I help her out of the car and walk her towards the porch.

"What, like Titania and Oberon?"

"I don't know who they are, but yeah, that sounds about right."

"Can you see these guys with faerie tale names?" she asks as Bud shoves his nose back into my crotch.

"I guess not."

I'm not saying she was particularly timid moving around earlier, but she gets way more confident as soon as we step onto the porch. I suppose it's got something to do with her being on home ground. If I were in her position I'd have memorized where everything is and all the steps in between.

She takes a key out of her pocket and fits it smoothly into the lock, using a finger to guide her. Swinging the door open, she reaches around the doorjamb to turn on an overhead light. I follow her inside. The dogs collapse back on the porch like they suddenly have no bones.

The room we're in is the kitchen—a big friendly and very cluttered space with rustic furniture standing shoulder-to-shoulder with modern appliances. From where we stand I can see another room past the kitchen. It's poorly lit at the moment but it seems just as welcoming and cluttered.

"Want to see my room?" she asks.

I laugh. "Maybe later."

When her parents are home.

"Okay. How about some coffee or tea?"

"Sure, I—look, I'm new at this, but I'm just going to go with the assumption that if you need help with anything, you'll ask for it. Is that okay?"

She smiles as she effortlessly finds the kettle, fills it, then takes a couple of mugs and a box of some herbal tea down from a cupboard.

"That's one of the things I like about you, Joey," she says as she plugs the kettle in. "With most people my disability is like a third person in the room that we don't really want to have hanging around, but there she is all the same."

"Don't you think that people are just being sympathetic? That they only want to help you?"

"Oh, I know that's most of it. But it also makes everything awkward because they can't forget about it either. So it never just feels normal."

I feel bad for her. I think about how few people there are in the world that I'm close to. But that's always been my choice—or if I'm going to be honest, the result of the bad decisions I used to make. The thing is, I never really tried to fix it. Juliana's had it pushed on her through no fault of her own.

When the tea's ready she leads me through the cluttered dining room into an equally cluttered living room where we sit together on a fat sofa. But for all the books and magazines and what-have-you scattered around I notice that the spaces between the furniture are all clear.

"So tell me more about faeries in Baltimore," I say to keep the mood lighter. "Or maybe this Bordertown you were talking about."

"Only if you'll tell me more about Jimmy Littlecreek."

"Deal. But you first."

"It'll be easier to show you," she says. "Are you coming back to FaerieCon tomorrow?"

"I hadn't really thought about it. Do you think I should?"

She taps her fist against my shoulder. "Of course I do. It'll be fun."

"I can't really get away until later on in the day. We're doing the set-up for a motivational speaker tomorrow."

"That's okay. Things don't get hopping until the evening. Everybody gets all dolled up and parades around the halls and then we all go to the Good Faeries' Ball. Mom says she's got some surprise outfit for me that she picked up in Eugene—that's where she's been, visiting a friend from college."

"I don't really do costumes," I tell her. "Even back on the rez. At the powwows, I was always the kid sitting under the bleachers swapping a bottle with the other reprobates and making fun of the dancers."

Her hand brushes my arm, butterfly light. "You really have had a hard life, haven't you?"

"It's just what it was," I say. "I'm working on making it different."

There's a moment of awkward silence and I wonder if I've said too much and who knows what's going on in her head because of it?

"So, let's forget about that stuff for now," I say. "What about this Good Faeries' Ball?"

She brightens up. "There's live music and dancing and just, you know, fun. But you'd probably like the dance on Saturday night better. That's when we have the Bad Faeries' Ball."

"You think I'm more into bad faeries?"

"No, but you're a guy and the girls wear some pretty sexy outfits."

"And are you going to have a bad faerie costume?"

She smiles. "I'm thinking about it. I guess it depends on if Mom's willing to help and Dad'll let me out the door."

I laugh. "So they're *that* sexy, are they?"

"You'll just have to come and find out."

I want to put my arm around her shoulders. No, that's not true. I want to lie naked with her on the sofa and forget about everything else in the world but her. But if I know anything, too much too soon is never a good thing if you want to stay in it for the long run. Doesn't matter how flirty she is with me. Except then she rests her head on my shoulder and I think the hell with it. I put an arm around her and lean down to where her lips are lifting towards mine and then headlights flash on the walls and we hear the tires of a car crunching on the dirt and stones of the driveway.

She sits up, though she doesn't move away from me.

"Perfect timing," she says ruefully.

I start to move my arm away but she lifts a hand to hold it in place.

"Come to the Good Faeries' Ball with me tomorrow," she says, "and I'll let you take me to the Bad Faeries' Ball on Saturday night. And no," she adds as I hesitate, "you don't have to wear a costume. You can be my mortal consort."

"I'll be there," I tell her.

The kitchen door opens and I stand up to meet her mother.

Alana Hill gives me a glimpse of the beauty that Juliana's going to grow into. She's a tall, striking woman with a spill of long reddish-gold hair that hangs almost to her waist in a waterfall of curls. After the introductions have been made she holds onto my hand and studies me for longer and with a more penetrating seriousness than her husband did.

"Mom," Juliana says.

Her mother finally lets go of my hand. I can't tell if I passed muster or not, but at least she smiles.

"Come on," Tom says. "I'll give you a lift home. And thanks again for helping me out."

"Can I come?" Juliana asks.

I figure that's not going to happen, not with her mother having just come home from being halfway across the country. Alana looks to her husband who gives her a helpless shrug.

"Of course you can go," Alana says.

Juliana takes my arm, but we all know she doesn't need any guidance here in her own home.

"We shouldn't be long," Tom says.

Uncle Herbert's building isn't much to look at, but I already know that the Hills are pretty casual when it comes to this sort of thing. They're not going to judge me on where I live. Tom pulls the station wagon over to the curb.

"Look the other way, Dad," Juliana says, then leans over and kisses me. "So, see you tomorrow?"

She sits back in her seat before I have a chance to react.

I nod. "Soon as I get off work. Thanks for the lift, Mr. Hill."

"Just Tom's fine."

"Then thanks for the lift, Just Tom."

Tom smiles and Juliana giggles as I get out of the car.

After they pull away, I stand there outside Uncle Herbert's apartment building watching until the taillights disappear. When I go inside, I feel like I'm walking on a cloud.

Uncle Herbert is still up, which means he trusted me enough to go off on my own, but he was still worried. He smiles at what I'm guessing is the goofy look on my face.

"You're looking happy," he says.

"Yeah, I—I just never had such a good buzz before that didn't come out of a pipe or a bottle."

"Funny how that works, isn't it?"

"What do you mean?"

"Come on, Joey. Do you think you're the only person in this family that ever had a problem with booze?"

"Are you saying—"

He waves the question off and pushes himself out of the chair.

"We can trade war stories some other time," he says. "Right now I'm going to bed."

I do the same. We've got a long day ahead of us tomorrow. But I lie in bed for a time, just grinning at the ceiling, and when I do fall asleep, instead of dreaming about being back in juvie, I dream about people who not only walk around with faerie wings, but they can fly, too.

As soon as we get finished up with the job on Saturday, I go home and take a shower. Afterward I'm standing there in my jeans looking at the half-dozen T-shirts I own when Uncle Herbert comes in. Maybe Juliana won't be able to see what I'm wearing in any kind of detail, but I still want to look good when I'm with her.

Uncle Herbert tosses a long-sleeved shirt onto the bed.

"I think this'll fit you," he says.

I hold it up. It's a soft, thick white cotton with a Kikimi pattern embroidered above the pockets in rusts and pale greens and browns. The colors of the desert.

"I can't take your shirt," I say.

"It's just a loan. But if you're going to be seeing much of this girl you might want to take a few dollars that you've got saved up for that truck of yours and buy a couple of nice shirts."

"Thanks. I will."

"How're you getting there?"

"The No. 12 goes right by the hotel," I tell him.

I didn't want to ask him for a lift.

He nods, then hands me the keys to his truck.

"I've found," he says, "that a girl likes a guy to have his own transportation."

"I don't know what to say."

It's not just the fact that he's loaning me the truck. It's that he trusts me enough to not screw things up.

He grips my shoulder and gives it a squeeze.

"You've been doing so well since you got here," he says, "that Tía Luba thinks I'm bullshitting when she calls to see how you are. You've earned a few perks, Joey."

I'm not much of a touchy-feely guy, but I give Uncle Herbert a hug.

I find Juliana sitting on the edge of a seat in the lobby when I come into the hotel—she has to, just to make room for her wings. They have to be three feet long, gossamer sparkling wings that lift above her head. Her hair is piled high, showing off her slender neck and the little pointed tips on the ends of her ears, and instead of sunglasses she's wearing one of her dad's masks—a slender green wave of leather with the tiniest of eyeholes.

Alana went all out with Juliana's dress. It's the color of a deep forest with a tight bodice that's all brocade and lace. There's more skirt flooding down from her waist than I've ever seen on a girl. All she needs is a crown to be one of those Faerie Queens she loves.

"You look gorgeous," I say when I reach her chair.

She jumps to her feet and throws her arms around my neck.

"You came!" she breathes in my ear.

"You didn't think I would?"

She kisses my neck, then lets her arms drop. She tucks her hand into the crook of my arm.

"I didn't know what to think," she says, "since we're just getting to know each other."

"Which I hope will be a long, fruitful journey."

I don't know why those fancy words popped into my head. I'm acting so weird I hardly know myself, but she squeezes my arm and rests her head against my shoulder for a moment. Then she gives me a tug.

"Come on," she says. "You have to come see the faeries and describe them all to me."

It's chaos in the hotel's lobby and halls. Everywhichway you turn there are faeries and goblins and I-don't-know-what-alls, and people taking pictures of them and each other. It's one thing to be checking out this kind of a scene from the back corridors where the crew and I are bringing in the tables and chairs, but a whole other to be right in the middle of it all. It's wall-to-wall people. The ones with wings sometimes have to turn sideways just to get through the crowd.

I do my best to describe them to Juliana. I think she gets a kick out of me stumbling over my descriptions, but come on, really. What can I do? After awhile you just run out of words.

But some stand out. A couple of scarecrows with straw sticking out of their hats and sleeves make me smile. A mermaid with blue hair. A totally wild woman, green body paint on every bit of skin showing, shrieking in a mad cackling voice. A gnome with a tall red, conical hat. A man dressed like a crow walking on stilts that lift him a few feet above the rest of the crowd.

But mostly it's faeries.

Faeries. Faeries. Faeries.

Baby faeries and old ones. Fat ones and skinny ones.

I think some of the bad ones are here a night early because there are more than a few girls and women wearing seriously sexy outfits. But here's the thing. No matter whether the people are going for a dark look, the vaguely

S&M look, or taking the flower faerie route, everybody just seems genuinely nice. They're respectful and appreciative of each other. Maybe away from a gathering like this they go in for the usual petty crap that everybody seems to, but they appear to have left it behind when they came here. And while I get what Juliana means about her disability being like a third person in the room, people seem happy for her to be here, even if they're wearing sympathy in their eyes at the same time.

I'm one of only a few people not in costume, but they're pretty welcoming to me as well.

When we get to the big room where the bands will play, there's already piped in music and people dancing. I see Alana and Tom across the room and give them a wave.

"Your parents are here," I say.

"What are they wearing?"

"Well, your dad looks like a tree and your mom . . . well, she's kind of got the leafy look going on, too, but she looks way better than the Green Men."

"She's a dryad."

"Which is?"

"The spirit of a tree."

"That makes sense," I say. "You can tell she's got a spiritual thing going for her."

"What she has," Juliana says, "is a gift for reading character. She can tell a lot by just looking at someone, but if she has physical contact, they're laid out for her like reading a book."

I think about how long she was holding my hand yesterday.

"Great," I say.

"Oh, don't worry. You likes you. She said if she had to sum you up in two words they'd be 'loyal' and 'kind.' She also said you could be dangerous, but never to me."

I don't know what to say to that.

"She's teaching me and Dad how to do it," she goes on, "but he's better than I am at it."

I smile, but she can't see it.

"So did you 'read' me yesterday?" I ask.

She nods and starts to blush.

"You know you're blushing?"

She ducks her head now.

"Oh, come on," I say. "What did you get?"

She mumbles something and I think I catch the words "soul mate." I don't push her, but I give her hand a squeeze.

It explains a lot. Her quick acceptance of me and the way I feel about her after knowing her for such a short time. I'm not sure what I think, or what I believe. But I know what I feel. It makes me happy and nervous at the same time and I can see she feels the same way.

Uncle Herbert would say the little thunders are whispering to us.

When the first band comes on they play music I've never heard before. It's somewhere between traditional folk songs and European dance music. I like holding Juliana in my arms but we listen as much as we dance. At one point a couple of very athletic faeries do a fire dance using long orange and yellow ribbons as their flames. In the flickering light, with the music throbbing, you can almost believe they're using real fire.

When the set's over Juliana's parents join us and Alana takes Juliana to the ladies' room.

"I'm glad you could make it," Tom says. "I've never seen Juliana so happy as she is tonight."

I guess this is the concerned dad talk.

"I know it seems to be going really fast," I tell him. "It seems like that to me, too. But I really like her."

"I can see that from how you look at her. But what I like better is how you look out for her—because I see that as well."

"I try. But she's pretty independent."

It's a little weird talking to a guy in a mask of leaves where all you can see is his eyes.

"Tell me about it," he says.

When the next band starts to play he claims his daughter for a dance so I partner with Alana.

"You've got strong, artistic hands," she says. "Do you play music or paint?"

"I do some woodcarving."

She smiles. "I envy you. I've never been able to do three-dimensional work myself."

"I'm not that good. I've just been figuring it out as I go along."

"Well, if you've ever wanted to try your hand at leatherwork, Tom's been looking for an apprentice for ages."

I just look at her.

"I know," she says. She pretends to be embarrassed and raises an eyebrow. "Step too far?"

I find myself wondering what it would be like to have parents that love you as much as the Hills love their daughter. My mother passed when I was twelve and the aunts took us kids in; no one knows what happened to my father. One day he just left the house and he never came back. He could be dead, or in jail, or living a whole other life somewhere. I'll never know.

But I do know that I feel like I'm in over my head. All of this *is* happening fast, but at the same time it doesn't seem to be happening fast enough. Mostly I find it hard to believe that it's real.

"I'd have to ask my uncle," I say.

"Well, think about it," she says.

My next dance is with Juliana and I tell her what her mother said.

"Wow," she says. "Didn't see that coming. What are you going to do?"

"I don't know. Making masks sounds a lot better than hauling around tables and chairs."

"Dad's workshop is at the house," she says, "and the way I hear it, apprentices usually live in their teacher's home."

She doesn't have to say any more. I can fill in the blanks.

"I'm getting tired," she tells me when the dance ends. "I'm not used to being around so many people for so long."

"What do you want to do?" I ask, willing to follow her lead.

"How did you get here?"

"Uncle Herbert lent me his truck."

"How about coming back to the house for awhile? I'll play you romantic songs on my ukulele."

"Really? You play music?"

She pokes me in the chest. "Don't sound so surprised."

"I'm not. I'm delighted."

She grins. "So let's find my parents and tell them where we're going."

Juliana does play her ukulele for me, and not only is she good on it, the instrument's got a lot more going for it than I'd have ever thought. In her hands it has a sweet, bell-like sound to match the bell-like tones in her voice.

We talk some, too, and drink a herbal tea that tastes like cinnamon and nutmeg.

But mostly we neck on the sofa until Juliana takes my hand and puts it on her breast.

"Want to see my room?" she asks like she did last night.

I have to clear my throat.

"What about your parents?" I say.

"They'll be hours still."

She squeals when I pick her up, but then wraps her arms around my neck as I carry her through the house to her room.

2.

Uncle Herbert says that sometimes things are exactly what they seem to be. Since that's how I want it to be with the Hills, that's what I choose to believe.

It's not like I don't get how everything's happening so fast. I do. But I'm almost eighteen now. I wasted so many years in a drunken and stoned haze that I need things to move fast just so I can catch up with what I missed—all the things that normal kids get to do. But it's not like I step right into the middle of a whirlwind. Connecting with Juliana and her parents happens quickly, but the day-to-day moves at a much more reasonable pace.

Still, before I agree to anything, I make sure that Uncle Herbert has a chance to meet the Hills. I owe it to him and Tía Luba for giving me the break I would never have had if I'd stayed in the desert.

A couple of nights after FaerieCon ends, we have dinner at the Hills' house. I help Alana prepare the meal, Juliana sits on a stool chatting with us, while Tom and Uncle Herbert are out on the porch with the dogs, getting to know each other. I don't have any worries about them getting along. Since Uncle Herbert was a medicine man back on the rez and Tom's got that whole Green Man thing going, they have plenty to talk about.

Uncle Herbert's easier to read than Tía Luba has ever been. So when he starts talking over dinner about growing up on the rez, telling funny stories about his brothers and their adventures, I know he likes our hosts as much as I do. But I don't get to know what he's really thinking until it's just the two of us in the cab of his truck and we're driving home.

"Well," he says, "that Juliana's a fine-looking young lady all right. It's not hard to see what caught your eye with her."

"It's not just that."

"Are you sure? You've only known her for a few days and here you are, already set on working for her daddy. Tom even tells me you can move into their house."

"It's hard to explain."

"Try me."

I look out the windshield and try to find the words.

"She's everything you said and more," I tell him. "She's smart and serious and funny and sexy. Anybody'd want to be with her."

"Even with her being almost blind?"

"I don't even think about it—I mean, not as a negative. It makes me want to look out for her, yeah, but it's only a small part of who she is."

I keep staring out the windshield, hoping to pull what I want to say out of the darkness and the lights going by. Uncle Herbert waits patiently.

"Maybe this is going to sound selfish," I finally say, "but beyond everything I like about her that's obvious, I also really like who I am when I'm with her. I'm not an addict or a recovering drunk. I'm not an ex-con. I'm not the guy just looking for someone to say the wrong thing so we can fight. I'm—I'm someone I never thought I'd get the chance to be: an ordinary guy. A *happy* ordinary guy."

"Do you think you make her feel better about herself?"

"I don't know. God, I hope so. But she's got so much going for her—that's the thing that worries me, I guess. What does she need from me?"

Uncle Herbert chuckles. "You don't see the way she looks at you?"

"What do you mean? She can't actually see me."

"I'm not talking about that kind of seeing. I'm talking about how whenever the two of you are in the same room her spirit starts to glow. You can almost see the light spilling out of her. She's always turned in your direction, or leaning toward you like a flower following the sun."

"I don't know about that kind of thing."

"That's why I'm the medicine man and you're not."

"I guess." I shoot him a quick glance. "You can really see that kind of thing?"

"Sure. I see all kinds of things. Like I see that there's something sad in that house, too—mostly I get it from Alana. I couldn't tell what it is and it's not polite to go digging for that kind of thing when you're a guest and no one asks you. But she's got some concern about something."

I nod, but I'm still thinking about what he had to say about Juliana.

"You really think Juliana feels that way?"

He gives me another chuckle. "Why don't you ask her?"

"She—she told me we were soul mates."

"I can see that." We drive for another few blocks before he adds, "That feeling you were talking about—how you feel you're a better person when you're with her? That's not selfish, Joey. That's what makes a couple strong."

I think about that the rest of the way home.

When we get out of the truck, I lean on the hood and look up at what I can see of the stars. It's not like back home, but the good here is outweighing the things I miss.

"I guess I'll call Tía Luba in the morning," I say. "See if she thinks it's okay."

Uncle Herbert leans on the hood beside me.

"You don't have to ask anyone for permission," he says.

"But—"

"Luba sent you here and I took you in because we wanted you to have a chance at a better life. But you had to choose to come. Just like you have to choose what you're going to do with your life. If I thought you were making a bad choice, I'd try to talk you out of it, but I wouldn't *make* you do anything."

I turn to look at him.

"So," I say. "Do you think it's a good choice to work with Tom and live there with them?"

Uncle Herbert grins. "With that girl? With a chance to have a real career instead of moving around dollies stacked with tables and chairs? Hell, yes."

We have a few years together. Amazing years.

There are lots of high points, but it's the little things that stick with you. The sweet routine of the day-to-day.

Family breakfasts. That's nothing I've had a lot of experience with—not unless you include a lot of drama and shouting, and usually several beers.

Juliana's home-schooled. She works with voice-activated computer lessons and Braille textbooks. She teaches me Braille. I put in the long hours of practice and it takes me awhile, but eventually I'm more comfortable "reading" with my eyes closed and a finger following the trail of words across the paper than I am otherwise.

While she does her lessons, I study with Tom in his workshop, learning his craft from the bottom up. Turns out I have a real aptitude for it—Tom says—but I have to admit that it all comes easy to me. I start with the faerie and Green Man masks that are his specialty, but he soon has me working on things from my own imagination. When we start selling them later, mine don't do as well at the faerie festivals—except for the bird masks: raven and owl, hawk and eagle—but there seems to be a huge market for them at the Renaissance Faires.

I dig deep into my memories of childhood stories to find the images I'm looking for. I get Uncle Herbert to tell me the ones I can't remember. Corn mothers. Deer dancers. Cacti spirits. When I do Green Man masks, the trees that come when I shape the leather are sycamore and mesquite, Palo Verde and aspens. I decorate them with Kikimi beadwork and feathers, strips of colored cloth—whatever works.

We have family lunches and suppers, too. Tom, Alana and I take turns putting them together, but it can get complicated for me, who's only ever really cooked for myself and Uncle Herbert, because there are almost always guests at those meals. The Hills know pretty much everybody in their community, it seems, and people tend to drop in throughout the day.

Unless there's something planned—like a music night when the visitor is a musician—evenings are when we go our own ways. Needless to say, I spend mine with Juliana. Sometimes we go visit Uncle Herbert, but mostly we find things to do around the house or walk through the neighborhood with the dogs.

At first I'm afraid that she's going to get bored with me, but that's never the case. It's sure not the case with me. More is never enough.

At night there are visits between our rooms. I'm sure her parents know, but no one says anything. There aren't even knowing looks in the morning.

One of the big things I learn is that Juliana can only get easily around the house if things stay the same. So while there's clutter on tables and the tops of cabinets, all the routes between and through rooms are kept clear. Nothing gets in the way, not even temporarily.

And there's more. Lots of little things. Like the kettle's always in the same place with the handle facing out so that she won't burn a hand feeling for it, and can heft it to see if there's enough water inside. The milk's always in the same place in the fridge. Her toothbrush, toothpaste, comb . . . well, you get the idea.

But that's only one routine. We have another on the road because it turns out there are faerie gatherings and Ren Faires all the time. Some are just for a weekend, others run a couple of weeks or even months. Unlike the one where I met the Hills, most of them are outdoors. The Faerie Festivals are the most fun but the Ren Faires are more lucrative. The ones in Maryland are in May and November, but there are others all over the country, throughout the year. They even have them overseas.

The first year we did a run along the east coast. The second year we hit the West Coast and the badlands: Colorado, New Mexico, and my home state of Arizona.

Packing up the van and station wagon. Driving to wherever the venue is. Setting up the booth and then our tents in the camping area if they have one. If not, we're in a motel, which cuts into profits.

Being away from the familiarity of home makes it a little harder on Juliana. It's the only time I see her use her white cane. But we all look after her. I also think she's a bit too touchy on the subject of how people feel about her because everywhere we go there's lots of care and genuine affection.

Though to be fair to her, there are also people who are overbearing. Some even talk louder around her as though she can't hear well either.

At times like that, Juliana gets annoyed—I can always tell—and later she'll talk about going to Bordertown and getting her sight fixed like it's a real place and it could actually happen. I don't interrupt her rants because everybody needs to chance to vent. And you know, at the Faerie Festivals I hear about Bordertown as much as I do Faerieland, so it's not like she's the only one who believes in it.

While I still don't do costumes, when we're at the fairs I trade in my jeans and Ts for brown pants and the puffy-sleeved white shirts that Alana makes for me. At faerie events, I go as Juliana's human consort. At the Ren Faires, I'm just Tom's apprentice.

That first year along the east coast—New England, New York State, New Jersey—is a real wake-up call for me as to how different my life is now. I get into it, but it takes some getting used to. By the time the next year rolls around and we head out west, I'm an old hand at it.

I'm looking forward to being on my home turf. Mostly because Juliana and I have a big surprise planned.

We get married at the Arizona Renaissance Festival. It runs weekends from February through April and it's a wild scene. The people are all dressed up in medieval costumes and there's jousting, feasts, the art and crafts fair where we set up, a circus, and a whole bunch of stages that are busy throughout the weekend.

I use some of the money I've saved up to fly Uncle Herbert down. Tía Luba and a couple of their sisters come up from the rez. My dad? I wouldn't have known where to send an invitation.

But Tía Luba refuses to dwell on the fact that I only have aunts and an uncle at the wedding and she does a good job of making me forget about it, too. I can tell she likes Tom and she adores Juliana. But her meeting with Alana is a little odd.

The two of them walk up to each other and hold gazes. Then Tía Luba enfolds Alana in a tight embrace as though she's comforting Alana. They stand together like that for a long moment. When they finally step apart, their eyes are glistening.

I'd never seen anything like it before. Tía Luba just isn't given to public affection—and certainly not with strangers.

I'm standing with Uncle Herbert and turn to him.

"What's up with that?" I ask.

He shakes his head. "I don't know. Some kind of spirit business."

I give him a puzzled look.

"Yeah," I say, "but Tía Luba would be Kikimi while Alana's spirits are faeries . . . "

"Spirits are just spirits," he says. "They don't care about the color of our skin. Just that we give them our respect."

I look at the two women. There's no sign of what I saw a moment ago. Alana is smiling and greeting my other aunts. Even the rare twitch of Tía Luba's lips is almost a smile.

An hour or so later, just before the ceremony, Tía Luba surprises me so much I forget to ask about what she and Alana shared.

"I never saw you on this road you're on, nephew," she tells me. "I just knew you could be more than you were. But now . . . all of this. You have embraced life and I am so proud of you."

I tell you it's really something, saying our vows to each other as we stand in the Wedding Chapel in front of all our friends with Uncle Herbert and my aunts beside me, and Tom and Alana beside Juliana. There's always some crossover between the faerie events and the Ren Faires, but today we have a full contingent from both groups—some people have even come from the other side of the country. There's a full hedge of Tom's Green Men, a flood of faeries, and then a bunch of the Ren Faire folk.

The organizers of the Faire comp us the wedding chapel and also the reception in the Feast Hall. After that, the party moves to the ranch of a friend of Tom's outside of Florence Junction and there are still people dancing a couple of hours before the sun comes up.

When you're around anything long enough, I suppose it just gets in your blood because it comes to the point where I can sit around with the Hills and their friends and talk about faeries and spirits and I'm just as interested as any of them. I think about the guys back in the Kikimi County Young Offenders Correction Facility and what they'd say if they could see me now. I realize I don't care.

One of my favorite visitors—to either the house or the campground at one of the fairs—is Seamus Moore, an Irishman who at seventy-four is the oldest of Tom's Green Men hedge. He's a wiry little man with blue eyes like sapphires and a shock of white hair. He has a voice that could carry across a battlefield and he's full of songs and stories and tunes from the Celtic faerie traditions.

I first met him at the Hills' house and I totally dug these long rambling stories he had, but then on one visit he pulled a weird set of bagpipes from this long wooden box he'd set by the door when he'd first come in. After telling us the story of how a boy learned "The Faeries Hornpipe" from the faeries themselves, he then played the tune.

I'd never heard or seen anything like it. He strapped himself into the instrument, bellows under one arm, bag under the other, wooden pipes seeming to stick everywhichway and played this gorgeous music that sounded as though three people were playing.

"What the hell are those things?" I asked when the tune was done.

"Uillean pipes," he said.

"But where did they come from?"

"Now it's funny you should ask," he said, "because there's a story in that."

Tom laughed. "With you there's a story in everything!"

"And wouldn't it be a sorry world if there wasn't?"

Magic seems not only possible, but probable, whenever Seamus is around. He's at the wedding, and he's at the party after, still going strong when so many younger participants finally drag themselves off to bed. Finally the only people who are still awake are Seamus, Juliana and me, the Hills, Uncle Herbert, and Nikki and Steve Hutchings, who came down from Portland for the wedding.

There's a fire pit behind the stables that Tom's friend has let us use. Sitting around its coals, with the dawn beginning to pink the horizon, Seamus told a new bunch of stories that I'd never heard before and I'd heard a lot of them.

"Where do you get all your stories?" I ask him.

"Well, now," he says. "I've lived one or two, and some I got from others who did the same, but most I heard during the years I wandered in the Perilous Realms."

"Faerieland," Juliana whispers helpfully in my ear.

"You've been to Faerieland?" I say, when what's really going through my head is, Faerieland actually exists?

Because the thing about Seamus is he makes you believe. You may have second and third thoughts once you're out of his company, but when he's telling stories or playing his music, you can almost feel something *other* sitting right there in the periphery of your vision, listening along with you.

"Many times," he says. "There used to be a city that straddled the borders between the two realms—a rare place that made the crossing easy if you were welcome to visit. If you weren't and somehow made your way across . . . " He shook his head. "You never got the chance to make that mistake again."

"A city . . . " I say, thinking about the place that Juliana talks about.

He nods. "I say it used to be, but perhaps it still exists. I only know that these past thirteen years any passage to it from these fields we know is no longer possible."

"You're talking about Bordertown," Steve says.

Seamus nods again. "But the borders on our side of the world are no more. Or perhaps the city itself is gone." His eyes get a faraway look. "I'd always thought I'd make one more trip . . . "

That bright blue gaze of his settles on me and he shrugs.

"But," he says, "it was not to be."

Aside from Juliana, the mention of Bordertown from time to time over the past few years has been much like that of Ys and *Brocéliande and Avalon* and Lyonesse and all the other places that figure in faerie lore. I always thought of them the way I did the lost mysteries associated with the old pueblo people in the mountains near the rez: good for stories, but not places anyone could actually go. Or if they could, once upon a time, they can't anymore.

Bordertown's supposedly more contemporary, but no more a reality than the any of the others. Except . . .

Tomorrow morning I'll probably feel the same way, but right now, at this moment in the morning with Seamus' steady gaze on mine and the echoes of his music still ringing in my ears, I believe.

"I've been to the Realm in dreams," Juliana says in a soft voice from beside me.

I know those dreams. She whispers them to me in the morning when we wake up. As always, the best part is she can see in those dreams.

"And so it is with me now," Seamus says.

His pipes groan as he fills up his bag, right elbow working the bellows.

"Have I ever told you the story of the left-handed fiddler and the goblin?" he asks.

We all shake our heads.

"It's a good story that gave us an even better tune," he says, "and what better way to finish off a night as grand and blessed as this?"

Then off he goes, and we all follow his words into the morning.

3.

It seems so small a thing, so *pointless*. Just a misstep on some concrete stairs.

But it changes everything.

I don't even see it happen. Tom and I are loading the van while Alana and Juliana are inside packing things up. Except for whatever reason, Juliana comes out to where we are, white cane in hand. Halfway between the hotel door and where the van is parked by the curb, she misses a bottom step and falls backward, cracking her head on the top step.

She never regains consciousness.

"We'll be together forever," she said to me last May.

We're in the camping area of the Spoutwood Faerie Festival, lying on the grass and staring up at the stars. There are a *lot* of stars, but there are always a lot of stars when you can get out of the city.

"Even when we die," she goes on. "Whichever one of us goes first will be waiting for the other."

"I don't like talking about stuff like that."

"What? Romance?"

"No, dying."

She give me a gentle nudge with her elbow.

"It's just another journey," she says. "Don't the Kikimi believe that?"

"Yeah, It's just . . . I don't know."

I can feel her smile when she cuddles up to me, face pressed against my neck.

"You're not sure you do," she says.

Her breath is warm on my skin.

"I don't know."

"Well, *I* believe," she says.

I think about that as I sit in the intensive care unit, holding her hand, praying to whoever might be listening that she not be taken away.

God. The ancestors. The faerie spirits.

They don't help.

No one can.

Nothing does.

I don't know how I get through the funeral. I can't go to the wake. I sit outside the hall the Hills rented, off to one side on a bench under some trees, not seeing anything.

At one point Uncle Herbert sits with me for a while. He puts his hand on my shoulder but he doesn't say anything. Tía Luba called last night but I couldn't talk to her, either.

Whoever goes first will be waiting for the other.

I want to hit something. Or someone. Instead I go to a bar down the street. I order a double whiskey. I stare at the amber liquid for a long time before I put some money on the bar and leave the whiskey behind, untouched.

—•—

Sometime later the Hills find me sitting in another park not far from the hall, staring at the ground. I have no idea what time it is, just that it's dark. I don't know how they found me. They sit on either side of me. For a long time we don't speak.

"I knew her life would be short," Alana finally says. "I didn't know how or why, but I knew. It's the curse of this gift of mine. Sometimes you don't want to see things, but you do all the same. And some things you can't change. But if Juliana's life was going to be short, I wanted what time she had to at least be happy. You made her happy, Joey."

I get a picture in my head of the first time she and Tía Luba met. Tía Luba saw it, too.

"Why did no one tell me?" I say.

"To what purpose?" Alana asks. "Could you have loved her any more than you did? Could you have treated her any better?"

I shake my head. "But now she's gone. I didn't even get to say goodbye."

I said it in the ICU but she was no longer there.

Tom nods. "But she's waiting for us in the Summer Country. That's what I believe."

"The Summer Country," I say. "That's part of Faerieland, isn't it?"

"No, it's beyond Faerieland."

"So how do you get there?"

"It's not a place the living can visit," Alana says.

Our voices—this conversation—seems to unfold in some faraway place.

"I don't feel like I'm living anymore," I tell them.

"You won't feel like that forever," Alana says.

She doesn't understand. None of them do. Without Juliana the world's gone gray. Without her, there's just no point to anything.

I let them comfort me. I let them take me back to the hall. It's almost empty now. The only ones left are the Hills' closest friends.

"Go ahead," I say. "Talk to them. I'll be okay."

I stand at the back of the hall. I'm thinking of leaving again, but then I see Seamus and I remember the campfire on the morning after Juliana and I were married. The stories. What he'd said.

He looks up, the gleam in those bright blue eyes of his dimmed by the loss we all share. I sit beside him.

"I'm an old man," he says. "It doesn't seem right that I'm still here and she's gone."

I nod. "I'd trade places with her in a heartbeat."

"I know," he says. "I felt the same way when my Emma passed on."

"Don't tell me it's going to get better."

He shakes his head. "I won't. Because it doesn't. The loss is always there. The hole in the world where once she was. Mine and now yours."

We fall silent. I look across the hall where the remaining people are gathered in small groups, speaking softly.

"I have to go to her," I tell Seamus. "I have to find her. Like in the old stories where the guy goes down into the underworld and brings his true love back."

"And if she doesn't want to come back?" he asks. "Your people speak of the wheel of life, how it turns as it must, not how we'd will it. What if she has accepted the turning of her wheel?"

"Then I'd stay with her."

Seamus nods. "I don't think it a worthwhile endeavor, but I understand how you feel the need of it."

"Is it possible?"

"They say anything is possible—somewhere."

"I thought . . . if I could get to Bordertown, then I'd be close to the Faerie Realms. And the Summer Country . . . it lies past them, doesn't it?"

Seamus is quiet for a long moment.

"In the old days," he finally says, "you would have been a perfect candidate for entry into Bordertown. It always welcomed those who had nothing left for them here in the fields we know. But there's no way back to Bordertown—not that I've been able to find in thirteen years."

"But if could get there . . . "

"You would get no further. They are very strict about who can cross and who can't. It's not like it was when I was a boy and strayed beyond the fields we know. There was no Bordertown then—at least none that I knew. There was only a music, late at night as I came from a hoolie with my pipes in a bag hanging from my back. I followed that music into the Perilous Realms—not once, but many times. I followed it until I heard it no more and that was when I found my way to Bordertown. But I never crossed over from Bordertown. It wasn't possible."

"I have to try."

"I know you do. And I wouldn't hold you from going. But something is blocking the way. Or maybe the city just doesn't exist anymore. It isn't mine to say. I only know that anyone I've met who was here in the fields we know when things changed, has been stranded here. And I've talked to many of them, if not all."

"I don't understand. How can a city be destroyed and it not be on the news?"

"I didn't say it was destroyed. It's . . . sometimes I think it's more an idea than a place—though it was certainly real for me at one time. It's where magic works—sometimes. It's where technology works—sometimes. But mostly it requires some curious amalgamation of the two.

"Bordertown has always been a paradox. You can get there if you really need to be there—or you can't. You can stumble into it by chance—or you don't. It could be right there—" He points at a mirror on the side of the hall. "Just past our reflection—or it isn't. At one time there was even a *Rough Guide to Bordertown* available, but the truth is the city's always followed its own rules and they can change with a shift in the wind. Or they don't."

"So what do I do?"

He gives me a long serious study.

"Here's what I think," he says. "The old wisdom tells us that ancient power spots and sacred sites are gateways. And maybe that is true, or once was true. But I believe that the true openings lie inside us. In our own hearts, minds, and lives.

"It's occurred to me on more than one occasion that perhaps the reason we can no longer enter Bordertown is because we, as a people, have no longer allowed for the possibility for it. We simply don't believe anymore—even those of us who have crossed over once and twice and more times still.

"If that is true, perhaps all you need to do is set out on a journey in search of it, believing that when the journey ends you will be there. Not perhaps. Not maybe. Leave no room for doubt. Go with the understanding that the path you take will bring you there. And if it feels like you need a ritual, then make one up. But don't make it easy. Easy doesn't earn you anything."

"Just like that."

Seamus gives me a sad smile. "It's never 'just like that,' Joey. Even you know that much."

When I was a kid, home life was a horror show. Dad left, Mom died and we kids were on our way into foster care until the aunts came and brought us back to the rez, but it was probably too late.

My older brother was heavy into drugs and living on the rez didn't stop his intake. He OD'd when I was eleven.

My sister ran with a gang and six months later got caught in the crossfire of a drive-by.

Like them, I abandoned the idea of family pretty quickly, too, and you saw where that got me.

Tía Luba and Uncle Herbert gave me a chance, but I didn't really understand the idea of family until I met Juliana and her parents.

But now I'm abandoning them, too.

After my conversation with Seamus, I don't talk to anyone about it. I go back to Baltimore with the Hills and Uncle Herbert. I go back to the rambling house, to the room I shared with my wife. Just before dawn, I pack a knapsack and leave a note on the kitchen table:

I'm sorry. I have to do this. Don't look for me to come back because I don't know if I will.

—Joey

I'm waiting outside the bank when it opens. I close my account, stash the money in a bag under my shirt, and then I set off.

4.

Where do you go when you've got a destination in mind but no idea how to get to it?

I do what I did when I was a kid. I ride the rails. It was tough enough when I was a kid because things had already changed from the old days when hobos crossed the country on the old freights. It's changed even more now, but it's not impossible. And there's no better way to travel unnoticed. Hitchhikers get noticed. Take a bus, a train, even if you pay with cash, someone notices.

I don't want to be noticed.

I feel it's important to just disappear, like it's the first part of a ritual I have to make up. I don't see the other pieces yet, but this first one feels right.

I eat off the land—fishing, setting snares before I go to sleep—or from fast food outlets. I clean up in public restrooms. I take a few bad spills coming off the trains. Sprain my arm once. My ankle another time, which has me hobbling for a couple of days, unable to catch another train. Dislocate my shoulder. That was a bitch to reset, pushing myself up against a pole until the damn thing finally popped back into place.

I manage to avoid the security guards in the freight yards. I'm not always so lucky with the other guys on the road. But I grew up fighting and it's not something you forget. After awhile word gets around and the would-be toughs stay out of the way of the crazy Indian.

Most people I meet on the rails don't want to fight. Most of them don't even want to talk. That's fine with me, too, because I've got nothing to say.

The loss is always there, Seamus said. *The hole in the world where once she was.*

That doesn't begin to describe the emptiness I feel.

I ride the rails.

I start carving acorns out of found pieces of wood. When one is done, I toss it from whatever train I'm on.

Seven months go by.

I'm on another train, sitting cross-legged in front of the empty boxcar's door, watching the landscape. It's desert country again. Badlands. New Mexico, maybe. It doesn't matter. It's just one more place where I am and she's not.

I finish the acorn I've been carving. I hold it up to my eye for a long moment, studying the smoothness of the nut, the tough texture of the cap with its little stem. I toss the carving out the open door, snap my jackknife closed and stow it back in my pocket.

"Didn't like that one?" a voice says from behind me.

I turn and look for who spoke. I find him sitting in the shadows, an old man with a bedroll under his butt. He's got a battered tweed cap on his head and he's bundled up in a greatcoat. I can see how you might want something like that when the sun goes down, but right now it's got to be in the high eighties. He has to be melting in that thing.

"I didn't see you there," I tell him.

The old man smiles. "I get that a lot. Maybe I should change my name to Surprise."

"It's as good as any other, I suppose."

"Think I'll stick with Rudy. What's yours?"

You don't meet many talkers on the old hobo trails and I'm not used to having conversations anymore. But we've got a ways to go before the train will slow down enough to jump off and I've already carved my acorn for this ride.

"I'm Joey," I tell him.

"Nice to meet you, Joey. So you like to whittle?"

I shrug. "It passes the time."

"That's one way of looking at it. Another might be that it's a piece of a ritual."

"What?"

"Did you know that when you work magic it shows? It puts a charge in the air. How strong the charge is depends on how close you are to finishing what you started."

"Who *are* you?"

"I already told you. My name's Rudy. I'm like you. Just a guy riding the rails. And like you—like every one of us living this life—there's more to me than the homeless guy you see when you look my way. Come on. This can't be anything new for you. You know none of us were born doing this. We came to it because we've got nothing else left. Or in your case, because it's something you need to do to make something else happen."

I glance out the open door but we're still going too fast for me to survive a jump.

"I don't know what you think you see," I begin, but he waves a hand to cut me off.

"And I don't know," he says, "what's happened to you that makes you treat everybody as an enemy. But it doesn't have to be that way. I've got knowledge. I've got skills. Maybe I can help you."

"Why would you?"

He smiles and throws my words back at me.

"It passes the time. And really, what have you got to lose?"

Nothing, I realize. So I tell him. Not what brought me here. Not about the hole in my life that can't ever be filled.

"I'm trying to find a place called Bordertown," I say.

"Bordertown? Yeah, now there's a place. It can fill up your spirit and it can break your heart—sometimes both at the same time. Being in Bordertown is like mainlining a drug. Go there once you don't ever want to stray because all you'll ever want to do is get back. Problem is, sometimes it's just not there anymore—or at least it isn't for you."

"But it is real?"

"Define real."

"You know what I mean."

"Man, how would I know what *you* mean? My real's not necessarily the same as your real. Don't look at me like that. I'm not just being cute. The thing is, we all live in the world that we see and expect. They don't always match up—you understand what I'm saying?"

I shake my head.

"Let me put it this way," he says. "You look out that door and you're seeing New Mexico go by."

"So?"

"So what if I told you I see Alaska? Or India? Or the heart of Moscow?"

"I'd think you were either yanking my chain—or you're crazy."

"Sure, that's the easy way to look at it. But what if I'm *really* seeing a landscape you don't?"

"That's impossible."

He nods. "Right. And if you keep your mind closed like that you'll never get to Bordertown. I mean, think about it. Is Bordertown, or even the Perilous Realm, any more probable?"

"I guess not . . ."

I look out the door, trying to see something other than mesas and badlands. Mountains in the distance.

"I can't see it," I say. "I just see New Mexico."

"Did I say it wasn't New Mexico?"

"But—"

"I was making a point."

"Okay," I say. "I get it. And I've been trying to open my mind. But I'm just not seeing any differently than I ever did."

"I think you've been doing pretty good. You can see me, can't you?"

"What's that supposed to mean?"

"Come on, Joey. You're a smart guy. You're walking around under the blessings of a dozen or so Green Men. You were married to a Green Man's daughter. You've been whittling acorns and tossing them out of trains from one side of the country to the other. Did you seriously not expect to call something to you?"

All I can do is stare at him. I never told him any of that stuff.

"Let me show you something," he says.

He stands up and what I thought was a bedroll is actually a pile of leaves. His eyes, I can see now that he's moved out of the shadows, are a mix of gold and green. His face is ruddy and round, with deep laugh lines. He comes to where I'm sitting by the door and waits expectantly until I stand up beside him. He puts his hands in the pockets of his greatcoat and pulls out two fistfuls of carved acorns. Smiling at me, he lets them fall from his hands to the track bed that's speeding by below.

"Where did you—how . . . ?"

I don't have the words to finish my questions. All I can do is stare at his hands.

"I think I liked the earlier ones better," he says. "You seem to have put more intent into them. Now you're kind of doing it by rote, but it doesn't really matter. They still fulfilled the boundaries of your ritual."

"I . . ."

"Don't talk," he says. "Listen. Look at those beautiful mountains."

We stand in the doorway watching the landscape continue to go by.

"You know it's not going to be any easier in Bordertown, right?" he says after a few moments. "Being there's not going to make things better, or help you to forget—unless you drink some of that Mad River water and then you're only going find out why they call it that."

"If I can get that far then I can—"

He points out the door.

"Pay attention here," he says. "Listen to the wind. Look at that mesa. Smell the clean air out there. Isn't it so much better than the diesel fumes and the metal and wood and grease of this boxcar?"

"I guess."

"Sure it is. Now here's where you get off."

I start to turn to him, but his hands are on my back and he pushes me out the boxcar door.

My years of drinking left me one positive thing. I know how you don't get hurt as badly from a fall if you can be totally relaxed before impact. Tuck in your head and roll with the slope. You get banged up a bit, but if you pick a gentle grade, or when the train's starting to slow down before a station, you can get through it without injuries. Usually. It's like a Zen thing. You clear your mind, shake all the tension off before you make your jump.

I don't get that chance here. Rudy's push sends me flailing into the air. I know I'm going to hit hard and badly.

Except the air seems to catch me. I'm floating. Bright sunshine all around me, the train wailing by.

And then it's dark. When I touch the ground, I land like a leaf. There isn't even an impact. I feel gravel under me and I roll over to see a night sky above. It's filled with constellations I don't recognize.

The train, Rudy, New Mexico—they're all gone.

When I sit up, I see I'm in a train yard. I don't know where, but I can guess. In one direction I can see a fence, beyond it blocks of dark buildings. In the other direction it looks like a dump, cars and trash piled high.

I get up and start walking across the tracks to the fence. I was planning to climb over but then I see someone's already cut a hole in it that I can squeeze through. On the other side I find out why the buildings are dark. The city's been abandoned—or at least this part of it is. I can see lights in the far distance so I start to walk through the deserted streets.

I'm almost to the lighted area when I hear the sound of wheels clattering. I see a white kid on a skateboard, rolling back and forth on a little patch of asphalt that must've been a parking space back before everybody left this area and nature made its come back. As I get closer I don't see anything unusual about him. No elf ears. No big wings sprouting out of his back. He's maybe sixteen with a rat's nest of hair, baggy pants, a Green

Day *Dookie* T-shirt and a pair of Nike Air Max. He stops goofing around with his skateboard when he sees me and waits for me to approach.

"Hey," I say. "Think you could direct me to a hostel or a flophouse?"

He laughs. "Just get here?"

"Yeah."

He waves his hand to take in the empty buildings that surround us.

"Take your pick," he says.

"I was hoping to clean up and get something to eat."

He pushes back his hoodie and gives me an interested look.

"You got any money?" he asks.

"Not much."

"Worldly money?" When he realizes I don't know what he means, he adds, "You know, from the World. Where you came from. The reason I ask is it's not worth as much here. You got any coffee or chocolate?"

I nod. There's probably a half-pound of French Roast and a handful of chocolate and granola bars in my knapsack.

"Then you're cool." He steps on his board and it jumps into his hand. "Buy me a meal and I'll show you the ropes."

"What's your name?"

He was starting to turn, but he looks back at me.

"That can be a loaded question here," he says. "Usually you wait until someone offers it to you. And," he goes on before I can say anything, "be careful handing out your own. Just give up something like a nickname."

"And that would be because?"

"Magic's unpredictable here, but that doesn't mean it's not potent in the right hands. Names are power. If someone has your full true name, they can make you do stuff that maybe you don't want to."

"Are you serious?"

"But if you need a tag, you can call me River."

Full true names are power? I don't really buy it. But to be safe, I just give him the shortened version of Joseph.

"I'm Joey," I tell him.

He smiles. "Baby kangaroo."

"What?"

"Nothing. Come on. Let's get you something to eat. Me, I'll have a sandwich and a beer."

"Yeah, right," I say. "How old are you?"

He laughs. "You think anyone gives a shit about that? You're in Bordertown now. We've got our own rules and how old you are isn't part of any of them."

"I guess I've got a lot to learn."

"You have no idea," the kid tells me. "No idea at all."

He's right. I don't. Bordertown's shabbier than I expected, rundown and wearing at the edges, but it's also got that makeshift cool that you'll always find in a certain part of any city. The place where the stores, restaurants and clubs are all just a little hipper.

Most people look as human as you'd find anywhere, though they've got a more individual and varied fashion sense that seems vaguely out-of-date. I was expecting something like a FaerieCon with everybody dressed up in their faerie gear. But it's more like a mash-up of a punk rock concert with a hippie festival.

But the elves. I get a real pang in my heart when I see my first honest-to-goodness one. Tall, slender and pale, with the high pointed ears and the silvery hair. I just think about how much Juliana would have loved to see one. To be here.

They don't call themselves elves, or faerie, River informs me. They're True Bloods, which I've got to admit, sounds a bit too White Supremacist for my tastes. I didn't imagine Bordertown to be racist, but apparently there's a real hierarchy here starting with high born and low born elves, through to halflings with humans at the bottom. Which would make a guy with my skin color at the bottom of the bottom.

River shrugs. "You can get all in a twist about it, or you can just let it go. So long as you stay out of the way of the True Bloods, and don't piss off one of the gangs, no one's going to care."

Says the white kid.

He never asks me why I've come and I don't volunteer the information. I do tell him I'm interested in the Realm—which is what they call Faerieland here—and he just laughs.

"No kidding?" he says. "You and every other newbie. But forget about ever getting over there. I mean, seriously. Forget about it. You might be thinking, 'Hey, I made it to Bordertown, which is like a miracle all by itself. Getting into the Realm is just one more impossible thing I'm going to do.' But it's never going to happen. And if you try, you'll just bring a world of hurt down on yourself."

He doesn't know about the world of hurt I carry around inside myself every day, but I just nod in agreement.

River hangs around with me until about mid-morning, which is about when he realizes that the flow of free food and drinks has dried up.

"I've got to motor," he says the third time he's unsuccessfully tried to get me to buy him something. "I'll catch you around."

"Thanks for the tour," I tell him.

He waves a hand, then disappears into the crowd, skateboard under his arm.

I spend the rest of the day getting the lay of the land, staying out of the areas River warned me about. I still get a kick out of seeing the True Bloods, though I can't pretend that what they stand for doesn't irritate me. You have to have been on my side of the race issue to really get it, I suppose. It's just not something I can ignore.

As the sun goes down, I sit on a low wall by the Mad River whittling an acorn and considering what I've been told about the water flowing by below. I know the river has its source in the Realm. I've been told that drinking it, or even swimming in it, messes you up worse than any bad drug trip and there's no coming down from it. I haven't decided how much of it I believe but I'm not ready to try that route yet. Sneaking onto one of the boats that plies its trade between here and the Realm is an option that I'm liking better and better after everything else I've seen.

I had a good look at Elfhaeme Gate earlier in the afternoon. The damn thing's huge and there's no way I'm getting through it—not with how well it's guarded. I also scouted the Nevernever—the Borderlands between the Realm and Bordertown. When I stepped out into them I thought I was having an acid flashback. Seriously. The landscape seemed to change underfoot whenever I turned in a new direction. Pastoral woodlands became a wasteland more barren than anything in my home turf, which in turn became wheat fields, arctic tundra, redwoods, you name it. It felt like it was going to snow, then it was sunny, then it rained.

It gave me vertigo but I trudged on until I finally saw the shimmering curtain that divides the Realm from the World. I stared at it for a long time. It was beautiful, but it made the vertigo so bad that I could barely stay upright. Trying to make my way through that shimmer was going to be a last resort. Especially when these boats seem like such an easy option.

The problem is, none of them appear to be going anywhere right now. The barges are all empty with no place to hide. I have to wait until they start to load them in the morning.

With that decided, I stick the finished acorn in my pocket. I close up my jackknife, shoulder my knapsack and head back into the part of Soho where I first met River. I'll get some shut-eye in one of the abandoned buildings. Have an early breakfast. Maybe find a place where I can grab a shower or at least wash up.

Walking down Ho Street feels like Mardi Gras in New Orleans. There are kids everywhere, music spilling out of the clubs, everyone having a good time. I get lots of friendly nods and invitations to join in on the fun, but I just smile, or say no thanks, and walk on. Fun's not a word that's in my vocabulary any more. It's been seven months, but it still feels like yesterday when I was sitting in the ICU holding Juliana's hand as she drifted away.

I'm not alone in keeping my distance. I see kids in the shadows, skulking in the mouths of alleys, or in the doorways of businesses that are closed for the night. They shrink back when they see me looking at them. Street kids. Some of them are younger than River. One pair of girls I'm sure can't be more than twelve or thirteen. I don't know their stories but I'm guessing that actually being here in Bordertown turned out to be a whole lot different from what they thought it would be—and maybe not so different from whatever they were trying to escape in the World.

I turn off the party street and find a quieter avenue that's heading in the same direction. The buzz from Ho Street still reaches me here so I almost don't hear the whimper in the alley as I pass its mouth. It's followed by the sound of rough laughter. I pause, and take a few steps back to peer down its length.

The light's not good, but I can make out three guys clustered around a body on the ground. They're taking turns kicking it. I reach into my pocket and pull out my jackknife. Then I step into the alley.

As I get closer I see it's a dog that they're tormenting. It's a mid-sized animal, shorthaired with a long face, big shoulders and trim hips. There's blood on its yellow fur. It keeps trying to crawl away but whenever it does, one of the guys gives it another kick.

Except they aren't guys—they're True Bloods. Tall and handsome, maybe, but with a cruel light in their eyes and knives in their hands. Now I know why the dog's bleeding.

"The big thing to remember," River told me this morning, "is you won't get in over your head if you mind your own business. You especially don't want to get on the wrong side of the True Bloods."

Screw that.

I open my jackknife and snatch up the metal lid from a garbage can.

"Get away from the dog!" I call to them.

They start to turn in my direction and I can see them smiling at the thought of some new entertainment. But I learned a long time ago that if there's going to be trouble, you don't stand around and talk about it, working up your courage. You just go for it.

I'm already in motion when I call out to them. By the time they turn around I'm close enough to hit the front guy in the face with the garbage can lid. I'm not ready to cut yet, but I aim the hilt of my knife at the head of the guy on my right. It never connects. He's fast. They're all fast. It's like nothing I've ever seen.

The guy on my left moves in and his blade punches me in the side, going in up to its hilt before he rips it out. The guy I missed ducks under my swing and he stabs me in the chest. The one I hit slaps aside the lid. I have the momentary satisfaction of seeing the blood spilling from his broken nose before he knifes me as well.

Fast.

So fast.

The jackknife drops from my fingers to clatter on the cobblestones. My mouth fills with the taste of copper.

They each get a couple more stabs in before I'm falling to the ground beside the dog. The one with the broken nose drops down, sleek as a panther. His face is inches from my own.

"You think this was a game, human?"

He spits the words into my face. I'm trying to focus on him but my gaze is swimming. I know I should be in a world of pain, but I can't seem to feel my body. I think he's licking my blood from the blade of his knife, but that doesn't make any sense.

"No one interferes with us. Too bad you had to die to learn that."

Except he doesn't look sorry at all. Then he's standing again—so fast I don't see him move. They kick me a few more times before I hear them leaving the alley.

I drag myself to the wall. I'm bleeding out, but there's nothing I can do. I've been cut too many times. I still don't feel the pain. I pull the dog's head onto my lap and stroke his bloody fur.

"Sorry, buddy," I tell him. "I wish I'd gotten here sooner, but it probably would have ended just the same. Though maybe you could have had time to run off."

I would have had your back, a voice says in my head.

"The hell . . . ?"

I look down into the dog's face. His big brown eyes are looking up into mine. I know it's ridiculous, but it's like the dog was talking to me.

Their generosity is legendary, the voice goes on, *but so is their cruelty.*

I look around. My vision's been fading in and out, but there doesn't seem to be anybody else here but the dog and me. I look back at him.

"Are you—are you talking to me?"

I think it's just the two of us here, so I must be talking to you.

"Yeah, but dogs can't . . . "

What makes you think dogs can't talk?

"I didn't—I mean, it never occurred to me one way or the other."

Maybe the ones you knew didn't have anything to say. Or maybe you just didn't know how to hear them.

"I never thought about it. They were just always around on the rez."

And yet without stopping to consider the consequences, you gave your life for me.

That brings me right back down to earth.

"So we're dying . . . ?"

I'm afraid so.

"I don't feel any pain."

Some of the Bloods coat their blades with poison to guarantee the death of their foe. But it has the side effect of numbing the pain.

"I can't die. I mean, I'm not supposed to die. Not yet. I was supposed to rescue her first."

Why don't you tell me who she is and what you were rescuing her from?

"I wasn't there for her when she fell," I say.

Time is crawling by in slow motion. I don't know if it's from shock, or something in the poison. But somehow I manage to tell him about Juliana and how she died.

What makes you think she wants to be rescued? he says when I'm done.

I remember Seamus asking me the same thing, but I still say, "What do you mean?"

Death is only a passage to another world. We leave this place and go to what you call the Summer Country, but eventually we leave it as well and go somewhere else. That is how it is forever. Your mate has finished the journey she had in this world. Why would she want to return to travel the same road again?

"She said we'd be together forever," I say. "She said whichever one of us went first would be waiting for the other."

And you doubt it?

"I—I don't know what to think. It doesn't matter. Nothing does now."

I will tell you what always matters, the dog says. *Shining a light into the darkness. Standing up to injustice. Just as you did earlier this evening. There aren't so many willing to offer help as selflessly as you have.*

"Except we're both dying."

It doesn't have to be that way.

"I don't get it. And Juliana . . . "

No matter how long you live, she will always be waiting for you. You do believe her, don't you?

"I still don't get what you're saying."

Just as your friend pushed you from the train into Bordertown, I can push you back from death. Choose life and see what happens.

"But without her—"

She will be waiting for you. She promised. But go only when your work is finished.

"What work?"

The work of living, and showing other how to survive. They come here to this city because they have nothing left in the World to comfort them, but they don't always find comfort here, either. You saw it yourself this evening. Bordertown can be a harsh mistress to the unwary. You can stay and be a strength for others, or give up and go to her. But ask yourself, will you be proud of your choice? Will she?

He's right. Juliana would want me to stay and make myself useful. I know that because it's what I'd want for her. I'd want her to live.

"So how do you push me back?" I ask.

There's no reply for a long moment, and then I realize that the dog's gone. He passed away between one breath and the next. I stroke his fur.

"Thanks for the company, buddy," I say.

I shift my position a little and something digs into my back. My jacket got twisted around when I pulled myself up to lean against the wall. What I'm feeling is the acorn I carved while watching the Mad River.

Choose, the dog told me.

Now I know what I'd choose, but it's too late.

I pull the acorn out of my pocket and turn it over in my hand a few times. Then I toss it away and listen to it bounce down the alley.

Either it's gotten completely dark now, or my vision's gone. It's really quiet, too. My tongue feels thick in my mouth. I'm falling. I'm in the alley, propped up against a wall, but at the same time I'm falling.

I try to find something to hold onto, but I can't feel my fingers anymore.

Falling . . .

Something the dog told me . . .

Falling . . .

Then I remember.

Will you be proud of your choice? Will she?

And as soon as I remember, I think I hear it. I hear *her*. That familiar bell-like laugh. Delicate and intoxicating.

I reach for her with hands I can't feel, stretching farther and farther until I can almost imagine her fingers close around my own.

The soft laughter is all around me now, just like my Juliana, sweet and happy.

Choose life and see what happens.

I want to be with her so badly.

But I remember walking down that party street. Everybody having fun, laughing and dancing and filled up with the music. But I also remember those kids I saw standing just beyond the noise and light. Came all this way but they're still just as much on the outside as they were before they got here.

I think of the True Bloods, and the gangs River told me about, pushing their weight around.

If the dog hadn't died, if I could still make the choice, I know what I'd choose.

I'd do what I could to make things right. That's what would make Juliana proud. That's the guy I'd want to be.

But it's too late.

The sweet laughter grows softer and I hear something else. I don't realize what it is until the acorn I threw away bounces back against my leg. I reach for it, close my fingers around it.

I can push you back from death.

I open my eyes. I clutch the acorn tight and lift my free hand to my chest. My shirt's still all cut up and it's soaked with blood. But the wounds are gone.

Juliana's presence has completely faded.

I sit there for a long time, aching to be with her.

Finally, I tuck the acorn away in a pocket. I get up and cradle the dog's body in my arms and go looking for a place to lay it in the ground.

I know that Juliana's waiting for me, but that's not going to be for a while.

I don't know what's going to happen next.

The start of something, I guess.

A new turn of the wheel, Uncle Herbert would say.

The promise of hope, Tom Hill would probably say.

Maybe I'll see if they have any Green Men in this place.

⊰═⊱

About the Authors

JOAN AIKEN (1924-2004) British writer and daughter of Conrad Aiken, Joan Aiken worked as a librarian for the UN Information Committee and as features editor for *Argosy*. Her many books for children include *All You've Ever Wanted*, *The Kingdom and the Cave*, *Tales of Arabel's Raven*, *Voices Hippo*, and *Dangerous Games*. Among her adult novels are *The Silence of Herondale* and *Mansfield Revisited*. A 2011 posthumous collection, *The Monkey's Wedding and Other Stories*, published by Small Beer Press included six never-before published stories.

KELLEY ARMSTRONG is the author of the Women of the Otherworld paranormal suspense series and the Darkest Powers YA urban fantasy series. She grew up in Ontario, Canada, where she still lives with her family. A former computer programmer, she's now escaped her corporate cubicle and hopes never to return.

ADAM CALLAWAY was born in 1989 in Madison, Wisconsin, and has slowly migrated north to his current home in Superior, where he lives with his wife and two small dogs. He read Gene Wolfe's *The Shadow of the Torturer* when he was nineteen, and it has driven him to write and write and write in his attempt to reverse-engineer genius. You can find him at www.adamcallaway.net.

TANANARIVE DUE is an American Book Award-winning, *Essence* best-selling author of *Blood Colony*, *The Living Blood*, *The Good House*, *Joplin's Ghost*, and, most recently, *My Soul to Take*. She is also co-author of the NAACP Image Award-winning Tennyson Hardwick mystery series. She lives in the Atlanta area with her husband and co-author Steven Barnes. Visit her at www.TananariveDue.blogspot.com.

DENNIS ETCHISON's stories have appeared widely in magazines and anthologies since 1961. He is a three-time winner of both the British Fantasy Award and the World Fantasy Award. His collections include *The Dark Country*, *Red Dreams*, *The Blood Kiss*, *The Death Artist*, *Talking in the Dark*, *Fine Cuts*, and *Got To Kill Them All & Other Stories*. He is also a novelist (*Darkside*, *Shadowman*, *California Gothic*, *Double Edge*), editor (*Cutting Edge*, *Masters of Darkness I-III*, *MetaHorror*, *The Museum of Horrors*, *Gathering the Bones*), and scriptwriter. In 2002 he began adapting the original *Twilight Zone* television series for radio, followed by further scripts for *The New Twilight Zone Radio Dramas* and *Fangoria Magazine's Dread Time Stories*. Forthcoming are a career retrospective from Centipede Press's Masters of the Weird Tale series and a volume of new short stories from Bad Moon Books.

PAUL FINCH is a former cop and journalist turned full-time writer. He cut his literary teeth penning episodes of the British TV crime drama, The Bill, and has written extensively in the field of children's animation. To date, he's had twelve books and nearly three hundred stories and novellas published. His first collection, *Aftershocks*, won the British Fantasy Award and he later won the award for his novella, *Kid*. He is also an International Horror Guild Award-winner for his story, *The Old North Road*. Most recently, he has written four *Doctor Who* audio dramas. His horror novel, *Stronghold*, was published in 2010, *Doctor Who* novel, *Hunter's Moon*, in 2011, and 2012 will see the publication of his novel, *Dark North*. Finch has also written scripts for several movies. The most recent of these, *The Devil's Rock*, was released in 2011. He lives in Lancashire, UK, with his wife and two children. His website is paulfinch-writer.blogspot.com.

JEFFREY FORD is the author of the novels, *The Physiognomy, Memoranda, The Beyond, The Portrait of Mrs. Charbuque, The Girl in the Glass, The Cosmology of the Wider World,* and *The Shadow Year*. His story collections are, *The Fantasy Writer's Assistant, The Empire of Ice Cream,* and *The Drowned Life*. His new collection, *Crackpot Palace*, will be out in August 2012. Ford is the recipient of the Edgar Allan Poe Award, the Shirley Jackson Award, the Nebula, the World Fantasy Award, and the *Grand Prix de l'imaginaire*.

LAURA ANNE GILMAN is the author of the Cosa Nostradamus books for Luna (the Retrievers and Paranormal Scene Investigations series), a YA trilogy for HarperCollins, and the award-nominated The Vineart War trilogy from Pocket. She also writes paranormal romances for Nocturne as Anna Leonard. Some of her short fiction was collected in *Dragon Virus*. In 2012, she will be dipping her pen into the mystery field, as well. A former executive editor at NAL, Laura Anne is an amateur chef, oenophile, and cat-servant. She lives in New York City, where she also runs d.y.m.k. productions.

ELIZABETH HAND (www.elizabethhand.com) is the multiple-award-winning author of twelve novels and three collections of short fiction. Her most recent novel, *Available Dark*, was named as one of the Top Ten Best Mystery/Thrillers of the year by *Publishers Weekly*. A *New York Times* and *Washington Post* Notable Author, Hand is also a longtime book critic and essayist who frequently contributes to the *Washington Post, Salon, Village Voice,* and *DownEast Magazine,* among many others. She has two children and divides her time between Maine and North London.

GLEN HIRSHBERG's awards include the 2008 Shirley Jackson Award (for his novelette, "The Janus Tree") and three International Horror Guild Awards, including two for Best Collection (for *American Morons* in 2006 and *The Two Sams* in 2003). He is also the author of two novels, *The Snowman's Children* and *The Book of Bunk*. "After-Words" appears in his new collection, *The Janus Tree and Other Stories*, just out from Subterranean. With Dennis Etchison and Peter Atkins, he co-founded the Rolling Darkness Revue, a traveling ghost story performance troupe that tours the west coast of the United States and elsewhere each October. His fiction has been published in numerous magazines and anthologies.

STEPHEN GRAHAM JONES is the author of ten novels and two collections. Most recent are *Zombie Bake-Off* and *Growing Up Dead in Texas*. Next are *Flushboy* and *Not for Nothing*. Stephen's been a Stoker finalist, a Shirley Jackson Award finalist three times, a Black Quill finalist, and has been an NEA fellow and won the Texas Institute of Letters Award for fiction. He teaches in the MFA program at UC Boulder.

CAITLÍN R. KIERNAN is the author of several novels, including the award-winning *Threshold*, *Daughter of Hounds*, *The Red Tree*, and, most recently, *The Drowning Girl*. Her short fiction has been collected in *Tales of Pain and Wonder*; *From Weird and Distant Shores*; *To Charles Fort, with Love*; *Alabaster*; *A Is for Alien*; and *The Ammonite Violin & Others*. Her erotica has been collected in two volumes, *Frog Toes and Tentacles* and *Tales from the Woeful Platypus*. Subterranean Press published a retrospective of her early writing, *Two Worlds and In Between: The Best of Caitlín R. Kiernan (Volume One)* last year. She lives in Providence, Rhode Island with her partner, Kathryn.

STEPHEN KING has since published over fifty books, many short stories, and has become one of the world's most successful writers. King has won numerous award and the National Book Foundation has honored him the Medal for Distinguished Contribution to American Letters. He lives in Maine and Florida with his wife, novelist Tabitha King. They are regular contributors to a number of charities including many libraries and have been honored for their philanthropic activities.

MARGO LANAGAN is an internationally acclaimed writer of novels and short stories. Her fiction has garnered many awards, nominations, and shortlistings. Her *Black Juice* was a Michael L. Printz Honor Book, won two World Fantasy Awards and the Victorian Premier's Award for Young Adult Fiction. *Red Spikes* won the CBCA Book of the Year: Older Readers, was a *Publishers Weekly* Best Book of the Year, a Horn Book Fanfare title, was shortlisted for the Commonwealth Writer's Prize and longlisted for the Frank O'Connor International Short Story Award. Her novel *Tender Morsels* won the World Fantasy Award for Best Novel and was a Michael L. Printz Honor Book for Excellence in Young Adult Literature. Her latest novel is *Sea Hearts* (Allen & Unwin, Australia), known as *The Brides of Rollrock Island* in the UK, it will come out under that title the US in September. She lives in Sydney.

JOE R. LANSDALE is the author of over thirty novels and numerous short stories. His novella, *Bubba Ho-tep*, was made into an award-winning film of the same name, as was *Incident On and Off a Mountain Road*. Both were directed by Don Coscarelli. His works have received numerous recognitions, including the Edgar, eight Bram Stoker awards, the Grinzani Prize for Literature, American Mystery Award, the International Horror Award, British Fantasy Award, and many others. *All the Earth, Thrown to the Sky*, his first novel for young adults, was published last year. His most recent novel for adults is *Edge of Dark Water*.

TANITH LEE was born in 1947, in London, England. She worked at various jobs until in 1974-75 DAW Books began to publish her science fiction and fantasy, beginning with *The Birthgrave*. Since then she has published over ninety books and over three hundred short stories, written for TV and BBC Radio. Her latest novels are available from the Immanion Press and reprints—such as Flat Earth sequence and The Birthgrave Trilogy—via Norilana Books. Much of her work will soon be available in ebook form via Orion, and other houses. She lives on the Sussex Weald with her husband writer/artist/photographer/model maker John Kaiine.

YOON HA LEE is a Korean-American writer of science fiction and fantasy. She majored in math, and it is a source of continual delight to her that mathematics can be mined for story ideas. Her first collection of short fiction, *Conservation of Shadows*, will be published in 2013.

CHARLES DE LINT is a full-time writer and musician who presently makes his home in Ottawa, Canada, with his wife MaryAnn Harris. His most recent books are *Under My Skin* and *Eyes Like Leaves*. His first album, *Old Blue Truck*, came out in early 2011. For more information about his work, visit his website at www. charlesdelint.com. He's also on Facebook, Twitter, and MySpace.

MAUREEN MCHUGH has published four novels and two collections of short stories. She's won a Hugo and a Tiptree award. Her most recent collection, *After the Apocalypse*, was named a *Publishers Weekly* Top Ten Best Book of 2011, was a Philip K. Dick Award finalist, a Story Prize Notable Book, and named to the io9 Best SF&F Books of 2011 List as well as the Tiptree Award Honor List. McHugh lives in Los Angeles, where she is attempting to sell her soul to the entertainment industry.

SARAH MONETTE lives in a 106-year-old house in the Upper Midwest with a great many books, two cats, and one husband. Her first four novels were published by Ace Books. Her short stories have appeared in *Strange Horizons*, *Weird Tales*, and *Lady Churchill's Rosebud Wristlet*, among other venues, and have been reprinted in several Year's Best anthologies. *The Bone Key*, a 2007 collection of interrelated short stories, was re-issued last year in a new edition. Her non-themed collection, *Somewhere Beneath Those Waves* was published in 2011. Sarah has written two novels (*A Companion to Wolves* and *The Tempering of Men* and three short stories with Elizabeth Bear. Her next novel, *The Goblin Emperor*, will come out from Tor under the name Katherine Addison. Visit her online at www.sarahmonette.com.

Naomi Novik's first novel, *His Majesty's Dragon*, the opening volume of the Temeraire series, was published in 2006 and has been translated into twenty-seven languages and optioned by Peter Jackson. She has won the John W. Campbell Award for Best New Writer, the Compton Crook Award for Best First Novel, and the Locus Award for Best First Novel. She is one of the founding board members of the Organization for Transformative Works, a nonprofit dedicated to protecting the fair-use rights of fan creators, as well as one of the architects of the open-source Archive Of Our Own. Naomi lives in New York City with her husband, Edgar-winning mystery novelist Charles Ardai, and their shiny new daughter Evidence. Her website is naominovik.com and she can be followed as *naominovik* on Livejournal, Twitter, and Facebook.

Paul Park lives in Berkshire County, Massachusetts, and teaches at Williams College. He has written eleven novels in a variety of genres, and numerous short stories. His most recent work includes *Ghosts Doing the Orange Dance* (nominated for the 2010 Nebula Award) and *Ragnarok*, a post-apocalyptic pseudo-Norse edda (nominated for the 2011 Rhysling Award). Under the name Paulina Claiborne, he has also written a recently published Forgotten Realms novel called *The Rose of Sarifal*.

Norman Partridge's fiction includes horror, suspense, and the fantastic— "sometimes all in one story" according to Joe Lansdale. Partridge's novel *Dark Harvest* was chosen by *Publishers Weekly* as one of the 100 Best Books of 2006, and two short-story collections were published in 2010—*Lesser Demons* from Subterranean Press and *Johnny Halloween* from Cemetery Dance. Other work includes the Jack Baddalach mysteries *Saguaro Riptide* and *The Ten-Ounce Siesta*, plus *The Crow: Wicked Prayer*, which was adapted for film. His work has received multiple Bram Stoker awards. He can be found on the web at NormanPartridge.com and americanfrankenstein.blogspot.com.

Tim Powers is the author of twelve novels, including *The Anubis Gates*, *Declare*, *Hide Me AMong the Graves,* and *On Stranger Tides*, which was adapted for the fourth Pirates of the Caribbean movie of the same title. His novels have twice won the Philip K. Dick Memorial Award, twice won the World Fantasy Award, and three times won the Locus Poll Award. Powers has taught fiction writing classes at the University of Redlands, Chapman University, and the Orange County High School of the Arts. He has been an instructor at the Writers of the Future program and the Clarion Science Fiction Workshop at Michigan State University. Powers lives with his wife, Serena, in San Bernardino, California.

Norman Prentiss recently won the Bram Stoker Award for Superior Achievement in Long Fiction for his first book, *Invisible Fences*. Previously he won a Stoker in the short fiction category for "In the Porches of My Ears," which originally appeared in *Postscripts 18*. His fiction has also appeared in *Black Static, Commutability, Tales from the Gorezone, Damned Nation, Best Horror of the Year, The Year's Best Dark Fantasy and Horror*, and in three editions of the Shivers anthology series. His poetry has appeared in *Writer Online, Southern Poetry Review, Baltimore's City Paper*, and *A Sea of Alone: Poems for Alfred Hitchcock*. His essays on gothic and sensation literature have appeared in *Victorian Poetry, Colby Quarterly*, and *The Thomas Hardy Review*. Visit him online at www.normanprentiss.com.

ALAN PETER RYAN (1943-2011) was the author of four novels and two collections of short fiction and the editor of five anthologies. He was nominated for the John W. Campbell Award and three times for the World Fantasy Award, and won a World Fantasy Award for *The Bones Wizard*. He also edited five anthologies of travel writing for which he won a Lowell Thomas Travel Journalism Award. As a journalist, he wrote for all the major newspapers of the United States and for many magazines, including *Smithsonian, The American Scholar, Islands, Travel & Leisure*, and *Playgirl*.

PRIYA SHARMA is a general practitioner in the UK, where she spends as much free time as she can devouring books and writing speculative fiction. She has a computer but prefers a fountain pen and a notebook. Her short stories have appeared in publications such as *Albedo One, On Spec, Alt Hist, Bourbon Penn, Fantasy*, and *Black Static*. She is currently working on a historical fantasy novel set in North Wales, not far from where she lives. More information can be found at www.priyasharmafiction.co.uk.

ANGELA SLATTER is a Brisbane-based writer of speculative fiction. She is the author of WFA-shortlisted *Sourdough and Other Stories* (Tartarus Press) and the Aurealius Award-winning *The Girl with No Hands and Other Stories* (Ticonderoga Publications). Her short stories have appeared in anthologies such as *Dreaming Again, Strange Tales II* and *III, 2012*, and *A Book of Horrors* as well as journals such as *Lady Churchill's Rosebud Wristlet, Shimmer*, and *On Spec*. Her work has had several Honorable Mentions in the Datlow, Link, and Grant-edited Year's Best Fantasy and Horror series; and six of her stories have been shortlisted for the Aurealis Awards in the Best Fantasy Short Story category, winning in 2011 with Lisa L Hannett for "The Febraury Dragon." She blogs at www.angelaslatter.com.

TIA V. TRAVIS was a finalist for the World Fantasy Award and the International Horror Guild Award. Her fiction has been reprinted in two volumes of *The Year's Best Fantasy and Horror* and *Poe's Children: The New Horror*. A native Canadian, she now lives in Northern California with her husband, author Norman Partridge, and two-year-old daughter, Neve Rose.

LISA TUTTLE was born in the United States, but has lived in Britain for the past thirty years. She began writing while still at school, sold her first stories at university, and won the John W. Campbell Award for Best New Science Fiction Writer of the Year in 1974. Her first novel, *Windhaven*, was a collaboration with George R. R. Martin published in 1981; her most recent is the contemporary fantasy *The Silver Bough*, and she has published around a hundred short stories, as well as books for children and non-fiction works.

CATHERYNNE M. VALENTE is the *New York Times* bestselling author of over a dozen works of fiction and poetry, including *Palimpsest*, the Orphan's Tales series, *Deathless*, and the crowdfunded phenomenon *The Girl Who Circumnavigated Fairyland in a Ship of Own Making*. She is the winner of the Andre Norton Award, the Tiptree Award, the Mythopoeic Award, the Rhysling Award, and the Million Writers Award. She has been nominated for the Hugo, Nebula, Locus, and Spectrum Awards, the Pushcart Prize, and was a finalist for the World Fantasy Award in 2007 and 2009. She lives on an island off the coast of Maine with her partner, two dogs, and an enormous cat.

KAARON WARREN's short story collection *The Grinding House* (CSFG Publishing) won the ACT Writers' and Publishers' Fiction Award and two Ditmar Awards. Her second collection, *Dead Sea Fruit*, published by Ticonderoga Books, won the ACT Writers' and Publishers' Fiction Award. Her critically acclaimed novel *Slights* (Angry Robot Books) won the Australian Shadows Award, the Ditmar Award, and the Canberra Critics' Award for Fiction. Angry Robot Books also published her novels *Walking the Tree* (shortlisted for a Ditmar Award) and *Mistification*, which was released in 2011. Her stories have appeared in Ellen Datlow's Year's Best Horror and Fantasy as well as the Australian Years Best Horror, Science Fiction and Fantasy anthologies. She has recently been named Special Guest for the Australian National Science Fiction Convention in 2013, and has appeared at Readercon in the USA as an invited guest. Kaaron lives in Canberra, Australia, with her husband and children. Her website is kaaronwarren.wordpress.com and she tweets @KaaronWarren.

GENE WOLFE worked as an engineer before becoming editor of trade journal *Plant Engineering*. He retired to write full-time in 1984. Long considered to be a premier fantasy author, he is the recipient of the World Fantasy Lifetime Achievement Award, as well as Nebula, World Fantasy, Campbell, Locus, British Fantasy, and British SF Awards. Wolfe has been inducted into the Science Fiction Hall of Fame. His short fiction has been collected over a dozen times, most recently in *The Best of Gene Wolfe* (2009). The most recent of Wolfe's numerous novels is *Home Fires* (2011). His novel *Peace* will be published in December 2012.

Acknowledgments

"Hair" by Joan Aiken © 2011 by Joan Aiken Estate (John Sebastian Brown and Elizabeth Delano Charlaff). Used by permission. All rights reserved. First publication: *The Monkey's Wedding & Other Stories* (Small Beer Press) / *The Magazine of Fantasy & Science Fiction*, July/August, 2011.

"Rakshasi" by Kelley Armstrong © 2011 by KLA Fricke Inc. First publication: *The Monster's Corner: Through Inhuman Eyes*, edited by Christopher Golden (St. Martin's Griffin).

"Walls of Paper, Soft as Skin" by Adam Callaway © 2011 by Adam Callaway. First publication: *Beneath Ceaseless Skies*, Issue #73, July 14, 2011.

"The Lake" by Tananarive Due © 2011 by Tananarive Due. First publication: *The Monster's Corner: Through Inhuman Eyes*, edited by Christopher Golden (St. Martin's Griffin, 2011).

"Tell Me I'll See You Again" by Dennis Etchison © 2011 by Dennis Etchison. First publication: *A Book of Horrors*, edited by Stephen Jones (Quercus).

"King Death" by Paul Finch © 2011 by Paul Finch. First publication: *King Death* (Spectral Press,).

"The Last Triangle" by Jeffrey Ford © 2011 by Jeffrey Ford. First publication: *Supernatural Noir*, edited by Ellen Datlow (Dark Horse).

"Crossroads" by Laura Anne Gilman © 2011 by Laura Anne Gilman. First publication: *Fantasy*, August 2011.

"Near Zennor" by Elizabeth Hand © 2011 by Elizabeth Hand. First publication: *A Book of Horrors*, edited by Stephen Jones (Quercus).

"After-Words" by Glen Hirshberg © 2011 by Glen Hirshberg. First publication: *The Janus Tree and Other Stories* (Subterranean Press).

"Azif" © 2011 by Lynne Jamneck. First publication: *Fantastique Unfettered*, Issue 4 (Ralewing).

"Rocket Man" by Stephen Graham Jones © 2011 by Stephen Graham Jones. First publication: *Stymie*, Vol. 4. Issue 1, Spring & Summer 2011.

"The Maltese Unicorn" by Caitlín R. Kiernan © 2011 by Caitlín R. Kiernan. First publication: *Supernatural Noir*, edited by Ellen Datlow (Dark Horse).

"The Dune" by Stephen King © 2011 by Stephen King. First publication: *Granta 117*, Autumn 2011.